THE
DEMONS

HEIMITO VON DODERER

Translated from the German by Richard and Clara Winston

ALFRED A. KNOPF · NEW YORK

1 9 6 1

Malevolence wears the false face of honesty.   TACITUS, *Histories, I, 1*

THE
DEMONS

VOLUME TWO

L. C. catalog card number: 61–92364

This is a BORZOI BOOK, *published by* ALFRED A. KNOPF, *Inc.*

FIRST AMERICAN EDITION

Originally published in German as DIE DÄMONEN. *© 1956 Biederstein Verlag GmbH München.*

Contents

VOLUME TWO

List of Principal Characters

Edouard Altschul, *a bank director*
Rosi Altschul, *his wife*
Countess Claire Charagiel, *daughter of Baron von Neudegg*
Prince Alfons Croix
Anna Diwald ("Didi"), *barmaid, underworld character*
Emma Drobil, *a beautiful stenographer*
Captain von Eulenfeld, *leader of "the Düsseldorfers," former hussar*
Alois Gach, *commissioner of markets, former sergeant in Ruthmayr's regiment*
Georg von Geyrenhoff, *the narrator, a retired civil servant*
Anny Gräven, *prostitute, friend of Leonhard Kakabsa*
Josef Grössing ("Pepi," "Croaky"), *a boy, Frau Kapsreiter's nephew*
Hofrat von Gürtzner-Gontard, *Geyrenhoff's former superior*
Renata von Gürtzner-Gontard, *the Hofrat's daughter*
Imre von Gyurkicz, *newspaper cartoonist and painter, friend of Charlotte von Schlaggenberg ("Quapp")*
Beatrix K. ("Trix"), *daughter of Mary K.*
Mary K., *a widow who has lost a leg in a streetcar accident*
Leonhard Kakabsa, *a young factory worker who educates himself*
Frau Anna Kapsreiter, *widowed sister of Mathias Csmarits, keeper of a dream-book*
Cornel Lasch, *brother-in-law of Grete Siebenschein, associate of Levielle*
Financial Counselor Levielle, *the villain*
Meisgeier ("the Claw"), *a murderer*

Hans Neuberg, *a student of history*

Géza von Orkay (the "bird Turul"), *a Hungarian diplomat, cousin of Geyrenhoff*

Alois Pinter ("Pinta"), *son-in-law of Franz Zdarsa, a pro-Hungarian conspirator*

Frau Friederike Ruthmayr ("Fritzi," "Friedl"), *an immensely wealthy widow*

Frau Camilla von Schlaggenberg ("Camy"), née Schedik, *Kajetan's estranged wife*

Charlotte von Schlaggenberg ("Quapp," "Quappchen," "Lo," "Lotte"), *Kajetan's sister, an aspiring violinist*

Kajetan von Schlaggenberg, *novelist*

Grete Siebenschein, *René Stangeler's girl friend*

René von Stangeler ("the Ensign"), *a brilliant young historian*

Dwight Williams, *an American lepidopterist*

A complete LIST OF CHARACTERS will be found at the end of this volume

Part Two 🏵

CONTINUED

Part Two

CHAPTER

SUDDENLY a Fräulein Agnes Gebaur had got under Jan Herzka's skin. Hitherto he had paid absolutely no attention to her—
and the word "absolutely" is used advisedly, to convey Herzka's
total unawareness of the girl. But at last he saw her, and for the
first time, after he had looked at her some three hundred times,
by fair estimate, for she had been working in the office for a year.
That first act of seeing took place on Monday, May 16, 1927,
shortly after eight o'clock in the morning—in other words, at the
beginning of the week following the table-tennis tea at the
Siebenscheins'. It happened as Jan was striding across the long,
very bright front office to reach the private office of the firm he
headed. In front of it was a smaller room for his secretary. There
was no one sitting there. For a week there had been no one there.
Herzka had been forced to sacrifice Frau Schnabel. The fat
manager of the Graz branch, who like the office attendant Moser
was left over from the era of Herzka's father, had suddenly
suffered a stroke. He had been a rather overbearing old fellow
who preferred doing everything himself. After his unexpected
departure from this world, there had been no one among the staff
capable of taking over the Graz branch of the firm. And so it
had been necessary to sacrifice Frau Schnabel, shortly before her
sixtieth birthday. At least for the present. She herself was not
reluctant to move to Graz, where she had relatives and would
be enjoying a considerably higher salary.

When an employee suddenly gets under the boss's skin, she usually becomes his receptionist—which means a promotion, pecuniary as well as titular.

Agnes Gebaur was informed of her promotion on the morning of May 16. Put another way, the receptionist, object of so long a search and so much study, had suddenly been found in a trice. It was a real discovery.

The first telephone call she took and transmitted to the boss's room was one from a lawyer, Doktor Krautwurst.

At his desk Jan Herzka was still busy with the morning mail; he had fallen into arrears on it because he had needed some time to recover from his initial contemplation of Agnes, and to compose himself again. In which effort he was singularly unsuccessful.

"Krautwurst?" he said on the telephone.

"Yes, Doktor Krautwurst, attorney-at-law."

"Don't know him. Connect me, please."

Agnes Gebaur's voice had a dark resonance (perhaps only to Jan). Dark as her undeniable connection with the day before yesterday, with the conversation at the Siebenscheins', with what those young historians had been saying. . . .

"Herzka," he said to the telephone; and then he listened while the lawyer spoke in a quiet voice, and at some length.

"Permit me, Herr Doktor," Jan said in the friendliest tone, when Krautwurst finished, "permit me to remark that today is May 16, not April 1."

The lawyer revealed no annoyance. Rather, there sounded through the telephone that tranquil, evenly gurgling and dignified laughter which might be called the laughter of colleagues, for that is the way such gentlemen laugh when they are among themselves, discussing a curious case or telling a joke which is no doubt amusing but from which they like to preserve a certain distance.

"So I'm getting a castle?" Herzka said.

"A castle. No castle in air. Assuming that you accept the inheritance—which, by the way, I scarcely doubt, hahaha. When would you be able to do me the honor of calling at my office?"

"Will you be there this afternoon at three, Herr Doktor?"

"For you, at any time."

"All right then—I'll be along."

Grotesquely, Jan suddenly thought of the verses from Schiller's *William Tell:*

> "To Death man swiftly falls a prey;
> No time is granted for delay."

And he involuntarily added:

> "And Life treats us the selfsame way."

But this was getting too silly. His face felt covered with cobwebs or veils, dark red in color; they had been beclouding his mind since early morning.

The mail. Everything seemed polished smooth, perfectly sleek; he skidded and lost his footing on it. It was as though the substance he had to work could not be roughed up, offered no friction to check his thoughts, no holds by which he could flash from one to another, making rapid progress, which was his usual way. Ordinarily many ideas occurred to him, leaped at him when he read his mail; and a good many of these could usually be carried out. For the businessman and the writer a kind of sober but vigorous imagination is necessary. Jan had no such faculty today. As he looked through his mail he always had a large writing pad beside him, to note down his ideas in brief phrases. Today the white paper remained blank. Jan was on the point of calling Fräulein Gebaur in to help him.

He did not do so.

All right, his mother had been a Baroness Neudegg. But how did old Neudegg in Carinthia, who had never bothered about him at all, come to make him heir to his castle? Mama had been only his cousin. A medieval citadel it was, near Toitschach or Foitschach, or whatever the name was (Herzka did not know the region), with tremendous foundations and underground rooms, but otherwise comfortably equipped for modern living, the lawyer had said: baths, electric hot-water heating, electric kitchen, guest rooms, overseer, telephone. What nonsense. How could anybody be named Krautwurst? The whole thing must be a joke.

But Herzka found the name of Dr. Philemon Krautwurst, with the address he had given, in the telephone book.

Nevertheless, all this might be some mediocre joke on the part of friends.

The thing was connected with Fräulein Gebaur: deep down, that was perfectly plain to him. It was connected with her, and equally with everything that had been said Saturday night at the Siebenscheins'.

He pictured Fräulein Gebaur again as he had seen her that morning. As he spoke to her—he had asked her for some data from the files—she had held her arms lightly crossed over her chest, head tilted, as she listened attentively to him. She was probably about thirty, he thought. Her hair was pale as moonstone—and in 1927 that color stood in extreme contrast to the prevailing fashion—and her face had an oddly antique shape. It might have been called a madonna face. A shawl over the head would have suited it well. (As outsiders we can observe that Agnes Gebaur simply represented a Slavic type; but Jan Herzka's mind swiftly transformed the shawl into a black veil, a kind of widow's veil.) Strikingly deep shadows set off her eyes. She kept them lowered, fixed upon the cardboard folders she was removing from their rows in the filing cases. But all that was nothing, and all of it taken together was still nothing. The abrupt, the instantaneous effect of Agnes Gebaur came from the quality of her physical existence; and yet Jan did not even know whether she was really tall or short, fat or thin, strapping or frail. He had not yet come so far. He had instantly looked away from her, in alarm. But there was no doubt in his mind that her body was something supremely unknown, not only something he had never seen, but that had never been seen by others: an indefinite cloudy structure above which her head hovered or floated. . . .

And there was something else underneath him, like the great dark back of a whale, that threatened to carry him off. It was a

crazy unity compounded of this girl, that old castle, and also—
very much also—of the night before last at the Siebenscheins'.
. . . He jumped to his feet and snatched up the telephone on the
desk.

"The mail is done. You can take it all. Connect me with Herr
Köppel, the head bookkeeper."

"At once," Agnes said. The dark voice was far less effective in
its reality. Perhaps that would also prove to be true of the body.
He would have to seize an occasion to look at her, calmly, when
she was not aware of it. Köppel answered. Jan asked him to
come over to the office. He entered in a few moments, slow
and broad of beam. Köppel had full powers-of-attorney; he too
was left over from the old regime of Jan's father. The son's regime, by the way, did not differ in essentials. Jan asked Köppel
bluntly whether he could go away for a few days; something had
unexpectedly arisen. The man produced a calendar from his
pocket, looked it over, reflected. Nothing too important coming
up, he said. Could he draw six thousand from the till, Jan asked
then; it was one o'clock; the bank was already closed. No trouble
about that, the bookkeeper replied. Jan wrote out the receipt.
Then he called in Fräulein Gebaur—while he was under the
protection of Köppel, so to speak. There she stood now. But her
physique remained impenetrable. She was wearing a loose-
fitting dress; moreover it was long, likewise in contrast to the
prevailing fashion. At any rate, she was certainly not slender.
Or at least not small and frail.

"I must leave for a few days," he said. "Transfer all calls to
Herr Köppel, Fräulein Gebaur, and keep track of everything for
me. The mail is to go to Herr Köppel, of course. All right? I
must leave," he repeated. "A matter of an inheritance. That was
the call from the lawyer with the silly name." Agnes smiled with
lowered eyelids; her lashes were very long, and the shadows
under her eyes deep.

The money was brought. Jan shook hands with Köppel and
Agnes, and left.

He went out as though he had just fired himself from his job. On the stairs he could still feel behind him the pressure of his own decision, which he had not even entertained fifteen minutes before, and which, now made, prohibited him from returning to his office that afternoon.

Yesterday had been fearful. Yesterday, Sunday.

Alone, at home.

Those young historians with their tales of witches had produced a shattering effect upon him, a kind of constant explosion, if anything so contradictory is conceivable.

All that without the addition of Agnes Gebaur.

But now! Now it was all coming down on him at once.

And now the blast was working backwards, into his own past: to his onetime amour, Magdalena Güllich. It was drawing fuel from her.

The weather was dreary. It weighed on his head like a hat pulled down low over the forehead. It had rained, or perhaps was still raining (but delicately, like spray from a child's watering-can). In this dampness and warmth a sense of steamy, sticky captivity arose. Nevertheless, Jan felt very well physically, his body charged with strength. He settled his shoulders under his coat. The feeling of being in possession of his own body, of a springy gait, of pleasure in motor and muscular processes, all that was bursting out of him into this sultry, imprisoning environment. This hothouse. There was a hothouse inside him also. It was trying to shut itself off again; yes, that was what it was really trying to do; it wanted to see and hear nothing around him, to concentrate on the vision of the woman. Agnes. Now the torturers had shut themselves into the room with her. They led Agnes toward the rear, into the dimly lit recesses of the chamber, and there began to undress her. The long black gown fell to the ground, and then the veil. The linen she wore underneath gleamed like the white down of a swan's breast.

He ought really to have shot up into the air like a skyrocket going off. But he walked quietly on.

The thing had fallen upon him. What he needed was perspective. To Death man swiftly falls a prey.

Swiftly. Overnight. Actually, from night before last to today. That damned fellow Stangeler!

A combination stirred in his mind. . . . Forget about that! Still and all, it might be worth sounding him out.

Restaurant. Savage hunger; weak in the knees. Then a quick stop at the café; look through newspapers; only the financial section really. The commodities exchange. Hemp. Especially jute. A vital raw material to the Herzka firm. For they sold belts, belting, webbing, Venetian-blind cords. Including those made by —it is obvious: we mean, of course, Leonhard Kakabsa's place of work.

Nothing much was happening in this market at the time. The big upswing came later, around 1930 or 1931, when in any case everything was happening, to put it mildly. Now, however, these affairs went their way quietly, with only unimportant fluctuations.

Magdalena Güllich . . . That had not been here. Not in this city. What luck! There was no spot here he had to avoid, no district to keep away from, no living grave. No, a distant metropolis, far to the west. Her home: 16 Boulevard Népalek. But it had not happened there; elsewhere. He had literally attacked her. Well, that was five years ago now. Shortly after his father's death, it had been; the old boy had sent him there to take over the firm's branch, partly because of his excellent knowledge of French. Moser, the office attendant, had come along with him; oddly enough, he also knew French well. Was the son of a minor official in the Imperial Court. Yes, she had lived at 16 Boulevard Népalek. The house would certainly still be standing—in fact she must be living there still. Certainly. He ought to have married her. He could have trained her to comply with his desires. But the way he had done it! What stupidity! After that it had been all over—for good.

No damned Stangeler at that time.

But instead an old book. He still owned it.

He had spent the day before, Sunday, with this book.

That time, too, circumstances had come down upon him like a closing trap door. In the afternoon he had come across the book. That same evening he had gone to the circus with Magdalena Güllich. The trained white mares. One of them was named Halka. Like the Polish national opera. It had happened after the circus. He had bustled her off to some hotel of assignation, right near the circus. Then a plain and brutal mistreatment of the girl which wasn't at all what he had meant or wanted. But she had not understood. He ought to have shown her the book.

Marry Agnes Gebaur.

Now the lid of the trap door smashed down upon his head. Time to be off! To the lawyer. Quarter to three.

Doktor Krautwurst was a smooth-shaven, bespectacled, prudent, and prolix catastrophe who performed his work of wreckage with the greatest complacency. For him, naturally, the business came down to the proper handling of technicalities, such as a statement by Herzka that he accepted the inheritance, and other formalities of that sort. All in all it appeared that there could be no question of immediate transfer of the inherited property; only the preliminaries for that transfer could be cleared out of the way right at the moment. But since Herr von Neudegg's will had not been contested and there seemed to be no other heirs besides Herzka—at least no one had put in an appearance—the legal steps would be simple and would not take too long. Doktor Krautwurst therefore thought that Herzka might as well inspect the property which was virtually certain to be his. Wasn't he the least bit curious? A castle was nothing to sneeze at. Moreover, one in perfectly livable condition. The old baron had invested a great deal in it.

It turned out that the lawyer himself had already gone down to the castle twice, immediately after the baron's death, to see to things; this was an obligation he had gladly assumed toward the testator, who had moreover been a friend of his, when they drew up the will together; all the more an obligation since he was also functioning as executor of the will. The will, he informed Herzka by the way, was of very recent date: March 2, 1927.

And so on. And this and that. Of course the lawyer was interested in altogether other matters than Jan Herzka, at least at the moment.

"I'll go. This very evening. I want to see the castle," Jan said.

Doktor Krautwurst was somewhat overcome by this sudden resolve and the rush to depart. "Why . . . ?" he said.

Herzka thought it wise to put the matter in a more sedate light. "You see, it's this way," he added. "During the next few weeks and months I shall probably not have a chance to get away; all sorts of things are coming up at the office. I have an important appointment, for example, three days from now. If I want to see the castle I'll have to do it at once; that is, leave tonight."

Krautwurst seemed reassured.

"In that case you would take the night express to Villach. You change there and are on the spot in the morning. But I'll telephone to let them know of your arrival. The overseer is a pleasant chap. He runs the place beautifully. He'll meet you at the station in the car. I'll put the call through right away. But first let us go over the schedule once again."

He was a lively and obliging person, Doktor Krautwurst.

Immediately after he had placed the call, however, he abruptly became solemn.

"Finally, here is one thing more, Herr Herzka. A letter from the old baron to you. Would you have the kindness to sign this receipt for it?" He handed Herzka a statement typewritten in advance. "Of course there is no need for you to open the letter right here and read it. But I should be obliged to you if you would care to do so, since this letter—whose contents are unknown to me—might contain information of significance to the winding up of the affairs of the inheritance. However, it is of course entirely up to you whether you wish to give me any data in your interest that the letter contains, or not."

The lawyer gave Herzka a perfectly ordinary, cheap business envelope without any imprint. Written with a soft pen, in large, rounded, spreading, and extremely flowing letters, were the words: "To Herr Jan Herzka, Vienna, to be delivered after my decease by Doktor Philemon Krautwurst."

Inside the envelope was a sheet of foolscap largely covered with that big flowing hand. The writing was no smaller than that on the outside of the envelope—most people write an address larger than the body of a letter. The letter was headed by the same text as the outside of the envelope. Immediately below the letter began; the legible writing could be read without the slightest effort.

My dear boy,

Everything goes to you. Don't worry about details. Krautwurst will take care of it all; splendid fellow. I'm alone; there's no one left. Just as well. They were all a pack of idlers, rascals, and cheats. Your mother was a Neudegg; my cousin. Didn't like me, by the way; we scarcely saw each other after her marriage. You're a decent, hard-working boy; you've carried on your father's business properly. And you're financially in a position to keep a property like Neudegg. I know all about you. Have made inquiries. What makes me hit on you? S. A. Slobedeff (really Alexander Alexandrovich S., but he always called himself Sasha) was here to see me last year. Great man, but you know that. Played for me on the organ in the chapel here. Genius. Told me about you. He met you four years ago; gather you made a kind of general confession to him. Well, I don't have to tell you anything about that. My wishes are these: leave everything unchanged. Keep the servants, too. The tenant-farmers are decent fellows. I'd appreciate your leaving my writing room unchanged, too. Sit down in it now and then. Think that old Neudegger used to sit here. One more thing. When you come here, sometime, take along a person who knows about old books, especially manuscripts, Middle Ages and the like. There's a remarkable library in the place. Get some such person to explain it to you; you need only ask at the University—they'll recommend someone. You wouldn't even be able to read the stuff by yourself. No one has ever had a chance to examine the manuscripts. While you're here you'll of course look at the vaults also, and the tower, and what is behind the heavy old foundation wall too, the place where you get the best view of what is left of the old moat. Don't crawl around there too much, even though everything's been ventilated and electric light installed. You'll understand better what I mean later on. A sum for an annual requiem on the anniversary of my death has been deposited with the church; permanent foundation. When you happen to be here you'll attend, hear the Mass, pray for me, won't you? All right. Enjoy your inheritance, live a healthy life, marry. Heaven protect you.

Ash Wednesday 1927

Achaz Neudegger

While Jan carefully reread the last part of the letter, the lawyer was talking over the telephone with Carinthia. When he was finished Herzka handed him the letter. Doktor Krautwurst read it through and then said: "Same date as the last will and testament. In agreement in other respects, also—that about the servants—there are five of them, and they're needed in such a big place—is even set forth in the will, as you have no doubt noticed."

Doktor Krautwurst made no comment on the second part of the letter.

With astonishment Herzka realized that a distinct worsening of his condition had taken place in the last half or full hour. He had not felt the fresh wound as so painful. In other words, while his head was still throbbing from being bashed by that trap door, Jan had been more himself than he was at this moment. But ever since he had arrived here, something had been cramping and tightening inside him; a whole set of gears seemed to be overheated, and at the same time he was eager to preserve this condition, did not want to let it escape him; it was a kind of pleasant fever; yet simultaneously he felt as if he had jumped the rails and were drifting at random off the track.

"Then that would be about all," he said.

"Yes," Doktor Krautwurst replied, handing him a slip of paper on which he had written the departure time of the night express.

"Would you mind telling me one thing more, Herr Doktor?" Jan said. "When exactly did the baron die?"

"On March 23. Most old people die in the spring or fall."

"Yes. To Death man swiftly falls a prey. Would you mind if I used your telephone for a moment?"

"Why, certainly, Herr Herzka, go right ahead," Krautwurst said. "Here is the telephone book. Would you excuse me for a moment?" He tactfully left the room on the pretense of busy haste.

Herzka looked in the telephone book: Im . . . Installation . . . there: Institute for . . . for Austrian Economic Studies. . . . How many Institutes there were! Wasn't the Institute for Austrian Historical Studies in the telephone book? Or was he, in his haste, passing it by? Wait! Old Achaz had mentioned the University. Universal Construction Corp. . . . Universal Transport . . . University! Buildings Administration . . . Dean of the Philosophical Faculty . . . Library . . . Concierge . . . that would be it. . . . "Hello, can you connect me with the Institute for Historical Studies?" . . . "Extension A 25–4–30." . . . "Institute for Austrian Historical Studies, Library Attendant Pleban speaking."

The voice sounded easygoing.

Herzka was holding the mouthpiece very awkwardly. He brought his other hand to his aid, straightened the thing out. His hands, too, seemed to have slid off the rails. As had happened that time with Magdalena Güllich. Then he had "confessed" to Slobedeff. . . .

"Please, is Herr Doktor René Stangeler there by any chance?"

"Yes, sir. I'll fetch him at once, sir."

"Herr von Stangeler," Herzka said after René had answered

the phone, "this is Jan Herzka. You remember, we met the night before last at the Siebenscheins'. I have a matter I should like urgently to discuss with you. Would it be possible for me to meet you somewhere in about twenty minutes—perhaps it would be best if I came to the University?"

Very well. In twenty minutes in the arcade court.

The car. He suddenly recalled that he had a car. How odd. Stangeler would have to go home to prepare for the trip. Splendid. Then they would dine together. . . . Think of the arrangements. Agnes . . .

With a start, such as one sometimes feels when half asleep, he fell into a deeper substory of his interior, and observed in it— while for a second a vacuum of fright lingered in the pit of his stomach—that the torturers had continued their procedure (all this time, while he had been with the lawyer!). Agnes stood turned away and bent over. She was half naked.

"Johann Herzka and Company."

The reality of the dark voice rescued him from the vision which had imposed itself upon him in an overpowering, an altogether brutal manner. He ordered the car to be waiting for him in front of the ramp of the University, and laid down the receiver. Simultaneously it occurred to him that he could have had the car come for him here. Well, there was time enough. He could walk the short distance. It would help give him perspective. . . .

The lawyer returned. "Finished telephoning?"

"Yes, everything is fine," Jan said.

"There was one thing more I wanted to say," Doktor Krautwurst remarked. "The decease of a certain person has relieved us of a complication, in fact of a considerable lien on the inheritance. Around the middle of February the testator's daughter died in Switzerland, a childless widow. She had been the wife of a French count. Old Achaz did not care much for her. He said so quite frankly. Still, we would have had to set aside at least the legal portion for her; in practice she would have been co-owner of Castle Neudegg. I believe that her death was the direct cause of the old baron's sending for me and making out a new will.

Just in time, as it turned out. Apparently the passage at the beginning of the letter to you, Herr Herzka, in which he says: 'I am alone, there is no one left,' or something of the sort, refers to the baroness's death. The result is that the only burden upon you, as the heir, is the legacy I showed you in the will."

"Yes," Herzka said. He shook hands with the lawyer.

"Do let me know, when you get back, how things struck you down there. And once again, my congratulations!"

"Thank you very much. Yes, I'll certainly let you know, Herr Doktor. Good-by."

To Death man swiftly falls a prey. All that was silly nonsense. Jan walked along the Schotten Ring. The pavement had dried. Four o'clock. On his right the sun broke through the clouds. Agnes was now naked except for a loincloth. The devil take Stangeler. With the appearance of Slobedeff in this whole affair, everything became deadly serious.

But the very fact that Slobedeff appeared was proof that he had not jumped the rails at all; that he was by no means traveling along some remote branch line or siding of life. Rather, this express train had been racing along the main line ever since this morning, or rather since Saturday night. Only he had not noticed the track for a long time. And concerning this very point Sasha Alexandrovich had been in error—after Herzka had "confessed" to him, as old Achaz called it, on the day after the disaster with Magdalena Güllich. "That sort of thing, Jan, will lead to no good. You'll go through hell. You'll see red, be always reeling and falling. . . ." Not at all. No hell, no reeling, no falling. Everything swallowed up, blown away. For five whole years. He had completely forgotten the whole incident; nothing around him tended to bring such things to mind. And now, along with all the rest, Slobedeff came back. What to do? The torturers would not be stopped. Now they were taunting the patient woman, leading her to a broken column in the middle of the chamber, and tying her to it by the wrists. The widow Agnes. The chaste Agnes.

Sasha was terribly present now. On the following day he had conducted a symphony in the royal concert hall. Herzka, who did not often go to concerts, had attended.

After the disaster with Magdalena there had been a night full of rows and brawls and other excitements such as Jan had never before been involved in. These had finally come to an end far on the outskirts of the town, by the river. He had jumped aboard a freight train slowly toiling uphill (with the sole thought of getting away, getting away from the region where the thing with Magdalena had happened). And jumping off the train again, he had nearly landed on Slobedeff's back. The composer was resting from his labors at this little village on the outskirts of the city, and thus, sunning himself on the railroad embankment in the morning, had made the sudden but very thorough acquaintanceship with Jan Herzka.

In the torture chamber they seemed to have called it a day. Nothing more to be seen there. That was a relief. The sun came from the right, very strong now. Across the street was the University.

The cool hall with the high smooth shafts of the columns. Stangeler, without a hat, having just come directly from his desk, sauntered up from the rear of the hall as Herzka entered the arcaded corridor that René had appointed for their meeting place.

"Herr von Stangeler," Jan said as they walked slowly along side by side, "I need your professional services. Unfortunately this matter has come up rather suddenly. Do you have anything urgent planned for tonight, tomorrow, and the day after? For I wish you to leave on a trip with me this evening, around ten o'clock. At my expense, of course. To recompense you for your trouble and the interruption of your studies, I should like to offer you fifteen hundred schillings as an advance payment. More, of course, if the affair should call for more work on your part, which I am almost certain it will."

After this preamble—René had replied that he had no pressing obligations—Herzka explained what the matter was about. He did not come to the real point; he spoke of looking over the old castle which had come to him as an unexpected inheritance, and in particular of a preliminary survey of a library—"a collection of medieval books and documents" was the way he put it.

"Neudegg," Stangeler said, and stood still. "Yes, we know that one. I'll go upstairs later and look it up. So then—manuscripts, you say, Herr Herzka? Are there archives there? I've never heard of any."

"I gather the things are in the library."

When he was in a good mood Stangeler could be obliging, modest, and completely at his ease. Anyone who knew him well would have noticed from far off that he was in such a good state of mind today; it was evident in the way he entered the arcades, the way his hair was combed, his whole casual manner. . . . Jan Herzka did not know Stangeler well; there was no reason for him to, for they had met for the first time the Saturday before. Thus he was unaware of the fact that in favorable circumstances René was capable of manifesting virtues which he ordinarily lacked completely: among these were prudence and presence of mind. Herzka, who was after all a businessman, therefore took the conditions that Stangeler promptly made quite as a matter of course, without thinking René especially clever for having posed them. They were in the ordinary line of commercial prudence. But for a person of Stangeler's character (as anyone who is like that knows well!) they represented a considerable achievement. Stangeler replied that he was ready to accept the work, at the terms offered, but only if he were given a guarantee in writing that the rights of publication for all the Neudegg manuscripts were his alone; likewise scholarly exploitation of the examination of the castle; furthermore, that no one else would be drawn into the consultation as long as Stangeler was occupied with the material. At least, he would have to be given one month's notice if another specialist were to be consulted.

"Agreed," Herzka said; he was pleased, for these reservations gave him the impression that he was dealing with a thoroughly substantial person (and so he was; everything about René Stangeler was substantial when he was in a good mood). "I'm delighted that you will take this on—because of your special knowledge of certain questions. And I see no need for a second specialist."

At this point, however, his lordship René proved stupid, in spite of his excellent state of mind. He did not realize what Herzka was referring to. The subject of Saturday night's discussion did not occur to him.

They had been walking slowly around the entire courtyard, whose quiet was broken only now and then by echoing noises from the stairs, while the lawn in the center remained peaceful as a pond. Meanwhile, however, the whole affair began to give Jan Herzka great trouble again, in spite of his interlocutor's obligingness, willingness, and matter-of-factness. He had landed here like a missile. But the force of the shot had passed, and the aura of this building was dampening. The cryptlike chamber within him seemed dead. Agnes had melted away—as witches are sometimes said to do. Jan felt like a cracked nut. He wanted to close around the sweet kernel again. But there was no kernel. It lay beside the shell like a parched, tasteless core. What remained now was money and property. What remained of this precipitate visit to the University was a justification: old Herr von Neudegg had recommended such a step. After all, it was necessary to determine the value of these old books and manuscripts, the money value, or at least the scholarly value; and it could do no harm to undertake this step at once. And in general to inspect his inheritance. To show himself there. To manifest interest. To see to rights. If it were not done at once—who knows what affairs might not come up to interfere? The business was worth some speedy action. A castle is nothing to sneeze at. Where was Agnes?

The whole thing now—it was as if he were really hearing Agnes Gebaur's voice.

"Herr von Stangeler," he said, and it was difficult to speak

against the waves of languor, "would you have the kindness to
come out in front of the building with me? I'd like to point out
my car. So that the chauffeur will know you. It must be here by
now. . . ."

"It ought to have been here before me," Herzka thought, suddenly taken aback. "Did I really fail to see it?"

"I shall be driven home to Döbling now. In half an hour the
car will be back, and is then at your disposal. You will have to go
home, after all, to get ready for the trip. Where do you live, Herr
Doktor?"

"In the third district."

"Well," Herzka said, "that is quite a distance."

Stangeler was the soul of prudence today. He did not decline
the offer of the car.

"May I expect you for dinner at eight o'clock?" Herzka asked.
"With the car, it's nothing to drive out to Döbling. This should
leave you a decent time for your preparations. It is now only
half-past four."

"Many thanks. On the way out to Döbling I'd like to be run
over to Althan Platz, to Fräulein Siebenschein, my fiancée,"
René said. "To let her know I'm leaving and to say good-by.
Would that be all right?"

This again was solid, correct, substantial. Thoroughly winning.

"That goes without saying, Herr von Stangeler," Jan said. "You
have only to tell the chauffeur where you wish to go."

They descended the stairs outside. The chauffeur, seeing his
employer coming out of the building, started the motor, intending to pull up toward him. But Herzka signed to him to stay
where he was.

"When did you come, Franz?" he asked.

"A few minutes before you went up the big staircase, sir,"
the chauffeur replied; he had got out and was holding the door
open. He was a middle-aged man. His strong workman's hand
with a wedding ring rested on the nickeled door-handle.

"You'll take me home now," Herzka said. "And then be back

here to wait for this gentleman. Herr von Stangeler will need
you until this evening. At eight you will be bringing him out to
the house."

Stangeler had by now drawn the connection between the talk
they had had on Saturday—after all, Jan Herzka's intense interest had not been lost on him—and the impending journey.

He walked slowly back through the arcades, drew the tinkling
bunch of keys from his trousers pocket, and ascended the stairs
at a somewhat faster pace. The broad corridors were deserted.
He pressed the latch of the door, which sprang open with a noise
that, in a sense, he had heard too often. Each time a drop of
discontent fell, and there had been so many of these that they
had already hollowed out the shallow trough of habit. René had
been working in the library corridor ever since he had completed
the three-year course and passed the big examination with fairly
good results. The main room was frequented by those who still
had the examination before them. The next examination had
been set for the summer of the following year, 1928. Consequently the nervous tensions in that room were still moderate,
discussions were often begun, and there was a good deal of
studying together. But here where René was, all was quiet. The
smell of the oiled floor also tended to produce nausea; the smell
had long since found a specific spot in René's interior and infal-
libly generated a certain repulsion. Life consumes. Steady dropping wears away the stone.

A second outsider met him in the deserted corridor: Doktor
Neuberg.

They greeted each other cordially.

"Have you anything yet?" Neuberg asked.

"Yes," Stangeler said candidly, "from the fall on. A real stinker
of a job. In the administrative library of the Federal Chancellery."

The University obtained posts for its graduates. But often
that meant years of waiting.

"There still isn't a thing for me."

For a moment a touch of despair flickered across his broad open face, and anger leaped forward like a spark from a damaged spot in an electric wire.

"Everything comes in time," Stangeler said affably. "What good is it anyhow? Your days of freedom are over, and you can't possibly live on the salary. Of course my father always says that the thing is to get on board and the rest will take care of itself."

"Your father is probably right there. But what do you do if you can't even get on board?"

"It strikes me that the two of us have as much place in business as a hedgehog in a salad bowl."

A friendly spark flashed from Neuberg's eyes. "Right again, I imagine," he said. They shook hands and went to their desks.

Well then, put away the Merovingian documents for today. First look up the castle. René carefully jotted down the data he found. There was not a word about archives. The article on Neudegg stressed the citadel aspect: here was a prime example of a castle on a height whose original defenses could still be recognized. One distinctive feature was that Neudegg had been in the possession of the same family since the fourteenth century. That was all. René took his magnifying glass from the drawer. Then Capelli's dictionary of abbreviations. The book was René's own; he was free to take it away. He put glass and book into his briefcase. "Though what good will Capelli do me?" he thought. "There will be mostly things from the fifteenth century, if there's anything medieval at all. And by that time they are all making whatever abbreviations come into their heads. Still, Grotefend will have to go along too, on account of the chronological stuff, the datings. . . ."

The library attendant Pleban came in. "Going already, Herr Doktor?"

Stangeler showed the contents of his briefcase, as prescribed by the regulations. "Two books of my own."

"Thank you, thank you, Herr Doktor."

The door shut behind him; he crossed the corridor, went down into the arcades; he began to feel a sense of release. Now, too, he thought of the tidy sum awaiting him. The money suddenly rose like a lid over his head, and he crawled out of the box, stretched his back, and slipped into a larger, roomier, and more suitable cubicle; all this, moreover, took place in his mind as he stepped outside onto the stairs and saw the car waiting down below.

The chauffeur opened the door and saluted. René climbed in at the rear, briefcase in hand. The car leaped gently forward, and began to cover long stretches of the Ring Strasse with its smooth motion, the wind it created generating something like coolness.

The sudden impetus that life had unexpectedly given to René was appropriately expressed by the rapidity of his present movement. Like an arrow from heaven, a tangible sense of well-being descended upon him: it literally struck him from outside, penetrated him. Now they had already reached the avenues and streets in the vicinity of his parental home. The thought of driving up to the house in this big car suddenly startled him. Like a rich son; one who had amounted to something.

He bestowed a good tip on the chauffeur Franz, so that he might refresh himself somewhere in the neighborhood; there was time enough for that. It was half-past five. René went up to the third floor. First he called up Grete Siebenschein. She herself answered the telephone: in a bright mood, and her voice was very warm. "Yes, yes, come right over, I'll wait for you."

Ever since Saturday she had been happier. Körger's maliciously conceived table-tennis party had had a result radically different from that intended by Körger himself and the other impresarios of that glorious farce: namely, to demonstrate "the untenability of the situation." Moreover, Grete was beginning, quietly and after many a revolt, to submit of her own accord to the laws of her love. From the party she had drawn the conclusion that everything would go well, if only she wished it so. And undoubtedly that conclusion was, within limits, justified by the event.

Above all, however: that evening, and in the course of the discussion of the witch trials, she had been defeated by René in a way in which she wished to be defeated.

The questionable victor now reached his own room.

A window stood open.

In the treetops of a wide adjacent courtyard innumerable sparrows were producing a piercing, jangled evensong which lingered in the ear like one powerful single note.

René washed up with care and dressed in a somewhat rustic sporting mode. He packed a suitcase with everything he would need for overnight, then added the two books, the magnifying glass, and a clean notebook. His jottings on Neudegg were thrust into his briefcase, his fountain pen filled, his mechanical pencil seen to. . . . At last. He found it difficult to leave his room to-day; every moment there seemed something new to do. He sat down and surveyed his situation. There could be no doubt that Herzka was under some serious emotional stress. There were therefore reasons, beyond those stated, for his having offered so high a fee. René closed his eyes. What did the man really want? An assessment, an inventory? "I'm not an appraiser," René thought. What was awaiting him?

It was time to be going to Grete. Also he would have to drop in on his parents on the second floor for a moment. Open the box, close the box, pop in, pop out. He took up his suitcase, hat and coat.

Once there had been a spiraling central staircase in the house. But it had been blocked off by the new inhabitants of the second floor. René had to go outside and around.

The doorbell rang.

A red-cheeked country girl opened it.

René entered his parents' apartment.

With eyes clear of their veil for just a few seconds, while his little mother joyously came forward to him, René noted his father's remarkable handsomeness: the strong clear forehead; the fiery dark eyes. It had been years since the old man could rise from his armchair and walk without aid. His joints were stiff; his hands and fingers too. The hands, finely shaped and with the fingers stretched straight out, rested on the crook of a cane that Herr von Stangeler held between his knees.

The maid brought a tray with coffee for the young Herr Doktor. It was very welcome to René; he felt, in fact, that this was exactly what he needed at the moment. His own state remained incomprehensible to him, as if tremendous exertions lay behind him. Had Herzka put such a strain on him? At the same time the exertion seemed to have purified him; he saw things with less distortion. Everything could turn out well, if you were so disposed. Even "box visits." If you only wanted it that way. In spite of the perpetual rattle of latches or the smell of oiled floors. Why offend the boxes, why rummage angrily around in them? They lay on the ground, half buried in mud, helpless and innocent. They rattled their lids, these mussels; after all, they had to have their water for breathing. It passed through them. . . . Grete would come forward to meet him in the vestibule. The thing was to know how to carry off these "box visits."

He said what there was to say. Since his own words now disturbed him—their resonance and content blocked his new view of things—he made the story very brief and matter-of-fact. The modesty with which he spoke was not deliberate; it emerged accidentally as a sham virtue from his desire to say as little as possible.

His father had sat up in the chair with obvious benevolence, and was now leaning forward slightly, hands on the crook of the cane. He listened very closely. René's mother, sitting at table with her son, seemed overjoyed that something new and stimulating had taken place.

"Quite right," the old gentleman said. "You must enter practice, so to speak. That would be old Johann Herzka's son. I remember, he took the boy right into the business. Decent and substantial people. Now an indiscreet question: is the fellow paying you?"

"Yes."

"What are you getting for this consultation?"

"He has offered me 1500 schillings for the present."

"What does that mean: for the present?"

"He says that if more work should be involved, he will pay still more."

"Fifteen hundred schillings? How do you happen to know young Herzka?"

Now the name of Siebenschein would have to be placed "in the box." Which meant stirring up the box. The thing was to break away cleanly at this point, without clouding the respiratory waters. . . . Not that René wanted to deny anyone or anything; nor was it necessary to deny what his parents had long known about. But striking that particular key at the present moment would introduce an awkward and altogether needless complication.

He replied: "Herzka came to see me this afternoon. I hardly do know him. He once heard me talking in company about medieval matters."

"He certainly must have inquired about your qualifications. So high a fee is not paid to anyone who chances to come along."

The old gentleman nodded his approval.

René sensed that he had caught himself. But he decided to remain quietly in the noose, not to struggle and draw it even closer. Moreover, his mother also spoke in tones of great encouragement and delight. The affair stood in the altogether false light of professional success and there was nothing to be done about it. Simply impossible now to say anything to the point about Herzka. The thing to do was to conclude, leave.

"I don't understand the size of the payment," René said. "If I were through with my studies, or an authority of any kind, it would make sense. But as it is . . ."

"Take it and don't worry about it, my son," the old gentleman said. "If you receive 1500 schillings for looking through a collection of old books or manuscripts, all is well and good."

The leave-taking was hearty and warm.

Open the lid.

Suitcase in hand and coat over his arm, René went down the stairs.

The car was waiting again. "Number 6 Althan Platz, opposite the Franz Josef Railroad Station," Stangeler said as he got in.

Again the rapidity of movement. It was twenty-five minutes after six. The sky had been rent open, the clouds scattered; it was fair weather. During the ride René smoked greedily. All this had been strenuous—above all the changing boxes.

With Grete, the strategy was different from the start. "Do you remember how Jan Herzka was so keenly interested in witch trials the other night?"

"Yes, of course. Incidentally, you spoke wonderfully."

Now, as he told her about the impending journey to Carinthia, René again recalled Herzka's manner during their conversation under the arcades, and returned to his initial idea that this façade of Herzka's had not been altogether normal. In retrospect there was something uncanny about it. And nevertheless he had seen the like before. Nevertheless! Somewhere . . .

He lost the thread. For Grete—who was also struck by the size of the fee—was saying gaily: "Really, you know, it's all nonsense. What makes him so certain that down there, in that library or somewhere in the castle, you're going to find something connected with witch trials . . . ?"

"I think it's this way," René said, slowly pacing back and forth in front of the sofa on which Grete sat. "Some kind of fixed connection has been established in his mind between the talk the other night and the castle he inherited today. Perhaps there are other elements involved which I don't know anything about. Which perhaps he doesn't know about. But he can no longer keep these things apart. A kind of rut has formed, and he is stuck in it. And so there has to be something there, as far as he's concerned. . . ."

He broke off. The idea he had been on the track of was trying to return now. But still indefinable. Not to be put into words. Doktor Körger, Geyrenhoff's nephew, came to his mind. . . . And Schlaggenberg, too, with his discourse on fat females. Körger's expression had been somehow related to Jan Herzka's. . . . The thing remained tormentingly vague.

But here now, this box visit . . . Why offend the boxes, cloud their respiratory waters?—they needed the water. He halted his pacing.

They heard the front door close.

"The folks have just gone out."

He dropped down beside her. As he opened her blouse, he heard a clear attack on the piano on the floor above.

"That's Mary," Grete said, smiling. "She's playing again. To-morrow she and Trix are going to Semmering."

Lid open, out of the box. In good time, well-satisfied and once again freshly washed and brushed. Down the stairs with coat, hat, and suitcase. The car in front of the door. Departure at seven-forty. A swing to the left, past the railroad station.

Off to adventure.

A good farewell. More than that: deep and intimate. A barrier had fallen away. Only now did this become apparent to René, now as the car roared on straight ahead. Grete's conciliatory temperament—ordinarily merely a bird's vain fluttering against a windowpane, against an invisible wall—had finally reached him. The crystalline wall of his reservations, the wall parting two worlds and realities, had been penetrated. It had dissolved. Not that the fluttering had banished it. Rather, it had vanished because of a new clarity which was on the verge of exposing the common denominator among Körger's views, Schlaggenberg's rigid look as he listened to them, this same Kajetan's propaganda for fat females, and Herzka's inflamed sphere of interests. These were "ruts which absolutely must terminate in something sub-stantial"—such was René's clumsy but vivid way of putting things.

"And will terminate in something substantial," he added. It briefly occurred to him that actually it was not so preposterous to expect that Castle Neudegg might contain information of the sort Herzka meant. It would be a kind of test case. A highly significant test at that. . . .

At this point the finely sharpened point of his thinking, which had been pointing in one specific direction, broke off. The car was hurtling uphill. Spacious gardens to left and right dominated the receding sides of the road. What a neighborhood! Here was the place to live! Façades of big villas, set far back from the street behind stretches of lawn, terraced; vestibules, resplendently white. Off to adventure. Perhaps this adventure would lead away from all the present, past all the dreariness. He only had to hold his own.

And right now René was really in an excellent state of mind.

To Death man swiftly falls a prey. When Herzka reached home, the almost total vacancy which had oppressed him during the ride out to his suburb began to assume frightful forms. He was hit hardest as he passed through his garden.

The house was new and small; Jan's father had built it after his wife's death, when he withdrew from his larger house and a more active social life. By that time the son was already in the firm. When people build anew, they usually do so at a riper age; and then they make things comfortable, for they are acquainted with their own needs. Thus the distinctly modern house, in which Johann Herzka had spent his last years alone with his only son, provided all the little things that make life more effortless, the small comforts which are always more palpable and important than the large ones, which are directed toward the outside world, existing more for the guest than for the owner.

The house, set in the midst of a sunny flat garden, scarcely harbored guests nowadays. Herzka gave no parties. In this respect a bachelor has few obligations.

Jan told the servant that he was expecting a gentleman for dinner at eight: Doktor René von Stangeler. He spoke the name slowly, so that the servant would not miss it.

"Tea in the library," Jan said. "Also, I am going on a trip this evening. Pack a small suitcase for three days."

He went up to change.

Agnes, then, had vanished for the time being.

Which meant that the trip no longer had a point. For all the rest was sheer pretext. Jan already understood that. Damn Stangeler.

Since Agnes had disappeared, he had to get back to where he had been before she suddenly emerged. In fact, back to before Saturday night.

It was impossible. An irresistible sleepiness overwhelmed him as soon as he tried. Sitting over the tea he had ordered, he dozed off for a few minutes. With a single numbing blow the strain he had been enduring caught up with him.

The room in which the man now sat in front of the tea table, sagging and asleep, was distinctly impersonal. It scarcely merited the name of "library." There were two glass-enclosed bookcases, but with few books visible; if any were there, they were pushed far back from the glass. At any rate, they lent no character to the room, provided no aura. The presence of books is ordinarily an assemblage of many silent persons who have their backs turned upon us, but are willing to turn to us.

There was a desk, and a number of chairs, all upholstered in light olive-green, even the leather armchairs, although these had darkened somewhat; the prevailing color was the same as that of the paneled anteroom of Stangeler's parents. This struck René when he came later. A large window looked out on the lawn.

The sun, breaking through the clouds, was now addressing itself to that lawn.

The lawn replied with an intense glow.

A bird piped two idiomatic and artful cadences. Then it fell silent. The sunlight reached through a corner of the window.

Herzka slumped motionless, a thing among other lifeless objects.

The sweetest slumber is involuntary. As though he had passed through a lovely and invigorating valley, Jan awakened now with that unmarked freedom of the will that only the very first moments of wakefulness confer upon us, as though it is a gift of sleep alone. Now, as he sat, still half dreaming, a narrow crack opened between him and the dreamlike confinement that his waking life had been this day. Through the crack he could envision possible escape from that confinement by a slight, ever so delicate twist. (So that, to couch it in Stangeler's phrase, the rut need not terminate in anything at all.)

Around his waist there was a slight tension, perhaps from his fashionably cut trousers. He was not exactly sitting comfortably, and had not altered his position since awakening.

It was tangible, the way the white linen of the loincloth (or whatever it was, perhaps her undermost petticoat, bunched up and knotted) lay about her curving hips. It was tangible, the way the cloth was impregnated with the warm vapors of the otherwise naked body.

She was back.

He had called her.

Only now did he really recognize her again: his Agnes, Agnes Gebaur, the virtuous widow. Virtuous? Widow? Virtuous! Widow? He had called her forth from the book. This book was tucked away far to the back of one of the bookcases, and it was not at all intended in the way Jan Herzka took it. During the seventeenth century a well-known group of Jesuits had engaged in the collection and critical examination of source materials for the biographies of saints. They had produced a monumental treatise in many volumes, including documents of the trials of all the martyrs—far more of such documents have come down from Roman antiquity than might be imagined. The collectors and students of this material are called Bollandists, after their founder, Bolland. Condensed editions were later put out for devotional purposes, often in one or two small folio volumes, and of course illustrated with woodcuts or copper engravings. These later editions are valuable—and not especially so—only to rare-book dealers. One of them was in Jan's possession. It was incomplete, for he had only the second volume; the first was missing. The oddity about this work was that it was not divided chronologically or according to the church calendar, but into male and female martyrs and saints. The second volume dealt with the women.

One of the engravings was indubitably a picture of Agnes Gebaur. Jan—his mind's eye suddenly wide open—now felt absolutely convinced of this. He had spent the previous Sunday over this book which had once had the power to bring about the disaster with Magdalena Güllich within a few short hours. Entering the secondhand book dealer's late one afternoon—to choose a gift for Magdalena, who liked books but had no literary inclinations whatsoever—he had been offered this volume by the bookseller; as a single volume of a set, it was an item hard to get rid of.

The rest is history. Three days later the books—both the *Passional* and a small volume bound in tobacco-brown leather stamped with golden flowers—came back in the mail without an accompanying word. He had presented the little book to Magdalena when he called for her at her home to take her to the circus, but had left the big book lying there, wrapped up.

Now that something resembling a reality was appearing at the terminus of the Sunday rut, it snapped him out of his chair as if an outside force were being exerted upon him. But he also experienced a violent and novel reaction. He went to his desk instead of the bookcase, uncovered a small portable typewriter, sat down, rolled in the paper, and began calmly and collectedly drawing up the agreement René Stangeler had demanded, with each point neatly stipulated.

As he was finishing he noticed the dusk, for the light was by now almost insufficient for writing. He switched on the lamp and drew the curtains. But every occupation, like all motion, contains a precise moment of inertia; such was the case here. He also wrote out a receipt for 1500 schillings. He put aside the copy of the agreement. He placed the money in an evelope. He then took out his fountain pen, signed the document, folded the sheet of paper, and placed it in the envelope with the money.

Wrote the name on the envelope: Herr Doktor René von Stangeler.

By then his self-control was exhausted. He was not able to put away the typewriter. For now Agnes entered. Ponderously. The ordinary tasks made possible by briefly regained composure had merely served to hold back the landslide and allow it to gather force. Now it broke through with greater intensity.

He took out the book and opened to Agnes. It was she. It was that loincloth and no other that he had felt around his own hips on awakening. She was neither especially beautiful nor shapely nor young. Above the bundled, much-folded cloth, the belly protruded. The knees were pressed together, one above the other, the thighs too broad; she held her arms in a humble position, crossed in front of her high breasts, and looked sidelong with half-averted face and downcast eyes. On the floor to her left lay the clothes which had been stripped from her; to the right stood a column with a rope wound around it and dangling down.

That was all that could be seen on the engraving. It was a feeble work of art; you might consider it a rather ridiculous representation of an elderly, sour-looking female with a blubbery body, with lean feet showing every sinew and big toes turned absurdly outward. Perhaps the preposterous appearance was due to the incompetence of the artist or the engraver, or both. And yet a special, inexplicable principle dwelt within these forms rendered so excessively third-dimensional by the strong deep shading. It was there, a principle of the flesh, for all that the expression of it seemed crude and tasteless and on the whole silly.

There was no similarity in the ordinary sense between the woman in the engraving and Fräulein Agnes Gebaur. Yet there was a kind of analogy. To judge by size, by approximate stature, it might have been the unknown, not properly conceivable, still heavily swathed (by the standards of our modern age) body of

Agnes Gebaur. Moreover, this patient sufferer in the picture wore her hair tied up in a cloth, not hanging loosely. But then, when had he ever seen Agnes with a shawl or a veil?

Herzka did not know that before the torture the hair of witches was always shorn, or at least tied up. Though why should the artist—who was supposedly representing a saint and not a witch —have hit upon this shawl? There could scarcely be any basis for it in the legend of the saint.

But enough—it was Agnes.

With a body pale as moonstone.

Revealed, depetaled, white as the down of a swan's breast.

Herzka closed the book and locked it away. Like someone who had looked through a reference work and found confirmation of his assumption. He leaned against the bookcase. He actually had to support himself. His breath was short and shallow.

There was a knock on the door. The servant announced Herr Doktor René von Stangeler. Stangeler entered. Herzka went up to him. Before they shook hands, both men stood facing each other motionless for the briefest of moments. Right now René seemed to Jan a key which was about to open a lock in him, unlock his life for him. And so he attributed to him a function which he himself was to fulfill in Stangeler's life. Sometimes we assign topsy-turvy places to ourselves as well as to others.

AROUND eleven o'clock on the following day—Tuesday, May
17—they saw Castle Neudegg appear above the moderate hills
characteristic of the vicinity. The driver of the light carriage
which had awaited the two men at the small railroad station
pointed out the dot upon the landscape with the handle of his
whip. Then the road curved and the castle disappeared again.
They had not seen much, aside from a rather massive tower.

Herzka and Stangeler were by no means worn out from the
journey, and had breakfasted well in Villach. René scarcely
recalled the trip itself; it seemed to him that he had fallen asleep
even before they pulled out of the South Station in Vienna.
Herzka likewise; each of them was exhausted, although in a very
different fashion. The first-class compartment had been large
enough for them to remove their shoes and jackets and stretch
out on the upholstered seats.

And now Neudegg reappeared. This time, however, they saw
the castle from a different side.

This time it showed its face.

The face was that of a tower; the tower which they had seen
before was the rear of the narrow side of the main building. The
front was topped by the rectangular stump of a tower, but this
rose above the roof only slightly, perhaps no more than half the
height of a story. Stangeler had seen a photograph of the building, but this had given the wrong impression. It had been taken
from above the site on which the castle stood with wooded hills

rising steeply behind it. "It looks almost like a Norman keep," Stangeler thought; he was familiar with such defense towers from reproductions.

But as they drove nearer, this one-sided impression of a hunched-up shoulder vanished, and the whole castle looked more spread out. Then they entered the shade of leafy trees and began crawling uphill.

The road cut through sheer woods on a steep slope, wound around two serpentine curves, curved once again, and then they were close up against the massive structure: heavy foundation walls rising above rocky cliff. The horses stepped out again in a brisk trot; the trees dropped behind; and they were facing the castle broadside. Now it looked rather oblong, with the stocky stump of tower to the right, the hunched-up shoulder.

It stood braced against a blue sky.

The day, which had been dull, began clearing. The sun came out.

An ascending ramp ran along the length of the main building, turned to the left—at this point separated from the corner of the castle by a deep moat—and reached the bridge, which was level with the lowest story. They drove through the stone arch which had once housed the mechanism for drawing up the bridge. Above René saw a gallery roofed with wood, the so-called round-way. Probably some recent lord of the castle had had this onetime archers' stand restored.

The carriage entered the yard.

To the right you looked up and out into space, over a crenelated wall that bounded about half of the spacious courtyard. Running along it were broad, well-tended flower beds. Stables filled the narrow end at the rear. To the left stretched the main building, with a modest staircase leading down from its portal. However, portal and stairs were not placed in the center of the building, so that the two wings were of uneven size; the side toward the tower was by far the longer. Quickly reconstructing the medieval layout in his mind, Stangeler decided that the castle had originally been symmetrical and the tower free-standing. The manor house must then have been much smaller and squatter, and had probably been set farther from the edge of the slope, so that it would be more easily defensible. Some later owner must have enlarged one wing—since there was no space to enlarge the other. Thus the "keep," whose foundations and lower stories were probably original, had been included in the building, so that now only the top of the tower protruded above the new wing, forming its corner post. The old outside staircase might very well have occupied its present position. At a first casual glance, Stangeler dated these changes at around 1600, certainly not long after that. For there was no trace of baroque arrangement of portal and façade. The prevailing note was that mingling of remains of native Gothic and haphazard ornamental elements of a northern Renaissance which occasionally turns up in Austria, and which one art historian has called "character of which lack of character is the essential feature." At any rate, Neudegg was not a ruin frozen in its medieval form. And as a living building inhabited right up to the present, it constituted a rare exception among the manor houses of this southern province, where the elaborate forms of the seventeenth and eighteenth centuries had almost everywhere overgrown, displaced, and replaced the older elements.

Meanwhile the steward—or to use the name more appropriate in this case, the castellan—had come up to the carriage. He welcomed the two gentlemen and ordered their baggage to be taken to their rooms. Both Jan and René felt the need of a shave and bath. Castellan Mörbischer was a man with silvery-gray hair, a smooth face, and that courteous, confident manner that old, well-trained servants preserve even toward persons of the middle class. He preceded them up a narrow stairwell, showed them their rooms, and made it clear how to manipulate the electric water heaters in the bathrooms. He let them know that lunch would be served in half an hour; he would send a chambermaid to guide the gentlemen.

René was alone.

The spacious room looked out upon the courtyard.

Ever since the day before he had been wondering continually at his own assurance, and his own good sense. Many things were coming closer together, so that they could be seen whole, surveyed.

Like a picture reduced in size.

Though that also made it seem farther away.

He would return to Vienna very much changed.

Curious that there was no village around this castle, or attached to the castle.

But now he saw a church tower, beyond a nearby wooded hill. Perhaps the village was so far off because there was no water here, while over there was a brook or small river.

Of course the castle would have its own water supply. All castles do. Often the wells were dug to incredible depths. Probably the baron had installed a pump.

There! Sure enough, he could hear it. An electric motor was humming. Beyond the steeple of the church tower, higher mountains could be sensed. The sky was a silken blue. The silence was complete: the hum of the machine vibrated in it, as though a gentle breeze were blowing.

Jan Herzka was alone.

He sat in the bathtub as though suspended over a thin false bottom of his own inner being. A fine scab was just beginning to form over the wound.

He could not understand why this inherited castle would not enter his mind, why it was assuming no reality, why he could not begin to grasp this piece of unexpected good fortune.

And yet he was a businessman. The businessman is a person who within his own environment is always the first to see where profit offers.

Jan did not see the profit. He had only been informed that it existed. But inwardly he had not taken part in it, he had not participated. Not so far. He was like a person whose leg has fallen asleep or is paralyzed and seems no longer to exist.

Beneath him, the possibility of a monstrous breakthrough opened up. He sprang noisily to his feet, rubbed his firm tanned limbs dry, and in the midst of this activity paused, completely lost to the world, hands resting on the bath towel around his waist. Now he too heard the humming electric motor. The pitch rising and falling. It vibrated like a candle flame. The humming was truly a song; there was almost an element of feeling in the tone of the insensate machine.

After lunch, which they took in the simple but comfortable breakfast room, Herzka decided first to glance at the library and at the deceased baron's writing room, which he had mentioned in his letter. Preceded by Mörbischer, they passed first through the adjoining dining hall—which was not much larger than a very spacious dining room in the summer home of some prosperous person of the middle class. The castellan stepped to one side of the door and let them enter the library before him.

It was utterly different from what they might have imagined such a room for books in an ancient castle to be. The brightness of the light, the colorfulness and casualness of the furnishings, produced an atmosphere reminiscent of a painter's studio. Yet the source of the light was not a large, slanting glass surface. Quite the opposite; it came through three enormously high and wide Gothic windows arranged side by side, separated only by slender pillars. The style of these windows was late and distinctly flamboyant, with chamfered "fishbone arches." The tracery at the top framed red, blue, and yellow panes of glass. The whole effect was of something installed during the eighties of the past century, in keeping with the antiquarian tastes of the period. These enormous glass surfaces, big as a city shop window, admitted a great excess of light, and at the same time framed an impressive view of the distant hills, gracefully divided by the slender pillars.

The room contained scarcely a single oldish piece of furniture. Reclining chairs of light wood, several big armchairs with blue, red, and natural-colored cane seats, a couch, three club chairs, and several small low tables with glass tops stood about in no particular order. The room was so big that the furniture did not matter; the impression was of emptiness. Along the rear wall a high wide tapestry in electric blue glowed brightly; upon it golden birds in flight were embroidered in oriental style.

The hoard of books filled only a fourth or fifth of the room. Starting in one corner and running along the two adjacent walls were rows of those useful, modern-type bookcases with glass panes which close dust-tight and to which units can be added at will.

As they slowly walked across the room, Stangeler brushed by the bookshelves and glanced at a few titles. He whistled softly between his teeth.

Where the bookcases ended, directly opposite the high windows, stood a plain, finely worked, very smooth and simple piece of furniture of light, veined birchwood. It was about the height of a wardrobe, but of slighter depth. On top of it stood nothing but a turquoise-blue glass bowl, placed exactly in the center.

Stangeler at once guessed that this cupboard must contain the manuscript collection.

Now, however, there was the baron's study to look at. Herzka had already entered, and Mörbischer was waiting at the door for Stangeler to follow.

This room was quite ordinary. Dark wood, dark leather, wide desk rimmed with an old-fashioned carved grating. Beside the blotter lay a horse's hoof, framed in silver and inscribed:

Halka L. U. R. 5 Zurawince April 4, 1916

Stangeler bent over it and read the inscription.

"Was the late baron in the Landwehr uhlans?"

"Yes," Mörbischer replied. "Halka was shot under him at Zurawince."

René looked over at Herzka. He was standing with his back to the desk, studying a portrait on the wall. René went over to his side. Together they approached the painting.

Possibly Herzka took longer than René to recognize that this was a frightful picture—both in its execution and the person represented. The brush of a fashionable painter well known in Vienna before the First World War, guided by neither instinct nor inspiration, had licked and dabbed away at a personality until a kind of oversized rubbing of this personality emerged. It contained the whole frightfulness of its subject, and the painter was as little responsible for it as a photographer—whose function he was fulfilling in this case. It was a portrait of a young woman in ball dress. Her face and expression were such that Stangeler wished he could smash the canvas as you would smash a pane of glass.

She was a pretty thing, with black braids wound around a white forehead. But the expression of scorn, of insolence, and at the same time of utter nullity in this face—in which the eyes were set very close together—had been simply copied by the painter. He had not tried for any improvement, had reproduced what he saw entirely without reservation, with a sublime opportunism. For that reason the whole face fell out of the painting, assaulted the onlooker—out of a painting that was no picture but was certainly a likeness to the point of vileness. "He did not even try to caricature her," Stangeler thought. "Probably she was not even repugnant to him. He may have been the same way himself."

Out of the corner of his eyes René observed that Mörbischer was by no means pleased to have the guests linger in front of this painting.

"Who is this lady?" Herzka asked.

"Baroness Charagiel," Mörbischer said. "She is dead. She was the daughter of the late baron."

"Did the baron have any other children?"

"No."

To himself, Herzka thought: "Wouldn't she have been a pleasant co-owner of Neudegg!" Aloud, he said: "Isn't there any portrait of the late baron?"

"No, sir," Mörbischer replied. "Our master never had himself

painted. We have only a few photographs. In this little chest
here."

René opened it. There were three or four pictures on top. He
handed them to Jan, keeping one in his hand and studying it.

The daughter resembled the father. That was obvious, but only
that and nothing more. For the resemblance was altogether
superficial. What new element had come between father and
daughter, whether an inheritance from the mother or from
remoter ancestors, there was no way of telling. But it must have
been a powerful element, splitting the body of the paternal
heritage like an axe splitting a log. Or perhaps, more gently but
no less effectively, the heritage had been dissolved as if by an
acid. Perhaps, too, it had offered no resistance. Achaz von
Neudegg's head and face were of the type that can still be
found among vintners in Lower Austria: a strong, self-contained,
long and narrow face, but not at all with that inaccessibility, that
sharpness and closeness of a bird of prey, which is typical of
alpine peasants. Rather it was humane and lyric, like wine itself,
with wide-open eyes which seemed used to gazing on a milder
landscape in a milder manner. It was the face of an open-
hearted, open-souled person, susceptible to influences, perhaps
even endangered by them. Moreover, Achaz von Neudegg had
had the face of a nobleman, and the last of his line. His countenance was no longer carved out of the heartwood of that line.
But there was an immediate appeal in the simplicity, the total
lack of embarrassment, with which this particular physiognomy
confronted the world. It had nothing to conceal because it
wanted to conceal nothing. That was a sovereign quality of this
face; it imposed on its beholder a similar honesty, it enjoined
him to drop all falderal. . . .

René handed this picture to Herzka along with the others.
Then he rummaged a bit in the chest.
But it held nothing but photographs.
Old photographs. When they are new they never look so fortui-
tous, ridiculous, or utterly ugly—for otherwise no one would keep
them, no one would allow himself to be photographed. The raw

uncomprehending naturalism of the apparatus tears a tiny piece
out of the elaborate ornamentation of a lifeline whose unfinished
streamer is directed toward the future. The lens ignores the
streamer; the snapshot is alien to biography and portraiture; it
arrests life. To photograph a person means in a sublimated fashion to shoot him dead; and whether this is done "artistically" or
merely for a passport photo is six of one and half a dozen of the
other.

Now they emerged from the chest, empty gray sausage-casings
of consumed life. René scarcely looked at them. Having had his
lunch, he was beginning to grow sleepy. He listened, riffling the
photographs idly, to what Herzka was saying to the castellan,
who at Jan's genial request had taken his seat in a chair facing
him, but who sat with a certain reserve. He did not lean back,
rather bent forward, looking attentively across the intervening
distance at Herzka.

"Herr Mörbischer," Herzka said, "I am as yet far from being
the master of the house here. The master of the house at present
is the estate as such. I must therefore ask you to draw up a
statement of all the current expenses—we are staying until the
day after tomorrow. I shall pay these expenses before my departure and give the receipt to Herr Krautwurst in Vienna. Naturally, until you hear further, Herr Krautwurst's instructions will
continue to be followed in all matters."

Mörbischer bowed slightly.

"So much for incidental matters. Now for something far more
important. I have a letter from the late baron in which he gives
me various instructions and expresses his wishes—among others,
that this writing room in which we are sitting is to remain unchanged. I intend to follow his wishes to the best of my ability;
and I therefore want to ask you, Herr Mörbischer, to see to it
that everything here, down to the smallest object, remains precisely where it stood or lay during the baron's lifetime."

"Very well, sir," Mörbischer replied.

"In general I am not overfond of changes. There are people who
must always be turning everything upside down. Every three

months all the furniture in the house is rearranged or switched around. It must be a kind of disease. Such people must be ill at ease in life. It's as if they have to wave their arms wildly in order to clear the air. I don't care at all for that sort of thing. In all these years since my father's death I have changed nothing in my business. I am already dreading the day when our old chief book-keeper, who was with us in my father's day, finally decides to retire. . . . And I've just had to give up my receptionist and let her take over the Graz branch. . . ."

But he did not fall into loquacity. He braked abruptly as soon as he realized that his talk was approaching warmer regions. Pulled himself up and became more concise.

"In short, I prefer not to change things, and will have no desire to later on, when I formally take over the inheritance. That the staff is to remain is already set forth in the will, at least as a recom-mendation, as Herr Krautwurst has probably informed you. . . ."

Mörbischer nodded. In his aged, smooth lackey's face a friendly light was beginning to glow.

"Herr Krautwurst also feels it would be wise to keep on with present tenant contracts. I understand that these are to run for several years. But would you tell me one thing that I forgot to ask Herr Krautwurst, Herr Mörbischer: were any of these rental agreements arranged through the Austrian Lumber Industry Bank?"

"No," Mörbischer said. "I am quite sure about that. The baron refused to enter into any business arrangements with that outfit."

"Was any such arrangement proposed to him?"

"Yes," Mörbischer replied. "In fact Herr Levielle, the financial counselor, came here in person."

"Little Victor!" Herzka exclaimed, laughing. "Well, everything is fine then. Herr Krautwurst told me, by the way, that this castle lies on the extreme edge of the estate."

"Yes," Mörbischer replied. "If you will look out this window, sir, you will see the boundary, out toward the railroad there—that is looking north—where the road runs by, from which our private road branches off. It is right at the foot of the castle hill."

Stangeler, meanwhile, had again begun rapidly looking through the photographs. He had fallen prey to the kind of catatonia that afflicts the "reader" of an illustrated magazine: the man becomes a pipe through which the pictures flow, a pictorial intestine. Out of the depths of this condition he asked: "Why did you say 'Little Victor'?"

"Because he's still far from being one but would like to be," Herzka replied, laughing, and the old castellan permitted himself a restrained smile of sympathy.

René, in his sleepiness, gave no more thought to the matter; yet a core was forming in the center of his sleepiness, made excessively sharp by the surrounding aura of an increasing craving for a nap. He observed Herzka and Mörbischer entering the initial stages of a mutual good relationship whose basis was prudence on both sides; prudence and restraint. This first conversation was like the eye of a needle through which the conversational threads of all that was to follow would be drawn. Both men seemed conscious of the importance of these minutes. For the first time in his life René recognized the serious, the sublime importance of prudence: prudence right from the start of things, at the very first leap into an affair. And yet hitherto prudence had been among the virtues he despised. Now he knew better and thought, after his own fashion: "It keeps the respiratory waters clean." With this thought still in his mind, he plucked out another photograph, and saw a picture of Quapp, Kajetan von Schlaggenberg's sister.

This, however, was the photograph of a child of eight or nine. He therefore refrained from showing Herzka the picture, or from obeying his first impulse to ask the castellan about it.

It might not be Quapp after all.

The eyes, wide apart, were flaring in surprise. The mouth stretched almost from one ear to the other. This was a little face of the utmost receptivity, as wide open to the world as the beak of an infant bird as it waits with simple-minded avidity for its mother to bring it food.

No, that could not be Quapp after all. It was a completely silly little creature. Quapp could never have been so silly.

This reasoning seemed so convincing to René that without more ado he tucked all the photos back into the chest and returned it to its place on the table.

Meanwhile the subject of the conversation had changed. Stangeler paid more attention.

"Let us postpone all that until tomorrow. In any case I want to see the chapel and above all hear the organ on which Slobedeff played."

"I can about manage a hymn," Mörbischer said modestly. "When the dean said Mass up here—he was friendly with the baron—I used to do the playing."

"Did you hear Slobedeff?"

"I did," Mörbischer said. "The baron sat up in the organ loft. I sat down below in the nave."

"And how was it?" Herzka asked, leaning forward.

"Beyond description, sir," Mörbischer said, solemnly and firmly.

"What did he play?"

"Variations on 'Whither shall I turn?' "

"How long?"

"About half an hour. It wasn't something written down—an improvisation, as we say. So I suppose it is lost forever."

"How do you mean that?"

"Six months later we read the news in the newspaper."

"What news?"

"Of his death, sir," Mörbischer replied.

"What!" Herzka exclaimed. "I didn't know," he added after a pause. "When was Slobedeff here?"

"It must have been about a year ago, or somewhat earlier. End of winter. He had come from Brussels. He was teaching there toward the end."

"Hm—tell me . . . in 1905, when Princess Mazunov brought him out of Siberia, he was a very young man, wasn't he? He couldn't have been even fifty . . . ?"

"Yes. And looked much younger. People say—it wasn't a natural death. He's supposed to have done it himself."

"Anything more that you know about it?"

"No, sir."

Herzka had sagged. He seemed suddenly struck down by a tiredness even greater than René's. The conversation had ebbed into silence.

"Herr von Stangeler," Jan said at last, "don't you think we ought to lie down for an hour or two? I must say I'm feeling the effects of that all-night ride. And we'll ask Herr Mörbischer to have tea served for us in the library next door at five o'clock; then we can have a look at the books and manuscripts. The late baron"—Jan turned to Mörbischer again—"suggested in his letter that I bring a scholar here. Doktor von Stangeler is a historian."

"Very well, sir," Mörbischer said, rising. "Tea in the library at five o'clock."

He bowed and departed.

They went upstairs. When Stangeler had closed his door behind him, Herzka crossed the wide arched corridor. His own room faced approximately north; it was on the same side of the castle as the library. Through the arched window he looked down over the treetops of the steep castle hill and far out across level land to where the highway ran.

He stepped back from the window. At the rear of the room stood a broad couch. Fatigue made him shiver with sudden coldness. He took off his jacket and shoes and wrapped himself in the soft camel-hair shawl laid out on the couch. Sleep came to him instantly, and with it a sense of gladness at the dissolution of waking relationships, at the passage through that region in which briefly sheer nonsense reigns because the laws of the dream have not yet intervened and those of waking life have lost their force. He dropped, deep down. Immediately it became clear to him that he must heat up the caverns below. So he did so. But the stoves were no longer in good condition. It was too cool to remain here any longer with only a towel around the waist.

René fell asleep at once.

When he awoke again, after what seemed a very short time, he had swum in one breath through an hour of sleep, like a diver who plunges headfirst into a green pool at one end and reappears on the surface at the other end.

All his tiredness was gone. And that "circumspection" which so amazed him again filled him to the brim.

He looked around. He was afraid of nothing. He realized, in the light of this, that hitherto he had always lived in states of anxiety.

Here was a wonderful chance to look at the library undisturbed and alone, to see whether there might not be a few crabs hidden under the stones there. Best to pull them out alone.

René washed his hands—as is only right when you are about to handle valuable books. He applied some lavender water, brushed his hair and clothes, and went downstairs.

This bottleneck of a stairwell with its stubby pillars was depressing.

He passed through the dining hall.

The library's double doors stood open before him, with an electric-blue flash from the tapestry at the back; the room spread itself before him like opening wings.

René lingered in front of the big windows, looking out at the view. He was aware of the altogether novelistic quality of his present situation; but he did not pursue the experience in greedy amazement; rather, he comprehended it, quietly, with a self-possessed inner force. The situation was his completely; it belonged to him. Interior and exterior fitted neatly together.

It is not easy to communicate the utter lack of bias Stangeler felt toward whatever motives and impulses had brought Herzka out to the castle. Had he been asked his opinion of the moral aspect of the matter, he would have had no answer; nor had he any inclination to form one. For him, the whole accent of the situation fell elsewhere, upon another plane. To use his terminology, he had come to the end of the rut, and to the beginning of a new era in which the delicate membrane which had hitherto separated exterior from interior in this whole affair of Herzka's would have to be rent at last. And what would become visible then? The empty space of an exterior world bearing no relation to wild dreams?

Stangeler heard a step behind him.

It was Mörbischer. Carrying a tray of coffee.

"Is the young gentleman already at work?" he said. "I noticed that neither you nor Herr Herzka had more than a drop of coffee at lunch. I thought a cup might be bracing."

A nice idea. Stangeler promptly asked for the key to the birchwood cupboard. Mörbischer took out his key ring. "Down here," he said, "are the household books. Up above, the historical items."

"I'll go through the library first," Stangeler said. "I don't suppose there is a catalogue?"

"No," Mörbischer replied.

"Wouldn't really be necessary, of course. There isn't so much here. And easy to go through."

The castellan bowed and left.

René felt as if he were postponing a decision as he now proceeded to open each of the glassed-in compartments in turn. The nature of the library soon became clear. There were no items of belles-lettres at all. The collection was devoted entirely to the late Middle Ages, with demonology as a central feature. Just as there were no belles-lettres, so there were no modern studies of witchcraft or witch trials. There was no copy of Soldan, or Hansen. On the other hand there was a well-preserved copy of Bodin's *Démonomanie*, the Paris printing of 1581. René was surprised to find alongside it a contemporary, Ambroise Paré, the reformer of surgery; but when he opened the calf-bound small folio volume, he found bound in with the *Opera chirugica* (it was an early seventeenth-century edition translated from the French into Latin) a treatise: *De monstris et prodigiis*. And alongside this volume there now began a weird row of books. The first was an altogether modern work, one of the strangest in existence: the *Histoire des monstres* of Ernst Martin. It contains the life-stories of all the known monstrosities of modern times, from Siamese twins to creatures of far more shocking nature. There followed older medical works by Maximilian Markwitz, Otto Luther, and Catin on monsters. There was also a dissertation of 1854, written in Latin: *De monstro quodam,* by Albert Georg Luecke. The final volume was Choulant's *Bibliographical Handbook* for older medicine.

Among the books were many items of considerable worth. There was the first and comprehensive edition of the collected works of Paracelsus—Huser's of 1616. In addition René found a very small incunabulum that would have excited any rare-book dealer: the Viennese doctor Bartholomeus Steber's *De malfranzos morbo gallico praeservatio ac cura,* one of the oldest scientific works on syphilis produced in Europe. Dr. Steber, dean of the Vienna medical school in the late fifteenth century, was an old friend of Stangeler's, for our scholar had studied the medieval texts that the Vienna College of Physicians had published around 1900.

There was a great deal more. On further shelves was a whole "scholarly apparatus," including a complete *Dictionnaire infernal,* and the many-volumed glossaries Stangeler had used in his studies. First editions of the *Thesaurus linguae latinae* were represented. ("So these must all have been bought by the old baron," René thought.)

Stangeler took out a number of small volumes for which he might have looked in vain in many an eminent library. Thus there was the work published by A. Fournier in Paris in 1843, Fernand Denis's *Le monde enchanté, Cosmographie et Histoire naturelle fantastique du moyen-âge*—a book which has become so rare that it compares in price with incunabula. Furthermore there was Count Luigi Bossi's treatise on basilisks and dragons, of lesser value, but a charming curiosity, an octavo volume bound in leather.

The subject of dragons was somewhat in the news at the moment. *Natural History,* the organ of the New York Museum of Natural History, had recently published the results of Dr.

Douglas Burdon's Komodo expedition, *The Quest for the Dragon of Komodo*, and it had struck Stangeler that the gigantic *Varanus Komodiensis* corresponded quite well to the description Albertus Magnus had given of the Indian dragon. The great Dominican, treating of dragons in his *Historia Animalium*, comments that "instructed and serious writers" have handed down no traditions of flying dragons; moreover, he adds, stability in the air would not be possible with so elongated a body structure. . . .

Suddenly Stangeler became conscious of a strong odor of lavender, and a touch of that charcoal aroma which is spread by a samovar. . . . It entered his nostrils from inside his head. And was followed by a very light, fresh, slightly bitter odor; that came from the American professor of zoology who had sat beside him near the samovar. At the "foundation festival" in Kajetan's place. René saw it now far away and reduced in size, as if he were looking through the wrong end of opera glasses. He had talked with Williams about that passage in Albertus Magnus; the American seemed to have been much interested.

René still stood holding open Count Bossi's treatise, but no longer reading the Italian text. Now he closed the book, put it back on the shelf, and took the next one. This was thicker and had a handsome eighteenth-century binding. Nevertheless it too was a fifteenth-century printing: the Carmelite Farinator de Vyena's *Lumen animae*. Stangeler knew the book and remembered a sentence from it: "The dragon is a symbol of envy; it is consumed by envy because it has no venom." An idea altogether consistent with the zoology of the Middle Ages, according to which the dragon belonged to the third order of serpents, those "whose bite may be fatal even without venom."

Enough, enough. René now had an over-all view of the library, rich as it was. He could make his report to Herzka.

However, he could not estimate the value of the books. He was no rare-book dealer.

The time had come to verify suppositions. He approached the wall cupboard of fine-grained birch wood and peered into it.

This cupboard had obviously been designed specially for its

purpose, and very well made. It was completely lined with aluminum; the three slatted shelves were of the same metal. The whole could be locked so that it was airtight.

On the lowest shelf, as the castellan had said, the household books were lined up, year after year, to 1926. These, then, constituted living archives of the affairs of the estate. The two upper shelves would be the historical archives: a collection of manuscripts. They were uniformly bound (an ill-fated procedure, Stangeler knew, which often resulted in the loss of characteristics and tipped-in pages). There were also several file folders, of the same leather as the volumes. Altogether, there were about ten items on each shelf; no problems of unearthing here.

Stangeler stood for a while inactive in front of the cupboard.

He was now confronting his own question: what rational justification did he have for the assumption, which he had cherished since yesterday, that the Neudegg collection of manuscripts would contain some material of the sort that interested Herzka?

And why should he expect to find it in the manuscript collection? Why not in the collection of books?

To this latter question he could now give some sort of answer. The actual documents of witch trials had been printed only in scattered fashion, here and there, as appendices and examples in treatises, or as curiosities. During the period of polemics against the whole matter, few documents had been published. Nor had there been accounts of witchcraft based extensively upon documents, nothing like the dry recitals of the procedures of the Spanish Inquisition published in the nineteenth century by Llorente, who had been the bitter enemy—and last secretary general—of the Inquisition. Llorente's work, in a four-volume German translation, was in the library. There was also an Augsburg printing of as late as 1731 of the *Cautio Criminalis* by the Jesuit Spee. Stangeler reflected: where could documents of this sort be found, reproduced in full? When he thought about it, there were very few, especially for the alpine countries. Old Ludwig Rapp, say, in his book on the witch trials in Tyrol, had printed seven "Confessions." And Stangeler thought he recalled several references to sources of this type in the fifteenth volume of the *Archive for Criminal Anthropology*. But on the whole most of the material would be found only in manuscript.

But why here, in this particular castle of Neudegg?

Herzka had already infected him with his mania!

For Jan had made a clean breast of it, in the course of their dinner last night, before they left for the castle.

Stangeler set to work and opened one manuscript volume after another. There was a great deal here, and much of it remarkable. Of course it was impossible to know at first glance whether part of it might not long since have been published on the basis of older and better manuscripts. That was true of the copies of judicial precedents; of land registers; of a description of the fear of the Turks in Carinthia, which might turn out to be only an extract or an addendum to the chronicle of Pastor Jacob Unrest, who lived near Pörtschach in the fifteenth century and reported on those events. This Turkish chronicle probably explained the presence of a 1904 dissertation by F. R. Ebermann, *The Terror of the Turks*, which Stangeler had noted as he was looking over the shelves.

He had already made a quick review of two thirds of the manuscript collection.

René took a swallow of the coffee, which by now was cold.

Suddenly it struck him—like an arrow falling from the ceiling —that in the improbable case that the remaining six or seven codices contained something "for Herzka," Herzka would be robbed of a far grander opportunity: to have made a fruitless stab in the dark. Stangeler actually put this idea in the following words: "Fall off at the end of the rut . . ." and: "Break through a partition wall . . ." and: "Get himself out of his damned second reality. . . ."

But if he now found something "for Herzka," that would mean that the whole affair was going smoothly and according to schedule, just like Körger's *pot-au-feu* the previous Saturday.

Here Stangeler smelled a rat. Usually slow-witted, in certain critical moments he was capable of forcing himself to think quickly. This was one such moment. Under its propulsive force he came to the surprising conclusion that such a find, if it did turn up, would represent altogether the more likely case, a far less surprising occurrence than the absence of such a find—paradoxical as this notion at first appeared. A verdict would be pronounced on Jan Herzka, who would thus have arrived at his desired goal overnight. With no delay, with nothing intervening. "If what is wanted is attained exactly in the preconceived manner, then the direction and object of the desire were unimportant and not worthy of discussion."

After this last sententious observation, our historian dropped off his rapidly grown tree of knowledge like a ripe plum. He lifted his hand from his knee at last; the hand held the next codex to be examined. It was in quarto format, but very thin, more a notebook than a book.

A manuscript, written on paper, also dated before 1500. The first words: "Specyfyeth of how the sorceresses were delt wyth atte Neudegck whan that they were taken Anno MCCCCLXIIIJ."

It was growing dark in the room. He could not go on reading. As he stood up to switch on the light, he heard footsteps in the dining hall.

The door opened. It was Jan Herzka. Behind him came a girl with a tea tray, although it was not five but seven o'clock.

"I've overslept," Jan said. "But let us have a cup of tea anyhow. Supper will be served a bit later."

The girl smiled. She was an adolescent country girl, no more than thirteen or fourteen. Stangeler had the vague impression that Herzka was cultivating good will among all the domestics with whom he came in contact by means of generous tips. Probably Mörbischer was no exception.

After the light had been switched on, the girl pulled the drawstrings at the windows. Curtains of the same blue and with the same embroidery as the tapestry at the back of the room flowed across the tall windows.

She arranged the tea things, poured, and left.

Stangeler vanished behind his teacup and cigarette.

"Been down long?" Herzka asked him.

"Yes," René said. He seemed to be imbibing the tea and inhaling the cigarette smoke simultaneously, as another person might consume the tea and biscuits (which he left untouched). It was an extremely intense proceeding.

"I slept only an hour or so," he said. "In the meanwhile I've looked through the whole of the library, and the greater part of the manuscript collection. But before I give you a report and, so to speak, an official opinion on it, Herr Herzka, I would like to put one question to you: how did you know that among the medieval manuscripts preserved here there would be one referring to witch trials at this castle?"

The shot struck home. It was well aimed. René saw Herzka pale.

"I . . ." Jan said at last, after a prolonged silence, "I knew—that it must be so."

"Good," René said. The wave of confidence in which he was swimming bore him up buoyantly—the confidence of the expert and specialist, and of a sharp psychologist as well. "Good," he said. "This manuscript here"—he took the codex from the table where he had placed it—"is it. I found it just before you came in. So far I have not read a line of the manuscript. But it may very well interest you—at least to judge by the title."

And he read with some pleasure: " 'Specyfyeth of how the sorceresses were delt wyth atte Neudegck whan that they were taken Anno MCCCCLXIIIJ.' "

Herzka reached out for the volume, and Stangeler handed it across the table to him.

He observed Jan, who began to leaf through the pages, found he could not read the script or the language very well, and let the book fall to his knees.

"I can't make head or tail of this," he said.

"With your permission I'll retire to my room with the manuscript right after supper. I'll go through it and will, I hope, be able to read it all to you by tomorrow afternoon."

"That would be very kind of you," Herzka said. "I really wanted to inspect the underground rooms of the castle, the caverns, sometime today. But I suppose it is too late now."

"You would be mistaken if you thought those caverns particularly interesting or romantic, Herr Herzka," Stangeler said. "Castle subcellars were often very large, and of course served to store supplies, but their chief purpose was to give shelter to the inhabitants of an unwalled village, and to their possessions and their cattle, in time of danger. Of course there were also dungeons, usually under the tower. In regard to these, this manuscript may give us some useful clues."

It was late at night, nearly one o'clock, when Stangeler stopped work. Since the neat cursive script of the codex offered scarcely any paleographical difficulties, he had already read through the entire manuscript, finding only a few obscure passages to transfer to his notebook.

The work itself had been relatively easy; it was not that which had exhausted René. He had to stop at one o'clock for other reasons; by this time he had almost reached the limits of his endurance. In view of the subject, he had prepared himself for cruelty, for horrors, for atrocities—although his general knowledge of the field would of course temper his reactions. But now, while he had encountered no bloody deeds whatsoever, the content of the manuscript had affected him in an entirely different fashion. A fearful miasma seemed to rise up out of these pages, springing from an inordinate lust that was like a tree of steel thrusting fiery-hot roots deep into the ground, cracking open bedrock. What had happened here at Neudegg was by no means a tragedy; it was a ridiculous farce of the passions. This manuscript overturned many traditional ideas. And it confirmed René Stangeler in many of the views he had long quietly held.

The man who signed himself as author and scribe at the end of the codex must have been old; by his own testimony he had written the account at Augsburg in 1517, in the sixty-ninth year of his life, and this statement was borne out by the script, which was distinctly fifteenth century; the author had probably learned to write around the middle of that century. On the first page was a note in a later hand:

Emptū Aug. Vind. magno p̄tio quadragintarum lib. den. a.s.
MDXVIIJ eodem i. domo ubi tum vixit obiitque abjectissimi
huĩ libelli auctor profligat'. Joann. Chrys. de Newdegck.
(Bought at Augsburg for the high price of forty pounds of pennies in the year of salvation 1518, in the same house where the profligate author of this base little book lived and died. Johannes Chrysostomus von Neudegg.)

This statement, and especially the enormous price paid for the manuscript, seemed to indicate that Baron Johannes Chrysostomus must have had an interest in obtaining possession of a document which might well dishonor an ancestor and the bearer of his name; perhaps the Neudegg of the manuscript had been his father, grandfather, or uncle. Stangeler had no way of telling under what circumstances Johannes Chrysostomus had been able to purchase the manuscript from the author or the author's heirs.

The name of this author had been Ruodlieb von der Vläntsch, and in 1464 he had served in this very castle as a page, along with two other sons of knightly tenants of the estate. Their master had been the then lord of castle and district, Achaz von Neudegg—the same name as the last scion of the line.

Nevertheless, Ruodlieb was no "profligate," as Johannes Chrysostomus saw fit to call him. It was rather a case of his character's having been poisoned, and perhaps that of the other youthful page as well.

That much Stangeler knew, having read the manuscript. But he had had enough; he could not go on with his note-taking.

René stood up, rather stiff of limb. Ordinarily he was not much of a drinker, but right now he wished with all his heart for a glass of hard liquor. The room was streaked with cigarette smoke. The silence was absolute. The noise he had made in moving his chair as he rose sounded like the snapping of a taut membrane.

He wanted to open the window, but was checked by a sudden thought. It occurred to him that Herzka might be insane. There he was, sleeping across the corridor. His mother had been a Neudegg.

René felt intensely disgusted with everything and everyone. Nausea came crawling in upon him from all sides. Perhaps Herr Achaz of 1464 had likewise been insane. Jan and Achaz both. Each in the style of his age. Likewise Körger. Probably Schlaggenberg too. A piano was struck. How she smiles! "Mary is playing again."

There was a knock at the door.

René started so violently that he almost dislocated his joints. Breathing hard, he called: "Come in!"

It was Jan Herzka.

Under his left arm he held a bottle with two traveling cups of silver nested over the cork. His hair looked tousled from his having lain in bed. He looked very handsome, and at the same time somehow changed, perhaps because of the uncombed hair and light blue pajamas he was wearing. Stangeler grasped this whole picture as Herzka paused in the doorway.

"I saw your light under the door, Herr von Stangeler," he said. "I was in the corridor—haven't been able to sleep, I suppose because I took so long a nap this afternoon. So I thought I might venture to look in on you. . . . You surely don't intend to go on working any longer, do you! In any case I brought a little strengthener along. . . ."

"That's splendid," René said. "No, I'm done for today. What have you there in the bottle?"

"Cognac," Herzka said.

"Wonderful!" René exclaimed. "The very stuff I need now. The thing is to have the magic power of making wishes come true.

Ten minutes ago I was violently wishing for a drink. And here it is. Although—I'm still far from being a master of wishes like you."

"How do you mean that?" Herzka asked. He sat down on the couch beside a small low table and carefully poured the cognac. The gilding inside the shining silver cups glowed to life.

"Because back in Vienna you wished something, and at Neudegg a Herr von der Vläntsch had long ago attended to the matter."

"And who is he?"

"The author of this manuscript. Tomorrow you'll hear it—a monstrous performance that—really leaves you nothing more to wish for."

Without drinking, Herzka replaced his cup on the table. He looked at René. The expression on his face was that of a man who hears the whistle of an arrow or the whine of a bullet close to his ear. Stangeler observed very closely. He had become acutely observant, and was once more happily in possession of faculties normally denied him, such as a clear grasp of situations and real circumspection. Although Herzka's knock had so startled and frightened him, he now felt a compensatory stability and well-being. The situation was to his taste; he felt that he controlled it as surely and firmly as a cork kept the contents of a bottle within bounds.

He tipped up his glass and drained it. Then he held it out to Herzka for a refill. He was much too exhausted to summarize the contents of the manuscript, he explained, but he would complete his work the next morning and read the complete thing tomorrow afternoon. They should first have Mörbischer show them the caverns of the castle.

"Is there something about them in this manuscript?"

"I should say so," René replied.

"You must have an enormous knowledge of your field, Herr Doktor," Herzka exclaimed.

René, with his present acuteness, clearly recognized the embarrassment and near-timidity of this attempt to change the subject.

"Not a bit," he replied. "Any student at the Institute could handle this sort of thing in his sleep, and most of them more fluently than I. Be that as it may, it's only natural for a postal clerk to know much more about postal matters than the two of us put together."

"Well, I consider myself fortunate to have you here, Herr Doktor," Herzka said. "Without you I would not have been equipped to . . . to find my way about."

He broke off. His own phraseology appeared to strike him as somehow amiss.

At this point René Stangeler hit on something rather remarkable. It was a new talent of his and consisted in his being able to respond in detail to something that had been said, without voicing a syllable of his real thoughts. But for this procedure to be effective, the response really had to be complete, and intensive: the inner resonance of it almost reaching the outer ear. It became a matter of thinking at rather than talking to his companion.

The process did not interfere with his actually saying things aloud, censored remarks, but not without content.

Mutely, therefore, René said: "You will probably find your way about very soon, and that may be the nub of the whole trouble. For out of the disaster which came upon—or rather came out of —your ancestor, Herr Achaz of 1464, you are going to make an institution. A little kitchen garden of eroticism. And how your plants will flourish in it! How lovingly you will tend them! A real romantic you are, prepared to devote yourself to the leftovers of the past. In the end you will send for a tile stove repairer and a chimney sweep to fix the heating system down there—for there is one—and romanticism requires warmth. Perhaps the best thing you could do would be to marry a female who can play the whole show for you. Though she'll need a seamstress who can make a costume of the times. I'll describe it for you. In general I am ready to assume the job of lecturer at a fixed salary on pseudo-witch trials—which will not take us too far from the historical reality, since I have long suspected that a good many of the witch trials were conducted this way, without damage to body or lethal outcome. *Prosit!*"

Aloud, he said: "I should like to return to your powers of making wishes come true, Herr Herzka. If, for example, while you are walking in the street you vividly think of someone, it may happen—this has surely happened to you, to you of all people, at least once—that you suddenly see the person in question coming along the sidewalk toward you. You are on the point of greeting him—and then you realize that it is not him after all, only someone who looks like him. That process may be repeated several times, two streets farther on, say. . . . And then—this has happened to me—just a few minutes later, I do actually meet that person I've been thinking about. On such occasions I've always been tempted to say: 'Well, well, my dear fellow, here you are—I've been expecting you for the past half hour.' Of course it's impossible to say that to anyone, but it would be the complete truth."

"I know exactly what you mean," Herzka said. "I've had the same experience myself, more than once."

Mutely, Stangeler continued: "But that sort of thing can happen only once. If more than once, then each time it's the one time, so to speak. You could never arrange anything like that. In sum: only what comes along is first class. Everything aimed at and attainable by aiming at is second class."

Aloud: "It is exactly the same with your foreknowledge of this manuscript here. The whole affair has what you might call a heightened degree of reality."

Mutely: "The question is, what are you going to do with it? Unfortunately I suspect that the ridiculous details in which this suddenly heightened reality of your life has been manifested are far more important to you than the heightening of reality itself. For which reason, my friend, you're going to go grubbing around in the details instead of so shaping your life that similar heightenings of reality—of a worthier sort—may enter it."

Then he himself was gripped by it. He was concealing the essence of the whole business from Herzka with a certain malice. The reason he gave himself, in his own inner language, was that "the verdict has already been pronounced" on Herzka and the man would have to be "given short shrift, since he can't be helped anyhow." But even while he remained stubbornly laconic, there floated before him, in the same bluish glow as the tapestry on the library wall had at dusk, an image of something he had seen a hundred times: the image hit him as though he had never seen it before, as though never before had it been possible for him to penetrate its nature. For now he was regarding it from within a life in which "happy chances" could become a daily routine.

As if it had been yesterday: the evening still glowed greenishly behind the tower, and into the waning daylight emerged the first glowing spheres, floating over the street in front of the shops. . . .

It was the Graben in Vienna.

In the blue light of dusk.

The same street he had seen and walked upon hundreds of times.

And still he saw it as never before in his life. He saw himself walking there, walking far away from himself, in past years; but he was walking on it now as if for the first time. For he himself was there, altogether himself, and circumspect, and quick-thinking, examining things in perspective, prudently checking all possibilities. Prudently—for prudence came easy to him now, had become natural and proper. "That is the true order which supports a person, the real order, not some chancy fabricated one. These fellows all want to live in a prolongation of their own imaginations. Just like Herzka. Otherwise they hold their hands over their eyes. An embryo in the womb. To whom did I say that? Oh yes, to old Gürtzner-Gontard."

His abstraction had lasted no longer than the time it took Herzka to fill the little cup again.

"All right, then, tomorrow afternoon, Herr Doktor. First we'll go down to the cellars and then you'll read me the manuscript."

"Yes," René said. He went to the casement window and began opening it. "You'll want to bring a large flashlight along. We'll probably need a hammer too. Not too small a one; something good and heavy."

"What would that be for?"

"To detect hollow spaces."

"Righto," Herzka said. He had stepped up behind René to the now open window, which admitted the cool night air into the cigarette smoke. The moon, which had been full the Monday before, was no longer visible; but after a few minutes of peering into the darkness they made out the subdued blue radiance of distant woods which seemed to rise gently upward in the moonlight like a noiseless wing.

Late the following morning Stangeler entered his last notes on the manuscript into the notebook. It was a day of brilliant sunlight. René was sitting by the open window, which looked out nearly due south. He had slightly drawn the lavender-blue-patterned curtain in order not to be dazzled by the sun. The curtain hung still; there was no wind. Only now and then a gentle movement riffled the pages. René once more read the concluding words of the manuscript: "*Explicit. Hoc est verum et cetera* what hath ben called fals rumour. *Actum sexagesimo nono aetatis meae anno Aug. Vind. MDXVIJ* on Tuesday byfore Ascension Daye. Ruodlip von der Vläntsch."

Out came Privy Councilor of the Archives Grotefend from René's briefcase, from whom René could quickly ascertain that the "Tuesday before Ascension Day" in the year 1517 had fallen on May 19. The *actum* evidently referred to the completion of the writing, not to the events narrated, which had taken place in 1464.

René screwed the cap on his fountain pen, closed manuscript and notebook, and put both away carefully. He had had enough for the present. But there was no getting away from it—the rest of the day would have to be spent upon the manias of Herr Achaz von Neudegg and Herr Jan Herzka.

There still remained some time until lunch, he thought.

Following Ruodlieb's account, he had drawn a little plan of the caverns, for there was no drawing in the manuscript, helpful as it would have been. René now tucked this drawing into his portfolio.

He drew the curtain fully open. The sunlight washed over him and fell deep into the room, while outside in the distance its glow laid a sheet over everything and dissolved outlines. The view from up here was more generous than from the ramp or the courtyard; one saw out beyond the glittering steeple of the church tower, and far beyond the woods René thought he could discern the whitish wall of distant and far higher mountains.

There were purer joys than crawling around in caverns where honorable widows had been tormented.

He heard the rumble of an organ. Soon it grew louder. Now came the choral hymn "Whither shall I turn?"

Herzka, then, was conducting a little service in memoriam for the dead composer Alexander Alexandrovich Slobedeff.

And Mörbischer was playing for him.

A crazy castle! You could give a play here, René thought, entitled *Le donjon des fous*—"The Madmen's Keep." The whole gang of them belonged here: Schlaggenberg, Eulenfeld, Körger, Orkay. They would hold foes at bay—until there was really cause to do so.

In the end Herr Achaz had also had to hold foes at bay. René pictured him speaking from the gallery over the gate to the lords and men-at-arms who had marched up to the other side of the moat (on account of the widows!). Only the menacing cannon had come to nothing; the clumsy things could not be brought up so steeply pitched a road. Herr Achaz spoke with great self-assurance, impressively and successfully: "Moste noble lordes, I muste alas balke your plannes. . . ." All in the very words of Ruodlip von der Vläntsch. It seemed to René that he could actually hear Lord Achaz's voice. Speaking well and skillfully ("damned wymmenfolke; we ryde forth with fyve score horse and not one canon nor bombarde, where sixe or seven be nedeful"—thus must have run the thoughts of one after another of the attacking party, until, with common accord, they all withdrew, blaming the widows themselves, who had come forth from the castle and announced "publickly" that no harm had been done them and that they were well). Yes, Herr Achaz spoke well and skillfully. And yet he was insane. Like the others.

The gong clanged. René went downstairs.

To Death man swiftly falls a prey; nor is it always physical death. Whither shall I turn? Jan Herzka wheeled behind Mörbischer down a somewhat narrower staircase below the main stairs; the vaulting was supported by those same stubby pillars, only they were less smooth here, and of darker stone.

Stepping off the last steps, they stood in a corridor that ran off to either side. On the left, obviously along the longitudinal axis of the building, it approached the great tower; toward the right, however, it deviated ever so slightly from its previous direction, and also sloped gently upward like a ramp. Mörbischer said that this corridor led straight to a gate in the rear narrow side of the castle. It was said that in times of war or the Turkish peril the peasants roundabout used to bring their cattle and possessions into the cellars of the castle through this gate. René thought that all this might well be part of the old substructure of the castle; but his knowledge of such architectural matters was too meager for him to be certain. The corridor was quite wide; an ox or even a cart could have been driven through it comfortably.

Everything down here was clean and well lit; at intervals of four yards an electric bulb glowed beneath the vaulting.

Mörbischer showed them several large chambers on the right of the corridor, which had supposedly served as shelters. Conditions were not bad in these rooms; you could look out through loophole windows to a great distance, in the same direction as from the windows of the library. In one of the rooms there was a tremendous, though ruined, fireplace of the kind that can still be found in the comfortable kitchens of French farmhouses. Another vault had obviously been intended as an emergency stable; it was equipped with stone feed troughs.

To the left of the corridor lay several cellars which were still in use.

Unexpectedly, they found themselves stepping through a small arch between the foundations of the tower and then over several steps into the tower's lowest story.

Seeing the narrow winding staircase, Herzka announced that he would not bother to climb the watchtower now. Perhaps he said this out of consideration for Mörbischer's old bones. Mörbischer, at any rate, seemed quite content.

For René there was enough to see here, though Jan Herzka might not be finding it too interesting. The stairs had perhaps been built in at the time the manor house was extended and joined to the "belfroi." For the most part these final refuges of a castle had their only entrance at the height of the second story, accessible only by ladders; everything underneath would be solidly walled up. On the other hand, down here in the substructure of the tower were defensive arrangements of such excellence that they could scarcely have gone unused in times past.

The room reminded Stangeler vividly of one that he had seen at Narva, when he was returning from Russia. It had been in the old citadel there, too; part of the fortress was separated from the rest, forming an outwork, and so encircled by the river Narova that at first glance you thought the water ran back upon itself, for it washed almost entirely around the foot of the castle. In the Cyclopean walls of one tower there had been another rather lentil-shaped room similar to this one in the substructure of Neudegg's *belfroi.*

The position of the loopholes and the view from them told the whole story. Every loophole in the thick walls widened out inwardly in such a manner that the crossbowman could comfortably draw even a wide and heavy weapon. Before each of these niches were two steps for the archer; if he stepped upon the lower step and put his weapon into position, the line of fire passed over the moat and cut across the road about half the height of a man. If, however, the archer posted himself on the upper step, he could tilt his weapon so that the bolt would fall into the moat. The four loopholes, each with two different angles of fire, were arranged to cover particular parts of the terrain outside. From the first loophole the road before the bridge and the corresponding strip of moat along it, or rather diagonal to it, could be placed under fire. The second loophole's range included the strip of road directly opposite, and the moat in front. The third aimed at the road and moat where the access ramp dropped and turned around the corner of the castle to its longitudinal face. Here the moat had, in modern times, flattened out and almost disappeared. The fourth loophole looked down on the road and moat on the longitudinal face: these latter two loopholes at sharper and sharper angles.

Enemies could get around this powerful corner tower only by advancing in the moat close up to the wall of the castle. But a well-preserved pitch gutter suggested plainly what they would be up against. One could picture the hot black serpents of pitch running out of the six spouts distributed around the tower, splashing down below and sending out a fiery spray in all directions. Under such conditions the devil in person might have been able to make his way around the *belfroi*, but no one else. Which meant that an enemy had to run straight ahead into the bolts from the crossbows. Moreover, if the attackers from the road or moat did come up to the tower, they could be shot at from the gallery over the portal of the drawbridge; and if the advancing enemy made his way still further, he would soon have a crossbowman from the substructure of the tower at his back, not to speak of the bolts flying from the numerous loopholes in the battlements between tower and bridge. Here, too, more deadly spouts were visible. This weakest side of the castle, near the road and drawbridge—for everywhere else the cliff dropped precipitately away from the walls—had been given the strongest defenses. Stangeler was once again struck by the thought that by no means at all ages had the weapons of offense matched those of the defense—as the time-honored cliché held. During the Middle Ages—at least until the creation of practical artillery that could readily be aimed and transported—the defensive obviously had the upper hand. It must have been a determining factor in the course of events; indeed, in the whole aspect of the age.

In the meanwhile René had appropriated the hammer and was tapping away at the floor, especially in the center of the room. But here, as he had expected, there was nothing but solid bedrock. No romanticism, no dungeons. Herzka was now watching him with interest—whereas while René had been pursuing his leisurely inspection of the loopholes, Herzka's boredom had been only too evident. As if he were locked up in a veritable dungeon of the emotions which permitted him only impatience toward everything outside. René, in his exceptionally liberated condition, felt walls of ponderous stone intervening between himself and the enclosure that held Jan Herzka prisoner. He himself was moving about freely in open spaces, enjoying the new ease and grace which had been conferred upon him. But he was aware, from frequent incarcerations, of a similar walled-off segment within himself, like that which now held Herzka captive. The captivity was self-willed, and he had dug and grubbed around in it— though its nature and tensions had doubtless been altogether different from and far more innocent than Jan Herzka's private dungeon. . . . But it helped him to understand Herzka now. He partook fraternally of Herzka's experience; for he had a part of Herzka in himself. It was as simple as that. At the dividing wall— which perhaps Herzka did not feel at all, but which cut sharply through Stangeler—there was even a sense of burning pain. Suddenly Stangeler felt that his association with Schlaggenberg, Eulenfeld, Orkay, Körger, was harming him all the time. The damage we derive from a friend is often as great as the benefit we derive from an enemy; but the infantile host of emotions, of sympathies and antipathies, tumble about so wildly that like unruly children they have taken the name plates from their proper places.

In these few moments René largely broke with the life he had led in Vienna. Or rather, it fell away from him like a layer of superficial scales. And he knew that he must leave it behind, must remain where he was—not in this *donjon des fous*, but in the position of inner security he had attained. During these few seconds he struggled, with a cold savagery, to hold the ground he had gained.

Then he recalled Brother Herzka, and determined not to climb the tower at this time; for he had been on the point of doing so alone, without putting Herzka and Mörbischer to the effort. The castellan had stepped under a narrow arch which led into the second underground passageway of the castle. Switching on the light, he preceded Herzka and René down some forty steps. It was not only light here, but dry also. That seemed surprising, for at one point in the narrow corridor they had seen living rock rather than masonry.

Although narrow, the passage was of more than twice a man's height; its form was actually that of a deep crack. Just above the heads of the three men the width doubled, for here there was a continuous archers' platform which could be reached by a short stairway on the side. Several loopholes admitted the daylight from above. René instantly reasoned that these permitted firing at the edge of the fosse. The rampart up above, as René had already seen, was likewise arranged for defending archers. This meant that two rows of crossbowmen were stationed here, although the lower row had to be shorter, whereas up above the rampart continued as far as the bridge. For this corridor here ended abruptly.

René, who had noticed the loopholes in the fosse wall when the two of them arrived the day before—the inner wall towered over the other somewhat—realized now that any enemy who attempted to avoid the *belfroi* and advance through the woods as far as the road would come under an annihilating hail of bolts just as soon as he appeared above the edge of the road. For the archers from the portal could likewise participate in the defense. When they were driving up in the car the previous day Herzka had wondered why the moat should have holes on the inside; if water were let into the moat, he remarked, would it not flow right out? René had explained that the fosses of castles on heights had never been filled with water. Where would the water have come from?

But René's attention was now drawn away from all these matters and concentrated upon quite another point. They had reached the end of the corridor, which probably lay outside the foundations of the manor house. Now they were standing in front of a cellar wall smeared with old flaking plaster. Not far from the end of the corridor was a low doorway on the left. Mörbischer stepped through this and switched on the light in the room beyond. René, after glancing into the room, took from his wallet the drawing he had made, based on Ruodlieb's data. He lingered outside in the corridor, near the door. After studying the diagram for a moment, he turned to Jan Herzka, who was standing at his side.

"We have reached the very spot, Herr Herzka. Notice everything carefully now."

They stepped through the arched doorway and into a chamber about sixteen feet long and thirteen wide. Above their heads, at about the height of an outstretched arm, ran a shelf from which at intervals pilasters descended to the floor. In the center of the room stood a solitary stub of a pillar that reached only halfway to the ceiling. But it seemed never to have been a pillar for supporting the ceiling, since the latter arched away above it. On the wall toward the main body of the castle there was another large, collapsed fireplace; next to it a number of steps led up into a second but smaller room in which there were also remnants of a fireplace. Everything was brightly illuminated by the electric lights on the ceiling.

"I suppose these too were emergency shelters—casemates, I believe they were called," Mörbischer said.

"And the pillars?" Herzka replied.

"Perhaps hitching posts for horses," Mörbischer suggested.

René, standing behind him, smiled for a moment. "Herr Mörbischer," he said, "may I have that hammer again for a moment, please?"

He stepped out into the corridor and went to the end of it.

There he studied the narrow terminal wall for a few minutes, stooping and apparently looking for something along the sides of the passage. Herzka and Mörbischer stood behind him.

"When I strike the wall now," René said, "you will hear the sound of massive masonry."

He struck the wall in front of him chest high. It was as he had said. Fragments of the dirty plaster fell, and the clear sound of solid stone rang under the blow.

"Now listen carefully, Herr Herzka," René continued. "If I am correctly informed, there is a room behind here." He pointed to an area of wall somewhat above his head. Then he tapped lightly with the hammer. The sound was unmistakably hollow. At the same time all sorts of small particles of stone and lime fell from the wall.

"How did you know that, Herr Doktor?" Mörbischer asked in amazement. He had evidently taken a liking to René from the first; but now he was enormously impressed.

"Yes, that's our Herr Doktor for you!" Herzka said with a nervous laugh.

René returned the hammer to Mörbischer. "You never knew of it?" he asked.

"No," the castellan said. "The late baron never wanted me poking around down here. I've scarcely been here more than two or three times. We used only the cellars over there. I always thought we could raise mushrooms down here. Herr Achaz was very fond of them, but he wouldn't give me permission. But how did you know that the passage extends further, sir?" He pointed to the wall.

"From my work in the library, Herr Mörbischer," René replied. "It is mentioned in an old manuscript there. And now we must do a bit of violence to this place, Herr Mörbischer—in the interests of science. Up there in the wall there is a door. There used to be steps leading up to it; you can even see traces of them here. The masonry sealing it up appears to be very brittle. As you saw, so much of it fell when I tapped it lightly with the hammer. Might we please have two of your men with a short ladder and a few tools? I think a few blows with a pickaxe will be all we need. Behind it there is a corridor which leads around the two rooms here. I want to enter that corridor."

"But, Herr Doktor, do you think it advisable—mightn't the wall collapse somewhere . . . ?"

"I'll make it worth your men's while, Herr Mörbischer," Herzka said.

Mörbischer bowed to Herzka, with a faint smile. "Certainly, certainly, sir, no question about that. . . . I am only concerned for the Herr Doktor's safety."

"No need to be, Herr Mörbischer," René said. "I'm sure that everything behind there is built of just as solid stone as here; in fact, part of it is probably bedrock. Only the rectangle of the door seems to be closed up with some crumbly material."

"Well then—may I leave you for a little while? I'll fetch the coachman and the gardener."

He left.

René took out his cigarette case.

The smoke floated about like something utterly incongruous. One was forcibly impressed by the fact that it was out of keeping here. Perhaps this was the first time anyone had ever smoked in these caverns, Herzka remarked.

They stepped into the first of the two chambers. René studied the pillar in the brilliant glare of the electric lights on the ceiling. It seemed to him that it did not belong here at all, that it was a fragment of a building carried in from somewhere else, and possibly of very great age. The foot of the pillar had obviously been sunk deep into the ground; it stood with iron rigidity.

"No, there was another kind of smoke here," René said while he examined it.

"What do you mean?" Herzka asked.

"Incense," René replied. "Before the torture of a witch, incense was always burned. And this was a torture chamber. In the adjoining room the victim was undressed and examined for the witches' mark, though not in every case. Then she was led out, tied by her wrists to the pillar, and scourged, sometimes, no doubt, only for form's sake, in order to intimidate her. Almost every interrogation began that way. Here, at this pillar, the widow of a mayor of Lienz was scourged—a beautiful woman, so it is said, though about fifty years old. And another woman also."

He looked hard at Jan after these revelations. Now Herzka in his turn produced his cigarette case. He said nothing, however, but turned away and walked slowly over to the steps which led to the smaller room, stepped under the low arched doorway, and remained standing in the room for a while.

Some time passed while René once again studied the pillar carefully, by now inclining to the belief that it might even be of Roman origin.

Then he heard footsteps on the stairs into the cellars.

René went out to the corridor again. The two men, armed with crowbars and wrecking bars, came along carrying a short ladder, which they leaned against the end of the corridor. René went up it and traced the outline of the doorway with the hammer. Then Herzka, Stangeler, and Mörbischer stepped back into the chamber and left the men to their labor, so that they would not have to look out to see where the fragments were falling. Moreover, in the chamber they were not bothered by the dust.

With dull blows, thuds, rumbles, and pattering of rubble, it was soon done. Through the arch of their doorway they saw dust floating in the sharp electric light and sinking down to the floor of the corridor.

Herzka distributed large tips. This was more than generosity, it was lavishness. Mörbischer smiled. A general air of good humor prevailed. The men left the ladder leaning against the wall, picked up their tools, and left.

High at the end of the corridor a small doorway yawned like a black open maw, the last rung of the ladder projecting into it. Under the dust-powdered ladder were heaps of broken masonry.

"May I have the flashlight now?" Stangeler said to Herzka. "I'll climb into there. Will you be good enough to stand near the pillar in the first chamber? And when I call to you to switch off the light, please do so."

762 / THE DEMONS

"I don't understand," said Herzka, who seemed to have become rather distraught. "We won't be able to hear you."

"You'll hear me very well," René said. "As if I were standing right at your side."

He first returned to the front room with Herzka and Mörbischer (the castellan was now regarding Stangeler with a mingling of mute admiration and concern). There he removed his jacket, looked around, and seeing no hook on which to hang it, or any other place to put it, tossed it with a certain conscious pleasure over the stump of the pillar. It was an act of insolence toward Herzka—the only one which René had permitted himself in the course of this whole affair. The jacket on the pillar was a ludicrous touch, not to say a crass violation of the spirit of the place. Then Stangeler went out into the corridor again. Herzka and Mörbischer followed, steadying the ladder while René climbed it. He flashed his light through the opening. They watched him as he stepped off the ladder and slowly disappeared to the left. Then they returned to the front chamber, where René's jacket hung like a hood over the pillar. Herzka regarded it with unconcealed distaste. But there was nothing to be done about it. He would have to put up with it, much as it disturbed the romance of the place.

For a while Herzka and Mörbischer stood motionless beside the pillar.

Everything was sharply illuminated by the electric lights on the ceiling.

On the floor at the foot of the pillar lay a cigarette butt Stangeler had discarded—although that had not been an act of brazenness. To Herzka, however, this relic now supplemented the impression of the jacket draped over the pillar.

"Would you put the light out now, please?" came a voice from just over their heads. Both men started. It was inevitable, given the charge of tension that had somehow come into the air. Mörbischer went over to the switch. A moment later the little room was plunged into total darkness.

Above their heads, but from the wall, not the ceiling, emerged the beam of the large flashlight René was carrying. The light came from an opening they had not noticed before, and played over the pillar and the two men. Looking closer, Jan saw that the aperture through which the light fell consisted of two narrow slits which together formed an inverted T (⊥).

"Now would you please go into the next room?" Stangeler's voice said. At the same time the ray of light turned and lit the way to the steps and the arched doorway. Then darkness fell again. Inside the second room, Herzka and Mörbischer took another two steps and stood still. They imagined they heard a noise, which was probably Stangeler; and then the ray of light struck them again, from similar slits. Then they heard Stangeler say: "Switch on the light again; I'm coming back now." The beam moved and lighted Mörbischer the way to the switch.

The two men stepped out into the corridor, and immediately afterwards René appeared in the opening above the ladder. Laughing, he clambered down. "Long live Ruodlieb von der Vläntsch!" he said. "Incidentally, I'll never believe that the fellow really bore such a name. Perfectly ridiculous. Probably it's a cryptogram—they were fond of such games in the fifteenth century. Perhaps I'll figure it out sooner or later."

He dusted off the palms of his hands, stepped quickly into the front chamber, and took his jacket from the pillar; the jacket, too, had become somewhat dusty.

Well, the drapery was gone, but the cigarette butt still lay on the floor. Jan would have liked to pick it up and dispose of it, but of course that wouldn't do; he had got rid of his own at the fireplace, covering it with a few fragments of crumbled mortar.

"Incidentally," Herzka thought, "these glaring electric lights must be removed from the ceiling. There must be some other way to arrange the lighting, and not with exposed wires."

"Now let us consider the stunt from out here," Stangeler said happily. "When we were standing here before, I could not find the slits, although I knew they were there. You see"—he pointed overhead—"the pilasters have a kind of bracket on top, and the slits are next to them. In the other room the arrangement was similar, but perhaps even more cleverly installed."

Mörbischer seemed to have been struck dumb.

Stangeler's behavior revived in Jan Herzka a distinct recollection of his childhood. He lay in bed with fever, quite hot, perhaps perspiring a little. The doctor came in, accompanied by his father. The cool hands touched and tapped the small patient's chest and stomach; then his hot wrist lay between fingers taking his pulse; then the gleaming stethoscope was applied to his heart and he saw the doctor's close-cropped, silvery-gray hair close above him (hair similar to Mörbischer's). To sum it up: he was inside, locked up, caught, hot and perspiring; but the doctor had stood outside, with cool clean hands and close-cropped hair, which smelled good, and with the clean shining stethoscope —belonging to a world of infinite order and perfection. But the main thing was the doctor's being altogether outside, unimaginably free. Toward Stangeler, Herzka felt a total impotence, perhaps even the remote possibility of impotent fury. For Jan had no way of knowing the extent of René's tolerance; nor could he grasp the fact that René's attitude contained not the slightest hint of criticism.

For fleeting seconds Herzka was obsessed with rage at those two trivialities: the coat draped on the pillar, and the cigarette stub that still lay at the foot of it.

But that was passing.

Stangeler invited Jan to inspect the newly discovered chamber.

Mörbischer was glad to be excused.

Already René was removing his smart jacket again and draping it once more over the pillar.

"Isn't it cold back there?" Herzka asked.

"Not a bit," René said. "No more than it is here. I want to spare my jacket. You can't help brushing against the walls."

This left Herzka no choice but to remove his jacket and hang it over René's; he slammed it on top of it, rather. Oddly enough, that act discharged his vexation, relaxed him. They left the pillar behind them under a doubly thick hood.

They climbed the ladder, René leading the way and almost immediately switching on the flashlight. They did not need to stoop. The floor seemed to be firm and hard, but not completely level. After a few yards it turned the corner to the left, and from here on the passage was wider. A band of light fell diagonally across it. It came from the front chamber, where the pillar stood. Now the perpendicular slits could be discerned. Herzka stepped into the comfortable niche and peered through the slits. He could see a large part of the torture chamber. Alongside the incongruously swaddled pillar stood Herr Mörbischer, looking equally out of place.

"Why has it this particular form?" Herzka inquired, drawing the inverted T in the air.

"To allow room for aiming a crossbow to the sides and up and down," René replied.

"You mean crossbows were used in here?" Jan asked, in a tone of some disillusionment.

"Yes," Stangeler said. "You will hear about that this afternoon."

Herzka said no more. They walked a few steps farther and looked down into the second chamber through the same arrangement.

When they had returned to Mörbischer and once again donned their jackets, Stangeler said that before tea he wanted to climb the tower—not through the house but via the tower stairway itself.

"You can go straight up, Herr Doktor," Mörbischer said. "It is all in good order, stairs, banisters, railings, everything is firm and solid."

"I'll return through the long underground corridor and from there to my room to wash up and fetch the manuscript. Then I'll come to tea in the library to read aloud, if that's all right with you, Herr Herzka."

"Certainly. We'll see you shortly, then."

Mörbischer bowed, smiling.

He and Jan slowly climbed back into daylight.

"An extraordinary young scholar, Doktor von Stangeler," Mörbischer said in that discreet tone of which he was a veritable master.

"Yes, he is stupendous," Herzka replied. "Though he says that every student at the Institute for Historical Studies can do the like, and that most know far more than he."

"I can scarcely believe that," Mörbischer replied.

"It is possible," said Herzka. "Our Austrian scholars are amazing fellows. Think of the medical men, for example. . . . Herr Mörbischer," he continued, "I should like to have a few alterations made down here. Above all we must have a proper door installed in the hole that was broken open today, of dark wood, with a small stone staircase in front of it. And the corridor behind ought to be provided with electric light. On the other hand I'd like a different kind of illumination in the two rooms. The electric bulbs ought to be concealed. I must think that part of it over. Perhaps they can be installed in niches. The way it is now—it violates the style." (Herzka was astonished at himself. The things he was saying seemed to him suddenly the outermost brink of daring. Mörbischer, however, took it all for granted. An old lackey is never astonished, never even mildly surprised; he is *nil admirari* incarnate.) "But the most important thing," Jan continued, "is the question of heating."

"We would only have to have the two fireplaces rebuilt," Mörbischer said. "The chimneys are perfectly in order. The chimney sweep has told me that. He was inside. They are big enough to creep into. The flues of open fireplaces almost always are."

"Good. But then the newly discovered corridor remains unheated. I suppose that would have to be done with electric radiators."

"I don't think that would be necessary, sir," Mörbischer said (absolutely impassively). "While you two gentlemen were examining the passage, I happened to think how the flues of the

chimneys must run in relation to the corridor, because I remembered what the chimney sweep had said. If the fireplaces
were repaired, the same flues would serve the room behind.
Still, the most practicable thing might be to install electric heating everywhere down there. Open fireplaces—they're really more
for the looks, you know. You need a wagonload of wood to keep
them going. And as for preserving the style—that shouldn't be
too difficult. Everything could be done with hidden installations.
Radiators in niches also."

"Idiot!" Herzka thought. Aloud, he said: "Yes, you are right,
Herr Mörbischer. I'll have both kinds of heating installed."

He turned toward the stairs. Where else was there to turn?

Meanwhile Stangeler had reached the top of the tower—and at
the same time plunged, for fleeting moments, into the depths of
recollection of certain dreams which sometimes troubled him:
of being exposed high up on a tower, irresistibly conveyed thither
by an elevator, a tiny cabin, ascending from one dizzying landing
to another still higher.

Here it was a matter of turning innumerable times around the
axis of a narrow staircase.

In order to avoid a trap door, the exit to the platform had
been protected by a wooden hatchway in the shape of a weather-
tight little cabin.

During the climb René had entered several of the tower rooms
—they were empty—and made some further observations concerning the defenses. But his interest in this had slackened.
From the various floors of the tower, none of which were exactly
on a level with those of the manor house, doors with small steps
up or down led into the wide corridors of the house. René thus
discovered a short cut to his room, and decided to return this
way from the top and so avoid traversing the long underground
corridor again.

When he stepped out of the cabin onto the massive broad
platform, which was surrounded by a high rampart, he heard,

borne by the gentle south wind, the Angelus tolling from the church whose steeple he could see from his window.

He walked around the rampart, without really paying attention to the impressive view. He had no need to study its details now, and perhaps for that very reason its presence had a powerful liberating effect upon him. Here, properly speaking—and not while he was bent over the manuscript, or studying the loopholes, or delving about the cellars—he sensed fully the reality in which this Herr Achaz had been rooted. The castle explained the man. Impregnable as it was, its lord must have felt himself the master of things to a degree which in our times would be inconceivable even to the most powerful. Let the south wind blow hot, let evil stars shine, or the scum from the mingled remains of long-forgotten forefathers rise to the surface—in this place the next step would have to be over the brink to excess. If a man lived the whole of his life without once going over that brink, it was at the price of heroic self-conquest. What a thing it was for a man to live in this bastion under this sky, high above the countryside, mighty of arm, as certain of the devotion of his yeomen as he was of the bolt from his own bow or the stroke of his own sword-arm. "My yonge lorde was in those dayes a worthy knyght and right glad in his armures [armor]." Evidently this Ruodlieb, or whatever his real name might have been, had been familiar with Hartmann von Aue's *Gregorius*, for the phrase "right glad in his armures" was a quotation from that poet. Stangeler had recognized the phrase in his first quick reading of the manuscript. A point that shed some light on the reading habits of young noblemen in the fifteenth century, he thought. . . .

Though perhaps Ruodlieb had read the *Gregorius* in later life.

In any case: all really profound thinking seeks distance—in time and in space. There can be no profound thought about things close at hand, only brooding. And in this case Herr Achaz was very close to him.

His feeling as he stepped out on the platform and heard the Angelus had been quite different; much had changed in a few minutes. By climbing the tower he had raised himself up, leaving

Herzka and Mörbischer far below him, and also the touch of self-importance and brashness that had afflicted him once or twice in the cellars. Now the tolling bells died; a single tone concluded the Angelus, frail, muted, as though heard through walls, as you might hear a distant piano in an apartment house.

"It's Mary. She's playing again."

The adolescent girl brought the tea.

Stangeler crawled into the teacup. He seemed to be imbibing the tea and inhaling the cigarette smoke simultaneously. It was an extremely intense proceeding. Herzka sat by, forcing himself to be patient. Suddenly he recognized that sitting opposite him was a man who knew more about him than even Magdalena Güllich—and who was at the same time virtually a stranger to him. Only late recognition of the obvious produces such a shock as Herzka now experienced. Obvious things are monsters that have slept at our side. Now the monster awakens, stirs. We have recognized it. Only obvious things can be the subject of real acts of thought. What is original and interesting is always second class. That is why there are only second-class anecdotes.

At last René spoke up. "Before I read the medieval manuscript to you, Herr Herzka," he said, "I must make a few brief remarks. Not on the nature of witch trials—that is, on demonology and whether or not it existed. We talked about that on Saturday, after all. Moreover, not all witch trials fall into any such category. Modern 'enlightened' literature on this subject is, most of it, quite impossible. Such enlightenment is, in my opinion, the most arrant stupidity. Nor has much consideration been given to the fact that the hunt for witches often had motives lying outside the matter itself: motives such as money and power. Accusations of witchcraft were a fine way to dispose of burdensome members of the family; and some persons might have had a whole flock to dispose of. In the second place—and this point is always prudishly passed over or barely touched on by so-called scholars —it was a way for men to lay hold of women who could not be obtained in any other way. In such a case the routines of a witch trial offered rich opportunities for amusement. It seems that a good many powerful and lesser lords indulged in such practices. One such was your forefather, Achaz von Neudegg.

"These things were no doubt an abuse of power. For in the views of the times, a mixed spiritual and secular commission should have been called in to examine the crime of sorcery. But even after witch trials were put on an official basis, no clear delegation of authority was ever made. Effective and comprehensive regulations were lacking. The medieval world as a whole lacked such regulations—and this went on into later centuries. Our ancestors did not have that drive for thorough organization, for regulating literally everything, which stamps our age. According to the views of those times, the bishop, or at least some spiritual adviser, should participate in sorcery cases. For witchcraft was always regarded as heresy as well. Nevertheless, the spiritual authorities were frequently evaded or passed over. Secular lords and committees of townsmen continued to preside over such trials even after the church had set up machinery for trying witches, both in Catholic and later in Protestant countries. This must be considered in connection with Achaz von Neudegg's proceedings, if we want to see them in the right light. He had to pretend to be acting in the general interest of the countryside by taking instant steps against sorcery—for fear of sorcery was a mania with the people. He maintained that he was laying hold of the mischief vigorously and directly. Of course it remained an outrage that the widow of a mayor and a kinswoman of hers should have been seized by him—and outside the limits of his judicial authority, at that. Incidentally, it is not clear whether Lord Achaz ever actually possessed judicial authority—here at Neudegg, I mean. It seems probable to me, but rule of the land and judicial authority did not always coincide. I shall be able to track down these details fairly easily later on. It appears that he was infringing upon someone else's jurisdiction in seizing the two women.

"But enough of this. The man whose story you are now going

to hear gives his name as Ruodlieb von der Vläntsch. He was a 'squire'—that is, a boy of knightly birth who had not yet received the accolade. Squires were a social grouping, distinct enough to be represented at district diets, for we read that these were composed of 'prelates, lords, knights and squires.' Achaz, on the other hand, was a 'lord,' a baron. At the time of the events described Ruodlieb was somewhat more than fifteen years old. He took notes of the events, but did not write this account until fifty-three years later, at Augsburg in the year 1517. When I come to copy the text for scholarly purposes, I shall reproduce the original in all its peculiarities. But I thought I would make a typewritten copy especially for you, Herr Herzka, modernizing the text somewhat, putting *v*'s and *u*'s in their proper place, for example, though leaving the charmingly chaotic spelling of the time and many of the expressions which give the thing its character. In general, clarifying the text as I shall now do when reading it aloud to you."

Once again Jan was reminded of his childhood sickroom, of the slight odor of disinfectants which came from the doctor as his close-cropped, silvery-gray head bent over the young patient. It was a faint, fine, cooling odor of carbolic that he sensed, the disinfectant which in a figurative sense proceeded from every scientific field, not medicine alone, and drew a sharp line between itself and unfumigated unscientific life.

"Here goes," Stangeler said, opening the old manuscript.

A TYME after duke Albrechts deth, he dyed the Friday after
Seint Andrewe of last yere ["December 2, 1463"], the noble lord
Lienhart von Felsegk had wreton to my lorde from Tyrol where
the same was wyth duke Sygmund that he had lettres from
Vienne sayyng the duke of Vienne ["Albrecht, that is"] had been
poysoned, as hath ben ofte bruyted ["rumored"], and sayying it
was true and not that he dyed of the pestyllaunce as the Imperyales saye ["the Imperials were the partisans of Emperor Fred-
erick III, who was Duke Albrecht's brother and his bitter
enemy"]. For that he had receyved a longe lettre from Hans
Hierzman, the whiche was doorkeeper of the duke and sleped
alleway wyth him in the same chambre and with him Achaz
Neudegker also. The same was a cosyn of my yonge lorde, who
hyght by lyke ["whose name was the same"] and served that
tyme the duke. Hierzman kept a nyght cap in memoriam of the
duke, the same whereon the poor noble lorde vomitted in his last
maladye, and otheres kept other thinges of no worth albeit the
maistres of medicines advysed ayen ["against"] it. But none toke
seke from the pestyllance, nother Neudegker nor Hierzman, the
whiche had layn in the bedde of the duke and in his swete after,
whan he wold be layd in an other bedde. And they had to slepe
therin, as he had commaunded theym, and he layd him self in
their bedde and sleped therein shortly byfore his deth. The
whiche was wel proof. The surgyens who opened ["autopsied"]

the duke after, sayde playnly he was poysoned and wist well to name the poyson, but were ordred not to speke.

My lorde was wood wrothe ["furious"] that this noble lord in suche wise was piteousely brought from lyf to deth, sith he had alleway ben good frende and bounden to duke Albrecht. And my lorde spake therof that yf any coud fynde the traytors whiche gaf poyson to the duke they shold be cut all to peces.

Thenne he wrot to his cosyn atte Vienne to go to her grace my lady margrave, that he myght lerne more. ["Katharina, wife of the Margrave of Baden, was the sister of the murdered duke and was living in Vienna at the time of his death."] But his cosyn dyd not answer and was doutles that tyme no more in the cite of Vienne. My lorde dyd chafe and wayte but message cam there noon.

My yonge lorde was sore angry who to fore was alleway glad and plesaunt, and rode alone in the weald ["woods"] and we ["the squires"] durst not ryde wyth him. And he waxed the more sad and wroth and ofte sayde yf suche a noble lorde myght be murthered, the which was nyghest frend to him, thenne no mans lyff was safe. For, sayde he, the murtherer muste have ben one nyghest to the duke. And Lorde Lienhart had wreton it was lorde Jörg vom Stain, so men said. But my lorde wold not bileve that and sayde that certaynly it was the Imperyales whiche gaf the poyson to his lorde duke Albrecht.

But if it had be lord Jürg, so sholde all the dukes and erles come togidre, not alone from Ostryche ["Austria"] but theym from Carinthia also, with men and coursers, to fynde and take him, that he myght be brought to jugement.

On Sunday after the Fast Weke ["February 26 in that year"] my lorde sayde he wold ride to lorde Lienhart in Tyrol that he myght lerne the more aboute duke Albrecht, for he was right sorowfull and his herte sad. We therfore made us redy toward our waye. My yonge lorde was in those dayes a worthy knyght and right glad in his armures ["armor"]. The tymes were peasfull and so he wold take onely Wolf wyth him, the which was a squyer

also, as was I. I knowe wel his ryght name but wold not
write it. Beside Wolf he had six horse ["that means: six mounted
mercenaries"]. Atte that tyme we kept a score of theym, men fro
Almayne or Beme ["that is, Germans or Bohemians"], they cam
from Ostryche for that theyre wages were not payd them, what
tymes had be the bataylles betwen his majesty the emperour and
lord Gamureten of Fronau, whiche contencion was tempred
anone ["settled by negotiation after a while"] in the yere Lxii.
These souldyours ["mercenaries"] were ynoughe for the defence
of the castell. Six of these he toke and also stedes for the packes.
Byfore the sonne rose up they rode on theyre waye on the laste
daye of Feverer, the nyne and twentyth, the which I have therfore held in remembraunce bycause it was an annus bissextus
["leap year"].

Atte the castell remayned onely sir Tristram Hamlecher,
knyght, who was my lordes captayne and burgrave, and sir
Oswalt Trittmang, knight, his stewarde, and two squyers, the one
named Heimo, a knyghts sone, and the others name I wyl not
saye, and I. And otherwyse onely servaunts and maides.

We thought to prouffyt us wel ["make good use of"] of the
tyme for to renewe all my lordes chambres and the stables also
and to put in ordre two arblastres ["crossbows"] and the
quareylles ["crossbow bolts"] therto, in the whiche we all employed our self and kept of good chere foure dayes.

The fourth daye, it was al redy ryght late night and alle on
slepe, I herde rollyng of wheeles and hoofbetes of mony ryders,
and sprunge from bedde and into my dresse in the darknesse.
And herde the horn of the keper of the tour ["tower"] and toke
my arblastre and ranne to the ramparte and ranne others also
armed wyth me. Then herde I a horn from the rode, whiche I
knewe was my lordes tone that he was wont to winde atte the
hunte. I cam to the ramparte and herde my lorde calle, 'Ho, is
not Ruodl there?' 'Here am I, Sire,' I crye, and, 'what wold ye
comaunde, Sire?' 'Let doune the brigge, Ruodl,' he sayes, 'we
are come home ayen.'

I ranne anon ["immediately"] to the brigge, but were two

souldyours alleredy there that let doune the brigge. And cam a bigge wagon wyth hevy stedes, and sittyng on the wagon one of the Bemes ["Bohemians"], and the wagon was all yclosed. Thenne rode my lorde in and behinde him Wolf and the Bemes wyth the packe horses and also ledyng one horse withoute ryder which longed ["belonged"] to him that sat on the wagon. And seeyng me my lorde calleth out tyl me: 'We cam well to the lande of Tyrol and then to Apfaltersbach and have made a goode capture.'

But I knewe not what he mente therby and me thoughte who myght be wythin the wagon, so folowed them to the bayley where stode the wagon and the Bemes, who stayed mounted, onely my lorde alyghted from hys courser and sette fote on grounde. And Wolf and Heimo were there also and all wayted upon my lorde's wyll.

'Ye there,' he sayde, 'ye, Wolf and Heimo and Ruodl, take care and guarde you wel, for that here in this wagon sit two sorcereses whiche I have taken prysoner and wyl keep. Putte the tweyne in a chambre and wayte upon them, givyng them what it nedes them or they wyll, but see that they do not enscape you. Fecche two maides to attende upon them. But alle the nyght one of you two muste watch atte the door to the chambre.' Thenne he tourned to the wagon and called inne: 'Ryse up, ye wymmen.' And tourned hys backe and wente in to the hous. The Bemes yet satte upon their stedes, but whan the one of the wymmen nowe cam forthe from out the wagon, they tourned quyckly to the stable ward ["toward the stable"] and trotted awaye as faste they myght.

The affaire seemed us right straunge, and Heimo called tyl the souldyours, 'Wold ye leve wagon and horses in the bayley all nyght?' But al the whyle we were there wyth the two wymmen, none cam oute ayen.

Theraftre we broughte the wymmen up to the chambre, but noughte of them we sawe by cause of theyre mantles and wympels ["hoods"]. And Wolf, byfore he wold telle us aboute them, made the kytchen maides to go uppe. For that none wold

go he had to kicke them in the arse that they bringe mete
["food"] and wyn and fyre wode for the sorceresses.

Therafter Wolf recounted the affair to us, fyrst of how they
rode slowely two dayes to Apfaltersbach and there entred an
inne. Atte the inne were the two wymmen whiche cam fro
Lientz and thoughte to ryde ferrer ["farther"] to Paszriach by
the lytyl lake, and had the wagon and were alone, for that the
servaunt who drave them was runne awaye, bycause of what
Wolf sayde he knewe not. And otherwyse were al alone, the
which he thoughte straunge, that they shold go their waye by
them self. Atte Paszriach lyves the daughter of the one whiche is
soone to come to childbedde, she wold be wyth her in her oure.
The two wymmen were not yonge, sayde Wolf, but in no waye
ill of countenaunce ["ugly"], rather fayre ladyes. In the chambre
where they satte at bord, our yonge sire made merry wyth hem
and we alle dranke muche wyn and the lorde made fayre and
curteys speche with hem. But it was wel to see that they were
honeste ["honorable"] and wel manered, the whiche mayhap my
lorde was not alleweyes. For, saide Wolf, I saw him right
chaunged and ful of good chere, and wold not take his eyen fro
the wymmen and looked at the one more than tother and thenne
at tother more than the one. And I wyt ["knew"] not where al
that wold ende.

Therafter, sayde Wolf, the one dame went to her chambre, she
sayde she had a good spyce to putte into the wyn, the whiche
wold strengthe us, for that we had all drunke to muche of the
wyn and the spyce wold help us. But my yonge lorde followed
her withoute no noyse, and was still as eny mouse, and we alle
laughed and made a grete clamour that she myght the lesse here
him. What happed thenne in the upper chambres I knowe not,
nor wether lord Achaz gaf her to knowe that he was there, but
onely wot that they were goon ["gone"] from table lenger than it
taketh to telle slowely from one to hondred. The ladye cam doune
the stayres ayen, and the lorde had alleredy retourned to table.
And she broughte a dissh wyth nought but herbes in it, but suche
that the chambre was filled wyth the odoure therof. Which she

thenne mixte in a canne of wyn and saide we shold let stond a
whyle and thenne drinke. So we dyd and felt better in the hed
therfore, and soone as clere in the hed syth ["as if"] we had a
longe slepe and were sobre and had not drunke immoderatly.
And we stayed yet a whyle togidre.

In the mornyng my lord sayth to me in secrete that he had
looked in to theyre chambre, for that they had not shut the dore
behynd them, and that from the chambre of them there cam an
odoure an hondred fold mowe swete than fro the spyces whiche
they brought to table, also that he had there seen glas of venyse
["Venetian glass"] and other wares of grete pryce, al shinyng
bryght.

We breke thenne our fast with the wymen, and whyle etyng
my lorde saide he wold give them companye, and sith they ne
had no longer eny cocheman one of the Bemes shold sit and ryde
with hem. I herde this wyth grete merveyll ["was greatly surprised by this"]. And after we tourned backe in sted of kepyng
oure waye in to the lande of Tyrol, and rode we up the grete
ryvere ["the Drau"] ayen and to the lefte in to the othre valeye
and atte the last rode doune in to the valeye of Gail. My lordes
hors wente wyth empty sadell for muche parte of the waye, syth
he satte in the wagon by the wymen, and had plaisaunteryes with
hem. Also we alyghted from our stedes sixe or seven tymes and
toke reste and drank muche wyn, tyl that my lord sayde that we
alle soone wold have nede of those good spyces, but may hap
we wold kepe wel withoute. One of the wymen laughed and
saide the spyce was to depe in the chestes whiche they had in
the wagon.

Thenne, sayde Wolf, my lord drewe on his waye a whyle more
and I looked secretely atte hym from the syde and sawe that he
was pensefull ["thoughtful"] and sore troubled atte herte. And it
seemed me that it muste be bycause of the two wymen. For may
hap he had alleredy understonden that they were honeste wymen
and despyte al plaisaunterye he wold not get them into hys
power, though he were a lord and yong and wel-spoke and payd
them complimentes. For he sayde al the whyle lady to them

wiche ne were lady ne damoyselle ["that is, they were of the burgher class"].

Aftrewarde he gaf the spores ["spurs"] and rode to the wagon ayen and parleyed ["chatted"] wyth the wymen. And syth we halted severell tymes, the daye cam to an ende.

We were thenne at a place called Perg, but coud not be lodged for that there were of us eight and the two wymen also. But the Bemes were of good chere for that the wyn had coursed wel thurgh ["through"] their veynes, and sayde: 'If it plese you, sire, we wyll contente us wyth slepyng by the horses in the stable.' So thenne a chambre was gyven the two wymen and my lord and I made do to slepe in the parlour where we had sat with the wymen alle the evenyng, drinkyng and makyng muche plaisaunterie, and they had fecched theyre spyce from the cheste. And us seemed it sorcery that we dyd not have to slepe awaye the wyn but in a lytyl whyle felt wel and rested. I marked that my lorde was alleredy sore enamoured on the wymen and al afyre, but whiche was more tyl hys taste I knowe not to saye. For he made sporte wyth bothe, but they wyst wel to kepe theire honestye ["honor, good behavior"] the whyle they dranke.

The daye folowynge we rode on not swiftely, for that the wether remayned fayre. And halted six tymes wyth muche drinkynge, and the Bemes sang theyre owne songs that go strayght to the herte, for that they singe with swete melancoley. Theire singing liked wel my lorde and he gaf each of hem a good silver grote ["groat, a large coin of the time"], whiche them liked wel. And with haltyng and eting and drinkyng even cam and it grewe derk ["dark"]. And we cam to the street ["road"] that renneth under Neudegck where we wold soone see the castell but for the derk-nesse. Thenne onely the wymen marked that we were ne lenger on theyre waye. But I wot not, said Wolf, wether my lorde gaf the Bemes commaunde to sing or wether they dyd so of them selfe. The lorde satte in the wagon wyth the wymen and had muche plaisaunterie wyth hem and there was loude laughter.

Anon ["immediately"] the wymen wyshed to be conduited ["conducted"] to their inne, and cryed loudly to the Beme at the

reynes. But he halted onely at my lordes beheste. Thenne my
lorde sprang lythely fro the wagon and to my syde, I leding hys
horse, and right swiftely mounted he and called to the Beme:
'Drive fast as thou canst!' The Beme smote the stedes and we
rode lyke the wynde. And I, Wolf saith, tourned and herde the
wymen callyng and sawe in the derknesse the five Bemes and the
pack horses rennyng behinde us. And my lorde tourned up the
waye to Neudegck, to his owne grounde, and then sounded the
horne from the tour, and I sounded my horn, sayeth Wolf. And so
Wolf had tolde his tale.

Therafter nothing more happed for a whyle, and the wymen
satte in theyre chambre in comfort wyth al they had nede of and
a good fyre, and the servaunts were ne lenger so sore frayed
["afraid"] of the sorceresses. But the wymen demayned ["uttered"] stronge complayntes and wyshed to see my lorde that
they myght reproche him for detayning them and lettyng ["hin-
dering"] them to go theyre waye, the more syth the daughter of
the one certaynly laye in childe bedde alleredy. But my lorde
wold not go to theyre chambre, for all they called loudely for
hym. That wente so meny dayes. Menewhyle I sawe carpenters
and masones goying aboute the castell, but whyst not what they
dyd ne sawe eny of them at werke. I knew them wel and axed
them what they dyd, but wold none answere me, so thenne I
troubled me no more syth my lorde had given hem commaundes.

Al this tyme my lorde had meny devyses ["talked a great
deal"] with Sir Tristram and the stewarde in secrete, and that
they were advysing them in some bigge affaire, I marked wel.
And one mornyng my lorde called me and axed: 'Ruodl, ye
mowe ["can"] write wel, mowe ye not?' And I answered: 'Yea,
sire.' 'Lyst and here me wel,' he sayde; 'I have mynde to hold a
courte ayenst these sorceresses, of lordes, knyghtes and squyers.
Of prelates have we no nede. Ye wyll be the scrivener and write
the playntes and enquyres and what els there shal be. And this
even we wyll begin wyth the one of the two, wyth the widowe of
the bourghmaistre.'

Whan I herde that I was ful sore dolaunt ["grieved"], for how

shold that be withouten a bisshop for to endoctryne ["instruct"]
us, and me seemed erst ["at first"] that my lorde was come to
lese his corage ["had gone out of his mind"]. But I durst not
speke ne contradicte hym.

My lord sayde that Sir Tristram and Sir Oswalt wold sit wyth
hym on the courte. Now muste I telle of Sir Tristram and Sir
Oswalt. Sir Tristram was a good captayn, talle and lene ["lean"]
and allewaye pale as a talow candel and ne laughed never nor
made grete devyses ["not much of a talker"], more lyke to a
ghoste, me seemed, than a man of flesshe and blood. Tother, Sir
Oswalt, hym seemed eting and swillyng to plese hym more than
alle els, and was no ghoste for that he had a bigge stomak and
muche fatte and coud ete for three. And he wold ryde al daye
out in to the contre and press the chorles ["churls, peasants"]
and bringe in daye and nyght what longed ["belonged"] to my
lorde.

I wayted right troubled and soroweful tyl the even and menewhyle sought to speke wyth Heimo of it, but coud not fynde
hym, for that he muste ryde thre stedes of my lorde that were
overstonden ["had been standing too long idle"], and he cam
late back over the brigge wyth the thyrd horse. Anon I ranne to
hym and tolde hym that I muste have spech wyth hym in secrete.
Whan he cam fro the stable agayn I tolde hym what my lord hath
said and that he wold bringe the bourghmaistres widowe to tryal
and wold have me as scrivener. But he onely laughed and sayde:
'I wot that alleredy, ye be the scrivener and I the beadel, and we
wyll have muche plaisauntery therby and may hap come to the
peine forte with the bourghmaistress and the other.' And he
sayde also that my lord had alleredy spoke wyth hym and that
was al prepared. 'How meen ye that?' I axed, and he sayd: 'As
my lord and sire meeneth it.' And said I shold go wyth him and
he wold shewe me the preparacions. So thenne we wente to the
tour ["tower"] but not up to the batelment, in sted doune a
stayre and to an other seler ["cellar"] not where the wyn lay,
but one where I ne had be no more than ones ["once"] or
twyce.

Heimo toke candels from the lowest room of the tour, and we wente in to the low passage where the lyght shyneth from over-hed, for that an arblastrer ["crossbowman"] mowe stonde and shote atte the fosse. At the ende where the dore is, with stepes afore it, it was bolted and barred. I axed Heimo whither the dore ledde. He sayde he wyst not, but had herde that from here renneth a way under the grounde oute of the castell. I saide I wyll not beleve that, syn we be so hygh on the mountain, it muste be ne more than another seler, may hap Trittmang keepeth wyne there also. 'He myght have lefte it here,' saith Heimo, and pusheth open a dore and sheweth me a bigge chambre. 'But my lorde hath given the kegges feet, whyche is to saye he hath had them moved in to the bigge seler under the hous.'

Menewhyle we wente wyth the candels in to the vaulte, that was not lytyl, and Heimo sheweth me another chambre whiche was smaler. And in the bigge chambre I see in the mydde a pyller. 'What is that?' I ax Heimo, for me seemeth I ne had never seen the lyke there. 'A stake,' Heimo saith, and he laugheth as he was woned ["accustomed to"] these dayes. 'Yf ye wold knowe more, I saye: a martris ["torture"] stake.' 'How mene ye that?' I say, right wrothe. 'Whom wyll we martir here in Neudegck?' 'The sorceresses,' saith Heimo. 'We wyll martyr them yf they wyll not confesse.' 'Hath the devil alleredy taken you?' I crye. 'Ne me,' saith Heimo, 'but the sorceresses withoute doubt, or els may hap oure sire hym self.'

I sawe also one or other wyde benche in the chambre, and eke in the lytyl chambre, alle newe, so that now I wyst what werke the carpenteres were doyng in the castell. But I wold not beleve that Heimo sayde, for that he was oft a jestre and had also a careles tunge. But yet I grewe more frayed, the whyle I still thought all muste be a jeste and plaisauntry of said Heimo and knewe that he coud lye lyke ten paynemys ["heathens"].

I satte me doune on a lytyl cheste whiche also had not be there afore. What is in the cheste, I axed Heimo, and he saide: 'All that pertayneth to torture and peine forte.' But I yet dyd no gyve hym credence and poynted my thum atte myn arse and sayde:

'Heimo, ye mowe—ye knowe what.' But he laughed and sayde: 'Ye be the scrivener and I the beadel, and bothe muste there be for the peyne forte.' And saide ferrer ["further"]: 'Telle me, Ruodl, have ye ever behelde a woman sterk nakyd?' 'How so?' I sayde; 'I ne have never had to do wyth the kytchyn wenches.' 'Ne have I,' he saith, 'in no wyse. Syn they long ["belong"] to Sir Oswalts scope and are a knyghts laydyes, an it were, let hym kepe them. But none other women have ye ne behelde sterk nakyd?' Say I: 'None have I seen and by what cause sholde I have?' Saith he: 'Thenne wyll ye soone sette your eyen upon the bourghmaistress thus.' 'How so?' say I. Saith he: 'Thinke ye we shall dresse hir in mantel and wimpel afore the torture?' 'How mene ye that . . . ?' axed I, but sayde ne more, for that I marked suddaynly how that my herte beat harde, and becam fereful and me lyst to go awaye, so I stode up fro the lytyl cheste and we wente awaye.

Whan we cam up fro the tour, it was alleredy sore derk, and not long afore the tyme to souppe. The winde had tourned and now blewe hard over the bayley, fro the south—a winde from Venyse I wold call this winde by tymes. It was warm and not good and smakked of foulle leves of the forest. For snow ne lay no lenger, so muche tyme had passed syn that we had the wymen atte the castel. Soone it wold be Josephi ["March 19"]. And wythin a fortnyght wolde begin the payring of heth hennes, but my yong lord spake no worde of the hunte of heth cockes, the wiche was othirwyse his gretest joye alle the yere. Nor dyd he ryde no more, I me remembred now, for sooth, my lorde hath not rydden over the brigge in al this whyle. That me made sadde and the winde wayed me on the herte.

Whyle we soupped, Sir Oswalt Trittmang him stuffed ful hys belly and sware enfamousely atte the chorles ["peasants"] with displeysaunt devyses. And Sir Tristram honored hys name, for that he sayde no worde and loked atte the bord ["table"] as yf hys nose him dryppeth. My sire was pale of countenaunce and his hair unkempt, whiche was wel growne and the colour of rede gold. May hap he had a hawten ["proud"] loke, whiche came fro

hys strayght, short nose. Whyle etyng I caste secrete lokes at my
lorde, for that I was right fonde of hym, he beying a strayght,
good knyght, and I sawe too that he wente a crooked waye now,
whyche me muche greved.

After we had dyned my lorde saide we shold us betake to the
halle, whiche coud hardely be called suche, for that it was onely
a bigge chambre. There were somme tables and stoles in one
rowe, and one lytyl table wyth a candel and alle that pertayneth
to writyng, atte the whyche I muste me sette. And more candels
were on the othre tables. There them sette Sir Tristram and Sir
Oswalt and Wolf, and Heimo stonde by syde of them. And my
lordes chayre remayned emty, for after that he sayde to Heimo,
'Bringe the bourghmaistresse,' he wente outen the halle and cam
not backe. And Heimo wente for to bringen the bourghmaistresse, and my herte bete so hardely that I coud fele it in my
throte. Menewhyle it begynneth to rayne, and thondreth and
lyghtneth, but ferre awaye.

Efte ["afterwards"] passed a longe tyme and none sayde eny
worde, and Sir Tristram had the semblaunt ["appearance"] that
he were made of waxe, and Sir Oswalt fel on slepe in his chayre
and begynneth to snore, and Wolf stareth at the walle, tyl that
I thoughte he beleveth in this mummery ["farce"] and taketh
it ernest, thinkyng the women be sorceresses and that here was
a courte sittyng in right and lawe. For Wolf was an honest soule,
but ne ware nor wyse ["not very clever"].

Thenne openeth the dore and in cometh Heimo and bringeth
the bourghmaistresse and leadeth her in a straunge waye, for that
she walketh with her back to fore and he holdeth her by the arm
and ledeth her in suche wyse to us, as men be woned to do wyth
sorceresses whiche are to take ["to be taken"] to tryal ["this was
a general practice in witch trials"] lest they smyte theyre judges
wyth theyre eyen. Thenne he tourneth her right gentilly, and
thenne Sir Oswalt waketh fro hys halfe slepe and saith: 'God's
wounds, is the wenche here alleredy?' And as he saith that I loke
atte the bourghmaistresse, who stayeth silente, and I see that she
be whyte in her contenaunce, and I loke atte her fully and see

erst that she be a right fayre and beauteus woman in her dress of red taffet, and see her hygh brest and caste myn eyen incontynent ["immediately"] doune. Thenne I marked well and understode wherfore she had bere feet as men do wyth sorceresses ["that, too, was a general custom in witch trials"]. Me was somwhat atremblaunt in the handes. Her red goune fel to her bere feet. Sorceresses be so led for that men thynke they ne mowe scape yf that they stonden wyth bere feet on the erthe.

Sir Oswalt waketh atte laste and axeth a question, albeit hym seemeth not to take no grete interest. 'Bourghmaistresse,' saith he, 'now speke the trouth and lye not, confesse and knowleche ["acknowledge"] what ye be, for that we alleredy knowe.' 'What charge bringe ye ayenst me?' 'Ye be a dampnable sorceress,' crieth he, but seemeth hym to nede muche strengthe, for after holdeth he hys hand afore hys bigge mouthe and yawneth wyde, as yf he wold begynne to slepe ayen. I merveylled at the gentilesse of this woman, that she ne gaf hym no angre replye. May hap she thought stil to come oute of the ado ["affair"] by fayre wordes and modere ["temperate"] conduyte.

And Sir Oswalt saith she shall not lye and shal knowleche anon that she be one, for that she hath given our syre a drynke of love of whyche pocion he is becomen right madde.

Saith she ne can do make any drynke for love and suche drynkes there be not, and yf that she ever knew suche scyences she had wel used hem in hir yonger yeres, but never had ne wyst suche scyences.

Thenne axeth Sir Oswalt what she bere in her chestes wherwith she maketh so swete odoures in roumes ["rooms"].

Those be onely herbes whyche be to fynde of eny one who spareth hymself not trouble and goeth to the hilles but not beyonde the snowe ["not above the snow line—alpine mountain pasture flora, in other words"].

'What maner of herbes?' Sir Oswalt axed, alle bloted with pryde for hys sagacyte ["cleverness"], albeit bothe he and Wolf loked as folysshe ["foolish"] and wantyng of engyne ["wit"] as two asses.

'Meny maneres and kyndes,' sayde the bourghmaistresse, 'there be of suche herbes. They muste be lerned by children, for that later none mowe kepe them in mynde. Nor do alle growe in the hilles, but some eke in othir places, lyke henbane behynde the hous.'

'Henbane, ye say?' axed Sir Oswalt in hys sagacyte.

'Henbane, saye I,' hym answered the bourghmaistresse.

Now from this answer I had not canne understonde aught but that she was certaynly no sorceresse, othirwyse she had not named henbane, for by that she nameth it she proveth that she wyst nothynge of suchlyke materes, syn it be well knowe that sorceresses tofore they go aflyeng ["fly through the air"] putte henbane in the oyntment wherwyth they anoynt theyre bodyes. And yf the bourghmaistresse had be coulpe ["guilty"] therof, she had doubtles named alle other herbes onely henbane not.

But wyse Sir Oswalt grewe ever wyser and spake: 'Now have ye betrayd your self, minyon of helle, for henbane is used of the sorceresses ere that they fly thurgh ["through"] the air to danse on the mountayn.'

'Of suche henbane I ne have never herde.'

'Thenny we wyll reforce your remembraunce, Burghmaistresse. Have ye also putte henbane into the love drynke? Do not saye fals!'

'I have never sayde fals. But your devyses ["talk"] be lyke a foulle smell.'

This was the frist ["first"] sharpe worde she spake to Sir Oswalt, may hap because she had now understonden what maner of man he be and that he dyd not suffer overmuche fro wyt and had lever ["liefer, rather"] slepe now.

But Sir Oswalt gaf her a vilaynous ["boorish"] replye to this her first sharpe worde, whyche also abode her laste, aboute the evyll smell fro hys devyses; and in sooth he dyd let forthe an evyll smell that was not to here ["to be heard"] but wel to mark by that the bourghmaistresse reculed ["recoiled"] a steppe to Heimo ward, that stode there al the tyme as helde he the woman by a cow chayne. And Wolf also tourned awaye, and it cam to me, and sodaynly Sir Tristram cam on lyfe and spake: 'Oswalt, be we in the secrete ["outhouse"] or the halle?'

But Sir Oswalt onely mutered somthyng and ayen begynneth to ax the woman aboute the herbes and al the whyle I had to do wyth the wrytinge, and it cam alle to nothyng. And atte laste Sir Oswalt had the woman brought to her pryson ayen and Heimo wente awaye wyth her.

But more was yet to come, for that it wente so everich even a hole weke, and the even before midde Lente, of Gertrudis daye ["March 17"], Heimo brought the othir woman also, wyth bere feet too, and al begynneth ayen. She too was a fayre burgayse ["burgess"], albeit smaler than the bourghmaistresse and had light, fayre hayre and her body was full rounde. She begynneth to crye and wepe whan she herde this hevy charge, and ex-claymed : 'Holy Cross, what wold ye of us, we have never done no evyll and do no more sorcery than ye lords tred the spinnyng weel, so lat us go hence and do not hold us caytif ["prisoner"], for that my doughter in Pasriach hath certaynly long syth given berth and shall I not see my owne grandchild?'

But by this she was not holpen ["helped"] and the folye wente on a weke more. And I writ alleways the same thynges that were said, aboute the love drynke and the odour and the glas of Venyse, and atte the laste, that theyre chestes be alle loked in and nothyng founde that was werke of the devyl, but onely medi-cines and scentes. And in secrete Sir Tristram bought for hym-self one suche bottel of the glas of Venyse right fulle of the good scente, and payed muche money therfor; bycause, saith he, he must shelde hymself ayenst Sir Oswalt whan they satte in judge-ment, for that the assaut upon his nose be too myghty and he wyst not els to defende hymself.

Menewhyle alleredy at that tyme, whan I satte wyth the court and the same thynges were sayde ayen and ayen and I had right plenteus tyme, I began to write doune how alle was come aboute and happed, syn that I had afore me all that was nedeful for the wrytyng. And so I thenne began and continued it in my chambre by candel lyght, so that I have not muste write this ["this manuscript, of course"] fro my remembraunce onely, for that the moste part was alleredy wreton at that tyme.

In suche wyse the affaire went on from Gertrudis to Josephi ["from March 17 to 19"] and ferre ["further"], and a whyle I hoped that soone the heath cocke wold soune his calle and thenne wold my syre recovre and go to the weald, for it was styll too erly. And ones ["once"] Sir Oswalt and Sir Tristram were in the halle and Heimo had juste brought the othir woman agayne to her pryson, her name was Maria and the othir name I marked not; and I wot that had Wolf be there they had not talked so, for that he beleved alle aboute the sorcery and thought that it was juste and the court a juste court. But that tyme Sir Oswalt saith: 'It passeth understondyng what he wol wyth the olde wenches; yf he had taken yonge wymen it wold make right good sence.' And I thought that hys kytchen wenches were doubtles yonger but for my part me lyked beter the bourghmaistresse and the othir called Maria. And ferre Sir Oswalt sayde: 'For that is clere, that he hath so do make this matere that the women must do hys wyll, and Heimo wyll telle you it is sooth, for that he ["meaning Lord Achaz"] hath severell tymes sent hym to theyre chambre to talk gentylly wyth hem and saye that yf they wol do hys wyll he wol lat them go, and afore ["before their departure"] he wol treet them kyndly and give them a goodly amounte in money and gold. But, the damned olde wenches dyd make refusal, from what spyte is not to knowe, and the bourghmaistresse hath verayly no raison to playe the chaste pucelle ["virgin"], syn she bereth a good fyfty yere on her fatte backe, it maketh to laugh.'

'Styll they be fayre women,' saith Heimo.

'Ye lewde yonge buck,' replyeth Sir Oswalt. 'Ye wol allewaye knowe more than your beters. The milkesop wol wette his breches for a woman that myght have putte hym to the breste. What aboute the peyne forte? Thenne wol ye see a praty ["pretty"] choys ["sight"], ye and your scrivener. For my parte, I had lever kepe bothe myn eyen close than see eithre.' So saith Sir Oswalt, and hymself shaketh as yf he shuddre wyth dradde ["dread"].

Saith Heimo: 'Alle is prepared and redy, and lord Achaz hath given ordre that we mowe onely make them afryghted.' So saith Heimo. And Sir Oswalt replyeth: 'I wyll wel beleve, for that our syre wold not have ne damage nor harme come to the delyghtes of his eyen. Hath he thenne spoke so openly wyth you?' 'He hath in secrete devysed wyth me aboute it,' saith Heimo.

I was sore troubled and penseful that our syre had more trost in him than me, albeit in thynges evyl, for he had spoke to Heimo in secrete but never once to me.

Saith Sir Oswalt: 'See to it that ye make progres wyth your peyne forte, then, for that it is hygh tyme. They of Lientz ben not sluggerds and may hap the matere hath alleredy be brought to the Diet. For that this thynge is not ne ryght nor juste, ye alle wel knowen. And meny a vassell wold it muche plese to apprehende our syre in a snare, the more syn he hath never payd right heed to the lawes of the chase and laste wynter shote his shammy whan he had not the right, for that the buck was in rutte ["the rutting time of the chamois buck is November and December"] and it cam all oute and muche talke was made therof, as wel ye knowe, and of othir materes also. And that in materes of sorcery is not to be acted nor aught doon withoute the doctryne ["instructions"] of the bisshop is wel yknowen. Wot wel that our syre hath said no worde even to the dene that cometh here to saye mass in the chapelle on sonday, for els he wold have talked right strycte to hym. The good olde man redeth the mass here and ne wyt nought therof that we have the wymen in the hous, and our syre giveth hym report in no manere nor wyse. But soone enow he wyll have myckel to fyll his eres. For suche materes fynde theyre waye to his grace the bisshop in Gurckh. Me seemeth afore muche lenger we shall have the lords fro there and Lienz gadred ["assembled"] wyth myght and power under the walles of Neudegck, and thenne shall we have toyl and swete, Tristram. Therfore Heimo, and ye, Ruodl, whan it cometh to the peyne forte, ye be wyse if ye ne handle the women over tendre, lest it bringe us alle muche trouble and vexacion. See that the tweyne wenches be quicke holpen to reson, but not so that our syre's plaisure in the syght of them be spoyled, as ye ben commaunded, Heimo. And for aught I care have your joye of these grandmoders withoute sherte or shifte, but doo that we here mowe ["may"] soone comen oute of this foles paradyse in the whiche our syre be more incarcered than the tweyne wenches. For certaynly he shall comen oute of it as soone as he hath had his wyll. For there ne is none othir waye that we shall alle escape from this folye and from no smale danger and eke trouble.'

Theraftre I wente to the stable, and my knees dyd shake and sodaynly was I alle aswete for fere and thought it be hungre, but that I coud not understond, for that we had lately dyned. The evyll winde of Venyse blew ayen, and to south were lyghtnings, as some tyme it dyd soone after snow. Sir Oswalt's foule and right wicked devyses ["talk"] wente to and fro in my mynde and me gaf muche commotion within my herte, and I thought of the bourghmaistress and her red dresse and white bere feet and me seemed I muste also crye oute for that I was in the same derke dongeon and pryson as my power ["poor"] syre. Thenne prayed I an ave but our lady herde me not and well I wot coud not here me, for that I was too far awaye from hir even for her grace.

The Sonday folowyng, Judica ["March 18"], I served atte the offyse ["that is, he was an acolyte at the Mass"], and sodaynly was remembred how that the tweyne wymen in theyre pryson were restrayned from heryng mass on the Sonday, and the whyle this thought was in my mynde cometh the tractus and saith the kyng ["that is, King David in the psalm"]: *Prolongaverunt iniquitates suas: Dominus justus concidit cervices peccatorum* ["They have prolonged their iniquities; the righteous Lord hath broken the necks of the sinners"].

From that Sonday hence were we sezed of grete distresse, and more than alle my syre, for he was sore besyde hymself and nyghe thre days ne had no more eten and was pale as a white shete. And toward even on the fourth daye Sir Oswalt commaunded us, that be Heimo and I, that a whyle after etyng we shold take the bourghmaistresse doune and do wyth her as our syre hath given us ordre. Our syre came not to table that even, ne dyd Wolf neithre, and me liste not to ete but I dranke of the wyn. And at table Sir Oswalt made devyses ful mockyng and withoute shame of the syght that wold plese our syre and our self, and that we muste take care not to spoyle the fayre semblaunce ["appearance"] of the old wench, but muste not be too tendre, and so forth whyche is not to write ["which cannot be written down"]. And I see wyth herte in my throte how that Sir Tristram fel aslepe the whyle Sir Oswalt spake, for that he cared so lytyl aboute al these materes, but that Heimo laughed and answered shameles and wickid thinges to Sir Oswalt, and bothe laughed lyke verray madmen. But Heimo in his wickidnes refrayned fro drynkyng, the whyche he othirwyse never dyd, albeit Sir Oswalt urged hym to drynke, sayeng: 'Wherfore wilt thou not drynke, boye, wilt thou ne see duble whan the bourghmaistresse weareth no sherte? Thenne thou sholdst have twyce the delyte of the eyen!' et cetera. And saith Heimo: 'I had lever see single but clerer.'

What cam theraftre and the dayes folowyng hath remayned in my remembraunce alle the dayes of my lyf and therfrom is a venym comen doune to this present daye an ["as if"] I had be poysoned for alle tyme. And therfore have I never wed.

Saith Heimo: 'Is every thynge redy doune there, so come now, Ruodl, we shall fet ["fetch"] the good bourghmaistresse, the wedowe Agnes Stoecher, for so she hyght ["is called"].' And rose up from table, and I also, and made our bowe to Sir Oswalt, for that Sir Tristram alredy was fast on slepe, and so we wente to the wymens chambre. And Heimo knockd full bold on the dore, but dyd not open, onely called, 'Bourghmaistresse, wol ye come,' as he was woned, for that he had don so ofte. Passed a lytyl whyle and thenne the woman cam oute, and with bere feet also, as she was alleredy woned, yet atte frist were bothe wymmen sore angred that they muste stand without shoon tofore the court, so Heimo had recounted to me. And so we led this same bourghmaistresse doune and cam to the longe passage where aforetymes, so men saye, the chorles ["peasants"] brought in theyre kyne and alle theyre goodes, whan were divers peryls and daungers. Thenne wente we to the stayres from the lowest roumes of the tour to the said two chambres, and the woman axed us, 'Whither take ye me?' 'In there,' saith Heimo, and pusheth ope the dore to the nerer chambre. Thenne afore the woman seeth where she be and whither we have taken her, Heimo hath alleredy closed the dore behynde her and bolted it fast. Me seemeth, seeyng how the same bourghmaistresse be so meeke and milde, that she beleveth to come well and by mildnesse out of the affayre, for alle that she be now come to no milde place; me seemeth, she thynketh mayhap she wyll escape withoute harme to her body yf she behave wyth gentilnes and humylyte, and may be the wymen have taken counseyl eche wyth other and decyded so to do, and may hap even Heimo knewe of this secrete counseyl, for in the ende I wel sawe that he was fals and ful of secrecy and also spake wyth our syre in secrete but wyth me never sayde what he thought or knewe.

But alle thoughtes wente fro my hed whan Heimo toke the womans arm and led her to a corner where was less lyght; al els in the roume was bryght wyth meny candels on the walle. And now marked I also the stronge odour of insens the whyche had be brent ["burned"] here, and sawe the glowe of fyre on the harth, and felte my visage growe hot. Thenne cryed the bourghmaistresse: 'What wold ye doo wyth me?' and I see Heimo drawe her arm behynd her, and she fyghteth, but not sore ["not too much"], and cryeth ayen: 'What wold ye doo wyth me?' She coud ne lenger move hir arm for that Heimo held it so stronge, and she stode there thenne with eyen closed. 'Wol ye be ydle, Ruodl, and muste I do alle the werke alone?' Heimo calleth to me, and says to the bourghmaistresse, 'Yeld ["yield"] thee, woman, or we wyll write on thy backe: too muche vertue bringeth wo.' And thenne he calleth to me ayen: 'Doo your parte and drawe off hir dresse!'

I loked at the bigge white bere feet of the woman, and sodaynly I stept to her ward and dyd as me was commaunded. She had underneth a white shift that also had longe sleves, and I

sodaynly pulled it off, it fel to the flore and lay there. And in my
wildeness I saw only white over white of her arm and sholders,
and swiftely drew down hir sherte to the middel of her body,
whan Heimo cryed: 'That is enough, more durst we not.' And
sayeng this he thruste her afore hym to the piller, but I for my
parte could not restrayn me and toke her breste; it was hevy and
she scremed, for Heimo held her handes on her backe the whyle,
but soone tyed them to the fore of her ayenst the piller. And
stoopt doune and lifted the shert up to hir middel, and there
tyed it. Thenne he tourned to the cheste, that muche I sawe,
albeit I was nyghe oute of my mynde, and me gaf into my handes
some thyng and sayde I shold smite the woman wyth it, and I
coud see it was alle velvet and smote hir a lytyl on her whyte
backe and elswhere, but she dured ["endured"] it withoute
playnte and onely syghed for shame; for wyth the velvet thyng
she coude not be hirt, even were the blowes stronge. And Heimo
also smote her a lytyl, but more made mocke of her wyth wordes
that I wol not endyte ["write down"]. And I ne coud not nor
was able to kepe on my feet, and stopt and lened ayenst the
walle, and my knees were atemblaunt and aflutter under me, and
yet I loked allewayes atte the woman by the piller, her whyte
body, and waxed hotter and the stronge odour of the candeles
and incens toke awaye my breth and sens, and I was all yfilld of the
woman and me thought I coud even taste her.

Aftre Heimo losed ["untied"] her and called me ayen, but I
coud not obeye and go nyghe her. So he led her awaye from
the piller and putte her wyth her backe to the walle, and I was
sore amazed atte the bourghmaistresse how she conduyted
herself wyth suche humilite and made no defens, and thought
ayen the wymen had taken counseyl eche wyth other so to doo.
Thenne he drewe her armes hygh over he hed to a hoke on the
walle. And wente arounde her and loked atte her there, and
swiftely cam I also nyghe and coud not wythdraw mine eyen
from her, so passynge beauteus seemed she me. She helde her
eyen shutte and her countenaunce tourned awaye. And at the
ende we layd the bourghmaistresse on a benche and tyed her

there and made pretens we wold now strech and racke her and hirt her sore, but dyd nought; thenne gaf we her leve to putte on her clothes ayen and broughte her backe to her chambre where the other woman, the cosayne, may hap was sore afrayed. But that daye we dyd not take her.

But her, this was the same whos grandchild was to be borne in Pazriach, her we toke to hande the nexte even, for that so Sir Oswalt gaf us ordre from owre syre. But I ne sawe the syre alle these dayes never ones ["once"]. And so we led her doune the steyres and to the chambre where stode the piller, and all was ayen lyghted well and myckel incens had be brent, and the fyre had be heped wyth wode to make a grete hete. The othre woman conduyted her more meker than the bourghmaistresse and made no defens neithre whan we losed her garment. But then whan it fel and the othre also and Heimo tyed the sherte arounde her body in the middel, and she stode shamed and wyth eyen caste doune, bigan she ayen as she had don at the courte to crye 'Holy Cross,' and sayde also, 'Dere sirs, harme me not, doo me no herte.' And thenne was don wyth her the same as wyth tother, and me happed lykewyse that ayen I scars ["scarcely"] coude drawe breth. And Heimo made mocke of her in the same wyse and she had to stand wyth her backe ayenst the walle, alle naked but for the sherte tyed arounde her middel. Me seemed this woman more beauteus than the bourghmaistresse, albeit some smaler, for her body was even fuller and al whyte as snowe and her longe hayr fel to her bere sholdres and nyghe to the whyte linnen that covred her extremist shame. But Heimo sayde him plesed Agnes Stoecher beter, and sayde meny othre evyll and shameles thynges. The wymen had not be shorne afore the torture, as otherwyse is don wyth sorcereses, and Sir Oswalt sayde that shold not be don for that theyre apperence be not spoyled, et cetera, et cetera, the whyche were shameful to write.

Fro that even whan we had the other woman in the torture coude I ne lenger slepe; and every daye we broughte one or other of the wymen to the piller, and Heimo bethought hym of meny spytes and mockt the wymen sore in theyre shame and humilite. And I was lyke sicke and atrembel of handes and feet as even drewe nyghe, and yet coude not wayt therfor.

Alle that tyme were we onely foure at table, for that owre syre cam not to dyne, and I shold make mencioun that Wolf had ryden off with two soldyours and wel armed, for that the syre had given him commandement and muche money, for he wished hym to go to courte where Duke Sygmunt sate, for Sir Lienhart von Felsegk was that tyme there as was alleredy wryten ["meaning: see above"]. My syre had wryten hym in the same lettre that spake of Duke Albrecht, as afore recounted ["see above"] that he had a fine yong squyer whom he wold doub knyght, and was sendyng hym to sir Lienhart who coude bryng him to the duke, that he myght serve the duke a whyle, who wold then doub him knyght. And so my syre had Wolf ryde to that ende, but me seemed that he ment in trouthe to have that good soul and honeste boye from the hous ere werst cam here to werst and dyd not want to have hym as knowyng what befel at Castel Neudegck. For til thenne Wolf doubtles had thought al wente by right, so that my syre wold not trouble this his beleef and was hymself ashamed afore the good and strayt boye. For our syre muche hym lyked yong Wolf.

Sir Oswalt was sore dysplesed bycause that we had not yet swayd the wymen in theyre myndes, and spake ful rude and harsh ayenst Heimo and me, what dyd we wyth the evyll wenches, he complayned, that we cam not to eny conclucion wyth them, and were not suche olde wymen sore dyspleasaunt to hym, he wold come self and helpe us the beter to caresse them, and we shold harder beset theym and write theyre vertue stronge on theyre bare backsydes or stryng them up wyth a rope, and more in suche wyse, et cetera, et cetera. And wel may it be understonden that he made like devyses, dyd Sir Oswalt, to our syre, advysyng hym not to forbid us to herte the wymen. What sayde our syre, I wot not, for that his commaundes he gaf to Sir Oswalt, and wold other tymes make Heimo come to his roume, but never me. And Sir Oswalt saith we muste fynde a waye to make the wymen sore afrayed, but withoute herte nor harme to theyre bodyes.

And one daye whan Sir Oswalt had ryden muche arounde pressyng his chorles and may hap lystenyng here and there at one or othir place, cam he to table and began incontynent: 'Now meseems the thyng hath come oute, and ye two berdles boyes see that ye brynge the wenches anone to raison, the whyle I wyll todaye hold speche wyth our syre, that we be soone free of these women. For the matere hath alleredy be bruyted aboute, it hath doubtles be spred by the damned Apfaltersbach or Lientz. So axeth me todaye the steward from acros the border wether we hold eny ones prysoner in the hous, so hath he herde. I tell hym I wot nought therof. But mayhap soone shall we have them of Lientz and others also come doune upon us, and atte the laste the high bayliff too and them of Villach also, whyche allewayes ben myckel leef to putte theyre handes in to affayres that ben no concerne of them. And ayenst Neudegck wyll they gadre the lever ["all the more gladly gather their forces, that is"] for severall resons, the whyche I have tolde you.'

So cam we to Estre Weke. Sir Tristram began to shewe a diligence that hym was not woned, and the soldyours of Allemayne and Beme wente muche aboute, and the same Sir Tristram had muche to do wyth them, loking atte al theyre arms, armures, swerdes, speres, and holdyng dryll in the bayley wyth them; also was eche given what hym lacked, so that in short whyle the castel was made redy for alle that myght hap; they shote also wyth the arblastre in the bayley, wherby was to see that this same Sir Tristram was muche the bedre shot than alle his soldyours and at twenty paces shote an egg shell wyth the fyrst bolt, the whyche sore amazed his soldyours. And were these same right devoted to Sir Tristram and sayde wyth hym wold they go thurgh helles fyre unafrayed. We had eke, syn that I have not afore made mencioun therof, a maystre of ordnence and two canon men under hym, they had three good pieces of artylery whyche were brought oute and made redy wyth muche care and solycytude.

Also rehersed Sir Tristram and his men severall tymes as yf we were beseged and commaunded eche soldyour his place to whyche he muste haste whan the watch on the tour soundeth his horne, and suche was not rehersed three or four tymes, but ten and more tyl that it alle wente wel. Eke provyded Sir Tristram wel for pytch and all that wente therwyth, suche as pannes, kettels, and fyrewode, and the kytchen wenches had to make redy all suche stuffes under oversyght of a Beme, so that the wenches also cam not unscathed but had muste werke for the tocomyng werre ["the coming war"].

Whyle we were thus armyng, in the whyche Heimo and I dyd werke wyth muche diligence also, albeit I had lytil herte therto, the peyne of the two wymen wente forth as byfore, and we biganne to take bothe togedre eche even. That Heimo myckel plesed, he beyng a right grete vâlant ["a late medieval expression for 'devil,' obviously something our scribe had picked up out of books, for the word had long since died out of speech"], for he sayde the wedowes now were shamed one part byfore us and one part byfore eche other. And he laughed wyth muche spyte. But we coud onely take them lyghtly to hande, the wymen, for that so had commaunded our syre and eke for that they were now allewaye right humble and gentil and ne made no lenger eny defense, but were full sore shamed. So that atte the laste the peyne and tormente becam almost a thynge woned to them. And Heimo toke the bourghmaistresse and I the other. And Heimo bethought hym new spyte and made the bourghmaistresse ryde on a wide benche, et cetera, et cetera. And alleredy me lyked full wel and muste confesse and knowlege ["admit"] that atte the laste dayes I toke muche playsure in suche werke and wolde not refrayne therfrom and yet had allewayes fere and dred therof, the whyle I in secrete craved and desyred that it continue, so that when even drewe nyghe I had no mynde of the taskes I shold doo, tyl that one even Sir Oswalt saith to me: 'Boye, go and joye thee of the syght of thy wymen, for here dost thou nought.'

That tyme abode I nyghe withoute slepe and lay wakyng alle

the nyght, halfe the nyght allewayes byfore the wymens dore, for that I shared the watch wyth Heimo, the whyche our syre had us commaunded, as was afore wryten. Heimo and I had made us a bedde byfore the wymens dore and allewayes one of us lay there al the nyght. And that tyme, it was begynnyng of Estre weke, was the mone full and the lyght fel me upon the face, but for that rayson ["reason"] shold I not have slept pouer ["poorly"], for that the mone had not in past tyme troubled my slepe; more the wind of Venyse, as I called it thenne, whyche cam ayen and blewe warm, and I lay on my backe halfe on slepe and dremt I could here the cocke ["heathcock"] crye. And I shold steppe swiftely, for the cockes be blinde and deef whan they be in crye, so that I wold come nygher for the shot. And coud not lifte my feet from the flore and stode there an ["as if"] I was of wode and me coud not do move ["was unable to make myself move"]. And the cocke ceaseth to crye, and thenne bigynneth ayen, but am I yet of wode as yf bounde by sorcery. Yet knowe I that it were me good yf that I coud hunte this cocke and wold me save and my syre also. And it was like a border goeth thurgh me, on one syde am I Ruodl and on tother am I al wode and I ne mowe go thurgh this wode and oute to the forest where the cocke cryeth. And was alle of wode and sore afrayed and full of dred for my sake and my syre. Thenne wol the cocke flee, and I crye loude and wake and fynde that I lye in my chambre and the mone shyneth the more. And it was nyghe to mornyng, for that I had the watch the fyrst halfe of the nyghte and now was Heimo there. Thenne herde I a cocke from the forest, and herde hym tryllyng, but no more. Yet coud it not bee that I coud here hym so ferre, albeit some were in the forest beyonde Neudegck. Then ceased the cocke to crye and I was sore distrest, and sodaynly sawe us wyth the pouer wymen and sawe the other under my handes, wyth whom I had behaved eke as shameful as Heimo with the bourghmaistresse, and thenne the same border ranne thurgh me and I was one halfe of wode and cloven in tweyne like a logge, and cryed aloude and thought I were in helle, and axed myself yf we were not alle here of a trouth in

helle, and putte my handes to my hed and knewe sodaynly what
helle muste be lyke, and knewe it for certayn and was fylled
wyth sore dred as yf I were alleredy dampned. And as soone as
I coud ayen take breth, prayd I an Ave. But She coud scarce
here me.

The laste Tuesdaye before Estre saith Sir Oswalt acros the
table: 'Now lyst, boye. I have had speche wyth our syre and he
commandeth that todaye ye take the wymen more stricte, notwythstandyng that ye yet muste not herte them. But yf they
styll be stuborn, and ye wene wel how that be ment, not that they
wyll not knowlege theyre sorcery but in their spyteful stubornnes
and refusell to be complaysaunt to owre syre—yf, saye I, they
styll be stuborn, thenne take not bothe togedre on the morrow,
as ye now are woned, but eche after eche. Thenne muste ye
serche and seke for a mark, the lyke hath evry sorceress on her
body, how be it on the moste hydden partes, for there marketh
the foule fiend that he hath layn wyth them. That wyll ye seke
wyth care and dyligence on eche of the wymen, evrywhere on
them, be it understonden. For straunge it is that wyth all the
peyne they wyll not yeld them, for the whyche reason we mowe
beleve that they ne feele nor sense the smarte in the peyne forte.
Now shall ye bothe seke and saye wether suche a mark ye have
seene on the wymen, for that wold mene that the fiend hath
made them senseles ["insensitive"] so that they feele not the
peyne forte et dure. And what ye saye, it shall be so, wether they
have suche mark or no. But yf they be in trouth sorcereses, so
wyll owre syre now conduyt hym more stricte wyth them and if
nede be give them ovre to the bisshop his handes, that a confessioun be brought from them or otherwyse don wyth them that
the lande be made free of suche wymen that in these tymes do
spoyle and wreke harme to people and wares, as is wel yknowen.
Now that ye have herde my speche whych is a commaund from
oure syre, see that ye belabour the delyght of your eyen wyth
dyligence and make syn your accountyng whyche none wyll
challynge. Suche is oure syres wyll. But fyrst on this nyght make

the wickid wenches to dance bedre ["better"] than ye have be woned.'

'Now it groweth hote,' saith Heimo whan we were ayen alone. 'What think ye, Ruodl, we wyll yet doo them but lytil harme; I wene it be so commaunded onely that we may have bedre cause for what cometh the nexte even. This thyng approcheth an ende, I wot. Late ["let"] us delyght us the bedre and afryght them tonyght for what awayteth them on the morrow, but not so sore that in theyre dred they yeld to owre syre and we therby lose the sport.' Et cetera, et cetera. I dyd not lyst to hym. Yet was I eke wel plesed that he wold not harme the wymen no more than I. But I sawe also in these thynges the shamefulnes and duble tonge of Sir Oswalt, for that in the one parte he wel understode that it was alle for oure syre and for the othir parte he dyd make beleve the wymen were in trouth sorceresses and withoute shame he toke the name of His Grace the bisshop of Gurk in his stynkyng mouth.

Theraftre it wente so that same even as alleredy wryton, we toke bothe doune and my breth dyd stop as afore whan I dyd strip the sherte and shifte from the beauteus cosyne, how be it not alle; and thenne eche dyd muste ryde on a benche 'to the mount and to the dance' as Heimo saide, and he made meny other shameful and scornful sayengis, and toke hold of the wymen, but only made a semblaunt of harshnes, and smote them wyth the velvet eke, but that now troubled them nought.

The nexte even toke we fyrst the cosyne and Heimo wente forthwyth in to the smale roume wyth her, where were alleredy lyghtes placed and it smelled of incens and a fyre was brennyng. 'Why here?' I ax Heimo, who replyeth: 'That wyll ye see anone, so hath oure syre commaunded, that this tyme we shall be herein.' And spake: 'Bigynne!' And we moved a wyde benche to the myddel of the roume. 'Be not so coye, cosayne,' saith he, and thenne to me: 'Take holde, Ruodl, do off her dresse.' And wente it as we were woned. But whan the woman lay on the benche and marked how that we bounde her therto, she cryed: 'What do ye,

what do ye?' but coud ne lenger move, and thenne screamed she
and I sawe how that he toke from her the shifte, and knowe no
more for that I bigan to tremble and me tourned to the walle.
'Ye can loke here,' Heimo calleth to me, but I wold not obey hym,
and herde the woman crye: 'Holy Cross, ye shameles wight.'
Then laughed Heimo and sayde: 'Wel, cosayne, now wyll ye be
losed and can do on your dresse,' and aftre a lytyl whyle I
tourned me and saw that she was free and had alleredy covred
her self. Saith Heimo to me: 'Ye folysh lout, wherfore wol ye ne
loke, ye have myssed the beste.' But I coud not gyve hym no
replye. 'Wel thenne, have your fyll of loking atte the bourghmaistresse,' saith he, and laugheth. The woman had menewhyle don
on alle her clothes and strode to one syde and tourned her self
awaye from us. Thenne we toke her backe to her pryson and
brought doune the bourghmaistresse.

I marked atte ones that Heimos breth cam harde whan we
wente in to the smale chambre wyth the bourghmaistresse. And
I had muste helpen hym, but atte the laste I me ayen tourned
awaye and to the walle, and as I stode there herde I the bourgemaistresse screme, more than she had don, and cryed so ferefully
that I swiftely loked and see that Heimo hath clomben on the
benche on top of her and wold putte to her. Thenne shouted I:
'What dost thou, Heimo, what dost thou, thou muste not,' and in
the midst of the noyse cam a grete crash in the chambre and a
bolt shote ayenst the walle and brake peces oute of the stone,
and in reboundyng fro the walle the bolte crossed sharp by me
but een sharper by Heimo. And he late the woman free and lept
off the bench and was atremble in handes and knees, and was I
also thus and founde neithre of us wordes. Tyl that atte laste
Heimo toke up the womans shifte and covred her and losed her
thenne and spake to her: 'Dresse yourself, Agnes Stoecher.' And
we toke two candels and blewe oute the other and wente awaye
with her; and we cam to the lowest tour chambre ["you remember, the lowest room in the tower, where the loopholes and pitch
runnels are"]. And thenne this same Agnes Stoecher stode styll
and spake to us and saide to Heimo and me: 'Yonge sirs, now

here my worde, for me as also for my cosayne wyth whyche I have taken counseyl to speke in suche wyse wyth you and make concordaunce ["come to an agreement"] and allyance wyth you. Syn ye knowe for trouthe that we be in no wyse sorcereses, ne have ye founde aught on oure bodyes the whyche ye shamefully serched, and no marke suche as have sorcereses, whereof we have herde and whyche is wel yknowen in the lande; yf ye wyll confirme and saye that for a trouthe, and yf ferre ["furthermore"] ye wyll not assaut us more strictely in the torture and peyne than ye have don hitherto, how be it mayhap ye have had commaundes to tormente us more than ye have don; yf yet we wyll late be in suche wyse as hath be tofore, so that no confessioun was forced from us by reson of grete peyne, whyche had been falshood and ayenst trouth and whyche we myght have don from overgrete smart ["pain"]; yf so ye wyll do and saye that no mark nor signe was founde upon us of sorcerie, so that we may hope yet to come livyng from this place and withoute harme nor damage to oure bodyes—thenne shall we on oure parte yelde us to your wyll and in alle thynges shewe us kynde to you and make endeavour you in all thynges to please, in suche wyse that we wyll not locke the dore of oure chambre to you after nyght falle; but rather shall one of you kepe watch by the dore as ye be woned, but the other shall come in to us and share the bedde wyth whichesoever hym liketh, and we shall late hym so do.'

'Agnes Stoecher, that is good speche!' cryeth Heimo incontynent. 'And ye, Ruodl, ye wol doubtles give your consente and not oppose.' And whan he so spake, sayde I anon ["at once"] that this allyance me seemed good and wel bethought; and in parte was this bycause that I had stronge lust for the cosayne and in part me seemed it a waye to staye yet greter evylles, that none myght come to grete harme in this affayre. And so we made agreemente wyth the two wymen as sayde, and brought them to theire pryson.

Yet had she spoke no worde of the shote in the chambre doune belowe, the whyche eke the bourghmaistresse muste have be ware of. And I had taken this same bolt wyth me, and whan that we were alone Heimo and I talked and devysed concernyng this same bolt, as wel may be understonden, and I sawe and knewe withoute doubt that this bolt cam from oure syres arblastre. That made no smaler oure fere and dred; and we crepte in secrete to the roume where hung all the armes, and there we founde two arblastres of our syre on theire hookes, but the third not, and was the same to whyche longed the quareylle ["quarrel, crossbow bolt"]. For they were boltes speciall suche that my syre had for the buck, they can not overtourne so esily as do the forked quareylles whyche have an yron pece wyth two endes, the whyche be used and employed for the huntyng of the chamois. But my syre hunted the chamois wyth sore hevy strayt boltes that had fetheres, not bone as meny make them, nor the chepe ones of wode; but my syres boltes had right good fetheres, and not them of swannes as moste are made, but them of buzzerdes, and he shote wyth a crown bolte ["a bolt without a tip, but with a strong, four-part iron crown at the end"]. And were the fetheres placed on the hinde parte of the shafte in such wyse that the same bolte tourned in ayre lyke a twirl and so helde its course well and so coud ye shote ayenst or acros the winde and dyd not muste come so nyghe whyche wold starte the bucke whan he standeth wyth the winde. My syre wold hunte the bucke hyghe up and dreded not the rockes and wold late doune the bucke, so soone that he smote hym, wyth ropes, yf that there were none other waye to have hym doune from suche a hyght. These same boltes wyth that he shote the bucke be called, whan they have fetheres, in Burgondy viretons, that was tolde me by my syre. For he coud meny tunges.

It maye wel be understonden that we sore fered oure syre aftre suche hap ["after what had occurred"] in the smale chambre, how be it we coud not rightly see how that had be and that he had shote from the walle thurgh a slit and unmarked by us. Yet dyd we not see our syre that even, eny more than tofore. But at nyght we dyd not for alle oure fere refrayne us, syn was agreed wyth the wymen how that they sholde awayt us in theyre chambre and sholde not locke the dore. So wente Heimo fyrst, for

that he had drawen the lenger lot, for so had we made agremente
eche wyth other. And I sate withoute on the bedde by the dore,
but slept not; the whyche may be esily understonden, and had
herte in throte and lysted wether I mought here eny thynge but
ne herde nothyng, ne from wythinne for the dore was myckel
stoute, ne other wyse in the hous. And thought of the cosayne,
yet not alone of her but eke of the bourghmaistresse her bigge
bere feet. And I was sore affrayed and had dred also of oure syre,
that he myght come, and lykewyse of the two wymen that I shold
soone go in to them. And menewhyle abode alle styll as in the
kirkyard and I sat on the bedde and durst not move.

In the middel of the nyght, I had notwythstandyng slept a
lytyl, oped the dore and Heimo clomb over my bedde and
sygned to me that I shold go in to the chambre, and wente I in
and saw a lytyl lyght from a candel and thenne saw I the fayre
bourghmaistresse sittyng on the bedde in a longe shifte and wyth
bere feet, and I layd me on the flore and pressed my face ayenst
her fete, and cam the cosayne and stroked me ovre my hayr.
And more wot I not and eke can not write that. In the morn,
when the lyght cam, I lay on my backe and bothe wymen slept
and I loked besyde of me and lysted in my halfe slepe wether I
coud here the cocke but herde no hethcocke crye. And was come
anothre tyme and as yf alle were longe past and me had dremed
it, not onely the wymen that slept besyde me but all my lyf that
I had hadde to that tyme ["this, incidentally, is unmistakably a
paraphrase of Walther von der Vogelweide"]. Thenne rose I up
and wente withoute noyse from the chambre and waked Heimo,
that styll slept, and it was alleredy full daylyght and so oure
watch by the pryson atte ende, as is wryton byfore. And so
wente we to oure roume and lay doune bothe, and he loketh
asyde and saith: 'Those be in trouthe right wundrous wymen, me
thought I was in Venus's mount.'

'Dyd ye not ax by what cause they have conduyted them wyth
suche obstynate mynde to oure syre and yet have so wyllyngly
yelded them to us and that in suche mesure?' So saide I; for I
had forsooth axed them in suche wyse; but they becam incon-

tynent sore angred and were full wroth wyth my syre and spake harsh wordes, sayeng they wold never have yelded them to my syre, for that he helde them caytiff here and by force and they wolde suffer werse martyrs ere ever they yelded them to him. And what we had don unto them had we muste do, that beyng atte commaunde of our syre and not of oure owne wyll.

That daye wente I aboute in half slepe; yet after we brake oure faste Heimo and I coud not refrayne and secretely clomben wyth candeles doune the stayres from the lowest tour roume and wente fyrst to the smalle chambre to fynde the hole thurgh whyche the bolt had be shote by oure syre. And soone founde the same when we clomben on a benche; behynde the shelfe the whyche renne arounde the walle. This same hole or slit was so made that a bolt coud be aymed hygher or lower or to bothe sydes, I shold bedre saye there were two holes one over tother. So that our syre had doubtles chused ["seen"] us in alle we dyd and had shote his quareyll by Heimos hed to affryght hym, so we now thought, notwythstandyng that bolt had nyghe kylled me in reboundyng. Thenne went we in to the grete chambre to see wether we myght fynde suche a hole, and founde it in lyke wyse and the same place, and so cam we to knowe that our syre had watched us atte alle oure werke wyth the wymen and had stonden over us wyth arblastre atte redy. That seemed us hard and we were sore affrayed of our syre. We coud esily reken that he had comen behynde us thurgh the same dore whyche was over the steppes, whyche dyd thenne not go oute of the castell as Heimo had thought, but behynde and arounde bothe chambres, and wherfore this had so be bilt we ne dyd knowe nor understonde the cause.

Cam the nexte nyght and Heimo wayted withoute and I was inne wyth the wymen and was my madnesse greter than afore and the wymen laughed atte me and had theyre playsure wyth me and shewed them so kynde and amourous that ne can be wryton. Whan atte laste I cam thurgh the dore and clomb over the bedde and Heimo wente in swifter than I coud sygn to hym, overcam me slepe incontynent and yet coud I not slepe and sate me up on the bedde. Thenne herde I foot steppes and knewe oure syres step, wel knew I it. And stode my herte al styll. And he cam along and wente paste me, and was full dressed, had on even bootes and veste; and in passyng, when I stode up from the bedde, he tourned to me and laughed and sygned me wyth his hande to folowe hym, and so dyd I and wente after hym and up the stayres and to his bigge roume. There bade he me sit and laughed ayen and gaf me a cuppe and pured wyn in the cuppe and the same for hymself; and bade me drynk and he dranke wyth me and sayde to me:

'Ruodl, ye have wel don, Heimo and thou, and I am sory that he sitteth not here and drynketh wyth us, but we wyll in no wyse dyscommode his playsure. Ye have wel don for that ye have overthrown these same wymens fals vertue; for that same dyd I wyll do, that it shold hap so and nought els. Therfore dyd I shote atte Heimo, for I wolde not that they shold suffre force or compulcion but sholde them self shew and make playne theyre falshode as they have now don so lewdely and have seduysed ["seduced"] you wyth theire shameles concupyscence, the cun-nyng Heimo in same mesure as thou who art an innocint lamb. And so have brought forth what was hindemost in theire nature and shewn it foremost, wherwyth I am wel contente and they shall soone go theyre waye, not withoute paiement and recom-pence, the whyche I am full redy to grant wyth goodes and money, how be it they have receved no visible damege nor harme, but notwythstanding wyll I give them all that; and it nede them not to fere more peyne ne lenger nor that I shall trouble nor moleste them ayen. Tell them alle that in good con-fydence. But saye also that I wel wened of theyre vertue, what it is lyke, and that they have bothe not hydden theire con-cupyscence but have given it full swaye wyth two yonge boyes who myght wel be theyre sonnes or eke grandsonnes, and have behaved in shamelesse wyse so that they wolde doo wel to speke ne more of vertue lest they brenne theire shamles tonges. Tel them alle that, for I wishe not to see theire countenaunces ayen ere they fare forth and go hence from Castel Neudegck. And that shall be soone. Menewhyle have your playsure wyth them, as ye no doubt wyll, thou Heimo and thou Ruodl, and I care not yf otheres of the housholde wolde also take theyre share.' After oure syre had sayde thus, he laughed and we dranke ayen from the cuppes and he gaf me leve to go.

Thereaftre, and syn we muste ne lenger fere our syre, were bothe Heimo and I so overcomen and our wildenes waxed so stronge it was soone a Sodhom and Ghommorah, for we had afore not dared so muche as now we dyd and us happed syth our syre had given us leve. Other whyle ["sometimes"] I wened in erneste that I was in helle. And cam nyne or ten dayes after Estre, byfore cockcrowe I fel somewhat aslepe on the bedde and wyth eche hand held one of the wymen, and slept there; and in the slepe me seemed it best I ne wolde never wake but slepe ferre and so go from this werlde. There brent a candel that stode on a table. And I loked ayen in to this same lyght and woke alle and ne coud slepe more and lay there in dred and fere and grewe hote and thought wether nowe I myght not escape to my chambre and hence and awaye from these same wymen who slept so sounde there; and bothe dyd snore a lytyl; and inwards ["meaning here: within myself"] becam I soone sore hateful ["filled with hatred"] and thought what coud have happed that we were drawen in to such folyes bycause of these same wymen and helde thus so longe a tyme, and I thought eke that afore we had lyved a bedre lyf, the whyche now me seemed alle paste and loste and forsworn and as yf we had now deyed ["died"] and were trouly in helle, and the tweyne sorcereses had be given eternall and everlasting power to peyne and punisshe us, not we ovre them as we had beloved; and we ne wolde never come more from that place of payne even whan Castel Neudecgk stode ne lenger, but were certaynly alleredy in helle where it was moste deepe. And even more hote becam I but coud not move me and this second tyme ayen becam lyke a log of wode, onely alle thurgh, and had I coud ["if I had been able to"] I hadde ["would have"] screme loude in my fere and dred, but coud not and laye styll and loked in to the lyght. And the candel now had brent lowe and waved ["wavered"] and moved.

Then herde I from the tour the watch blowe loude upon his horne, and dyd not stop and continued to sounde, blowyng in suche wyse as to shewe that we muste make us redy for the defence syn we be in peryl of assaut. And joyned hym a second and blewe also, and continued both to sounde theyre hornes. That was a grete gladnes to me, and it is straunge and to mark that in the continuyng soundyng ["while the horn continued to sound"] that sweete scente of the waters ["perfume"] whyche the women used here in this chambre cam to my mynde so that I smelled it stronge, how be it they had used it alle the tyme and I had not notyced it afore, syn that I had smelled it so ofte tyl that I marked it not; but now cam the odour keenely to me. And I was wel ayen and sprange wyth joye from the bedde, and the two wymen waked, and I dressed quickely and called to them: 'Wake ye, women, ye, bourghmaistresse and ye, cosayne, and doo on your clothes and gathre your goodes. For now wyll alle bigynne anew and alle wyll chaunge.' And sayeng so, I renne wyth spede to my owne chambre to provyde me wyth armes. And I was gladde and joyouse in my herte that a newe tyme was comen. And armed my self wyth care in my armures and toke my helme and gerded on my swerde and toke my arblastre and quareylles also.

Thenne went I to the bayley where it was alleredy dayelyght and ranne as swifte I myght to my right place, as was my devoyer ["duty"]; my plase was on the rounde waye above the brigge. There were alleredy assembled the Allemaynes and Bemes on the brestewerke and stode wyth arblastres atte redy; and the gunner wyth his men stode by the thre peces and had his fyre brennyng. Sir Tristram was full wyde awake and laughed as I had not seen hym this longe tyme, and called a Beme and sayde to him: 'Vaclav, renne to the kichen, the wenches shall fyll a grete pot.' And soone retourned the Beme wyth the wyne, and as he dyd so cam my syre in ful harneys ["armor"] adoune

the steppes and laughed loude, and Sir Tristram lykewyse. Sir
Oswalt biganne to singe, but was a corse songe, and the souldyours alle sangen wyth hym, and my syre also, and the songe
was:

> The wyghtes, they wol breke doune
> Neudegkh of grete renoune.
> But we wol synge theyre hyde
> Lyke swine, tyl they abyde . . .

Menwyle loked I doune fro the rounde waye where I stode
wyth two Bemes, and loked over the fosse and rode to the wode
wards where I coud mark the movementes of meny men. For
they had not yet brought theyre engynes ["means cannon here"]
to the rode syn we coud covre the same wyth oure arblastres; but
styll I coud see them go to and fro now and ayen, and thought
may hap they were draggyng up theyre gunnes so that they
myght fyre upon the brestewerkes and so breke doune the same
that they coud venture the assaut. But they had sore swete and
trouble, for that the grounde sloped so sharpe doune from the
rode. But I sawe that they were sekyng to place theyre gunnes
and sheldes byfore them, and sente a Beme to make reporte of
the same to Sir Tristram.

Soone aftre, syth was more lyght, they whyche stoode on the
hyght of the tour coud bedre see in to the wode, and sawe it full
of men and gere ["gear"], but that they coud not brynge the
gere to the rode, how be it they hadde horses enough and meny
chorles to helpe. And from the tour was this reported to oure syre.
The same gaf thenne commaunde that none muste lose a shote,
wether by intente or that a bolt sprang of itself from the nut.
And our syre sente souldyours to go the whole lengthe of the
ramparte to loke that none cam secretely from othre sydes and
over the stone ["via the cliff"].

Thenne grewe it full lyght, al be it the sunne was not yet yrisen
at oure backes, yet coud it alleredy be marked that it was a fayre
daye wyth blyew skye.

Thenne herde we severall trumpetes blewe from underneth the

rode in the wode; and theraftre swung a baner over the rode and was helde hyghe, but for the swyngyng ["because of the motion"] I coud not descrye its heraldrie; and then called a loude voyce from doune belowe: 'His grace the baron Achaz of Neudegk is hereby axed and requested by his Grace the lorde High Stewarde here in Carynthia to comen in good confydence and stande over the brigge that his Grace the Lorde High Stewarde maye see hym and holde parly wyth hym and bringe hym a tidyng.'

For in these tymes we had no duke but a lorde hygh Stewarde who was hight Sir Sigmund the Crusader.

Then cam my syre up to the rounde waye. And atte same tyme Sir Tristram calleth wyth a myghty voyce, as he was els not woned to use: 'Late no one shote the whyle the lorde and his men stande in good confydence on the rode.'

They camen incontynent forth from the wodes and were a goodly host. Frist cam the high stewarde hymself wyth severall lordes and knyghtes, and the baner was planted by syde of hym and was the baner of the lande of Carynthia. And ayen were sounded the trumpetes. And the Hyghe Steward tourned hym then to the rounde waye and lifted his arme and greeted our syre, and he greeted hym in lyke wyse.

Thenne spake the hyghe stewarde and sayde how that they of Lienz had receved complaynt for that he helde here two women, one beyng the wedowe of a bourghmaistre, and they of Lientz had made appeale and so the thynge had ben brought byfore hymself, the hyghe stewarde, for that it was doubtles a breche of peas and justice and an acte of wronge and nyghe to treson the whyche our syre had don. For whyche reson in so grave a matere he had not sente a messager, for that it hym seemed that he, whyche is to saye our syre, wolde not have given answer to the messager; so was he comen hymself, albeit that was not usuall and the custome of the contre, and that he was comen wyth full gere and a stronge partye for to shewe that he ment in erneste to restore ryght and justice and to set free the wymen, and not withoute paiement and ful recompence, the whyche he muste give them wyth good and myckel money and muste late them eke go theyre waye, whither they wyshed to go, wyth alle theire goodes and horse and wagon. And yf these same wymen here at Neudegck had receved eny harme or damege to bodye or goodes, he muste make them speciall and meete recompence. And yf not, thenne the affayre muste alas tourne from the waye of goode feloweship and they wold incontynent make assaut upon the place, wyth employement of the canons and peces he coud see and other whyche they had also that he coud not see, and wold assaut and storme the castel tyl that they made caytiff oure syre and the justice of the lande myght thenne take its corse.

And the whyle the hyghe stewarde maketh suche speche, comen more and more men fro and appereth oute of the wode on the rode and helde up theyre baneres, lordes and vassels, and they of Villach eke were there, as Sir Oswalt had saide a whyle afore, and were also meny lordes from nyghe ["that is, from the immediate vicinity"], and the same lorde was there also wyth two knyghtes and a baner whose bucke my syre had taken the year paste.

Thenne my syre, standyng on the rounde waye, toke off his helm that it be convenable for hym to speke, and gave answer and sayde thus:

'Moste noble lordes, I muste alas balke your plannes; for yf we wel consyder what hath be saide by his Grace, the hyghe Ste-warde, and yf al shall be don in right and justice, then wol ye hardely bigynne to assaut and storme and try to wynne Castel Neudecgk. For I have in mynde and wyll to accept and obey saide condicions and even more than that; for I have given the same wymen of Lientz payement and recompence wyth myckel money, to eche one of them XV gulden. Notwythstandyng that neithre the one nor tother hath received eny harme or damege to bodye or goodes from me. And the same wymen shall go hence and take theyre waye withoute let nor hindrence from me or myne wyth alle theyre goodes, horse, and wagon yf ye wol give them a man to conduyte them and drive theyre wagon, for suche they ne can doo, theire owne man having runne from them atte Apfalterspach, albeit what reson he hadde is me uncouth ["I do not know the reason"]. And as for paiement and recompence, and that they have taken no harme or damege here atte Neudegck, so shall they them self knowlege and confesse it to his grace the hyghe steward, and telle hym that they have longe syn made them redy to departe and goe hence. Ne wol eny one beleve that I have had shameful intente or wyshes toward olde and honorable wymen, syn that I my self be yet in yonge yeres and wolde lever seke my lucke wyth them that be yonger. But that I have done them violence and made them caytiff and taken them here to this hous and helde them in pryson, whiche seemeth now ayenst right and justice, so dyd I this in belefe and bona fides that such be my devoyre. For by meny and hevy resones I thought these tweyne wymen to be sorceresses. And thought, as men saye evrywhere, what grete and sore harme and damege is done and brought upon people by suche wytches, warlockes, sorceresses, and magycians, what troubles upon cattel, fruit, men, springes, fishe pondes, and pastures; so that it was my devoyer to acte and take hande incontynent and withoute axyng or sendyng message to his Grace the hygh Stewarde or even his Grace the bisshop. For it is wel yknowen how suche sorceresses and sorcerers mowe and canne escape swiftely and are more pyght to flee ["adroit at fleeing"] than eny other foule criminell. And how be it I wel dyd knowe that all suche crimes and foule deedes are by right to be broughte tofore a courte of bothe the powers spirituell and werldely, neverthelesse had I mowe take cure ["care, from the Latin *cura*"] withoute delaye lest I neglecte my devoyer. And alle was proceded and conduyted in all right and justice, wyth deliberacion, and I dyd do write ["I had written down"] evry worde spoken therby. And by suche dylygent procedyng and conduytyng were alle suche sore suspicions and grevous charges lifted and the wymen acquitted altogedre; yet was there nede that those charges shold be made and consydered, for that both the same wymen shewed them self in merveyllous mesure and more than is woned in theyre skyll wyth makyng and preparyng brent and wel smellyng waters, in suche wyse that myght be called straunge; and had wayes and menes to change and altre the senses of a dronken man in the twynklyng of an eye and brynge hym to a sobre state, and othre artes and skylles as well. Notwythstandyng hath it now becomen playne that these artes and skylles have nought to do wyth magical fetes or sorceryes, not in eny wyse or manere, but onely wyth good and wholesom scyence in materes of medicine and of knowlege of herbes the whyche eny childe mowe picke or plucke; but that he lacketh the understandyng to werke so wholsomely and helthfully therewyth as don these tweyne wymen who knowe to hele and brynge improvemente to the sicke and playsure to the bodye of the well man. From suche remarkable causes be we redy to saye and confirme that no sorcery nor harmefulnes was founde in these wymen. And therfore have we of oure owne good wyll made them paiement and recompence, withoute eny compulcion in no wyse, and withoute that the same wymen have receved eny damege or harme to theyre bodyes or goodes. As withoute doubt these same wymen be redy to saye and confirme openly byfore the lorde hygh Steward yf he wyll lyst to them, and in lyke wyse to all other knyghtes and lordes here asembled.'

And whyle that he was spekyng I see how that the tweyne wymen come from the hous, accompanyed by Sir Tristram; and was no doubt agreed wyth the same that he sholde brynge them now aftre that my syre had spoken and made explanacion. And the same wymen cam up on the brestewerke and cam a Beme rennyng up and placed there a benche; then clomben the tweyne women on the benche and stode so that they coud wel be seen from belowe the fosse. And stode there the bourghmaistresse in her red dresse and spake:

'Hyghborn lorde Hyghe Stewarde, hygheborne noble lordes, that ye be comen to helpe tweyne pouer wedowes and have taken armes therfore, that has happed in trewe and loyale fulfillmente of your knyghtely vowes ["the protection of widows was one of the items in the vow made by every knight"], and we have you moste humbly to thanke and remercye. For the affayre dyd trewely seem that nought els had us happed and occasiouned than violence, thefte, shamefulnes, and harme and as yf we had be wronged and besette by injustice. Yet hath that not be so nor happed. And it muste plese and give ioye to me as to my cosayne that we be clered and aquitted of suche hevy charge and suspicioun of sorcery, and that the matere be wyth care and dylygence proceded and conduyted so that there be no taynt nor stayne upon us, as we now have testifyed therunto in writyng by his lordeship and baron here at Neudegck. And have we eke receved goodly and consyderable paiement and recompence, namely eche of us XV gulden. Also hath his lordeship and Grace given commaundes to late us goe oure waye from Castel Neudegck to Paszriach on the Lytyl Lake whither we wolde fare; yet lacke we styll a man for the viage ["journey"], and therfore moste humbly axe and requeste the lorde Hyghe Stewarde and all othre hyghborne and noble lordes as be ygadred here to graunte us one suche for the viage to Pazriach, wither we wolde fare wyth oure owne horse, wagon, and goodes. But we wolde make knowne ayen and knowlege clerely that we holde oure self in no wyse harmed or dameged by the noble lorde Achaz here in hous Neudegg.'

After the heryng of suche speche of the bourgemaistresse the Hygh Stewarde and severall lordes that stode by hym wente backe from the rode to the wode and there devysed and talked one wyth other. Therafter cam the Hyghe Steward fro to the fosse ayen and called up ayen to oure syre who styll stode on the rounde waye, and gave him replique ["reply"] and spake:

'Noble frend. Us seemeth wyth this witnesse of the wymen, that they have in no wyse received harme nor damege from you or thurgh your coulpe ["or by your fault"], that the matere is fynisshed and settled to satisfaccion, yf that ye be now redy to late the wymen go oute from the castel and from your power, wyth all theyre goodes, horse, wagon, and gere, withoute lette or hyndrance; then hath this oure assemblenge comen to a good ende and al be tourned in peas and feloweshippe.'

'So be it, your lordeship,' cryeth my syre wyth loude voyce.

And had no doubt ben lykewyse agreed wyth Sir Tristram that now the wymens wagon cam from the stall oute to the bayley and the wymen clomben on the wagon, and theyre chestes were borne oute of the hous, in the whyche were styll meny fyne spyces, and laden on the wagon and made faste. And Sir Tristram ordred the souldyoures to late doune the brigge; but ere that the brigge wente doune, I sawe this wel, Sir Tristram had three men of the Allemaynes and three of the Bemes step to the syde of the gate tour and stande belowe, some wyth bowe drawen and some wyth swerde bared, but these same men coud not be chused ["seen"] from belowe the fosse. Thenne onely dyd the brigge go doune and incontynent rode oute the wagon over the brigge, the reynes helde by a Beme. Thenne stopped he on the rode and gate hym off and gaf the reynes to an other man who cam forwarde, and wente the Beme back ovre the brigge to the bayley, but the brigge abode so as it was. Thenne spake my syre ayen and sayde:

'Your hygheborn lordshippe and Hyghe Stewart: Syn we now have don and satisfyed alle condicions that betwene us were consydered, I axe and requeste your Grace and the othir noble lordes whyche be gadred here to steppe on the brigge that we stengthen and reforce sayde agremente wyth hande claspe and a drynke, as is the good wonte and custome of oure lande.'

And whyle he spake thus, juste thenne wente the sunne atte oure backe hygher in the skye and shone full on my syres red gould hayre and it was as yf the same were alle brennyng. And my syre wente doune on the brigge and hys Grace and Stewarde cam forwarde and the other lordes behynde hym, and my lordes captayne, Sir Tristram, folowed hym. And as they now cam on the brigge, they on the rode swunge and waved the bannere of the lande ayen and ayen blewe full sore loude on theyre trumpetes, and oure men blewe lykewyse from the tour. And so was made and completed the hande clasp.

Thenne sawe I Heimo acomyng over the bayley and to the brigge ward. He had don off his helm and was dressed in a veste of my syres colores and his fayre haire wel kempt, and that same wyght was almoste playsaunte and good to beholde; and behynde the same cam a wench wyth a bigge sylver canne and a myckel cuppe, the whyche was alle of gold. And when they came to the brigge, Heimo toke canne and cuppe from this same wenche and wente up on the brigge wyth good demeenour and knelte byfore the Hyghe stewarde and other lordes that stode there; and poured the wyne, and in suche wyse was drunken and tosted to the hyghe Stewarde. The same smyled graciousely and in frendly wyse atte the yonge squyer, and my syre and Sir Tristram dranke also, tyl that the canne was nyghe emty. And the Hyghe Stewarde smyled and sayde: 'Give hym eke a mouthful,' and so Heimo was lykewise late to drynke.

Thereafter the lordes alle mounted theyre coursers, whyche had be led oute of the wolde where they were hydden, and rode hence, and amonge them was the bigge wagon of the wymen; and aftre camen the canons, how be it that toke a whyle afore they brought them out of the wolde and on to the rode; for it was sore werke, al be it they had no bigge and grete bombarde, but onely the same as we owre self had at the castel. And I stode by my syre who had comen up on the rounde waye ayen, and I loked at hym a whyle; and shone the sunne hygher and my syre's red gold haire was fayre to see. And they camen wyth theyre gere and horses all on the rode atte laste, and ferre, and mounted the maistre of the canon and his men on theire horses eke and rode awaye wich muche noyse tyl that atte last alle cam arounde the tour and from syght of our eyen.

Acros the bayley cam the sounde of footsteppes, how be it alle the souldyours were comen doune from the batelmentes; it was Sir Tristram lokyng ones more that al be well. Then my syre called doune to hym: 'Noble frend, be so good and see that alle men be given a bigge canne of wyne after breke faste ["breakfast"], eche man hys owne canne, and therafter mowe eche man slepe as long as hym lyketh.' And wyth that Sir Tristram wente in to the hous.

Therafter I abode alone wyth my syre on the rounde waye, and now alle was styll in the hous; and my syre loked over the wolde where it was lykewyse alle styll and no sounde coud be herde. The sunne had gon yet hygher and shone upon oure backes. Then saide my syre:

'Ruodl, it was an evyll winde, a winde of Venyse, as thou callest it, and it blewe hither and now is gon hence. And me seemeth I have ben made ayen whole oute of two halfe men, and the one half was of wode.'

Thenne was I affrayed, but knewe not by what cause I was affrayed. Sayde my syre ferre: 'A dreme, when that overcometh thee and thou art alone wyth it, wyth thy dreme and vision, alle els escapeth thee and thou art loste.' Then abode he sylente a whyle and thenne toke and putte hys one arm on my sholdres and sayde: 'When go we to hunte the hethcocke, Ruodl? Wol we try oure lucke on the morrow?'

'Yea, Syre,' say I, 'late it be soone, late it be the morrow!' And I lened ayenst my syre and helde my hed on his breste on the harneys, and he ranne hys hande a lytyl ovre my hayre. 'This yere shalt thou have the beste cocke,' sayde my syre. And he abode thereby and nexte mornyng we wente to hunte the cocke, and the thirde was the beste and my syre late me shote it self the whyle he loked on. *Explicit. Hoc est verum et cetera* what hath ben called fals rumour. *Actum sexagesimo nono aetatis meae anno Aug. Vind. MDXVIJ* on Tuesday byfore Ascension Daye. Ruodlip von der Vläntsch.

"NICE the way he describes this tower of madmen," René said casually, laying the manuscript aside.

Herzka looked up at Stangeler with the eyes of a man lying feverish in bed. At his bedside now sat a total stranger, more strange and incomprehensible than that doctor of his childhood had ever been.

The next day, Thursday, May 19, they rode back to Vienna in the same style as they had come. The manuscript was stowed away in René's suitcase. René had an inner aura today, a kind of lingering fragrance, as of an alcoholic distillation of herbs. It was connected with his feeling of great agility and lightness, a feeling that spread through all his limbs, but without foaming over. Everything within him was arranging itself with a quiet, airy distinctness.

Herzka's car was waiting at the South Station. The chauffeur saluted René as if he were already an established appendage of his boss. As they glided through the damp cool streets, René was keenly aware of his new condition.

Again the big car rolled up in front of his parental home.

Stangeler went up to the third floor. As he passed the second, he remembered how a few days before, just before his departure for Carinthia, he had looked in on his parents, enjoying momentarily the false glow of a success he had not yet reaped, lying by means of the truth.

He entered his room, disposed of his luggage, cleaned up—and above all put away Ruodlieb's precious manuscript, locking it up along with his notes in the drawer of his desk.

But he could not go down to the second floor to announce that he was back and invite himself to dinner with his parents, for he would have had to give them a little prior warning. That half lie which he had involuntarily left behind now impalpably blocked his way.

He went to the telephone in the vestibule and rang up Grete.

The moment he heard the bell ringing at the other end of the line, he knew that this, his telephoning now, was the right and proper act for the moment. Because all he wanted to do was to hear her voice, rather than make an immediate report to her.

And sure enough, she herself answered at once.

However, it took but a moment for Grete Siebenschein to open the tap on René's urge to communicate. She was not only highly interested, but as curious as a magpie. "Go out to eat somewhere," she said. "I'll meet you there."

Seeing her again, René sensed instantly that he had left some of the inner stumbling-blocks between them down there in the caverns of Neudegg. There they remained, moldering away, soon to molder away to nothing. He also felt more assured with her, and more self-contained. To put the whole thing into René's own peculiar language, we would have to say: "She acquired objective character." It was not often that René could say this of anything or anyone, for most outside things seemed like members of his own body—almost to the point of his feeling the smart of another's stings. Hence, true objective character was rare in his experience. (Incidentally, a number of philosophers deny that it is possible.)

Naturally, he now told her the whole story in detail. They sat in a small underground restaurant, the "horse-pond" of a grand hotel—that being the Viennese name for these moderate-priced offshoots of famous establishments.

Stangeler, then, told his story—recounting first what had come last, after he had finished reading the medieval text to Jan Herzka. . . . But what he said was not real narrative; rather, dry information. He seemed to be drawing up lists. At the same time he appeared not yet to have come to terms with these dubious successes; he had not yet warmed to them, for all that they promised to change his life for the better in so unforeseen a fashion. Herzka had offered him the position of librarian at Neudegg. He could consider the place his headquarters and would be free to go there at any time; but would be under no obligation to remain permanently at the castle or subordinate his studies in Vienna. His job would be to supply Herzka with information and bibliography on certain cultural-historical matters, and to supervise the stylistic details of the repairs to be done in the underground rooms of the castle. But above all he would be expected to expand the library in the direction of Herzka's interests by purchasing new as well as old and precious books; he would have sizable funds at his disposal for this purpose. All this along with an ample monthly salary that would mean for René nothing more nor less than complete independence. Tomorrow afternoon he would be meeting his employer at the office of the lawyer, Doktor Krautwurst, to make a formal contract.

"So I'm employed as an expert on witches," René said.

Grete, for her part, wholly grasped the extent of his success; she saw it vividly, distinctly, in all its details. Moreover she remarked that if Herzka were empowering him to purchase old and valuable books, he was placing René in a rather enviable position in that particular branch of business. For since Jan Herzka had no specialist's knowledge of the subject, what was bought or not, and from whom, would depend entirely on René.

Here was where the first practical confirmation of the change that had taken place in René Stangeler within the last few days came to light. For now he raised no foolish objections to her "business sense," launched no wholesale accusations against this sense with the accompanying looks askance (not to speak of blows below the belt) at Grete's racial stock. René was the soul of circumspection. There was nothing feverish about his views today; they had the coolness of sound health. He perceived at once that Grete was not thinking of profitable commissions, but of acquisition of influence and personal connections.

"There are only three specialty houses here in Vienna that can seriously be considered for such things. Vienna is hardly an important place in that respect. The center of the rare-book trade and dealings in incunabula is London."

She looked at him with more than a touch of astonishment. Her casual question was rather like the casting of a pebble at a sheet of ice to determine its thickness and strength. "You do know English, don't you?"

"Yes," he said. "When Herzka spoke to me about the book-buying, I thought at once that this might give me a chance to go to London sometime."

Her eyes flashed. "Mary, who lives on the floor above us, has a good friend in London. . . ."

She broke off, casually, trailing off unnoticeably. No. They had not yet come so far that she could tell him about Mme Libesny, with whom Camy Schlaggenberg was staying—a refuge had been found for Camy through Grete's intercession with Mary. If she said anything, sooner or later Kajetan Schlaggenberg would hear of it, and that was precisely what Camy did not want. Moreover, René was not in Mary's good books, and had made himself altogether unwanted recently by his rude conduct toward Trix.

"Yes," Grete said, "you must have a chance to go abroad sometime. Since your folks don't want to help you, it can be done this way, and it will be ever so much better anyhow."

Stangeler had always taken an angry tone toward such talk of travel and widening of horizons. He had acted as if there were things he had to do first, as if he thought himself not yet ripe and were being disturbed in some activity he considered had to be finished first. But this time even that familiar reaction was not forthcoming.

"It's high time I did," he said. "Everybody is traveling around constantly these days, even the fellows at the Institute. I think it will be possible to swing it—I mean, having Jan Herzka finance such a trip. Perhaps he will even go along, and I'll accompany him as his private secretary, so to speak."

"Bravo!" Grete cried. They touched glasses and drank their wine.

"Do you think he will put the matter of the books into the contract also?" she said.

"I've been wondering about that," René replied. "But I don't think it would be right to remind him directly of it tomorrow at the lawyer's. Perhaps it can be done indirectly, or else he will include it of his own accord. I'll telephone you at once as soon as the contract is signed, and tell you all about it—not from the lawyer's office, of course."

She rejoiced inwardly: "He isn't stupid, not stupid at all, not a bit stupid! They're all wrong! He's only been preoccupied. When he isn't preoccupied, he's clever and prudent. More than the whole bunch of them. We'll see one of these days how things turn out for Cornel Lasch, and whether they turn out so well at all."

Next day, at Herr Krautwurst's, it developed that Herzka laid special stress upon René's purchasing books, both old and rare ones and more modern "cultural-historical material"—that being the very phrase used in a special paragraph of the contract. René had already received his 1500 for the inspection of Neudegg; now he was to collect his first salary at the beginning of June.

Afterwards he telephoned Grete from a café, and they both laughed and were altogether silly over the telephone.

Going out on the street again, however, René now felt it impossible to return straightway to his desk in the Institute, where he had sat that morning over his documents. Impossible. The new element that had entered his life only now began to penetrate him, to rise into the fine branches of his being, the capillaries in which, it appears, the self-evident factors of our lives have their real seat; and if they have not yet penetrated to those vessels, they are not self-evident. Newness must trickle through to the true laboratory of the psyche, where the mysterious chemical transformation of convictions into qualities takes place. This is why newness takes time, requires a minimal incubation period, in order to become really new for us. Such was René Stangeler's experience.

It being impossible to travel just now, he felt the urge to travel within his native city: to take one of those journeys of which Paul Valéry speaks in his book *Tel Quel*. Old cities have frequently grown together out of various parts; such is the case with Paris and Vienna. The genius loci of these disparate portions of the city which have been unified and connected by modern institutions, lingers with incredible persistence in their air, and probably can never be entirely dispelled. It is as though such a quarter of a city were constantly contemplating its old days, remembering its origins, its original nature. Now nothing is more useful a tool to deep recollection than the sense of smell. Thus the relics of bygone communities continue to give off the odor of their origins. ". . . *Si ma sensibilité olfactive vient à s'accroître, je me promène dans Paris comme un étranger.*" ("If there has been a sharpening of my sense of smell, I walk about Paris like a stranger.") This was what René Stangeler now tried to do. He liked to go walking about Vienna like a stranger. Now and then, without any practical reason, he would visit remote parts of the city. No doubt there were elements of a silly romanticism in this recreation. Undoubtedly René would have been delighted with that passage from Valéry, had he been privileged to read it. It had, in fact, been written long before, in 1910, but did not appear in print until thirty-one years later, in the *Cahier B*.

After signing the contract at the lawyer's and after his telephone call to Grete, then, René found his way by drifting, not to an old part of the city, nor to the countryside on the outskirts

where the vintners' villages lie among the hills and the leaves of
the grapevine cut jagged patterns in the blue of the sky. René
was not seeking an idyllic landscape today. But where the river
intersects the edge of the city, great lumps of the edge are
broken off and block the view of the countryside with quays,
cranes, and warehouses, with railroad tracks, shipyards, and factories.

Now, after a longish streetcar ride, René stood in this vicinity,
truly a stranger.

The light here, too, differed from that in the interlaced greenery of the Prater meadows with their smells of plant growth and
earth, with their isolated pools and marshy tributaries. This area,
open to the wind that followed the rapidly flowing water, lay
under a comparatively bright and cold light. And the river did
not pause; it hastened along, washing the shores of the city.
Where buildings stood, they shared in that sober light which
streamed everywhere along their oblong lengths. The modern
complex of buildings belonging to the firm for which Trix K.
worked stretched out along the deserted sidewalk. It did not
occur to René, of course, that Mary K.'s lovely daughter might
be here. He walked slowly. Enjoying. Enjoying what? The for-
eignness of the place; partaking of the same enjoyment that
others—for example Titi Lasch and her husband, or even Grete
Siebenschein, if she happened to be taken along—would have
enjoyed in Genoa or Rotterdam, in Riccione or Brussels. René
had this same pleasure along the Danube waterfront.

He came to the corner of the Bunzl & Biach factory. The
factory receded here; there was a gap in the solid front of buildings along the shore. A multitude of paths crisscrossed a tiny
area of green. Here you could walk right down to the river. And
the current had almost vanished at this spot. The water stood
still. Only farther out from the shore did it continue to flow
swiftly, curling and curvetting, or advancing in smooth planes.
The other shore appeared like one compressed green strip. René
thought of the great rivers he had seen in Asia, the Amur and
the Ussuri at their confluence, for instance, looking like a vast

moving lake. By comparison with these the Danube at Vienna was small. But the comparison almost escaped him; he had no really vivid and self-evident awareness of the size of those other rivers, only some statistical data. This river was after all mighty. Especially when you looked across it at a diagonal, turned half in the direction of its flow. A train of scows moved rapidly past his vision, going downstream. The tug in the van, behind it the huge black scows. The smokestack of the tug puffed billows of sooty smoke. Stangeler watched the boats gliding rapidly away and had a feeling very like what he had experienced the night before when his train pulled into the station and he had regarded the branching of the innumerable tracks radiating in all directions away from the city. There was a process going on within him like the unfolding of a fan as he looked after the scows fading from sight in the center of the river.

Simultaneously, and flowing into this picture, there awoke in René awareness of an olfactory sensation, something halfway between the subjective and the objective; perhaps it was only the thought or recollection of a scent. But there it was! It came from the meadow behind him, but smelled not of grass, rather of still unripe fruit. He turned around.

A man and a woman were standing at the top of the steps. The man wore no hat; he waved his hand in greeting, laughed, and called out: "How are you?"

René clambered up the stone steps. He was incapable of striking off any contact in his memory, could not recognize this tall blonde man who looked extremely friendly and shone with cleanliness, as if he had not only donned clean clothes that morning but beforehand slipped into an entirely new skin.

"Long time no see," the man said. "Not since that evening of great discussions at Herr von Schlaggenberg's in Döbling, early in March. Samovar, Russian cigarettes . . . and you, Doktor, sat by the samovar all the time."

His speech was fluent, sprightly, and good-humored, but the accent, the Anglo-Saxon accent, came through.

"Ah—you are the zoologist!" Stangeler exclaimed. "The story

about the octopus in the South American port—that interested me enormously." They shook hands.

"May I introduce my fiancée—what was your name again, Doktor?"

"René Stangeler."

"Of course!" Williams said. "Well, this is Doktor Stangeler, and this is my fiancée, Fräulein Emma Drobil."

Emma and René greeted each other. René had the impression of vigor, self-possession, of a kind of splendor. All three now sat down side by side on the steps, close to the water, Emma between the two men, sitting on Dwight's jacket, which he had spread for her.

"What is this story about the horrible creature in South America?" Emma asked. "An octopus, did you say? You never told me about it. That's what we call a polyp, isn't it?" She was now speaking German with Dwight.

"Well—the term 'polyp' means something else in zoology. These octopuses are what we call cephalopods. Not the most attractive creatures. Sometimes they grow to fantastic size. I ran into one once, as I told Doktor Stangeler over the samovar in Döbling."

"Did you 'run into' it at sea?" Emma asked.

"No, not at all," Dwight replied. "In a perfectly safe harbor—right at the pier, in fact. A bizarre business. The way they dispose of their garbage there is to have refuse holes out on the pier, with gratings, like sewer gratings. They empty the slops pails into these. I was at a restaurant there, a place famous for its fish dishes. Suddenly a native gave a fearful cry; he'd gone to empty a pail, and this thing caught him. Right through the grating a long tentacle shot out and gripped him around the ankle. People came running up with knives and freed him, but one of the rescue crew was also caught by the foot. I saw it with my own eyes, and realized at once what was happening. I had a pistol with me, ran over and fired through the grating, kept firing as long as anything stirred. There was a tremendous splashing and crashing in the shaft. Nothing like this had ever happened in the port. Later they pulled out the dead creature; it weighed far more than a hundred pounds and had eight arms each about ten feet long, suction cups the size of plates. People said that the nettings over the outlets of the sewage system on the sea had long been rusted out."

"How ghastly!" Emma cried. "And did it try to grip you with its tentacles?"

"No," Dwight said. "It pulled back after those two tentacles had been cut off."

"What would happen if you met a thing like that in the water— when you went swimming, for instance?"

"You might well be done for, unless you had a knife or a large shears with you. But who goes swimming with such equipment? Incidentally, a specimen of that size would be strong enough to pull a person from the shore into the water. Divers know a trick to be used in extremity, I've heard. The octopus has a kind of beak, a horny beak like a parrot's or vulture's. The story is that anyone who can overcome his disgust and fear, reach between the writhing tentacles, pull apart the beak and turn it inside out like a glove, will kill the kraken. I don't know whether it's true or not—fortunately I've never been in a situation where I had to try it."

"I'm so glad that you specialize in butterflies," Emma said. "When I think that you might be constantly occupied with such octopuses and perhaps even have to go hunting them . . ."

"If so, it would be done with the right equipment," Dwight replied in all seriousness. "But no, since my undergraduate examinations I've not paid much attention to mollusks."

"That's really horrible, about the beak," Emma said.

"There is something even more horrible about the beast," Williams said. "The eyes. They are disproportionately large, very well formed—in fact they have a structure usually found in creatures of a much higher stage of development—even mammals. Eyes of that type, of course, have what we call a real gaze. And this very circumstance makes the big cephalopods—which are after all related to the snail and are only the top class of invertebrates—rather diabolical creatures. After we'd killed that monster, all sorts of stories sprang up about octopuses having penetrated into the sewerage system under the city. It was said that a woman had been attacked in her bathroom and another in a cellar, and similar sensational nonsense. I could not check up on it because I did not know enough Portuguese to speak with the people, certainly not in the local dialect. But probably these were all fables based on the one octopus we'd killed. I had to leave the next day, incidentally, and anyhow I'd come to Brazil to study butterflies, not sea monsters."

"Thank goodness," Emma said.

At this point in the conversation a boat of recollection in René slipped from the pier of the present and for a few seconds he glided off in this vessel, far out, to where he could feel far greater depths of water beneath him. At the same time he was filled with astonishment: why should this happen now? That time at Schlaggenberg's, sitting with Williams beside the samovar, no such association had come to him, although the American had told his story about the sea monster then. But now it came, bobbed up out of the bluish depths that one can feel, almost see, in old streets of suburban Vienna. And the image lacked all definition of time; it might have been this past winter, or perhaps a year before. On Liechtenstein Strasse, where it narrows down, just before the streetcar tracks turn off it: he visualized a small corner building with a blue enamel unicorn in a niche above the first corner. "Nearby, somewhere, there must be a tobacco shop," René thought, "for while I was buying some cigarettes I saw this newspaper displayed, with headlines about the great sea monster that had somehow 'crept under' a central Brazilian city, although one far from the sea. It was supposed to have swum up a river. And suchlike nonsense."

He now told Williams about the contents of the article: "It was one of those sensational newspapers—weeklies, you would call them in English; they're very popular here. The issue was just off the press, for several persons came in one after another and bought a copy. I also was tempted into buying one. It was illustrated by a fantastic drawing of people going around with knives, and a woman armed with a big pair of scissors. But I didn't believe a word of it."

"Why so?" Williams asked.

"Because I knew that cephalopods are completely salt-water creatures."

"Right," Williams said. "That is a kind of 'dogma' in zoology, insofar as a science can have dogmas. What is your field anyhow, Doktor?"

"History, especially the Middle Ages. I'm what you might call a medievalist."

"Oh yes, I recall now," Williams said animatedly. "We were talking about dragons that evening. Whether they might ever have existed. You quoted a sentence from Albertus Magnus to the effect that 'serious writers have reported nothing concerning flying dragons, nor can it be understood how an animal of such length could preserve stability in the air.' Smart old Dominican. I made a point of remembering it."

"Let's not sit by the water any more," Emma said. "I'm starting to feel nervous. Any moment I expect one of those tentacles to come reaching out. Besides, it's growing cool. Shan't we walk a little? Won't you come too, Herr Stangeler?"

"Gladly," René said.

They stood up. Williams donned his jacket again, and they went up the stone staircase. Stangeler was conscious of the river they were leaving behind, flowing incessantly on, with the evenness of a clock, almost stagnant by the shore, farther out hastening past, curling and curvetting, or advancing in smooth planes.

Beyond the green area crisscrossed by many paths René saw a small red automobile, a splash of bright color, like a painted Easter egg.

"That's our car," Williams said. "After our walk, I'd be glad to drive you back into town, Doktor, if you don't mind sitting in the rumble seat."

"Thank you, yes, that would be very nice."

"Any part of town especially?"

"To Althan Platz—near the Franz Josef Railroad Station."

"Oh, I know the neighborhood," Williams said. "I went to a party there with Fräulein Drobil at the end of April. Number 6 Althan Platz. That's fine, right on our way. We are driving out to Nussdorf."

"That is the very house I want to go to, Althan Platz 6," Stangeler said. "My fiancée lives there."

"And what may your fiancée's name be?"

"Grete Siebenschein."

"But I know her! A very pretty black-haired young lady. I had a long talk with her. Not only beautiful but intelligent. Later on, Fräulein Drobil told me her name. Well, I must offer my congratulations, Doktor!"

While they continued to stroll for a while in the region of large factory buildings and big bridges, exposed to the wind from the river, Stangeler became conscious of the extensive transformation which had taken place within him down at Castle Neudegg. It was almost physically palpable within his mind. At the same time he puzzled quietly over the way in which Fräulein Drobil's face had briefly darkened at Williams's remark: "I went to a party there with Fräulein Drobil at the end of April." She had looked alarmed, and her eyes, big and black as cherries, had retreated slightly into their sockets, become deeper and more shining. Since his return from Carinthia, René had acquired a new kind of perspective on himself and others. He saw more, and therefore saw differently. Not so long before, this bumping into Williams and Emma Drobil would undoubtedly have aroused disagreeable emotions in him; he would have been upset and possibly depressed by it, by the thought of a scholar so well situated, with a decent career, an automobile, and a fiancée. Though that time in Döbling, at the "foundation festival," he had not disliked Williams. Still, the man had had a rather depressing effect on him. He had at once started thinking: "I should have studied something else, something with a practical application." Whereupon all his usual feelings had started to torment him. But now he was discovering the practical possibilities of his own profession. His life, too, had been placed on an ordered basis. He could meet these people on an equal plane. Gradually the realization of the enormous success he had achieved down there in Carinthia was trickling through him; trickling through to the depths where he could really appreciate what had happened. He was profoundly astonished at his own lack of constraint. Never had he possessed such a degree of self-assurance. Why, he no longer had any insoluble problems. His sufferings were over—only he had not yet fully realized it.

He was due to be even more surprised at himself. For Dwight Williams went on: "A pity you were not there too at that very nice party at Frau Mary K.'s. How is it that you don't know the lady, although your fiancée is such a good friend of hers?"

"I have known her since last autumn," Stangeler said. "But she doesn't like me. And for good reasons—I mean, she's quite right not to. She disapproved of the way I was behaving toward my fiancée for some time. Also I once said some very tactless things to her daughter Trix. But that's another story. Anyhow, that's the way it is. Very simple."

In fact René found it very simple to speak the truth. It could, he discovered, also be put very briefly. Williams looked at him with undisguised liking. "Since you see the matter so clearly, Doktor, it should not be difficult to install yourself in their good graces again."

"I intend to," René said. "I'll simply go up there and say I see what an idiot I was and beg their pardon."

"Wonderful," Williams said. "But what was this awful thing you said to Mary K.'s daughter?"

They were now walking for a short distance directly along the river. Under the bridge they could see the vertical black line of a steamer's smokestack, far away and thin as a black crayon, pointing up out of the gray-green expanse of water. The train of scows seemed to be standing still, although it was imperceptibly nearing them. But a light breeze carried to them the noise of the engines, a steady low grinding and rumbling.

"What I said to Trix was," Stangeler replied, speaking in the same natural tone as before, and finding it easy and comfortable to speak thus, "that the parties in her mother's house made me want to puke. Which was not very nice of me, but happened to be the truth. In the first place, the whole company up there is threadbare, with a few clear exceptions: Herr von Schlaggenberg, Herr Kakabsa, the captain, and the students. But you know, Doktor Williams, I couldn't stand that circle of adorers around Frau Mary. There isn't any doubt that she is both beautiful and intelligent, and that she has also shown tremendous will power. Like our famous Baron Münchhausen, she's pulled herself up out of the swamp by her own pigtail, so to speak. And that is what is fascinating about her. But to my mind, the triumph she is celebrating there cancels out the victorious campaign."

"Every triumph is a cancellation," Williams said. "Every success in general. By the laws of compensation, the tension is relieved. And that produces an insipid aftertaste. At bottom there is something repellent about everyone who, after a long effort, is what you might call exonerated by success. It's a dubious stage in a person's life."

Thus it happened that René learned that even a well-situated scholar with a decent career, an automobile, and a fiancée, could sometimes have something to say. In his previous state of mind, only a week before, he would never have believed it.

"But I quite understand your reaction," Williams continued. "The one evening that I spent at Frau K.'s, I had exactly the same feeling as you." (Stangeler, with his present keenness of perception, caught an almost imperceptible nod on Emma Drobil's part.)

Stangeler therefore spoke briefly of his visit to the castle in Carinthia. He told them about Ruodlieb von der Vläntsch's manuscript and enlarged a bit on its implications for scholarship.

"Why," Williams exclaimed, standing still, "can you beat that!" Without moving another step, Williams said: "Doktor, listen to me. This matter interests me, and what I am going to tell you now will interest you. In London I stayed with a Mme Libesny, a Viennese, incidentally. She has two married daughters in America. The older girl is the wife of a Harvard professor named

Bullogg, a quite well-known historian and medievalist. His hobby, or specialty if you like, is the witch trials. And it has long been his thesis that the usual interpretation of them is absolutely wrong."

"I quite agree with him," René said.

"Just wait till I tell Professor Bullogg of your discovery in the archives of Castle Neudegg. He'll be wildly excited. From what you've told me, this source is a confirmation of his ideas—in short, grist to his mill. He'll see to it that you can publish papers on this matter in the best American journals. That is, if you don't mind my telling him about it. To be perfectly candid about it, Bullogg is very influential at the university. So that it would be a big boost for me, too, to be able to pass on this thing to him."

"Do by all means inform Professor Bullogg," René said. "I have not the slightest objection. You could also give him my address and tell him that I'll be glad to correspond with him on this subject."

He took out his wallet and handed Williams his visiting card.

"What's more," Williams said, "Professor Bullogg was planning to come to Vienna this year, toward the end of June or July. I'll telephone you as soon as he arrives; I know he'll be eager to meet you."

"If you call me, please don't use the telephone number on this visiting card. There's this somewhat cranky old lady who isn't reliable in transmitting messages, and can sometimes be extremely rude over the phone, especially if she is disturbed on my account. If you want to get in touch with me, would you just call my fiancée, Fräulein Siebenschein—I see her every day. Here, I'll write the number on the card."

"Splendid," Williams said. "And speaking of your fiancée, couldn't we four get together sometime—that would be nice, wouldn't it?"

"An excellent idea!" René replied. "Just call Grete and arrange it with her—I'll tell her you're going to."

"Yes, we certainly must!" Emma said.

They had reached the stone steps by the shore again. The water had risen high over the steps, for the train of scows was just passing by. In the midst of their lively talk, the three had not noticed the descent of evening. Now they crossed the trampled little meadow, in which the grass between the paths stood deep green and luxuriantly moist, and went to the red auto. "An odd neighborhood for walks," Williams said. "But we wanted a change. It doesn't always have to be the Vienna Woods or Schönbrunn or the Ring and Kärntner Strasse."

Stangeler packed himself into the rumble seat of the car. They roared off. The wide streets in this area turned and swung around like long oblong tablets; the speed at which they drove reduced the considerable distance to insignificance. In front of the house on Althan Platz, René vaulted from the seat. "And don't forget about patching matters up with Frau Mary!" Williams said as they shook hands. "Nothing to be done about it, now," Emma added, laughing. "They're both at Semmering." The car shot off, and René turned toward the door.

Evening with Grete. They had dinner by themselves—the parents had gone out. "Well, my sweet," she observed, "let me tell you one thing right off: if you ever start pretending I'm a chaste widow and want to play games of that sort, you'll get a couple of good hard slaps." By now their laughter was soft and somewhat languid; they were on the sofa, their arms entwined about each other.

She was completely attuned to René now. She felt the change in him, and the way he had changed toward her. On the strength of this, she came over to his side of the fence, and even prattled a bit about the family—with whom she was never in too great sympathy, even when René had hurt her and thrust her back upon her kith and kin.

Various things had been happening, it seemed, during the days René had been away. Namely, three quarrels: one between Cornel Lasch and Titi, one row between Cornel and Levielle, and still another row with a gentleman she did not know, a lawyer named Doktor Mährischl. All three scenes had taken place right there in the apartment. (Ferry Siebenschein must have been delighted.)

We will all, now and then, give way to loquacity, as though a wound were opening and beginning to bleed, after the long scarification of silence. Schlaggenberg, for instance, had talked at great length to Grete that evening in early spring when he and Laura had run into René and Grete. Ever since, his name for Grete had been "the young lady with the good memory."

Now as it happened, René's memory was not bad at all. He listened to Grete's story with right good will and close attention. But as usual in these matters, the thing was a closed book to him; he could not fathom the conflicts and the compacts, the way in which people made so much money or lost it again, or the reasons for changing one lucrative position for another. Titi, especially, and her ambitions, were to René a dark mystery. Lasch's scarcely less so. He was struck by the name of Mährischl only because it sounded somehow absurd.

For moments it almost seemed to him that all these matters were as unreal to Grete as for himself; that she as speaker was practicing the same kind of deception as his own when he played the understanding listener. For everything she told him remained intangible, signified nothing, would all be blown away like mist.

Lasch, it seemed, was in a bad jam. Levielle was supposed to help him out of it. There was something about capital "salted away" in England which Lasch was supposed to free from the restrictions that kept it there. But for that they needed Doktor Mährischl's services as a lawyer. Such were the odds and ends that Grete had overheard by sheer chance, for she was not in the least curious about the whole business.

At any rate, Lasch's affairs were plainly heading downhill. Grete had always expected that and had seen it coming. Now he wanted to sell the car. Of course Titi was outraged. And for other reasons also. Had René ever heard about an actress named Maria Orsetzkaya? No? A drug addict, a morphine hound, it seemed. Lasch often did not come home for three or four nights running; apparently he was now taking drugs too. He would end up by dragging Titi into it. It was always that way with married couples.

Grete's eyes suddenly filled with tears.

René was not in the least outraged on moral grounds. What would be so terrible about Titi's taking morphine? And what loss was it to them? Of course it wouldn't do to say this to Grete, and he did not say it. But with all this, reality slid altogether from under him. However, René promptly saved himself by a happy inspiration. He changed the subject and told Grete all about his meeting with Dwight Williams and Emma Drobil by the river; the amazing thing was that his find at the castle should fit in so well with his meeting with the American. For there was this Professor Bullogg at Harvard who would be so interested in the manuscript. And so on and so forth. It was astonishing: Grete was quickly consoled, forgot her concern over her sister.

"Wouldn't it be nice if we could live abroad someday!" she said.

"Mr. Williams will let us know when Professor Bullogg arrives in Vienna; I gave him your number because I might not get the message at home," Stangeler remarked. Grete appeared delighted to be included in the affair. "Fine," she said, and for the rest of the evening did not return to her unhappy preoccupations.

9 ⌐ *The Fall from the Hobbyhorse*

I HAVE not taken the floor for a long time. If I now venture to call the reader's attention to myself again, I must remind him that after leaving Hofrat Gürtzner-Gontard's apartment I stood still in front of the door as if under a canopy of contradictory thoughts, under a load that threatened to crash down upon me. And I felt altogether unable to cope with it. Standing on the threshold of the house as on the margin of a continent and looking out upon the street, I realized that the darkness had not yet descended as fully as had seemed from upstairs in the room. Twilight surrounded the street lamps, which had already gone on; and twilight was inside me also. Absurdly, my mind still held that picture of a child in the womb, hands over its face as if it were covering its eyes; that casual figure of speech which Gürtzner-Gontard had used to illustrate what he meant now seemed to me the sole argument with which to refute what he had said. For if the revolutionary does not want to see and accept the world as it is, then everybody in the world has acted the revolutionary within the womb, lying curled up and covering his eyes. Thus every revolution would be a legitimate expression of what was human and not only the efflux of weakness and degeneracy. For had not everyone held his eyes closed, refused to see? Thus the refusal to see receives an a priori legitimation; reform, revolution, is making oneself stupid, pretending to be more stupid than one is already. Without stupidity, no life.

Now, standing there, I thought through all these dubious

riddles. There is always satisfaction in thinking anything through without losing the thread. A ridiculous satisfaction, for in really profound thinking the thread is always lost.

I began walking at last, crossed Ring Strasse, entered the center of the city, and went on further. I reached the Graben. The evening tinged the sky behind the roofs with a greenish glow and the bright spheres from street lamps and store fronts bloomed forth into the oncoming darkness. A hat was doffed and waved in a wide slow arc, a white head, the little white brush of mustache —and I myself was already preparing a ceremonious salute when I recognized that the greeting was not directed at me, and that the gentleman was not Financial Counselor Levielle at all, except perhaps for the vulgar arrogance they had in common. Now, however, I realized what I had been thinking of all along— in spite of and beneath my dubious quarrels with Gürtzner-Gontard's arguments.

Almost as soon as the false Levielle had passed, someone who was walking right behind him called loudly: "Lieutenant von Geyrenhoff!"

I saw the pseudo-Levielle turn slightly toward the other, pre-cisely in the manner of such persons as Levielle or Baron Frigori: taking note with raised eyebrows of a phenomenon that has had the impudence to intrude upon their presence; such objects re-ceive only a hasty, indignant glance and are then brushed off, for they are not found worthy of further attention. The man who had called now came toward me, a dignified-looking person of about fifty-five, with a quality of rustic solidity. His hair, under his lifted hat, was white. After a second, I recognized him. He was the sergeant of that squadron of the Fourth Dragoons Regi-ment in which I had spent the greater part of the war.

"Herr Gach!" I exclaimed as we shook hands.

We had not seen each other since the war. As we walked on together toward Stephans Platz, I learned that he was not living in Vienna, nor in Wels, from which he hailed. I had forgotten his occupation in civilian life; it seemed he was a state employee, commissioner of markets—he referred to himself by the simple and rather old-fashioned name of "weighmaster"—in the town of Eisenstadt. The town had always had a large swine market.

While my good weighmaster and I were bringing each other up to date on things, I was actually constantly expecting Financial Counselor Levielle to turn up, since he had more or less announced his arrival beforehand, according to the law of such events. Once I felt sure I saw him coming straight toward us—but then it turned out not to be him at all. Immediately afterwards, however, striding down the street and apparently totally absorbed in her haste, came Quapp. She did not notice me, held her head down, and crossed the street in an extremely careless manner. However, on a Sunday afternoon in good weather there is not much traffic in the heart of Vienna; the street was at this time fairly deserted, although beginning to come to life.

Quapp almost ran into me, stopped at the last moment, exclaimed: "Oh, beg pardon," and in looking up recognized me.

I for my part immediately recognized once again her fine, really aristocratic manner, the brief flash of her true nature which momentarily broke through the clouds of her evidently troubled state. I introduced her to Gach, telling her that we had been in the war together; and she shook hands heartily with the old soldier, with the same degree of respect which would have been shown by a well-bred young man. In fact, she bowed slightly just like a man. It was almost imperceptible, that bow, but I saw it and I still see it plainly when I think of that Sunday in May of 1927. Ah yes, that was Quapp for you. That was how she used to be. A straight young chevalier. I observed how old Gach and she looked cordially into each other's eyes as they shook hands.

I would have liked to have her with us, and so I asked Quapp whether she could not stay in town a while longer, and where she was bound. But immediately the clouds gathered across her brow again. She was terribly sorry, she said, she'd be ever so glad to stay, but she had to go out to Döbling, she was expected there, was already two hours late, had unfortunately been held up. . . .

There are people who, if for once they are about to be punctual, will instantly find some diversion which immediately becomes a delaying factor, an insuperable obstacle to their keeping an appointment on time. Unpunctuality appears to be a genuine mental disease, an unconquerable phobia of punctuality; it manifests itself in an absolute inability to tear oneself away in time.

And off she went.

Gach and I crossed Stephans Platz, and now I asked him in turn where he was bound for.

He had to go to Schwechat today, he said; but it was still too early; he was expected between nine and ten o'clock in the evening; a friend was meeting him there and would take him back to Eisenstadt on the back seat of his motorcycle.

Then we could have dinner together, I suggested. And since he would have to take the Pressburg Railway to Schwechat, it would probably be most convenient for us to dine in some restaurant near that station. Gach agreed, highly pleased. And for my part I felt the company of this simple, upright, self-possessed person as a veritable blessing on this particular evening. As I walked along beside Gach I remembered how often, in the days when I was a young officer first serving in the field, I had in secret sought and found inner support in his calm and fearlessness.

Near the railroad station we found a comfortable restaurant. We raised our beer mugs and drank to old comradeship.

We spoke of the old days in the cavalry, of course.

"At the start I was with the Seventh, not with the Fourth Regiment—with the Brandeis" (he meant Dragoon Regiment Number 7, which had yellow insignia). "But then I returned to the replacement squadron and was later assigned to the squadron where you were, sir."

"So you rode out with the Seventh in 1914?"

"Yes. Third Squadron. Captain Ruthmayr. Did you know him, sir?" Gach asked, seeing that I had recognized the name.

"Yes," I said. "But not in the army, in civilian life. Georg Ruthmayr—he owned large estates."

"Yes," Gach said. "A big landowner."

He drank a glass of wine. I was beginning to feel uncommonly good. Gach smiled, and said in the tone of one making a small confession:

"I must tell you something that struck me just now, sir. Today on the Graben, when that young lady came along . . ."

"Yes?" I asked, as he hesitated.

"I was staggered. Such a resemblance . . ."

"What do you mean? To whom?" I asked.

Next moment I was seized by suspense. Not that I anticipated anything specific, but I felt eager to hear what Gach was going to say now.

"To Captain Ruthmayr, bless his memory," Gach said.

"Yes," I said. "You're right at that."

"Is she related to him?"

"Not at all, so far as I know," I said.

"Odd, how things are connected sometimes," Gach said. "Just before I called out to you, sir, someone passed by on the Graben whom I once had dealings with. He lives on Johann Strauss Gasse. I don't recall the name any more."

I could no longer make contact. There was a kind of vacuum inside me, as if waiting for the switch to be thrown, but for the present nothing happened. "Who was that?" I asked.

"Captain Ruthmayr once sent me to this gentleman on Johann Strauss Gasse. Just a half hour before the captain lost consciousness at the dressing station, he gave me orders to go there. It was just a little while before the end."

"What kind of errand was it?" I asked.

"I had to deliver a large envelope."

"And did you know what the envelope contained?"

"Yes, for I was right there at the dressing station when the document in the envelope was drawn up. It was the captain's will."

"So then you delivered it to this man on Johann Strauss Gasse?"

"Yes. They sent me to Vienna to deliver it. After the captain's death I didn't return to the Seventh Regiment, but to my old replacement squadron. That was where I really belonged. I'd only gone to the Seventh on account of Captain Ruthmayr. He fixed up the transfer."

"Had you known the captain before the war, then?"

"Oh yes. I used to be on one of his estates in Styria. I was in charge of the saddle horses, as trainer, and of the whole stud."

"Ah, I see. Now I understand why he chose you to go to Vienna for him. To Johann Strauss Gasse, eh? And what did you find there?"

"Well, there was this gentleman who came out into a big vestibule, and I handed over the envelope and told him that the captain had passed away. Then he asked me a few questions, what kind of wound it was, and how and where. All the time he kept saying to me: 'Tell me—Lach . . .' You'd think he might have said 'Sergeant,' for I was in uniform. Maybe he didn't recognize the insignia. He talked down to me from miles up above, I can tell you that; didn't even offer me a chair. Not a bit like the captain, bless his memory. And kept calling me 'Lach.' I didn't correct him; it didn't matter to me. Incidentally we did have a Corporal Lach in the Seventh; he was killed later, together with the clerk of the third squadron, who were the two witnesses to the will. For the captain dictated it and they wrote it down. Lach was trumpeter of the third squadron; he was a Viennese, and was right there on the spot when the captain breathed his last. The two of them signed it in his presence, because they happened to be closest to him. I wasn't able to sign because I'd had to hold up the captain while he put his own signature to the will. Then the captain told me where I was to go with the paper; those were the last words he spoke. For the chaplain had already been with him and given him the Sacrament."

"Then the captain didn't send you to see his wife?"

"Of course, that too. But first I had to deliver the envelope; that was my order, and then this gentleman . . ."

"Could you recall the name, Herr Gach?"

"No," he said hesitantly, with visible effort. "It was a foreign name. After all, pretty near thirteen years have passed since."

"Listen closely, Herr Gach. Wasn't he a man of good average

height, with a brush of a mustache; perhaps it was already white; talked condescendingly and as if he were a little irritated . . . ?"

I imitated the occupant of the house on Johann Strauss Gasse as well as I could, although I had never before tried mimicking the financial counselor.

"That's right," Gach exclaimed. "That's him to a T!"

"Was his name by any chance Levielle?"

"Right, that was his name!" Gach said. "I saw him on the Graben today, shortly before I spotted you, Lieutenant. Well, I didn't get to see Frau Ruthmayr. This Herr Levielle told me she was not in Vienna but in Bad Gastein, and that he himself would go there right away and break the news gently. So I went straight home to Wels that same day."

We should not count chickens before they are hatched, for there may be more than we think. Certainly this was so today. It was essential, I felt, to avoid all needless complications. That it had not been Levielle on the Graben this afternoon seemed of small moment. The point was to remain on the simple, straight track, and that meant not to muddle Gach.

"Do you happen to know what was in the will?" I asked.

"Yes, I can recollect quite a bit of it. I was going to add that I wrote to Frau Ruthmayr right away, to her address in Vienna—a pretty long letter, telling her as well as I could how it had all happened and saying truthfully that the captain scarcely suffered any pain and that he received Holy Communion while fully conscious. Later Frau Ruthmayr answered very kindly thanking me, and she sent me a silver cigarette case for a memento of the captain. I have her letter to this day; I keep it in the cigarette case, because the case is much too heavy to carry around in the pocket. In Eisenstadt I always have it lying on my night table, next to the clock."

He fell silent, his honest face showing a good deal of genuine sorrow for his former employer and superior.

There was still time for us to drink another glass of wine.

At last Gach returned to the track of his own accord: "Well, it was this way with the will. My impression was that the captain, to come right out with it, had a daughter out of wedlock somewhere whom he wanted to provide for in his last hour. A lot of his money was in England, and must have been frozen on account of the war, and in this paper the captain stipulated that a batch of securities were to go to this daughter as soon as they were freed again after the war. That's how I understood it. I gathered, too, that this batch had already been put aside, placed in a different bank from the rest of the funds. Yes, I remember that particular point. So the captain had already arranged things, only it had not yet been put down in writing."

"And the name of this daughter?"

"Hm . . . that I no longer remember," Gach said. He subsided into silence, and looked off to one side. I was sufficiently self-possessed to hold my tongue. Slowly, gradually, the rusty last link in this chain emerged from the deep shaft of time, rose closer to the surface, threatening every moment to sink anew and completely.

"The name might have been Lotte, but not the nickname, no. Maybe it was Charlotte. Charlotte von . . ."

"Charlotte von Schlaggenberg," I said quietly. For I thought this was the moment for it.

"Yes, Lieutenant," he said. "That's the name. How did you know all that?"

He clearly had not the slightest mistrust or feeling that I had been pumping him. From this point on I avoided saying anything more on the subject. I had his address in Eisenstadt, and he had mine and my telephone number. He promised to telephone me the next time he came to Vienna. We raised our glasses once again. It was already time for him to go; I accompanied him to the brown cars of the Pressburg train.

There I stood now, after the train had left, in a not very pleasant neighborhood, by the big bridge that led across the maze of tracks, in the vicinity of the big Market Halls. I was glad that at one point in Gach's story I had broken in to ask whether Levielle had not given him a receipt for delivery of the envelope. Nothing of the sort. That seemed odd. But Gach had been a young man

at the time and a soldier coming directly from the dreadful eastern front. It was not hard for me to understand, from my own
memories, his state of mind at the time: the state of a man on
furlough from the front, with that curiously overintense way of
regarding home and rear echelon, while the future vanished from
sight like a railroad train whose last car one has just seen gliding
into a tunnel. . . .

But the point was not to linger over details, but to recognize
all that this day had brought me. Fate had tapped me on the
shoulder—first on my visit to Gürtzner-Gontard (especially in the
vestibule), then most emphatically on the Graben. I began walking again and crossed the bridge.

Darkness had long since fallen; this was no longer a dead
Sunday afternoon but a lively evening. From the bridge I could
see far out over the illuminated railroad yards. Everywhere arc
lamps with slender swan's necks dipped their radiant light into
the retreating darkness which was dotted here and there with
green and red signals. This was an expansive, dreary, and utilitarian neighborhood. I walked past the market halls.

I refused to let my imagination play over what Gach had unexpectedly revealed to me at the restaurant table. I was no longer
a chronicler. My role as such had come to an end today. I had
fallen from my hobbyhorse. The fall was followed by a sense of
emptiness. I walked along, deeply absorbed, into the Third District, which is distasteful only along its inner edge where I now
was, but farther on contains several exclusive streets lined with
fine mansions—the so-called Embassies' quarter.

The fact is that since that Sunday, May 15, 1927, I have written
no further connected chronicles. The big neat volume with its
many white pages has lain untouched, as it was, only one quarter
of it filled; and at this point I shall confess that that notebook
was procured by me after I met Schlaggenberg on the path
between the bare vineyards in December 1926. But my chronicle
gathered intensity and bulk only after that conversation with
Levielle on the Graben, on Annunciation Day. During the subsequent period I wrote for hours every day—until May 15. In

other words, for a total of about a month and a half. Henceforth I only jotted down notes, though some of these were rather detailed, and occasionally numerous. Many years later, when I took up the matter again, they proved to be more useful for me and Kajetan than the coherent text that I had written previously, and altogether prematurely.

Still walking along lost in thought, I had entered that quiet patrician quarter, though without particularly intending to, for I had no destination there, and in fact no destination at all for the rest of this Sunday. Indeed I felt that it was a day more than full, and my direction was prompted mostly by the desire to escape from this vicinity of freight station and markets, and so I unconsciously drifted toward the opposite kind of neighborhood. I walked slowly. The dark streets were almost empty. Now and then the mansions were far apart, and I could sense the presence of a great garden.

Now, for the first time since the morning, I felt a sense of everything that had happened, was about to or could happen, stacked up beneath me. And I suddenly became aware that I would never fully understand the group whose activities I was attempting to chronicle. I was alone, meandering through these streets; and yet I felt as if each member of the group were with me.

"Everyone his own department head," Kajetan had once suggested as a possible motto.

Perhaps it was incipient old age that was crawling over my skin. I no longer sat tight as the kernel of a nut in its shell, within a surrounding world, within my own aims and interests. A crack had formed; the shell rattled. Indifference gripped me, but this grip was not gentle, not reassuring; it was icy, hinted at fearful terrors. I realized at once that indifference does not permit an objective view of things, as might at first appear. It blocks one's view. Indifference blinds. Nor does it remain indifference; it degenerates rapidly into disgust with life.

"What's the point of all this childishness?" I thought. "What's the point of this present setup? Why this assemblage: Gach and Quapp, Grete Siebenschein and Camy Schlaggenberg . . . ?"

They all grayed, churned through me in a spectral dance.

The squealing tires of a braking automobile on my right. On my left a high portal. Someone shouted from the car: "Georgy! Stop!"

For the third time that day I felt myself literally arrested, as if I were caught between the wall of the building and the car, for all that the sidewalk was broad there. Mucki Langingen clambered from the car. "Where're you going, where're you bound, what're you up to?"

"Nothing," I said, and instantly regretted it, "just walking." (As if a walk down Reisner Strasse in the evening needed justification.) Now Alfons Croix appeared behind Langingen. "Well, then, don't be dull now, come along with us; we were only going to have a drink at my place."

His voice moved me deeply. It changed my situation, saved me from an ennui such as I had never experienced before with such intensity. The prince's voice came like a pure tone from a well-tuned instrument. It was a tenor, not a bass. I could not resist it at all, and made no further demur; there seemed to be something irresistible even in his choice of words. We stepped under the arched entrance gate. Through the glass panes of the door I saw a servant hastening down the steps toward us.

The library, to which we repaired, struck me as being unusually large. I did not know this house and had not been aware that Croix was living on Reisner Strasse. Croix was a little older than Langingen, the antique hunter; he must have been about the same age as myself. My connection with the two men was only a casual one. We had gone through the officer's training school together. I was also acquainted with Count Langingen from government service. At the Siebenscheins' the night before, however, we had only greeted each other briefly.

"Why did you vanish so suddenly last night?" Langingen asked.

I said I had been invited to the opera.

I wished that I could hear the prince's voice again. But Croix now beckoned to the servant and gave him instructions in a low voice.

The walls of the room were lined with books from floor to ceiling. There were a number of movable ladders. At one end, where we were sitting, were a few armchairs and a round stool; at the other end, two tables. Otherwise it was empty. The glass-fronted cabinets for precious pieces, such as are often found in the middle of such rooms, were conspicuously absent.

I asked the prince whether this library was his personal property or belonged to the estate.

"All the estate's," he said. "But in practice the library belongs to me. No one gives a damn about it. The trustees are happy if they don't hear about it. The whole thing has to be put in order. But I've had this house only for six months. No one in the family wanted it. I took it chiefly on account of the library."

Never again have I met a person who for all the ease and simplicity of his sentence structure and choice of words so distinctly discharged his speech into space. It was as if he assumed a cleared area existed for it; and the assumption created the area. Even Mucki, by nature a loquacious sort, never once interrupted the prince; and in the course of the evening I was to observe, for I made a point of paying close attention to the matter, that the prince himself was absolutely free of the currently widespread vice of interruption.

Since I had always tried to behave properly on this score, and since Mucki's blabbermouth was kept in check by the prince, our otherwise light and casual talk gradually took on a distinctness and sharpness rarely to be found in conversations nowadays. It may be that the spacious room, whose stillness formed a brownish background to our meeting, contributed to this sharpness of outline, conferring upon this simple social occasion the etched quality of a scene on the stage.

"If you want to put the library in order, you will need someone for the job."

"True. I can't possibly do it alone."

"I know someone. A graduate of the Institute and doctor of philosophy. A young historian."

"I really would prefer not to have a trained scholar. I'm that myself, after all. And of course there is the household staff to take care of the physical work, including setting up card catalogues, and so on. I even have a man with the most beautiful calligraphy, absolutely like engraving. What I want is to train my librarian myself. I'd as lief have him start from scratch. Incidentally, what you see here is by no means the whole of it. There are two more rooms full of books. Come, I'll show you."

The prince rose. I followed him, and Mucki trailed after us. The curtains had not yet been drawn over two of the tall windows, and you could look out into the darkness of the extensive gardens. Here, in the main library room, the artfully inlaid parquet floor exposed its full gleaming expanse, unconcealed by any rug. I had an impression of solitude; the prince's surroundings did not bespeak any emphasis on domestic comfort. His bearing expressed the same asceticism. I thought it possible that when this man was alone he must possess an incomparably greater clarity of thought and ability to analyze his ideas than most other people, no matter how intelligent. In the matter of domestic comforts I must remember, of course, that he had not been living in this house long.

We now entered the adjoining room through a pair of French doors. When the light was switched on, it proved to be a cave full of books. The windows giving on the dark garden were high and bare, without curtains or drapes. Long rows of golden-brown leather volumes lined an angled passageway into still another room. We returned to the main library and drank, standing, two manhattans.

"Listen, Georgy," Croix said. "You may see more of people than I do. Mucki is absolutely indolent; the only thing he notices is old furniture." The count made no protest. "Perhaps you'll come across someone. Only not an academic. Do me the favor, will you? You have eyes in your head. Call me up if you find someone, or come to see me."

"All right," I said. The conversation turned shallow for a few minutes—largely the effect of Mucki's presence—and slid over into social matters (a euphemism for gossip). Then came hunting; later, in connection with hunting, Carinthia. The servant prepared a third cocktail and then withdrew across the whole length of the room to the doorway to the other two library rooms. This seemed to be the custom here.

"You did know Baroness Charagiel, didn't you?" the prince said.

"Brrr . . ." Mucki piped up.

"Idiot," Croix said. "That isn't the point. Did you know, Georgy, that she died this past winter? Her husband had been dead a long time. He was an old fool anyhow; she rode him to death and then had herself a good time."

I wondered at the crudity of his expressions. Here, too, solitude played its part; he was much alone and his speech was therefore subject less to the censorship of convention than to the desire for precision.

"Well, Baroness Charagiel was an attractive woman, as the phrase goes. At the same time one of the most horrible persons I have ever seen. Anyone who could see only her looks must have been a thorough bastard. She was a reagent, a touchstone. You could use her to diagnose anyone. There were people who thought her 'chorming' " (he imitated a manner of speech common in his social class).

"She was a Neudegg," I said, simply to say something, and perhaps also with the desire to blunt his sharpness—out of consideration for Mucki, whose good-natured face wore a dismayed expression.

"Yes," Croix said, "she was a Neudegg. Old Neudegg also died this year, in the spring. Once upon a time a fellow appeared who wanted to marry Claire Neudegg—a landowner named Georg Ruthmayr. The old baron took quite a shine to him. The story goes that he said to him: 'Georgy, you really aren't going to ruin your life by taking on this awful girl, are you?' "

"From whom did you hear that?" I asked. I was neither surprised nor excited; I had crossed a kind of threshold of sensation and could no longer react to stimuli. Moreover, ever since entering this house I'd had the feeling that I had come into a kind of central telephone switchboard where calls from every imaginable direction might impinge upon me.

"From someone who was present at the conversation. A factotum of the baron's, his steward in fact, a man by the name of Mörbischer. He told me about it—throwing in his own remarks concerning Baroness Charagiel. I'd been invited for hunting at the old man's place down there. The best heathcock hunting in Carinthia. Old Neudegg was so tetched by that time that he used to go shooting with an ancient crossbow."

"Did he ever hit anything?" Mucki asked.

"Never missed," the prince said. "I saw it myself. Click, swoosh —and the bolt was in. But then the daughter herself once shot Mörbischer's canary bird at an incredible distance, from the rampart across the drawbridge; he lived in the gatehouse, and had had the cage standing in the window. Still, I don't think that incident really tells too much about Claire. It's the sort of thing that could come over anyone when conditions are right—or wrong enough. All of us have committed acts of spite as children, and sometimes pranks that seemed malicious even though they weren't. Once when my governess was bathing me in the tub, I suddenly turned the shower on full force upon her. I was severely punished. But I hadn't done it out of meanness, or even boyish mischief; rather out of a kind of technical curiosity. During a recess at the Theresianum Academy one time we gave the Leyden jar battery in the physics room a heavy charge. The teacher came back rather suddenly and no one took the time to discharge the jar—perhaps we didn't know how to. You can imagine the consequences when the teacher attempted to demonstrate an experiment. That was like taking a shot at the canary bird. For Mörbischer, though, it was the last straw—for he must have detested the girl all along. He told me that story by way of making clear what a little bitch she was—and yet, compared to other things she had done, the killed canary had little to do with Claire Neudegg. She must have seen the moving yellow speck and wanted to hit it; one can feel tremendously drawn to hit just such a speck; and perhaps there had been some such speck in her dreams the previous night; perhaps it had to be struck and killed; and perhaps the weather was oppressive too. . . . All that was remote from Claire herself, I might say, since it was not an act of brazenness. Compared to the depths of brazenness in the woman's character, that shot was almost a warmly human element, an accidental slip. . . ."

It was impossible to make out what he was getting at or why he had brought up the subject of the countess at all, which had led in turn to his mention of Ruthmayr. . . . Thus it is that sometimes weapons we have not loaded are thrust into our hands; and nevertheless we fire the shot. Filled to the brim as I was by the many events of this one day, I had become almost totally insensitive. It would have taken a great deal to touch or move me. But behind my present stunned indifference a refined and deep astonishment was eating into a corner of my mind.

Effortlessly the prince talked on. Mucki was docile toward ideas; he did not know what to do with them, but swallowed them as a good child will its medicine. As far as I was concerned, I did not care whether what was said was more or less clever. *C'était pour moi particulièrement le ton qui faisait la musique.* The tone was everything. And not only the tone of the voice, but the brownish tone of the room with the splashes of red which were our leather-covered chairs. And that my day's drifting had ended here. That this room was saved out of the congestion of more or less incomprehensible matters that dwelt in my mind, and had been saved out until this very evening.

"Even the most impossible persons who do the most unforgivable things possess substantial reality; from their own points of view they are always right—for let them only doubt that, and they are no longer such impossible persons. And we must pay close heed to those who play such ungrateful roles, for these roles are indispensable. It is no small thing to be a monster or a spiteful idiot, and in the first case to think oneself beautiful, in the

second a highly intelligent person. Such characters must be represented. Someone has to do it. At the same time we see that
the person who assumes such a predetermined ugly role is by no
means blameless—such a role always suits his nature."

Having delivered himself of these thoughts, the prince raised
his left arm, and the servant came to our end of the room, opened
a door, and stepped back.

We had a rather peculiar meal. First black tea with toast and
butter, then grilled meat, and then cold lobster. After the tea we
had champagne; there was no other drink. I scarcely ate, but the
prince and Mucki fell to. However, I drank rather heavily, and
in this I was not alone. The room in which we sat was small,
scarcely more than a large closet, and virtually empty. A blind-
ingly white second French door led on into other rooms. I was
struck by the attractive setting of the table. In the center stood a
lamp with three electric candles, their dark red shades focusing
the light on the table itself, so that the servant had to work in
semidarkness at the small buffet, for there was no other source of
light. A few flowers were casually scattered over the tablecloth,
and oranges placed irregularly here and there. I had noticed this
latter custom only once before, at a ball in the home of Richard
von Kralik, when all the tables at the supper had been decorated
in this charming fashion. The glassware and silver at the prince's
table were smooth, heavy, unornamented except for the engraved
arms of the Croix family.

Our little gathering moved me strangely. I should not have
been able to say why. We knew one another only superficially,
as tends to be the case in the collective pot of army life. Moreover, throughout the evening we made no mention at all of this
common past. We were strangers in every sense; we were strange
to one another, and the prince and Mucki must also have been
strange to each other. More than that, the prince seemed to me
all the while a stranger in his own house. This evening, after a
day that had gathered in all the factual and imaginary substance
which then filled my life, gathered it together like a curtain—
this solitary evening was not without its sweet sadness; it was

itself like a hand that is about to grasp the curtain to gather it, and dispiritedly, rather wearily, does not trouble to do so.

Croix rose to his feet. "Please stay seated," he said. "I'll give you a little dinner music." The servant at once opened the white French door, and the prince went into the adjoining room. He began to play the piano. His playing was masterly, though his choice of music surprising. The music that floated back through the door was the funeral waltz from the ballet *Lazy Hans* by the once famous Bohemian violinist Nedbal.

Part Three

1 ⌐   *Fat Females*

WE SHALL see later how fantastically ill-timed was the moment in which Schlaggenberg handed me that long-threatened manuscript on the "Fat Females," his *"Chronique scandaleuse,"* or whatever he called it. ("Must go in. Must. Every bit.") After I had looked it over, my conclusion was—to put it mildly—*c'est impossible!* In order to convey some idea of what it was like I can give only small (and highly censored) samples; and I shall do so here and now. For we shall not again be free—in the rush of events— to waste time on these idiocies.

The whole thing was a strange idea to work reforms in a restricted but highly central field. All the same this minor insanity clearly exposes how utterly foolish so-called "ideologies" in general are, by contrast with the life they would hope to improve. For these ideologies all wear blinkers which blind them to the real constitution of the world. They are all as crazy as Kajetan's Theory of the Necessity of Fat Females to the Sex Life of the Superior Man Today.

FROM SCHLAGGENBERG'S TEXT

To go about this in an organized way means nothing less than discovery of a new dimension of life. Seeking sufficiently large area for encounters—five type-defining ads in the newspaper— elimination of all material not pertinent to idea. Now 10 FF.[1]

---

[1] FF in Schlaggenberg's text always means Fat Females.

The fifth ad most closely narrows down the type concept. Reinsertion refused by the newspaper.[2] In general, despite extremely varied characteristics, two fundamental types can be distinguished: convex and concave. Latter type harder to take (esp. No. 10) because of vinegary intelligence and enormous vigilance. No. 10 not from own ad, but through reply to one of hers.

None of the numbers of remaining stock wholly typological.

Two cafés by the Danube Canal and one in city center further sphere of action. Another insertion of more generally worded ad is of doubtful value. Still, must seek greatest possible area for encounters. But in this case atypical specimens must be rapidly excluded, in order to be able to deal with typologically potential remainder.

Remainder:

1. Hermine E.

Convex, dark. Intellectually not altogether out of range. Vigorous character outline, proud, dash of masculinity. Impressiveness only up above. Therefore to be ruled out (in general quicker work necessary!), although gracious and attractive. 183; 46½; 40; 44 (estimates).[3]

2. Rosi A.

Convex. Good type, auburn hair, medium height, no impressive upper story. Intellectually subnormal. Fatty, stupid. Extremely limited. Excellent "riding-breeches type," but without the frequent deficiencies of that type. Preserved youth. Insufficient poundage. Also telephones too much, especially in the mornings when I'm still sleepy and can't think of anything to say on the telephone. 169; 39½; 44; 45 (estimates).

---

[2] Clipping was attached. It was certainly specific enough. Astonishing that the newspaper printed this advertisement even once. Among other flights, the text contained this passage: "of extraordinarily full, corpulent, luscious, and extremely broad, massive stature."

[3] The figures mean, successively: weight, bust, waist, age.

3. Hanna W.

Concave. Too heavy, not by weight, but too monumental upper stories and contours carved out of wood. Tragic caryatid, without Konterhonz's stupidity. Not uneducated. Best so far, but impossible to manipulate. Hypertrophically fat legs. 242; 54; 54(!); 53 (measured, and according to weighing card).

4. Just had first sight of. To be ruled out at once. Grenadier with low bass voice and Slavic accent. Even letter aroused suspicions. Signed: "Not an ordinary spirit." I agree!

5. Fritzi G.

Convex-concave; mixed type, duck-beak nose. Smallish format, rather akin to the "riding-breeches type." Has an incredibly sterilizing effect upon me. Musically very well informed without any relationship to music. Simplicity combined with phenomenal frigidity (*sed non fundamentaliter*). Inhibited. Aura: dull. 171½; 39; 41; 51 (measured, weighing card).

6. Vilma S.

Concave. Snub nose; unusable facial type. Cowlike. Enormous specimen; vital statistics can hardly be estimated. Husband in prominent position. Stupendously ignorant. Did not know who Mozart was, associated the name only with a pastry. (Mozart torte.) Measurement here at my place shortly; she has already been here, like the others. Unprecedented stupidity engenders genuine tenderness. But must likewise be eliminated.

7. Gisela B.

By weight probably an FF. But well-formed, smart-looking woman. Mobile, acquainted with literature. We laughed a good deal, finally took the whole thing as a joke. Lacks the requisite helplessness of the FF. Should have been ruled out at once. Letter much too intelligent.

8. Elsa P.

Not through ad. Sent her my visiting card in the café. Concave. Very pretty, blonde, about 175 lb. Good type, but too strenuous, out of reach, contact scarcely possible. Husband furniture dealer ("My husband is in furniture").

9. Mela R.

Convex type almost perfect, also in weight and measurements. Unfortunately too crude and earthy in tone, no FF-type dignity and prudery. These traits indispensable, I see. Divorcee. Husband ran out on her with a Moroccan woman five years ago, in South of France. Would be perfect as far as the individual components go (estimates: 181; 46; 48; 48!). Unfortunately *encheiresis naturae* . . . etc. Lacks true FF elements; no ostentatious middle-class solidity as exemplified by "My husband is in furniture." The latter light blonde and too consumptive.

10. Lea W.

Physician's wife. Saw husband with her on the street. Stern close-clipped beard. Spends his leisure time tinkering with radios. Lea has grown son. Pleased that, as she says, women run after the handsome boy and he treats them badly. Lea is maximally concave type. Very brash, unfortunately almost normal figure, about 161 lb., fairly large, but without generous upper story. Not really sensational. Extreme vigilance, even sharpness. Complete complacency. In every respect valuable specimen, but will also have to be eliminated since a digression from true main type. Numbers 3 and 9 come closest to the hypothesis upon point-by-point study of the inventory. Nevertheless, neither 3 nor 9 really suitable. The true narrowing down of the type is proving more difficult than I assumed. It will be necessary [4] to seek out the true typol-

---

[4] "It will be necessary"—this is a typical phrase of all "reformers." They find necessary what others do not need at all; but the reformers are always trying to impose this necessity upon the others! Every reformist idea is nothing but a fig leaf to cover the weakest spot of its author.

ogy within the point-by-point restrictive analysis. Fresh acquisition of wide assortment of material no doubt indispensable, from which the result must ultimately be distilled as a kind of concentrate.

Close-ups of previous remainder, Nos. 1–10 (without 4): [5]

New flood of material in tremendous quantity, but all satisfactorily handled; have seen the writers of all 42 letters, with the exception of missives such as this:

If you will give me the opportunity for a personal interview I shall gladly introduce you to my friend, who fully corresponds to your advertisement except that the lady is a beauty, very cultivated, knowledge of languages, musical. In expectation of your reply in writing . . .

Among 42 letters a relatively small number indeterminable, relatively large number of better class. Many of them quite promising, for example (disguised handwriting, with a tendency to climb upward on the page):

Dear Sir:

Permit me to state that all the characteristics you list in your advertisement apply to me. Kindly inform me in a few lines what your intentions are, where to write to you, in short everything necessary to initiate a correspondence. My address: Thea R., general delivery, Nibelungen Gasse post office.

Forgive the writing. Not having a ruled blotter throws a person out of line.

Already thoroughly harried. Now very close to 80 interviews, all in all. Of the first batch 1, 2, 5, 8, 9, 10 are still current. Frequently have to take cabs between rendezvous to make them in time. Work: only stuff for Alliance. Whole campaign would have been impossible under previous financial status (before Alliance).

---

[5] The rest is unprintable.

Second batch after eliminations leaves meager remnant. Thea R. much too pretty and elegant (mondaine in the sense of the café on the Danube Canal, little finger outspread when spooning up whipped cream).

Close-ups of remainder Batch II: [6]

Curious, and I don't quite understand, what the whole campaign has to do with—Döbling. Yet there is a connection, although not a single rendezvous is taking place here—by chance not a single one lives in this neighborhood—and although I am doing no hunting in Döbling, restricting myself to the two or three cafés in the center. And yet I can conceive of the FF project only with Döbling as base headquarters. Probably could not have undertaken it from anywhere else. An antirational but nonetheless real relationship undoubtedly exists.

Envy the women their peace and orderly situations. I would have a better use for such than these women with their telephoning, bridge, Mozart pastries. Such consolidation in the case of almost all—in fact, all without exception. About time I put my own affairs in order, and therefore intensely wish to reach the goal (in a typological sense) in this business. Telephone, mail, cabs. For the present I have been unable to conceive of new methods with which to begin all over again at the beginning, naturally first liquidating remainder Batches I and II. Cannot hope to attain to the typical without first discarding atypical material. A clean sweep necessary. Specimens such as I/7 or Thea R. (II/3) simply do not belong.

Every letter swollen promptly with anticipated typological hopes. Then detumescence. Mechanical repetitions. The first phase of the affair was more euphoric. New momentum needed.

Walk with I/10; first conversations:
The way she strikes me, it is as if she were always humming

---

[6] Censored.

inwardly like a teakettle, warming with satisfaction, and with self-satisfaction as well. Enormous vitality. Constantly drilling forward, like a power drill.

A spring day bringing sudden gusts of heat. At once tiring and agitating. From the viaduct of the railroad the outer suburbs of the city and the hills beyond in sharp unshielded sunshine.

We got out in Ober-St. Veit and found our way between the houses into the countryside, without having agreed on our way or destination. Everything distracted and asthmatic. Our path was blocked by a whole sea of watery filth. There was no picking our way around it: plank wall on the right, trellis fence on the left. I offered to carry her to spare her fine shoes and stockings. "No," she said, "we'll just turn back." But I had already picked her up. No light morsel (more than 160, I should think). She had enough presence of mind not to struggle while I carried her across the muck. But she did hold herself so clumsily and leaning so much away from me instead of close against me that in the middle of this puddle I had all I could do to keep my feet on the slippery, oozing ground. For a moment I was afraid we'd topple—what a nice embarrassment that would have been. But I brought her across safely, and then it turned out that the thing had enormously amused her—she mentioned it repeatedly afterwards.

Out among open hilly meadows and untidy woods whose fresh glassy-green leaves do not yet conceal the damp black branches. Because of the dampness we couldn't sit down anywhere; that kept us moving, made us restive and talkative.

Asks my advice about her anteroom. She wants to have it re-painted. Color, pattern, or no pattern at all, just ocher tone with perhaps an ornamental border.

Discuss the anteroom in detail. I couldn't care less, of course. Maximum duplicity on my part. Therefore pretend deep interest. Slight pressure behind the ears.

Further conversation:

"I say, tell me, you're supposed to be a writer, but I bet you don't write anything worth bothering about."

"What makes you think so?"

"Oh—I don't know, I just think so."

Further:

"Are you really a Doktor? Or is that just a hoax? Do you make a lot on writing?"

"No."

"There, you see. Probably you don't have any talent. You ought to read the novels of Hugo B. That's the sort of thing that goes over big."

The landscape had surprisingly opened out, arched away in rolling hills to distant horizons, against which details stood clearly outlined, glowing in brilliant light. The inquisitive questions beside me, the pert chatter—it had already become thoroughly repellent.

Very well, she would simply have to be crossed off Remainder List I.

What troubled me most on this walk was not really my companion's fault but lay within myself. We continued on, loquacious and restive, in the bright sunlight, as if walking in thin mountain air, with wholly incredible widths of distances spread before us, and such deep rents in the background that this well-known neighborhood seemed entirely new in its spring gloss. Nevertheless, it was impossible for me to hold on to anything in the background. I fell away from it like a badly stuck stamp from an envelope; the hills before me were as unreal as Frau Lea W.'s fictional anteroom. At the same time I felt roughened, scraped, with flaring internal lights deep inside me, such as one sometimes feels in a state of incipient fever.

I have added these last remarks later, in what space was left on the page; they are therefore written in retrospect. I recall that I returned home from Ober-St. Veit in a state of complete exhaustion. As if I had been walled up, or parted by a heavy curtain. The wall ran straight through the middle of me.

Hunt: terrain, Danube Canal. The thing is wearing me out. But I can't let the whole enterprise go hang because of my lack of stamina! Everything is falling into a routine: the methods at the rendezvous (each time I formally return the letter to its writer), or on the hunt (visiting cards). All the old material must go, all the residual batches be liquidated! I must begin a fresh drive—and find sources of new momentum in myself. Newly acquired material, sorted out on strict typological principles. And put into order. Order above all is necessary. It has gone by the board.

Concentration and advance into the typological center is hampered by insufficient liquidation of Remainder Lists I and II. In one case—I/6—that has led to an untenable situation (Idiot's Hell, see below).

The typological center marked by Frau Selma Steuermann—from all Geyrenhoff has told me. Refuses to introduce me to the lady. Sheer meanness. Says: "Frau Steuermann will not be delivered up to your mercies." But I'll find her myself. Then: Victory! Watch the three cafés closely!

Hunt now chiefly concentrated upon Selma.

In course of it (at Danube Canal) I/2 and I/10 seen at one table. I give courtly bow in passing and make my escape. A third lady was sitting with them, at first glance typologically correct, but to the keener and more practiced eye off-center; brownish, rapidly moving mousy eyes, hands in cuffs of fat (the latter, of course, would in itself be entirely acceptable).

I considered possible consequences of contact between I/2 and I/10. Shortly before final liquidation of the leftovers of Batch I (though unfortunately I/6 has remained, see below, Idiot's Hell), I once more ran into I/10. How did I know Frau Rosi A.? "Oh, I've known her a long time," I replied. Did I know her husband also? "No," I said, "though of course I know who Director A. is." Had I noticed the third lady? Yes? "What about her?" I asked.

Then she told me that Frau M. was so thick with Frau Rosi A. only in order to keep an eye on the bank director. "She and her husband, a lawyer, are a regular detective agency as far as the A.'s are concerned. Doing it for a certain Herr Levielle. Who calls himself a financial counselor. Do you know who he is?"

"No," I said, at hazard.

"Come, come, do you live on the moon?"

"That's one place to which his fame hasn't spread, at any rate," I said.

Distinct feeling that here is my chance to learn something of importance about Levielle. At the same time complete paralysis, indifference, inability to grasp anything at all while I am dwelling on this plane of—of a second reality. Total unpreparedness for anything new. Nailed down, cut off. Levielle—simply does not belong in this sphere—rather like I/7. I stand behind a kind of wall, barred off from the rest of life. Although I should certainly take advantage of this lead (all this only three or four days after Levielle's second call on me!). I/10 would gladly have spilled the beans. Reason enough to postpone liquidation of remainder Batch I in regard to 10. (And yet—out of sheer laziness!—I kept on with I/6 and cut all the rest off cleanly.)

I: "Do you know Frau Selma Steuermann?"

She (visibly miffed, for she would have liked to continue gossiping about Levielle, the A.'s and the M.'s): "Yes, casually. But she hasn't come to the café for a long time."

And she immediately changed the subject.

Idiot's Hell: taken along by I/6 (clownish) to an afternoon coffee at a friend's: a blonde, lumpy, almost cube-shaped person; several atypical FF's; a municipal councilor. Insanely strong coffee with insane quantities of whipped cream. In best of neighborhoods (Reichsrat Strasse). The councilor engaged to the hostess. He is tall and gaunt. I ought to have been able to explain that I was there by mistake, or something of the sort, and not really present. I/6 stood square on the soil of her consolidated reality (envy on my part!); the episode was anything but annoying to her. Annihilating to me. I sat leaning forward, staring at the floor. "Why so pensive today, Herr Doktor?" To be truthful I should have replied: "Because there is no explanation for the fact that emptiness can become substance—and yet it does."

Now (in the evening) comes the clear realization that I find myself in such a fix only because of inconsistencies in my typological approach. Typology. Deviation. I/6 to be liquidated instantly.

Von Geyrenhoff recently: "So you have met Frau Thea R.? Pretty as a picture, isn't she? If you have any luck there—well, my congratulations!"

Nonsense. Typologically a blank.

Total liquidation completed. Now reconstruction must begin methodically. Keep strictly to the line without deviations. Everything hitherto only a preliminary study. Discovery of a new dimension of life is at stake.

Enough. Any more would be unbearable. Certain ever-recurrent pseudoscientific words ("typological") remind me of whalebone drawn out of the corset of an FF and used ("methodologically") to hold this flabby, jellylike potpourri together. In times to come, we would find similar words playing the same role in a different context: "Provocateurs," "saboteurs." Six of one and half a dozen of the other. The essential feature of the whole pattern—for it was that, as I now know—seems to me the fanatical craving for the ordering of a sexuality turned inside out. In times to come we would find altogether different things being turned inside out— among them, for example, conscience.

QUAPP hurried over the hill. It had long since grown dark. Wherever possible she took the stairway short cuts. The evening was cool: bushes and lawns exhaled none of the sun's warmth they had been absorbing all day. The darkness lay empty, without scents.

Gyurkicz had spent the day over his drawing board. There were some drawings he had not quite completed yesterday before the table-tennis party at the Siebenscheins', and which had to be done for a Monday deadline. He had worked hard since the morning, so that he would have the evening free for his Lo. Now he was waiting for her. On Monday one of the Alliance editorial underlings (one Herr Otto, and by far the brashest of all the insolent characters at the office) was to come for the finished drawings. Herr Otto lived fairly near and could easily drop by on the way to work. Imre's landlady was reliable. It would suffice to leave the drawings with her, along with a pack of cigarettes as messenger fee. This method of delivery had been used before; it was an established routine.

Come Monday, Gyurkicz wanted to ride out to the Burgenland, where he could work from nature again. On the whole, he was fed up with everything in Vienna, fed up to here—this remark accompanied by a horizontal gesture across his neck.

However, Lo contrived to introduce a complication into his projected trip. Introducing complications was one of her greatest talents. Someone—probably Stangeler or one of his cronies at the

Historical Institute—had told her about the Roman ruins of Carnuntum and the museum in Deutsch-Altenburg on the Danube,
containing finds from these. Quapp had listened in amazement—
she had never heard a word about these famous ruins—and had
taken it into her head to visit the sights. And of course the occasion
had to be Imre's next trip to the Burgenland, although Deutsch-
Altenburg was by no means nearby. But, after all, she could come
from Vienna and he from the Neusiedler Lake, and they could
meet at Deutsch-Altenburg, couldn't they, and look at the Roman
things together.

That had been agreed on, for Tuesday. The schedules did not
work out quite perfectly, for Lo's train would arrive in Deutsch-
Altenburg half an hour earlier than Gyurkicz's train if, as he intended, he spent Monday and Tuesday morning painting by the
Neusiedler Lake. This Imre was determined to do, since he was
expected back at Alliance on Wednesday. Lo, however, had already found out the name of a good inn at Altenburg—probably
from someone who knew the place. The informant might likewise
be Stangeler. She could meet Imre at this inn on Tuesday around
noon.

Every so often she could display a positively offensive efficiency.

Gyurkicz consented. Although, as we know, he was not very
keen on educational matters.

Today, Sunday, Lo had gone into town to see her aunt (the one
Kajetan neglected). Her return home was delayed. That was more
or less normal. Her lateness was not as enormous as that of the day
before, and had no such terrible consequences. This time it well
suited Gyurkicz, since he was able to finish his work in peace.
Now he wrote in the captions. Done—he packed up the drawings
and turned them over together with the pack of cigarettes to his
landlady. Her name was Joachim and she gave out that she was
related to the famous violinist. As he was returning through the
vestibule, the bell rang. Lo stood at the door.

Naturally there had been a reconciliation after their quarrel of
the night before—a reconciliation that was sorely needed after the

things that had been said while Lo made her toilette for the five-o'clock table-tennis tea at the Siebenscheins', running in and out like a mouse from living room to bathroom. We will remember that the quarrel continued all the way to the Siebenschein stairs and right up to the door (to the distress of Laura Konterhonz, who slowly followed behind the pair). This Sunday morning, too, they had talked the matter over a little; Imre had come over to Lo's for breakfast. All that did not amount to very much. Ordinarily Quapp was always ready to engage in fundamental discussions; in fact, with Gyurkicz she was always tumbling head-on into them and getting terribly involved. But today even Quapp let everything drift vaguely, in the muddy waters of a psychological depression that had been spreading ever since yesterday—or to be more precise, ever since her encounter with Herr Tlopatsch. Spreading and trickling deeper than she realized. It was linked with a positively painful weariness. And so she made no explanations of the vital need she sometimes felt to collect herself by having a cup of tea, even when the cup of tea, viewed externally, seemed a mere waste of time. She said nothing about her right to such habits and how that right fitted in with the whole business of respecting her personality, and so on and so forth (it was always difficult for her to wind up to a conclusion, once she got started on that track). Today, however, all that was omitted. She was prepared to stretch a membrane, no matter how thin, over the still open crevice of the quarrel, if only to cover the sharp edges which hurt her, cutting into her despite her profound exhaustion.

Gyurkicz, for his part, was eager to get to the drawing table and afraid of the endless explanations and talk which might ensue from this breakfast on Sunday morning in Eroica Gasse—a spring morning that had turned cloudy and misty, always on the verge of rain, after a brief breakthrough of the sun earlier. And so he confined himself to urging Lo to learn to be more punctual; it would be of the greatest benefit to her, too, and she would soon see how much pleasanter punctuality made life, and so on and so forth. Imre was never concerned about fundamentals. He was mature enough to know that between lovers only one way succeeds: muddling through. Couples can agree on nothing in the world, for the whole relationship consists in the fact that they are always twain—*ce mal d'être deux*, as Stéphane Mallarmé has called it. What unity they have is only in trivialities, shared jokes, cultural pleasures, "common interests," and similar nonsense. Imre Gyurkicz held this mature view, but he had not attained to it by long and sad experience; he had assumed it from the first.

As it was, Imre and Lo remained in a subdued mood this Sunday evening as well. Quapp's spirits had not exactly been raised by her visit to her aunt—whom, moreover, she was going to have to visit again on Wednesday afternoon. And so peace and harmony prevailed between the couple, although on the lowest plane— the plane of sheer weariness. They even went out to dinner—economically, for they were rather short of money, but in the confusions of the Saturday had not got around to buying any groceries. They decided on one of those small, excellent restaurants of which there are a great many in Nussdorf. Arriving there, they found that the mist had risen up from the Danube, just as it had the day before, and the ancient narrow streets lay wadded under seemingly independent, floating street lamps, for the wires from which these hung had become invisible. As the evening wore on, Quapp reached a state which might be described as one of agonized high spirits. She had three glasses of wine—a frivolous expense, in their present circumstances. Gyurkicz, however, soon called a halt to all this, declaring that he had to get to bed early.

Quapp slept too soundly. That, too, can happen. The deep sea of sleep with its cold dark bottom, to which one drops like a stone, has a lifeless quality. It is inimical to life; it does not release one easily, as do the higher levels in which the sleeper hangs suspended and moves with curiosity from one dream to the next. There is this kind of stony sleep that has a quality of temporary suicide: for a single night. Tomorrow—everything. Today—nothing, nothingness.

Tomorrow everything. Including the fact that one week hence, on May 23, she would have an audition to pass, her first perfor-

mance outside of private musical circles. She was to play for the
concertmaster of a symphony orchestra. In those days important
orchestras rarely included women musicians, except perhaps as
harpists. But the celebrated conductor of this orchestra was prepared to make an exception in cases of real competence. Quapp,
for her part, was only halfheartedly applying for this post, as a
temporary measure. What she wished and was working for was a
career as a virtuoso.

The deep night released her at last. Now Quapp was alone.
That was her first thought on awakening, that she would be alone
all day. Kajetan had probably left already, to visit their mother.
Or was he leaving today? She should have asked him for some
money. She was not in the least shy about that. But she had simply given it no thought on Saturday evening. Nor, for that matter,
had she had the chance. It struck her as especially annoying that
she should be so short of money just now, this week before her
audition. It was a depressing and restricting circumstance. She also
should have bought herself a few things. All right, the jersey dress
in tan checks would do; it was practically new. But she should
have a hat to go with it. Should she ask her aunt on Wednesday?
Was that at all possible? On Wednesday, too, Gyurkicz would be
paid for the drawings he was delivering. She was on the point of
becoming dependent on Imre; she could see it coming. He was to
be envied. He could live by his talent. She could not. True, she
had two or three pupils. Her teacher ("Is this method really based
on psychological foundations?" Fräulein Wiesinger had asked the
night before last, on Saturday. Away with her—never play with
her again!)—her teacher had turned these pupils over to Quapp
so that she could file away their crudest violinistic abuses and bad
habits. But in the first place he himself would soon be taking
them over again, and in the second place they paid too little. In
a city like Vienna, where a considerable portion of the population
could qualify as music teachers, it was not easy to find pupils
when you lacked all celebrity. Quapp had never yet given a concert. And she was a private student, not enrolled at the Academy.
In fact she would never have dreamed of enrolling there.

Her brother Kajetan certainly should have discussed such matters with her. But he hadn't bothered much with Quapp, except that he had brought her and Gyurkicz together; the meeting might have come about quite by chance, but still it had happened by way of Kajetan. Everyone is fully responsible for the people who are met through him. Kajetan also had never said anything to deter Quapp from her firm resolution to make a career as a virtuoso. She was too old for it. That was one simple fact which he should have known, even if he did not know that there were other weighty reasons why his sister was ineligible for the profession of soloist—reasons we shall learn in good time. Kajetan should have pointed out to Quapp the possibilities of chamber music, or of working in an orchestra, possibly even of studying in the proper official and public institutions. . . . He should have —how many sins of omission he was guilty of!

The day was overshadowed—with some of the shadows green. For now in mid-May treetops and bushes had come out into full leaf and laid long green shadows across narrow Eroica Gasse, so that you floated along, or rested as at the bottom of an aquarium. Or as in a hothouse; the past few days had been muggy and the rather steamy air suited well the climate of a hothouse. Quapp did not grasp the idyllic sweetness of the environment in which she stood, did not notice the flowering lilac; she did not flow into the surrounding stillness, the muting of all sounds from any distance, the gentleness of the green subaqueous light, the enfolding enclosure of the moment. Had she been able to grasp this, she would have been less vague, would have acquired definition and form; and then she might have been somewhat more "in form." After all, she knew something about form from her musical studies. But nothing of the sort took place. At the moment she had no clear direction within her. She was disoriented. And in this state she went to her music stand.

And the shadows within her were no soft ones, no dimness left-over from ambrosial night between which, by day, the scent of lilac can concentrate with an unworldly, excessive coolness. The shadows in Quapp were bolt upright, stiff, black lids which threatened at any moment to shut down upon her. Occasionally a glaring white daylight broke in upon them, revealing to her things that were all askew, things that she ought to have taken care of, such as money, such as the purchase of a new hat.

One black lid came from Saturday evening; the other towered up ahead on Monday, May 23: the day of her audition. In between these two black menaces were green Eroica Gasse here, like a precious fluid, cool and fragrant, inviting her to bathe in it.

Quapp practiced.

That, at least, was a victory. She had not remained sitting and brooding—her greatest danger.

The intonation was pure, the tone not bad.

So she managed tolerably well between the two lids. As far as the first was concerned, the things she had said to Herr Tlopatsch the night before last, Quapp was fortunately not entirely aware of how serious and irreparable her boner was.

The day passed, her work remaining fairly good. "One more like this," she thought, "and I'll be in fine form. She was profoundly astonished at her recent desire (which had suddenly come over her like an obsession) to meet Imre in Deutsch-Altenburg and see those Roman ruins with him. Now she wished only that she could stay home in Eroica Gasse tomorrow, all by herself as she was today.

Nevertheless, the next morning the journey seemed to her a sensible recreation. The way to the railroad station from Eroica Gasse was long and involved, but Quapp left the house in good time for once, and did not have to rush. Everything was turning out peacefully; she even derived tranquillity from her astonishment at the landscape to the east of Vienna, which she had not seen before. It had an expansiveness and brightness—a light quite different from that of the Vienna Woods. Seen from the third-class compartment of her slow-moving train, the country had a bleached look.

At the railroad station in Deutsch-Altenburg she inquired the way to the inn and set off. She soon became aware of footsteps following her, and then something struck her ear that sounded like a prolonged, muffled barking. It was some time before the noise dissolved, to her ears, into an endless string of vulgar abuse in which two words recurred at regular intervals: "tramp" and "slut." Quapp grasped first these two words, and then the rest. She stopped and turned around.

She saw at once that these recriminations were directed at herself, had been directed at her all the way from the station. For there was no one else on the street. A withered little woman of about fifty was following five paces behind Quapp. As Quapp now stepped toward her, she shrank back, and the stream of invective was arrested for a moment.

"What do you want of me?" Quapp cried out loudly.

Later, telling the story, Quapp said she could distinctly feel how her own face changed, how "an entirely strange face sprang out of mine, or dropped out; I must have looked altogether different; I suppose my eyebrows contracted, but the way it felt to me was as if my eyes had moved closer together. . . ."

Now the sewage eddied out again with redoubled fluency, and Quapp was able to gather that she was being reviled for coming here from Vienna for months on end in order to lead a decent husband astray.

In the face of this incomprehensible charge, her own stranger's expression "became stuck," Quapp said later. The woman's fury seemed to mount. Quapp took another step forward, and again the woman shrank back, though this time without desisting in her abuse. Then vigorous footsteps approached behind Quapp. A man's voice said loudly: "Off with you, go on home, Frau Öhler, stop molesting strangers here or I'll call the police." That was the end of it. The little woman's face contorted into a compact knot. She stared at the speaker, who had stepped up to Quapp's side; then, without another word, tripped off toward the railroad station.

"The things that can happen to a person in Deutsch-Altenburg —hard to believe, isn't it, Fräulein?" the man said to Quapp. "Don't let it bother you. The poor thing's off her rocker. Every few months or so she gets the idea that ladies are coming from

Vienna to make up to her husband. The fact is she hasn't got any; her husband died ten years ago. The county board says she doesn't belong in an institution because she's normal most of the time and when she does go off, it isn't as if she were danger-ous. . . ."

Quapp turned to face the man, her expression still frozen; but the pleasant voice seemed to thaw it—"Next moment it was as though a mask dropped from my face" was the way she later expressed it. And now she was recognized, and in a moment she too had placed the man.

"Fräulein von Schlaggenberg . . . ?"

"Why, you're the sergeant!" she exclaimed.

"On the way to the museum, are you?" Gach said. "It's odd, but Frau Öhler always picks on young ladies who are going from the station to the museum, usually students. Why, it was only day before yesterday, wasn't it, that Lieutenant von Geyrenhoff and I met you on the Graben in Vienna, didn't we, Fräulein?"

They had shaken hands cordially. Gach offered to accompany Quapp to the inn she was seeking. Meanwhile it had turned sunny, but the street was steeped in the light of the leafed-out chestnuts which hung above like a green sky; to look up into the higher reaches of this foliage roof was almost as dizzying as looking into the open blue heaven itself. And now Quapp saw the tall pyramids bedecked with their innumerable pink and white triangles, tier upon tier of blossoms. At the same moment she became aware that this was the first spring that she was directly aware of these ornamented green towers, more like mountain peaks than treetops. The narrowness, sparseness, and obsessive-ness of her life pressed like a yoke upon her neck; the interval between what she was and the vista she now beheld—so blissful, so vast, of such immaculate innocence—was so great that it filled her with violent alarm. Interval is feeling. Interval is also sorrow. Every feeling is likewise sorrow.

Perhaps the old sergeant of the dragoons had an inkling of what was going on in the mind of this child (for so she appeared to him). Perhaps also he remembered what else he had learned about this young lady the day before yesterday. At any rate, there was a note of concern in his question:

"Have you seen Herr von Geyrenhoff since, Fräulein von Schlaggenberg?"

"No," Quapp said. "Unfortunately not," she added with emphasis. "I would so much like to. I've seen very little of him lately."

They paused at the entrance to the inn's garden. Quapp looked at the scene under the chestnut trees: the tables covered with bright-colored cloths, some tables already set.

"I must wait for my friend here," she said. "He is coming up from the Burgenland. The train will be in soon."

"I am going to the station now," Gach said. "Perhaps I'll meet the gentleman on the way and direct him."

She was left alone again. The calm hand that Gach had laid upon everything within her—even upon provinces of her interior of whose existence he could scarcely guess—was lifted again as she recalled that terrible meeting with the madwoman and the discovery she had made of her own "two-facedness"—no, she could think of no other word for it. And yet there was something about the experience that was not entirely new. Where, when, had something like it occurred? Had it not, perhaps, always been so, never any different? Had she experienced today the thing that is hardest to learn—namely, what—what she herself looked like? For a brief moment dizziness overcame her, as at the sight of the treetops overhead.

An old waiter approached her table. She asked what there was to eat, and he placed a tiny menu card in front of her. "I'm waiting for a gentleman," she said, ordered wine and soda, and smoked. The cigarette made her feel immoderately good; she inhaled deeply and now actually became a little giddy. What was the meaning of the madwoman! By whom and why, so to speak, had she been sent? What message did she bring? For some moments Quapp was empty as a funnel which has just before been filled to the brim with some liquid. She drank her spritzer, and for a long time sat without stirring. Now the gravel spoke. Imre's footsteps. Yes, they were his. Quapp at last looked up—it was actually he.

"A nice old fellow showed me the way," Gyurkicz said. He set his handsome leather suitcase on a chair. Quapp said nothing. Suddenly she felt how altogether absurd was the necessity always to establish connections, make remarks. She felt oddly strengthened by her silence concerning her own acquaintanceship with old Gach. It did not even occur to her to tell Imre about the incident with the madwoman.

They had their lunch, and over coffee Gyurkicz showed her several water-colored pen-drawings of Neusiedler Lake. They were really extraordinary, and she told him so. But as she said it, she began to doubt everything, not only her violin-playing, not only her hoped-for profession.

They went on to see the museum; it was not far from the inn. Quapp was tremendously astonished "at all the things they had in those days." Her ignorance prevented her from properly apprehending what she saw—a wave, lapping out to the eastern rim, of that polished Roman civilization which had reached as far as here and had left behind as sediment much of its customary stock, from perfume bottle to stone memorial tablet, as well as a good many objects of art which in this remote outpost, so far from the metropolis and of only military importance, assumed distinctly provincial forms. Quapp was wonder-struck. An elderly curator pointed out one thing and another to the young people. Gyurkicz took no historical or educational interest in the objects, but promptly and directly viewed them as specimens of the minor arts. Some of the artifacts pleased him considerably, and he praised these things as if they were the products of living craftsmen being exhibited for the first time. "Likarz and those other women in Vienna might just as well pack up—the most they could do would be to imitate this." Quapp grew even more astonished. Her unawareness of many things ran, through the years, parallel with events that were going on all around her. But once she discovered them, she turned at right angles from the orbit of her ignorance and came right up to the object, all but pressing her nose flat up against it. It is a moot question whether this approach may not be more fruitful than that of so-called general education, in which everything is served up at once smothered in a single sauce. It must be admitted that Quapp's naïveté called for some patience on the part of her companions. Kajetan and Stangeler had this patience toward her; and Géza von Orkay later displayed it to an altogether amazing degree— as, for example, after the events of July 1927 in Vienna when he explained why the Palace of Justice had been set ablaze, and what all the riots were about—really telling her the whole story *ab ovo* (to use this favorite expression of Herr von Geyrenhoff). Quapp's lack of knowledge about the Romans was of the same nature and extent as her political vagueness.

Thereafter they visited the extensive ruins of ancient Carnuntum. They stood on the gently rising rows of seats of the former amphitheater (a second theater has since been excavated; it was a large garrison city, militarily more important than Vienna was at the time, even though the philosopher-emperor Marcus Aurelius had made Vienna his residence during his last years). The shallow amphitheater, strewn here and there with rubble and remnants of structures, stretched like a pale wing against the clear sky; it was as though this history-soaked earth were showing its light-colored underside, like a dead fish when it floats to the surface. Imre and Quapp found it hard to tear themselves away; Imre, too, began to feel the spell of the place. They walked here and there, covering several miles in the course of their strolls about the extensive ruins. In the so-called "Heathen Gate," a mighty arch of an old wall, stood a semicircular patch of blue sky, looking like part of the ancient stone—as if it had come down in time from those days long past, not Austrian sky of the present, but sky imported from Italy in the times of Marcus Aurelius.

They did not know how tired they were until they were seated in the train. Once they were in Vienna, the streetcar ride from the railroad station to Döbling seemed interminable. They ate ham sandwiches and drank beer in a Heiligenstadt restaurant. Just reaching narrow, dimly lit Eroica Gasse was like being received into a bed—a fragrant one, for the perfume of the lilacs reached their nostrils.

They paused in the street between where he lived and she lived. Imre kissed Quapp's hand. When he said: "It was interesting down there," she suddenly realized that that whitish light of the ruins was still present to her, that reach of sky, the bleached landscape, the blue in the gigantic old arch. All that was here still in the green street, under the different auspices of a neighborhood that was not bleached and stiffly silent, but rather whispering in the darkness, pressing close with sweet-scented questions, with fragrance of lilac and green foliage.

In her room Quapp saw a letter lying on top of the minute lady's desk which she had placed at her window but at such an angle that one sat at it without looking out into the street. That was how Quapp preferred it. Frequently, if you called on her in the evening, you could see her from the street, seated at the little desk, writing something in the open notebooks before her. At times it seemed she spent more time at her desk than at her music stand.

The letter came from a lawyer, Doktor Philemon Krautwurst, and was registered. Quapp had given her landlady written authority to receive such letters.

Each letter, as it lies awaiting us, jumps up like a little jack-in-the-box.

At first she did not understand the contents of it at all.

It was every bit as incomprehensible as that encounter with the madwoman in Deutsch-Altenburg.

She had received an inheritance. Or rather, a legacy had been set aside for her from a certain inheritance: a sum of money which she was now to receive.

Step right up, ladies and gentlemen, walk right in!

But it was more than a quarter of a million schillings.

And she was asked to call at the lawyer's, bringing identification, sometime in the next few days. Would she please telephone beforehand?

It took a while before Quapp grasped the facts of the matter. The testator—Baron Achaz Neudegg—meant nothing to her personally; she had at most heard the name mentioned socially. She was still sitting at the little desk, the letter spread out upon it. Her sleepiness was now so great that for a few moments she almost doubted that she would be able to cross the room to her bed. Imre had probably gone to sleep long before. She suddenly thought how awkward it would be if Imre and she lived on opposite sides of the narrow street so that they could see each other's windows. They had once even been sorry that this was not the case, for it would have been nice to greet each other from window to window. She almost fell off the chair from sleepiness. But if it had been so, Gyurkicz would see that she was still up, sitting at her desk, with a letter before her; perhaps he would have been able to see that from his bed, across the narrow street, from his already darkened room. Frightful thought. And yet such things could occur, and once they did exist it was hard to escape them. . . .

Quapp slowly folded the letter, put it in the top drawer, and turned the key twice. She rose with an effort, attended to her evening toilette, and went to bed—unusually early for her, incidentally, for it was but a little past ten o'clock.

She awoke very early next morning, feeling as if she were leaving tremendous quantities of sleep behind her. But it was a different kind of sleep from yesterday's. This sleep had in no way interrupted her life; life had continued during it.

Immediately after awakening she still felt utterly empty.

Then the second quiet day of practice approached her—the day she had decided she would need in order to be "in form." It approached, but stopped at a certain distance from her, would move no nearer.

Into the empty space leaped the letter from the lawyer.

Beyond the letter Quapp saw her aunt, whom she was to visit that afternoon.

Not until she was sitting over her morning tea did Quapp look
at the letter again. She took it from the drawer. It showed her the
smooth face of an official communication. This affair was—the
conclusion was forced upon Quapp—like yesterday's meeting
with the madwoman: an orbit from some hereafter in the here
which suddenly impinges upon us and becomes of concern to us.
With the difference that in this case no Gach could step forward
to put the lawyer to rout. Gach had been the awakening which
dispelled the dream image. But with this there was no awakening; wonderfully enough, she could go on dreaming. And Quapp
dreamed for a while, after replacing the letter in the drawer and
locking it up again. This time she even removed the key and
placed it carefully in a little box.

Then she practiced, pegging away at her normal daily stint. But
the unyielding distance that separated Quapp from that second
day of good work, which she had thought necessary to get herself
back into form after the depression induced by Herr Tlopatsch—
that distance remained. She could no longer revive her Monday's
concept of the "two good days," although on that day she had
actually wished she could practice on Tuesday instead of going as
arranged to Deutsch-Altenburg. She was practicing now. But it
was all secondary. News of an inheritance should have given her
day's practice an extraordinary impetus, enabling her to pitch
overboard many sacks of ballast full of needless cares. But that
was not the case at all. She realized this herself, and was profoundly disturbed by it, though she could not interpret the
meaning of it. This practicing that she was doing was obviously
self-deception.

Shortly after nine o'clock she telephoned the lawyer. To do so
she had to take the key out of the box and open the drawer to
check on Doktor Krautwurst's telephone number on the letter-
head.

First the office answered, then the professional voice: "Delighted, delighted, Fräulein von Schlaggenberg." He would call
back in half an hour and let her know whether he could be at her

disposal that very afternoon (Quapp had proposed three o'clock). He noted the telephone number.

Then Quapp returned to her practicing, her secondary, meaningless practicing. While she was at it, she heard the hall door shut. This meant that her landlady had just gone shopping and that Quapp was alone in the apartment. Five minutes later the telephone rang. It would be a pleasure, Doktor Krautwurst said, to see Fräulein von Schlaggenberg in his office that afternoon at three. Quapp said—in that quiet alto voice she had at times, and which together with her clear fine enunciation made an excellent impression—something to this effect: "My dear Doktor Krautwurst, I have a request which I hope will not strike you as too outlandish. It so happens that your letter reaches me at a time when I find myself in extreme embarrassment with regard to money. In view of this sum I am to receive—a sum which, for a person of my modest circumstances, is very large, it seems so useless for me to have this money difficulty. Would it be too much to ask you for a small, a very small advance on the legacy this very afternoon?"

The lawyer asked at once how much she had in mind. "At most a thousand," she replied. "Why, of course, Fräulein von Schlaggenberg," the professional voice said. "We can arrange that just between ourselves. The sum of a thousand schillings will be ready for you at three o'clock."

One hurdle had been taken, without even a running start. But with this sudden inspiration of Quapp's, she was done, and done in. That was clear to her as soon as she stepped back into her room.

The lawyer's readiness to accommodate her struck her as extraordinary. It made her think that something lay behind this whole affair, something which she did not know but which had some highly personal significance to herself. Perhaps she could find out from the lawyer who this deceased Herr von Neudegg was, and why he had left her money.

Doktor Krautwurst answered her first question that afternoon without hesitation, and in detail. But he said he could not answer the second because he did not know. However, he sat regarding Quapp thoughtfully for several minutes, and she had the definite impression that he knew more than he was entitled to say.

There Quapp sat, as if before a boarded-over archway in a wall. There was no way through, and yet the place where you were supposed to pass through was clearly indicated. She must ask Kajetan. But he was not in Vienna now.

The rest of it rustled by to either side of her: the signing of a statement, the validification of her signature. She also signed her name to a receipt for 1,000 schillings. Shortly afterwards, she stood in the street again with this amount in her pocket. She felt as if she had been whirled back and forth like a weather vane. Nevertheless, it remained clear to her that within a short time she would have at her disposal a bank account of 250,000—minus 1,000. A great expanse of time without cares stretched before her. As yet Quapp had not begun to reckon. That mood would not ensue until evening, at her little desk.

But what amazingly overcame her now was a sudden impulse toward, of all things, thrift. A resistance to spending money. Hairdresser—hat to go with the tan checks (she was wearing the dress now, but without a hat)—some flowers or candy for her aunt? She had an errand to do for her aunt, to pick up a package and take it somewhere. Old-lady affairs. Quapp did not consider how old ladies managed often with the smallest of means to get along respectably without being a burden upon anyone—that this was possible only by mouselike care in the pettiest matters.

The day was windily warm, changeable, blue at intervals, with the sun breaking through occasionally, growing cloudier toward evening. Quapp felt enormously enlivened, no doubt about that. She did go to the hairdresser, although she had undergone rather extensive operations along those lines only the week before: now her hair was given just a touching up, which might be needed for trying on hats. That did not take long. The milliner's name was Pauli, and her place was on Schuler Strasse. Besides her flair for designing hats, Frau Pauli had a clever tongue, and many of her remarks were bandied about among ladies' circles. On the oc-casion of the marriage of a distinctly elderly miss who possessed only a single, though very prominent, attraction, Frau Pauli had said to a customer: "Does it surprise you, ma'am? Not me. With that saucy balcony!"

In fact an ideal lid was found to cover the seething pot of Quapp's headgear desires: a small toque of brown felt. Frau Pauli was quite wonderful about helping customers choose the right hat for themselves, and besides the field was already narrowed down by the tan-checked dress.

Then to the flower shop and on to her aunt. This took more time than the visit to the milliner's. In regard to the hat Quapp had clung to the rationalization that she needed it for the audition on Monday—in spite of the violent wind from the new situation which seemed truly to have knocked her about like a weather vane. This clinging to the forthcoming ordeal of the audition was virtually all that was left to Quapp now. With dogged obstinacy she performed all her errands in the city on foot, without once using a bus; and this was done to save the fare, not because Quapp preferred walking to riding. In a momentary flash she observed herself with astonishment. A kind of mutiny had broken out within her, a revenge against all the life and tumult around her that had so often roared unfeelingly past her in her many melancholias and deep depressions. Now she herself was running past it: with brows slightly contracted and again with the sense that she looked different from the way she had looked, that she had a different face—as she had had the day before on the street in Deutsch-Altenburg. Yes, that was it, but today she did not feel it as unpleasant. An underground lake, concentrated out of her many despairs, had been tapped and was now streaming forth. Its waters were bitter. And whipped with waves from the new wind that was whirling her around.

She arrived in Döbling again, and in the green street, as dark-ness was descending. She had taken the tram out; she would have liked to do this stretch on foot as well, but it would have meant a tramp of far more than an hour.

She got out of the streetcar at the terminus, at the highest point above the park.

And went down over the hill in a way she had never done since she had lived here: descending as if she were walking alongside a gaping crevasse. Not solitary, not embraced by the sheltering enclosure of this hour here and now, under the high dark trees and along the big children's playground where the gas lanterns were always burning: not solitary but isolated. When she had reached home, and from the hall heard the footsteps of her landlady in an adjoining room, she was overcome by a strangely lordly feeling. In her own quarters she first took off her new hat and put it on the piano. She kept her dress on, contrary to her habit, for Quapp always wore a modest dark smock at home. She went to the kitchen to make a pot of tea. Then she installed herself at her desk, took out the miraculous letter and the papers the lawyer had given her (including a list of securities, for half of the legacy consisted of good stocks), and with pad and pencil drew up a summary, a kind of preliminary financial plan. For a long time she sat at the little desk, smoking and drinking tea. When she heard Imre's footsteps in the street, passing by her window just beyond the strip of front garden—yes, it was he— she carefully folded up all the papers and placed them in the drawer, together with the pad containing her calculations. She turned the key twice, withdrew it, and hid it as before in the little box. The bell rang. Yes, it was he. Quapp went out without haste to open the front door.

3 ⌋   *At the Blue Unicorn*

IT IS a long, wide, and animated avenue leading straight from the center of the city. At a certain spot the streetcar tracks which run along it turn away and the street itself becomes narrow. A bare hundred steps more and you notice that here and there the houses, formerly forming a solid and regular front, begin to protrude or recede. Moreover, one side of the street suddenly drops down in level a whole story, or even two. Here stands the house called the Blue Unicorn. But we need go only a block or so further to find ourselves already emerging from this curiously independent, lumpy area imbedded in the city—we are back once again on the normal long avenues where the lines of the roofs are high and level.

Below the house called the Blue Unicorn, however, lie several narrow alleys. The streets go downhill here, toward the Danube. In this quarter people stand around on the street on summer evenings, waiting for nothing and nobody in particular, and thus for everybody—for these bystanders speak to passers-by. And hence almost everyone knows everyone else. Here is the parish church called Zu den vierzehn Nothelfern. Here, only a few minutes from Ring Strasse (where we were all alike), we feel that we attract attention as strangers.

This whole area nevertheless seems only a few yards wide. It is like a crumb already disappearing into a huge maw. A cat looks out of a window. From the street people talk to others leaning out of windows in the lower stories of the houses. We notice the entrance to a house and see that it is really the gateway to an inner court, wide enough for a hay wagon and no doubt many a hay wagon has passed through it. Later on, a turn in the street confronts us with the moon; it hangs full and honey-colored in the sky, which is very open here above the low roofs. No one can say where this ancient part of the city really begins or ends—no more than we can say this of our own entanglements. These cramped alleys here are also only an entanglement into which one stumbles, and perhaps the little old houses are not always here; perhaps upon occasion we may walk right through them without noticing. They are a condition into which we fall, which comes into being only through a rare coincidence of many different components, as if we had continued to dream again something we had already dreamed once before. Such is the nature of our encounters with this quarter, which would ordinarily be only at long intervals.

We step around a corner and see, huge and wide, the illuminated side of the railroad station for the trains to Bohemia and Moravia. It takes a moment before we realize that there on the other side of the broad square, directly opposite the main façade of the old-fashioned terminal building, stand those huge bloated creations of the nineteenth-century real-estate boom in one of which, in apartment Number 14, lives the Siebenschein family.

By 1926 Renata Gürtzner-Gontard was often able to escape from her parental home, and under the best of pretexts. There were, in those days, various leagues and organizations for young people whose purposes were even then rather hazy and which by now have disappeared completely into the haze of the past. Only the Scouts are still scouting, although what they are scouting for and whether they will ever find it remains unknown.

The Gontards looked kindly upon such group-sponsored activities, and perhaps regarded them as an escape-valve for a growing daughter, since they no longer knew quite what to make of their Renata. She frequently went off on "camping trips" with girl friends: trips with all the trimmings, such as tents and alcohol stoves. When we think back hard upon such trips, an enormous loveliness will flash suddenly out of them and even today will cut sweetly across our spirits like a beam of sunlight cutting across tall woods, transforming the rows of tree trunks—in spite of all their ponderousness—into the strings of a harp from which the ray of light evokes a melodious cadenza.

And the tent, set up in the rocky gorge to be out of the wind! Here too was the right place for the campfire, far enough away from the woods so that no sparks could cause a fire. The girls had been taught all these points of woodcraft. How marvelous was the evening after a tramp that could go on ever so much farther than usual because there was no necessity to return the same day, none of that anxiety of the housebound to get home before the onset of darkness, to hurry, as though nature became spiteful with the oncoming of night and would snap at the walker's heels. No, nature is not like that, she does not bite. Nature for campers is not the same as "nature" for those who go on outings and picnics. Camping trips are something quite different from such feeble and superficial pursuits. It is like the difference between the real hunter and the sportsman out for a day's shooting. The camper, like the hunter, must come to practical terms with "nature"; the characteristics of the natural world cannot be altered or improved, but must be accepted, taken as they are. "Taken," in fact, as a boxer must sometimes take a blow. You must study the water situation. If, judging by terrain or vegetation, there is not likely to be any, you must take your water with you in big canteens. But it doesn't do to carry it too far. Someone has to decide what is really the last source of water before your tenting site. For in those days there did not yet exist camping places as crowded as railroad stations. Aside from the infrequent larger camp meetings of young people—youth camps, jamborees, or whatever they were called—the campers were mostly tiny groups of some six or eight boys and girls. They made their way by preference through unknown regions, woods and mountain pastures, scrub land and river bottoms—all the vast, almost untrodden regions that exist in

Austria, where you can tramp for days without seeing a soul. The campers did not fear solitude, and the bravest and most honorable of all were the littlest squirts. At times it would be necessary to post guards—in regions, say, where there were big herds of cattle, or in bottomlands where the sharp-toothed muskrat could gnaw his way into the tent in order to get at the bacon. Often air rifles or even bows and arrows lay ready to the hand of the alert scout.

How vital is the evening. The real camper knows what it means to wrest freedom from all that mere picnickers mean by "nature." That freedom begins with the many tasks to be performed. First there is the matter of erecting the tent, whose canvas must be drawn smooth and taut and every stake set just right. A ditch must be dug around a tent, and a drain contrived; thus even on nights of pouring rain it will be dry and warm inside. Cooking is quite an affair. Now this is needed, now that; and little cans of pepper or salt are almost invariably at the very bottom of the knapsack. But by the time real darkness falls, it is all done, and the two Scouts who have investigated the immediate vicinity are back from their tour. Everyone sits down at the fire.

Then evening really comes. It rises out of the earth like dark ground water in the woods, and the paling sky drops down upon the treetops. Beyond this dropped veil the night itself appears, and a few stars break through, flashing vigorously, even while the pompous spectacle of the sunset is drawing to an end in the west.

It is by no means wholly still. A jay chatters its cadenza. The regular whistling farther back in the woods comes from the goatsucker, whose real hours begin now.

Many had been the excitements and adventures of the day. Thus, as they were passing through a lonely pasture, a bull had made for them; but someone had hurled a spear, which stuck into the ground two paces in front of the charging beast and frightened it so that it tossed its heavy lowered head, turned aside in one leap, and fled. With a dog, on the other hand, the recognized procedure was to get down on all fours, hold a hat between your teeth, and crawl straight toward the enemy. And in fact one of the little squirts had been able to demonstrate the efficacy of this method against quite a fierce-looking hound. That afternoon Renata had proved herself master of the bow and arrow, and all had cheered the excellence of her home-made weapon as well as her skill in shooting. Drawing a feathered arrow from the leather quiver, she had struck at forty paces a small tree stump, so low that it barely showed above the grass. Afterwards everyone kneeled around this dead hit, no little surprised at the power the slender bow had imparted to the arrow, for it had gone deep into the wood.

But such Red-Indian feats were really incidental. The real point of it all lay hidden under the flickering campfire, round which the Scouts sat and talked. As by a wall far off, this troop of young people were surrounded by various parental homes, which on a single score were all alike: they were too much with them. Those homes formed a shell of basic experiences in which they were imprisoned, and out of which they must somehow struggle. And every one of these parental homes reeked of the last century. Herein lay a certain poetry; but this would not become apparent to the young people until later, in recollection. For the present these parental homes made themselves as heavy as possible. They became ends in themselves. They imposed far more ballast than necessary upon vessels which were only just starting out on their voyages. And the rigging they offered was too low, wholly inadequate. Everything was done to hamper the vessels, lest they should spin and whirl madly in the high winds of life. From the height and authority of their own mission (which they served ill), befuddled fathers spoke of themselves in the third person, employing phrases like: "What a way to speak to your father!"

To oppose this superior force, so unfairly used against them, the oppressed young people attempted to find themselves a center of their own, no matter how frail. It had to be situated outside, in space as well as mind, of the baleful family. For there is a certain diabolism about everything familial, and nowhere do evil spirits more freely roam than within the sanctity of the home. But a rite had been found to combat them, and its altar stone lay deep in the ground beneath each campfire. Of course the band of campers also included casual boys and girls who lacked the profundity of youth, fair-weather friends even now floating on their own surfaces like dead fish. But Renata and her friends knew about the altar stone under the campfire; seated about it, they could make their first stabs at still unsound but altogether indispensable critical thinking.

Perhaps immurement within the parental home had once offered security. But after the war even that began to look doubtful. As the young people took courage from their rites and altar stones, they sprang up and looked over the walls, which at once began to crumble into the disparate fragments of conventions and social considerations out of which they had been built, while their mortar turned out to be composed of nothing but ordinary timidity. And it became evident that the same was true for other parental homes. And since the young could see nothing in all this rubble that was worth preserving, their courage rose steadily as the prestige of the family sank.

Here now, around the fire, it has grown late. The fire dies down. The darkness is dense.

In the end they thought of a possible danger which made it imperative to post a guard.

This region, they knew, had once been stocked with ibexes, and the animals had increased and multiplied; some would even appear now and then in lower-down regions. The ibex is not so shy as the chamois; it is quick to take the offensive when it sees a strange phenomenon that incites its rage. The tents would surely not be to its liking. Caught unawares inside the tent, you would be helpless to defend yourself against the mighty antlers; in fact, a collapsing tent would pin you down.

Therefore, when all the others had crawled in to sleep, an experienced Scout assumed sentinel duty. He changed his broad-brimmed hat for a knitted cap, picked up the long sports javelin (perhaps in memory of the recent successful battle with the bull), and began slowly circling the camp. From time to time he stepped closer to the fire, which glowed a feeble red, and added a stick or two. Tonight they had not put the fire out: a glowing log, leaping to flame when whirled through the air, would certainly be the best defense against a fractious specimen of wild game. One such log lay among the quiet embers.

So the hours pass.

It grows cool at this altitude.

The Scout rolls up the turtleneck collar of his sweater.

The goatsucker is silent now. Regiments of newly rising stars advance sparkling into the sky. Late and secretly the crescent of the waning moon comes forth above a ridge. The sentinel's footsteps ring. Now, above a small outjutting rock, his silhouette appears against the sky, towered over by the shaft of the javelin. The boy's shoulders are already well developed, broad. The strikingly narrow hips run down into slender, excessively long legs. In spite of the chill, his knees are bare, and the shorts look like a skirt. Two and a half thousand years ago this same silhouette was seen, standing straight against the sky, only the stars over his head.

The stars of that time were already rising (for those who had eyes to see, at any rate), though some still lurked below the horizon and some were just barely appearing above the brink. But here in the camp they were already lagging minute by minute behind the stars, and they lagged until they were days, weeks, and years behind, and until it became obvious that anyone who in any way "leagued" himself with an organization and became part of it (six of one and half a dozen of the other) thereby lost the ability to cut the Gordian knot of the times in his own breast. For that is something which can never be done in conjunction with others. It was not yet known that everything would soon depend upon the individual, and that it was incumbent on the individual, for a time at least, to take his place exactly opposite every sort of collective. For individuals would be spewed out by their age, "exposed" in every sense as the indispensable adver-

saries of the age. This was a situation which could not be averted
—at most delayed. Meanwhile the young people let their own
Gordian knot be; for the time being they fled to the camp. The
cumulative weight of such postponements produced the momentum of historical facts; what the young would not admit into
their heads beforehand they afterwards received as a crashing
thwack of knowledge upon their backsides. But the backside is
not susceptible to education; it just hurts like mad.

We do not know, of course, whether the uneasiness that Renata
felt really sprang from some premonition of these matters. At
any rate, even when she was with her good friends, she was
frequently overcome by the feeling of being a clown in front of a
paper-covered hoop. The idea was to jump through somewhere;
you couldn't quite see where, but you knew that the pretty paper
would tear, and that almost inevitably you would end by landing
on your face.

It speaks for a certain flowering of instinct on the part of Renata
that she began to seek solitude, in order to consider how she
would make her leap. Not solitude for a few hours, but for some
days at a time. Such a luxury is not to be had, of course, in the
dear and warm parental home. Even if it were, one would be
instantly beset by all the evil spirits who would crawl out of all
the old cupboards, even while the beautifully grained wood of the
cupboard doors went on gleaming their usual polished gleam.

Renata had a close friend named Sylvia. Both girls, who often
outdid each other in bold exploits, were warm-natured and
helpful. In Renata's case especially, one often caught sight of
something like dark velvet when she opened her eyes wide.
Sylvia, who knew and understood Renata's moods of needing
solitude, although she herself did not have these moods to anything like the same extent, wondered how it could be arranged
for Renata. Sylvia was wide-awake; her alertness showed in her
light gray eyes, which peered with a certain sharpness out of a
pretty, rather birdlike face. She had the faculty of making acquaintance at the drop of a hat with all kinds of people; and the
tutoring she did brought her in contact with many. Occasionally

she went as a tutor to the house called the Blue Unicorn. Her pupil was not always in Vienna; he was still attending the last class of a village school in the Burgenland. Afterwards he was to take the examination for admission to the Gymnasium in Vienna. Not that there were no Gymnasia in the Burgenland. But Pepi Grössing had an aunt in Vienna who, in her loneliness, was more than happy to have him stay with her during his further schooling. She had set her heart on her nephew's studying in Vienna, and in order to make sure that he would pass his entrance examination, Frau Kapsreiter, née Csmarits, had the boy tutored by Sylvia during all the holidays in his last year of grade school. Frau Kapsreiter's brother, Mathias Csmarits, was always traveling between the Burgenland and Vienna, and would bring Pepi with him each holiday.

Frau Kapsreiter lived in the house called the Blue Unicorn.

In every class there are people who fall out of it, whether upstairs or down. Thus, there are high aristocrats who spend almost their full time in libraries and seem no better than humble scholars. There are industrial workers who climb to the heights of culture. There are bookbinders with touches of genius: consider Hirschkron of the Café Kaunitz. There are petty bourgeois with breadth of soul and magnificent human qualities. One such case was Frau Anna Kapsreiter. "Just bring your friend here, Fräulein Priglinger," she said to Sylvia. "She can have her peace here. I won't bother her. She can take the corner room. I understand just how she feels. I'm on good terms with the concierge; she won't say anything. Tell Fräulein Renata she can come any time. I'm looking forward to it."

Of course such visits were possible only during the holidays, since Renata, like her friend Sylvia, had to go to Gymnasium.

In the late summer of 1926, shortly before the fall term was to begin, she and Sylvia started out together from her parents' home "on a camping trip." But they "tripped" along on foot for no more than twenty minutes, and deposited their knapsacks in the house called the Blue Unicorn.

Frau Kapsreiter was an all-day coffee drinker; she drank only the best, prepared in the Turkish manner, and drop by drop, like a bird. The quantities were consequently infinitesimal; probably she took no more than a full cup in the course of a day. It certainly did her no harm. She was well preserved for her sixty-one years. Moderately slender, with white hair, she had a smooth pink face. Every day she smoked five cigarettes, of a cheap brand.

At bottom there was a mystery about this woman. She had never had children, and had lost her husband, who had been ten years her junior, a good while before. He had been a municipal official, occupying a rather high position, and had moreover received a promotion just two weeks before his decease. This had meant a tidy addition to her widow's pension. (In Austria, incidentally, people who receive no state or municipal pension, subsidy, or annuity whatsoever are extremely rare and looked down upon.) We may ask what Frau Kapsreiter had to do aside from drinking coffee all day long. The answer is: nothing. And therein lay the grandeur of her existence; for she did not fill this empty space, in which she had nothing to do, with mere nothingnesses. In this fact were fixed her stout links to Renata, for a strong chain of affection formed between the two almost from their first meeting.

Frau Kapsreiter, what was more, read no books. Thus, there was no knowing what her taste in literature might have been. Her reading consisted only of those weeklies which are manufactured especially for the readers of her class, and are so cleverly whipped up that there are two drawing cards for everyone in every issue. Frau Kapsreiter picked up her magazine every week at the tobacco shop, where enticing piles of the latest issue lay. The day the magazine came out, the shop, ordinarily patronized mostly by men, would have an influx of large numbers of elderly women from the whole neighborhood. One magazine would be put on display outside showing the table of contents and cover, whether the feature article concerned the former ruling house, or the rise of a poor orphan child to world fame as a film star, or even a fictional offering like the memoirs of Helen of Troy, or, say, the days of terror experienced by a city of Brazil when giant octopuses entered its sewerage system. With pictures.

Aside from such weeklies, Frau Kapsreiter read nothing at all. On the other hand, she kept a journal.

It was really a nocturnal, so to speak; a book of her nights, although written down by day. It contained all of Frau Kapsreiter's dreams; nothing whatsoever from her waking life. She dreamt vividly every single night. In this way she collected through the years voluminous notes on a second existence, inscribed outside that existence each morning. For she wrote in bed, immediately after awakening, in a big, thick, hard-bound book which looked like an account book. Renata inherited it from Frau Kapsreiter.

There was a second case of this type in Vienna at that time. The wife of old Hofrat P.—in his time the best chamber-music violist in Viennese society—always kept a pad and pencil on her night table, for her husband talked in his sleep, long and loud and saying the most curious things. His wife wrote it all down, and at breakfast the old parties would then amuse themselves royally, for she would read the text aloud. Among other things he was once reported to have said: "Frau von Stangeler rides a narrow-gauge track on a narrow-gauge schedule."

Frau Kapsreiter, however, was her own amanuensis.

The house was a tiny one, having only two stories. Frau Anna occupied the upper story. The rooms were small, but there were three of them, and a kitchen. Anna Kapsreiter's corner room, which Renata was to occupy, was situated in the middle of the apartment, but oddly enough had no connection with the adjoining room; perhaps the door was blocked by the huge wardrobe which covered the whole left wall. The room was exactly on a level with the unicorn couchant installed in a corner niche on the outside of the house. This was of blue faïence. Sylvia and Renata called it "the blue sheep," and accordingly referred to the house also as "The Blue Sheep." The room which Renata was free to use had this remarkable quality, that though its space was greatly taken up by the monstrous wardrobe and the couch, it nevertheless gave the impression of being far larger than it was. Perhaps this was because its other furniture was confined to a light table and two comfortable wicker chairs. There was also a bookcase. Its shelves were empty. Nor were there any pictures.

Just as well, for Frau Kapsreiter would probably have hung those which somehow delight people of her class, and not for lack of knowledge that other schools of painting exist, but because of a deep-seated affinity for this very type of thing, so that everything else is avoided, excluded. Here, however, no "Artist's Destiny" or "Beethoven and the Muses" looked down from the wall. Incidentally, it is possible that such paintings might have amused the girls immensely. Baudelaire remarks somewhere that from a certain intellectual altitude the reading of idiotic books can provide sublime pleasure. We are perfectly ready to ascribe that altitude to our two Gymnasium students. The girls might very well have been ravished by the abominations of pictorial art, and regarded "The Lover's Lament" with endless delight. But there were no lamenting lovers on the walls; there was nothing at all adorning them.

Altogether, the room gave an impression of emptiness.

There were two windows looking out in different directions. One looked out upon that long avenue from the center of the city which changed its character where the streetcar tracks turned off. The other window looked into a small side street. Both windows were provided with curtains of a rust-brown, roughly woven material; to judge by these, Frau Kapsreiter might have been possessed of superior artistic taste. Perhaps it was there, only unawakened.

It was the same here as everywhere: as though you had come to a halt after a long tramp and remained standing, sitting, lying; and by so doing you froze and preserved for the time being your circumstances. The street would go on; there would be other streets after it. But here you had set down your pack (there it lay, beside the big couch, untouched; you did not open it right away). Sylvia had just finished giving little Pepi Grössing a lesson and then was really "going camping." The gang were waiting for her at the nearby railroad station where one took the train to go upstream along the Danube (and also into Bohemia). This time they were going to camp for a few days in the bottomlands near Tulln. And then the gang would sail downstream in folding boats.

At the moment Renata was at loose ends. Nothing in her surroundings was firmly fixed, as in life things are ordinarily so firmly fixed, like teeth in the jaw. Everything was singular, and things fell out of their designations like dried nut kernels from a shell; they made a rattling sound. Here was none of that well-established bath in which everything floated at home: the parental amniotic fluid. Perhaps Renata was still far too young to have had practice in grasping any given surroundings, in lightly constructing new realities. She still possessed that high degree of genuineness which resists entrance into such fictional worlds. And in this uncertain situation Renata hovered as over an abyss, for the space of seconds anyhow, over the possibilities of absurdity.

The cognoscenti know this yawning gulf, and know too that it is a necessary component to life. But Renata was not so knowing. Consequently, this new situation bore down on her with an almost physical weight. She could not bear it and threw herself on the couch without even trying to find a comfortable position. It was—in medical terms—a veritably catatonic state. But in her innermost recesses dwelt a kind of inborn confidence in the functionings of the mind's mechanism, for otherwise she would have jumped up and given herself something to do, such as unpacking. But no: Renata was very intelligent in a higher sense. She did not writhe and struggle. She fell asleep. Sleeping, she landed on a new stage of existence, like Odysseus on Ithaca.

Something warm, still smelling of milk like a calf, crawled up on the couch, rolled up beside her, and likewise slept. It was little Pepi. He had sounded his signal at the door—the sawing, croaking tone of a jay or crow, because of which Renata had given him the nickname "Croaky." Then, having received no answer, he had quietly opened the door and found Renata asleep. Now two young creatures slumbered on the couch, both exuding the milky, calflike smell.

Meanwhile the Blue Unicorn sank deep into the afternoon, whose long rays already slanted in through the window. In Tulln the campers had reached their goal; they were tramping through the meadows, their folding canoes pulled along on small two-wheeled racks. Voices re-echoed under the high sunlit treetops that bordered the meadows, resounded across the winding arms of the river where the silvery twists of water snakes glided away each time the noisy party approached a shore. They found the best place for tents and set to work.

With afternoon's lengthening, the Blue Unicorn had also sunk deeper into the city and into the old ground hereabouts, as though the underlying morass of centuries of urban life were sinking slightly beneath the walls, and the walls sinking with it. Out of the soil, out of the cellars, out of ancient front halls, the genius loci emerged as evening descended and stepped out on the street, as if to take part in an untimely witching hour, for it found people still in front of their doors and old ladies at the windows and the street full of conversation.

Frau Kapsreiter opened the door a crack and saw the two sleeping figures. She tiptoed through the room, set down the coffee she was carrying, and moved the small light table over beside the couch. After she had transferred the coffee to it, she stood still looking down at the children. Perhaps the gaze was so intense, or else the surface of the two young people still so thin and porous that they could feel it; at any rate, they both at once opened their soft eyes.

Frau Kapsreiter took one of the wicker chairs and sat down by the couch. Voices could be heard from the street. Renata drank coffee and Croaky milk. "He already knows a little Latin, just ask him somethin', Fräulein Renata."

A large cardboard box had been resting in the pack. Renata took it out. After the paper and excelsior had been removed, a ship appeared. It was a small three-master, the latest specimen of Renata's handicraft and a very nice piece of work. "It's for you, Croaky," she said. "I've tried it out, it floats very well and doesn't sit too low or too high in the water." While Frau Kapsreiter cautiously took over the vessel, Renata produced a wooden base in which the three-master could stand in glory on dry land.

Croaky had not yet got up the courage to touch his present. He embraced Renata and kissed her repeatedly. "I won't take it down with me," he said—meaning back home, to the Burgenland. "The other fellows would break it. I'll keep it in the next room, where I'm going to stay when I come to live with Aunt Anna when I'm in the Gymnasium. It can stand in the middle of the big chest."

"You're right, Pepi," Frau Kapsreiter said. "That makes sense."

They solemnly carried the boat to its place. Renata saw that Croaky's room had already been fitted out for him. There was a new bookcase and a new table at the window, which looked out on the side street leading to the parish church. The three-master looked very handsome on the chest.

"Do you know what 'ship' is in Latin?" Renata asked as she stood with Croaky contemplating her work.

He did in fact know, and even the words for rope, sail, and rudder.

"How do you know all that?" Renata asked, and Frau Kapsreiter too regarded the boy with astonishment.

"From Sylvia," he answered, looking up at Renata. "I'll stay here—with the boat," he added, pointing to the three-master as Renata and Frau Kapsreiter turned toward the door.

"Of course, you stay," Frau Kapsreiter said. "It's your own room, after all." There was palpable satisfaction in these last words.

Croaky, then, remained alone. It was quiet; the voices from the adjoining room could not be heard. Croaky was in the grip of a profound emotion. He fetched a chair and sat down at some distance from the chest, facing it. That way he could see the ship best. So far he had not touched it even with his finger tip. What if he did not touch it for a long time? Or never? That was a wholly new feeling. That was something he had never had before, not once. It would be a secret: never to have touched the three-master. And how beautiful it would remain: just as he had received it from Renata's hands. The shining varnish. The brilliant paints! The frail taut rigging. There—it hovered, rocked along, against the sunset glow in the window. How far this ship sailed! Croaky could sail along with it any time he pleased. It was a secret, a secret of his love for Renata. He would keep it faithfully. The ship must stand right here, just the way she had placed it. Croaky slid off the chair and went up to the chest, but with his hands held clasped behind his back. He bent his head, moved it slightly nearer the ship, until he was looking at it from the same level, his head just above the deck. Then he became smaller and smaller, and the deck grew larger and larger; it was already about thirty paces to the tiny cabin of the galley with its smoke-pipe and little door, and a much greater distance to the fore-castle; and he looked simultaneously past the two foremasts. They stood stout as trees, and under the mainsails he could see the bow. The sails filled and stretched, the rigging creaked, the blocks—how beautifully they were made, how delicately, but now each one was as large as Croaky's head—the blocks took the strain; and as the ship now sped forward with slanting deck, a small fountain of foam shot up and the spray dashed over the bowsprit.

"Stumbling brings you luck, they say," Frau Kapsreiter was relating. "I only hope it's true. I almost fell flat on my nose today. Near the restaurant on Alserbach Strasse, the one called the Flight to Egypt, they were filling some tanks in a cellar from a wagon and I didn't see the hoses in time, they had them across the sidewalk going into the cellar window, and I came within an inch of falling, what with my shopping bag. It's funny how those hoses look. Like a black snake crawling out of a hole onto the street. You know, Fräulein Renata, it'll be a good thing for Croaky when he comes here for good. There are six brothers and sisters besides him and nobody to pay much attention to the boy because both the parents have to be off working and the three older girls too. My younger brother, I always used to call him my little brother, well, even now he isn't so big, Mathias Csmarits, he's the only one out there who does anything for the boy, and he's the one who always brings him to Vienna to me. But you can't say Mathias is the right sort of company for a child like that; for instance, he'll take the boy right along to the tavern when he goes to see his friends here in Vienna. And the way those fellows talk! It's nothing for a boy of ten. Other ways, of course, I've got nothing against Mathias. Poor fellow, he lost an eye in the war. So that means he has a pension. Besides that he does a little business now and then, like he buys wine in the Burgenland for a couple of Viennese tavern keepers, and other such little deals. Does pretty well at it. Of course he used to be a railroad man, but having only one eye he couldn't go back to his old job. Now he does something for a coal firm in Neufeld, in the warehouse or something, but it's one of these jobs where you just sit. Because of losing an eye and all, he qualifies for more than the ordinary pension, which helps. And besides that he has a pass so he can ride on the railroad for practically nothing. I tell him and tell him he oughtn't to take Pepi along to the tavern, but bring him right here to me when he gets into town. But there's no use talking to Mathias. 'It doesn't bother Pepi one bit,' he said. 'He drinks his raspberry soda and has himself a good time.' Pigheaded, that's Mathias. Even when he was a kid, the other boys used to call him 'the squarehead.' He really has a square head. Like a box. Years later somebody once said about him: 'That man's a squarehead raised to a cub. . . .'"

"Cube," Renata said.

"Yes, cube. And he looks that way to this day. To top it off, he's got that funny nose, like a bent handle on the box. Or like a nail that's been hammered crooked. Since he lost his one eye, poor fellow, he often opens the other just as wide as it will go. Last summer he fixed the doorbell here, in the vestibule. There's a kind of battery or 'element' to it, attached 'way up on the ceiling, it would be up there, why I don't know, maybe somebody wanted to save wire. There's a kind of box hanging there with the works inside. At the front there's a nail that's been hammered in and bent, to make a handle so you can open the door of the box. The whole thing looks just like Mathias. The spitting image. 'Mathias,' I says when he was standing on the ladder, 'will you be so good as to take away the wires, the old ones that are hanging around there and aren't needed any more,' I says. 'What for?' he says. 'They don't do any harm, the bell will ring just as good.' 'It's not that they do harm,' I says, 'but because it looks sloppy.' What do you think, Fräulein Renata, he left every one of those wires, and even took them apart while he was working so that they stick out in all directions like hair standing on end. You must see it."

Renata followed Frau Kapsreiter into the vestibule. It really was not apparent why the box with the "element" had not been placed in some corner of the vestibule instead of being attached to the low ceiling. Several crooked ends of wire streamed away from the thing in all directions.

"Looks like a spider," Frau Kapsreiter said.

Renata too thought it quite hideous. But she said nothing. It seemed to her that Frau Kapsreiter was placing somewhat too much emphasis on this matter. A momentary concern darted like a doe from the dim thickets of her inner self, a tender and affectionate concern for Frau Kapsreiter. Perhaps it was the future physician in her that gave her this awareness of something symptomatic. At any rate, Renata was prompted to lead Frau Kapsreiter to see the matter in another light.

"You know, Frau Anna, your brother would have had to check every one of those old wires to see whether they mightn't belong to the circuit after all and have to be there. He may have thought that too much trouble."

This was not altogether convincing, as Renata well knew. But since Frau Kapsreiter possessed no extensive knowledge of matters electrical, the little supposition had a soothing effect.

When they were back in the other room, Frau Anna took a tiny lamp from the top of the big wardrobe, placed it on the table by the couch, plugged in a long cord, and switched on the light. Renata was mildly perplexed by this circumstantial procedure. But of course she said nothing. Frau Kapsreiter, however, remarked: "I don't ever use the lamp, most of the time."

Because of the milieu from which Renata came, she could scarcely grasp such trivialities as part and parcel of a style of life altogether alien to her social stratum. In homes like hers lamps remained where they were needed—because, for example, people read, and because when dusk fell they wanted without fussing to be able to switch on a light while they read. Frau Kapsreiter never read, as we have said; and she did all her writing in the morning. A lamp represented to her an object to be used when visitors came. In the world of Frau Kapsreiter the requirements for comfort and good living were of quite another sort. Thus, for example, Frau Anna had feather beds of only the finest down, and in the kitchen six frying pans of graded sizes, so that no fat would be wasted.

"By the way, Fräulein Renata, I've just remembered something I've been wanting to tell you about for ever so long. My late husband knew an engineer, a professor at the Technical here in Vienna, who tried out some new inventions for supporting houses when the ground gives under them so that you start getting cracks in the walls and such things. You fill the ground under the foundation with concrete, but under very high pressure, you really spray it in; that way the concrete is pressed or pumped into the ground and goes into the thinnest cracks. At least that's how I understood it, anyhow. Well, this professor was at a building once, a real castle it was, that they were repairing the foundation of. While the work was going on he went to the bathroom there, a regular modern flush toilet and everything. And as he was sitting there, something cold touched him from down below, and before he knew it, it was lifting him up, and he jumped off, and then he sees rising out of the bowl a long gray arm, higher and higher, three feet or thereabouts it was. The concrete they'd been forcing in had run into a broken soil pipe and gone up through it until there it was growing out of the toilet bowl like the trunk of a tree. My husband told me about it. It sure gave me the willies."

"It would give me the willies too," Renata said. She was lying curled up on the couch, her big velvety eyes fixed on Frau Kapsreiter.

"Where can that boy be?" Frau Anna said. "Oh, he's still with his pretty ship. I can't thank you enough for that, Fräulein Renata. Shall we go in and see him?"

In the dusk of his room they found Croaky sweetly asleep on the chair which he had moved up opposite the chest and the three-master.

Renata had curled up again on the couch by the lamp, Frau Kapsreiter having gone to the kitchen to prepare supper. Croaky came over briefly to thank Renata again, and to cover her hands with many little kisses. Then he returned to his room and stayed there.

The solitude Renata enjoyed during the next hour was soaked through with the omnipresent qualities of this house and its immediate vicinity. It was a boundless solitude, for all that it centered upon a narrow old street; for all that its essence was confinement and restriction, a congealing of surrounding circumstances. She had thrown herself into it like a stone, scarcely considering the nature of the surface she was sinking through, falling to the bottom of, so that all the circumstances and circumstantialities of her ordinary life danced above like corks, growing smaller and appearing farther and farther away. Any sound that penetrated into this place, this solitude—the howling chromatic scales of a receding streetcar, a voice from the street—any such sound struck her directly; it did not have first to penetrate a ring of entangling circumstances which she herself had not created; it did not have first to pass through the aura of her parental home, to submit to examination and hold its own against the polished browns of gleaming wardrobes, or the sparkle of glass-faced cupboards in which sat all sorts of china figurines—demonic companions of early childhood. Here she lay alone because she had broken through, at a self-chosen point, that omnipresent smooth and gleaming surface, which parted, quivered in spreading rings behind her, subsided again.

Incidentally, it was not Frau Kapsreiter's way to sit in Renata's room for any length of time. Today she had been unusually loquacious. Her talk in any case was scarcely communication, scarcely addressed to anyone in particular. She simply thought aloud, or rather half aloud. She opened a drawer and let what was going on inside her be seen. Renata liked to look in. You saw no principles, no demands, no moral missiles, no dogmas or lessons. You looked into sweeping independence that depended on nothing, was sustained by no one. Though the substance of what Renata heard might be simple-minded or even banal, she felt every time as if some lower window of life were opening into greater depths; above life floated or rocked like a Noah's Ark; and when Frau Anna spoke, Renata looked down and out through the belly of the ship. Why Frau Anna affected Renata this way remains incomprehensible. At any rate, Renata responded with an affection that came from her inmost being. And when she compared Frau Kapsreiter with the other persons of her small circle of acquaintance, the woman seemed to her far and away more intelligent than any of the others, without exception.

Be that as it may, a few days spent in "The Blue Sheep" meant for Renata an inpouring of strength, an airing and relaxation from the tightness of her home. It seemed to give her a kind of protective moat which parted her somewhat from everything and therefore, oddly enough, conferred upon her a readiness to enter benevolently into everything. After a stay with Frau Kapsreiter it was easy for her to recognize, say, her parents' virtues; or perhaps we should say: to overlook those virtues. This was especially beneficial in her relationship with her father. The glow which had entered through the "lower window" each time left a lingering golden track that showed in her behavior. (Hence it was that Herr von Gürtzner-Gontard in the course of time came around to favoring such "camping trips.")

Now and then Renata would drop in on Frau Anna for shorter visits, partly when she felt she had to, partly when she took over the tutoring of Croaky, for Sylvia sometimes could not take care of all her pupils. When Renata was his teacher, Croaky learned still more nautical expressions in the language of the Romans, as well as the Latin words for bow, bowstring, arrow, arrow-feathers. At Christmas, Renata's handsome set of bow and arrows lay under Frau Kapsreiter's Christmas tree, and soon adorned Croaky's little room, hanging on the wall above the three-master and giving the boy's quarters an aura of the exotic and faraway.

On February 6, 1927, shortly after dinner, the telephone rang just as Renata was passing through the vestibule of her parents' apartment. She had the feeling that she had just been stopped and addressed, so certain was she that this ringing was directed at her, although she was not expecting anyone to telephone.

Sylvia was on the phone. "Come down quickly and wait for me in front of the house; I'll be along in five minutes. We must go to Kaps. I'll tell you the rest when I see you."

The girls always referred to Frau Kapsreiter simply as Kaps.

It was a gray Sunday, and not cold; scattered persons were strolling along, most of them slowly; perhaps some reasonably pleasant destinations awaited them. There was Sylvia already crossing the square. She had a more pinched look than usual.

The girls started walking.

"Croaky is dead," Sylvia said.

Renata did not answer. But her hearing had suddenly become sensitive, and the meager street noises sounded twice as loud.

"Last Sunday in Schattendorf there was some shooting between the Socialists and the 'Veterans.' Someone fired from a tavern on the Reds, who were marching in the street. Several people were wounded and two killed: Croaky and his uncle, the war veteran with one eye. Nobody has any idea what the boy was doing there. Kaps hasn't been able to find out. She went down on Wednesday, to the funeral. Croaky was hit by seven pieces of shot—big coarse shot—and his uncle by even more. They were both killed instantly. The shots came from close up; the street isn't very wide there. Of course no one was aiming at the two of them, but at the Socialists. Or maybe the shots were only intended to frighten. They say that the tavern keeper, Tscharmann, and his son and son-in-law were the ones who did the shooting. His tavern was the regular hangout for the 'Veterans.' The Reds came marching along from another tavern where they always meet; I understand there were about a hundred and fifty of them. Probably the Tscharmanns were frightened. Not that any of that matters. Croaky is dead."

"And how is Kaps?" Renata asked at last. She spoke only with her mouth, with the very skin of her lips, because it was impossible to keep silent any longer. The wall of facts that had suddenly shot up here out of nothingness found Renata not only perplexed but also constricted and guilty—because she had no idea what to do with these facts. Too young for the realization that every descending avalanche of facts always represents the end of a long earlier process, Renata felt turned to stone. For some seconds she doubted her capacity for normal feeling, for confrontation with life. She could not put the matter in its simplest form: that there no longer was anything to be done with it because the process had now wound itself to its end.

"Kaps," Sylvia replied, "is simply grand, and somehow mysterious, just the way she always is. You'd think she might be crying or taking on, but not a bit of it. She said to me: 'Fräulein Sylvia, the bottom's dropped out on me. I'm ringing and humming like a bell after it's been struck. Once that stops it's really going to hurt.' She's angry as she can be at her dead brother, Csmarits. But of course she suppresses that. *De mortuis nil nisi bonum.* Only every so often she comes back to the fact that Mathias always took the boy with him everywhere, no matter what she might say."

They walked on down Alserbach Strasse. Here as everywhere in the streets of metropolises, the fine dust of thousandfold pasts hovered over places beset by thousands of memories; the ghosts of sorrow and joy appeared in broad daylight out of the semi-darkness of entrances, emerged onto the street, and perfumed an already disintegrated present with the scent of autumn leaves, as if it were not February but late October. Life's terrible bulk came close up against the two girls' young bodies, and Renata felt how the remaining space was swiftly narrowing. Soon she would be tightly enclosed.

Upon the blue unicorn up on the corner of the house lay a wintry afternoon light, a characterless light which spread grayly everywhere here, incapable of brightening to any kind of glow.

But they found Kaps in command of the situation. She put her arms about each of the girls. "Stick by me for a little, children," she said. "You'll come and see old Kapsreiter now and then? She built herself a castle in Spain, and now it's fallen down. She oughtn't never to have done it. Come, let's go up to his room. And the ship and arrows, they can stay there for a while, can't they, Fräulein Renata?"

Renata was incapable of answering. They stood in front of Croaky's chest.

The tragedy led to more frequent contact between the girls and Kaps, and by the spring Renata already felt as if she were settled in this quarter of the city. They would go over to see Kaps in the evening, just about when dusk was falling. The small lamp became a more frequently used object; it was no longer stowed away on top of the big wardrobe. Renata and Sylvia both noted that Kaps was not given to repeating the usual clichés about what had come tumbling down on her. Altogether, she was not given to repetition at all, except for those reproaches against her brother for having taken the boy about everywhere with him. But by and by even these ceased. Only now and then she would say something about herself being like a bell, or would return to the idea of "the bottom's dropped out."

However, the whole picture was enough to make the girls anxious. "Most of all, you mustn't let yourself kind of petrify," Frau Kapsreiter had once observed, in the spring. But that was just what Renata thought was happening to Kaps. The world was hardening around the woman; she herself was acquiring grandeur but losing flexibility. It would have been much better if Kaps had poured out endless and repetitious laments. Her self-control had something alarming about it.

Renata and Sylvia grew accustomed to roaming around the neighborhood—along the narrow part of Liechtenstein Strasse and to Liechtenwerder Platz, which until now had remained unknown to them. The square is situated by the high viaduct of the suburban railroad that girdles the city. From the little square, as far as the eye can see, the view extends over railroad properties; everything is striped by tracks; farther out, the red-brown freight cars look very tiny as they line up alongside the loading platforms; there are mounds of coal, swaths of drifting smoke, puffballs of steam. In the square itself stand three small green trees; but thereafter the whole landscape is man-made; although there are a few trees even there, you scarcely notice them; they make no impression. Everything is a drift of smoke; only the fresh steam being puffed out here and there holds its shape for a moment, a white spot amid the gray and black. Liechtenwerder Platz lies raised above the freight terminal, commanding the view like a kind of balcony. You look down into an exposed nether world; scarcely ever is a human being visible in it.

The girls became acquainted, accustomed; the neighborhood captured them; they went there not only because they were visiting Frau Kapsreiter. For a few weeks and months these straight or winding avenues and streets, these high and new or tiny and ancient houses exerted an independent power over their lives: hunting-grounds that surrounded them with a density as great as woods and bottomland meadows. Though they did not know what the object of the hunt was. They had no aim, no purpose in this part of town. For Sylvia and Renata, these streets were more like a bit of countryside than a quarter of the city. Perhaps the chaotic intermingling of new and old, large and small, straight and crooked, wide and narrow, corresponded profoundly with the true state of mind of youth in those days.

With Renata you were never safe from sudden whims and startling leaps. Thus one day she suddenly decided that she had to have a drink—perhaps it was the first in her life and at any rate remained the last for a long time to come. She decided this in front of Freud's brandy shop ("Tea, Rum, Liquors"). If this experiment had to be made, it should undoubtedly have been undertaken in a respectable café, of which there were two nearby. But no, it had to be Freud's.

A well-meaning gentleman thought it wise to intervene and warn the two adolescent girls off when he saw them on the point of entering the brandy shop. He had a large, well-groomed face with blue eyes that in their depths held a pining, childlike expression; wore a dazzlingly white collar with wide four-in-hand, a light-colored overcoat and light-colored gloves, and sharply creased trousers that broke exactly upon the tops of his shoes. The shoes themselves were of a broad diagonal shape unusual for the period. Altogether, his dress gave the impression of being somewhat behind the fashion, but thoroughly substantial.

"I beg your pardon," he said, "but it wouldn't be right for young ladies to go into a place like this."

His patronizing air was too make-believe for the two girls to feel its force and take offense. Moreover, his accent was not that of a Viennese, but somehow foreign, and that fact accentuated his ironic tone doubly. And underlying his warm bass was the same good nature that seemed to lie hidden in his eyes.

Sylvia, who wasn't happy at the prospect of entering the brandy shop, hesitated readily enough. But Renata was checked only for the time it took her to say: "You ought to be a governess." Then she had the door open.

It was a door with milk-glass panes, the lower part protected by a dozen or so brass rods set at a diagonal. Such doors were then also in use at railroad stations and post offices.

"Then I shall have to go along with you, inconvenient as that is for me at the moment." He spoke the last half of this sentence as if to himself.

The almost obligatory reply, "No one's making you," was not spoken. The language of these adolescents had not yet become that barbarous jangle so universal nowadays. As for the stranger's last remark, it rang completely genuine—thus emphasizing the falseness of the way he had addressed them before. He appeared enormously put out at the task of guarding these awkward girls whom chance had sent across his path.

Incidentally, he seemed to place both of them accurately as far as family and class were concerned; his manner was perfectly in keeping with all of that.

The room which Renata entered first had the length and shallowness and the general air of inhospitability of a public booking-office; likewise the smell of an oiled floor. Contrasting with the oiliness, but equally numbing in quality, was the odor of alcohol. The gray, zinc-topped counter ran across the back instead of the side of the place. There were only a few tables and chairs. At first the girls saw no one; the room seemed empty. Then a young woman with a big snow-white apron emerged from behind the counter.

Out of the corners of their eyes the girls now caught sight of someone sitting at the farthest end of the room. The officious gentlemen who had entered with them seemed slightly perplexed; he merely stood and made no suggestion about sitting down. He said nothing at all. Of their own accord the girls took seats at one of the small specked tables, and their companion did likewise, but without removing his overcoat. The waitress had meanwhile come up to them.

Renata asked what kind of brandy she had.

"Treberner, Jeržebinka, Stanislauer, Slivovitz . . ." she reeled off.

"But my dear young ladies," the officious gentleman murmured, "you aren't really going to start drinking brandy in this place! Order tea with rum if you must have something."

The young ladies vouchsafed no answer. Three glasses of

Stanislauer—a regular firewater—appeared; one of them was placed in front of him.

The girls sipped the brandy.

The gentleman sniffed it and did not drink.

Didi, the bar girl, had stepped away. But she did not go behind her counter again; she remained standing a few paces off, frankly studying the three.

It was the big, stainlessly white apron that somehow brought out and made visible a kind of dirtiness about her. In herself Anna Diwald, otherwise known as Didi, was an attractive buxom woman of about twenty-seven with thick dark hair, round face, and greenish eyes. Her eyes could flash with sudden fury, and then the eyeballs would roll dangerously in the child's fat of her face, which seemed to have developed little beyond the baby stage. . . . Incidentally, her eyelids were cut somewhat on a slant; there was a kind of Mongolian fold to them. But this could be seen only when her face remained calm, when her eyes did not flash with anger and roll in their sockets.

It must have been the blinding white apron that made Didi's face appear gray and sallow. Her skin had a palpable kinship with the walls of the place; walls into which the smell of fusel oil must have sunk six inches or more in the forty years that old Freud had been occupying these premises. And rumor had it that even before his time a brandy shop had been located here. In Didi's case you had the feeling that no amount of washing would do any good; that the dirt lay not on or in the skin but under it. And even if Freud's brandy shop had been cleared out, and the walls scraped, plastered, freshly painted, ventilated, and dried for many days, and the whole place put to quite different use—the greasy essence of it could still not have been expelled. It was established back of the walls, as it was under Didi's skin. Not to speak of the back room which Didi inhabited together with the old man.

Such premises as these were analogous to the dwellings of Viennese concierges, to which the malignant, obstinate exhalations of the race inhabiting them clung diabolically, never again to be expelled—not by disinfection or plastering, not by torrents of hot soapsuds; the effluvia of a terrifying attitude toward life lingered on, whether in the walls, in the air, or if you will in some wholly immaterial realm, in the shape of a genius loci degenerated into a ghost and condemned to haunt the place forever. For that very reason such caves are always preserved for their original purpose, and anyone in Vienna would refuse with horror to move into a concierge's apartment, unless he himself were a member of the race or descended from it.

In the rear of the brandy shop was a room and a small kitchen; both, however, were also used to store supplies for the business: huge-bellied demijohns, their lower portions protected by wicker, which contained the alcohol which could be transformed, by the aid of so-called "flavors," into any desired beverage: into rum that had nothing in common with sugar cane, into slivovitz that had never been in contact with plums, and so on—the resultant products actually tasted a little like what they were imitating. Everywhere about stood sticky funnels and empty or half-empty vessels for mixing. It was a regular laboratory, though entirely lacking in order or cleanliness. Freud's suspenders and a pair of slippers were lying on a workbench which also held a vise and innumerable bottles, each of which left a dark ring on the wood when it was lifted. Here on the workbench, its handle held tightly in the jaws of the vise, hung Didi's large locked leather bag in which she kept all her documents, pictures, letters, and savings; in this way she had this precious object in one fixed place, where it could instantly be seen by her. She carried the key around her neck, and never left the house without the bag.

In the middle of the room was an electric light, a kind of chandelier in *art nouveau* style, which came from a former apartment of the old man; apparently he had once seen better days. That seemed to be indicated, too, by his occasional babble. Freud was a good old Hebrew, and not without devoutness. But senility was more and more overtaking him. Sharing the living quarters with the young woman, who behaved in an untrammeled manner in his presence, he experienced an occasional flickering of the lamp; but there was no longer any oil to nourish it. Didi took this matter entirely from the comic side. She would have had no qualms at granting him his will. But since he was no longer able to have any such will, she did what she could for him, and helped him to such small pleasures as still lay in his capacity. Incidentally, we must not conceive of all this as so terribly serious and sinister; the two did not know, after all, how miserable and unappetizing they were.

Didi stood there frankly studying the guests. With drooping nose and the silly expression of an offended female, the gentleman was looking down at the table. Renata was casting a cool look into the air, and Sylvia was watching Renata. During this tableau, about as lively as a scene in a waxworks museum, something stirred in a kind of cave formed by the end of the counter and a protruding wide shelf on which glasses were arranged. Now the thing crept forth and lithely stirred its limbs, moving so noiselessly that neither Didi nor the three at the table noticed its approach. It was Meisgeier, alias the Claw.

This creature could not have weighed much more than a hundred pounds. The creeping mode of locomotion seemed entirely appropriate to it. Indeed, it gave the impression of being quite well organized, although on a low level in the hierarchy of living beings. Thus, for example, there was nothing superfluous about the face, nothing of softness or spongy deception to obscure the structure of this physiognomy. Here everything was economically trimmed down. Nothing not absolutely essential to the function of crime softened the sharp edge of this face—which consisted chiefly of an enormous beaklike nose toward which the chin below grew up. The eyes, however, belonged to a higher order of life than the rest of the organism. The eyes were relatively overorganized, very light in color, very wide in the center and narrowing rapidly to damp slits. These eyes were terrible. They transformed the primitive creature into a kind of diabolic thing.

The Claw now slithered past Didi, who started—it was as if he had floated noiselessly through the air. Now a long arm swung forward, pointing at the seated gentleman, and the creature said in a language and pronunciation that contained surprising echoes of cultivated speech: "You were in Schattendorf on January 30. You sent the Reds to the station; you told them that Lieutenant-colonel Hiltl was expected there. You were in the Moser Tavern."

The gentleman looked up. He displayed remarkable composure toward this phenomenon that had suddenly appeared out of nowhere. His composure was probably genuine. Nevertheless, the cool and formal tone had something bogus about it, just as there had been something bogus about the way he had addressed the girls in front of the brandy shop.

"What do you want of me?" he said.

"Not a thing, not a thing. Don't play dumb. I know you."

Didi did not intervene. Of course she wanted peace in the tavern; she did not like people being molested. But at the same time she was curious to see how the fellow was going to take this. In any case, she could scarcely have come between the two men in time, now that Meisgeier had already slithered past her. He approached closer and closer to the man at the table. Sylvia's eyes were wide with alarm. Renata had half turned in her seat. She looked on bravely.

"Go away and don't bother me," the gentleman said quietly to Meisgeier. He remained in his seat. It must have been this which made the Claw pause at a distance of not quite six feet from the table, although he would have done better to attack at once, before his opponent had time to stand up. But the unconcerned manner in which the man sat at the table, and hardly turned to face him as he spoke, held the attacker off for a few seconds.

"Shut your trap, you dirty bastard," Meisgeier said then and leaped forward. Sylvia screamed. The gentleman, who had risen to his feet as lithely as a rebounding rubber ball, watched Meisgeier's left hand, not his right fist which was feinting an uppercut. Thus, he caught a glimpse of the tip of the knife which protruded no more than an inch between the thumb and forefinger of the little fellow's left hand. In one of those moments which are truly marked by inspiration, which cannot be practiced, which one may

never have attained before and will never understand afterwards—in one of those fractions of a second that come out of the
deepest nexus of our lives, that produce an almost incredible co-
ordination of senses with muscles—the gentleman in the light
coat landed a straight blow with all his weight behind it upon the
Claw's solar plexus. The feinted uppercut was diverted, the
knife aimed against the stomach missed its mark (later, incidentally, the light overcoat showed a rip). Meisgeier, with his
mere hundred pounds, flew back, stumbled back even past Didi.
But now the toughness of this creature was revealed. A straight
blow to the solar plexus, especially without gloves, can bring a
strong man to the ground. But not Meisgeier. He stumbled,
was almost knocked off his feet. But he struggled successfully to
keep his balance; leaning forward, he gasped for air, and was already gathering himself for a new assault, his wide colorless eyes
fixed on his opponent. The little man was a real fighter who did
not give up. The knife had not even slipped from his grasp. The
man in the light coat recognized all this at once, and likewise
realized that the little runt was undoubtedly superior to him in
rough-and-tumble fighting. For that reason he immediately
sprang forward toward Meisgeier, intending to knock him quickly
to the ground with an uppercut before he could recover. But
now Didi stepped forward and blocked his way. The gentleman
stopped. He did not press on past her. He had not been acting
out of anger but out of the instantaneous and clear conviction—it
too could be called inspiration—that the way to save himself was
to rush upon Meisgeier. And now he was blocked by Didi. Behind
her, the Claw had caught his breath again. Didi turned un-
hurriedly toward him, raised her arm slowly, and pointed to the
corner, the cave from which the creature had emerged.

"Back," she said curtly. "I don't want the cops here. Back, or
you'll find yourself in the clink for five years."

Slowly, Meisgeier retreated to his cave.

"You pay and get out," Didi said tersely to the gentleman in
the light overcoat, regarding him not without respect.

So they came out of it safely and onto the street again. The gentleman, however, seemed to have derived little satisfaction from this affair—which, after all, he had handled very well indeed in the presence of two young ladies. This failure to congratulate himself did not suit him at all; and Renata's acute sensibility told her so. Something was wrong with him; something was bothering him; and yet it could not be the adventure they had just passed through. Perhaps he knew that horrible creature in there better than he had let on. Such were the thoughts that passed through Renata's taut young brain, which still possessed the only real and effective intelligence there is: that of youth, as fragrant with thought as a fresh apple that has never yet been gnawed by a worm.

The unknown gentleman's face now looked very large and gray; its surface seemed strained by the effort to cover some mysterious despair. At last he said: "Now, you see, young ladies; I said that wasn't the sort of place for you."

"If you had let us go in by ourselves, nothing might have happened," Renata replied. She was deliberately provoking him, out of a kind of scientific interest.

But he seemed really depressed, for he did not trouble to pluck out this arrow, and merely said: "You may be right about that, Fräulein. However, I'm in a bit of a hurry and I must ask you ladies to excuse me."

He shook hands with Renata and Sylvia, lifting his gray hat as he did so; he replaced the hat straight and precisely centered, and took his leave. The girls watched him for several moments. Both realized that his gait—but this was only now; they had not before seen him walking—was by no means that of a limber and athletic person, although he had amply proved himself to be one. Nor was there anything elegant about it. Rather, he had the carriage of an old and rather clumsy man who plods along with bowed head.

IMRE VON GYURKICZ walked along Liechtenstein Strasse in the direction of Heiligenstadt. He walked awkwardly, with almost dragging footsteps. His shoe kicked against a bump in the granite pavement, and a few steps farther on he almost stumbled, but this time without any external cause; he had merely placed his foot clumsily, as if he were about to descend a step, and the sole of his shoe slapped hard against the pavement. The inspiration, that miraculous co-ordination, had departed from his limbs. Imre was not twenty-six. He was old and awkward, old and unhappy; far, far older than he liked to admit to himself.

When you listened to his stories of the war—Imre's favorite subject, we may remember—you could only gather that he had very quickly risen to the rank of officer. It so happened that Höpfner, the writer of advertising verse, and at that time in charge of the advertising department of a large transport firm, had commissioned a series of posters from Imre. In connection with the contract, Höpfner needed to have Imre's personal papers. After everything was arranged, Höpfner returned the documents to Imre and remarked with a casual laugh: "Enlisted at twelve and lieutenant at fourteen—my congratulations, Imre!"

Gyurkicz made no direct reply to this and merely murmured something like: "You don't understand this matter, my friend, and the whole thing is too complicated to explain." But since Höpfner did not dwell on the subject, it was quickly passed over. As for Höpfner, his almost unlimited liberality sprang from his being himself a man without a center. Tolerance came easy to him; profound sympathies or antipathies were alien to him. After all, he had nothing he could refer things to, and therefore took them as they were. This is probably the ideal state of mind for a publicity man. A person who is constantly endeavoring to arouse specific impressions in others would only be hampered if he tried to express something of his own. All propaganda is characterized by venality; it is addressed always to the mass, never to the individual; and its means are always adapted to the crowd. Thus Höpfner took Gyurkicz as he was, with the utmost casualness. At the same time he liked the Hungarian and was on friendly terms with him. Just by the by he had not overlooked the fact—how could he?—that Imre's papers were not made out in the name of Gyurkicz at all, but in the name of his supposed stepfather, who bore the altogether different name of Friedmann. But Höpfner let even that pass. Imre had volunteered some kind of complicated explanation of the business. It seemed these papers had been given him when he entered the Red Guard in Budapest on orders from the later regent, Horthy, when the latter was still living in Rumania. After the suppression of Béla Kun's regime he had been sent abroad with the same papers as an agent for "Awakening Hungary." After a while this secret-service work had rather soured on him. He'd indicated that he wanted to get out of it. This had not pleased his bosses. As a result, Lieutenant Imre von Gyurkicz had simply been dropped and had never been able to recoup his genuine papers. . . .

However that may have been, Höpfner took it all with the greatest of casualness. He was the only one of "our crowd" who reacted properly to Imre. Thus, he let the matter be, added nothing to its inherently low specific gravity—which was its outstanding quality. For there was little gravity about Imre's life; he took things easy—although perhaps he was not taking things so easy at the moment, after stumbling for the second time on the narrow part of Liechtenstein Strasse.

We are more upset by such slips than we know. As he steadied himself, Imre suddenly remembered that casual remark of

Höpfner's about his military service between the ages of twelve and fourteen. And though that remark had glanced off him at the time, it now struck him keenly when he was walking along by himself.

It struck him hard because he was moving along now in a figurative sense as well, and in a figurative sense too had changed his residence—just as in a literal sense he had moved from the Second to the Nineteenth District of Vienna. For he had really wanted to accomplish the move "over the hill" and not merely over that height called the Hohe Warte. Prater Strasse, where he had last lived with his mistress—who had passed for his wife— was somehow far closer to his Budapest past. That was true of the whole Prater area. You were, after all, that much nearer the Danube down there. The level bottomland flowed along with the flowing river, and as it were carried him along with it. Everything in that district had reference to these moving masses of water, which in their turn swept him back to those turbulent days in Budapest, when he had proudly stalked along Andrássy Street, dressed in more or less fantastic uniforms, in the company of other masters of the situation of those days. Of course, under Béla Kun the street had been called by another name— not Andrássy Street.

At this moment, then, Höpfner's remark came back to Imre von Gyurkicz and struck him as extraordinarily tactless and offensive. It burned like acid dropped upon the skin. "After all, I'm not a swindler; I make my way by honest work. Everyone commits youthful follies. As for my family, there really is noble blood there. The old man cannot possibly be my father. You only have to look at him to see that. Mother has been hiding the truth from me—it's only human. There are plenty of other people whose papers don't tell the truth about them."

So he thought as he walked along. It was more or less what he would say in his own defense to someone else—to Höpfner, for example—if the point should ever come up again. Perhaps he would once again fish out the story about the way he had lost his real documents. His private thoughts, then, did not differ from arguments he might have advanced or had already advanced; other people were present during the process of his thinking; it took place before witnesses, so to speak. Imre himself plumbed no deeper. Paul Valéry says there is nothing cheaper and more vulgar than to use in inner dialogues arguments that one would employ toward others. That was what Imre von Gyurkicz was doing.

But such thinking brought him no comfort. It did not create a center to which he might have retreated from the pressure on all sides, as pedestrians can flee to a "safety island" on a wide, heavily trafficked street. In large cities such as Paris or Vienna these islands are generally built around a lamp post. But there was no such haven for Imre. In the sea of troubles momentarily engulfing him there was no lighthouse, no saving beacon.

On the contrary, without benefit of any beacon light he could plainly discern the new waves that were bearing down upon him. Quite recently he had been invited to dinner on Johann Strauss Gasse together with the editor Holder and the "poetess" Rosi Malik—whose impudent, pug-nosed face gave him a pain, but it had to be put up with; she was a necessary appurtenance. Levielle sometimes extended himself socially to "talented youth" —as we know from the case of Doktor Neuberg. And there a wholly casual question on the part of the financial counselor had caught the "gifted young newspaper cartoonist" altogether unprepared. "You're living out in Döbling in a kind of artist's colony, aren't you?" Levielle had introduced the subject. "I mean, in that kind of set . . ." And then came a question about certain members of the "set," which had evoked from Imre an innocent, not to say brutishly stupid reply. He had said something like: "Yes, yes, Captain Eulenfeld and Schlaggenberg, nice fellows, awfully original." He had fancied that his tongue was on the right track, for hadn't he heard somewhere that Kajetan was quite in Levielle's good graces these days? Besides, he rather liked Quapp's brother, although he was bothered by the whole idea of "our crowd." All in all, he'd said what he'd thought was wanted. He had no sooner uttered the words, however, than Holder's and Rosi's expressions told him that he'd committed a blunder. A restrained, cool, or skeptical remark would have been more to the point. "You see a good deal of those people?" Levielle said, but the question was plainly rhetorical; no answer was expected, no correction possible. The financial counselor let the unwelcome answer rebound from his impenetrable surface. He was no longer listening to Imre; he was asking the "poetess" about the size of the royalties from her play *Captain Dash*, which was about to be produced.

Something else had happened around the same time—Gyurkicz was at the moment too fagged out to determine when exactly the thing had begun. The mere effort to remember the approximate date, in fact, drove him wild. At any rate, it had been several weeks after he moved to Döbling.

For the longest time Imre had been doing the title-page drawing for a satirical weekly published by the Alliance firm. His reputation as a cartoonist was largely based on the fact that he always did the lead cartoon for this highly popular humor magazine. It was so much taken for granted that he would do the drawing that Imre used to sit in on the editorial conferences. Now it had happened at one of the editorial conferences, just as Imre was about to explain his idea for the latest drawing, that a former "larva" broke in—to add insult to injury, the one with the goatee who, the reader may still recall, had succeeded after years of effort in boring his way into the nutritive jelly. This larva now turned to the editor and reminded him that young Weilguny was to do the title page this time. Thus Imre was informed of the name of the unknown youth who sat in at the meeting, who had appeared that day for the first time but had not introduced himself to Imre. Herr Weilguny then took the floor and made his proposals.

During the following weeks other cartoonists turned up; and henceforth Imre drew only every second or third title page. Or else the drawings he delivered were simply shifted to the inside of the issue and another cartoonist's work appeared on the title page. Imre could not very well object. Variety was essential.

The editor-in-chief overflowed with amiability toward Imre, and asked him his opinion of the young, up-and-coming talents who had to be "given space," and wasn't it right and proper to do this. Imre vigorously affirmed that it was. He had once seen Weilguny on the stairs with Levielle just as the latter came out of Wangstein and Oplatek's offices. (Incidentally, the financial counselor was never seen in the editorial rooms of the newspapers themselves. He called only at the offices of the management—and that very rarely.)

All this, to be sure, was as yet nothing very tangible or distinct, for Imre received the same payment for his drawings whether they appeared on the title page or further back in the magazine. What was really worrisome was Herr Weilguny's behavior, for he continued to regard it as unnecessary to introduce himself to Gyurkicz. Weilguny by no means appeared at every editorial conference. On the other hand, his drawings began to appear more frequently in other of the firm's publications.

Almost simultaneously, a few of the drawings that Imre sent to these others—for he did not work only for the satiric weekly— remained unused for a considerable time. And finally an issue of the humorous weekly came out which did not contain a single contribution of Imre's, neither large nor small.

Things had clearly reached an alarming point.

Imre's income had also taken a drop.

This was why Imre had been attempting, of late, to get out of journalism. Hence the business with the posters for Höpfner's transport company, and hence it had come about that Höpfner had seen Imre's papers and made the remark which struck Imre hard only many weeks later: right now as he walked on Liechtenstein Strasse.

Darkness had meanwhile fallen. The gas lamps were burning. Imre had come to a standstill. Very well, there was this contact through Höpfner. He had delivered some posters and was going to deliver more. He went to a great deal of trouble over these sketches; the people were satisfied with them and paid what had been agreed on. But by itself that was pretty small pickings.

926 / THE DEMONS

And no further prospects offered. Imre was known as a news-paper draftsman, not as a "commercial artist." Strong pressures tended to throw him back upon Alliance.

And yet he had left Prater Strasse down there, and his former mistress Anita, and a good many of his old associates, and had been stirred by rather profound hopes, when he teamed up with Quapp. He regarded her as a young lady of good (once great) family, as was her brother, whom he esteemed on these grounds, not on any literary ones. It was as though a rope were being thrown to him, as if he were being pulled aboard. And at first he felt all right among this crew. But after a while he noticed that the vessel was steering a different course from the one he had expected, even though a Herr von Eulenfeld and a Herr René von Stangeler were along. All well and good, this young man's Bolshevistic utterances didn't bother Imre much. Let the young man shoot his mouth off. But when, by and by, he found himself sitting in a boat with Quapp—his "Lo"—and pushing off from "our crowd's" big ship, he discovered that she was imposing a course he had really not intended to take.

For there was in him an honest desire for solidity and order (he said this now, in argument with himself). He was no swindler, and when he boasted that he made his way by honest work it was true. He really wanted to be an Imre Gyurkicz de Faddy and Hátfaludy. Therein lay the real secret of his existence. He wanted to be thoroughly proper, honorable, spruce, modestly distinguished. And—damn it all!—wasn't he like that, and hadn't he been like that for a long time! Sometimes he went too far in his quest for solidity. In order to keep in touch with the latest thing in fashion design—for this was a rich field for Imre—he sat down twice a week in a decent café and, spectacles on his nose, studied all the current fashion journals and a large pile of illustrated magazines. His note pad lay ready to hand. He worked hard and fast, timing himself. At a certain exact hour and minute he had to be back in his studio; by nine o'clock in the evening he had to have finished a drawing for the satiric weekly.

What more could you ask of a man?

He woke early in the morning.

Only Lo took up a great deal of time. Her endless explanations; her fantastic unpunctuality.

The place he lived in now was not really a proper studio. Not like his studio on Prater Strasse, with its huge skylight. Much as Imre had longed to go "over the hill," he now sometimes felt a kind of nostalgia for his old place, an easier world where people did not probe, demanded no proofs, recognized no real goals and therefore could not be aware of obstacles. Anita and he had long since gone their own ways in every respect, without interfering with each other, indeed without observing what the other one was about. His earnings had been more than ample for himself, and Anita likewise made her own money; she did various things on the periphery of the arts, an area where feminine sloth settles so happily and so becomingly. Such dabblings always pay better than work at the center does. Anita and her ilk, therefore, did some sculpting, did some drawing, did some writing or peddling of the writings of others with marginal notes of their own; above all, they did some dancing, taught gymnastics and eurhythmics, produced choreographies and figurines. In short, they were artistic. Those of them who enjoyed special protection were "active in welfare work" (it began in those days) and had remunerative positions taking care of somebody or something. Anita, for her part, taught gymnastics, danced (she had done one dance based on Johann Sebastian Bach's sonatas for unaccompanied violin); she also dashed off some fine specimens of pornoplastic art.

Since leaving all that, Imre no longer had a proper studio to work in but a garden room in a narrow two-story house that sat back from the street behind a small lawn. Imre's room, however, did not look out on the street. One whole side of it was window, against which the green of treetops pressed. It was an intensely cloistered room, dominated by a dense crystalline stillness, and green as an aquarium because of the light filtering through the trees. Imre had somehow managed to give the place a studio look. Thus the simple blue garden furniture was so arranged as to contribute to that effect. Water colors had been tacked lightly to the blue wardrobe. Other pictures, framed and of a moderately modern character, adorned the ocher-yellow walls. On a smoking table, likewise of softwood painted blue, various objects lay on casual display: three English pipes; a string of amber; a violet-silk tassel. The arrangement was random but quite pretty. By the window stood a wide blue garden table which Imre used for his worktable. Implements for drawing and painting were placed to the left and right; the center was clear and reserved for his drawing-board. A further supply of brushes and crayons lay on a stool to the left of the table. There was no trace of uncleanliness here: no dust, no caked pigments, no splashed paint. A polished, heavy brass ash tray in the shape of a wide shallow bowl stood on the table; but it seemed never to have contained any cigarette debris. A skull sat on a wall bracket. It had a cigarette between its few remaining teeth and wore a steel helmet. From this bracket dangled several wooden-headed dolls which Imre had carved; the faces were pronouncedly criminal types—one of them looked much like the Claw. They were dressed as convicts and had large numbers across their chests. The strings from which they hung were coiled around their necks. Tossed over a strong hook in the wall was a military belt, complete with handsome map case, and bayonet.

These, then, were the personal touches Imre gave to his room. They gave the place a curious character. The light furniture, the casual manner in which things were distributed here and there, gave it the look of an unstable headquarters; and that impression was underscored by the belt; it hung there as though at any moment there might be an alarm and orders to march. As for the skull, Imre had carelessly circulated two quite different stories about it. One story was that he had appropriated it from the anatomy class, back in his art-student days in Budapest. The other was that the skull went together with the belt, map case, and bayonet, and was the earthly remains of a war buddy, his best friend in fact, a lieutenant who died in action. But neither belt nor bayonet was of the officer type (as Eulenfeld once noted

when visiting Imre, for the captain had intimate knowledge of Austrian as well as German equipment).

The chances are that Imre von Gyurkicz believed both stories, sometimes one and sometimes the other.

Since, as we have seen, he possessed no real inner life, since others were always present at his interior colloquies, things of the outside world did not rest firmly upon their bases for him, nor did facts stay inexorably in their places. Rather, the outside world became a question of arrangement. Since he was incapable of changing himself, never made the least attempt to do so, or even wanted to (he never felt a feeling of dullness or depression after spinning one of his little tales), all his efforts went to altering the insignia. That, not any significant metamorphosis, was what Imre considered to be change within himself. Emblems had enormous power over him. He was, we might say, a believer in primitive magic.

Emblems were, in fact, his passion. He had a seal ring, which he had had made for himself—with the arms of the lords of Faddy (and Hátfaludy) engraved on the broad gold surface: an arm brandishing a scimitar. Yet Imre was really no swindler, no clever charlatan who knew out of his own venality that swindles can be put over best with the cheapest, simplest of popular devices. Had he been, he would have equipped himself promptly with the necessary stage props: title of count, monocle, borrowed automobile. Perhaps Imre would have pulled such tricks had the opportunity arisen. But in truth he was too infatuated with his emblems; he did not use them as tools for advancement but merged with them. And merged also with all the stories that he loved to tell: they were building-blocks of a world he wanted to enter, of a personality he wanted to become. Since no real inner life provided him with perspective on the outward facts of his past, he could not really absorb these facts into himself. Facts are not convincing in themselves; they must be taken in, grasped in the round. And that requires at least a degree of perspective. Gyurkicz had no perspective whatsoever on his "emblems." The skull, for example, was that of his best friend, was that of a

criminal, or had come to him via a girl medical student with whom he had once had an affair back in Budapest. Again it was Höpfner, as luck would have it, who had unearthed this whole story by chance on a visit to Budapest—and had never mentioned it to Gyurkicz. But even had he done so, the other two versions would nevertheless have retained a greater vividness in Imre's mind. He lacked not only perspective but the organs to grasp facts in the world of the actual; he was incapable of driving any kind of wedge between fiction and fact. Nor did he care to try. Rather, the emblem-economy of his interior self—insofar as he had one—required precisely the opposite: required fluid boundaries between what really was and what should have been.

To sum up the matter: Imre had no memory. Or he had only the kind of memory women have, who in hindsight misrepresent everything, including themselves; who are simultaneously deceivers and willingly deceived.

Imre's room, then, empty and still in its clear subaqueous light, gave, emblematically speaking, a fair account of its inhabitant. A pistol, for example, was among the props; the type "Parabellum" such as was used in the First World War. It too hung from the belt which was no officer's belt. But as an emblem the pistol belonged to a different category, to the division of: gambling debts, take the consequences, suicide. Imre and gambling debts! Actually he had never had any. The pistol was pure emblem. But it was needed to round out the picture. This room was a careful draft of Imre's fictitious life-history. At the rear of it, moreover, diagonally opposite the door, it had a second exit—though only in a figurative sense. That exit was formed by the water colors tacked to the blue-painted wardrobe.

There are Chinese legends that tell of great masters walking into their paintings and vanishing. Imre was no great master. But he succeeded nevertheless in vanishing for a time through his pictures, as through a back door, out of the ordinary symbolism of his life. Of course he had a command of the technical aspects of his métier; he had learned the craft, after all, and learned it very well.

These works were not exactly water colors, though we have called them so for lay purposes. Rather, they were colored pen-drawings; there was a solid graphic base to the little pictures. Imre did not shun difficult perspectives and overlappings; he mastered them. His drawings, done as a private discipline, were in no way like the work of Gyurkicz the newspaper cartoonist. They eschewed the latter's abbreviated, allusive techniques; there was no attempt at compression, at sharpening a point. These drawings were precise. They strove hard for the object; and since to strive is *studere* in Latin, they could quite justly be called "studies." They were not more than that, but also no less; and they had no greater ambition. Since Imre had moved "over the hill" he had taken to sketching bits of the neighborhood. When he sat on his folding stool or on a stone or a stump, with his spectacles on, working perseveringly and using his leisure well, he looked much as he did in the café over his conscientious examination of the illustrated journals. Incidentally, Imre had long before observed that his best and most peaceful hours with Quapp usually came about when he went to see her after such a session.

Naturally, Gyurkicz's commercial work benefited from his nature drawing; in a way, the latter was a welcome relief from the line technique needed for newspaper work, a technique that always bordered somewhat on fraud.

These private exercises in art, however, were not a matter of only yesterday for Imre. Nor had he begun them only after moving over the hill in the spring of 1927. He had in fact started at the end of the past summer, in the Burgenland. What had originally led him precisely to that district can scarcely be set down succinctly.

It may have been the semi-Hungarian landscape that attracted him—since his political past still barred him from crossing the "royal Hungarian" boundaries—the wide open villages, shoreless village streets lined by low houses and irregularly planted trees around which the wheel tracks go in flattened arcs, the waddling processions of geese. He would find this sort of thing in, say,

Fraunkirchen, which is nevertheless a German-speaking village in the vicinity of the big lake. At the tavern called the Stork's Nest, the stork appears twice over: painted on the sign; and directly above the sign, in the midst of a flourishing family life, arriving with prey, clapping its wings shut, stalking, feeding, clattering, flapping off again with tremendous energy. Opposite, like a puffy-cheeked baroque fanfare, stands the pilgrimage Church of Our Lady. The Mount Calvary to the left of it is a kind of nightmare, for all the stations of the cross are confined to a tiny space and arranged one on top of another; you walk in and around them through grottoes and arches.

Imre sketched all this, except for the specimens of baroque architecture.

In the south, in the region called "Angle of the Lake," he drew the curious barns built in age-old fashion entirely of reeds, their roofs almost touching the ground; many of these were destroyed during the Second World War, and many have since disappeared, replaced by modern buildings. In those days, however, they were relatively common, not only around the village of Apetlon but also in the vicinity of the body of water called "Lange Lacke," where immense flocks of wild geese would make a stopover in the course of their autumn migrations. Here one feels the great plains press in from Hungary. The sensation is strong at all seasons of the year but especially in the summer, when there seems to be a greater stillness over these prairies than anywhere else in the world. It is not an empty stillness, not rigid and static, such as we often find around and inside large buildings. Rather, this stillness is divided and accentuated and appears to hum audibly. It lures. It lures one out to the horizon and deeper into the *puszta*. In this region you are never entirely where you happen to be standing; you feel always drawn elsewhere; the feeling begins in the fibers of the heart, but the body wants to follow and remains frustrated by the small steps that the legs can take. It is country where only the mounted man can be entirely with himself and at the same time entirely with the world, even when his horse stands still. Galloping remains as a possibility: if he wishes he can thunder off toward the horizon.

Imre did not know this feeling. Nor did he succeed in entering entirely into his pictures and thus vanishing out the back door. For he was no great master. He could not produce metamorphoses. And no matter how he changed insignia and emblems, that back door remained widely ajar; through the opening, Gyurkicz drew after him a thread of the sticky stuff of his past.

Gyurkicz's little sketching trips to the Burgenland did not remain a secret to his colleagues in the Alliance offices, although Imre could not have said how anyone heard about them. He had never run into anyone in the Burgenland whom he knew or who knew him.

In the late autumn of 1926, Imre had been planning a trip to Drassburg and had been incautious enough to let this be known. Whereupon he had been casually requested to deliver a message to Thomas Preschitz—in other words, to plunge straightway into that deployment area in the political life of Austria where opposing forces tested their strength against each other; it was conveniently remote from the strong Viennese police force. The matter-of-fact way in which Imre was asked to perform this messenger service left him no choice in the matter. It was a form of compulsion. He was also asked to call old Zdarsa's attention to his son-in-law's politics. He had no choice, whatever his own sympathies may have been. His situation was not in the least changed by the fact that in the Burgenland he'd consorted— partly to speak his native language again, partly to act out his "emblematic" part—with persons who probably would have taken a violently different attitude toward him if they had ever met him on their own soil, "inside the royal Hungarian boundary posts." Fraternize as he might with fellow-Hungarians, he could not manage to change horses, much as he would like to have done so for emblematic reasons.

However, the time that Imre had come to Schattendorf on the eve of January 30, he had not been burdened by the slightest assignment, had no messages to deliver. All he had in mind was to do a certain view from the Schattendorf cemetery wall in winter, although it was hardly a real winter that year, scarcely cold at all and with no snow to speak of. He wanted precisely this view toward Hungary, whose rolling terrain began just beyond the wall—this view and no other. He felt as though a back door might be about to open for him (although he did not yet live in the blue room "over the hill"), a rear exit from the studio on Prater Strasse. That was what he had hoped to find at the Schattendorf cemetery in winter. He wanted to sketch: he was already that close to the border of real art. And on Sunday morning he had had his breakfast in Moser's Tavern while the two parties nearly came to blows at the railroad station. Of course he had had to take his breakfast at Moser's, the Social Democratic tavern; no other would do for a man attached to Alliance. But he had not known anything about the impending arrival of a Lieutenant-colonel Hiltl, nor had he said anything to anyone, nor sent anyone anywhere, nor informed anyone of anything. And Imre had never seen the Claw before and knew not a thing about the ugly creature who had almost stabbed him in the stomach today.

Renata had been quite wrong about all that.

Right now, walking slowly uphill toward Liechtenwerder Platz, Imre could find no rear exit from his cramped inner situation and his disturbing outer predicament. But there is an exit from such situations, and one can find it by going cautiously backward the way a crab seeks out its hole. Only one must know the background, must be willing to take cognizance of it—the background and grounds for one's own discomfort. One must look into it, as into deep waters, and without thrashing about; then the whole thing becomes clear enough. It takes a certain strength of character to do this, and such holding still is not exactly pleasant; but it is the only way to see the truth. Gyurkicz, however, was utterly incapable of such introspection, partly because others were always present at his inner converse, and partly because his system of emblems distorted everything.

Thus he was utterly at a loss to understand the cause of his present battered and buffeted feelings, his sense of having been suddenly, dangerously thrown off the track of his life, and of already lying in the ditch. What had so startled him and thrown him off the track? His consciousness could give it no name, no location, no voice. It operated only as a dull, shattering blow from below the level of consciousness. Its most telling sign was the entirely uncharacteristic mode of reaction which had appeared in himself. For it was certainly abnormal for him to have felt not the slightest trace of satisfaction over his brief fight with the Claw, over a test which he had passed so well in the presence of two "young ladies." It was as if half his life had been broken clear off, and half his pleasure in life. Renata had sensed some such process going on in Imre, and that was why she had felt the desire to bait him. Gyurkicz baited by a young lady! That was all he needed. Usually he was the one who did the baiting, as we have seen on the occasion of his first meeting with Charlotte Schlaggenberg. But this time he had simply "taken it," as the boxers say, taken it from Renata without covering, without parrying. He had been too damned tired. "What the living love, the dying hate." All he had wanted was to take his leave, to get clear of all that, to be alone. And that after a considerable athletic triumph. And even if this triumph of his, his instantaneous, smooth, effective response to danger, had come over him like an inspiration, as if it had been given to him from outside himself— when, in the past, would Gyurkicz have hesitated for a moment to claim full credit for the thing? With what gusto he would have told everyone about the incident in Freud's brandy shop, improving on it by saying that he had been well aware of whom he was facing: namely, one of the most dangerous professional criminals in Vienna. But now that kind of thing seemed very far from him. He did not know as yet that he would never tell this story, but that very fact was one of the underlying reasons for his discontent. He knew nothing of it. There was only the feeling in his bones of some ground-breaking change, some terrible burden that had somehow descended upon him.

In this state he came to the little square with the café on the left and the view to the right down into a man-made landscape of iron, smoke, and coal. But now, in the darkness, it was a black valley, only here and there defined by cold pale lights.

By now Imre really needed a brandy.

In the café he forgot to remove his coat. He sat down and dropped his hat on the upholstered bench at his side. He noticed the gash made by the knife in the light-colored cloth of his overcoat. The big coat must have helped deflect the thrust which he had so quickly parried. The tear was in the shape of a triangle. Here was a marvelous emblem for Gyurkicz, quite in the same class with the emblems he cherished, like a military cap pierced by a bullet or a steel helmet grazed by a shell splinter. But now Imre regarded the neat ornament on his coat with sulky distaste.

He was about to order a second brandy when someone approached him from behind. Gyurkicz had been aware of the person for several seconds before he managed to stir and look up— which meant that his weariness and his desire to be alone exceeded his caution, for the incident in the other café should certainly have put him on his guard. Now, however, a warm and friendly voice greeted him in Hungarian, and by name.

"Good evening," Imre said, likewise in Hungarian. He rose and shook the man's hand. One thought dominated his mind: he must pretend to be entirely at his ease and quickly find out who this person was. And so Gyurkicz gestured toward the upholstered bench opposite him and invited the man to sit down. He remembered this handsome, vigorous, black-haired man from somewhere; but due to the momentary constipation of his brain he could not think of how or where they had met, and so everything else escaped him, including the name.

However, the matter was made easy for him.

"I must thank you for your friendly warning at my hut, Herr von Gyurkicz," Pinta said in fluent Hungarian, though with a trace of a Croatian accent.

"Did the warning prove justified?"

"Absolutely, Herr von Gyurkicz. Except that the whole thing turned out different from what I'd hoped."

Pinta then described the two invasions: the relatively harmless visit of the "Republican Protective Association," and the attack of the "Magyarones" brought on by the accidental opening of the shutter. "Still, some of the Reds took a good beating," he added jovially.

Gyurkicz, who had listened with great attentiveness—overcoming his misery for a few minutes—looked at Pinta's forehead. "You can still see the mark," he commented.

"Oh, that's nothing," Pinta said. "About the worst of it was when I came home with the bandage on. I live in Stinkenbrunn, and my father-in-law is a Red. He's been kind of suspicious since then."

"How did you tell him it happened?"

"I said I'd tripped over the tools of the hut in the dark."

"Did he believe you?"

"I don't know. He didn't say anything, not then or any time since. I'm always careful not to talk politics with the old man. You see, we're in the same business; we own these vineyards. We have some out near Mörbisch too. That's why I go there."

As they talked, Gyurkicz regained his presence of mind to some degree. He leaned well into the curve that had suddenly appeared before him. It looked dangerous, but he had to drive through it. He was aided in this feat by the factor that ordinarily made him blind to his own inner states: his brash readiness to dismiss his own faults; in short, his sheer effrontery. There was an idea which was possibly beginning to germinate within Pinta; Imre perceived this idea and far from avoiding it, took hold of it, brought it out, called it by name. Real and effective effrontery differs from coarseness: coarseness is merely a surprise assault that batters the walls of another's body; effrontery is a surgical operation, a knife in the intestines.

"An equivocal situation for you, Herr Pinta," Imre said. "Both our people and the Reds could think you had lured them into a trap—the Reds because you acted so pleasant, inviting the whole gang to stay and have wine, and our people because there was that signal with the shutter."

"It was just as you say, Herr von Gyurkicz. But the Reds had to see it wasn't so, because I was the first and only one to be really hurt. They had to leave me lying on the floor, after all. And as soon as I came to, I explained all about it to our people. I also mentioned about your visit, Herr von Gyurkicz. If I may say so, I somehow got the impression that they weren't so sure about you, or hadn't been before. I don't know why that should be."

"Naturally," Imre said with utter calm. "If a man really wants to be useful to a cause, and not just parrot slogans, the ordinary followers will sooner or later suspect him, just because he isn't a dumbbell. By profession I'm a newspaper artist and political cartoonist, which means that I'm dependent almost exclusively on the nonconservative newspapers nowadays. The result is that I have connections with the Reds in the course of my work. If that weren't so—I'd never find out anything. For example, I wouldn't have been able to tell you what was up, Herr Pinta. The very position I occupy enables me to be useful to our cause, I think. If people suspect me, I can't help it and it doesn't alter my feelings. I'm ready to make this sacrifice. It wouldn't be the first."

Behold what cogent statements, what excellent arguments, what displays of loyalty effrontery can rise to.

"Do you know the count?" Pinta asked.

"Who wouldn't know him!" Imre replied cleverly. "You don't mean it's the count who doesn't trust me?"

"Unfortunately, yes," Pinta said. "Although I tried to put him straight. You did me a big favor that time, Herr von Gyurkicz, so I'd like to give you a piece of advice."

"And what would that be?"

"You ought to try to keep in touch with our people here in Vienna, not so much down there in the Burgenland. This is where it counts most. With those connections you mentioned, you could help us out quite a bit—supplying information. Then they'd see about you." Pinta had talked himself into a state of enthusiasm. His tone was frank, confidential. Imre saw a rope ladder being let down an otherwise insurmountable wall. However, he preserved his caution and deliberation.

"Could you mention any particular person I might contact?"

"Certainly. A fellow-countryman of yours. You may know him. I don't, but I've heard him mentioned by the count. He is Herr Géza von Orkay, and he's at the legation here."

That was a bit too much for Gyurkicz. He felt rather the way a horse might feel who reaches out and takes something from the palm of a hand, only to discover that it is not a lump of sugar but a slice of lemon. But Imre saw at once that there was nothing for it but to swallow the slice of lemon and seem to like it.

"Thank you, Herr Pinta," he said. "I hardly know Herr von Orkay, but I'll take occasion to speak to him someday. It was a great pleasure seeing you again, Herr Pinta." He paid for the brandies he and Pinta had drunk, laughingly fending off the Croat's protests. They shook hands vigorously and parted.

Imre emerged from the café and began walking again. Tramping manfully along, rather, at a steady pace, first gently uphill and then following along the streetcar tracks, down the principal avenue of this quarter. He walked easily, no longer stumbling. It was a spring evening, though not especially fair; but still, an evening in May—which means a constant teasing and querying of mild air against temples and cheeks, a being surrounded by gardens full of things in bloom. But Imre was in a state of utter inaccessibility to the whisperings of spring. Now that the rope ladder had been drawn up and he faced an unbroken wall again, a deep fury had gathered inside him, like black ground water in a hole. Suddenly he recalled that Quapp had only recently turned down, once again, his plans for their marrying and setting up house together. Very well, then! They didn't want him, neither here nor there! But he had other choices. Damn it all, he had other choices and would know how to uphold his honor even if they wanted to be nasty. He knew better what was right for a man of honor than did the whole rabble of them, all this swell-headed "our crowd" and "our people."

And yet at bottom Gyurkicz was a good-natured fellow.

Now he was crossing over the hill. He thought of Lo. He grew calmer. The shrubs and trees of the hilly park arched greenly toward the path, in the light of street lamps. Now the path leveled out again as it crossed the children's playground. Imre thought of Lo. Would she still be practicing now, or could he go to her at once? For moments there washed through him the violent desire to take her into his arms without delay. But she usually practiced in the evenings, and as he had long since discovered, not out of excessive industry but really out of laziness, because she had not practiced all day, had once again been "not in form" and had spent the day chasing after some trivialities that seemed to her of highest importance. Always in a hurry, of course, because she took too long over everything, went about her errands far too fussily, and wasted too much time in talk. In addition there were those all too frequent hour-long discussions with René Stangeler in some café or other. For Imre had long since found out about these meetings. That was the explanation for Lo's sudden fits of interest in this or that field, whether archaeology, history, or literature. Whatever the fad of the moment, the one constant about it was that it led away from the violin. Lo would spend her time running to libraries or poking around in bookshops.

Imre did not consider Lo a real, a born violinist. Some deep instinct told him that she did not really like to play but felt an obligation to do so, an obligation derived from some theoretical views altogether incomprehensible to him, which she would discuss for hours with René Stangeler instead of practicing. This was not the way to be or become a musician; Gyurkicz felt sure about that. He too, after all, was engaged in an artistic profession; if he had gone about things the way Quapp did, he would never have been able to learn his craft, much less earn his living. If, however, he hinted anything of the sort to Lo, she became extremely tormented, deeply depressed, treated him badly, and began to mutter what a pity it was that she could not communicate with him at all about the really important things in her life, and that it would be better if he would let her alone altogether. At this point Imre would usually placate her, partly out of a sudden fear of losing her, partly out of good nature, because he saw that she was suffering.

Thus, placating her, he would soon find himself taking a step or two further, and even indulging in philosophical conversations with Lo. These discussions were really dreadful. They were studded with ideas originally developed by Schlaggenberg's teacher Scolander. These ideas had been passed on in polished form from Kajetan to Stangeler, newly roughed up and then smoothed down again by the latter, and straightway applied by Quapp to her personal life, although our poor Quapp's life and thought dwelt on a plane far beneath all philosophical canons, not to say beneath contempt. Nevertheless, she would snatch up these canons and hurl them at poor Gyurkicz. Their philosophical talks were often amazingly silly, and the sole effect was that they wounded each other.

Of course the person to blame for all this was René, who was to blame for so much. Imre knew that, knew it with an intensity that seared his flesh. Stangeler was constantly spouting his theories to Quapp. He let himself go, in the first place because everyone likes a listener, and especially so respectful a listener as Lotte Schlaggenberg; in the second place because he used his long talks as pretexts to shirk his own work (which was really making Quapp drink from a poisoned well); and in the third place because our slant-eyed scholar seriously thought that what he said was valid. It is not for us to decide here whether René's opinions did or did not have any objective value. Quapp, at any rate, found them enormously convincing (at least in theory), simply because she had spent her whole childhood under a fictional obligation to a mission which lay within herself and which she absolutely must carry out. Possibly it had been in-culcated into her unintentionally by old Eustach von Schlaggenberg; it may be that he exercised his mind on some twisted private theology while he permitted Levielle to cheat him out of his forest lands. Kajetan was never willing to reveal anything substantial about his deceased father; instead he spoke of him with extreme affection, never judging him or attempting to sketch his character. Whenever Kajetan mentioned him, which was seldom enough, he gave the impression that he had put his father off to one side in a kind of niche, and that he had never compared him with anyone else—which comparison, after all, is basic to any evaluation. "My father," he once said, "was altogether a special case. He was a heart on legs, and a sensible heart at that. He didn't need to have anything in his head. It sometimes seems to me that he was the only real person I have ever known."

But about Stangeler. Our good René held forth, for example, on the theory that there was no such thing as being "creative." He would quote Gerhart Hauptmann, who once answered a question about how he invented his characters by replying that no one could invent a single character; all a writer could do was portray them. Everything "creative," René reasoned, was only imitation, and the whole "productive act" nothing but wholly free apperception, penetration of the world into a human being utterly without distortion. The thing was to remove every obstacle that tended to hinder this penetration. That was the fundamental achievement from which everything else followed, including talent.

This was the last straw for Quapp. Since René treated human "creativeness" only in a metaphorical sense, he leveled out the distinction which every sensible person makes between the productive and reproductive arts.

And for the present Quapp gladly accepted the elevation in rank implicit in such views.

What René permitted himself with this girl was almost a kind of experiment. And all the while he ignored her femininity, dismissing it as a detail that did not matter.

Gyurkicz, *simplificateur terrible* that he was, really saw the thing as it was. Quapp lacked the qualities of stalwart musicianship. Of course, Gyurkicz's image of a violinist had been formed by the gypsy—the natural musician. Still, Quapp could have used some such gypsy qualities. Technically, she was already far advanced. Her teacher had broken her of several faults and a number of rigidities; the results, after so few months, were distinctly gratifying. But what her teacher did not know, probably because he could not conceive of such a thing, was Quapp's incapacity to achieve real violinistic emotionality that she could count on to come again and again, that could easily be evoked, being nothing in the mind, only to a small extent in the soul, and for the most part in the muscles, in sheer pleasure in playing the violin. (In this respect, then, Imre saw correctly.) The interflow of all the many, highly complex, and rapid motions of both hands, the riding of the melody as if it were the crest of a wave, the sinking into the sparkle, the feeling of power over a whole hall full of people who might appreciate music up to the hilt, but none of whom could become at one with the music, as the player had become at one with it—none of these feelings had ever entered into Quapp's vitals. She played the violin correctly, precisely—sight-read excellently, by the way; she played with earnest and deep resolve—but that kind of violin-playing has never intoxicated anyone. The violin had no power over Quapp, and therefore Quapp with her violin had no power over people. She never felt herself, as the interpreter, far superior to her audience. She did not play, she recited. Perhaps for that reason, the two or three times she had given performances—always for a small group—she had suffered from extreme nervousness. More than that, and far worse than that: from tremors, as it is called. Her fingers trembled so that at first the tone was clouded, or at best characterless. This trouble left her only after she had played for some time and her hand had warmed up. Or perhaps it might be better put: when a terrible guilty conscience, which rose up out of her inner divisiveness, was at last narcotized and her heart took courage again. The onset of those tremors was the darkest and profoundest experience in Quapp's life so far. They were a danger that lay in wait for her as soon as she was supposed to exhibit her art. She never spoke of this. But she was aware of those tremors day and night, almost with every breath she took, and especially in all her dreams. They were a disgrace, a shame, a terror, a defeat. She could never forget the way the fingers of her left hand became like jelly, the knuckles soft and the finger tips furry and spongy; and the way the wrist suddenly vanished from her bow hand and her forearm felt like a hollow tube filled with nausea.

Stangeler knew nothing of this. Neither did Gyurkicz.

Gyurkicz now crossed Pfarr Platz. His longing for Quapp had suddenly faded. He felt this cessation of feeling as a loss, just as if something had fallen out of his pocket that he ought to have had with him—as if his hand were to fly in alarm to his chest where wallet or notebook were missing. At the same time he still hoped intensely that Quapp would no longer be playing this evening, that he need not hear those single thin notes of her bowing exercises as he neared the front door. . . . His antipathy toward those sounds, toward her always belated evening practice, became sharp and clear. He turned into the narrow lane with which Eroica Gasse begins, passed below Beethoven's windows. A green street on the whole, greener than ever in the glow of the gas lamps. Imre strode along past the big garden which belonged to a somewhat neglected house set far back from the street. Now he was nearing the house in which Lo lived. He stood still. It was still. No bowings in the various positions. He was being spared that. He was on the point of feeling relief, and then something entirely different overcame him. It was as if a total stranger had entered into him. It was a stranger who proceeded from Lo herself, emerged from one of the facial expressions she sometimes wore—namely, when she began to treat him with contempt, during one of those frightful, endless discussions that gave both of them headaches. But this contempt did not strike Imre von Gyurkicz at the spot at which it was aimed—the place where his false inner balances were drawn up, where he so easily discharged himself of blame, whence his effrontery was nourished.

Rather, it struck him where he was really sensitive, where the blinders painted over with emblems tried to hide the dubiousness of his origins and past. And when Quapp threw a stone at this region, the sound given forth was hollow, as if the stone had struck a cardboard lid. Then it was no longer evident that he belonged to her class; that assumption was shaken, threatened, without a word's being said about such matters. At times like that Gyurkicz was often on the point of demanding who she thought she was, anyhow! What else was she but the daughter of an almost ruined landowner, a girl who lived on a pittance here in Vienna, taking the bread out of the mouth of her widowed mother and preparing herself for—of all things!—a soloist's career. A career she should have begun on long before, if she were ever to amount to anything!

But Imre could say none of this, for she never extended a rapier at which he, in turn, could have slashed furiously in such a manner. And never, in any of their talks, did she actually aim in the direction in which her stones flew, to Gyurkicz's discomfort. These stones were not, in fact, even thrown at him. They went their way indirectly, like billiard balls; and it was precisely this which so infuriated Imre. Quapp herself seemed to become a stone, with that stranger's face from God knows where. This was the picture of her that he had now. A frightful picture: though she looked very pretty in it, with her hair in braids wound around her head. No, she was a really pretty girl, but the expression of scorn and hardness literally leaped at Imre out of the face, and along with it an enormous nullity and effrontery. (For that was what he branded it. To be sure, he enjoyed the good fortune of not knowing himself. Not only is the demonic force of effrontery based upon that lack of self-knowledge, but also the power of many whom history has called "great.") Visualizing this face, Imre would have liked to smash it as you would smash a pane of glass. Lo's eyes, which were very far apart, always seemed to move closer together when she was in one of her difficult moods. And it was this particular feature that most unnerved Gyurkicz—even now, when he was merely imagining it. For as an artist, he had to note this phenomenon, although it ran counter to all the principles of Imre's naturalistic drawing. . . .

But now, as he envisioned Lo, it was curious that in this "picture" she was not wearing her ordinary clothes but elaborate evening dress. She did have one such dress, he knew; she had happened to be wearing it during one of the first critical scenes he had had with her, and that was the first time he had seen it. It was that time, too, that he had first seen that strange repellent face of hers, with the eyes closer together. Now, as he stood alone in the darkness of Eroica Gasse, he tried to encourage himself (so strange did he feel and so unhappy was he!). He actually whispered under his breath: "It's rare, after all; it rarely comes out." And even as he became aware of his solitary whispering, he for seconds touched the lowest and darkest depths of his inner misery.

From every nadir the only possible direction is upward, and so Gyurkicz walked as it were uphill to the door of Lo's house. As he walked he had for a few moments a clear vision of the true Lo, and during those moments could recover the feeling for her that he had lost. Going by her lighted windows, which were on the ground floor, he saw Lo sitting at her little desk, papers spread out before her. The curtain was only half drawn. The tea tray seemed to be standing on the window sill. Lo's dark head stood out sharply against the whiteness of the papers.

Imre rang and waited a little while at the door. Then came the sound of her footsteps.

As soon as she opened the door, and then in the small white vestibule, she struck him as altogether different from what he had anticipated, different from the way he had been imagining her.

For just a few seconds the fear lingered that he would see again that "narrow look" of hers. But there was nothing of the kind. Rather, she seemed serene and self-assured. For just the space of a thought Imre was vexed by this—what right had she to serenity and assurance? She was also not wearing her usual smock but her tan-checked jersey dress. The dress became her; she always looked well in it—a really pretty girl. The dress emphasized her nice, high breasts and good figure. Moreover, her hair was carefully dressed. Others could envy you for possessing a girl like that—with this fellow Imre others were always looking on, even in such matters.

Would he care for some tea? she asked. She always asked him this when he came. His reply to it depended less on whether or not he had a desire for tea than upon the greater or lesser degree of tension between himself and Lo. She liked to offer him tea when he returned home from the city; she drank along with him, and enjoyed his company better than when she had to sit high and dry with him, so to speak. Moreover, she found it really dreadful that anyone could come from his work in the city without feeling the need for a cup of tea. That seemed to her inhuman; Lo felt very strongly on this score.

This time, however, Imre declined the tea. Very well. They sat. She took a cigarette. "Been to town?" he asked, regarding her appearance; he knew that she wore this dress when she went into town. "Did you wear a hat with it?" She gestured casually to the piano, where she had laid the little toque of brown felt. Imre stood up; best to set the specialist in motion, since otherwise everything would remain at a standstill. He picked up the little hat, went over to Lo and placed it cannily on her head, drawn down to the right. She held her head still and smiled. She even stood up and struck a pose, like a mannequin.

"New?" he asked.

She nodded.

"Very good," Imre said. "Just right for you. Bought it today?"

"Yes," she said, laughing. "At Pauli's on Schuler Strasse."

He was surprised. Lo had been worried about money all week. He had been racking his brains as to how to get a little extra to give her. But he said nothing about this. "Anything happen in town?" he asked casually.

"No, I went to see someone for my mother."

"Aha," he thought, "she must have got some money from that aristocratic aunt of hers, Baroness . . . what's her name?" His eyes wandered around the simple room. The desk was cleared;

no papers were visible. Lo had taken off the hat. She sat down beside Gyurkicz and asked about his affairs. Imre talked. He really wished to unburden himself, to explain that he intended gradually to get away from newspaper work and into advertising. He was beginning to be more and more repelled by his work as a cartoonist, he said—not mentioning the troubles he was encountering at Alliance. In the first place, for purely artistic reasons, and beyond that, because of the intellectual or ethical attitudes involved (whatever was possessing him; why was he venturing so far?). He had been feeling that way ever since the autumn, he said, ever since he had begun drawing from nature down in the Burgenland, and especially during the winter, doing views from the Schattendorf cemetery. . . .

"I can very well understand that," she said tranquilly. "A growing distaste—yes, I think I can understand. . . ."

She did not change in the least. Her expression remained perfectly tranquil. Apparently she was not in the least out of sorts with him. She did not attack. But there was something firm about her. Was she not acting out of strength? Suddenly he knew, with the certain instinct of all impudent people for the positional strategy of life, that hitherto she had always attacked out of weakness. Now she was not doing so. So it was better when she did attack. . . . Did she know something that he knew? What was it? Or had she found out something that he knew nothing about?

They sat together, but in fact there was no contact between them, as there was no contact in their conversation. He had really wanted to tell her some of the things that were moving him; he had wanted that with a kind of sudden inward softening. But now everything fell upon alien ground, like apples shaken from a tree that fall behind the neighbor's high fence; you hear the thump of them, but you cannot see where they have come to rest.

They did not talk much, Lo and Imre. For a good while they were silent. Gyurkicz clearly felt a firmness in her that was resisting him, with which she was literally forcing him away. He gave up. The gulf stretched between them. It was nothing he had created; it was all her doing. It hurt him that such a gulf could make plainly visible the thing he concealed even from himself behind all his emblems: the wound, the dark scar at the core of his being, his own "tremors," we might put it. (Quapp had no idea that he was a victim of "tremors," even as he knew so little about hers.) Meanwhile, all their conversation remained friendly. A thousand times better to quarrel than to lose sight of each other. A thousand times better to glare into another person's eyes and heart, even in rage, than into the blankness of a no man's land. There was nothing more to be done here. This evening they slid by each other like two passengers in different trains. A moment before, the windows of the cars have been exactly opposite; now they are both gone, one in one direction, the other in another.

He left. Their parting was most friendly.

In the darkness he crossed Eroica Gasse diagonally toward the door of his own house. It was like wading through deep green water. The water reached up to his neck.

So it was. And yet we must not imagine Imre as too lost in gloom and despair. We must remember his low specific gravity. Moreover, only we know, but he himself had no conception of how greatly he was alienated from truth, how blinded he was by his emblematic blinkers.

Not so the two girls whom he had left in front of Freud's brandy shop. In them the intelligence and profundity of youth stood as erect as tulips in a freshly dewed bed. Let a parching wind blow, let discontent oppress, and they felt it in its full force, everything affected them down to the ground, which was as smooth and pure as a sandy beach just abandoned by the water at turn of tide. The ground of their young souls was not yet scribbled over by the lines of innumerable comparisons, as is the case with grownups. Everything that happened made its mark upon them; these marks stood out, isolated and excessively distinct upon the clear surface, scarring it beyond reasonable measure.

For that reason the incident in the brandy shop went on

troubling the girls for days. It was not so much the scuffle in the
tavern that preyed on their minds, but rather the way their unknown protector had gone off, with bowed head and the tread
of a clumsy old man.

Kaps, too, began to walk with bowed head nowadays. Or
rather, to sit most of the time. The signs were ominous; Renata at
first only sensed this, then recognized it clearly. After a while
the doctor spoke to the girls: with a case like this they must be
prepared for anything at any moment. He added that the popular
expression "to die of a broken heart" was not just an empty
phrase. Anna Kapsreiter was already in a state of living death.
She "petrified"; it was really that, and there was no checking it.
For the first time in her young life Renata became aware of the
inevitable, irrevocable sliding away of a dear part of her own
existence. Henceforth, she knew, she herself would have not
only present and future, but also a past; for the first time the
Memnon's lament of the past entered the girls' lives—for Sylvia,
too, felt the same way. For the first time—while this having a past
paradoxically still lay in the future.

But not in the future for long. When the boy from the green-
grocer's opposite the Blue Unicorn stood at Sylvia's door, she
knew before he spoke what he had to say. She telephoned
Renata. But when the two girls arrived at Liechtenstein Strasse,
they found Frau Anna no longer living. She looked lovely and
kind; her white hair had been smoothed down. The priest and
doctor had already gone. The girls were left alone with the dead
woman for a short time. Both of them kissed her. Then they composedly prayed the *requiem aeternam*. There was a letter for the
girls there; it lay on the "night book," and had been there for
several days past, the landlady said. Frau Anna had asked her to
give the letter as well as the "night book" to Renata and Sylvia
"if anything should happen to me." Also the ship model from the
next room—and the bow and arrows, because these things were
Fräulein Renata's property.

The girls went into the other room, which had been intended
for Croaky. Even the box in which the boat had been packed was

still there. The landlady came in with a heap of newspaper and string. They made a package of the bow and the quiver, so as not to attract attention in the street when they carried these things. As they worked, the landlady mentioned that Frau Anna had drawn up a proper will in favor of her relatives in the Burgenland, the parents of Croaky. Her savings were quite sizable; moreover she had kept a large amount of cash here in the apartment right up to the last; it was mentioned in the will, and the money was all there. The landlady had been one of the witnesses at the drawing up of this last will.

The paper made a great rustling as the girls did the wrapping. The sound hurt their ears; a white emptiness had formed behind their brows, and the landlady continued to talk into this emptiness. She mentioned that she had already telegraphed to the Burgenland and someone would probably come today. Glancing out through the window, Renata noted with a strange sense of alienation that outside it was a bright sunny day. On the way here she had not noticed. Was she to step out onto the street into this sunlight, carrying the boat, the bow, the quiver, the night book—was this not a monstrous demand? She felt Frau Anna's letter in the breast pocket of her blouse.

They walked up along Alserbach Strasse with the box and the two long objects—these were awkward to carry, and the girls had to be careful that no one barged into them. Renata carried the big "night book" under her arm. Here, as everywhere in the streets of big cities, hovered the powdered remains of 10,000 pasts over the sites of as many memories; the ghosts of sorrow and joy came forth in broad daylight from dark cool stairwells out upon the sunny sidewalk.

And at last they themselves dived into a cool stairwell that was filled with the familiar miasmas, like all the theaters in which youth plays itself out, like all the stages of the way to school. The divisions were marked out here by stories: Frau Tarbuk's apartment on the second floor breathed out the suggestion of a clean perfumed fragrance. But when you passed Dr. Schedik's, something medical and disinfectant was distinctly evident on the stairs. Here, during office hours, an electric light was always burning, sharply illuminating the doctor's big name plate.

Renata's parents were not in, so the girls were alone in the apartment.

Sylvia went to Renata's room with her. They put down their bundles. Again the rustle of all the newspaper as they unpacked grated on the girls' ears. Both became aware of this with mild astonishment. Why was their hearing so sensitive to pain? Sylvia hung bow and quiver on a picture hook that happened to be unoccupied. Meanwhile the boat gradually emerged from its box and paper wrappings. The sheets of newspaper seemed to continue rustling, although they now lay still. Beside the quiver on the wall a red-gold band grew wider and wider from the glow of the setting sun.

Renata had taken the letter out of her blouse pocket and laid it on her desk. It had been lying there for some time. Now at last she reached out for it. Sylvia gathered up all the newspaper and took it to the kitchen. Renata read:

> *My dear child!* When Kaps is no more, take the book I've filled with writing and keep it. It lies on the night chest. Read a few pages of the book now and then. There's lots in it. My dear child, please take back the little boat, and the bow-and-arrows too, please take very good care of the boat, don't give it away or put it in the attic, but keep it with you always in in your room. Kaps is sailing with Croaky in the ship. We're happy. Put this note in the ship, too. I bless you, my good child. Anna Kapsreiter.

Irresistibly, a torrent of tears poured from Renata. It was as though an inexhaustible flood were rushing, gushing out of her. She swirled in grief as in rushing waters. The genius of youth— which deserves as much reverence as age—made possible such grief, which cut a course for itself like an unchecked mountain stream. Sylvia came in. Renata, without looking up, handed her the letter. After Sylvia had read it, she took a few steps toward the window and remained standing there, letter in hand. Outside, the distant prospect dissolved in the lavender-blue of oncoming dusk. It was curious how in an already indistinct distance here and there a green tree stuck up between the gray houses like a brush or broom.

We would be much mistaken were we to imagine that enmity prevailed between Didi and the Claw. To be sure, Didi knew a good deal about him—enough for more than four or five years in the "clink." She knew, among other things, who had really killed Hertha Plankl, on whose case the police had been working in vain since the previous summer. She not only knew but had the proof in her bag hanging on the vise—Hertha's last lines, with those few words from Anny Gräven scribbled on the note. But Didi and the Claw were strangely enough on the best of terms. They shared common principles. Once, while good old Freud was in the indescribable back room we have nevertheless described, taking his senile nap, Didi had asked the Claw . . . No, it sounds utterly idiotic. But it is a fact: she had asked the Claw why he was not a Social Democrat. Since he was always so mad at the rich.

Mad—well and good. But at this question, Meisgeier really showed what it was to be mad. "Those rats!" he screamed. "You horse's ass, Didi, you dumb slut. Those rats, those Reds, those brown-noses! We'd be sewed up good and proper if we had them. All they want is to fix things so everybody shares alike—like a bunch of sheep. And where would that leave me! Where would it leave you? Those mother ———. Aren't you ashamed down to your ——— talking such ———. The Sozis are the worst enemies we have, the worst anyone has who isn't a lousy stool pigeon and ass licker. In my book the Reds come right after the cops!"

Didi's green eyes glowed. The criminal, after all, is the only man who does not hold up to females those ethical ideas invented ages ago by the world of men and in the course of the millennia elaborated into ever more foolish and troublesome forms (right up to the "categorical imperative"). At most he holds up to them what it is proper to hold up to them. Hence he is on their level. For he too is oppressed. He is completely on their level.

"And what about Fittala?" she said cunningly.

"Fittala!" he roared. "That editor's lackey, that idiot! Sold out, that's what he's done, sold out. He once belonged to us. But now—he can stick it! Raises a stink at meetings whenever there's someone around the Reds don't like. Dirty bastard. Ought to be stepped on hard."

"You're right there," Didi said, smiling with satisfaction. "Want to come in?" she added, jerking her head toward the back room. "The old man sleeps sound, and if he isn't asleep he gets a kick out of it."

"Wouldn't mind," Meisgeier said, getting up.

TONIGHT I gave Kubitschek two slaps, I don't know why. I don't know anybody named Kubitschek except in my dreams. These slaps "petrified" him—that was the word that came to me in the dream. But it really meant that he shrank or condensed the way something does in cooking, so much so that he was only eighteen inches tall or so, and for that reason he left furious at me, and looked at me with terrible rage, but without turning around; he had a red eye in the back, like an auto, and he said out loud: "You'll see what comes of this when you go to the john, don't think I'm going to put up with anything from you. You'll be sorry." I felt just awful then (only in the dream, because when I woke up I felt fine). After I'd gone back to sleep again it started from the beginning again with the caverns. But this time the rooms were dry. I only heard knocking and was horribly frightened because I thought the knocking was again coming from those horny talons that sometimes move at the ends of the long arms. But this time nothing came. I went from room to room, higher and higher, and each one was drier and brighter than the next. Then I was standing out on the street in front of my door, so I must already have come through the sewer grating.

But I mustn't think we can be safe because it is dry up here: the next dream told me that, plainly enough. I'm so terribly worried about Croaky, because that must mean that something can reach up and take the boy from me. I couldn't survive that. This time I wasn't down below. I stayed here. But still I heard it down there splashing around and wallowing in the filth. When I was below, in the drier passages, but even in the damp and the wet ones too, where you could meet something like that, I didn't feel the danger as bad as I do up here when I have the boy with me. Though down below I forgot the big carving knife every time. And yet I went down into the wet caverns too. Caverns—that was the word I always dreamed. Once I stood right in the water. There was a noise. It's over, I thought, I'm done for. I was so filled with disgust that I would have died if the tentacles had really come.

But up here I'm really afraid, and the fear is more serious than down there, because here there's no adventure, while down below I'm curious. Just as I was falling asleep yesterday I thought of the knife, thought hard about it, and then I didn't have the dream again after all. It's a bad neighborhood here too, so close to the Danube, and I live only on the first floor. I didn't want to go down through the toilet; it isn't proper. I wish I could forget what there is down there, and that those things are crawling around, but we're all undercrept (that was the word in the dream); if they were only rats, it wouldn't be bad. But it's different when something creeps on such long arms, and on so many of them. Then I dreamed the boy was in the john and didn't come back. No, he didn't come back. He won't ever come back, because he should have been back here long ago. Here it's really safe too— that was my excuse for having let him go to the toilet alone. But what can I do, he's a big boy already, will be going to the Gymnasium soon. He hasn't come, he won't come back! I scream; it was horrible, and then I woke up.

Kubitschek has put in gratings, nets, so nothing can get through. I think to myself, how can he do that, he's too small, and he has no eyes up front. On the other hand he has lots of arms to make up for it. Tough as wire. That made me suspicious; I run as hard as I can so he won't net me in and make me have to stay down below all the time. Again I didn't have any shears with me. What will the boy do without me? But I made it through the sewer grating. Outside Kubitschek was standing, and he says: "What are you doing here, Anna? The nets are all finished."

Kubitschek tells me that if they set fire to a big building, that will flush them out; the things will stick up through all holes because the ground will become hot and they can't stand that. In the dream that made sense, and I asked him when they're going to start the fire so that everything will be cleaned out once and for all under the city. He says: In the summer maybe; it'll work better then because it's already hot. In winter there would be all the snow to be melted first, and that would make better moisture for them down below.

Kubitschek has taken the boy with him again; he winds his wire arms all around him. I can't stand that. He laughs and says the boy should go with him everywhere, it won't do the kid any harm if he sees something of the world, and no harm either if the boy drinks raspberry pop. "Do you want him to be drinking wine too?" I say. "What kind of crazy talk is that, anyhow? For all I know you've been giving him wine already." And I tell him he mustn't take the boy with him at all when the big building is burned. He laughs so dreadfully, and yet he's no bigger than a medicine chest. "You miserable chest," I say, "you mustn't take the boy with you when you start the fire, not down there either." "Who's starting any fire down there?" he says. "It's much too wet there." But when I said "down there" I didn't mean under the city, but out in the country where Croaky's parents live, near Schattendorf. But I wasn't able to say that in the dream; I couldn't manage to bring it out. It just wouldn't come, just the way I never could take the scissors along.

ON THE morning of Monday, May 16—I had spent the previous evening with Prince Croix and Mucki Langingen—I awoke in a manner that I can best describe as "at a distance." My room seemed to me larger than usual, and very bright. I lay in perfect order on my bed, as if it were a bier.

I was not yet wide awake. The sequences of my dreams had already fled and become tenuous; but the chain of cause and effect, on which our daylight day is strung, had not yet closed. But though I lay thus stranded on this shallow margin of the night, I knew one thing with utter clarity: that much had changed between my awakening yesterday, on Sunday morning, and this awakening today.

Yesterday I had thought of Cornel Lasch, and had been sure that I would have him as an enemy—but how, and why?

Today I thought of Renata Gürtzner-Gontard, whom I had seen in the dim vestibule when I went to see my old chief.

Everything that I had learned from Sergeant Gach seemed subdued, almost like a wound which has been properly treated and has now settled down under its clean bandages and stopped throbbing.

But the real gulf was formed by my evening with Alfons Croix and Mucki. That was the deepest part, a gently glowing hollow in which the previous excitements of the day had come to rest. But this hollow, shut within the great gray stony masses of surrounding existence, to which I had suddenly and accidentally penetrated, gave me assurance of unknown values in this world around me, of potential new fragrances—gave me for the moment real life, true hope.

With this new *élan*, I sprang out of bed. The *élan* remained with me for part of the day. I looked at my chronicle, my hobby-horse, and knew that I would never again mount into its ridiculous little saddle.

As I thus took leave of it, a refrain began in my mind: "Something must be done, something must be done." There it was: Gach, or rather not Gach himself, but the ancient news he had brought me. But what should be done? What was I supposed to do, or cause to be done?

So the day passed without anything's being accomplished. But musing, meditating, pressing, I circled and finally spun like a top around the matter of Quapp's legacy. In the process I used up that stock of composure, of untoward well-being, which had been infused into me the night before at the prince's. In fact, I still harbored a nonsensical certainty that the evening spent with Croix had settled everything very well, in some peculiar way in no sense related to outward action. Everything had seemed so well settled, and the sudden emergence of Ruthmayr—Quapp's father, as I now startlingly knew—and of that horrible Countess Charagiel, whom I had long since stowed away in a dusty urn of memory in some half-buried vault—the sudden appearance of these two had been unable to affect me the day before, because of that gently glowing hollow in which the day had ended.

But on the following day, Tuesday, the calm infused into me proved to be all used up. Even my long dormant jurist's personality awoke—Herr Dr. jur. Geyrenhoff—although his province was more questions of administrative jurisprudence than matters of civil law, including the laws of inheritance (though, of course, I had not too long before come into a tidy little inheritance myself, albeit with certain losses which Financial Counselor Levielle thought I need not have accepted so tamely . . .).

I therefore began mulling over the thing from that angle. Gach's story seemed absolutely without doubt. It checked, too, with that discovery I had once made when half asleep of the resemblance between Captain Ruthmayr and Quapp, his daughter. Gach, too, had noticed this resemblance, had remarked on it. Hence it was an objective fact, not merely an illusion on my part. Now the thread was drawn; now I saw the run making a pathway through the whole fabric; it stood out clear, all by itself. . . . The evening tingled the sky behind the tower of St. Stephan's with a greenish glow, and the first bright spheres from street lamps and store fronts bloomed forth. . . . A hat doffed and waved in a wide slow arc, the white head, the little white brush of mustache. . . .

And I had talked loosely and at some length to the financial counselor about that very resemblance.

"What? What's that you say?"

He actually screamed at me. His face was deeply flushed; he looked very vulgar. The careful folds of his "à la English lord" countenance became disarranged.

So there it was—I had fired the shot that sounded the alarm. I myself had fired it, on Annunciation Day, and curiously enough at almost the very same spot on the Graben where the day before yesterday Gach, at approximately the same twilight time, had made the same observation and the same remark—to me.

Here, then, lay the explanation of Levielle's sudden cordiality toward Schlaggenberg. This was it, not the accidental eavesdropping by four-footed and long-eared Herr René, upon a conference between Levielle and Cornel Lasch in the Siebenschein music room.

Perhaps the conference had dealt not only with banking transactions.

Perhaps there had also been some talk of an inheritance.

This occurred to me just by the by. But I did not pursue this thought just then. The key to the situation, to the sudden blessings from Alliance which had descended on Kajetan—that key which Kajetan and I had vainly sought during our long conversation in the café—was now right in my hand. More than that: I had fashioned it myself.

Plain as day: my chronicle was done for.

I was an actor now.

And immediately I plunged into action. First in thought. Legalistic thoughts. I mustered up all my rather rusty legal knowledge. The failure to execute Ruthmayr's will in accordance with his instructions—in short, the suppression of the document that Alois Gach had brought from Ruthmayr's deathbed—remained a fact punishable by law. If that was what had been done. Punishable even if the legacy had shrunk to nothing due to the devaluation of the old currency. Still, even the old currency had retained a certain value after the war. But had not Gach mentioned English securities, a special deposit of them? Clever of him to have noticed. Could it be that Levielle, as executor, had nevertheless suppressed Ruthmayr's very last will only in the interest of the widow? For according to Paragraph 601 of the General Civil Code, a last testamentary statement was inviolable. Had the will stipulated that Quapp's legacy be paid out of the fortune left to Friederike? And did Friederike know about her husband's illegitimate daughter? That seemed unlikely. For in the spring, that time we had been sitting in Gerstner's (later to be joined by the Edam cheese and that insolent fellow Frigori), I had perceived, by the expression on Friederike's face, that she was the product of a class which considers transmission of blind spots, and deliberate walling out of certain aspects of life, among the crowning graces of traditional education. Only the supercharge of exceptional intelligence breaks through such a background (as Leonhard, by grace of his intelligence, had broken through his); and there could be no question of such intelligence in Frau Ruthmayr's case. Levielle, then, could probably have assumed that she would not know about Quapp. I suddenly recalled a remark that Kajetan had made during that long conversation in the café: that Levielle had arranged "certain affairs" for the Schlaggenberg family concerning which both Kajetan and Levielle were obligated to keep silence "up to a certain point," in obedience to old Eustach von Schlaggenberg's last will. And that aside from the financial counselor and himself, only his mother knew. . . .

No doubt the "affairs" in question had to do with Quapp. And I felt absolutely certain that Frau Ruthmayr had no knowledge of her existence; I had only to think of Friederike sitting there in Gerstner's *Konditorei* to be sure of it.

There are people who by type are ignorant of things and who always remain so. Quapp, for example, was one such person. She was amazed that there were Roman ruins in Carnuntum. She was later astonished beyond measure when she learned what had led to the burning of the Palace of Justice in Vienna on July 15, 1927. She never found out anything of her own accord. She was never well informed.

It seemed to me that Friederike was likewise just such a person.

Of course she would not have known anything.

And in his last hour Ruthmayr had sent his will to Levielle. Still not wishing to confide any of this to his wife.

Ruthmayr's last will had been, according to Gach, a legally valid *testamentum militare*, as provided for in Paragraph 600 of the General Civil Code: a will set down "with a minimum of formality." It seemed obvious that the will must have bequeathed to Quapp some special fund, undoubtedly deposited in England, which had long before been set aside from the rest of the estate for Quapp's benefit. It would not have been mentioned in Ruthmayr's earlier will, either as a legacy or otherwise, for that earlier will would ultimately be seen by Friederike, if she were not already familiar with it before Ruthmayr's death.

But in order to make such a fund available, the military testament would not suffice, nor would the certificates of deposit— for these would merely confirm the existence of such a trust. In all probability these certificates were in the hand of the executor —in this case Financial Counselor Levielle. As far as my legal knowledge went, in order for anyone to draw upon the fund, there would have to be a court decree and a deposition by the

phone; you could sit comfortably while talking. I settled into the chair. Suddenly I felt abnormally aware not only of myself but of the nearer and more distant surroundings here, the villa quarter, the whole district, out over the hill and down as far as the Danube, and also down toward the center of the city and the close, unbroken rows of houses, to the Franz Josef Station, say, or to Liechtental, near the parish church Zu den vierzehn Nothelfern. I saw those streets as if from inside, looking out of the old houses, out of cramped rooms, so many of which had already been abandoned as an incessant and imperceptible migration took place from these antiquated and grubby quarters—into the enormous housing projects built by the city of Vienna, vast assemblages of humanity in Heiligenstadt, say, or out on the edge of the city in Margareten. It was better out there for children: they grew up in light and air and in friendlier surroundings, with playgrounds and wading pools in the summer. Certainly that was good. It would have been even better if the ages could have been cleanly cut off one from another. But the old streets and the "modern living conditions" overlapped because the people brought all their paraphernalia with them into the new apartments—cupboards and crockery, worn carpets and hideous old lamps—and in the end there was a great chaos of contemporaneity, everything jumbled and juxtaposed, and the new aged with the old and rotted along with it.

Filled with such melancholy visions, I sat for perhaps half a minute on the flowered chair without reaching for the telephone. At last I did so, with a considerable start, for I had been so lost in the gloomy images passing through my mind that I felt as if I were inhabited by an alien personality.

This happened in my home in Döbling.

Tuesday, May 17, 1927, in the morning.

For a few seconds I had been absent from myself, totally astray.

Schlaggenberg's landlady informed me that "the Herr Doktor" had gone away; to Styria, to see his mother.

Very well then, Quapp. "Fräulein von Schlaggenberg is off on an outing. To the Burgenland, I believe."

Rising rebellion in me. What was the meaning of this! Where-upon I made a telephone call that had no connection with the matter at hand, one that I never planned on making—to René Stangeler. Not to the Institute for Austrian Historical Studies, but to his home. A voice said in a Czech accent: "He went away last night, to Carinthia, he said."

All of a sudden everyone I knew was simultaneously departing to all four quarters of Austria.

All in all, I felt thoroughly rebuffed, as I sat by the telephone in my vestibule. I was on the point of calling Eulenfeld at his office, more or less to complain to him about this surprising set of cir-cumstances. Just as I was reaching out my hand for the receiver, the telephone's shrill ring sounded.

"This is Cornel Lasch. May I speak to Herr von Geyrenhoff, please?"

"Speaking," I said.

With my "activity," I had been beating the woods; now the fox leaped out. That was how this telephone call struck me. In the politest, friendliest manner Lasch asked whether he might see me for a quarter of an hour; he had something to tell me.

He came on Wednesday afternoon.

I had asked him for coffee.

It would have been senseless to be excessively aloof. I might worm something out of him. The whole point was not to keep him at bay, or even to act as if he were my opponent. Nonsense! He was coming, after all, because he suspected that I knew cer-tain things. He might think I knew far more than I really did; and that what I knew pointed in a certain direction, which in fact I could not even guess. He had been alarmed by Stangeler's silly "eavesdropping." That had happened twice over and must really have seemed intentional. There had also been those significant looks Kajetan and I had exchanged the Saturday before at the Siebenscheins'. And then there was the first, the real alarm shot which I had unwittingly fired on March 25 when I said something to Levielle about Quapp's resemblance to her natural father. Had this any meaning for Lasch? Did he know about it at all? That was the big mystery.

I had decided to improvise. If Lasch thought that I knew any-thing—very well, I had no intention of disillusioning him. I was not going to make any slips which would reveal that my actual knowledge lagged considerably behind his conception of it. Per-haps in this way I would be able to gain some ground, to add to what I knew.

It was half-past two. I was lolling on the window seat of the deep bay window when Lasch down below wrenched his car around the corner and came to a halt in front of the house, tires screeching.

As I watched him getting out of his vehicle and locking its door, I thought of something wholly dissociated from the affairs of the moment. First of the Stangeler family home in the Semmering area, of life there and the outings to the Höllental and over to Wildalpel. I had talked of all this with my old chief, Gürtzner-Gontard, when I'd been to see him on Sunday. Then my thoughts turned to Semmering itself, to the hotel terrace there (an asso-ciation with the luxurious appearance of Lasch's huge car?). The spotted limestone cliffs in the forest always had an autumnal look, no matter whether the season was spring or summer; the rosy sun-light so often laved them like a soundlessly breathed word, and the mountains looming up above the gentler hilly country had a southern sweetness strange for such high peaks. White table-cloths, well-dressed people. A hoot of the train disappearing into the tunnel, the brief salutation of smoke in the nose—smoke al-ready mixing with the discreet perfume of the woman at the next table, or the puff of a cigarette. . . . And in the end all of this to-gether seemed to point to faraway places, as did the sun-stained cliffs, like coral reefs glowing out of the mossy fastnesses of the woods.

For moments I was lost in these images and felt as if I were in-habited by an alien personality.

I heard the Czech maid in the vestibule.

I stayed where I was. She would let Lasch in.

Now he rang. I was still at the window. There was a knock at the door. I called: "Come in," and went toward the middle of the room. Lasch entered.

My first impression was: I liked the man. Quite unreservedly.

His physical appearance projected a stodginess, a clumsiness, which I was certain was not at all the truth about the man. The whole of his stocky figure seemed formed after the pattern of his wide firm jaws. The imitation was carried out even by the heavy horn-rimmed glasses.

"How do you do, Herr von Geyrenhoff?" he said slowly, bowing and smiling in a way that was quite winning; there was a kind of irony directed at himself far down in the underlying structure of that smile. The irony—it was plain to see—was concerned with his presence here, with the fact that he had come to call on me at all.

"Delighted, Herr Lasch," I said, shaking hands with him. Then we settled ourselves comfortably. The girl brought in a pot of Turkish coffee, which he greeted with pleasure, but asked to be excused from the cognac. He lost no time in getting down to business.

"I have come to you, Herr von Geyrenhoff," he said, "in order to entrust a certain item of information to a person of absolute and unquestionable integrity. You are all the more the logical person to hear it, Herr von Geyrenhoff, since you are already acquainted with certain other confidential matters—but no more need be said about that. I consider you a man of absolute probity, and therefore the very person who should know this."

I was extremely impressed by Cornel Lasch, so much so that I had a fundamental insight. I decided then and there that there are two kinds of people whom one comes in contact with. The first kind are those who remain completely captive to their established trivialities, their blind spots and walled-up places, so that despite all other excellent qualities they might possess, they could never quicken those blind spots, never pierce through the walls that confined their view. My prime example of that was

Frau Friederike Ruthmayr. She was entirely a social product, not in the economic sense of the phrase, but in the way her sensibility had been formed and conditioned. Her trivialities were quite fixed. They might equally well have been an altogether different set of trivialities, but those too would have been fixed for all time. When you talked with Frau Friederike or other women and men of her type, you had to pay careful attention lest you offend them. And that concern barred all possibility of real conversation. For every real interchange opens gateways into the here and now. But when you are with a person who is resolved to do anything but enter through such a gateway, the process of speaking one's mind can degenerate into the greatest impoliteness or even callousness. Thus there are people with whom it is impossible to talk, though they may be the dearest, most decent, most energetic and intelligent persons in the world. Talk is impossible because you have to be too careful with them. The opposite of such persons are the completely open individuals. With them you may talk about anything you like, though they may be the most cunning, the most corrupt, the most questionable persons in the world. Lasch was one such. Nothing that might be said to him would embarrass him.

With Lasch it was possible to talk.

Not that I was going to be tempted to that. Still, there was something beneficent about his personal aura. Such is sometimes found among big businessmen, and also among physicians.

"And what is that item of information?" I asked, amiably and casually, coffee cup in hand. "I shall certainly respect your confidence."

"I am not asking that at all," he said pleasantly. "On the contrary. You are entirely free, Herr von Geyrenhoff, to pass this on to anyone and everyone. Moreover, you may even say that I gave you full permission to do so."

"This is more or less a news release, then," I said.

He laughed heartily.

"But I am not operating a news service," I parried.

"I am aware of that," he said, still laughing. "I merely want you to know. It is this: that I am not identified with Financial Counselor Levielle, or no longer identified with him. That is all. I know that people think otherwise. That theory was never altogether right. Now it is not so at all. There is a well-known Jewish expression for the temple servant and for subordinates in general. I am not—to use that expression—Herr Levielle's *'shammes.'* "

"May I ask an indiscreet question?" I said, laughing; the whole conversation, in fact, was conducted in a mirthful tone.

"Fire away, my dear sir."

"Have you had differences or any unpleasantness with the old fellow?"

"Easy enough to have them. There's that business now about the lumber for Australia—you know about that from the newspapers, of course." (I had no idea, had never heard of the matter, and of late had scarcely been reading the newspapers). "Well, to put the matter in the language of the financial page: 'No agreement could be reached on the methods for obtaining the capital.' Or as I have already said, I am not Herr Levielle's *'shammes.'* "

Naturally I was perplexed; I was quite up in the air. Once again I saw that I knew nothing at all (and I had set myself up as a chronicler!), that I had nothing to go on but a vague suspicion, based on nothing but my own wild imaginings.

"I understand," I said in a benevolent tone, really as though I were deeply sympathetic.

"Wood can be used for building, and paper too—newsprint, for instance. I wouldn't want to think that Herr Levielle and I have become so much involved in wood products that we are both on the skids. There are people who look much alike, because of the material out of which they are made, but who nevertheless are not related to each other. It might seem that Levielle and I are closely associated. But the fact of the matter is that our ways are parting for good. That is all I wanted to say."

"And how do you feel about it?" I said, only in order to gain time, for it seemed that he already wanted to take his leave. I was struck by the double meanings in his last speech. Were they involuntary—a welling up of subjects just under the surface of consciousness—or were they deliberately planted there, to sound me out? But I am sure I gave no sign of being alerted. Nor did he seem to be observing me in any narrow way.

He seemed satisfied; he stood up and said: "My dear Herr von Geyrenhoff, this talk has done me ever so much good. One doesn't often have a chance to speak frankly—especially with you. Thank you very much, too, for the great friendliness with which you have received me."

He bowed slowly, laughed, we shook hands again, and I went with him as far as the vestibule. As the door closed behind him, I was left standing in front of it—the way one stands in front of a closed door. Blocked. Even though it was the door of my own apartment.

For today I had had enough. I took care of some correspondence and then went out. It was still light. I wanted to take a long walk, to get myself into motion. The visit from Lasch, my thoughts and speculations, all lay lumpily within me, like some coagulated liquid. I was filled, not with melancholia now—that can be a kind of animation, if it is powerful and deep—but with a sense of staleness and depression. I felt as if I had lost my grip on everything. Here was the deep subway cut. I walked along it. Normally, this whole neighborhood still held some of the charm of newness for me. Those who travel a great deal become dulled in this respect; they can no longer find novelty in such modest matters as a change of neighborhood within the same city. Foreign countries fly toward us on tracks and roads, whirl through us, and often leave very little behind. But for me, ever since I had been living here, a new radiance had lain beyond every line of villas that ascended a hill toward the sky.

Still, wouldn't it be nice to take a trip?

After all, I was a well-to-do bachelor.

The next moment I saw that any trip was out of the question.

How could I abandon the field, when Levielle had suppressed a will and Lasch—who had perhaps been meant to pull the chestnuts out of the fire—could "reach no agreement on the methods for obtaining the capital."

So that I really could not go off on any trips, not in the near future. That was clear. Or was I only making myself important? I walked down the main street of Döbling. I should have stepped into some pastry shop or café, but I felt rejected everywhere, by house after house; I walked as if I had been turned out. If there had been any She to walk beside me, arm in arm, I would have been carrying a house with me, a snail's shell. As it was, I crawled along naked, slow, with waving antennae. Such are the low points in the life of the bachelor, of a well-to-do bachelor who does not travel, who really cannot travel. Every status has its snares.

Twilight began to fall. Here and there the first lights appeared. I came to the end of the Döbling main street, to that border region where a new span of my personal life coincided with a new neighborhood in which I dwelt. An enchantment that had held me spellbound for nearly half a year was coming to an end.

I wanted to make a turn somewhere, do something that would let me step out of the rut, something that would interrupt the too predictable course of the years. (At bottom, elderly people are always walking their own death like a puppy on the leash. . . .) In short, I wanted to get out of all this. It was this which must have made me turn left rather than right after I passed under the viaduct. I was drifting about like a wild animal in the forest; and I suddenly became aware of that; we were all wandering about in a forest which could not be seen for the trees. I had come into the neighborhood which is still called Liechtenwerd, which means a meadow full of light. The terrain dropped off sharply; I could see far out over the tangle of rails of the railroad station for the trains to Czechoslovakia. I was standing there on a kind of belvedere, with balustrades, fifteen or twenty feet above the freight terminal.

No, it was no longer a meadow full of light; it was a sooty expanse, and the eye followed long rows of rusty-brown freight cars parked on sidings as far as the ocher-colored viaduct.

I turned away from this scene and plunged into the city again, walked down Liechtenstein Strasse, sank beneath its surface. Here was another neighborhood I had seldom entered. Among a group of dreary tenements I saw a low yellow building some centuries old, judging by its lines. It may once have been a stopover inn in the days when the open highway ran there. A sign announced "Hotel," and what kind of hotel it was could easily be guessed. But the building itself—solid, shallow, two-storied—stood out as superior to the other buildings around there, in spite of its possibly unsavory uses. Anyone reasonably familiar with the various ages and architectural styles of the city could not fail to notice it.

I saw this happen. A gentleman on the other side of the street, dressed in a light topcoat, light-colored gloves, and gray hat set most correctly on his head, stopped and looked across at the old building. He simply stared toward it, not really studying it; his pause was too brief for that. Already he began walking on. Slowly, rather clumsily, with bowed head. I recognized the man as Imre von Gyurkicz only after he had passed. He seemed not to have noticed me at all.

The street narrowed and tilted, with the right sidewalk, on which I walked, lying far higher than the left. I strolled by small old houses. I saw one entrance which surely belonged to the period before 1800, and drifted on. I also went by the Blue Unicorn, which at that time I did not know; I failed to observe the faïence figure set into the corner of the building. Now I came to a region of traffic, streetcars, tooting horns, and ringing bells. I turned to the right. By the time I reached Ring Strasse, darkness had fallen. The street roared evenly like a waterfall.

When I reached the center of the city, I walked down a number of quieter streets to Bank Gasse. There was the Hungarian Embassy. I went through the portal of the onetime palace, stepped up to the illuminated glass cubicle of the gatekeeper, and placed my card on his counter. Was Herr von Orkay at home? It seemed he was; the man telephoned, and a moment later Géza came running down the wide steps. "*Gyuri bacsi!*" he exclaimed. "How delightful."

Would I like to come up? he asked. "Have you anything planned for this evening?" I asked. "Not a thing," he said. He sprinted back upstairs for his coat and hat, and we went out to eat in the old cellar restaurant three stories below the Hofburg. They had a ridiculous clock set in the wall which marked the hour with old-fashioned hunting fanfares instead of the usual "cuckoo, cuckoo." Amid such clangor our meal was brought, and we burst into laughter. To add to the jollity, we had ordered venison. I had the illusion that I had jumped out of my fatal rut.

Soon after we had done eating, I observed that Géza wanted to tell me something. You can almost always sense that sort of thing beforehand; a bulging area of high pressure within a conversation, which yields when the person speaks at last.

"I'd been wanting to call you, *Gyuri bacsi*" (that means "Uncle Georg," although I was not his uncle but a cousin; still, I was so much older than he); "I've been wanting to talk to you. You know, I've been thinking of changing my post, leaving Vienna. How does that strike you?"

"It amazes me, Géza," I replied. "Vienna is a preferred post, after all. You were lucky to be sent here."

"I know, Georgy," he said. "I was lucky. But I have no luck here and I'm unhappy."

"But what's wrong, Géza?" His expression startled me. "You know you can talk frankly to me."

"I know, and thanks," he replied. "I'll do just that. First of all, to make it short: there's my position here as attaché." We both looked around to make sure no one was sitting within earshot. "The position carries with it certain political burdens. I need say no more about that. You know what I mean. The ambassador keeps free of them, as far as he can, and so I'm delegated to handle these things. The result is that I've been thrown into contact with certain circles here in Vienna which make me more and more want to puke. Especially since last January when the whole crew showed their real face and some poor kid was shot in Schattendorf. Well, that was about the end of it for me. I've come to see quite a few things differently. You'd have to be deaf, dumb, blind, and besotted not to see that these butchers—I mention no names, but you know who I mean—just because they were once needed to restore order, now want to take over the whole show. Their methods aren't anything for a civilized state, and their affairs are nothing a diplomat has any business being involved in. That's the first reason I want to transfer."

"Any openings likely?"

"Yes."

"Where?"

"Berne. No such monkey business out there. Here the ground is hot underfoot."

I did not comment. I was not entirely unacquainted with the matters he was discussing.

"And what would be the second reason?" I asked at last.

"Reason number two," Géza continued, "is that I'm miserably unhappy here in Vienna. An altogether hopeless love. There. Now I've said it. It's been killing me. I must get away."

"And who is she?" I asked. "May I know . . . ?"

"You may," he said. "Quapp."

I leaned back. I felt literally smashed in the face by the sense of utter failure—I had never noticed the slightest sign! Not a thing. Only now that I had been set wise, a few items came to my mind . . . Géza's markedly respectful treatment of Quapp, for example. . . . "But you never noticed a thing!" I cried to myself. To think that I had wanted to be a "chronicler"—but no, I no longer dared even to think of that.

We both sat silent.

Out of the violated and exposed caverns of my nonknowing there arose—a kind of creation out of the void—a ready-made picture, consisting of an ideal match, implemented on the one side by a sizable fortune and on the other by the distinction accruing to a legation secretary at the Royal Hungarian Legation in Berne. Poor Quapp.

I was stuck; I did not want to say anything at all. At last I managed to bring out a question, to fill the gap. "Have you said anything to Kurt about your wanting to transfer?" (I meant my nephew, Doktor Körger.)

"No," Géza said. "I hardly think he would sympathize with any of my reasons. The captain and Kurt are thick as thieves these days. Similar views. In regard to Schattendorf, for example."

"And about Quapp?" I asked.

"Naturally not. Altogether unthinkable. In his sausage-shaped way, he's so damned down-to-earth and so lacking in the least sensitivity. Oddly enough, that's why Kurt has been a kind of support to me all this time. But I can't stand it any longer. No, I can't stand it any longer."

Suddenly, faced with this predicament without exit, this walled-up gateway—for so every passion of others appears to us, and how terribly wrong we are!—faced with this, it struck me that I had to act. This was the second time that I had felt this urgency—the previous time being the Tuesday before when I had fallen off my chronicler's hobbyhorse. I was also astonished to learn of the role my nephew Kurt had been playing in Géza's life of late. But then it is well to realize that everyone fulfills a function for everyone else, and that we present as many faces as we have functions to fulfill.

I was impressed by the way Géza said nothing further about Quapp herself. He did not allow himself even a single one of those observations which pretend to be objective but whose real purpose is to linger over a sweet and painful image. He did not even take to psychologizing. He had himself in a firm grip—but was already admitting defeat and preparing for flight. Poor bird Turul!

He himself reverted to the earlier, more general subject, thus sparing me the necessity of saying anything about his personal plight. "The child was shot," he said. "But the exploitation of such an incident to further the ends of the class struggle is indicative of an abyss of shallowness—forgive this contradictory metaphor, *contradictio in adjecto* as our humanistic captain would say with his classical tag for every emergency. But shallowness can be abysmal—that's the real secret of it, that it is so shallow and yet has such a force. Two-dimensional in the midst of three-dimensionality. Sorry, but I must turn philosophical. In the view of certain highly placed personages a Hungarian has no right to a brain, but only to a dumpling heavily spiced with paprika inside his skull. That seems to be the official view. So that they too are no more scrupulous than the Reds when it comes to grinding a child's corpse into propagandistic hash. You may wonder at how well informed I am—I've spent the last week in the library, looking over the newspapers since the beginning of February. The leftist papers and the rightist ones. If anyone thinks there is the slightest ray of hope in either one of these two movements, he deserves to have a roofing tile fall on his knob. As indeed one will when the roof over all our heads collapses all at once, as it's bound to do, in the near future. My pessimism for personal reasons fits in very well with my pessimism for general philosophical reasons. I really see no way out. *Impavidum ferient ruinae.*"

We left the restaurant and slowly climbed the many ancient stone stairs.

Out on Schaufler Gasse, I found it hard to take my leave of Géza. A man in his fix, as I knew, does not feel solitude fragrantly surrounding him like the springtime air; rather, it perilously besieges an asthma of the heart.

The following day, Thursday, I tried again to call up Quapp and this time got her at once. She greeted me delightedly, so exuberantly that I could picture her wide mouth grinning from ear to ear. Yes, it seemed she had actually been to the Burgenland. And now she threw at me a jumble of words concerning Carnuntum, which is not in the Burgenland at all. I didn't set her straight on this geographical point, and waited until her ebullience subsided somewhat, which it did after a while. It seemed to spring from some excitement whose source I did not know. When would Kajetan be back in town? I asked. Not until next week, she replied, he was visiting Mother.

When she ceased to bubble quite so much, I was able to get around to the purpose of my call.

"Quapp," I said, "listen to me for a moment. I need some information from you which is important to me. I want you to answer a single question, even if it strikes you as extremely silly."

"Yes, yes, of course, go ahead."

"Tell me, Quapp my girl, has anyone recently told you of some legacy you are to receive?"

"I should say so!" she shouted into the telephone and burst into laughter. "Glory has descended upon me in my hovel! The most amazing thing! Won't Kajetan be surprised! Our tough times are over!"

"Quapp, my dear, my heartiest congratulations!" I said. "But you must tell me about it in detail. Not over the phone. When and where can we meet?"

"Wonderful!" she boomed. "Incidentally, something else: guess whom I met on the street yesterday in Deutsch-Altenburg. That nice sergeant you were walking with Sunday on the Graben—I can't remember his name. . . ."

"Alois Gach," I said.

"Yes, that's it. Imagine, he saved me from a most embarrassing situation in Altenburg. I have to tell you all about that too."

"Did you know about the legacy when we saw you Sunday on the Graben, Quapp?" I asked.

"Not at all," she said. "I only heard about it Tuesday night. But how in the world do you know already?"

"I can only tell you that when I see you, Quapp. But when?"

"Hm, that's a complicated nuisance," she said and her tone drooped, grew weaker, sounded almost broken. "On Monday I have an awfully important audition with a conductor. And here it is Thursday. I have hardly four days left to practice. I'm not ready yet. I really wouldn't like to so much as step out of the house before Monday. Please understand! It would give me such enormous pleasure to meet you now. But I'd better save it up till afterwards, as a reward. Do you understand?"

"Why, of course, certainly, I fully understand, Quapp," I said dutifully. "Only I don't see what sort of reward it could be, meeting me. . . ."

We agreed that I would wait for her to telephone on Tuesday —May 24. All very well and good. I had pretended to be understanding concerning her pressing need to practice, but in reality I did not understand it at all. Did she expect to learn to play the violin in those four days or to reach a higher stage of violinistic development? The few instrumental artists I had known would have been capable of displaying their full brilliance at any hour, even if they were roused all of a sudden out of their deepest sleep.

There I stood with all my speculations, my resolutions on a "higher form of action," like the cow in front of the barn door. For everything had settled itself. I was a ridiculous ass. There was not a thing to stop me from traveling.

From what Alois Gach had told me, I had come to the conclusion—could I be blamed for this?—that Quapp was Kajetan's half sister. For the time being I had no idea that there was not the slightest blood-relationship between the two. Even now, as I thought about Levielle, the same thing happened to me that had happened during my first hasty theorizing: I lost touch with the ground underfoot. All my guesses and deductions had been in vain. I had reached the end of my efforts both as chronicler and as actor. My total bankruptcy was exposed. I soon came to the curious conclusion that I had had no right whatsoever to resign from my civil service post. "Pensionism" inexorably tests a man by providing him with a perfectly round, unlimited horizon of freedom. So far as I knew, I had never really failed as an active civil servant. But now I was failing—as a pensioner.

MARY awoke. At first it seemed to her still completely dark. Then she observed that the darkness was already graying. She lay on her back with eyes open. Beside her slept Trix. They lay in twin beds, as at home, here in the small pension at Semmering. Mary had been firm about not wanting to stay in a large hotel. But almost every afternoon they had their coffee at the Panhans, on the terrace, surrounded by "everybody," looking out over the last receding curtains of mountains against the hilly uplands. Often a rosy glow lingered on individual limestone reefs that jutted out of the mossy forests, and the clouds stood still against the warm southern sky like thoughts that someone had failed to pursue and that now hovered there, frozen, as though they were going to float above the horizon forever.

Mary listened with tenderness to Trix's breathing.

It had scarcely grown any brighter.

The French doors leading out to the balcony stood open.

Mary felt a pain, or rather only a sense of discomfort, where there was no longer anything, where her right knee had once been. She groped under the blanket with her hand and touched the warm stump of her thigh. This movement was nothing unaccustomed; usually it sufficed to dispel the vague pain, to prove it mere imagination. That happened now. The stump was smooth. She could feel scarcely any scar. It was smooth and warm. During her whole stay up here at Semmering, Mary had been walking well. She scarcely gave a thought to the leg and even did a good deal of climbing.

Now the dream returned, which waking had for a moment snuffed out. First only a fragment of it came to the surface. The courts of the Augarten Tennis Club, to which she had once belonged. The reddish sandy clay. The white lines. She was running. Actually, she had wanted to achieve all that again; that had been the meaning of her concentrated efforts, especially during the crucial time in Munich. Enough that she could now walk again, even walk very well. A lack had been remedied. She had accomplished what she had had in mind. At bottom Mary had believed that this accomplishment would bring about the second great change, would partly balance out the disaster of September 21, 1925. Enter Leonhard. So that was it. She suddenly understood that every real change consists not only in the elimination of something. Now, in inextricable involvement, Leonhard literally occupied the space where the missing limb had been. So that was what had really happened in front of the Franz Josef Railroad Station on September 21, 1925. The misfortune was only a part; Leonhard made it a whole; it was all interconnected. She tried to assail the iron ears of life with a question, interrogating these moments of semiconsciousness: would she have been happier keeping her leg but never having seen Leonhard? The iron ears did not open; silence followed her question, and at last the question itself dissolved. It was nonsensical. For there was no choice; both were part of one and the same complex; and this consolation held overwhelming power.

Now it was graying inside the room. The three-legged Secessionist stool in front of the equally old-fashioned dressing table began to emerge from the dimness. Mary swung out of bed without difficulty. She reached for the artificial leg; she stepped into it. The straps and bands slid smoothly and obediently through her fingers; it had all been practiced hundreds of times. She stood. She walked. Throwing a kimono over her nightgown, she stepped out onto the balcony. It was still night. But in the east, a growing pallor was appearing among the tree trunks. Out of the darkness of the mountain forest, frail whistling chirps at regular intervals slit the stillness. As more and more detail emerged from the rent velvet of the night, the chirping swelled rapidly; complex cadenzas began to accompany it. The concert grew louder until the moment that the glowing globe of the sun edged over the sweep of the forest in the east. Then it was as if a brief intermission were being observed; for as the orb lifted itself into the sky, the woods were for a few seconds utterly still.

Weilguny appeared on the terrace every afternoon. The saxophone and clarinet of a small band playing inside the hotel could be heard out on the terrace. Mary sat comfortably. Trix accepted Weilguny patiently; no more than that. He remained a feature of the foreground. She looked over his shoulders, and not only while dancing; she was always looking beyond him. And all the time she knew what was going on in her mother's mind and feelings. She knew all. When Williams and Emma Drobil came up, it was a relief; with five of them there, real and serious conversation became feasible. The talk digressed to London, and it came out that Williams knew Mme Libesny. Trix occasionally danced with Williams and Emma with Weilguny. One pair always stayed with Mary, and finally Williams remained alone with her. He told her briefly about the picture in Mme Libesny's drawing room on Albert Road in Battersea—told her, that is, only that he had seen the photograph there, and that Mme Libesny had spoken about her. A train whistled: a cry from far away. At some deeper level of intuition Mary knew of her importance to Williams, though he had said nothing about it. But she was altogether without curiosity. In her own way, she too was looking over Dwight's shoulders, though without the contempt that underlay Trix's treatment of Weilguny. The sky was dizzily blue and high. A pink glow laved the distant cliffs. Mary's predicament was like a thin grating, easily seen through; yet you could not be altogether sure of what lay behind it, though whatever it was pressed forward, imposed itself upon Mary. What it was, still, was the oneness between Leonhard and the accident in front of the Franz Josef Railroad Station. That oneness was plain, and yet its meanings could not be assessed. The real, the actual goal had not been her triumph over that fearful emptiness where her right leg had formerly been. And the past weeks with the parties, with Captain von Eulenfeld and the students, all that lay behind like a brief intoxication, already embarrassing in retrospect. Probably her son Hubert had been right with his cold rejection of all that. . . . Emma and Weilguny came off the dance floor. Again a train whistled, rushing away now in the opposite direction. Swiftly, a streamer of steam formed, as if drawing a line under everything that Mary had just been thinking.

About this time, toward the end of May, Leonhard in Vienna made the acquaintance of an upright handsome policeman, a Sergeant Zeitler. He was about the same age as Leonhard. Zeitler made a hobby of local history—the history of the Brigittenau district of the city. But he did not know Latin and so could not decipher a certain document. Leonhard came to his aid; old Scheindlerian that he was now, the simple medieval Latin gave him no trouble at all.

The acquaintanceship had been struck up at a soccer game at which Karl Zeitler—in civilian dress—happened to be sitting beside Leonhard. The two men left the field together. As they did so, Leonhard casually remarked that highly disciplined practice in running and the ability of men to throw themselves into battle with unimpaired strength after a run had once been of crucial historical importance—had in fact affected the birth of Europe. He cited the Battle of Marathon, repeating much of what he had once heard from the bookseller Fiedler (and his daughter Malva, but Leonhard did not think of her at all now). In so saying, he touched upon Zeitler's ever-alert interest in matters historical, for this interest was not limited to local history. And so the two scholars fell into a conversation that went on for some time. And Leonhard learned a good deal.

Leonhard passed this whole period—we are referring to the month or so during which Mary was absent from Vienna—very quietly, in a state of contemplation of which he himself was scarcely aware. Not until it was over did Leonhard become fully aware of the value of these few weeks, of their sustaining and up-lifting force.

About a week after his return from Carinthia, Stangeler ran into Leonhard at the university library. It was evening—Leon-hard rarely missed an evening in the reading room. Later, the two turned their steps homeward together; that is to say, Stangeler went to Grete Siebenschein's (whether he was really at home there need not be discussed now) and so could walk as far as Althan Platz with Leonhard.

This walk soon became a daily habit with the two of them. And curiously enough, when Leonhard later thought back upon those weeks without Mary, the walks with Stangeler proved to be the really significant development of that period. Soon they waited for each other down below at the library steps; they would then leave the university building through a small door that gave on Reichsrat Strasse. If either one were missing of an evening, the other really missed him.

Daylight lingered much longer those days. At the hour that Leonhard and René walked down Universitäts Strasse and Alser Strasse, then to the right and uphill into Spital Gasse, twilight still hung in the mother-of-pearl sky, though the street lights had already been turned on.

Between the two young men there existed a relationship which joined them, far beneath their more or less technical conversa-tions, like the meshing of precisely fitted gears. Stangeler's recent good luck had made it possible for him to earn his livelihood by his profession. His prospects were very good; he was busily evalu-ating the find made at Neudegg; and in the offing were also the various things hinted at by Dwight Williams. René was gradually growing accustomed to having solid ground underfoot, and stepped more lightly.

Had René associated more often with Leonhard in the past, he would surely have been deeply impressed by Leonhard's ability to support himself through practical and useful labor. He would have looked upon Leonhard's choice as a sensible course he himself had failed to take. As it was, luckily for Stangeler, no such regrets occurred. Leonhard, for his part, was growing more and more passionate about his studies and was feeling the pressure of lack of time. He therefore regarded the man at his side as the embodiment of desirable freedom. Candid René had made no secret of the terms under which he was living and working. And although envy was unknown to Leonhard, he nevertheless found it harder these days to defend his own situation and the relationship between occupation and inclination as ardently as he had once done to the bookseller Fiedler—in the days when something still "remained to be proved."

Yet it was René himself who vividly, fervidly, sang the praises of Leonhard's own situation in life. Every really heroic achievement—this was how René put it—had to be made under superpressure and compression; if every effort is given the space it needs in a person's life, the first thing that happens is loss of tension. Thus René. "Every triumph is a cancellation," he said. And fell silent at once. For he could not help recognizing that the words of another had fallen from his lips—and moreover the words of a well-situated scholar with an assured career, an automobile, and a fiancée; in short, Mr. Dwight Williams.

"On the other hand," he then continued, the egocentricity of a young man returning in close spirals upon itself, "on the other hand, every so-called success restores equilibrium again. We are rehabilitated, throw off our obligations. What that really comes down to is the opportunity to see the world anew. That way we can more easily get away from ourselves, escape from our own gravitational field, so to speak. That is the spirit in which a success must be pursued, it seems to me; only through this does the success become a success. Not in our wishing for more success of the same sort. I'm sure you will eventually experience that in some shape, Herr Kakabsa, and I hope you'll remember me then. At any rate your initial situation is almost ideal."

And here we may see how the egocentricity of youth aims beyond itself, at least in any halfway normal mental apparatus. It is as in archery when the bowstring is stretched to the limit, almost to the full length of the arrow; then, at the moment of release, it loses its tension and vibrates with a melancholy sound like the plucked D-string of a cello—such is the tone that lingers after the bowshot and after all heroic achievement on the part of youth. But the arrow has flown with full force, and perhaps it really hits its mark.

So it went. Sometimes they stopped and sat somewhere, or they wandered into some café and Stangeler telephoned to Grete that he was with Kakabsa and would come a little later. Grete was sensible enough to approve of René's new friendship; she even knew that if she did not, René would be endlessly scornful of her. Once she suggested that René bring Leonhard along to see her, and the evening turned out quite well. It proved, in fact, to be highly educational, for Kakabsa modestly but firmly contested a good many of Grete's enlightened and socialistic views. Not that he had any idea of the weight the opinions of a "man of the people" carried in those days for such "cultured" persons as Grete, who belonged among those who had been swimming with the stream for nine years, since 1918, often keeping 'way ahead in a passion of contemporaneity that was already going too far.

It was half-past nine, that evening, when Leonhard left the house on Althan Platz and went home. He had felt, there on the Siebenschein floor, below Mary's apartment, as if the house were a nut without its kernel.

But the bridge across the Danube Canal arched high in the middle, and high above it the new moon flew freely along in the blue night sky. Up from the water the odor of moisture rose, cutting into the dusty air: a heavy ripe fragrance of thick grass along the embankments.

Until a year before, Zeitler had not been in Brigittenau; he had been assigned to the Alsergrund precinct. But he lived with his parents fairly near Leonhard. His father was a "certificate holder" —such was the term for police officials of the lower ranks who, having completed their term of service in the police, were entitled to a salaried civilian post. In the latter post he had won promotion and then retired. His son, Karl Zeitler, took pride and pleasure in being a policeman. The good tradition of the Viennese police force fell upon fertile soil; old Zeitler—who had also served in the glorious Royal and Imperial Austrian Army—had a special way, earnest and emphatic, of speaking of the "comradeship" of the force. To his mind, comradeship was the heart and soul of the service. The same opinion was held by the Viennese police commissioner's office—and is held to this day. But we must keep in mind, lest we endow those times with ideas arising from a later time, that the police force then was no military organization. We have in the meanwhile known a good many types of police forces, which grew more and more to resemble the military, until ultimately the difference between a hundred soldiers and a hundred policemen virtually vanished. And yet this difference is fundamental. A hundred policemen are one hundred individual officials acting with full responsibility, even though occasionally they may obey a unified command. But a hundred or two hundred soldiers are always a single body moved by its head, the captain: a *syntagma*, as the ancient Greeks called it; not a sum of individuals, but a being of a higher, though not more sublime, order which incorporates the individual. Hence its impetus, its brute force. In 1927, however, the Viennese police were still devoted to the pure idea of a police force. They were entirely an instrument of peace, a corps of responsible individuals, although well trained in the use of arms. They lacked the uncompromising either-or of the military, the smashing destructive effect. In those days a police force was not there to suppress; in those days the police were still guardians of the peace. But to their misfortune, the door to a new age was just then turning on its hinges. And it opened in July 1927, while the flames leaped out of the windows of the Palace of Justice: a hot summer day with not wind enough to transform the smoke into streamers.

Karl Zeitler seldom spoke of his work, even though he was entirely devoted to it; only of certain incidents which seemed to have become really personal experiences for him. One such was an accident that had befallen a lady in front of the Franz Josef Railroad Station on a warm day in September 1925. Zeitler had gone on duty at his post in front of the old-fashioned station only half an hour before. The woman had been extremely beautiful—so Karl related the story—and she had for no apparent reason run straight into an approaching streetcar. Right leg cut off above the knee. Her life had been saved only by instant and skillful action on the part of a man—a major, probably seen service in the war —who had immediately made a tourniquet around her thigh with his belt, tightening it by twisting it with his cane. Otherwise she would surely have bled to death before the ambulance arrived; there had been a whole pool of blood. A young girl had pluckily come to the aid of the major—and Zeitler himself, of course. He often thought of this man, almost as a kind of model. One of those types of the old Imperial Army—really first class. Afterwards he had had to get a cab for the major, because his clothes and the clothes of the young lady were all stained with blood; they could not very well go walking down the street in that state. He often thought of the man, Karl remarked. That was the kind of person to be, that was what you had to strive for.

Karl told this story to Leonhard one Sunday in the Danube meadows, near Kritzendorf, where he and Karl had gone for a swim; the weather turned warm early that year. They had tramped along wide arms of the river that wound through the woods, the tops of the trees almost touching overhead, the sun slanting down through the foliage and lighting the gleaming brown river down to its bottom in shallow places. Voices echoed through the vaulted woods; the smallest branches, far up, seemed to dissolve in a golden glow. People sprawled about here and there in groups, near tents, on a peninsula, in a clearing. As they followed the path along the stream, Leonhard saw at intervals small ring snakes unwinding their slender shapes and fleeing into the water. More frequently, a frog hopped and splashed. The

path climbed up and down the embankment of the uneven shore.
Trix had once told Leonhard of the circumstances of her mother's accident. She had even mentioned the major whose quick action had made such an impression on Karl Zeitler. The young lady had been his fiancée. Mary had later called on her rescuers occasionally. Leonhard said nothing to Zeitler about recognizing Mary in the story. His mind flew back, however, to Alois Gach's description of the cavalry charge, the inn called the Stork's Nest in Fraunkirchen, and the motorcycle trips to Wallern. These days he no longer went to Stinkenbrunn but to Kritzendorf, and no longer with Niki but with Karl, and no longer by motorcycle but by train, on a line that started at the railroad station where Mary had lost her right leg. But Sergeant Gach, too, was a type like that major. These people of the old days. They all had a secret. They were not stupid; even the warehouse attendant's widow was not stupid. "I'll do your prayin' for you." Leonhard became conscious of the spacious depths of the woods. Far back there, amid the impenetrable greenness, lay something like his past. Stinkenbrunn was there too, Elly Zdarsa, old Goatbeard, the bookseller, Malva. He had a past now; it was all scarcely a year old; this past was still brand new, but it lurked back there in the depths of the woods, a layer of density in itself. The present, too, had grown more dense, denser than the green thicket here. This struck Leonhard particularly when he recognized that the woman of Zeitler's story was Mary. The net! What net? The net in which he was caught, and which held him ever tighter. He was walking up Alserbach Strasse. It was almost deserted: a Sunday. The Café Kaunitz. The encyclopedia. Pico della Mirandola. There had been a time, not so very long before, when the university library was still unknown to him. That time too lay back in the depths of the woods, one layer among others: his rapidly accumulating treasure. "I am about a year old," he thought now. "With that one year, I have shaken the dust from my feet."

He felt elevated. His still nameless potentiality elevated him. He dearly wished he were able to grasp it and compress it into a single decision, as you grasp something and compress it in your clenched fist. The forest came to an end. Here was the river. The wind. The water flowed evenly. The view was far-ranging.

The two girls, Lilly Catona and Fella Storch, had long since resumed their watch at the window on Thursdays at six o'clock—once they were done with their drilling and redrilling of mathematical formulas, of aorists, of the Battle at Chaeroneia (lion, monument!). For the warm days had come again. Only Trix did not appear down below these days, never got off the streetcar. She was away in Semmering with her mother. And although she was not staying at the "Südbahn Hotel"—she had made a clean breast of that before her departure—Lilly and Fella were still profoundly impressed. It was horrible to have to go to school!

Leonhard, too, was hardly ever seen these days. The girls had no idea why. Of course Fella had treated "the Sailor" rather aloofly soon after they became acquainted. But now she would gladly have spent a pleasant half hour with him and Lilly Catona at the Freudenschuss pastry shop. And Lilly eagerly wished for something of the sort.

Because she clung to the wish, it came true. Though only after some time.

For Leonhard spent every evening at the library.

To waste no time, he had formed the habit of heading for the library just as soon as his shift at the factory ended. He slipped out of his blue work smock and into his jacket which he had hanging in the nearby office of Krawouschtschek, the factory carpenter. The good-natured Czech would be having coffee at this time, and Leonhard was always obliged to gulp down half a cup, standing. Then he ran for the streetcar. At the library, later, he noticed the salutary effect of the coffee. All tiredness had fled. The stimulation was even more effective when he had a few puffs of a cigarette along with Krawouschtschek's strong coffee. In order not to sponge on the carpenter, Leonhard one day brought him two pounds of the best Mocha mixture. The Czech thanked him cordially. *"Nasdar!"* Leonhard would greet him each time he entered. And Krawouschtschek laughed. As we can see, international relations were excellent.

But one Thursday, after the requisite coffee, Leonhard did not feel in the mood to rush off to the library. He was still too little experienced with the mechanisms of the intellect to know that our constitutions set certain limits by which to prevent us from depleting the mind's resources. Otherwise Leonhard would have recklessly plundered those resources. We must consider that at the library he was not engaged in the scholarly pursuits of leisure. His daily stint was a distinctly creative affair, though compressed into a mere hour; its purpose was to bring out into the light the sprouts which had been germinating in his mind, during sleep and waking, for the past twenty-four hours. When the attendants in the hall called out: "Closing time, please, closing time!"—Leonhard was often thoroughly exhausted. Perhaps a kindly fate operated in those days to give him but that one hour in the library.

It was inevitable, therefore, that one evening the tension deserted him even as he was standing in Krawouschtschek's office, and even before he had had his cigarette (which the carpenter always finished to the end, for Leonhard did not take the time for it). And so this evening he sauntered slowly along, and his fat, hard-bound notebook remained in his coat pocket. Taking the route he had customarily walked in the past, he saw Lilly and Fella at the window. Involuntarily, he stopped. They waved. They signaled that they would come down. Leonhard had not been prepared for that. Now they joined him. Now they were walking together as they had in the past. Now, out of the forested depths of a short but highly personal past, an already existing layer broke free and floated up, drifted forward. Moreover, Malva Fiedler was standing in the door of the bookshop. Leonhard greeted her as he passed by with the girls, but without in the remotest way glancing into that province of life to which Malva must have directed her gaze when she saw him approaching between fragile little Fella and rather massive Lilly Catona. It is appropriate to remark that in this particular passage through the realms of Venus, Leonhard was completely blind to an extremely lovely belly which once upon a time, at the Danube Canal and then on the bridge, had almost lured him to a sublime and sublimated form of suicide.

Nowadays as he rode the streetcar along this route, it never entered Leonhard's mind that he had just roared past the Fiedler bookshop; nor did the corner house on Jäger Strasse come to his mind—not even on Thursdays.

Well, now they were walking. The proprietress of the tea room recognized Leonhard as well as the girls. Fella had to pay the bet, at high odds, for Lilly Catona had recklessly gambled upon one who had become a total outsider, had wagered that today, today of all days, he would pass by, down there on the street; and along had come Leonhard. Three doughnuts and two rum babas with brandy-soaked cherries! Imposing Lilly stowed away both pastries with ease. Without a doubt she possessed magical powers of wishing; she had proved that today. Unfortunately she lacked the time to enjoy the situation to the full, for she was going to the theater with her parents that evening and needed to primp a bit. But for the time being she plashed away with a gay rapid flow of chatter. In high good spirits, Leonhard offered to treat Fella to another doughnut, which offer was straightway accepted. Actually, he was the only real, true-to-life child here; with the girls, this sort of thing was only an affectation nowadays.

After Lilly had left, Leonhard accompanied the "clearwing" toward the bridge; they even went down the steps and walked along the embankment for a while. Things were lively down there; people had taken off coats and jackets and spread them on the grass; there were even card games in progress. The sun was still shining. Walking along here with Fella, Leonhard felt as if he were on a flat roof, on a level plane with her; thus had all the vaultings and arches collapsed. Malva, Trix, Elly Zdarsa above all: he had become as indifferent to them as to Fella. He walked along beside her as if tramping upon the roof of an entire year.

They ascended again. Leonhard was ready to walk Fella all the way home. But midway on the bridge—as though she amiably wished to release him from any such obligation—she smilingly shook hands with him, turned, and flitted off.

At home, Leonhard found a card from Mary awaiting him. He recognized at once that the address had been written by Trix. The card stood propped against the short row of books which adorned Leonhard's desk. In this way, "I'll do your prayin' for you" had signalized the rare event of the arrival of mail.

"Most cordial regards from the lovely mountains here. Faithfully, Mary K."

Underneath her signature: "Trix."

A wildly surging wave of burning fidelity: such was Leonhard's response to the one little word that danced between the conventionalities and a longed-for deeper meaning, danced back and forth like a point of light in a moving glass. He took in the lines on the little white card as if he wanted to drink them away, leaving only a blank surface behind. The "K." was scarcely defined. But the name "Mary" stood out boldly. The handwriting was altogether different from Trix's sharp, easily flowing script. It was an open handwriting, almost like a child's, the letters marching along side by side in orderly fashion; a sturdy, good-souled handwriting.

Leonhard leaned forward, more and more. Finally his forehead rested upon the desk top, his lips upon Mary's lines. His heart, as healthy as that of a three-year-old horse, pounded.

Géza von Orkay had just accompanied his superior in the car from the embassy to the East Station—the chief was going to Budapest and wished to use the ride to give Géza a few instructions—about matters, by the way, that made Géza no happier.

Now he left the platform. Against the background of the broad square stood the embassy car, and beside it the driver, Raymond Szilagi, in his livery. "Drive into town," Orkay said as he got in. "Drive slowly down Kärntner Strasse." The breeze of their movement felt good. There was a hidden pressure in the warmth, as if this afternoon suffered from an internal tumor: it was not something outside.

The weather was sultry.

It was as if you were surrounded by pillows, bedded in.

It was a state of intensified involvement, a psychologist might have said, with a relatively low degree of consciousness. Very well. All right, the matter is plain.

The speed of the big car ate into the distance; the blocks of houses of this quarter of the city near the railroad stations fell away and behind like great crumbs. The wind blew. An artificial wind, but it brought some coolness. The massive structure of St. Charles's, humped high, a columned tower against the partially blue sky. The thronging and clamor of more crowded parts of the city began, ringing of streetcar bells, tooting of horns; Géza could see down as far as the Ring, and farther still. On the right side of the Opera a multitude collected—where did they all come from? Too many, really, too many. The assemblage of so many people looked like a hanging tapestry, full of crawling movement. Géza looked straight ahead in alarm. For the first time he recognized his own condition, saw the consequences of repeated enforced restraint, holding himself in. Saw that it emptied him, wore him hollow, inescapably and utterly hopelessly.

He did not know that the chauffeur, Raymond Szilagi, who heard many a word of what was said in the back seat of the car, was a close friend of Pinta's; and so information in the end reached the count, who however made no use of it. The same cannot be said of Pinta. Behind the heavy eyebrows his whole nature lay compressed like the kernel of a hazelnut in its hard shell. He and the others never put down Géza von Orkay for "unreliable"—

no one had as yet heard the sound of her violin and had any opportunity to judge it. For had she played anywhere, the false note of that Saturday evening—her bad beginning, her failure to make contact with Tlopatsch—would have rung louder in any critic's ears than any true notes her violin might produce. But Quapp was unaware of this situation. Nor had it come to her ears that the conductor of popular symphony concerts, before whom she was to play today, was perhaps the one person in musical Vienna who did not care about the Czech pope of music and privately took it as a recommendation whenever someone came to him without a recommendation from Tlopatsch. This conductor had actually succeeded in making a good name independently of the Siebenschein domestic idol. The strings pulled and manipulated by Tlopatsch did not affect him; they could not cut into his flesh, even by way of the music criticism of the daily newspapers. For, naturally enough, the popular symphony concerts given every Sunday were not considered worth reviewing. Such a musical organization was regarded as second-rate, no doubt about it. Nevertheless, it stood on firm ground, for these popular concerts were always very well attended. A violinist in that orchestra would likewise be standing on firm ground. Quapp, to be sure, thought of the first chair. With a tone such as she had produced this morning, that would not have been out of the question. At any rate, however, she would have had to rearrange her life through and through, provided that she could obtain such a position after a certain probationary period—no matter in what chair. However, Quapp thought of the whole business, including the first chair, only halfheartedly. Her mind was fixed on a virtuoso's career. Yet a seat in that orchestra would have given her a firm basis, a professional outlook, and even considerable instruction. The conductor—a somewhat venturesome fellow who even within the sphere of popular concerts took many risks and came off successfully in regard to both programs and interpretations—this conductor was noted for his readiness to aid his men, and the few ladies in his orchestra. He gave them a lift, he promoted their careers. The orchestra was famous for its esprit de corps—and the whole thing stood outside the mysterious realm of Tlopatsch's power. To sum up the whole matter with brutal bluntness: after the disaster of Saturday, May 14, this was Quapp's last chance in Vienna. It was as simple as that.

Quapp did not know this, and her ignorance was at least one advantage.

Just now incidentally, it did not occur to her that she had often envied Gyurkicz because he was able to "live on his art," or however she put it. For here was her chance to do the same. With a job in the orchestra, and with the small Neudegg legacy in the background, she could have attained a position in which she would be free of the uncertainty and breathlessness of her existence, which so often haunted her dreams—and that is always a sign of the relative gravity of a situation! There is no doubt about it; the door was open now, and she could have slipped through.

At the moment she was still sitting over breakfast. Without any sense of comfort. On the run, as the phrase is. Gyurkicz had been banished for the day. She was free of him. That much she knew about regimen; she took it for granted, with deepest conviction, that in serious cases all false associations must fly out the door, and true ones as well. But she ought to have been comfortable, sitting over her breakfast, to have felt easy and free from care after so successful a dress rehearsal. Instead, she was inwardly driven, violently urged, to her violin; she outlined a practice program for the morning, but meanwhile dallied over her tea—fortunately.

That much at least was fortunate. But because she was so often in arrears on her regular stint, because her practicing was so often delayed or only half done, she could not skip it altogether now, proper as it would have been. What she was undergoing now—for Quapp was still sitting on the sofa—was at bottom an artificial and extremely subtle process of guilty conscience, while outside the morning padded itself in sultriness and transformed the empty street into the interior of a hothouse, a green tunnel. Gradually her earlier brilliant playing took on an unreal aspect; she felt it as a transitional state, one of the many to which she had always been exposed, like the transition that was coming later in the day. . . . As yet, she still dominated the situation. But the practicing on which she spent the rest of the morning was unnecessary and superfluous. Deep within her, like a dark flash of lightning, played the threatening insight that her trouble was not the violin playing alone but her way of living, which only seldom allowed her to come near real violin playing—whereas it should always have been ready to hand, so that she could spring upon it and ride away from all anxiety, all misery. Most of the time, however, she fended off any such possibility, and resorted instead to the most variegated means for such an escape, whether the means were called Imre, or money, or an aunt. Today she had not resisted, and out of the wisdom of sleep and dreams she had carried over into waking life the assignment that had been given her. But the impulse sufficed only for this room, for this green tunnel of a street—where she wished she could stay all the rest of the day. And scarcely for that any longer. She had happily crossed the first frontier. But beyond the second appeared an outside world which parched and wilted everything, all the fresh greenness that she had carried across the frontier of sleep, and whose reality she had proved earlier that morning.

At last it was time to have lunch, to get ready, to ride into the city.

All that went swiftly, with almost disturbing smoothness—for Quapp. It was as though she were rapidly falling through some substance of light density which scarcely bore her, which allowed her to sink down through it with the acceleration of a fall. It was upsetting. Nothing was holding her up—she could get ready so quickly—and that was just the trouble: that nothing was holding her. Yet everything was filled with anxiety in a fine suspension; an anxiety that remained nameless, that precipitated itself nowhere as a distinct accent, though for a moment it might take the face of a spiteful-looking old man on the streetcar, or spread out over the monotonous gray façade of a many-storied house. Quapp still felt herself in her own street, in the green tunnel, and already she was standing, stripped of that protecting enclosure, in a big waiting room where a considerable number of persons had already gathered, all with violin cases like herself. As soon as she entered, her eyes focused upon the face of a very young woman —though when Quapp looked closer the face proved older than she had thought, and was already underscored by the beginning of a double chin. But this did not diminish her strikingly pretty appearance. Her prettiness was only too obvious. The girl sat with a very straight nose stabbing the air before her, sat perfectly still, did not look around, talked with no one; she sat quietly beside her violin case, fitting smoothly into the row of the other aspirants, among whom, Quapp now noticed, were also several young men.

Quapp joined the row. It was warm there, too warm, and quiet. Through an upholstered door she could hear occasional strokes of a violin. At intervals of five to seven minutes one wing of the green-upholstered door would open, discharging the aspirant with the violin under his arm; he would put the instrument back into its case, which had been left outside, get ready, say good-by to the others, and leave. People were taking out their violins; Quapp did likewise. Names were called in an extremely polite, distinctly friendly tone, and the person called went into the adjoining room. What order was being followed remained unclear; it was at any rate not alphabetical. You had to be there on time and ready. Quapp at any rate was there on time—a considerable achievement for her!—and was also ready. For some time she could not make out who it was who opened the door and asked the next person in, for the wing of the door blocked her view; she did not know whether it was the maestro himself. But the sixth or seventh time he came somewhat farther into the waiting room. She saw him greet the candidate with a short vigorous nod, then close the door himself. Quapp's turn was next.

The room into which she stepped was very big and wide— why had she expected a kind of tiny cabinet? Far at the back stood a number of music stands. A single stand, metal, of the collapsible type, stood beside the maestro. It was a little askew. The conductor at once placed music on it, said: "Please," and took a few steps backward.

For almost every instrument there are collections of the most difficult orchestral passages. Quapp knew that, of course, and also knew the passage which the maestro briefly tapped with his finger. It was nothing special. She could have sight-read it even if it had been entirely new to her. But now she no longer had hands. The fingers of her left hand were spongy and swollen, the right hand was on the point of failing her altogether. Moreover, part of her right arm was missing. It consisted of nothing but air. With a truly fearful and desperate effort, she began. She was able to get the intonation purely, but her bowing was a nullity; she had almost to start twice; between the first note and the next one there was a tiny vacuum. She knew it, she felt it, even as her playing gathered some strength. She was actually in command of the subsequent passage—staccato—but the almost hoarse, sickly initial stroke had the aftereffect of poisoning everything through and through; at one point she came within a hair of playing something altogether false, or doing something altogether senseless, letting the violin drop.

Gradually the blood re-entered her fingers and arm. The passage was over. She stopped, wondering that the conductor had let her play so long. He must have observed everything. Her body was covered with sweat, but she felt it as a kind of shameful slush running down inside her underwear.

"No, that won't do, Fräulein von Schlaggenberg," the conductor said. He was standing close to her. "You are playing on the brink of the abyss, I might say. That is violinistic epilepsy."

"Tremor," she said, speaking to the page of music, not turning her eyes from it.

"Yes," he said. "With that, you cannot practice this profession. It is absolutely impossible. You must realize that. I'd like you to listen to the next candidate here; please take a seat back here. I'll give Fräulein Gagler the same passage you had—I've heard her once, incidentally. She will no more play false than you did, but she will—play. That is what counts. I rather think she is the best."

Then the girl with the sharp straight nose came in, attacked the orchestral passage without any special effort—the held whole note at the beginning did sound a little harsh, rather cutting, as if it were being played on a wind instrument; and the staccato was only a kind of walk, a Sunday stroll. "Have you a telephone, Fräulein Gagler?" the maestro asked. She handed him a card. "I want to hear you at the rehearsals too; I'll telephone you—all right?"

Fräulein Gagler left. Quapp had risen to her feet. "I'm very sorry," the conductor said. Quapp went out. She slowly placed the instrument in its case, tucked the bow into the lid, and slipped the little wooden fastener over it. For a second, while passing through the door, she had wished she could stay a while longer with the conductor. Now her violin case was closed, zipped into its green canvas cover. She thought of the manner in which two black strands of hair had fallen over the maestro's forehead when he made his curt brisk movements. Still accompanied by this image, she stepped out onto the street. She walked, carrying her violin case, but in a wrong direction, not toward the stop where she would have to take the streetcar home.

Now, suddenly, she felt how warm it was, and at the same time she felt a curious coolness on her skin; she became conscious of her skin as something slippery. Stepping around a corner, suddenly plunging into a swarm of people, she realized that she had stumbled into the dense stream of traffic on Kärntner Strasse. She drifted on in the crowd, dully, slowly, hampered and padded within a warmth which had already increased to outright heat. There was a squeal on her right; a massive something stopped; she did not look. A car door sprang open, intruding upon the sidewalk. "Fräulein von Schlaggenberg!" Orkay called. "Greetings! Where may I take you and your violin?"

At that moment she realized, as she had not done before, that the conductor had cleanly cut something out of her, a thing like a goiter or a tumor or something of the sort, which all her life, ever since her childhood, had grown with her, had been a part of her. She extended her hand to Orkay, who kissed it. Now she was free. Logically, she should simply have left the violin case standing on the pavement. But she took it along with her into the car.

"To Döbling?" Orkay asked.

She nodded.

Very soon the rapid cooling ride moved on to another plane, not only for Quapp, but also for Géza. Both these young people had been blown together by the winds of chance, each in his own way having just suffered considerable tribulation. In truth, two hereafters in the here bordered one upon the other in this automobile that glided through a hot May afternoon and through the turmoil of the center of town. Two hereafters: each was that for the other. For each was so uniquely embedded in circumstances of which the other knew nothing; and even had each known, the knowing would have been no more than a mere naming of what filled the other's soul. Not real knowledge, then; merely information. But they did not have even this in relationship to each other; there was only the contact of borders, the present situation of each: in Géza seething and then again controlled beneath a perfectly smooth though alarmingly thin surface layer. Not far below this surface there stuck, like a barbed arrow, Imre Gyurkicz of Faddy and Hátfaludy. And Quapp was stunned, stupefied, and for the time being grasped only the fact that she was being transported farther and farther from that spot on Kärntner Strasse where she had left her violin case on the sidewalk—which nevertheless was here in the car with her.

Nothing came of the ride back to Eroica Gasse, to the green street, the green pool from which Quapp was slipping away like a trout darting off to other pools through a crack between stones, turning once more, just once more, then shooting off. No, there was no point to limiting the ride to Eroica Gasse. The ambassador had let Géza have the car for the rest of the day; for pleasure trips, as was the custom, Géza had only to pay for the gasoline. That, and a princely tip for Raymond Szilagi—which said Szilagi gladly accepted, even from those gentlemen of the legation whose political attitudes he and Pinta did not thoroughly approve. The streets straightened out, became longer, emptier, greener on both sides. Now they were rushing down Grinzinger Allee, and then at a more moderate pace through the old vintners' village of Grinzing itself, and past the old church which like no other stands up to its windows in wine and tumult, against which a wild stream of casual pleasure surges and flows by, sometimes with a raging current (high water every Saturday night). And yet, in the small, frightfully ancient nave of the church it is just as quiet as in any other. With a martial roar the motor began making the curved ascent up the road to Kobenzl. Because Quapp so wished, they stopped at the "dairy," and did not go as far as the luxurious terrace of the castle.

From there they could see the city spread out below them like the palm of a hand. It was just as hot up there, but the surrounding greenery and the nearby wooded mountains made the heat less oppressive. What was sultriness down in the streets could be called fair weather up there under a blue sky. The clarity of the sky, as Géza sat there facing Quapp, made him feel the pain of the barbed arrow more acutely, as if it had just entered him, as though he had just learned of Quapp's relation with Imre von Gyurkicz. Of course he had known of it for a long time, and the wound of it was long since inflamed and swollen. But now it was a new pain again; and a pain, when it strikes, can also produce anger. That came, a bitter rage, and Géza wanted to knock Quapp from her pedestal, to overthrow the memorial he had erected to her in the center of his heart—because she insisted on living with such a horrible slippery fellow. That being what Imre was to Géza. Even the best and most beautiful of women can suffer so great a devaluation on such grounds that the loss is irreparable—except for the man who loves her. Indeed, such devaluation can last for a whole lifetime—and with a certain justice, in the final analysis. Quapp sensed his gathering gloom. But good soul that Quapp was, if she ever did finally gather what anything was all about, it was always too late. Meanwhile, the two tapped lightly at each other with questions, civil questions, casual questions; but in asking them they were already entering the crackling underbrush on the fringes of the unknown wood like the one which began not far from their table, an ever so dense and woody hereafter in the here.

The crackling was betraying. It gave a hint of many things. These first noises in the leafy margins were already incipient confidences. Géza retreated in alarm when he observed that incipience in himself. In the first place he was anything but crude, never one to trample straight ahead, and in the second place he had good reason for retreating. Moreover, the arrow hurt.

With a remarkable freedom and matter-of-factness, which surprised Quapp herself, she told him about the crucial event of the day, her failure.

His attentiveness gaped like a devouring maw. The thought flicked across his mind that these minutes might be decisive. Géza did not utter a peep, did not stir. He was like a hunter who does not dare to make a movement, but whose eye roves restlessly over the terrain beneath his sights, awaiting the proper moment to press the trigger.

First of all he reflected that Quapp, at the particular low point she had reached today, would not permit herself to be caught by the first casual comforter who knew how to interpret and exploit her momentary predicament in some vulgar fashion. Anything of the sort, Géza imagined, was far below Quapp's level—from which we see that even a diplomat can be naive.

Since, however, as things had fallen out and he had been elected for the part of sympathetic listener, he unexpectedly slid into sympathy itself; and so gently and without much noise he strode through the leafy margin of the unknown woods; it closed behind him and he saw now that he was inside, not inside the woods as a whole, but standing among a goodly grove of trees.

"This must mean a kind of turning-point for you," he said. And now it became plain that an assumed attitude, a pose like this one, of altruistic interest on Orkay's part, can unexpectedly pass into the very attitude simulated. Pose as a larval form of attitude! A gentle touch and parting of the bushes; you act as if you are entering the wood, and before you know it you are actually walking in it. Thus Géza realized that this tadpole before him had had a fictitious backbone, a kind of swallowed stick, as easily extracted as the bone of a sardine. To understand this meant that he was already walking quite deep in the woods. But of course he was at the same time suffering from the suppressed expectation that another poisonous arrow would come whizzing along and strike him.

Quapp, however, was now beginning to understand at last, because she felt herself understood with such kindness, and perhaps she wanted to return a kindness when she said: "In many respects. No, in every single respect. For only then would it be a turning-point. It would have to make everything different. That's what we mean by a turning-point, isn't it?"

Perhaps at the moment Quapp was only tossing those words before her with the intention of catching up to them later on. But enough, there and then, in that late afternoon hour, with the gold of evening overflowing its banks. A flood that could no longer be checked had begun to surge—whirl the inky lake of the city, lick up into the landscape, begin to cool to a steely blue down below there. For the first time, Quapp thrust her nose over the edge of a new horizon, whereas until now, ever since she had set the violin case down there on the sidewalk, she had been under the impression that she had lost an old horizon.

They rose from their table. Raymond Szilagi shot out of the tavern and ran to the car. But Géza advised him to take his time over another glass. They wanted to walk a bit. (So now it was to be a real walk, in a real woods; or was it after all also a hereafter in the here?)

The crimson setting sun addressed a lovely but incomprehensible speech to the real wood, which said no word and remained profoundly silent among its soaring trunks. Here, with the same trees enclosing both of them, they spoke more candidly. Quapp even mentioned Imre's name. She said straight off that, as far as she was concerned, it had become a name belonging to the past, and that it had been such for some time. She also remarked that she was thinking of moving. Orkay spoke. Nothing against Imre, although Quapp had said some things in his favor, referring to the good and sincere sides of his personality—for perhaps she was trying to fend off the verdict which Géza might well have pronounced upon her because of her relationship with Gyurkicz. Gradually, she had become aware of the peril of that verdict. And so now she twisted and turned Gyurkicz around as if he were a prism on an axis and she were trying to bring all the better facets of him to the fore, where they could show to best advantage. Orkay spoke, but of something else. As for her failure at the audition, "There are no negative events," he commented. And when something ceased and broke off, as the violin—in her opinion—had just now broken off from the rest of her body —when that took place, the impetus of the event was by no means exhausted, and the transformation of which she had spoken was still far from complete. "In life there is no such thing as a mere amputation. Not as long as life is still there, or rather, to put it another way, procreation."

He spoke calmly, with a sympathy that had long since become genuine, behind which, however, he gently put forward his own intentions. Quapp felt this, and with an extraordinary clarity and distinctness that had suddenly been given to her. When Géza spoke quietly and slowly, he made scarcely any mistakes in German, and was even able to express himself with considerable effectiveness. But the Hungarian accent, which has a homelike and familiar ring to every educated Austrian, remained with Géza no matter how well he spoke. Quapp loved that accent. And while the sun sank low enough to the horizon to pierce through a gap in the foliage and fire to a blazing red a low alder bush by the path, Quapp listened, listened really only to that Hungarian intonation in Géza's speech; and it seemed to her that for the first time she was hearing that tone, that coloration, in its purity, in altogether delightful purity. Listening back, feeling her way back, it seemed to her that Imre's way of speaking was muddied, that it came from some baser, some almost repulsive source; that it was inauthentic and unsound. All this while the sunset fire consumed the alder bush; all this while

Quapp could not turn her eyes from the spectacle, from the slowly fading crimson fire. A fire had burned down inside her as well.

"Would you please," she heard the voice saying beside her, "not call me Herr von Orkay any longer? Please say Géza to me. Please." And he had pronounced those Hungarian names as only a Hungarian can. (Incidentally, it is futile for a non-Hungarian to pretend to be a Hungarian in Vienna. Most Viennese speak no Hungarian, but they know the tone. They are in general very sensitive to differences in tone, though in other respects they can be quite deaf.)

"Gladly, Géza," Quapp said, "but you must say Quapp to me—everyone calls me that."

"Quappchen!" he cried, and now his smooth and ever tauter surface broke, and into the ridiculous name there shot a protuberance that filled the tadpole plumpness with a heated core— "Quappchen! Everyone calls her that!" He took her hand and gave it a long kiss.

The sunset had meanwhile finished its performance. They left the woods. Géza remained silent. The drive down the serpentine curves took place in the already bluish light of dusk. Quapp asked to be dropped off at the parish-house square. She did not want the car to take her all the way to Eroica Gasse. This little stratagem cast a deep and darkening shadow across Orkay's face as he helped Quapp out of the car and reached in again for the violin case. But they stood for a few moments at the door of the car, which Raymond Szilagi held open; a look joined them again, a look of understanding which the handshake only confirmed. "May I telephone you?" Géza said; and even as he said it, the question seemed superfluous to him, and in a way a break with the kind of communion they had had together till now which needed none of these conventional tropes. But just before their parting he had suddenly been struck by the fear that it could all vanish again, fade out like an improvisation.

She nodded. "See you soon," she said. While he drove off, she remained standing there, waving a bit to him, for he sat facing around and looking out the back window. Then she turned into her street. She cast a glance up at that window where washing usually hung. It was a very brief but curious look, as if she were imploring, for the span of a heart beat, kindly forbearance and understanding.

Doktor Neuberg could not remain entirely in ignorance of what Stangeler was engaged in, these days. Surrounding desks here at the Institute were peopled by a spirit equally alien, if not hostile, to both of them; for our two scholars did not belong among the ranks of the local historians. They were both, therefore, outcasts, and could make common cause on this basis, if on nothing else.

Upon his return from Carinthia, Stangeler had had two photo-stats made of the Neudegg manuscript. Now he was working from one of these, and making two copies: one an exact transcript, and one somewhat modernized, for Herzka. As for the original of Ruodlieb's manuscript, Stangeler had placed the precious thing in a safe-deposit box at a bank.

René had already made considerable progress with his transcription and explanatory notes. However, he had not yet been able to solve what he took to be the cryptogram in Ruodlieb von der Vläntsch's name. Of course the name might be the real one, after all, but René's first instinct had been to smell a cryptogram, and once an idea lodged itself in our good René's head, he did not willingly let it go.

He was hard at work, then, partly at home and partly at the Institute, and had good reason to be pleased with his own industry. True, he was a little dissatisfied with himself for jabbering about the manuscript to one of the *"troupistes"*—it was the jazz pianist, Bill Frühwald, of the thick-soled shoes, who always wore his clothes with such a jaunty air. They had run into each other in a park near the University. Asked what he was doing, what he was working at, and full of his discovery, Stangeler had simply said too much. They had been walking along a broad path through the green lawn, which held at bay the noise of the streets; the quiet alone had promoted communicativeness. Stangeler's remarks were greeted with an enthusiasm which instantly put him on his guard and made him hold back everything that had not yet slipped from his unwary tongue.

"A knockout!" Frühwald said. "That's just the sort of thing you could really put across. Why, there's a pot of money in it. If I could suggest something—there's a series being put out called the 'Library of Sexual Science'—as it happens, I even know the publisher. . . ."

"No," Stangeler said—he was anxious to break off this somewhat slimy thread he had himself unfortunately spun, "that end of it has already been taken care of—there's no difficulty there —and first of all, of course, I must see to the publication of a scholarly edition of this important source."

"That's just it, that could be best done within the framework of the Library of Sexual Science. Besides, they pay handsomely. Have you made any final commitments in the matter?"

"No," René said (another example of his often pointless conduct; he should have said "yes," since all he wanted was to get rid of Bill Frühwald, but he spoke the truth where it was unnecessary, and then lied where there was no need to).

"In any case, I'll mention the matter to the publisher, Director Szindrowitz. Don't be surprised if he calls you up."

René finally escaped from Frühwald, who sauntered longlegged on down the wide park path. Stangeler turned back to the university building.

For the past week, René had been aware, Doktor Neuberg had been missing from the adjoining desk. Now René saw him mounting the steps somewhat ahead, and caught up with his friend. Neuberg seemed plainly pleased as he turned his broad face toward Stangeler. But the impression he made upon René was alarming, and struck Stangeler the harder in that he was himself somewhat shaken up after his ill-advised conversation in the park. Neuberg's expression revealed such torment, such conflicting forces, that it seemed as if his face were being torn apart. That was Stangeler's first impression, and the very breadth of his friend's countenance, the very sturdiness and openness of it, deepened the impression. Moreover, Neuberg seemed exhausted from lack of sleep. There were dark rings under his eyes. He looked at René, but without speaking.

"What's bothering you?" René said, reaching up for Neuberg's arm.

"I thought I'd go up and try to work for an hour or so," Neuberg replied, making no effort to dissimulate his despairing look. "But I can't. Are you going in?" he added, jerking his head with a weary movement toward the entrance to the Institute.

"I was going to," Stangeler said, "but now I'd rather talk to you."

"Have you a little time?" Neuberg said.

"Of course," René replied. "I just have to close my desk in there and get my briefcase. I was out for a bit of a stroll in the park. Will you wait here till I'm back?"

"All right," Neuberg said, and remained where he was, arms dangling helplessly, without stirring. René ran down the echoing corridor, pulling his key from his pocket as he did so.

When he returned, they descended the wide stairs again. The arcaded courtyard was almost deserted, and here they stayed. Back and forth they went, passing repeatedly by the busts and memorial tablets of famous university scholars. The evening sky cast an intense blueness into the green of the garden. This yard was a bit of the South, of southern manners and southern moderation. But there was none of that in Neuberg now.

"I've broken up with Angi," Neuberg said. He meant his fiancée, Angelika Trapp.

Stangeler was only too experienced in such partings—there had been enough of them between him and Grete! Hence these words stabbed deeper than even Neuberg had expected, although like every young person he assumed far too much sympathy and interest on the part of his companion. Here, for once, the assumption was correct. On the basis of his own experience, René was really alarmed and disconcerted. "For heaven's sake!" he cried. "What was the cause? Whatever happened?"

"Basically only one cause and nothing at all happened. It's just that I can't stand the incessant quiet needling of that family of philistines. Especially when Angelika herself goes over to their side. Better for her to become a Frau Dulnik."

"Dulnik? Who's Dulnik?"

"Head of a paper factory. Prints that toilet paper, you know, with ads all over it."

"Oh, him!" Stangeler exclaimed. "But really, there's nothing out of the way about such a situation. That's the way it always is —with every girl."

"Always," Neuberg agreed, "with every man and every woman. For that very reason, I had to take a stand. Just for a change."

"I beg your pardon," René said. "Am I to understand then that you acted simply out of principle? That nothing happened to precipitate this break?"

"Of course not," Neuberg exclaimed. "Things came to a crisis, naturally. To be perfectly candid, Herr von Stangeler, the final straw was—your fiancée, Fräulein Siebenschein. You know that I have the very highest opinion of Fräulein Grete and see her now and then. We met by chance on Ring Strasse—I guess that must have been in April—and sat down in a café to chat. . . ."

"Yes," Stangeler said, "she told me about meeting you. But what has that to do with Fräulein Trapp?"

"I'm coming to that," Neuberg said, slightly annoyed at the interruption. "At any rate, someone saw us there in the café. . . ." He hesitated, then interjected: "Well, it doesn't matter who it was. In any case, Angelika heard about it. She made a bit of a fuss to me. But how Trapp *père* came to know that I had gone to a café with your fiancée, Herr von Stangeler—I simply don't know. It could only have been Angelika herself who complained to him, don't you see?"

They were still circulating under the arcades along three sides of the yard and back again. René now recalled that not long before he had walked there in the same way with Herzka. ("The *dernier cri*," he thought. "At tense moments people walk around the arcade court." And then: "Kakabsa will soon be leaving the library. A pity.") Darkness had almost fallen. Dim electric light fell under the arches here and there. The sky above the yard turned deepest blue-black.

"Trapp *père* said to me," Neuberg continued, "said to me: 'Listen here, Neuberg'—that's how he talks to me—'you need not think I blame you if you have an intellectual exchange of ideas' —those were his very words—'with Fräulein Siebenstein, or whatever her name is. Perhaps you find her intellectually more interesting than my Angelika. You can speak quite frankly to me. After all, it might be that this Fräulein Siebstein, or whatever, might be a more suitable connection for you for, well, for more than one reason, if you know what I mean.' . . . And that phrase, 'intellectual exchange of ideas'—he could only have got that from Angi. In short, I can tell what kind of wind is blowing there."

"I know that kind of wind," René said sadly. "I know it in the reverse direction, so to speak. At the Siebenscheins', for example, they call me the 'death's head.' Not to speak of what Titi Lasch calls me."

"Sneer and snicker, that's all the bunch of them knows what to do with us!" Neuberg burst out. "Oh, forgive me, you're, you're, if I may put it that way, still engaged—aren't you?"

"Yes, I am," René replied. "Things have more or less straightened out for me. Winds like that can change overnight. The Siebenscheins seem reassured."

"Then sooner or later you will be getting married?"

"Yes," René answered.

"And what kind of wind is there in your own family?"

"Somewhat the same as at the Trapps', perhaps harsher."

"And probably you'll be a professor somewhere after all, with that manuscript you've discovered. It's a good start, anyway, a good beginning for a scholarly career, I mean. How far along are you with the thing?"

"Another three weeks," Stangeler said.

But Neuberg gave short shrift to this subject—in fact, he had all along displayed little genuine interest in René's project. ("I don't know much about the late Middle Ages," he had said upon first hearing of it, and had turned back to his Carolingians.) They exchanged a few more remarks with regard to the Trapps and Stangelers on the one hand and the Siebenscheins on the other. Then they left the building. Neuberg took the streetcar. Stangeler, looking after him, felt for a few seconds that he himself had drawn an easier lot. Neuberg was unhappy. He himself was a lucky boy, even a successful one; brilliant though he was, Neuberg had still achieved no such success. Of late not only the Siebenscheins but also René's parents had been more content with him. (For six years Stangeler had been acquainted with the Siebenschein cosmos—in itself a hereafter in the here!—without having discovered that it was not success which was needed to make that world circle in friendlier fashion around him; all that was needed was a happy face on the part of Grete. And for Grete to be happy, all he had to do was not bait her and plague her. Actually, the Siebenscheins were very modest in their demands. The only demands they made lay in a dimension that his lordship René had not yet discovered: the dimension of feelings.)

René walked slowly down toward Alsergrund, cutting across the wide square in front of the strait-laced neo-Gothic votive church. The building was connected with his family, with some uncle or great-uncle who had been the architect. Evidently something of the sort was expected of him; Neuberg, too, seemed to expect it. Hm, he'd turn right now, down Alserbach Strasse. This time he'd taken a different route from the usual one when he walked with Kakabsa. What would Grete have to say about the breakup between Neuberg and Angelika Trapp? Something new was always going on, usually sheer nonsense. Neuberg was free now. He could throw everything over and start afresh. That was the great thing. . . . René became perturbed. Yes, circumstances were simply the things that stood around you. Let everything stand or be as it was, and they ceased to bother you. No need to throw things over. He felt easier. And wondered at himself as he walked along on his way to the Siebenscheins', past the rear entrance to the Liechtenstein Park. On the other side of the park the narrow streets began. René knew them well. At this moment he felt completely indifferent to Grete. Here was the house called the Blue Unicorn. These old parts of the city seem to stand deep in a swamp, or in a kind of guano: soil that has been heaved up a thousand times. Overinhabited, rotted through. He must get out of this, out to brighter parts, where the big new buildings stood. "Careful. Here's the front door. Pull yourself together. Look friendly. Then everything goes well."

Not long after Stangeler's meeting with Williams and Emma by the Danube shore, Grete Siebenschein gave a little tea to which she invited the American and his fiancée, and also Neuberg—because she had heard at once of his misfortune from René, and knew from talking with him that he was 100 per cent committed to the Carolingians and therefore was no rival to her René in this business. If Grete had a halfway rational reason for giving a party, her parents were more than co-operative. Frau Irma would even dispense with her usual illnesses—and all that sort of thing. A gathering such as this was always put on with skill and chic at the Siebenscheins'.

Williams, whom everyone addressed in English until it developed that he had no trouble speaking German, was in fine fettle; he brought a veritable cloud of fresh pear scent into the room with him, and behaved very properly toward Grete's parents —who were briefly visible. Frau Irma was in fact well worth seeing; her dress set off her slender figure, and her lively intelligence—equipped with an estimated several hundred quivering antennae—made interchange with her remarkably easy. If only our Mama Siebenschein had been able to control the mouse-like darting of her pretty eyes, she would have been a charming lady to meet in any drawing room. As it was, however, everyone at least recognized the gravity of the situation.

"I have written to Professor Bullogg," Williams said to René as they shook hands. "He'll probably shoot off a long letter to you."

Frau Irma Siebenschein expressed curiosity and was told what this was about.

After the parents had left, the conversation lingered on the Neudegg manuscript.

"Herr Achaz von Neudegg was a highly modern man," René said.

"How so?" Williams asked.

"Because we find him exemplifying the dominant factor of our time: a second reality. This is something which is set up alongside the first, actual reality—it is a question of ideologies. Herr Achaz's ideology, his second reality, was a sexual one: mature women, chaste widows, bringing about the end of their chastity, and so on. Sadism is only a word. But the purpose of psychology is not to distribute sedatives in the form of technical terms which one has only to use in order to imagine that one has the whole thing under control. Achaz was an ideologue simply because he reached out his hand for experiences which—which can only be given to one. That's what all ideologues do. Reformers go out directly for a change of circumstances, instead of beginning with themselves; if they did the latter, a new reality would accrue to them, a reality of the first rank, not a phantom reality like Achaz's artificial, arranged sexual experiences. Achaz had a program. It's nonsense, of course, to maintain that political programs are a form of sublimated sexuality, or an outgrowth of it. Ideology does not come from sexuality; it is no substitute for it. Still, it stands under the same pale phantasmal light as Achaz's *idées fixes*. That is why I said he was a modern man. Incidentally, I know someone today who has also developed a kind of sexual ideology, and one in some ways akin to Herr Achaz von Neudegg's."

"Who is that, René?" Grete asked. She was listening with the greatest attentiveness. Perhaps she did not actually understand his argument, as we mean understanding in the philosophical sense. But she felt, and quite distinctly, that there was something behind his remarks. There was substance there. Her not understanding did not affect that substance—and its existence sufficed her.

"Kajetan," René said simply.

For a moment Neuberg raised his head.

"Consider," René went on, turning now to Williams, "that passage in the manuscript which I told you about, where young Ruodlieb von der Vläntsch—or whatever his real name was—dreamed that he was made half of wood. There you have the collision of two realities. He could still remember the first, but already the second reality possessed him. At the end of the whole story Ruodlieb stands beside his sire on the 'round-way' over the drawbridge and Achaz says to him—I remember the very words, because they strike me as so significant: 'Me seemeth I have ben made ayen whole oute of two halfe men, and the one half was of wode.' Which made a shiver go through Ruodlieb, because he had had the same experience as his sire. Or to put it differently, here was a general experience become visible, become an experience valid for all. That is the modern experience, the clash between a first and a second reality, between which no bridge exists, and no common language, although all the individual words that make up the two languages are common to each. Lord Achaz expresses it in the following words: 'A dreme, when that overcometh thee and thou art alone wyth it, wyth thy dreme and vision, alle els escapeth thee and thou art loste.'"

"In those days it was called a demon," Williams said.

"And rightly so. Today such a thing is falsely called a philosophy. As if it were of rational origin! But the mutual hatred that constantly breaks out between these rival philosophies should tell us something. That alone should indicate that their real source has nothing to do with divergent opinions on how 'humanity' can be helped, or on this class or that race, six of one and half a dozen of the other, and suchlike idiocies."

Williams, however, paid scant attention to what Stangeler was saying, although unlike Grete he was quite well able to follow the course of the argument. In those days the New World still stood far from the diseases of the old. It still smelled well groomed and of unripe pears or other fresh and slightly bitter substances, and had not yet made direct acquaintance with that boundary in itself which separates health from illness or, if you will, life from wood—that boundary along which vital feelings are created and vital pains are felt.

Thus the subject of Neudegg was soon abandoned. For several minutes Grete sat deeply absorbed and even forgetful of her duties as hostess, the noblest of which is to entertain the guests by putting as many and as pointed questions to each of them, all aimed at their presumptive interests, and displaying a detailed knowledge of what each person has on his chest (except for Neuberg, with whom it would not do to bring up such intimate matters). Instead, our Grete sat in silence—and even before had expressed neither disagreement nor assent to all that Stangeler had put forward. Her silence, however, went unremarked. Her guests all spoke at once, and although there were only three of them, they created a kind of babel. In that babel the germ of Stangeler's thought—it was no more than a germ—was submerged. Neuberg remarked trenchantly that it was high time we stopped using the single label "Middle Ages" for periods with such entirely different psychological foundations; the term had been conceived by a German professor in the sixteenth century, at the time people first began looking into old documents, not for scholarly reasons but to find legal grounds for combating traditional rights . . . and so on and so forth. Neuberg likewise argued that behavior like Lord Achaz von Neudegg's would have been beyond the bounds of possibility in the eighth or ninth century. Williams refused to see that.

Well, that was more or less the gist of it. The talk was thoroughly intellectual, and the two ladies, Grete and Emma, said nothing to detract from its high level. In honor of the American guest, whiskey and soda were served; but Williams showed more interest in Viennese pastries. When the company had withdrawn from the fifteenth century and condescended to consider the present, politics crept into the conversation. But only lightly and somewhat feebly—comments on internal conditions in Austria, say. No one so much as mentioned the incidents in Schattendorf during the winter; by this time they had long since been forgotten. Neuberg, incidentally, made some very peculiar remarks on the current situation.

It was already June when this tea at Grete Siebenschein's took place—without table tennis. Mme Libesny was not mentioned; there was no cause to bring up her name. The name of Schlaggenberg entered the conversation only in connection with the monstrosities he cultivated. By this time, incidentally, he had abandoned this particular perversion. The "Fat Females" were short-lived, as we have already said. A telegram from Kajetan's mother, arriving shortly after the table-tennis tea, had sufficed to exorcise the last of them. A few days later, when Kajetan stood in the garden room whose glass doors gave on the terrace—it was scarcely a foot above the totally overrun and neglected garden—the second reality had already burst. His recent mania had become incomprehensible to him. Every second reality must burst; Plato's model republic would have done so too, had it ever been put into practice. The garden room in Kajetan's parental home was green: not only the leather armchairs, the wallpaper, or a gigantic punch bowl that stood on the heavy sideboard, encircled with many green glasses like so many offspring—not only these individual items, but the room itself swam in moss and water, sinking deeper and deeper into them with the passage of the years, so it seemed. For the trees in the garden grew higher and denser each year, and through the lofty windows scarcely any sky could be seen nowadays. Frau von Schlaggenberg, Eustach's widow, also seemed overgrown with moss, though she was still a lovely woman.

At any rate, Kajetan was back in Vienna on Tuesday, May 24.

In Grete Siebenschein's room a slanting streamer of smoke eddied toward the windows. The windows of Grete's room had arched tops, which was not true of any other windows in the apartment; that was a fact which could not be overlooked, which remained even though no one referred to it. The streamer of smoke came from the last of Williams's British cigarettes, and smelled sweet.

Neuberg said that he had the clearest feeling that in recent weeks a curter rhythm of life had secretly come into being. Everything was moving in shorter, sharper curves, he said, changing rapidly and not sliding tranquilly on through the weeks and months. Things that had long been nearing their end, he went on, were ending now, or would soon end; and everything destined to completion or perfection would be perfected now or never— and this rhythm certainly included "public affairs." Grete Siebenschein observed, of course, that Hans Neuberg was speaking *pro domo,* or at least *ex domo.* What did such a discovery or intuition amount to? Such an intuition as this depends upon the house, the *domus* from which people are talking—which may be a shed at the edge of the woods, or a castle on the heights. And in Neuberg's case it was certainly no shed, at any rate. Stangeler, who had no aptitude for dismissing anyone's proposition with psychologistic, *ad hominem* arguments (which is to say, he was a miserable critic)—Stangeler seemed to be struggling with some confused image in his mind. Now he softly burst out with it. For our good friend Stangeler belonged to the type of person who always tramps around loudly when the ice is thin underfoot— that is, when they are lying; while, on the other hand, they always put forward the truth with the utmost discretion, probably because of its relative rarity. Truth seems to stir them to a shy embarrassment.

"That is true, Neuberg," Stangeler said. "It is like a pond in summer. Little creatures shoot around on the surface. All making short rapid dashes. Then one such creature will stay perfectly still. Sharp curves. Good. Shooting around. I once stood looking into such a pool. It was not very deep, hardly two feet. The pace of the dashing around grew livelier. I could see right down to the brown bottom. Then I noticed that a big crab was crawling around at the bottom. The little creatures on the surface had no reason to fear it; crabs don't feed on them They weren't fleeing.

They were only darting about more hurriedly. Just because it was there. They were revealing something that was coming, something unknown down there in the depths. You're right, Herr Neuberg."

Emma Drobil regarded René as if he himself were a crab crawling up to the surface. "Never mind," Williams said in English. He reverted to German: "That can be taken symbolically. In zoological terms, it is not really valid." Perhaps Williams privately thought he had fallen in with utter madmen. Nevertheless, he seemed to feel very comfortable in this company. Grete spurted soda into the whiskey and set the siphon back in the ice-bucket, creating a guttural rattling and scraping like a mess of shellfish being shaken together. The daylight, the long day of approaching summer, still held, already turning bluish but still bright. Anny Gräven, for example, was going to work later and later these days. From the Prater Stern came a rumbling, then the vulgar rattling of a hay-wagon's iron-bound wheels lumbering into Franzensbrücken Strasse. Anny Gräven lay on the sofa. She was drunk. Ever since Leonhard had stopped coming she had been sliding down somewhere, she herself did not know where. She went about with people she would formerly have avoided. Of course she steered clear of monkey business such as stupid Hertha had been involved in. Meisgeier, incidentally, was little seen these days.

"I hope no crab pinches us," Grete said, releasing the bottle after she had wedged it deep enough into the ice. No one took up this remark. The whiskey played a greater part in the ensuing conversation than any of the speakers realized ("*quam quisquam ratus esset*," says Sallust). That was true even for Williams, but most of all for Neuberg. It gave him an assist and lent him strength, for the duration of this gathering anyhow; it held him above the abyss of his separation from Angi.

But absolute inability, if suffered long enough, may ultimately be the beginning of real ability; that has often been noted (and not only in love-affairs). For Jan Herzka, however, this principle did not apply at all. While the protracted evening of this season

slowly receded before the people of the city, like the background
of a spacious hall which, upon entering, one had not thought to
be so big and long—while the twilight lingered rather than
descended, Herzka had gone home from town and his business
and refreshed himself with a bath.

Herzka did not intend to call it quits at this point. He had had
a rather weird adventure, what with the castle and the manuscript found there. Was he now to stow this adventure away in
some cupboard of the mind and try to regain his equilibrium?
Not Jan Herzka. Rather, he went forward with the thing, creating
for himself a kind of private sphere, a subject peculiarly and
professionally his own—a sphere he had hired René to adminis-
ter. Thus a single explosion had been transformed into something
continuous—which seems paradoxical enough in all conscience.
But Jan Herzka was a businessman with a talent for organization.
Moreover, he saw Agnes Gebaur at the office every day. But for
the time being he did not take this hurdle, did not even fall back
for a running start at it. Agnes remained only a kind of picture-
symbol for the whole, a hieroglyph. It did not occur to him as yet
to attempt to decipher her. For that, Herzka had first to experiment a little.

We do not wish to follow Jan all the way into these experi-
ments. Strolls in a second reality are never profitable (except for
those who would make their name as technical experts, the way
René did in Carinthia). And it is characteristic of all matters
connected with the demonic that although they create a tremendous stir and a great deal of motion, they never leave anyone
with anything substantial in his hands afterwards.

Herzka stood in his upstairs bathroom. The garden lay below
the window, flat, sloping only slightly toward the back, where
the property reached up to the slope of the hill. It consisted of a
big meadow with small fruit trees at wide intervals—they had
been planted by his father. There were no flower beds or borders.
No gardening hobbies, responsibilities, or chores were in evi-

dence; no one ran around with watering-cans. Jan, standing there in the bathroom, had the feeling that everything outside was brown, as it would be in the fall. He was not really conscious of this idea; it was only a by-product of his profound isolation. In reality, the first and valid reality and not his private second reality, the garden was lush with spring; the birds were making a great din in the treetops, and two titmice darted down and flew with lightning turns across the meadow and in among the small fruit trees, almost skimming the ground. In neighboring houses people had their legs under tea tables and were holding conversations which, without whiskey, were nevertheless as interestingly aimless as the talk at that moment going on in Grete Siebenschein's room.

But Herzka was altogether cut off from sense-perceptions of the outside world. He had plans, ideas, considerations, measures in his head. The alterations down at Neudegg were not progressing as rapidly as Jan would have liked. Moreover, the heart was still lacking down there, in the sense of a real center, as we may speak of the "heart" of a cable, as opposed to the many layers which merely form its wrappings. The heart of things, Agnes Gebaur, had become Herzka's secretary in the meanwhile. A man of the middle classes like Herzka is always characterized by discontinuity. These are the born week-enders—business Monday to Saturday, then "higher things," enjoyment of nature, cultivation of artistic interests, or whatever the particular phrase may be. On Monday at eight o'clock in the morning the cuckoo steps out of its clock again and it's all been for the birds. Anyone who imagines that there are "higher things" is by that token unable to practice the life of the spirit in everyday affairs. For there is only one life; except for it, there is nothing at all; we must make our stand in the here and now. Fine and good, if there really could be such "higher things." But anything which could possibly be called by that name is suspect.

Jan, then, had this bourgeois capacity for shifting from weekday to week-end existence. Thus, he was able to behave like a boss toward Agnes when he sat facing her, and at the same time to hold her as a hieroglyph he was feverishly determined to decipher. Why did he avoid any hint of this when he was with her? Why did he extend no feelers? Perhaps he would have been met halfway. Sometimes he was sure he could sense something coming from her, striving to make contact. Was it only timidity toward an "employee"—only the businessman's prudence, then? Much as every businessman is governed by that, even in his wholly unbusinesslike parts, the explanation does not seem to be quite credible here.

Rather, he was inhibited by something else entirely: timidity toward reality, toward the first and real reality of which we have spoken. Had he not maintained the strict separation between his role as boss and his private inclinations, everything would have slid abruptly into the tracks of that first, real reality. And perhaps that would have happened not only to Herzka but to Agnes also, for various crude and subtle reasons. But very simply: he liked her, over and above all that, aside from all that. As it happened he even knew a few things about her. The girl's father had been a lieutenant colonel, killed in the war. Once Mama Gebaur had telephoned the office, and by chance was connected with Jan Herzka; she wanted her daughter told that her wage-tax card, which had been lost, had just been found. The voice and speech of Frau Gebaur were those of a lady; that much was clear to Herzka from the few words she spoke. And apparently a very likable lady at that. Perhaps Agnes resembled her.

Yet all that led, if the slightest contact were attempted, out of the airtight isolation in which Jan was developing, ordering, systematically furthering his new concerns, plans, practices, and arrangements. The caverns of Neudegg seemed to lie outside the world and life, as far as he was concerned (though this was not really the case, which was just the trouble), just as "higher things" lie outside life for the average man.

If Herzka now began roaming around at night, he was doing so in a deliberate attempt to evade Agnes Gebaur. Oddly enough, Anny Gräven thereby became a matchmaker between Jan and

Agnes, as we shall see—although of course she had not the slightest inkling that she was doing this, and would never have guessed it even had she been less stewed than she usually was these days, every day.

Anyone who roams around a big city at night, either aimlessly or pursuing such vague aims as Jan's, literally falls from step to step down a steep incline, like water falling in cascades: the tendency to drop, which is characteristic in life anyhow, is accelerated. Pursuing his own fancies, a man inevitably runs his keel into the bottom; that is to say, comes afoul of a world which has nothing whatsoever to do with those phantasmagorias of his. Only Agnes really had anything to do with them. But to become involved with her would have been binding—and here we have caught Herr Herzka. For he wanted no binding ties; he wanted to isolate himself in the caverns of Neudegg, to be alone with those caverns. A cavernous man. (Something like Pinta or Pinter, the son-in-law of old Zdarsa at Stinkenbrunn, though on another plane—six of one and half a dozen of the other.)

Stangeler, of course, was not drawn into these predatory expeditions. What use would he have been to Jan on them? Jan saw no sense in bringing the "expert" so close to the intensely personal heart of the matter. But it was not because Jan Herzka in any way feared shocking his historian. In this regard Herzka had come to a better understanding; in hindsight he had recognized and come to appreciate René's boundless tolerance. The jacket on the pillar in the caverns of Neudegg had been forgotten; in retrospect it was regarded as just as harmless as that cigarette stub tossed on the floor. After all, there had been neither ash tray nor clothes hook down there. We, for our part, are not so convinced as Herzka of René's harmlessness—at least in regard to the jacket. Still, it was just as well that Jan took this view.

Anny Gräven listened as Herzka tried to make his intentions plain to a fat woman with popping eyes—he was going on a good deal about culturo-historical matters and still keeping pretty far from the point. He had brought the two women to a room in

Anny's building—such rooms could be rented by the hour. At the women's request, a number of bottles of wine had been brought up; it was stuff from the Burgenland and adjacent Hungarian regions, and seemed to be greatly to their taste. Herzka thought it wretched, but needed something to wet his gullet, for he had been talking a great deal and there was no water at hand— although there was a spigot above the big washbowl, and two water glasses even stood on the glass shelf, probably intended for toothbrushes, although no one had ever brushed his teeth in this room—that much was fairly certain. But Herzka was so horrified by the room—though it was large, clean, almost hospital-like in appearance—that even the spigot seemed to him suspect, and he would not have cared to use it even for washing his hands. The tall window was shielded by closed, heavy wooden shutters. Unpainted, these were gray, and their effect was to shut off the outside world so completely that the room might as well have been deep under the ground. The silence was perfect. That was just as well. Aside from two beds, which looked fresh and white, and the table around which he and the women sat, there was also an ancient sofa covered with leatherette, on which a sheet had been newly laid. The sharp fold from ironing struck the eye; it looked as if a surgical operation were being prepared for.

Anny Gräven listened to Jan Herzka's queer lecture on witch trials and certain situations that might develop in the course of them—he knew what he was talking about, after all, since he himself had a professor specially working on the subject. But Anny simultaneously was listening to her own reactions, for once with singular acuity, and discovering that the change that had taken place in her had begun immediately after the death of Hertha Plankl. Since that time she had also been drinking harder. More precisely: she had changed while Meisgeier was climbing, while she had watched. The inner transformation had taken place at that very moment, and for that very reason she had taken the note left by the dead woman and sent it to Didi. Thus she had at last deliberately taken a path on which hitherto she had only slipped and slid by chance. Admiration for Meis-

1029 / Sharp Curves (I)

geier, a deep inner sympathy with his boldness, had been the decisive factor, for all her fright of him, and in spite of his having murdered her best friend. Even her sometimes violent longing for Leonhard, who had stayed away completely ever since the autumn, faded and vanished along this new path she had taken.

She remembered the man with whom she had spent the night when Hertha was stabbed—his story about the sister who in reality was the child of other parents, and who therefore could be cheated out of her inheritance. For Anny knew, with a sense of utter certainty, that it hadn't been the usual battery of lies which clients told. This time she felt sure it had all been true and that that nice fellow was probably a stupid idiot who let people make a fool of him. For Anny knew only too well what lying was like, how people talked when they lied—using what amounted to a different language. After all, she herself lied most of the time. The recollection of that night with the gentleman in her room was not unpleasant. The wineglasses on the tray by the couch. She had lain there looking out the window on the Prater toward the scattered blue lights of the railroad outside. He had paced back and forth across the room, hands in his pockets. She had known other such gentlemen; but in the past few months they hadn't been coming around, somehow. This man now, who sat rather than paced, and talked a mile a minute at that dumb cow who wouldn't ever catch on, was the same type. Anny had caught on long since. It was so simple. He wanted to take a few poses, to do "living pictures," or something of that sort. Nothing to it. You could go anywhere this man wanted, even to his own apartment, without worrying. He wouldn't do you any harm. Perhaps he'd already set up his whole stage somewhere. And besides, he wasn't the kind to short-change you. There was good business here. Anny saw that. But she remained numbed, although Herzka now glanced over at her, seeking help. Anny even knew that right here and now was her last chance, that here was the last "gentleman" she would ever have. She could have drawn Herzka to her with her little finger and wound him around it.

But she no longer wanted to. She no longer wanted any gentlemen of this sort, or even like that nice fellow with the sister. She
also no longer wanted Leonhard. That was what she suddenly
realized. It was amazing!

She downed the full glass of wine at one draught. What she
really would have wanted was to drink herself down at one
draught. And then finish, over with! Hertha was lucky. These
fine gentlemen could all go to the devil, and Leonhard with them.
At most she wanted to lie down flat on her back. In the café,
where she spent hours playing "bucki dominoes" and "twenty-
one," there was a Greek who was teaching her how to really
gamble and make big winnings. She was learning. She liked the
Greek—not that he was handsome; he was young, that was all
—but because he knew these tricks in games, and was so good
at them that nobody caught on. He really cleaned up. Sometimes,
for instance, after he had been winning, he'd start to lose. His
opponents would get it all away from him, and there he'd be
sitting with a foolish expression. So then they would give him
"revenge," and two hours later there he'd be with all the cash in
the house in front of him. And by then it was usually closing
time.

While Anny, without really wishing to do so, sluggishly glanced
out the corners of her eyes, as it were, into the anatomy of a
few decisive moments in her life, peering between the warm veils
of the wine that swathed the inside of her head, Herzka plodded
on with his explanations. He hinted that he would make it worth
their while. He hinted that it wouldn't hurt them any. He went
on endlessly, drawing back like a rock-drill to get a fresh start,
turning now and then to Anny in the hope of getting aid from
her. But while the popeyed fat girl only gaped and goggled,
smart little Anny remained altogether unresponsive and impenetrable. She only smiled, like a Chinese, or like someone from
another planet; she smiled toward him out of her hereafter in
the here and said not a word. Herzka's state was altogether
indescribable, and our Anny knew that, recognized it. Talking
incessantly like an agitator trying to pound some slogan into the

thick peasant skulls of his listeners, Herzka trotted in circles on the thin ice of his second reality, the sounds of cracking in his ears, while the outside world would not cease to remain what it was, to insist upon its first reality and threaten the second. But Herzka saw nothing; he had really been stricken deaf and blind, though not dumb. He saw nothing and therefore could not hit any mark, could not even aim properly. But he could be hit. Anny knew that too. He could have been hit by, say, the sight or smell of the spilled wine here—after all, his senses continued to receive impressions. But just as easily, something could hit him which would directly oppose his mania—such as, for example, the fact that his fat listener was dead drunk. Herzka had not yet grasped this; he did not want to. Anny thought a step further, and grazed the notion that he really ought to be given a shock. It would not take much.

And then it was given, though not by Anny.

"Go on," fat Anita said thickly. "I'm just fascinated. You learn the damnedest things in hist'ry. Give me the lowdown on Napoleon."

She rose, lumbered to the big washbowl, half sat herself on it, and relieved herself. Then she turned on the spigot, still sitting there.

Anny was looking at Herzka. He had gone pale. He thrust his hand into his jacket as if he were groping for his heart. At that moment, seized by a fierceness and hatred incomprehensible to herself, Anny added her bit to the liquidation of the situation. When Jan had come up there an hour before, he had asked the women, in the pleasantest manner, to avoid that singing and humming of songs which is the habit of all streetwalkers—a not altogether meaningless matter, for it is a kind of whistling in the dark; no doubt the humming and trilling helps to assuage initial uneasiness. It has a kind of biological basis. And up to this moment both women had refrained from singing. But now, as Jan Herzka produced his wallet from under his jacket (he had not reached for his heart, then, but for his money) and handed a large bill to each of the girls, though keeping his head turned away from Anita, who still sat on the washbowl—at this point Anny launched out into: "How could I live without—out—without you . . . ?" She eyed Jan for the effect of the song. It was really as if she had spat at him and the spittle were running slowly down his face. He clapped his hat on his head—he had kept on his light coat all the while—and went to the door. His movements were not rapid but stiff, awkward, glassy, brittle. Anny sang at his retreating back. She knew that she still could have called him back. She knew that she still could have drawn him with her little finger, only by revealing that she knew what he was after, by exposing her extensive and detailed understanding of his fantasies, with which she could so easily have complied. Her thin blanched face would have been very well suited to such a role. "I would've had to put on a little white powder and rub the mascara around a little under my eyes. And comb my hair out." She had this thought even as Herzka opened the door. He left. With him went Leonhard, the nice fellow with the sister, and several others of the kind. Whole years filed out with Herzka. But that was all over with now. Anny wanted no more of it; she was sick of these fine gentlemen, undrinkable as lukewarm water. She had a horror of them. She wanted to go straight to the Café Alhambra. The Greek was there. She wanted to play. Lately they had been working together, not only at the Alhambra, but at other cafés also. They made a good team. He always knew just when the time had come to lose again, for a change. The only time Anny felt good nowadays was when she was with him and his crowd. She despised Herzka. Now he was gone. She stopped singing.

Anita, still perched on the washbowl, gaped at the door which had closed behind him. "Hey, Anny—what the devil did he go away for? He must be screwy!"

"And you're dumb," Anny said. "Why'd you let him go? Now it's too late. You could've got a couple thousand outa him without half tryin'."

"C'n ya beat that! Him giving me the dope on Napoleon an' . . ."

"He wasn't telling you a damn thing about Napoleon," Anny said.

The popeyed girl finally slid down from the bowl and stood unsteadily on her feet. She fixed her clothes. Anny Gräven had suddenly lost all patience—not only in regard to Anita, but in general, with everything. She flared up, burst out, fired away at Anita as if telling off the world. "You dumb cow, you!" she shouted. "When for once ya get a gent what's a real gent and would pay up without a peep and just has a few screws loose, instead of listenin' to what he says, you get tight and have to go and piss in the washbowl, you pig. You're the one that's screwy, not him. If I was him I would've scrammed too."

"Then why di'n't you give him what he wants?"

"Because I'm your friend and not goin' to grab a catch from you!" Anny called back over her left shoulder and marched out. Her departure was brilliant, insofar as anything can be brilliant in such a gray lower world, gray as the dirt-ingrained shutters and gray as the unpainted floor. Only the sheet on the operating sofa gleamed white with its sharp folds from ironing. The fat girl sat at the table. She drank down a glass of wine and leaned back. Her knees fell wide apart. She went to sleep. After half an hour the night concierge came in through the unlocked door— the room was needed again. He woke Anita and requested her to abandon the field. The field with the sharp folds from ironing. The sheet was not changed—after all, it had not been used. Only the wineglasses and the bottles were removed, and the ash tray emptied. The chambermaid finished the rest of the wine.

With that last shot, fired off over her shoulder, Anny falsified her whole past and her future as well, for later on, in spite of a vivid memory of Meisgeier's clambering feet and her own feelings in regard to it—later on she seriously believed that she had given up that fine gentleman and all fine gentlemen in general only on Anita's account. Swiftly she tripped on her high heels down the old, dished steps, sauntered through the tavern, darting a look around (but there was nothing there worth so much as a glance), and stepped out into the street. A weak spring rain of scattered droplets had begun. The wide deserted roadway of Prater Strasse glittered slightly with the wet. Anny went diagonally across its expanse. She was heading for the Café Alhambra, for her Greek and the cards.

She found both in the card room at the back. Its air was as stale and smoky as that in the front room, where a gypsy band was busy, but it was far less crowded. Anny's arrival was noted, in spite of the prevailing atmosphere of rather brutish tension, and someone moved over to give her a seat beside the Greek, Protopapadakis. Her friend had just been cleaned out. Anny volunteered to lend him a stake, but he refused her money with some indignation and just looked on for an hour or so. At last, after a good deal of persuasion, he accepted a small sum from Anny, won, lost again, and so worked things around to their usual pattern; half an hour before closing time he had divested himself of part of his money again, as the result of several bets so foolish that they produced a kind of shudder around the whole table.

The players here were scarcely "professionals"—that would have been out of the question, for who would have taken money from whom? There was, for example, the pianist from a restaurant across the street, a stubborn old music teacher on a pension who suffered from insomnia and usually spent the night playing cards. Here was a man who seemed to be guided by an entirely sober, almost disgusting carefulness; he kept watch over the whole table (though of course he was easily hoodwinked by our Greek) and sweated all the while. That is to say, he actually came in soaked in sweat because he had been banging away at fox trots, two-steps, and Viennese waltzes all evening. His brownish skin was always damp. His head and face were well formed; in his youth he might well have been quite handsome. But his wariness had risen to the surface, dissolving everything else. No one liked him here, but he simply belonged, and was one of those who came every night. There were other players who appeared more rarely. Protopapadakis did not come every day. He also played in other cafés, and in a secret club. When he ran into his fellow-countryman Xidakis in this café, they both pretended not to know each other. But they would go together to Anny's apartment after closing time. Xidakis, who was called Kaki for short (the far more unpronounceable Protopapadakis went by the name of Prokop), was by far the better-looking of the two; his proportions were almost that of a classical Hellene, with his medium height, narrow waist, and broad chest. Moreover, he possessed something resembling a Greek nose, though when you first saw him it was hard to decide whether it was quite that and not rather a sheep's nose; when in fact you looked closer, and especially when you caught sight of the young man in profile, your doubts were resolved in favor of the sheep.

Then there was also Herr Rucktäschl. He was extremely small, but stocky, equipped with enormous hands which he never knew quite where to stow away, so that he often swept them about over the table—a trick nobody liked. By profession this little fellow was a typesetter for a newspaper—and so did not turn up at the café until after the page-proofs were in, a little while before midnight. He would bring with him some of the oily smell of the printing plant. One of his peculiarities was that he would never meet anyone's eyes, and whenever in danger of this would instantly begin waving his hands around and looking away. His fingernails were edged in deepest black.

Beside Rucktäschl, usually, sat a middle-class couple in their fifties, the Hadinas; they entered the café like two moons rising together over the horizon. They brought with them an aura of nutritious smells, not only of cheese but also of smoked meat, sausage, herring, anchovies, butter, salami, chives, and what not —individual odors which were mingled in their store into olfactory chords. This aura always palpably interfered with the petroleum odor of Herr Rucktäschl. It was sharpest when they first came in; by and by it became overlaid by the general smell of the café.

Then there was also Ria, an elderly prostitute, well set up—she was extremely frugal, never wasted money, at most spent it on something sensible, a new coat, say. But when she began to tire of tramping the streets, she dropped in at the Alhambra, and played a few games for the smallest stakes. The thought never entered her head to let the gambling make any inroads into her quite respectable savings. Ria looked almost elegant when seen in the street from a bit of a distance; in reality she had long been a rattling skeleton. The Greeks sometimes let her win sizable amounts, whether they were playing "deuces wild" or "twenty-one"; in the latter game Xidakis almost always kept the bank.

There were still others. In conversation with Georg von Geyrenhoff, Prince Alfons Croix had once remarked: "Even the most impossible persons who do the most unforgivable things possess substantial reality; from their own points of view they are always right—for let them only doubt that, and they are no longer such impossible persons. And we must pay close heed to those who play such ungrateful roles, for these roles are indispensable." All very well. Though it is to be doubted whether our good Geyrenhoff really understood the prince. He was always rather slow-witted. Moreover, he had few contradictions in himself from which he could have derived some knowledge of human nature, and probably was unaware of the boundary within himself which separates health from sickness or, if you will, life from wood—that partition which alone produces essential feelings and essential pain. The essence of Geyrenhoff was ordinary common sense, pared down to ultimate respectability. He simply did not have it in him to behave in an importunate or overbearing way. Easy enough to be just toward others when you have that kind of mind. But enough. Herr von Geyrenhoff has been much troubled over cheekiness in this manuscript.

There were still other phenomena in the back room of the Café Alhambra. Should anyone ask how it was possible for honest business people like the Hadinas to sit down at the same table as "females" like Anny Gräven or Ria, it must be said that suspense and greed easily drive away status-consciousness—although it is well known that the latter grows more insistent, the more one descends the social ladder. In people like the Hadinas, status-consciousness is very strong, and they never miss an opportunity to inform virtual strangers that they have a nephew who was an officer in the reserve, or that the wife's sister owns whole sets of classics and a very fine library altogether. An academic from the provinces must let the world know of his "honorably earned degree," whereas the above-mentioned Herr von Geyrenhoff did not even have his title of doctor of philosophy on his visiting card—if only because in his day people in certain high positions (like the Foreign Service, for example) avoided academic degrees and concluded their studies at the University by taking state examinations. Geyrenhoff acted as if he were not a "Herr Doktor" at all—a pose, by the way, to which he was scarcely entitled, for he had not been a diplomat, only an administrative official. But we do not want to annoy him again.

There were, then, other phenomena, including one such academic from the provinces. He was the son of an innkeeper in Troppau and had satisfactorily completed the engineering course at the Technical Academy of Brünn. A certificated engineer, then, or "full academic" as the phrase frequently goes nowadays. This fifty-year-old bachelor (it is worth remarking that the Hadinas were the only married people in this circle) had held a secure position in Vienna for more than twenty years. His income was quite appreciable. What then was he doing here? You had to look closer at his good-looking and also good-natured face to understand his presence. That face was grooved with deep furrows, and there was dirt in them. But nonsense, the man was well shaven and well washed. Nevertheless, it seemed as though in the course of time something of the atmosphere of so many different cafés over so many nights had settled into the folds of his face, a precipitate of the café smell, which, we have remarked, proved to be stronger than the various professional odors of the Hadinas and the typesetter Rucktäschl.

Not all who suffer from falling-sickness can be medically classed as epileptics. This was true of Herr Riedener from Troppau. What is more, mere falling is really normal, for people can be blown like leaves diagonally across the field of vision. The fall is usually gentle. Such a person imagines he has only to put his hand on the imaginary levers of his will to stop the gentle fall. But he does not make this little gesture. Why should he not go to his regular table in his favorite café at night? To be sure, for a long time he has been unable to go to sleep without drinking beforehand. And then one day the liver acts up, interferes in the interior monologue. Of course there are some who do not fall, who have never fallen, and who also conduct no interior monologues (as Herr Riedener did all the time, only these monologues grew more and more similar; they subsided into one single interminable one, gray and dusty, full of breaks and cracks). There are some who have always sat down below on the firm ground, on the rocky soil which may give those who fall too rapidly some surprising bruises, at the very least. For those dwellers down below, grubbing about among the flinty rocks, nothing but their own sparse cultural medium has any real existence. The innumerable new arrivals seem to supply constant confirmation of its reality. And it must be granted that this particular cultural medium has always existed, through all heroic and unheroic times, through all changes. As for "the gallery," it too has always been (the same is true for bureaucracies too), whether its headquarters are a Roman tavern or the Café Alhambra. Someone is always being taken, whether it is the stupid peasants from the Roman countryside, or Pop Rottauscher and his admiring pupil Zurek, who, clever though they were in other things, were no match for the firm of Prokop & Kaki.

An elderly member of "the gallery" and a raw youth.

It had been Pop Rottauscher who by virtue of a single genuine gold watch performed the feat of selling fifty counterfeits in the course of two years. These had been picked up by mistake on a punitive expedition directed against a jewelry shop, and then assigned to Pop Rottauscher, along with that one real one on which the whole deal hinged.

Zurek once remarked to a gentleman (the very one who sometimes takes a jab at Herr von Geyrenhoff, from which it becomes clear what kind of company novelists keep): "You know, sir, as far as technique goes, I think I'll catch up to old Rottauscher someday; I've been studying with him for three and a half years now, and I've been in on lots of things. But with that business of the watches I really saw where we young fellers can't compete. We have the nerve all right. But we don't have the sureness of these old guys, the way they know how to look solid and make themselves trusted. He knows right off just how to talk to everyone. And then there's something so respectable about him—it ain't nothing you can imitate."

"Where does Herr Rottauscher come from?" the novelist asked.

"From Imst. That's in Tyrol."

"Aha."

"The thing for us young fellers would be to figure out different methods that fit us and our special abilities. But all I can do now is learn the old tried-and-true tricks, and that's just as well, I guess. As far as Pop goes, I'll lay you anything that lots of the guys who bought the fake watches off him believe to this day that they're the real article. Why not? They're all solid citizens who wouldn't dream of taking their watch to the pawnbroker. . . ."

"Hm, hm," the novelist said.

Zurek was a big strong boy of about twenty-one. Had served a few minor sentences. His forehead was broad, his vigorous face rather rounded in shape. Some of the phrases he used sounded quite cultivated, but he could not keep up this style of speech for long. You had the impression that he was always perspiring, even when the weather was cool. But it was not that. Rather, he had an exceedingly oily skin—what is called an "unctuous face." Some psychiatrists claim to have observed this characteristic in mental defectives, and are inclined to regard it as in some circumstances symptomatic. But the author of these pages is acquainted with quite a few individuals who are mentally far below the level of Zurek, and yet have entirely dry faces. Among them have been several full academics.

These, then, were the scenes and the characters of that segment of her life into which Anny Gräven plunged, once she had
blocked and destroyed Herzka's last attempt to evade Agnes
Gebaur, and had left Anita behind alone in the hotel room. And
as she stepped out into the spring rain whose scattered droplets
fell from the airy spaces above the city upon the damply glittering street, and as she crossed familiar Prater Strasse diagonally,
Anny Gräven was in fact already walking on a different plane
from that of her previous life.

New elements entered, old ones vanished. From that night on,
Anny no longer thought of that sheet of letter paper which she
had once sent to Didi, to Anna Diwald, Freud's brandy shop,
Liechtenstein Strasse . . . (she even knew the number of the
building)—that sheet of letter paper which recorded Hertha
Plankl's last words and on the back of the second fold: "Take
good care of this, Didi. Tell you more when I see you. Anny Gr."
Formerly, Anny had occasionally felt the desire to possess the
letter, to recover it. Without any special purpose. Or did she
have such a purpose? Did she want to give it to someone? Or
destroy it, together with the envelope and the postmark? Why?
The impulse to go to Anna Diwald to fetch the thing had once
become so strong (though so puzzling) that Anny actually took
the streetcar out to Liechtenstein Strasse in the afternoon. And
found Didi there. "Of course you can have it any time," she said,
and went to the back room where old Freud was sleeping the
unappetizing sleep of the just, and returned with that old briefcase which Editor Holder had once mentioned, during that walk
of "our crowd," as a typical appurtenance of hers. "Here," Didi
said after she had found the letter among the assortment of
documents, letters, and photographs with which the bag was
stuffed. "Here it is. But don't do nothing foolish. Don't give it
to nobody. Don't let it out of your hands. And don't think to
burn it. Be smart. Tell you what, why don't you come around
again tomorrow? Leave it here with me till tomorrow; I'll take
good care of it for you. Sleep on it once more, Anny." Anny

found this advice good. That night she drank heavily, slept all day, drank again the next night, and so for three days. But she clung to her intention; she wanted to have the thing. Now, however, she no longer wanted it. She completely forgot about it. It had become a matter of indifference to her.

The "veiled quality" of Agnes Gebaur was a fact, not one of Herzka's wild fancies. She really had something rather considerable to veil, not only in a physical sense (though she had that too), but in quite another. For a good long time she had been fervently in love with her boss, who had first taken notice of her on May 16.

Since then, as we have already related, she had become a hieroglyph for him, the black central sun of a second reality. After the fiasco with the two whores, and the collapse of his last hope of arriving at satisfaction in some oblique way, Herzka for the first time became aware of the distant possibility of using the immense power inherent in Agnes to lift himself from a second into a first reality. When this thought first came to him, it was likewise a shock, but one that healed the earlier shock which had persisted with him for some time, even though he had not allowed his thoughts to linger on it.

Not long after this, Agnes was descending the steps ahead of Herzka one day after closing hour when she sprained her foot. She was pretty far ahead of him, more than a story below, and could not have known of his presence. Or so we might think if we did not know better—know that women also have eyes in the back of their heads (almost like Meisgeier!) and can see around all corners with them just as well as with the eyes in front.

She clung to the railing and was holding one leg off the step when Herzka came down. He reached her side in a moment.

Jan carefully helped Agnes to the elevator and then to his car. The district in which Frau Gebaur lived was almost entirely strange to Herzka—a very old part of the city—Kandl Gasse. They drove past a large church and a park that Jan had never seen before; it surprised him that Franz, the chauffeur, was evidently familiar with this neighborhood and knew the way.

Even as he sprang to Agnes's aid, Herzka had been literally pierced by a consciousness of her physical being. And while they were still standing in the elevator, he had realized everything. Realized that he was caught. That you could not practice things outside of life, neither on Prater Strasse nor in the caverns of Neudegg. Now he had been brought back into life. Now he was clambering into the boat again. He felt that everything was starting to move once again, not just circling around a single spot as in a closed vault. From the first moment that he had stepped swiftly to Agnes's side to hold her up, he bore a burning wound and he remained aware of it despite the balm that soon began to surround it on all sides.

At the house on Kandl Gasse he brought Fräulein Gebaur, with the chauffeur's aid, up to her apartment.

Frau Gebaur, the lieutenant colonel's widow, was greatly alarmed.

Franz slowly descended the stairs and waited in the car.

Herzka found himself standing in the middle of a rather small dining room. Agnes had been bedded down on a couch in the next room, and her mother was busy wrapping the ankle with cloths soaked in a solution of alum—Herzka had stopped en route at a pharmacy. The family doctor had been called and was on his way.

The room here, modest as it was, did not belong to the apartment of ordinary people, nor did the vestibule, nor the air in the vestibule—that least of all. The sideboard was probably Biedermeier. The whole room smelled faintly of old wood, perhaps also of floor wax, with a trace of some perfume, possibly heliotrope, the kind that elderly ladies love. Above the sideboard hung a large reproduction of Liotard's "Chocolate Girl" in a narrow mahogany frame. Frau Gebaur, however, was not an elderly lady; she was already old, in fact somewhat bowed and shrunken, extremely tiny, very thin and frail, a little gray mouse. That had surprised Jan; he had expected to find a far younger mother.

Agnes was his own age; he had seen her official papers, after all. So she was a late-born child.

Now the doctor rang. Jan went to open the door, since no maid appeared.

The doctor, an old general practitioner, laughed at the diagnosis of a "sprain," said: "Oho!" and declared that the foot would have to be set at once. An X-ray too would be needed. (Agnes had done her work much too thoroughly; the slip on the stairs, then, had been a bona fide accident, though doubtless guided by profound feminine wisdom.) The doctor said that someone would have to hold the patient a bit, and "I don't think you're up to it, Frau Gebaur. Who is the gentleman in the other room? . . . Well then, we'll have to trouble your boss a bit." He went out to Jan, introduced himself, and asked for his assistance. Agnes, whose eyes had followed the doctor, stared in alarm at the door through which Jan Herzka was about to enter. Herzka saw her lying on the couch, veiled and swathed as ever, but with one foot bared. The foot was lean and delicately formed, the ankle appeared somewhat swollen, and the leg above it, of which Jan saw only a small part, emerged smooth, white, and strong. Now Agnes had to sit upright on the couch. Herzka posted himself behind her, and under the doctor's direction she leaned against him, her trunk bent somewhat forward. "Would you grasp Fräulein Gebaur around the waist and hold fast?" the doctor said. "I must give this a little pull." He took the bare foot in both hands and raised the leg slightly. Agnes uttered a suppressed groan. "Done," the doctor said. No click or snap had been heard. The doctor felt the joint. "There, that's back in place now," he said. "Take this pill, will you—what's the use of suffering pain? And now we put on a tight bandage, and tomorrow off we go for an X-ray." He wrapped the bandage, then took out his pad and wrote instructions for the X-ray. Agnes's right foot was now wearing a kind of short cuff—a frail lean foot with long thin toes; the big toe was turned sharply out of the central axis of the foot. Before, when the doctor had lifted it, a good deal more of round white leg had appeared as the long skirt slid back. That foot of

Agnes Gebaur's was known to Herzka; more than that, it was deeply familiar—from the old book which he had bought the night he had gone to the circus with Magdalena Güllich. One of the martyrs had the same feet as Agnes Gebaur.

And the same, slightly excessive shapeliness of the hips; he had felt that while Agnes was enduring her little martyrdom.

A man in an advanced stage of drunkenness could scarcely have been less in control of himself than Jan when he took his leave—saying he would come again the next day to drive Agnes over for the X-ray. He managed to reach his car, however, and found the doctor's auto standing just behind it. The doctor thanked Herzka and drove away.

This is the place to compare two couples: Mary and Leonhard, and Agnes and Jan. There was something extraordinary about both of them—and we do not mean Herr Herzka's little peculiarity, which was basically rather harmless. What we regard as most extraordinary was the complete lack of that questioning, in the case of Mary and Leonhard, with which so many people contrive to shrivel their already meager inclinations—the question: what is to come of it, where will it lead? As if the god (the rascal with the quiver) first requires legitimation for his appearances, calls for the possession of three rooms and bath, or a substantial pension. Second only, then, to the extraordinary valor of Mary and Leonhard, the most remarkable of the couples whom we have met, comes the first-rate performance of Agnes Gebaur.

Now it is clear that the affair could only run on toward an engagement (on such feet! not to speak of other imposing attributes). Matters moved very fast; soon Grete and René were offering their congratulations, and the newest couple had tea at the Siebenscheins'—a little gathering once again distinguished by vivacity and chic, with the assistance of the two elder Siebenscheins. The foot had long since healed. Its primary purpose, aside from walking, had been fulfilled. The second mission of the two feet was drawing nearer. And here Agnes proved that she was magnificently capable of doing her whole duty. Which was well. She stayed on at the office a few weeks longer, for Herzka's sake; for Agnes Gebaur had become as difficult to replace as the former secretary now residing as branch head in Graz, Frau Christine Schnabel.

And wonder of wonders, when Herzka told Agnes his story—in the form of a virtual confession—and the stories connected with it, she declared in all modesty and all tranquillity: "Why not? I shouldn't think I'd have any difficulty with that. No, really, it's no problem." Scarcely were these words spoken when Jan had the feeling that all his strange preferences were deserting him; for a few moments they became utterly incomprehensible to him. Then he looked at Agnes. She smiled. The future mistress of Castle Neudegg smiled. Gradually, the fire returned to Jan, the wound he had received burned anew—but now deeply embedded in balm, enclosed in a kind of cavern which surrounded it on all sides with the healing balm of reality, protecting it against that emptiness which seems to have its site outside the emptiness of space.

This talk took place some two weeks after Agnes wrenched her ankle.

It had probably been in connection with this that Stangeler had been asked by Jan to take a trip to Neudegg—Herzka himself being too busy at the moment to go—to give a bit of guidance to Castellan Mörbischer and to see how the work of restoration was going. But above all, since Herzka was contemplating marriage in the very near future, someone had to see what needed doing down there at the castle for a lady's comfort, since no member of the sex had occupied the place for a very long time. And who should go with Stangeler but Grete Siebenschein, at Herzka's request. The thing was clear: Stangeler's functions were already extending beyond the field of his specialty. He was beginning—this time with Grete's help, moreover—to play the role of private secretary. "The castle is really worth seeing," Herzka said to Grete by way of coaxing her to go along.

And so, two days later, René and Grete saw Castle Neudegg looming up above the gentle hills of the district. The coachman of the gig which had awaited the couple at the railroad station pointed out the sight to the lady with the handle of his whip. Then the road made a turn, and except for an impressive tower, Grete had seen little.

Grete privately and from the start had called this expedition "the honeymoon," although they had not yet married or even settled upon a provisional date for the wedding. Ever since René had swung the rudder around and abandoned his fundamental resistance, Grete had become extremely unconcerned on this point. Remarkably enough, the same thing had happened to her parents. They were content to see Grete happy, not just happy every so often, but in a more substantial and lasting fashion. Moreover, they decided that things were just beginning to move in Stangeler's case, and that the time was not yet ripe to go into the details of a program.

Yet Grete with her "honeymoon" had hit the essence of the matter, had recognized and named, if not struck the fundamental note of, these days. Even the weather was perfect. As they rode up the steep little road through the leafy woods, there was a spicy odor all around them: the dense plant growth exhaling the warmth of the day.

Mörbischer, the polished old lackey, received them. The inaugural softness and breadth of summer washed over the courtyard, spilled down from the ramparts. They went up into the "manor." Grete was given the room that had been Jan Herzka's, and René, as before, was lodged in the room opposite, a few steps down the corridor.

"Anyone should envy you this post. To think you actually belong here, in this dream."

"The only one who will do any dreaming here will be Herzka, with his virtuous Agnes. I have work to do. You can come out here with me whenever you like. Jan has said so, several times. The finest of summer resorts."

Grete was particularly taken with the library, with its light gay furnishings and brilliant blue tapestry. They sat there after lunch. She reclined on a chaise longue in front of the tall glass windows that reached almost to the floor and looked out on the road.

They had inspected the portrait of Countess Charagiel, and Grete, quite without René's prompting, had been horrified by the face. René had also dug out the old photograph which he had fancied might be a portrait of Quapp as a child. Grete, however, could discover no resemblance. It was, she said, a silly plump child's face like a million others.

Now, after she had seen the beauties of the castle, Grete also wanted to make the acquaintance of its underworld. For a moment she seemed to experience a shudder when René led her down the famous steps. He had himself already been down there with Mörbischer and had been quite amazed at how the work was going. The castellan had planned things cleverly. The bare bulbs and exposed cables were gone from the ceiling. There were now two recessed lights to either side of the entrance; some traces of the operation still remained, dust and bits of pried-out masonry. In the center, near the pillar, stood six large new electric radiators, awaiting installation. They struck a far less disturbing note (from Herzka's point of view) than had Stangeler's jacket draped over the pillar.

"Excellent," René said to the castellan.

"A question of understanding the place," the old lackey replied. "The two fireplaces are also being repaired, here and inside," he added, pointing to the entrance to the smaller room.

Stangeler could not help feeling that he now stood on rather dubious ground, and would have to stand on it for a while longer at least. A brief thought of Professor Bullogg and of all that Williams had said flitted through his mind. That was where the backbone of the whole affair lay, not in Herzka's vagaries. They stepped out into the corridor again and Stangeler examined a little flight of steps built of stout planks and a brand-new wooden door to the opening he had discovered. "The corridor at the back will also be heated and illuminated," Mörbischer said. René almost shook his head, but recollected himself in time and forbore to comment.

Over lunch he spoke to Grete of his passing thought concerning Herzka and the Harvard professor. She quite agreed with him; but her view of the matter was not the product of a momentary mood; it was more reasoned. As far as his present relations with Jan Herzka were concerned, she remarked: "What you have, you have. You've already earned quite a bit, and will probably come in for quite a bit more, on the strength of your contract. Of course Herzka will want to call the whole thing off fairly soon now. You can't very well blame him for that, since he launched the affair when he was in another world, so to speak."

"In a second reality," René said.

"Yes," she agreed. "Probably that is the best way to put it."

After lunch and black coffee they went down to the caverns.

They traversed the long, broad, electrically illuminated corridor and the lentil-shaped room between the foundations of the tower. René held a powerful flashlight similar to the one that Franz, Herzka's chauffeur, always kept in his car. For he wanted to show Grete the corridor that ran behind the two rooms, and had learned from Mörbischer that the lights were not yet installed in there. They descended from the tower room and saw above them the platform on which Sir Tristram's Bohemian mercenaries had once been posted with crossbows.

René switched on the lights and showed Grete the entire layout.

She was taken aback at first, intimidated by a world so utterly strange to her that even her curiosity rebounded from it.

René led her into the corridor behind the rooms and let her look through the slits. That was a bit too much for her; she was visibly upset. When they returned through the door and back into the room where the pillar stood, with the six radiators beside it, the commonplace sight restored her.

"Why, he was crazy, the old knight!" she exclaimed. "Staring through peepholes at undressed old women—what an idea of fun!"

"Programed sexuality. Sexual montage and tinker-toying. Kajetan with his fat females is doing exactly the same thing. Setting up a secondary sexuality. Quite aside from sexuality, it's a way to double other things: two languages, two laws, two literatures. . . . So this is where Fräulein Gebaur will officiate."

"How awful. Somebody ought to tell her."

"He's already done so."

"How do you know?"

"He's told me so himself."

"Filthy character, this man Herzka! And you're nothing but the venal servant of his lusts."

She exaggerated her indignation charmingly. Stangeler entered into the game.

"Terribly venal," he said with pleasure. "To the tune of 400 schillings a month and a special fee of 1500. And incidental emoluments. And the manuscript, to do what I like with. As for Fräulein Gebaur, she's simply a victim of science. It is to be hoped that her first torture can take place soon. Besides, she's not to be tortured; it's only a game. Incidentally, one of these days when they have this place fixed up, I'm going to put on a torture rehearsal."

"With Fräulein Gebaur?" Grete asked, bursting with laughter.

"No. With you."

"Then I'll slap you so hard you'll forget about torture for the rest of your life!"

Doubled over with laughter, they dropped down beside the fireplace. They whimpered and gasped, but softly. Obstinate, humorless, and silent, the nether world surrounded the couple. But their banter broke all the charms and terrors of the caverns and left them utterly ineffectual, fit only for ridicule.

They left this grim nether world, where they had behaved so unsuitably, and slowly climbed up to the platform of the tower, which Grete had not yet seen.

The summer day spread vastly before them, cooling and receding into enormous distances. The scene was rather more a lesson in geography than a poetic experience. No vesper bells rang—it was four o'clock in the afternoon. What was going on within Stangeler would no doubt have been called "intestinal symbolism" by Kyrill Scolander. We call it "unorthographical thinking." In fact he felt as if he contained within himself the vaults of this castle, down to the lowest caverns, and as if in climbing up here he had risen out of the depths of his own bowels to get a freer view of the world. The relative importance of this moment, and the final completion of a turning-point within himself, was not something of which he became conscious. At most he was aware that something had closed behind him like a sliding wall.

There was many an admonitory knock upon Mary's walls. But her suffering—which it would be impertinent for us to try to measure—had finally thrown her out of the narrow-gauge track of anxieties. Once a person has experienced catastrophe, he will, if capable of development, never again be prey to petty worries, never fall back into the trivial lotto of life, into a succession of improvised stratagems.

It was summer when Mary returned from Semmering to Vienna.

The breakfast room was light. The windows were closed on account of the dust, which otherwise settled heavily on the polished surface of the furniture. Everywhere, throughout the rooms, the past stood on two legs of its own. Leonhard was to come in the evening. The children were going out.

The bell rang. He lingered long over her hand, as one bows over a pain, or under a load.

"Well, Leonhard, how are you?" Mary said. She looked at him; there were cracks in her smile, through which unspoken words trickled.

"Thank you, very well," he replied; but his voice was too brittle for him to say even these few words properly. Marie brought the tea and left them. It is worth noting that Mary did not even ask

Leonhard to sit down, that she did not set foot on this little bridge which was there for the using, which would have made it possible to step over these moments when the ticking flow of time came to a halt. And so she lay in his arms and yielded her lips to him. Even during the kiss he gave utterance to a deep sigh, and then slowly sank to his knees before her, and remained so, kneeling, without touching her. She took the chair, and then his head in her lap, while his hands groped for hers. Next moment he was shaken by sobs, and then he talked wildly: "It's too much—always the library—Stangeler. You're never there. Always being without you. 'I'll do the prayin' for you.' *Eripe me e necessitatibus.* Down Spital Gasse with Stangeler. Always without you. The grass so green under the bridge." Pause. Then: "I love you."

She: "I love you."

TOWARD Brigittenau and the Danube, Lower Döbling pitches steeply down, a slope which can only be descended by long stairway-footpaths. From the river, it looks like a tremendous escarpment, well suited for fortification purposes. But so far as I know, it was never so used, not even in the days of the Turkish invasions. The section which particularly interested me is conveniently reached from above by a few side streets that run off from the main avenue of Döbling—on the right when your back is to the city.

I discovered this section not long after my move out to Döbling.

There are days when you wake unusually early, without having gone early to bed the night before. You wake, and it is still dark. But the faintly glowing hands of the wrist watch on the night-table surprisingly inform you that it is already morning. In the darkness you lie on your back in that curious state of almost perfect freedom of choice and will, as though you had overnight got rid of all your habitual weaknesses—or as if these weaknesses are still asleep while you yourself are extremely wide awake. You have really had a full night's sleep, are rested—and feel as if you have leaped abruptly out of all the nasty tracks on which you daily move in the scheduled trains of your character. You are alert, and have left your petty "suburban line." Now you venture to take hold of the new day and of this new opportunity; you quell the objection, "It's only half-past four," throw off your habits along with the blanket, and jump out and onto the bedside rug as if into the center of a new horizon opening out before you. And you derive the sharpest pleasure from the sharp glow of the lamp within its still-dense surrounding darkness.

Ah yes, everyone has his potentialities.

You have truly arisen like Aegidius, who "rose early, concerned for his salvation."

Perhaps it is due to age also, and happens only to elderly persons. I cannot recall that as a young man I ever lay wide awake at half-past four. Getting me out of bed at such an hour would have required main force. Later the task was accomplished by the usual horrid methods that the army has devised—in its folly, for it might more easily train horses out of the habit of breakfasting before the crack of dawn.

It was, then, not long after my move to the garden suburb, when I could already be considered an elderly person and had even been pensioned (though somewhat prematurely, especially in the opinion of Financial Counselor Levielle), that I for the first time "discovered the escarpment." Or rather, first paid attention to it, for it could scarcely have been entirely unknown to me. That had been in the late winter of 1927. And on May 24 I actually lay wide awake in my bed long before half-past four, and finally, concerned for my salvation, arose energetically, quickly made my toilet, gulped down some black coffee, and went out into the still-dusky streets—the glowing tip of the cigarette I was smoking stood out sharply against the darkness. The streetcar tracks were quite deserted.

This, then, was the beginning of my walks on the escarpment.

For this morning, incidentally, I was expecting Quapp's telephone call.

Well, plenty of time to return home by then.

Echoing footsteps down Pokorny Gasse. The sky in the east was inflamed; full morning light fell into this street, because of its situation. I reached the end of it. The view dropped away. The sun was not yet visible. It seemed to me that the din of the birds practicing their various airs in the gardens all around had briefly stopped, that it had suddenly become completely silent, as if some signal for a general pause had been given. A moment later they were again trying to outdo each other in their piping. The sky was pure as lacquer. The sun shot a first ray across a line of houses, converting the edge of a roof into a strip of red-hot coal. Between the trees of the park here, and diagonally across the broad path, a ribbon of red was stretched.

I looked over a battlefield. Why I felt that at the time is a mystery, for I could not have had any forewarning of events which were later to take place there. But the noiseless tumult created that impression: lines of houses thrown slanting across the center foreground; church steeple on the right, and behind a gas tank; here and there flashes of bright green like flames; the steep fall of the terrain before me; everything with outlines sharpened by the fierce arrows of light. This quiet matutinal scene was furiously turbulent.

It was as if the rising sun were about to cast its light upon some gravely decisive arena. As at the battles of Lützen or Königgrätz.

Before these battles, too, the sun had risen on a certain day at a time that could still be exactly calculated, had drawn aside the shroud of night under which the loaded guns stood ready. And Wallenstein had had the roadside ditches deepened in which his squadrons of sharpshooters crouched. At Vercellae the legions had advanced as if on parade (following the new regulations of Marius) in solid formation into the morning mist.

And there he was, the enemy! In rows of gigantic figures.

How much an hour had decided, in certain places, at certain times!

How many an hour, how many uncounted hours, one had lost in indecision, conversation, and boredom. And then again, suddenly . . . At Vercellae and Lützen quarter hours had counted.

I stepped forward to the balustrade, a masonry wall. From the railroad yards farther off rose a pillar of steam, came a long-drawn-out whistle. Now the sunlight included the whole of the little park here. The day had come. And I went home.

After shaving, bath, and breakfast, it hit me, with a feeling of utter certainty, that Cornel Lasch's call on me had been a mistake, from his point of view; that from the first it had been conceived in error. By now he must already know this. Lasch had by no means come to see me solely on rational grounds and after prior reflection, but because he had been startled, worried, perhaps driven to fear. Of course his visit had given him the chance to sound me out—and perhaps he had pretended to himself that that was what he had come for. But he was deceiving himself. An old deceiver thought to do a little deceiving and was instead deceived. The apparatus of association had run away with him, had been stronger than himself and all his cleverness—because it was after all obeying a law of nature. That remark of his about resemblances: "There are people who look much alike, because of the material out of which they are made, but who nevertheless are not related to each other"—that should not have slipped from him. People like Lasch easily underestimate our sort. To be sure, they are much more securely in possession of themselves and conscious of their own interiors as familiar vaults closed in on all sides, from which nothing incomprehensible to themselves, nothing absolutely new, can escape and confront them (that was how Camy Schlaggenberg had once put it!). Nevertheless, this interior space, however well known and well secured, contains its dangers.

If the "methods of obtaining capital," a point of issue between Lasch and Levielle, concerned Quapp's legacy—then I had actually made Lasch my enemy, though at quite another sector of the front from the one I had hitherto imagined. For all along my suspicions had been resting on Altschul and his bank. No, now I saw the matter clearly: we were opposed to each other, not in any objective sense, but in the depths of personal life. It was not some banking deal or business swindle which was at stake. The enmity stemmed from my friends, from our entire circle here, the "colony," the "Döbling Montmartre" (so short-lived, as I now know!): from my relations to Quapp and to Kajetan. Director Altschul—"Let him fall! Ruin him!"—I had run into him quite by chance on the Ring after leaving Friederike Ruthmayr in Gerstner's *Konditorei*. And so that item, too, formed part of the whole, for later on that afternoon I had had that long talk with Schlaggenberg about Alliance affairs—and once again Financial Counselor Levielle had come into the story—as he came into it at many points.

Quapp failed to call. Toward eleven o'clock, however, there was a call from Kajetan. He had got back to town that morning. Could he come to see me at three? Would I be so kind as to telephone Quapp and ask her to come too, but later, around five? He had been unable to reach her and was in a hurry. Had something to discuss in private. All right? He had to leave for the Alliance office right away.

Very well.

At three o'clock—exactly three, for unlike his sister Kajetan was extremely punctual—he arrived at my apartment, looked around, as was his habit, took from his briefcase a stack of papers at least 300 pages thick, and laid it on my desk, saying: "I won't insist that every line of this be included in your chronicle. A certain censorship is unavoidable, I grant. But don't let your prudishness run away with you."

He had lingered in front of my desk and was looking thoughtfully down at the desk top and the manuscript. It did not occur to me that Camy von Schlaggenberg's letter from London also lay there; it had been on the secretary for days, and was still unanswered. Since the "fall from the hobbyhorse," since the collapse of my chronicle, I had been avoiding the desk altogether. I scarcely sat there at all, and even now I continued to avoid it. "Let me see the stuff, would you, Kajetan?" I said from my armchair.

Yes, there were at least 300 pages there, although many of them were half empty, or contained only a few penciled notes.

The more finished pages showed the neat corrections character-istic of Kajetan's manuscripts. I leafed through them. Then I said: "A fine hodgepodge."

"Certainly," Schlaggenberg replied promptly and easily. "It rather reminds me of a fat sausage that has burst. Every achieved second reality must burst sooner or later. It holds together only as long as the partition wall, alias sausage skin, sustains the pres-sure. Once brought into direct contact with life, it falls apart im-mediately. Even becomes incomprehensible. Every burst second reality is incomprehensible."

"I told you so myself, Kajetan—not long ago, in that café—you remember—though the way I explained it was a good deal simpler."

I was wondering, incidentally, at the way René Stangeler's views and expressions were transmitted to others. He literally infected his surroundings.

"In simpler words, no doubt, but a good many more words too, my dear sir. That lecture about pedantry alone was five times as long. And then came that business about 'life' and 'You hate life!' In short, you were solemn as a funeral. Solemnity is for those who cannot achieve precision; and anyone who has to speak in conventional terms needs five times as many words as a person who can manage epigrammatic conciseness. Two proper screws hold a shelf better than fifteen little nails. I am speaking purely formulatively."

"Formulatively is good," I said. "Epigrammatically too, for all I care! You seem to have a special deposit of long words that you can draw on at will."

We laughed. It had not taken us long to recover our own par-ticular tone. I opened the title page of the manuscript and read:

FAT FEMALES

Jottings for a *"Chronique scandaleuse"*

Well we have seen samples of that.

"And where do you stand now in your campaign?" I asked.

"It's over," he said. "That loophole is closed off. I am turning back to—to 'life,' as you so solemnly put it. *Merde!*"

"*Merde!*" I repeated, and as if to signalize the conclusion of all that nonsense, I laid the batch of papers on a small table near the wall.

"There are more important things," he said—and so he really seemed to want to leave the "Fat Females" lie like empty sausage skins—"there are more important things we have to discuss. Something has happened—I've just found out about it, from my mother—and it relieves me of that obligation to secrecy which I once mentioned to you."

"What is this thing that has happened?" I asked—and now I was really alarmed.

"Countess Charagiel died in Morgins—last February, as a matter of fact," he replied.

"What's that!" I exclaimed. "I know that already. But what is the connection?" And I sprang to my feet. Maruschka, the pretty Czech maid, came in at this moment with coffee, whiskey, and soda—I knew Schlaggenberg's tastes. I had not even heard her knock. She stood startled in the doorway holding the tray—apparently Kajetan had called: "Come in." "*Postav to a jdi pryč,*" I said (Put it down and please go!). She set the tray on the low table between the armchairs, curtsied to us both, and left.

"Quapp's mother," Kajetan said calmly.

"I see," I said, collecting myself. "I thought you had the same mother. Quapp's father was Captain Ruthmayr, of course."

"And how do you know that?"

"First I dreamed it, though with open eyes, on that Sunday morning last winter when you opened a new chapter in your life, so to speak, here at my place—and behaved with your usual rudeness. For example, when I asked you whether you would care for tea, you answered: 'Of course I would care for some tea. What do you think? Kindly spare me such frivolous asides.' Very nice. Well then, first I dreamed the thing—that is, I was struck by the remarkable resemblance between Quapp and the deceased captain, two persons between whom there was not the slightest link, as far as I then knew. Did you ever know Ruth-mayr?"

"No, neither him nor Claire Neudegg, later Charagiel."

"Aha," I said. "Well, on top of this resemblance, which re-mained a subjective matter, there later came—to be precise, on Sunday, May 15, of this year—an objective substantiation."

I told him in detail about my encounter with Alois Gach. I also mentioned the appearance of the gentleman on the Graben whom I had briefly mistaken for Levielle.

"That must have been the chief surgeon or surgeon-general or whatever he was, the financial counselor's brother. As a matter of fact they don't look too much alike, but their bearing, their way of walking, is almost identical and that's why they're often taken for each other. The two Levielles once turned up at my parents' house when I was there. Those arrogant faces—they ought to be smashed in like a windowpane. You really ask your-self how people like that do it, who they think they are and where they get such brazenness."

During these moments I once again looked deep down into the shaft of the past, far below me, and paradoxically enough I looked into a still-open wound down there. Yes, it had scarcely begun to heal; it still ached. Once, in my mother's house, I had had to accompany Claire Neudegg to the door, and schoolboy that I was had followed respectfully along behind the per-fumed beauty. And then it had come, that horrible, senselessly arrogant look. . . . It seemed to me now that on the evening of May 15, when I had encountered the pseudo-Levielle, Claire Neudegg had likewise been present.

Kajetan listened with the greatest attentiveness to my story. For a while thereafter, he remained silent. I too said no more.

From my armchair I looked down to the end of the main avenue of Döbling. Now and then the red-and-yellow street-cars appeared beyond the boulevard trees, coming into view at the subway cut, as bright as scarlet easter eggs in a nest, cradled by the bright green of the May foliage. Now I was entangled with the secret details of this affair. Yes, really entangled. I could feel the tug all the way down to the fundamental fibers. Here was a network that I had wanted to control. Now it had caught me. First I had simply moved out to Döbling and run into Schlaggenberg on the wintry path between the vineyards, and now . . .

"I suppose you want to know the story of Claire Neudegg," Kajetan said. "Very simple. When she was a girl she got into trouble with Ruthmayr, who of course knew what his duty was; he went to old Neudegg and asked for the daughter's hand. The old boy, who must have known what the girl was like, is supposed actually to have advised him against it—whether or not that's true, I don't know. I have the story from my father. But it does seem highly improbable. At any rate, that's not important. The main thing was that she, Claire, wouldn't marry him. Because he was not a member of the nobility. Imagine! Stupidity is like iron. Not even *force majeure* can bend it. My kindhearted father, who always helped everybody except himself, took the matter in hand, just in time. My parents set out with the girl on a long trip—to Morocco, Egypt, and such places, from which they sent all their friends cards and letters, so that 'society' was well aware of their travels. And finally, in a tiny place in southern France where nobody ever comes, a daughter was born to my parents, and announcements duly sent out all around. That was Claire Neudegg's child—Quapp. Of course all the documents of the birth had to be made out properly—they couldn't go so far as to falsify them; that wouldn't have been any more possible in France than here. But adoption proceedings were put through at once. My father could never have managed such affairs—Levielle helped to stage and put across the whole business—not exactly as a *maître de plaisir* but as a *maître de complication* or *de camouflage*. And successfully, I must say. I understand that no doubts were ever raised, no whispers ever circulated. At least so my parents said; I wouldn't know. I was a boy at the time, and had not been taken along on their trip. A few weeks after her confinement, I believe, Claire Neudegg captured old Count Charagiel in Menton. He didn't survive the marriage very long.

Now, of course, Quapp is officially a Schlaggenberg, and the only ones who know the real story are my mother, Levielle, myself—and now you."

"What about the French birth certificate?" I asked. "Does it still exist?"

"Yes," Kajetan replied. "I saw it only a few days ago at my mother's. Things seem to be going better for her—financially, that is. The debts my father left have at last been cleared up. I am firmly convinced that my father was ruined solely by that lumber business with Levielle, and no one can tell me different. Mother's chief concern at the moment is Quapp's career. Well, Quapp swears by her teacher. He limps like Hephaestus, has written a fearfully clever book about the technique of violin playing—but he can't sign any testimonials that carry weight in official quarters. That was more or less how my mother put it. She told me all this while pacing up and down in the garden room, and I sat in the center of the long room drinking Styrian plum brandy. Outside the room is a small terrace with columns and a roof, a loggia or pergola, or whatever you call it, and then the garden slopes downhill slightly. It's completely neglected. The trees in front of the house have grown so tall that they cut off all the light from the room. I even imagined it was damp, which it could scarcely be, since the house is built on a hill and the ground is largely sandy. But the light in the room was green as moss, and at odd moments I found myself seeing moss everywhere, sprouting from the walls and from a huge oak sideboard. And on the sideboard itself everything was moss-green, especially a huge punch bowl with innumerable glasses around it, a generation or several generations of green glasses. . . . My mother, too, seemed moss-covered. She is still a lovely woman, tall and straight. But there was this green mossy light on her also—the light you see in a forest pool whose top is coated with algae. . . ."

He broke off.

I carefully let the soda water hiss into a glass of whiskey.

Outside, the afternoon sun, precisely divided and distributed, emphasizing or ignoring, falling between trees and buildings, spread radiantly upon flat surfaces, paling in the distance. The sky had been cloudless since morning. One window of my room was open. The growing warmth of the season could be felt.

"I remarked to my mother that, as far as money was concerned, I would do what I could for Quapp," Kajetan continued at last, "at which she said that she too would be able to give her a bit more than she had been doing. 'But,' she said, 'regardless of what we do for her, the poor girl was entitled to better things. Here she had a rich grandfather—I mean Neudegg—a well-to-do mother, and a father with an enormous fortune—and has had to get along on a pittance. I don't understand Ruthmayr, God rest his soul. Claire left everything to foundations—well and good, nothing else could have been expected from her. Her own child never existed, as far as she was concerned. She was a reptile on two legs. And from all I hear, old Neudegg, who died just this spring—was perfectly dotty toward the end. I wonder who will inherit all that—the castle, the title, the money. As for Claire and her foundations, I learned of that from old Gürtler of Vienna— he was once Papa's lawyer. It seems he's contesting Claire Charagiel's will at the moment in behalf of a Vienna firm: there are still some liens on the estate. Gürtler was here in the neighborhood and dropped in on me; we talked of this and that. Your Papa thought very well of him.'

"I can scarcely describe my feelings while my mother said all this and I sat there in the green underwater light, drinking down the slivovitz, with towers of guilty conscience rising all around me. And the worst of it was that I couldn't pick out any specific omission for which I could blame myself. Only I did not, as did my mother, think that Ruthmayr had showed an incomprehensible indifference to his daughter's future. Rather, I thought Financial Counselor Levielle a scoundrel. But how the devil was I even to approach this whole affair? After all, I'd promised my father to keep the secret. As long as this damned Charagiel woman was alive, I had been virtually paralyzed."

Kajetan fell silent. I took occasion to tell him about the shot I had unintentionally fired on the Graben on Annunciation Day, when I made my remark to Levielle about the obvious resemblance between Quapp and the deceased Captain Ruthmayr.

"Then it must have been that," Kajetan said, speaking with more animation, "and not the fact that René Stangeler twice happened to overhear conversations between the old scoundrel and Cornel Lasch. Although that too must have entered in. Actually that ass Stangeler didn't listen at all. But perhaps the two were discussing the matter of the inheritance. In that case your magnificent chance remark and the supposed eavesdropping sufficed to bring down upon my head a shower of blessings from Alliance, more or less as a bribe. Remember that Claire Charagiel was no longer alive by then, and old Levielle knew that the ban on my speaking out was lifted. My father had bound Levielle to silence too, which perfectly suited his book. But when you said those things to Levielle on the Graben, he undoubtedly thought you my agent, just as he considered Stangeler my spy—that much he told me himself. He must have thought he was being threatened, especially after that priceless remark of yours—which, incidentally, since it was the key thing, you clean omitted to tell me during our memorable conversation in the café. It lay below the horizon for both of us at the time. Though if you had mentioned it by chance, it would probably have clarified everything for me. Though I would still have had to hold my tongue."

Still I made no comment. I did not mention what Quapp had told me over the telephone. I wanted to listen. Passionately— though I was no longer a chronicler—I was seized by a violent craving to get beyond myself, into the hereafter in the here; to make my way into this other man before me, into the fabric of his reticences.

"And so I went around, with this thing in me," he continued, "and as time passed the whole situation seemed to me more and more abstruse and monstrous, swollen and callused. All the more so since I couldn't talk to anybody about it, could never air the affair in a reasonable manner with a rational person, the way I'm doing now. Just once I did do so—as a kind of check—

in order to find out whether I myself was not a little dotty, like old Neudegg. I could do it without naming any names. It was during my worst period last year, in the midst of the crisis with Camy. Must have been late summer, I think—I recall that the weather was still mild. I told the whole story to a likable and clever little prostitute—Anny by name—in her apartment. The fact that I could do so at all, that it was even possible to communicate this hodgepodge to someone who had no bias one way or the other—that fact alone reassured me. It transferred the whole wretched story back to the ground of reality which bears all such wretched stories and where the laws of reality sooner or later have to operate. No, there are no really abstruse matters."

He had finished and fell silent.

His experiment with this girl Anny struck me as really quite understandable and sensible.

"And what did this girl say about the whole story?" I asked.

"She went straight to the heart of the matter. What she said was: 'Somebody's doing some cheating there.'"

"Bravo, Anny," I exclaimed.

"Bravo, Anny!" Kajetan echoed. I reached for the bottles and we both drank to Anny.

"Well and good," he continued then. "But that sterling opinion nevertheless supplied no key to the affair, no *clavis rerum*. For what was I going to do? What ought to be done? That 'reptile on two legs,' as my mother had called her, was still alive. Besides, it once occurred to me that Levielle for his part must feel a kind of affinity for that woman, and that was why he devoted himself so eagerly and successfully to her affairs. . . . And who can say what other reptilian rewards may not have glimmered in the distance for him? Enough. Incidentally, the story goes that several years ago old Neudegg showed Levielle the door when Levielle turned up there in Carinthia to rope him into that Austrian Lumber Industry Bank of his. Which means that old Neudegg was far from being off his rocker; then, at any rate. Well, Claire was still alive. Nevertheless, even at that time I realized that there might be a certain contingency under which I would feel justified in flatly ignoring my promise to my father. I admitted that to myself. The contingency did not occur. But out of pure love of science, out of love for the science of life, shall we not let our imaginations play over that contingency, if only for a moment?"

"I don't understand what you're getting at, Kajetan," I said.

"You'll understand in a moment," Schlaggenberg replied. He left his chair and began to pace back and forth—there was ample room for such activity. I watched him. Usually when a person talks while pacing back and forth, it is a sign of a constricted, obstinate, or even manic state of mind. But with Kajetan it was quite different. The very *élan* with which he sprang from the chair had a grace, an elegance, a real pleasure about it. Such pleasure is never felt by those temporary maniacs; their souls rattle the bars, but let anyone attempt to open the door and they will retreat quickly to the depths of the cage. Kajetan, however, was enjoying his movements now, was taking pleasure in each of his relaxed paces, in every gesture, and especially in the words he spoke, or rather let drop, scattering them on the rug to either side of his course. This was one of his improvisations. When he did this sort of thing, I would feel that there was something irresistible about him. I would put up with a great deal from Kajetan for the sake of this.

What he brought forth was surprising; it reminded me of that type of movement which is called "traversing" in skiing. He first described how he had "made Quapp's acquaintance"—for, as we have seen, after his return from the war in 1918 he had been home but briefly, and seen her there only as an adolescent. Then, suddenly, a couple of years before, this "female person to judge by the clothing" had turned up in his room in Vienna and addressed him as "brother." Although he knew better, it was at once clear to him that he was essentially her brother and nothing else. It had been a winter morning; snow covered the roofs, a train puffed uphill along the subway cut. But what—here his exercise in casuistry began—what if he had felt this young person to be feminine in other respects besides clothing; what if the little god had released the arrow from his bow, in this first moment which is always the decisive one?

"Or whatever metaphors there may be for that situation—I can think of some indecent ones. . . . At any rate, if that had happened, I tell you that I would flatly have broken my promise to my father—if it had come to that, and for all that Countess Charagiel might have been very much alive. I wouldn't have given a damn about her. I would have smashed the legend that Quapp was my sister by blood, would have smashed it to smithereens, convenient as this legend had been for Levielle all those years. I wouldn't have given a damn about breaking my word, not if I had really been concerned about a connection between Quapp and myself. And what a salvation that would have been, what a rescue from the entanglement with Camy! Then, too, I would have fought for the legacy I always suspected was due Quapp. I might even have found ways of putting the screws on the old scoundrel. 'Somebody's doing some cheating there'—that's what I thought too. But as things were, I lacked the motive force. And when a person doesn't really want to come to grips with a problem, he never sees where he could effectively do so. This is one of those rare cases where we've been privileged to find out what did not happen, where we passed the switch and had a glimpse down a stretch of track that was destined never to be traversed. We can recognize now, too, what we've been spared."

I pointed out to him that Levielle probably had also at one time or another considered that possibility.

"Oh, undoubtedly!" Kajetan exclaimed. "As a matter of fact, he came upon us when we were living together in one room because we were so broke. He even mentioned that nastily to you, so you've told me. That too gave him a scare. Naturally he considered this eventuality. Whatever I've thought, he's thought for a long time. But mostly, I suppose, he was pushed to the brink by that 'spy' and complete ass Stangeler—and still more by an enormously sagacious gentleman named Geyrenhoff."

"Yes," I thought, "weapons that we have not loaded are forced into our hands."

And still we fire the shot.

Kajetan went on to say a number of very pessimistic things about Quapp. I had not realized that he was capable of taking so sharp, not to say acid, a view of his sister.

For example: "If something doesn't happen to Quapp which somehow patches her up—I don't know what will become of her. She cooked her goose with Tlopatsch, you know, and that's fatal. She's on the downward path now. It's as though she had a curse on her and ought to be avoided like someone with plague."

"A bit exaggerated," I said. "But to return to what you were saying. What was that about being able to recognize what we have been spared? It's not a question of being spared anything. In the first place, Quapp as a woman is inconceivable to you. . . ."

"Conceivable, as you see, but only in the mind."

"Aha."

"Yes, yes, aha. Moreover, when one really does not want something, one does not get involved in it. And then, you see, the mechanisms of life stand still. Much of what the church calls virtue is based on that fact. There is a quiet and almost nameless abstemiousness that comes long before all asceticism; the latter has never been in my line. There is an abstemiousness in regard to words that one might perfectly well say, and in regard to movements that one could make without more ado; even in regard to one's personal property, which can be arranged one way or another—that is the abstemiousness of taking for granted and security in possession. The result may be that everything is left just where it is, unarranged, never put in order. But what is gained by that kind of conscious abstention is a kind of fine gap between us and the physical world, the beginning of perspective—in itself an enormous intellectual advance which, if prolonged, could confer new insight upon a man. Such a gain would more than compensate for any loss that might result from the neglect of rearrangement. Any type such as the one you projected that time in the café, when you were drawing your portrait of the pedant—not badly, by the way—any such type would forever remain miles away from that kind of gain because he cannot practice discretion in regard to his possessions, to his physical surroundings. That pedant of yours would be a crude and ponderous ascetic. Never someone practicing discreet and light-handed abstinence."

I must admit that I was a little surprised by him; he was really "worth his keep," as the phrase goes, and had answered me quite well—with a neat little stab, too, not with a heavy-handed blow. In reply I had only an argument *ad hominem,* and out I came with it.

"But you know, Kajetan, if the well-known arrow had struck you at your first sight of Quapp grown up—if the devil had got into you—I can well imagine that you have plenty of indecent expressions for it—then your 'discreet and light-handed abstinence' wouldn't have done you a damn bit of good. Besides, it's more than strange to hear you of all people talking about abstinence. That thing lying on the table there—I mean your *'Chronique scandaleuse'*—is nothing but a piece of pornography. . . ."

"On the whole, yes," he tossed off easily and serenely. He dipped the straw into the glass and sucked.

At such moments I really liked Kajetan. You could say anything to him; he listened, accepted, gave it thought. He was one of the most talk-to-able people I have ever known—in fact the only person I could really talk to without any hindrance.

"Since you admit it," I replied, "I shall include only a few sample pages of this glorious elaboration in my chronicle—if the work is ever to be brought to finished form. And we'll do without 'strong passages' and 'grand situations,' understandibus, M'sieu Kajetan? The odd views you sometimes have of the 'grandeur of the moment' and of 'grandeur' altogether . . ."

"Oh, well," he said with a really winning smile. And pointing to the little table on which his manuscript lay, he continued in the most modest tone: "Oh well, around here, of course, people have such high standards. . . ."

"Enough!" I cried. "Enough. Not another word. I don't want to hear it. Enough of your stupid sexual pedantry. What I would like to know is why you think that you would have been spared something. You could easily have escaped from Camy; you did not have to marry her. As for you and Quapp, there was certainly a strong affinity there. Such an affinity might well have sustained a marriage and the responsibilities that marriage brings. Certainly it was a better basis than the one you had with Camy."

He had halted right in front of me, glass and straw in his hands, both swaying gently as he listened. I finished. Kajetan remained silent. He "ebbed." I too said nothing. I waited for him to begin to speak. For whenever he did not answer at once, but "ebbed" beforehand, what he said was interesting—I knew that from much experience. What he said now, however, was extremely concise and did not seem to come easy. He spoke as if he were sparing his words, as if each one were too much for him.

"Affinity, marriage, responsibilities—devil take it all. Much like 'life' and 'You hate life!' Well, you know. No decent person can regard the relations between the sexes optimistically, not even if his own are the happiest. We are nailed to a cross, and to attempt to make a couch out of it is a business for boneheads. For them, of course, the world of sex is a kind of enhanced pastry shop."

"Oh well, of late you yourself have been picking up some good plump cream puffs there."

"And in the course of doing so, learned the lesson I have just recited. Incidentally, you have withheld from me the fattest cream puff of all. I have still not met Frau Steuermann. All right, that's over and done with. I suppose you think I would have been 'happy' with Quapp. Aside from the paltriness of this whole concept of 'happiness'—'I take a dim view of a world populated by happy people,' my teacher Scolander once said to me—aside from the dubiousness of all that—I would never have been happy with Quapp."

"How can you be so sure of that?"

"I have been sure of it since the late fall of the year 1918," he said, sitting down again, finishing his drink, and holding out his empty glass to me. When I had refilled it, he continued, but in a wholly different tone. Now he spoke as if he were talking to himself, in a low voice, without looking at me, leaning far back in the chair.

"I had a long furlough, back in the summer of 1918, and spent it at home, and then the war ended before I was called back. We had a Miss Rugley working for us—she'd been my governess, and then Quapp's—and as it happens she is still with Mother, as housekeeper. A nice little mouse. One day she had been reproving Quapp for something or other—her unpunctuality or some other foolishness—Quapp has those faults even to this day. Anyhow, I came along in the course of the little scene. I didn't know what it was about. But Quapp was answering back. All right. The thing was how Quapp behaved—with a haughtiness and a senseless and hateful arrogance—masterfully offensive it was, somehow—that struck me as . . . as if some horrible foreign body had suddenly appeared in the house. The girl was seventeen at most, but still almost a child. Her face—that good, broad, round, childish face—seemed absolutely to disappear, and a stony stranger emerged from behind it. And yet in those days Quapp had a rather babyish look about her. She has changed a great deal. Perhaps she has developed herself too consciously. Geyrenhoff, if you could see a portrait of her as a child—I don't have any, unfortunately—a photo of her when she was six or seven, you would find it hard to imagine that the picture represented our Quapp. She was such a silly little tadpole at the time —though uncommonly sweet. Well, then, her face was still pretty much the same at seventeen. And out of that face I suddenly saw leap the maximum of icy impudence. For days afterwards I was conscious of that look down to the marrow of my bones."

"I can't imagine it," I replied.

"Of course not. Quapp has never turned on you with such a face. Nor me either—not so far as I know. And if it had ever happened, I would know. All of us are prisms with many facets; we have as many different existences as there are people who know us. After all, it's a common enough phrase: 'I never knew that side of so-and-so.' What I saw just once in Quapp was like the other side of the moon. Still—and now listen carefully, because this brings me back to the main track of our conversation—still, I can conceive of circumstances in which Quapp would be able to present this other side of the moon to the world."

"Heaven forbid!" I exclaimed.

"Oh yes," he said. "If Quapp were to become rich, that's what she'd do."

I said nothing. I restrained myself. But a foreboding, a suspicion, rose within me and ran like sheet lightning over a certain fabric of facts, without yet illuminating the details.

"Yes," Kajetan continued, "that's how it is. You and I can see what we've been spared—from Quapp, that is. Because she loves us. It's very simple, and it applies to you and to me. Love or sorrow carry to extremes the best that is in a person; the side that Quapp turns toward us is the most advanced side in her nature. But don't imagine that Quapp consists of that one side alone. Especially not when she's alone, when we don't see her. Under certain circumstances the moon would swing round on its axis and we would have a view of its other side. Or to put it differently: we would see something like a second biography of Quapp, one that had not yet come to fulfillment. And I firmly believe that wealth, or at least prosperity, would be part of it. I never knew Quapp's father or mother. Ruthmayr was rich. But from my parents' description, I can imagine this man without his enormous fortune—and picture him as quite a pleasant person without it. But not the mother; money, quantities of it, was certainly a part of her. Moreover, she knew how to go about obtaining it; she had a talent for inheriting. What I saw in Quapp that autumn of 1918 was my picture of Claire Neudegg."

I rose slowly to my feet, stood still, and in a loud distinct voice said only: "Yes."

The afternoon light had undergone a transformation, was beginning to modulate through all its keys, was falling through its entire circle of fifths toward evening, with the aim of reaching the beginning again in the darkness of the night. Now a wide golden-red track fell across the green of some treetops, linking them with things entirely different from themselves. Part of the meadow, and a park wall farther off, were included. Kajetan lounged in the chair, holding his head raised and looking up at me.

"Yes," I said again after a few moments of silence. "It was Baroness Charagiel's face that you saw. I know it."

So it was that she caught up with me, coming toward me out of my fifteenth year; caught up with me far more effectively than Gach, who had put an end to my chronicling. For after meeting Gach, I still held the belief that I could act with sovereign independence. But now I had to see with what a delicate thread I had been sewed to the whole fabric from the start; now the thread had been pulled out, and I felt, deep and painfully, the sharp tug at the seam; it ran back to the time of my youth, the only truly decisive period that a man passes through, no matter how he writhes and thrashes about later on.

I too was one of "our crowd"—nothing more.

"Permit me to digress," Schlaggenberg said quietly, lowering his eyes again to the dun-colored rug. "My father-in-law, Dr. Schedik, one of the best and most just persons I have ever known, said to me in the course of our last talk: 'Kajetan, I don't want to blame you, I don't want to act the judge. But one thing I must say: you have made my good Camy into a frenzied, fanatical Jewess. That is the harm you have done; that is what you are guilty of.' "

"You didn't tell me that last December, when we met after so long an interval on the path to the vineyards. Yes—it was still in the old year. But what are you getting at when you quote Dr. Schedik? What he said is true."

"It was not at all true. Absolutely not. Camy was never 'frenzied and fanatical,' not even in her worst period. She was only peace-loving. She was so constituted that she had to buy her peace at any price, even at the cost of inner and outer compromises that went against my grain. She had to buy her peace that way. Had to—understand? The poor girl simply could not cope at all with ambiguities. The nature of intellectual tension remained a complete mystery to her. She could not understand it; and if she had understood, she would not have wanted it. Her doctor—her father never treated her when she was sick—once remarked that Camy had, anatomically speaking, too small a heart for her body. Oddly enough. But now I am just coming to the essential point, and so to Quapp. It seems that I have the faculty—or call it a mania, if you will—to cast other people back upon what they really are, ultimately, in their very depths. I construct what I imagine is their real selves, and then I want to force a decision. In Camy's case my construction was false, and her final 'showing her true colors,' as I put it, was nothing but a desperate convulsion—whose manifestations were taken too literally by her father, to my mind. . . . In any case, I am convinced that I have been on the right track in Quapp's case since that day down in Styria in the late fall or early winter of 1918. Ever since then I have been lying in ambush, so to speak. It won't do to forget about Claire Charagiel. It's not my purpose never to catch sight of her. On the contrary. I feel that she must be driven out into the open. Everything else must be pushed aside someday, the violin and fraternal affection. That is why right at this moment I intensely wish that Quapp would stumble into money—so that she shows her true colors, even if those should turn out to be the Charagiel colors. Rest assured that in this case my egoistic desires play only a very subordinate part. Although I know that if she were rich Quapp would not forget me, in spite of everything. Quite the contrary."

I was still wondering at what he had said about his estranged wife; something seemed to have happened to him. . . . Almost solely with the aim of gaining time, I said: "Your mania for casting people back upon what they really are, Kajetan, strikes me as operating largely in a negative way."

"Yes," he retorted. "Only the full presence of the negative state, without any touching up, permits a decision."

I shrugged. What could I say? He had an answer to everything.

I was still standing in front of him, two steps from his chair, hands in my pockets, looking down at him.

"So Quapp ought to become rich. Yes, she must. Yes!" Kajetan stood up. His voice took on strength and animation. We stood facing each other. "I tell you, Herr von Geyrenhoff, wealth is simply indispensable to the completion of her personality. Away with the incipient character. From now on my interest in the matter will be stronger than my sluggishness: I have found my motive force. But tell me just this one thing: we now know far, far more than we did a few weeks or months ago. Moreover, I can now speak openly to you. And besides we have Gach— probably the most important witness of all. But what should we do now? What can be done that will be really effective?"

"Nothing at all," I replied slowly. "Absolutely nothing. Quapp already knows about the legacy. She told me so herself over the phone on Thursday."

Schlaggenberg said not a word. The telephone rang in the hall. I heard Maruschka's voice; then she came running to the door and knocked.

"You're wanted on the telephone, sir. A Herr Kak."

"What kind of name is that!" Kajetan called after me as I went out.

It was Alois Gach. He was calling as he had promised to do a week before, since he was briefly in Vienna again. Two details had occurred to him in regard to his story about the financial counselor; he'd like to tell them to me. Unfortunately he was rather short of time. I begged him to take a cab at my expense and come out to my apartment at once; he could ask the cab to wait downstairs for him. That way we could have half an hour together, anyway.

Gach agreed.

"That was Alois Gach," I said, returning to Kajetan in the room. *"Lupus post fabulam.* I've asked him to come. I hope you're pleased."

"Well, of course," Kajetan said. "I certainly must meet him."

"One thing now before he comes, because Quapp will be here soon, although we may well reckon on her usual unpunctuality. How much ought Quapp to be informed of, Kajetan? How much should she know?"

"Everything. Probably she already has the story from the lawyer. And if not, then we'll tell her everything. Incidentally, that's just what my excellent Anny recommended. In this whole affair her advice seems first rate."

"Quick, before Gach comes: you really haven't told me anything about how your damned 'Fat Females' came to an end so quickly. Or how this sausage skin of a second reality suddenly came to burst, to use Stangeler's language. I hope you know that you were employing Stangeler's phrase for such a situation."

While I was talking I put two bank notes into an envelope— an amount covering the average cost of a cab from the terminus of the local rail line to Schwechat and back—Gach had told me that he was in that vicinity.

"Of course I know it," Schlaggenberg said. "Now and then René has that epigrammatic brevity that you lack. Your style is fearfully circumlocutory at times, like oral narrative. Why should I not use a phrase invented by Stangeler? I don't place any exaggerated value upon originality."

"Good," I said, "formulatively speaking." (He made a rapid movement of his finger around his neck, with an upward prolongation.) "But tell me this: did the change of heart take place while you were at your mother's? I didn't even know you were planning to go. Did you have it in mind last Saturday, at the table-tennis tea?"

"I did. You probably didn't hear when I mentioned it. My mother wrote, asking me to come. She had heard about Claire Charagiel's death only shortly before, and evidently wanted to talk the whole matter over with me."

"And there, with your native ground underfoot, united once again with the soil, you freed yourself of the 'Fat Females'?"

"Drivel," he said. "My mother's letter merely arrived *a tempo*

—it was all I needed. She also mentioned that Charagiel woman in it. In general I had the impression that Mother expected me to do something on Quapp's behalf; evidently she thought the coast was clear, now that the countess was dead. That idea came out every so often in her talk, although she did not speak about it directly. Incidentally, she did not say a word against Levielle. Not that it matters now—nothing remains to be done, since the inheritance is on its way. You, my dear sir, took care of the matter with your shot on the Graben on Annunciation Day. But to come back to the fate of the 'Fat Females'—a postscript to the '*Chronique scandaleuse.*' I'll be brief: there is a lady named Mary K. who lives in the same house as the Siebenscheins and is a friend of Grete's." There now followed a characterization which I later was able to confirm. "Incidentally, I'll wangle you an introduction to the lady; it's a rewarding experience, I assure you. I myself happened in there some time ago, when I was still pre-occupied with my fat females, had my hands full. . . ."

"Kajetan," I interrupted, "your phraseology—sometimes *c'est impossible.* If that is what your manuscript is full of, I'll have to delete almost everything."

"Delete all you like," he said. "Most of it is far worse. Close-ups —understand? And after all, the objects in themselves are not exactly infinitesimal. . . ."

"Stop it!" I cried.

"All right. Delete. You can throw the whole thing into the wastebasket, for all I care. The work was its own reward. When I first caught sight of Mary K. I was conscious of a bad clouding of my sight. I recognized her excellence, recognized the sort of person I had before me—and yet I could not really see her. Do you understand that? Apperception remained shallow, like shallow hasty breathing. The object perceived did not penetrate, did not penetrate into me. I felt as if I were callused, covered with a horny skin. Every real apperception is not only a contact and superficial mingling of inner and outer; it is an interpenetration of both—more than that, a chemical process, a compound, an 'alchemical marriage' between us and the world, in which we are playing the feminine role. . . . But in those crucial moments I lacked the capacity to be penetrated. I was capable only of a kind of bordering, fringe contact; only in that limited way was apperception possible for me. And I had to recognize that I had lost my sexual impartiality and was living in a second reality" (Oh, Stangeler!) "as everyone who pursues a 'type' becomes the idiotic scarecrow of his own displaced sexuality: a constant anticipation that is never attained. There is a meaning in my never having been allowed to make the acquaintance of Frau Steuermann. Probably—assuming that she really is an ideal, or better a real image of my desires—I would have had exactly the same experience with her; I would not have perceived her in the true sense; I might not even have recognized her at all. 'The bridge of frozen lusts leading to the outer world,' as Scolander once put it, would never have been built. For sex is the greatest window of our apperception, and if this window clouds, all the others will soon suffer from cataracts. Half blind, you will peer out at all things only through the narrow slit of some program or other, always anticipating what ought to be. And in the end you'll call it an ideal. No, I shall never meet Frau Steuermann, and no longer want to. And no, I have disgracefully failed in the struggle with Camy. My efforts at escape have been the worst failure of all. Meeting with Mary K. taught me all this. Of course the silliness went on for a while, out of a kind of pedantry, a mania for completeness such as obsesses stamp collectors. And toward the very end it really became bad. I had stumbled into a kind of idiot's hell—see manuscript! Oh, Scolander! How does he put it? 'There is a deep lesson to be learned from the basic attraction between materialistic unteachability and spiritual intelligence.' And then came my mother's letter. With that the bubble burst completely. Not that I was finished with the whole thing all at once, or am yet. I often think of Frau Steuermann. But only as a goal. I myself have blocked the way to it forever."

"I told you all this one spring day in the café," I was self-righteous enough to remind him again.

"Yes," he replied. "But instead of being precise you were

solemn, and a person of my type cannot bear that under any circumstances."

"That may be," I said. I really saw that it was so.

At that moment a car drove up down below, and shortly afterwards Gach rang. I went to meet him in the hall, and after pressing my envelope with the fare upon him, led him into my room.

I introduced Schlaggenberg as Quapp's brother—and as they shook hands I observed Gach looking keenly at Kajetan. Perhaps he was struck by the absence of any family resemblance.

Since the sergeant seemed little attracted by the whiskey, I gave him a glass of wine.

Over the wine Gach related two details—insignificant in themselves, he commented. But the first of them did not seem so to me. A few years after the war, he said, at those innumerable clubs formed by the members of old regiments, inquiries had gone the rounds about fallen, missed, or captured cavalrymen. He now recalled that there had been one such inquiry by an officer of the surgeon-general's staff who had the same French name as the financial counselor. This officer had asked about a noncommissioned officer of the Seventh Dragoons named Lach; no precise rank was given. During a get-together Gach had reported to the club secretary that he was certain this man had been killed; he remembered some mention of this in a letter, when he was back with his old regiment, the Fourth. The secretary, Gach said, had shortly afterwards passed this information on. Thinking over his interview with Levielle, it had struck him as odd that Levielle had constantly addressed him as "Lach," and that then another Levielle had inquired about a Lach who, as it happened, had also been one of the witnesses to the will. This Corporal Lach, a Viennese, had been the bugler in Captain Ruthmayr's squadron.

Kajetan, naturally, listened to all this with the greatest attention.

Then, Gach continued, something else had come to mind: how Levielle had put away the will, and where. Gach had been able to see this while he stood waiting in the anteroom, for the door, which had not been entirely closed, had swung slightly wider ajar. Through the crack he had seen Levielle standing before a huge, old-fashioned secretary desk—"a real genuine antique piece," Gach said. He had been struck by the way a tiny drawer sprang suddenly out of the secretary when Levielle touched a place along the side panel. "Those old pieces are sometimes regular wonders. It must have been one of these hidden compartments."

Very well. His time was up, he had to leave, and we bade him good-by with the greatest cordiality—I asked him to telephone me again next time he came to Vienna. As I stepped out into the hall with Gach, there was a ring. Maruschka opened the door for Quapp, and curtsied.

Quapp and the sergeant exchanged hearty greetings— they had renewed their acquaintance only recently, after all. When the front door closed behind Gach, we went into my room and found Kajetan standing with his back to us, at my desk, apparently deeply absorbed, for he ignored our entrance for a moment. When he turned around and caught sight of Quapp, he began to laugh, went up to her, embraced her, and asked: "Well, Quapp, old frog, how much have you inherited?"

"Two hundred and fifty thousand schillings," she replied promptly, grinning from ear to ear. Kajetan threw a questioning look at me, obviously wanting to know my opinion. But I had been thrown completely off kilter by the extreme smallness of the sum, compared to what I had assumed.

"And from whom is the bequest?" Schlaggenberg asked.

"From someone named Baron Achaz von Neudegg—whoever he may have been."

"The *lupus* was not *post fabulam* after all," Kajetan said to me. And to Quapp: "Baron Neudegg was your grandfather."

She began to laugh resoundingly. "Let him be my great-grandmother, for all I care. The main thing is that we are clear of our worries for a while."

We were all three still standing. I urged them to sit down and poured drinks. The ice, most of which had already melted, produced only gentle, clinking sounds in the cooler. Quapp had actually contrived to stretch her lateness almost till dusk. She downed one glass at a single draught, and then another—she had always liked whiskey. The room began to gray. I switched on the light but left the window open.

Then we told her everything. It seemed to make no special impression upon her. Perhaps it was still too intangible, rebounded from the surface-tension of the present. News has to sleep with us before it becomes real—the good and the bad both. Her mouth did not open wide in astonishment—as was her wont. She said to Kajetan: "But you'll still go on being my brother?"

"Why, of course, Quapp old frog," he said, getting up. He went over to her and kissed her.

What should be done, if anything? The whole matter was now discussed anew, and without result of course. Quapp, although everything had apparently rebounded from her, was already beginning to act as if she were sitting under a cold shower. So were we. She asked me how much the hypothetical legacy might amount to. How could I know? At any rate it must be a matter of millions—perhaps many millions—twelve to fifteen, for all I could guess.

Now the thing began to take effect. The fantastic notion of real wealth seemed to blow like an icy wind across her mind. Her features froze slightly; it was as if she had come to a halt like a pendulum clock that has been momentarily stopped. Perhaps there was something else behind this, a secret thought unknown to me.

"Kajetan," she said, "you tell Alliance they can whistle for your articles. You finish your big book, the one you already have a publisher for in Germany."

"I won't have any choice," Schlaggenberg said. "Because Alliance is going to let me whistle for my salary before long. In fact they're going to pipe me a tune, as the Germans say, namely, play me a rousing exit march. Herr Levielle will see to that. And even if he didn't specifically order it—without support from him I'd be done for there in any case, and I'd go flying out quicker than I blew in. I think that will happen. As a matter of fact it would be a valuable confirmation of our theory."

"Absolutely," I said.

I then asked Quapp about her yesterday's audition—how it had gone and what had been the result. It was as though my question had switched on a different kind of light in her round face. Quapp became dreamy, in fact elegiac. She told me flatly, and rather casually, that she had had a total failure, in fact experienced a kind of breakdown; that all her previous violin playing was buried in the ruins. (This seemed to make little impression upon Kajetan.) "A great deal changed for me yesterday," she said, and fell silent for a while. Then she added that she wanted to move, to leave Eroica Gasse. "This Eroica Gasse was nothing but an alluring dream."

"The same might be said of the whole 'Döbling Montmartre,' " Schlaggenberg commented.

"And of your Fat Females," I remarked bluntly.

Quapp laughed.

"Where do you want to move to?" Kajetan asked. "Oh, well, I suppose there are plenty of rooms around here."

"I don't want to stay in Döbling," Quapp replied. "I'd like to be in the Hietzing villa quarter."

"Aha, perfectly respectable middle-class neighborhood," Kajetan said, laughing.

"That's right," Quapp agreed, putting an end to the subject. A few months before, such a remark of Kajetan's would have startled her, roused her to contradiction and defense, even made her angry. In truth she seemed to have changed a great deal.

I took occasion to bring up a few matters in regard to the legacy of which Quapp, of course, had not the faintest idea—the valorization of unblocked funds in England. Kajetan seemed almost equally ignorant of this subject. I, however, had had to deal with such affairs. As I have already explained, my rather favorable material situation rested upon a settlement made during 1925 and 1926. Underlying the entire question was an Austrian law of 1921 which in its turn was based upon Articles

248 and 249 of the Treaty of St.-Germain—a law which today, in hindsight, may almost appear as the beginnings of totalitarianism. . . . But enough of that. Fortunately there had been a Graz jurist by the name of Doktor Kornegger—a benefactor to all involved in such affairs!—who had issued a commentary on the text of this law and thus for the first time clarified this "still extremely fluid legal matter" (that was his term for it in his treatise) for the benefit of practicing attorneys. The treatise discussed England first of all; I had it at hand and brought it out for my friends' benefit.

At one point in my explanation I could do no better than quote good Doktor Kornegger: "'The clearing system adopted by England is based on Article 248 of the Treaty of St.-Germain. The essence of this clearing system consists in drawing up a balance from the debts and claims of the nationals of one state as against the debts and claims of the nationals of the other state. Each state then settles the debts and claims of its own nationals. By this arrangement, the contact between native debtors or creditors and foreign creditors or debtors is rendered superfluous. Instead, the two governments act collectively, and settle any outstanding debits between themselves. Private debtors or creditors thus become the debtors and creditors of the state to which they belong. . . . Citizens are required under penalty of law to report prewar debts and claims. The Austrian government has the greatest interest in obtaining full information especially in regard to prewar claims, in order to achieve a better balance . . .'

"And now, Kajetan," I said, "I would like to know how our financial counselor is going to squirm through that. Even if he got himself onto the Board of Trade, or the Austrian Comptroller's Office, or the devil knows where else. Squirm through to a private clearing arrangement, I mean. He has hesitated for years, to study the way these matters are being handled; that we may be sure of. Undoubtedly he also has his confederates in England. But I tell you, it would take more than a few forged documents to swing this thing. Even though he has the tremendous advantage of being executor of the will, and curator of the estate, or whatever the term is. . . . Of course a court decree can be forged, a testamentary declaration can be forged; technically, the thing is possible, and probably not very difficult. But although I do not have the pleasure of being intimately acquainted with Herr Levielle, I think I know for a certainty that Herr Levielle would never release any document that could ultimately be used against him. If anything of that sort has to be done, a straw man will have to do it—a desperate straw man, I might add, because only such a one would do it. Lasch, when he was here, gave the impression of being nearly desperate enough. But he couldn't possibly be the one. Only a practicing lawyer would be in the right position. And at this point I am at the end of my rope—all the more so since I know, from what Gach said, that Quapp's legacy forms a special reserve fund, deposited elsewhere, and is mentioned as such in the supplementary will. It therefore was not valorized along with the main body of Ruthmayr's fortune and credited to Friederike, his widow. I can't see a single loophole for Herr Levielle to slip through."

Kajetan had followed my reasoning very well, as was apparent from a few remarks he made when I finished. But he soon fell silent. Quapp had her mouth open now, but in sheer amazement. She did not say a word, did not understand a thing. Her habitual ignorance withstood all assaults.

Thereafter we said little more; that is to say, we did not talk the matter to death. We could scarcely have done so, for we had no more to go by. We found ourselves facing the yawning black pit of our own lack of information.

Kajetan and Quapp left, with the intention of going out to dinner somewhere. I preferred not to join them; I wanted to be alone. I accompanied the two to the door and then returned to my room.

Through the open window the whine of a streetcar could be heard; it was climbing the hill toward the Hohe Warte. A gust of wind slightly stirred the papers on my desk.

The air was warm.

I looked up toward the ceiling, where it met the wall—toward that upper emptiness of the room at which we seldom glance. And as I did so I felt something at once alienating and deeply familiar, like a memory out of the depths of my childhood. In my parents' home, next to the big laundry and the drying room, there had been two empty rooms in which the ironing-boards were usually set up. When I was a small boy I had dreamed about these rooms. In the dream there were innumerable such chambers, through which I wandered hurriedly, seeking something. In one of them I knew there must be—like the minotaur in one of the corridors of the Cretan labyrinth—a creature that clung like a gigantic spider to the ceiling where ceiling and wall met. But the creature was made of wood and wires. It had a name. I struggled to recall it, but vainly. But I began to feel more and more that something utterly foreign had entered into me, something that did not come from me at all and therefore could not be a childhood memory. A foreign excursion. Ah yes, that was the name René Stangeler gave to his odd walks in remote sections of the city. This thought submerged the whole recollection. It disappeared again.

At my desk a stronger gust of wind riffled the leaves of my writing-tablet. As I stepped over to the desk, I saw lying beside the tablet, the letter that Camy von Schlaggenberg had written me from London. The envelope lay, not with my address up, but turned over, so that it showed the return address: Camy von Schlaggenberg, 110 (or some such number) Albert Rd., London S. W. 11, England.

So now he knew her address. Oh, very well. He had never asked me for it. Nor would I have given it to him.

The following day a note from Frau Friederike Ruthmayr reached me, inviting me to tea on Monday.

On the morning of that day—it was the thirtieth of May—I stood on the escarpment very early. Although we were almost at the summer solstice, at this hour it was still not yet full daylight. I stood by the balustrade and looked out into the distance.

But what my eyes saw was more a memory of my first morning visit there than the actual scene that presented itself. This time the sky did not have that lacquered clarity; the sun finally broke through curly little clouds that appeared wonderfully compact and substantial. Again it was as though the voices of the birds made a general pause at the moment the sun rose, only to resume more vigorously after.

That, incidentally, was the last of my walks on the escarpment.

Standing in the first rays of the sun, I noticed that I was not alone. About thirty yards off to my right, someone else was watching the sunrise.

The spectacle fading, the man moved slowly along the escarpment toward the end of Pokorny Gasse, where I stood, and passed no more than ten paces from me. He did not notice me. It was Stangeler. I called to him and received the impression that he was pleased at this encounter.

What was he doing here at so early an hour? I asked.

"And you, Herr von Geyrenhoff?" he retorted.

"Oh well," I said, "I live nearby. But you have at least an hour's walk from the Third District. . . ."

He would have a nap after lunch, he said; there was no reason not to; as a matter of fact he had gone out shortly after midnight. There were times when you had to seize the moment (what kind of moment it was, he did not say).

The sun had broken fully through the clouds by now, and in its pleasant warmth we began to walk back and forth along the balustrade. The ribbons of smoke from our cigarettes smelled peculiarly fresh and clean in the morning air.

I knew, as the result of my vain telephone call, that he had been away, and asked him about it. René brought me up to date about Herzka, the castle in Carinthia, the manuscript he had discovered, the fee, and his contract. In regard to Jan Herzka, whom I remembered quite well from the table-tennis tea, he spoke quite candidly and objectively—perhaps "clinically" would be more like it. Among other things he remarked: "This business cannot possibly last; it will burst when it has attained its maximum of detailed arrangement and what might be called phantasmagoric order." He then spoke of Williams and of Professor Bullogg. And finally of Grete.

Here too a great deal appeared to have changed. "Things are heading downhill with Lasch," he said. "He was constantly being held up to me, silently of course, as a shining example of business efficiency and of the capacity to support a daughter. So it's an advantage to me that his affairs are really going to pot."

During his absence, Stangeler continued, there had been several first-rate rows at Number 6 Althan Platz—with Titi, of course, who was all upset because Lasch wanted to sell the car, and then between that old horror Levielle and Lasch, who had asked Levielle to finance something or other, and so on and so forth. . . . There was also a lawyer called Doktor Mährischl—weird name, wasn't it? Really a diminutive. They wanted something in England, or were supposed to get something from England, and would not or could not. . . . "How do I know? Grete picked up a whole lot of such stuff. She doesn't understand it herself."

We left the escarpment. I congratulated him heartily on his professional and financial successes. The news really pleased me. At bottom I was quite fond of Stangeler. The new road he had set out on already seemed to possess a good solid base.

René turned toward the city and marched off. It was still too early for the streetcars. I watched him go. His gait was slow, swaying, leisurely. Perhaps this was the selfsame pace with which he had once tramped across the Kirghiz steppes on his flight from Siberia. He vanished from my sight.

I did not take the shortest way home. But out here it was too early for breakfast; all the restaurants were still closed. I walked toward the Hohe Warte. The air was windless, warm, almost steamy: already a characteristic summer morning. The lilacs in the gardens were, some of them, still at the very peak of their bloom: foam and puff in white and purple; frozen explosions. I turned left, walked along an almost level, narrower street, across the "Haubenbigl," and then along the "Hungerberg." Here it was that I had met Schlaggenberg toward the end of the previous year. Now everything seemed so entirely different, and for all of them: for Quapp, for Géza, for Stangeler and Grete Siebenschein, and for Kajetan also. But I still felt the common aura that surrounded all of us. We still belonged together—even Körger and Höpfner and Gyurkicz and Neuberg and Angelika Trapp; we had not yet been scattered, not yet cast into total lack of relationship to one another. All together we still formed a kind of constellation in a space which was enclosed by a fine, transparent, membranous skin.

It was still nowhere near six.

No factory whistle sounded, no streetcars tinkled their way up from Grinzinger Allee.

I walked home very slowly.

The action that I planned to carry out that afternoon, before the tea at Frau Ruthmayr's, had been clearly and decisively in my mind since morning.

After my bath and breakfast, I waited until a reasonable hour and at half-past eight telephoned Quapp. As always she was delighted, greeted me with a cry, and hurled the news at me that she had already found a charming apartment in Hietzing; the landlady had just telephoned and said she might have it. She seemed tremendously excited about this move. I asked her whether she had time to spare for me at four o'clock that afternoon. At exactly four o'clock—"give me your word of honor, Quapp, that this time you will be punctual; it's about the matter we discussed yesterday. Yes?" We agreed to meet at that hour on the corner of Schotten Gasse and Helffersdorfer Strasse. I had found Doktor Mährischl's office address in the telephone book.

I decided then—to go to sleep. The night had been too short. And in the afternoon I would need all my wits about me.

I settled down on the couch and had Maruschka remove the

tea wagon with the breakfast things. She was looking particularly quaint that day, with her Czech child's face. How quaint she would look if she were wearing her beautiful Czech national dress —Maruschka owned a very handsome outfit which I had seen her wearing once when she was leaving for the dance given annually by her fellow-countrymen who lived in Vienna.

If I were a seigneur, I thought, I would have all the servants wear nothing but national costumes, instead of the livery that made them all alike. The forester would wear Styrian, the chambermaid Bohemian, the groom the corded Hungarian tunic. . . .

Such trivialities passed through my head as I lay comfortably on my back. I did not think at all about what I had planned for that afternoon. Here no amount of thought was of any account. The sun fell upon the meadow outside. It was utterly still. I had closed the windows. The garden suburb outside, with every street and path lined by sunlit shrubs and trees, the room here, the couch—it all bore me up like water. I slept. I floated like a leaf over the quiet depths of a woodland pond.

Quapp was punctual. "When it is a question of money, people suddenly become serious," I thought. For the span of a thought I recalled Baroness Charagiel, Schlaggenberg's story of Quapp's adolescence, and his opinion of her future face and fate.

I explained to her that we were now going up to see the lawyer. That she would not have to say or do anything, merely be there.

Doktor Mährischl, I added, would probably say that he knew nothing about the matter and had never received any such commission.

In preparation for the interview, I put on my stupidest expression—which was not difficult, since I really knew nothing, except that I knew of my ignorance. Yet knowledge of one's own ignorance does result, all things considered, in a kind of superiority.

The lawyer came forward to meet us, massive but rather flabby;

he belonged to the class of people with low skin-tension, whose exterior always has something drooping about it; in corpulent individuals this becomes a pronounced tendency to folds. This was the second time I was seeing him—the first time I had noticed him at the Burgtheater with his wife and Frau Rosi Altschul by the wrought-iron fence around the gardens of the Hofburg, and walked along Ring Strasse with him. This time I had the impression that Doktor Mährischl was by no means an unlikable or in any way repugnant person. Rather, he looked intelligent and cultivated (later I learned that he was a great collector of prints). But everything about him was washed in resignation and melancholia. The deep, dark rings under his eyes gave the impression of standing pools in which his gaze floated.

Today, too, he was wearing the gold chain around his wrist.

I introduced him to Quapp and reminded him casually of our own first meeting. I had brought the young lady up there, I explained, because sooner or later she would have to be coming to that office, "since you, my dear sir, are in charge of that business of the posthumously found will or postscript to the will, or whatever it exactly was, of Captain Georg Ruthmayr. And Fräulein von Schlaggenberg here is in fact his daughter."

There was really nothing whatsoever to observe. The pools remained absolutely stagnant. I realized that this melancholia and resignation represented a perfect device for remaining aloof from everything and everyone. Only the small gold chain quivered slightly.

"Amazing," he said. "No, I do not have any such document, Herr von Geyrenhoff. That must be a misunderstanding."

He did not ask me about the source of my information; he refused to become involved in any way.

"Evidently it is a misunderstanding," I said, rising. "I beg your pardon for disturbing you, Herr Doktor."

He bowed Quapp and me to the door, and we took our leave of him in the friendliest fashion.

It was barely twenty minutes after four o'clock. Quapp was eager to go out to Hietzing to make the final arrangements with her new landlady. I saw her into the streetcar at Schottentor, she waved animatedly, and the three-car train glided away.

I had plenty of time.

I was due at five o'clock at Frau Ruthmayr's.

I went slowly, on foot, choosing a roundabout route.

My second warning shot, this one deliberate, had been discharged.

Nothing more could be done. The recoil threw me quite out of the affair and back into my own personal life. I was on my way to see Frau Ruthmayr. But this was odd: all my actions and attitudes of late branched off in some incomprehensible fashion from this single channel and ran back into it: my sympathy for Director Altschul, whom I had taken to be, perhaps mistakenly, personally endangered; my interest in Lasch, and in this whole matter of the legacy. It was all one and the same thing.

It was, of course, Levielle: my competitor, my rival, my personal foe, though on quite another plane, not at all in matters legal and financial. And I had wanted to be a chronicler! "Every man his own department head!" Rot! It seemed to me that I had come to life again for the first time in many years. A new game was beginning inside me, a new rhythm, a new timidity; and turning myself around inwardly, and looking down the series of rooms of my past years, I abruptly recognized that it was the old timidity, the same that I had felt as a fifteen-year-old, walking behind Claire Neudegg on the garden path, in her perfume, accompanying her to the gate to open it for her, on my mother's orders. That was how I was going to meet Friederike now. I was truly falling into my own peculiar track and out of all others.

Yes, Friederike alone, she alone could heal me, could draw out the wasp's sting that had been imbedded deep in my youthful soul, that time. She, Friederike, would have the maternal hand to grope for and find it, the sting which was unnoticeable to others but which still upon occasion smarted bitterly in me. Now

I knew why I had so long remained a bachelor. And a crystal wall, a glass pane, was receding from me and dissolving into thin air, and from behind I felt the breath of a warmth I had never experienced, warmth that for seconds rose to a burning and then was swiftly repressed again.

I had entered the quiet streets of the quarter in which the Palais Ruthmayr stood.

I did not hesitate, did not procrastinate, even speeded my pace, and pushed aside all reflections. This thing had fallen all complete out of me, like a solid kernel out of the shell, just as complete as my decision that morning to go with Quapp to see the lawyer—aiming into the air a second time, but now intentionally—and who knows, perhaps hitting the target. The black bull's-eye at the center.

Her hair was black as ebony. I thought of that now.

It was not in the captain's room that she came forward to meet me, but in a salon that was too small for her, so that it was as if Friederike were wearing too tight-fitting a dress. Such was my state. She floated up to me like a noble ornamental fish out of the green background of an aquarium: now it stops behind the pane of glass and looks at us out of its element, mute and good to its very essence.

So the glass pane was still there, transparent, but firm.

Incidentally, there was also a real glass pane present, but not between me and Frau Ruthmayr. It divided this small room from a much larger one that lay in semidarkness—probably a large reception hall of which this Empire salon formed a kind of annex. Across the large room the maid (Ludmilla) now came, bringing the tea. She entered through a noiselessly swinging glass door.

And so we sat at the tea table, and Friederike seemed pleased to have me there. For a few moments I was really what is called "happy" (that happiness of which Kajetan seemed so contemptuous), and floated with Friederike in a kind of unmoored balloon above everything and everyone. It was a delicious feeling.

As though my fleeting thought of Kajetan's cranky denial of

"happiness" had summoned up his very name, it now entered our conversation: Friederike asked whether I knew Schlaggenberg.

"Yes," I said, "he is one of my friends."

She had read some of his things, she went on, and would like to meet him. Before midsummer—she was staying longer than usual in Vienna this year—she was giving a little garden party, and so on. She would like to invite Schlaggenberg, if that would be agreeable to him; if it were, would he leave his card?—that would be quite enough. Would I tell my friend?

A whirlwind of contradictory emotions rose within me.

"Of course," I said.

She was wearing a dress of dark, gleaming steel-blue, perhaps not quite right for the color of her hair. That minor circumstance made me feel that her womanly power lay sleeping within her. She was ignorant of it. Her wealth of hair held an inexpressible darkness. From the short puffed sleeves her arms emerged, soft, full, flawless, and dazzlingly white all the way down to the delicate wrists, where a bracelet terminated this glacial flow. Above, the throat, a similar whiteness of ancient ice. Scarcely any décolletage. The dress was on the whole unfortunate, but could not entirely quench her impressive endowments, which here and there made their presence felt. I recall that while all these perceptions were taking place, and in the midst of the perturbation caused by the thought of Kajetan, I became aware of a very faint fragrance of camphor or varnish—this instead of some perfume that would have been suitable to Friederike, like heliotrope; for she seemed to be wearing no perfume at all. The fragrance was probably in the furniture. It was very fresh. Now, in retrospect, it strikes me as the odor of a newly begun chapter of my life.

Meanwhile Ludmilla came in through the glass wall, as noiselessly as if she were wearing felt slippers, and said that Doktor Mährischl was on the telephone and wished to know whether Herr Levielle would be coming to see Madame this evening, since he was unable to reach him anywhere.

"Yes," Friederike said. "In half an hour. Tell him to call again."
That was the second cold shower.

I shook myself inwardly like a poodle coming out of the water.

No turning back. My resolution was inexorable; it had come into me like a finished product entering from outside myself. Moreover, I realized that here too I was sitting in a kind of central telephone switchboard where the call might arrive at any time—the same feeling that had swept over me at Prince Alfons's place. We talked about Döbling—"where you're living now," about various stately homes and their inhabitants, all members of a society I had long ceased to frequent. And during those minutes my whole garden suburb had acquired for me, in a curious foreshadowing, the golden-rust patina of something already antiquated. The long, green, straight avenue up to the Hohe Warte, where the tram whined as it toiled uphill, sloping Heiligenstadt Park, Nussdorf with its small houses and big, still peasantlike gates—all of it gleamed rustily. Down to the river! It hurried, quivered with slanting, gray-green streaks, floated its coolness along and thrust the opposite shore far away toward Spillern and Jedlersee. You stood still and looked out across the water, on your left the Bisamberg, which turned its back on you and addressed an altogether different horizon.

After about half an hour Doktor Mährischl telephoned for Levielle a second time; Ludmilla came in to report this.

"It can't be much longer," Friederike said. "Herr Levielle is always punctual. Would you tell the gentleman to try again in a little while?"

A few minutes later Levielle arrived, and seemed not surprised to find me there. So Friederike had informed him that I was coming. For a few moments this little insight aroused in me a veritable rage. That meant she was in constant contact with him. She told him everything. Like a wife. Not that I had ever remotely assumed that there could be more intimate relations between Friederike Ruthmayr and Levielle—nor did I think so now. Somehow the impossibility of that was self-evident, just as there could have been no question of that sort of thing between Quapp and Kajetan. It is significant that although Frau Ruthmayr and Levielle were so frequently seen together in public, there was no gossip about them in Vienna (and that means something!). *In puncto puncti* society usually senses aright; and society placed Levielle as a kind of elevated lackey of Friederike's—though perhaps a lackey with expectations.

We greeted each other with considerable formality. Levielle had scarcely tucked the teacup under his white brush of a mustache when Ludmilla came floating through the glass door once again to inform Levielle that Doktor Mährischl was on the telephone and wished to speak to him; the gentleman had called twice before because he had been unable to reach him anywhere. . . . Levielle's expression seemed to show that he considered this report too long and too public; he rose abruptly, stepped through the glass door, which Ludmilla held open for him, and strode down the full length of the adjoining room. The telephone seemed to be at some distance. I remained alone with Friederike for a while.

Friederike had dismissed Ludmilla's breach of form with a faint, benevolent smile. The girl was obviously treated more like a protégée than a servant.

I happened to glance through the net curtain and the wide window, and became aware that this salon looked out over the garden. I turned my gaze down into the thick greenery and the winding paths among a few belatedly flowering lilac bushes, white and purple. Closer to the house stretched a green tunnel, an arbor, on which the first rambler roses were already showing, for it was in a sunny spot.

I had risen and was now standing by the window, holding the curtain slightly apart.

Friederike came over to me. "The arbor," she said, "was getting rather rickety. But Ludmilla's brother fixed it beautifully last year." I felt that she was looking at me while I gazed down into the garden. And I wanted to catch her expression. With this intention, I turned abruptly toward her. She blushed. I could not believe my eyes, and stared down at the rug. Then I looked up. She stood before me and said nothing, while the pinkness vanished from her face and its ordinary tranquillity was restored. Just then Levielle returned from his telephone call.

He took his seat again and made some trivial remark—but I recognized at once that he had reached the extreme limit of his self-control. He was furious at something. I thought of how he had screamed at me on the Graben on Annunciation Day ("What? What's that you say?") and I knew that in a moment his face would show the same expression it had shown then.

Fortunately, there sometimes opens between us and the present situation a gulf out of which coolness rises as from a crevasse in a glacier. I did not have Quapp's legacy in mind—not at all. My own situation, unexpectedly cracking open—how long and under how many forms had I concealed it from myself!—now demanded cool reflection. Given the tension here, any unwary word could cause a crisis. I definitely wanted to avoid any open conflict with Levielle, any "difference of opinion"; anything of that sort, especially in Friederike's presence, would have been extremely undesirable. And so I decided to decamp. I rose, made some pretext (a meeting of officers of my former regiment, I think; in my haste nothing else occurred to me), and took my leave of Friederike. I shook hands in the friendliest manner with Levielle, who really seemed to have reached the end of his rope and whose expression during the last few seconds made it clear as day that it was high time for me to be going. Even as I descended the steps and passed the doorman, I painfully missed Friederike herself. But as I left the house I felt strongly that my inner being was made of firmer stuff than it had been two hours before, when I entered the Palais Ruthmayr.

IT CAN no longer be determined who first brought Prince Alfons Croix up to Mary K.'s. But in all probability it was Count Langingen, who after all had already been seen leaning against a doorjamb at the Siebenscheins' on May 14. From there to Mary's it was only a step, or more precisely, a story.

At any rate, Mary had returned from Semmering on June 10, and around the middle of June the prince was seated there in a corner with Leonhard Kakabsa and René Stangeler, the three obviously engaged in a deep talk that lasted almost an hour. No one else was able to endure it for long. Trix had sat with them for only a few minutes. Hubert stretched his stay to a full quarter hour. Frühwald had no more endurance than Fella Storch. The latter specimen of *Sesia myopaeformis* L. had fluttered up soon after the prince's appearance, but had been quickly repelled. It must be said that Croix was a disappointment for certain people.

Mary, however, saw very well (how could it have escaped her!) that Prince Alfons had fastened his attention upon Leonhard. She even lent an ear for a time, and discovered to her astonishment that the two were employing René Stangeler solely as an information bureau, and referring to him as they might to a handy lexicon of ancient and medieval history, and occasionally of Latinity. In which capacity the slant-eyed scholar did not fail them.

Finally, however, it was the prince who put an end to the

conventicle by rising and taking a seat near Mary. She now observed two curious things about him. The first was that he displayed toward her the modest, almost shy manner people have toward a person of extraordinary accomplishments. And secondly he employed a gentle but irresistible force to induce Mary to talk. She saw this, was quite conscious of it, and nevertheless succumbed completely. Prince Alfons achieved his end, for that evening Mary told him her story, the story of her accident and its consequences. She related it in detail, though belittling it somewhat, and with a faint touch of irony, as far as such a subject could be treated ironically.

Finally Leonhard and René also came over. Mary had not been back long when Stangeler did as he had pledged and apologized for his previous rudeness. The ladies had been more than mollified, and so René and Grete were once more guests at Mary's. Grete was at the moment sitting in the music room, chatting with the butterfly expert, his fiancée, and Count Mucki, who felt no obligation to play a miniature Boswell there, waiting upon every word that fell from the prince's lips; instead he talked as much nonsense as he pleased in German, English, and even Czech (with Emma Drobil). Grete was much taken with him, and even flirted a bit with harmless Mucki.

Stangeler, meanwhile, was observing Prince Croix's method of drawing out Frau Mary, but could not get to the bottom of it. The prince would first ask a question, very sympathetically, with overtones almost of tenderness; then he would listen to the answer with the greatest attentiveness, and for a while intersperse only purely matter-of-fact questions. But before the thread of this interrogation could break off, Croix would approach the subject from an entirely different side; with great circumspection and gentleness would ask a personal, psychological question— and the game would begin anew. It was really difficult for anyone to resist. René had the feeling that Prince Croix was constantly promoting what he later called "a clarity outlined with a drawing-pen." As he listened to the prince, he thought: "The man wants to see everything stereometrically, so that you'd literally have to walk around it. Exemplary, real. He exudes distinctness like an aura. You almost feel that the room here is deepening and the objects in it being defined with sharper contours."

That morning René had received a four-page typewritten letter from Professor Bullogg in Cambridge, Massachusetts. The professor wrote in considerable excitement, and in a fluent and natural German. (Later it turned out that his name had been Balogh and that he had taught history and German at a Budapest Gymnasium.) His views in regard to the whole witch-trial business appeared to be virtually identical with the ideas that Stangeler had briefly outlined to Jan Herzka at Castle Neudegg, and the manuscript René had found certainly offered welcome support for a theory of this sort. Professor Bullogg was therefore anxious to see the whole text as soon as possible, and equally eager to have René Stangeler's commentary on it. This latter point was emphasized; perhaps the professor wanted to form some opinion of the technical qualifications of his Viennese correspondent, and such qualifications can, of course, be deduced from the manner in which a specialist supplies such a text with elucidations. Moreover, an essay of this sort would reveal the scholarly and intellectual qualities of the author. René was intelligent enough to realize that Bullogg was in this way offering him the opportunity to present himself properly. And the letter contained some hint of practical prospects: the possibility of publication in a journal of the first rank, and of a fellowship—just as Dwight Williams had indicated.

Grete had already been told. Which accounted for her gay mood this evening.

The letter concluded: "I had intended to be in Vienna by now. But I have had to let my wife precede me to London, where she has visited her mother (who is Austrian by birth, incidentally), for one thing to acquaint her with her grandson—our ten-year-old boy. My wife then continued on to Paris and will probably be in Vienna by now, together with my sister from Chicago, Mrs. Garrique, and her children; they had arranged to meet in Paris. But I do not yet know where the ladies are staying in Vienna.

My mother-in-law, however, has remained in London, although she too was planning to visit her native country, together with a Viennese friend who is staying with her; for some reason this trip has been indefinitely postponed. My brother-in-law, Herr Franz von Gürtzner-Gontard, will be traveling directly from here to Vienna, with his wife, to visit his parents there. I am giving him your address in any case. I myself will be held up—I have examinations to give and various meetings and congresses to attend, so that I cannot possibly reach Vienna before the middle of July. The chief purpose of this letter is to ask you to remain, if at all possible, in Vienna until after mid-July, since I naturally have the most intense interest in seeing the original of Ruodlieb von der Vläntsch's narrative, which is in your keeping. I shall try to get in touch with you immediately after my arrival in Vienna; probably that can be best managed through Professor Williams, who writes that he will be staying in Vienna throughout July. I am awaiting your manuscript with a good deal of suspense, as you may well imagine. . . ."

So far, so good.

The whole matter had been discussed with Grete and Williams.

And René had already made such progress in his work that he would be able to dispatch his material to Professor Bullogg within a few days.

The gathering at Mary's broke up a bit after ten. For a few moments everyone stood around in front of the door. Hubert had gone down to unlock it, and Grete, Fella, and Trix had tripped down with the others, although all three lived in the building. But they had decided to walk Lilly Catona home. Lanky Bill Frühwald seemed to welcome this idea, for he had thrown in his lot with calf-milky Lilly this evening. The others were probably counting on Leonhard to enliven their party, since his way home led in Lilly's direction. But Leonhard quickly said good night, and was off and away toward the Danube Canal with rather surprising haste.

The prince looked after him. "A man of remarkable distinction," he said.

But Hubert K. found this untenable. "Do you know what his occupation is, Prince?" he said.

Now something terrible happened.

"Yes," Croix replied, "the gentleman is a workman." He gave Hubert a curt glance as he spoke, then turned his eyes away as one might look away from a sausage dropped into the gutter by a dog. That look ran down Hubert like cold, sticky porridge. It was as though Croix had flung a bowl of porridge in his face. Then the prince lifted his hat to the others, turned, and set off toward the bridge.

The reaction of the various members of the party differed. But the silence which remained behind like an empty bowl showed that something had really happened. There was no concealing it. Count Mucki had the foolish look of a person who has discovered his trousers falling. Whether Williams, in spite of his excellent knowledge of German, knew what had taken place, seems doubtful. He had paid no special attention to Leonhard during the evening, and for that reason may not have understood. But Emma did. Hubert had repelled her from the first, repelled her à la Santenigg. . . . René, too, approved of the noiseless slap in the face that the prince had administered to the young man— a slap after which no one said anything for several moments, as the twittering and chattering of birds in a wood stops for moments after a shot has been fired. Bill Frühwald made no attempt to hide his grin. Grete's and Trix's eyes widened. Hubert himself had turned pale; that could be seen by the light of the street lamp. And one person interpreted the matter quite differently, on another plane, from all the rest. That was Fella Storch. Croix had avenged her. This time Hubert had run afoul of the wrong person! Any disappointment she might have felt in regard to Prince Alfons evaporated. (She had come to Mary K.'s only because Trix had told her they were expecting a prince.)

Nothing came of the little group's planned evening walk. The three girls and Hubert went back into the house; the others went their ways. Bill Frühwald escorted plump Lilly home alone, which pleased him no end.

When Croix had gone about thirty yards from the group in front of the apartment house, he filled his lungs, pressed his elbows to his sides, and began to run, keeping his pace moderate for better endurance.

He had already lost sight of Leonhard. But when he reached the bridge, he saw him already on it. Leonhard was sauntering along with that somewhat rolling gait which had once given him the nickname of "the Sailor."

"Herr Kakabsa!" the prince called before he had quite reached him.

Leonhard stopped.

"Have you a little time for me?" Croix said. "Or is it too late? There is something rather important I'd like to discuss with you."

"Gladly," Leonhard said. "Tomorrow is Sunday. I can sleep as long as I like."

"Splendid," the prince said. "I'll send for my car and we'll drive over to my place, if that's all right with you. Tonight being Saturday, all the cafés are full; no quiet anywhere. And I must talk with you, Herr Kakabsa. Let's drop into some bistro now, drink a slivovitz—I need it after so much exposure to youth— and from there I'll telephone for the car."

"Yes, sometimes a slivovitz is really a necessity," Leonhard said gravely.

They had been walking along Wallenstein Strasse. They found a café, downed their plum brandy, and the prince went to the telephone booth.

"The matter is this," he began as soon as he returned to the table. "I have long been searching for a librarian. I don't want a middle-class academician reeking of general education. I want someone with native wit—he can go ahead and study and attain his doctorate—of course at my expense and with my assistance. His interests should lie within the fields of history and philology. You, Herr Kakabsa, fill my bill. It is difficult to find someone who does, or I would long ago have found him. I am offering you what is called a lifetime position, as estate librarian, and with it the requisite education for that position. You will have two rooms in the palace on Reisner Strasse, your board and service taken care of, and above all, plenty of time and a reasonable monthly salary. We will then work out together the initial plans for handling and arranging the library here in Vienna. There are two more, one at a castle in Lower Austria and one in Czechoslovakia. After six months, if you are satisfied, we'll draw up a regular contract. Right now you would have nothing to do but give notice at your job and move over to Reisner Strasse. That shouldn't be very difficult for you, since you have told me that you have no ties. This, at any rate, is my proposal. When we go home now, we'll see to some better refreshment and consider the matter from all sides. It's an effort to talk here in all this noise. If any questions occur to you, we'll discuss them. Besides, you can look over the library and also see the quarters you would occupy."

In spite of the din of the café, the prince's speech effortlessly conquered its environment. That was the first thing Leonhard felt; he had a keen ear for such linguistic matters. The prince came through. Leonhard even had a rather exact idea why: the prince came through because he did not force his way, did not force himself upon his listener, was not in the least forceful. He merely made an experimental cast, without in the least disturbing his own balance. In fact, this maintenance of equilibrium while he spoke—so, for a second, it seemed to Leonhard—was in a way the principal aim of his speech, far more important than anything he actually communicated.

"There is only one real objection," Leonhard said, after a considerable silence—during which the racket in the café, from which the prince's speech had shielded them as with a stretched canvas, crashed down upon their heads. "And this is a purely subjective one. Up to now my thought has been that I must present an example—namely, that freedom was possible under the existing circumstances of my life. If I change these circumstances, that principle falls by the wayside. To change my occupation would be, for me, disloyalty. Not toward my occupation as such, but toward that situation in life within which I feel I have been called to present an example, small as it may be."

No—he did not think back to that walk with the bookseller Fiedler by the Danube Canal just a year before, and to a conversation in which the parts were similarly assigned, although on another plane. Leonhard's gymnastic exercises in German grammar: "It remains to be proved. . . ." Well, since then it had all been proved; Prince Croix, as we shall see in a moment, likewise thought so. Those days, and the language of them, already belonged for Leonhard to prehistory. Primordial sounds, mythic struggles of ancient ages. Now he stood in the light of history, and within the orderly realm of formal speech.

Leonhard's speech, too, held the din at bay.

Perhaps Prince Alfons was as conscious of that as Leonhard had been when the prince spoke.

His reply was cautious, judicious: "It is not you who will be changing your circumstances, nor I; the circumstances will simply be changing of themselves. You never saw them as the ruling forces. You've never said: 'If only I had the time, I would study.' Far from it. A person who does not make anything dependent upon a change of his circumstances is in no way the sport of changed circumstances. Another thing: an example must be unique, must form a single point. *Exemplum docet, exempla obscurant.* Once the example has been made, nothing is gained by repeating it innumerable times, or by stretching it out."

Leonhard considered and said: "I acknowledge the force of both arguments and withdraw my objection; it is not cogent."

(In tribute to Leonhard's character, the author here rises from his desk for a moment. Karl Zilcher had spoken truly when, standing in front of Leonhard's new table, he had said: "So our Herr Doktor is going to be studying." He has already reached that point for us. We have no hesitation in awarding him his degree, Leonhard Kakabsa, Ph.D., estate librarian and curator to His Highness Prince Croix. For all that he was later to become. To make your way in the world you do not necessarily have to discover indecent fifteenth-century manuscripts.)

Leonhard had scarcely spoken these last words when a man in the Croix livery entered through the revolving door, looked quickly around the café, and coming up to the back of the prince's chair, reported in a low voice: "Highness, the car is here."

It was Mary, not Leonhard, who instantly recognized the significance of this turn in all his affairs. But her gaze remained fixed upon the displacement of external factors. Here it became apparent that Mary, for all her intelligence, could really derive conclusions only from facts, from the facts which come tumbling like an avalanche of broken stone when what they have produced has already happened and is actually past. For in reality Leonhard had won his real fame long before. The average numbskull sees something in things only when they are on the point of being broken up; he solemnly dubs such situations "a historic moment." By then, however, the historic moment has already gone by. We, however, remember the momentous night when Leonhard Kakabsa crossed the dialect frontier.

Now, moments came when he feared falling into a new entanglement—this was his character, after all; feared the involvement which would begin with the prince and with all the new elements in his life. He still had that false fear for his "freedom" (really only for a faded conception of it) which affects many a person who is about to step out of something and fancies that he is stepping into something else which is going to imprison him. René Stangeler's feelings about his involvement with Grete had been of the same order. But Leonhard saw himself once more walking upon that suicide bridge, as he had envisioned it more than a year before, on the verge of sliding like so many of the living suicides into some opening maw. At that time its name had been Malva Fiedler: suspended like a wall of water above him, full-breasted, cat-eyed, Venus-bellied, inhabited by icy tempests. No, there was no question of such temptations here, or of Elly Zdarsa with her dark places, or of Trix and her rosy glow. This new life was no entanglement; it was a link. Quite suddenly this perception came to him; and it applied to Mary as well as to the prince.

Meanwhile, in that manner which we later find so hard to reconstruct (how did we ever do it?), Leonhard shifted the mechanism of outward life into neutral, stopped its carrousel, and dropped off. Moving out is a kind of dying, at least for the district in which one has previously lived. Leonhard quit his job, resigned from his union, since he was changing occupations, and gave notice to the warehouse attendant's widow.

"And here you've only just had yourself a desk made!"

Soon Leonhard was floating free in space, in a kind of unstable equilibrium, without the bonds and tensions that had previously held him. He continued to live for a while in his room on Treu Strasse, but he was inhabiting it as if he could just barely remember the place. It was as if he were becoming his own echo.

Just as his last week at the job came to an end, he received a summons from police headquarters, a printed form that looked somewhat as follows:

Honored Sir

you are hereby requested to appear at the above station within the next week to provide certain information.

When Leonhard presented himself and this form, he was directed to the office of the criminal police. He entered a small, rather pleasant-looking office and found himself confronting a middle-aged gentleman in uniform, with several gold stars on his collar, who was smoking a Virginia cigar. The gentleman gestured to a seat beside his desk. Leonhard sat down.

"Well, Herr Kakabsa," the official said, "we have a denunciation against you—anonymous, by the way—in which you are charged with having relations with minor girls. I must ask you for a statement. Can you, for example, tell me what such a denunciation might be based on?"

Leonhard was merely astonished; he had no other feelings about the matter.

"I must think that over," he said. And then, after a pause: "I have it."

He told the official about Trix—"but she looks quite grown up, like seventeen or eighteen"—and of the house on Althan Platz to which he was sometimes invited. He also mentioned Trix's friends, the daughters of Professor Storch and of Dr. Catona on Wallenstein Strasse. He himself, he added, was part of Trix's mother's circle of friends; he had the greatest respect for the mother (at this point he briefly mentioned her accident). He had indeed gone walking now and then with the girls, and had sat with them in Freudenschuss's pastry shop. On the whole he seldom saw the young ladies, only at parties in Frau K.'s house. That was all there was to it. He knew of no other young girls that he associated with.

"How old are these girls?" the official asked.

"I couldn't say exactly," Leonhard replied. "But they are in the sixth class at the Gymnasium."

"Well, then. I remember Frau Mary K.—she had her accident in September 1925. A young sergeant was there at the time; he's in our precinct now."

"Yes, Karl Zeitler."

"Quite right. Do you know him?"

"Yes, he is a friend of mine. We sometimes study together. He's interested in history."

"Right you are! That's Zeitler. A most ambitious young man. Herr Kakabsa, I'll tell you something confidential now. We have made a few investigations, unobtrusively, into this matter, for after all this is a grave charge against a young fellow of excellent reputation. We have observed nothing more than what you have just told me. That seems to settle it. If I may give you my opinion, though, it's this: it looks to me as though there's a woman behind it. Some woman with a grudge against you. If you think the matter over, you'll no doubt be able to figure out for yourself who it might be. But the best thing would be not to give it another thought."

The official laughed. Leonhard rose. "Anyhow, I'm moving away from this neighborhood, to the Third District," he said and mentioned briefly his new position and his plans to become a student for a while.

"Aha, I see!" the official said, likewise rising. "My congratulations. Well, good luck for the future, Herr—Herr Doktor!" Laughing, he shook hands with Leonhard.

But in spite of such constabulary wisdom and profoundly Austrian insight into the nature of human relationships, Leonhard did give the matter another thought. Outside in the street and the bright sunlight, he felt the touch of the dark sting that for a moment had stabbed him and then immediately been withdrawn into a hereafter in the here, without having really injured him, but leaving behind on his skin a drop of the venom of hatred. In his new life, there was nothing to propitiate, nothing to appease along the straight line of truth and loyalty; and for a second now he felt this line within himself, in quite the same manner as he had the year before when he had declared in the tavern that he was "satisfied" and an elderly workman had had to take him under his wing. But this wall of misunderstanding between Malva and himself could no longer be broken through, nor could it be rebuilt out of softer material as that decent fellow in the tavern had ultimately succeeded in rebuilding it in Leonhard's favor. He thought now of passing by Fiedler's bookshop with the girls. Malva had seen him with Fella and Lilly. That was the clue that had come to his mind as he had talked with the police official.

All this was a part of leave-taking too. Arrows were already flying out of the hedgerows in this neighborhood. He no longer belonged here, and lingering any longer in what had already become his past would lead to trouble. *Exemplum docet, exempla obscurant.* The prince saw the matter correctly.

Yet no evil had ever come to him out of that really ugly darkness in which Anny Gräven lived.

He stood still, remembering her with sincere affection and good wishes—but also as a point from which he was already separated by many bends in the road, a truly past point that was now only a fading dot of light.

By next day he was ready. His friends turned up. They helped pack.

The warehouse attendant's widow watched.

"And here you've only just had yourself a desk made!"

The desk was to be left behind as a present for her. But first, the packing already done, the three young men sat around it once again over a bottle of wine.

Leonhard wanted to take along Krawouschtschek's book-ends, in spite of the lead plates screwed underneath them. Likewise the desk-lamp he had bought cheaply from Karl Zilcher. These were not packed, merely put in a paper bag; they could be taken right along in the cab that way. For it had been decided that the quickest and simplest way was to make the whole move at once, by taking a cab and going right along with the baggage. There was not much of it, only a suitcase and a small chest. In the course of packing, Niki had remarked that Leo had few but all good-looking things: shoes, shirts, the dark suit. The two sets of work clothes had been washed, mended, and ironed; Niki and Karl could make good use of these uniforms.

And so they had one more drink.

"Well then, here's to our Leo—now he's really going to be a Herr Doktor!" Karl said.

And Niki recalled the motorcycle trips, and their talk with the old sergeant in Fraunkirchen.

Leonhard looked through the window at the façade of the house across the street. No sunlight fell upon it; it lay dull and locked within its grayish-yellow color. There was something parched about the façade, it suddenly seemed to him. It was as though all this neighborhood were vanishing. From now on he would be looking out into a garden. His rooms, which he had seen that night at the prince's, were small, white, shipshape, and modern. They floated like the gondolas on water above the old rooms of the Palais Croix. The story was a new addition. The windows were on a level with the tops of trees. For a moment Leonhard was grazed by the feeling that he was losing a standard, a good counterweight; he would be able to maintain his equilibrium in the new situation only with heightened caution. He had to cling to Pico, to return to Pico della Mirandola, and start out from him again. Back to origins, to the small, precious treasures of a still-brief past.

They took the things. Niki ran ahead to the taxi stand and in a trice was back with the cab. The warehouse attendant's widow stood at the front door. "Drop in at church sometimes, Herr Kakabsa," she said. Leonhard shook her hand without reply. "Well, no matter, I'll do your prayin' for you." The door shut; the old woman could be heard shuffling away. They descended the steps. The baggage was stowed into the cab. Standing at the cab door, Leonhard shook hands with his friends. At this moment, the very last, he felt his first pain at parting from Brigittenau; there was a little scratch, a drop of blood.

"You'll be coming around again soon, won't you, Leo?" Niki said. There was a somewhat anxious overtone to his voice.

"Why, of course, of course I will."

But his own words did not reassure him, did not reassure his conscience. Already he had been drawn too deeply into life— without the slightest entanglement!—not to sense how great was his parting from all those to whom he had belonged in this quarter of the city, from Karl and Niki and the warehouse attendant's widow, from the carpenter Krawouschtschek, the bookseller Fiedler, and even Malva. He was falling out of the margin of the universe into a different space, had burst out of this afternoon as out of a constellation, and was now dying a local death here. As the cab turned the corner of Treu Strasse, and he looked back out of the rear window, he saw the somber look on Karl Zilcher's face, as though his friend were watching his funeral procession.

The summer afternoon sunlight overflowed everything on Wallenstein Strasse, and as far as the bridge all sharp outlines were blurred by the dazzling light. On the bridge itself the thought suddenly hit Leonhard that Malva had been the only one to try to place a monstrous stumbling-block across his path from the brief past to the widening future. So be it! He had escaped her. Not through his own strength. "*Alea iacta est,*" Leonhard thought. The inevitable Caius Julius had crossed the Rubicon. Sitting in a cab, Leonhard drove over the Brigitta Bridge and so crossed the Danube Canal, taking care the while that the lamp, lying on the seat beside him, was not jounced to the floor. In a moment the cab was passing Mary's house. And here, on the other side of the Rubicon, the sense of permanency returned.

During the first half of June I had several visits from Kajetan. I told him, of course, of my call on the lawyer Mährischl and transmitted Frau Ruthmayr's invitation. He was most prompt about leaving his card at her house.

There are periods which in retrospect offer no holds for the memory. They have no denominator, no handle our recollection can grip. Nevertheless, precisely such periods can be vessels in which anonymous deposits have accumulated which we are not yet allowed to touch (*loci intacti*). Some time or other they will be poured out, and perhaps prove to hold a more brilliant history than others which from the very beginning offered a handle to memory, but a handle which in the meantime had long since been worn out.

We waited. There was nothing else to do. While the oncoming summer leaned against the sky, I ran over the whole affair in my mind, for the last time. Then it faded, vanished from sight, and the more the days passed, the less reality remained to the whole business of Quapp's legacy. It flew away from me like a child's balloon, and joined the summery wisps of cloud which I could see resting motionless in the blue sky, off in the direction of Heiligenstadt—for my windows looked in that direction. There were two windows. One stood open. On its window sill, feet resting on a chair, sat Schlaggenberg on the afternoon of June 22, with his shirt sleeves rolled up and a stubby pipe in his mouth.

We did not speak of the matters just mentioned, although I would have liked to hold on to them. For what emerged from behind them was a new power that threw everything else overboard. Behind, stood Friederike. I stood confronting her, often racked by shudders that reached to the marrow of my bones, as though a hereafter were breaking through into my here. She floated up, she swam up to the glass pane. She came through it . . . ! She had blushed when I looked at her. I plunged into the glacial flow of her arms.

It was only for moments that the sensation lasted. But during them my heart drummed, healthy as it was.

But really, since when? I asked myself.

Since I had sat with her at Gerstner's?

And I had to answer: It has always been so.

Since Claire Neudegg stabbed me when I was a boy of fifteen. Yes, ever since then, I had to admit to myself. Here, in Friederike, was my only comfort, my only chance for healing.

She had blushed when I looked at her.

I had to lean forward in the chair, hiding my face from Schlaggenberg.

Then I busied myself with the whiskey and the siphon.

Outside all was sun and summer, a congealed cataract of light.

From the street below came a short whistle, the kind made by placing two fingers in the mouth.

Schlaggenberg, at the window sill, turned around, leaned out a little, and called down in English: "I'm coming in a few minutes. Go up this street, please." He gestured with his left hand uphill along Scheiben Gasse.

My room was on the second floor. From it you could easily call across the narrow front garden to someone standing in the street. I stood up and approached the window, and keeping out of sight, peered out. On the other side of Scheiben Gasse a small troop of young people started moving off. Leading the line was a plump boy of about ten; then came a lean, long-legged young fellow in a gray sweater; beside him a much smaller girl with raven-black tousled hair; then Renata von Gürtzner-Gontard with a second girl (Sylvia, as I was to learn in a moment). Beside them walked a boy of about fifteen, in scout uniform, with the broad-brimmed scout hat. This adolescent was extremely slender, but broad-shouldered. He carried a long sports javelin.

They all had their backs to us and marched up Scheiben Gasse toward Wallmoden Strasse.

Without waiting for me to question him—which I would certainly have done—Schlaggenberg slid from the window sill and said: "That's my gang now, my 'team' as we say in Vienna. I'm called 'the Chief.' One of the girls is called 'the Falcon.' *Noms de guerre.*"

"And how did you pick them up?"

"Through Stangeler, as a matter of fact. I went to look him up at the Institute for Historical Studies because I hadn't seen hide nor hair of the fellow for ages. There he was, sitting at a desk covered with folio volumes and papers, concocting something. Told me it's something very important for him, and that he's almost through with it. 'Also means cash in hand,' he told me. But was somehow so mysterious about it that I didn't press him for details. He was highly pleased with himself, seems to be in better circumstances. . . ."

It turned out, then, that in spite of his great respect for Kajetan von Schlaggenberg, René had not said a word about his discovery in Carinthia or his contract with Herzka. So the fellow had learned how to hold his tongue lately, even toward Schlaggenberg—whom, moreover, he scarcely saw. Then things had changed somewhat, here too. Ah yes. "For among friends the same spirit does not remain the same," as the Greek tragedian says.

"It's some kind of manuscript René is working over," Schlaggenberg continued. "He mentioned that a university professor in America has taken an interest in it. Just by chance I was given proof right then and there that this wasn't just bragging. For while I was talking to him a medical doctor from Chappaqua, U.S.A.—it's in the state of New York, I think—came to see him. I gathered that the doctor's brother-in-law, a professor of history over there, asked him to look up Stangeler at the Institute—in fact, I had the impression that the visitor was kind of checking up on René. He kept asking whether the stuff was ready yet. Stangeler said he would be mailing it to America in three or four days."

"René's a good fellow," I said. "But what has all that to do with the young people across the street?"

"Patience, my good friend, patience. Yes, René is a good fellow. Also good and sewed up now—in other words, properly engaged. May make an ass of himself yet. Grete will be after him to make a career. Women poison everything, even the purest aspirations. But to me the most repulsive thing on earth is a woman who 'makes' her husband. As for the man who lets himself be 'made,' he belongs on the manure heap. . . . Well then, this American doctor—Viennese by birth, incidentally, the son of a Hofrat von Gürtzner-Gontard—went down with us to the philosophy faculty's buffet and we had a cup of coffee together. Hard to say how one thing led to another so rapidly, but the upshot was that Gürtzner-Gontard and I fell into a lively conversation; we got on swimmingly, and he also seemed much taken with René. I have an excellent impression of Doktor von Gürtzner-Gontard. Baudelaire says somewhere in one of his late jottings, written when he was already in Brussels, that a man who is worth anything will keep the soil of his native country on the soles of his shoes even in foreign lands. He would have been pleased with Doktor Gürtzner on that score. The way the man wore his hat, for example, was a dead giveaway of his Viennese origins. And sure enough, the gripes came: this thing or that used to be a lot better here. 'Why the devil did they change it?'— he was referring to the milk bar in the Votiv Park. And: 'Look at those horrible ads—it will be as bad as America before long.' There are people who after two years in England are already swallowing their r's in German too, you know, and fumbling for German words at the slightest provocation—you know the sort. Doktor Gürtzner is just the opposite. But of course, what counts is where a person comes from, what box he comes out of. He invited René and me to dinner, and we went to the Hotel Krantz at the Neuer Markt with him; he's staying there with his wife and several relatives. Really curious dinner we all had together. His wife has a Viennese mother who lives in London. The wife's name is Price, originally Miss Libesny. Swallows her r's and fumbles for words when she speaks German. Then there was her older sister, Professor Bullogg's wife—both women pretty, the elder the mother of a roundish, comical ten-year-old boy. Also Mme Garrique, the professor's sister. Fairly certain to be from Budapest and Jewish, extremely sweet, fat, intelligent, and jolly. My type—you know what I mean. *Passons,* as Counselor Levielle says in such cases. All that is over. I confess I didn't straighten out all the interrelationships among these people until afterwards. M. Garrique was there too. Frenchman with an Henri-quatre beard, a wine-dealer from Bordeaux who moved first to Canada and then to the United States. I found it hard not to begrudge him his nifty wife. Picturing her with that beard—oh well. A few weeks ago that would have hit me very hard. Not at the heart, but still—cut me to the quick. The beard would have stabbed right into me. The Garriques have two almost grown children: Gaston, a gangling longshanks of sixteen, and his sister Lilian, a petite type with thick black hair. When we arrived at the hotel, Renata von Gürtzner was also there. She's about sixteen, I'd guess; a tall strong girl with something daring about her: velvety eyes, handsome, intelligent nose. She had her friend Sylvia along. So it was quite a party that sat down to dinner. The Garrique children speak no German. Mme Garrique speaks fluently, with a Hungarian accent and no fumbling for words; she's too intelligent for that sort of thing. Professor Bullogg's fat little boy speaks a perfect German—learned it from his mother. But on account of the Garriques I talk English to my 'gang.' Renata and Sylvia are pretty good at it, and so is the scout out there. You must have noticed him—the one with the javelin. The dinner was a boisterous affair; the young people were shouting all the time. We adults hardly had a chance to say a word. Still, it came out that the Garriques and Mrs. Bullogg wished there were someone around who would be able to help the children find their way around Vienna, who would introduce them to 'things cultural' (*sic!*), someone who was knowledgeable in such matters. René did not bat an eye. But oddly enough, I had already so endeared myself to the young folks that Lilian gave me an encouraging kick in the shin under the table. I caught on right away, and volunteered to take the youngsters on a few hikes and rides. Afterwards Lilian said to me: 'We'll take Little Bully along— he's very useful sometimes.' She meant the ten-year-old. . . . Doktor Gürtzner thought Renata and Sylvia ought to join the party. That's how it started. The girls brought the boy scout along. For the sake of appearances we've actually visited the Hofburg, Schönbrunn, and the Museum of Art. But otherwise we just knock around, go out to the Vienna Woods, for example. We've had some roaring good times, and done a bit of mischief."

"I can imagine," I said. I didn't like the sound of the whole business. "Well, well. First you want to be a kind of pasha with a harem full of fat females, and now you seem to have decided on the career of Indian chief."

"I have to run along now," he said, laughing. They're waiting on top of the hill for me. Is it all right with you if I call for you tomorrow night at half-past eight on the dot? I may as well come right off in a cab, to save our fancy duds."

I was agreeable. Kajetan could be counted on to be punctual, after all.

He left. I went to the window. From the street he waved to me once more, then padded like a panther up the hill. My eyes probed his back. Evidently Kajetan had not recognized Renata at all. This was, for me, the most amazing aspect of his recital. She had crossed our track on skis, she had stood near him on the brow of the hill when he had waited up there for us; she had passed by us and right between us, parting our whole company.

And then she had appeared once more by the rickety, battered gray benches when Stangeler was in the midst of his peroration! . . . Yet Kajetan had not recognized her when he met her among the Americans at the Hotel Krantz. How odd that was. I could feel his blindness as if it had once been my own. And he had himself described this very state, in regard to Mary K. Though this was not the same kind of experience, for here he did not know that he was blind. I thought of his talk about Quapp and about what he had "been spared." This again was different: Kajetan was seeing nothing at all, just as we cannot see the brightest star that rises when the mist hangs heavy on the horizon.

Now I felt the burden of summer weighing down upon me as I looked out the window and uphill along Scheiben Gasse into the incessant hail of light; I could almost hear its rattling impact. As we grow older the summers seem shorter; winters form the measure of time, with only intervals between. These summer intervals are often terrifying; they seem to surround the heart with a padded silence. The selfsame summer which in youth seemed endless now assails us with a mute pressure, so that we feel we must stop and grab at something, grasp something. But what is there to hold on to? Where can the hand find support?

I was not thinking of Friederike during these minutes—that was it. Though surely she stood somewhere behind, stored up, a ponderous force. But at the moment I did not see her. I myself was blind. Gnawing within me was a certain concern over this little gang Kajetan had taken up with. I knew his mania for the scandalous: "Everything must be carried to extremes." But then, I thought, he always stopped short of actual misdeeds. No, it was just a mild mania. He liked to play with grotesque whims. In the case of Grete Siebenschein he had certainly intended to stage some sort of scandal, and in conjunction with the captain and my nephew Körger, no less. Right now, and in retrospect, I was more ready to expect something dreadful of Körger than of Kajetan. But nothing had come of it; or rather, it had all turned out contrary to expectations. The Alliance. And the Fat Females.

Away with them! Stop it! Standing here at the window, I felt first one and then another part of this garden suburb within myself: the deep gorge down in Wertheimstein Park, say, with the little brook that gathered in a pool and the birds splashing in it. . . . Oh well, what harm could Kajetan do with his little gang? Nothing much more than harmless follies. I caught one last glimpse of Kajetan; then he vanished up there, turning into a narrow street which was lined on both sides by rich gardens.

The reception at Friederike's took place the following day, June 23. It was a Thursday. The weather had suddenly changed. In the morning it rained violently, and while at noon it had been 86 degrees in the sun, the thermometer now dropped precipitately to 55. The sky did not begin to clear until half-past four, when the rain stopped.

To my mind, Friederike had luck with the weather; for since it was unmistakably dreary and cold, her own gathering was saved from a certain ambiguity which might otherwise have been present. (I did not learn until afterwards the real meaning of this fête.) For it could never possibly have been called a garden party—quite aside from the fact that even before 1914 garden parties in Vienna were given mostly at the tail-end of summer, when everybody had returned to the city from the spas and mountains. It could never have been called a garden party because the note in the corner of the invitation had indicated evening dress. Technically, too, a large garden party would not have been practical in the park behind Friederike's palace, for it was surrounded by apartment houses, so that outdoor music and dancing would have been out of the question after ten o'clock.

As it was, everything worked out well. The weather alone would have driven the company from the damp lawn into the illuminated house, while at the same time it was not so hot that wearing full dress became a burden.

Exchanging remarks to this effect, Kajetan and I were whisked by cab through the still wet streets of the garden suburb and out toward Wieden. It was somewhat after nine o'clock and already dark when we pulled up in front of the Palais Ruthmayr, whose windows were all brightly lit.

Almost simultaneously others arrived, cab after cab; the doorman stood outside, opening car doors, helping the ladies, signaling.

While some of the new arrivals lingered in the vestibule, Kajetan and I went forward into a small empty salon, which was mainly white; I still recall the oval violet cushions on the dainty chairs that stood about in it. Before us was a second French door with many small panes. Beyond, all was excessively bright, not to say glaring; you could almost feel a pressure through the glass door from the intensity of light and movement. Now its two wings opened, drawn apart by two maids—neither of whom was Ludmilla—and we took our first step into the lower end of the hall, where there was no one but us and the two servants. I glanced up at the red stairway, arched like a lyre, and into the density of movement in the upper part of the hall, between the columns. Kajetan and I ascended. In the middle of the landing, at the head of the stairs, stood Friederike in a cataract of white silk.

The moment crystallized and became a scene. It was a matter of chance that there was no one ahead of us on the red steps; chance also that at that moment a musical ensemble, which I could not see, began that rousing march which in the *Tales of Hoffmann* accompanies the entrance of the guests into Professor Spalanzani's house. There was no turning back: I had to mount these steps with Kajetan, with Kajetan of all people, and the steps led us up to her. There we were. I introduced my friend to Friederike. He lingered over her hand a second, perhaps a second and a half, beyond the fine margin of etiquette. It was then that I looked at Friederike's feet, at her innocent girlish feet. Then it was my turn. When I straightened up again, I saw that Kajetan was on the point of greeting Levielle, who stood behind and to the left of Friederike, turned slightly to one side, exchanging a few words with someone. Schlaggenberg contented himself with a slight bow in Levielle's direction.

The financial counselor greeted me ceremoniously, however; but immediately afterwards turned away with a shade too much emphasis. I was content and promptly dived into the turmoil, already parted from Schlaggenberg. Someone took my arm and said to me: "Imagine, Georgy, I've already found my librarian, a man who's really first-class." It was Alfons Croix. For the moment I did not realize what he was talking about, and said only: "Congratulations." Then, as he began telling me about his librarian, I recalled his mentioning the matter the evening I had spent with him. I found myself looking at Director Altschul, who for a moment stood there with his face altogether unprepared for an encounter; then we greeted each other. He had been standing leaning against one of the columns which supported the ceiling; here, in the upper part of the hall, the ceiling was lower, and consequently the columns were not very high and not so thick. For that unguarded moment the bank director's face had fallen so completely that I half expected to see it on the floor; in the place of a proper social countenance were formless bundles of images and emotions: indecision, grief, care—"Perhaps something is wrong with the bank after all," I thought.

Then we were shaking hands. Almost immediately his wife Rosi came over, inquisitive, childlike, laughing. She instantly barraged me with questions, why I no longer came to their bridge games, and so on. It was fortunate that she talked so much and so rapidly that I did not have to answer, for I should have been hard put to it to reply. But with horror I glimpsed in momentary flashes the stone within her breast, the hard core of this good-natured, innocent stupidity. And then the Trapps were greeting me, together with their daughter Angelika. The Edam cheese, barbarically hung with jewelry (perhaps these brooches, diadems, pearl necklaces, and bracelets were necessary to hold it together, to keep it from falling apart), immediately introduced me to Angelika's now official fiancé, Director Dulnik, the future son-in-law, big as a stove, his boiled shirt like a snow-covered roof.

So it went. I had to grind up people by the bagful; they were poured into me as if I were a mill. I shall not speak of Levielle's sons, of Baron Frigori, of Mucki Langingen. At some point Schlaggenberg introduced me to Dr. Franz von Gürtzner-Gontard and his wife. I thought with warmth of my old department head; so now he had his boy back again, and I was informed that the other, Anatol, would soon be coming on a visit also. It was a benefaction to hear something of this sort for once; at the same time it was a benefaction, there and then, amid the grinding to flour or sausage-making of people and relationships, to encounter a genuine fact, a real result.

But while my disappointment grew as it became apparent that amid all this I would not again catch sight of Friederike, the essential content of rapidly passing time remained something different for me; and today that essential content forms the board on which I place all the miniature figures of that evening. It was this: I had already left the upper part of the hall with its thinner columns and had gone through two other salons which were almost empty. . . . Then it came: I was stirred to uncomprehending surprise because during all the meeting and mingling with people I had been looking up, as if under a compulsion, to the ceiling between the columns, as if I were searching for something at the very point where columns met ceiling, in the upper emptiness of the room, at which we seldom glance. Now, while acting under this irresistible compulsion, I left the small salon through a door open at the back of it and entered a room that was new to me. It was really a corridor, a kind of oblong den; it might have been called the library corridor, for on both sides it was lined by tall black bookcases of an old-fashioned type, in which, however, the backs of only a few big dark volumes showed. There were niches and small arches; the bookcase on the right displayed a whole gallery of them, masterpieces of the joiner's art, excesses of the "old German" style. The light was gentle and muted; it came from the ceiling. The open French door at the other end led to further public rooms. I heard a babel of voices. But no one came in. I had stood still and was looking up at the ceiling, at the spot where it met the wall. This room, it seemed to me, did not belong at all to Friederike's house; it was as though it had only just opened up for me alone, an unknown chamber which I had discovered. I sought something on the ceiling, while I thought of empty rooms of my childhood, the rooms not generally in use, which were not seen often—rooms such as those in which laundry was hung or ironed. At bottom those were rooms I had only dreamed of as a boy, through which I had hastened only in dreams, and never without fear.

This room, too, was dreamed.

I never saw it again, never entered it again, never found it again.

Toward the end of July in that year of 1927, Friederike had a minor structural change made in the house. She had never liked the dark windowless library corridor. But it took some new stir in her life—the first in the carefully cultivated stasis since the death of her husband—to open her eyes to the possibility of simply changing what had long displeased her.

Before, she would never have been able to carry through on such an impulse, she said to me at the time.

Exactly twenty-eight years have passed since I stood in the "library corridor." Today is June 23, 1955—also a Thursday, for after twenty-eight years the days of the week again fall upon the same date.

In the "library corridor": enter, from right, coming from the small salon, Kajetan. Strikes an attitude:

"Ha, wretch, art caught—at last I find you here,
Who secretly delighted in a star,
While giving me, with Selma, a bum steer!
Kept both to yourself, your dearest friend betraying!
Summa summarum: we'll go no more a-Maying."

No doubt he considered these to be iambics. And then: "Off with you to the buffet, Herr von Geyrenhoff; they've already opened the dining rooms; I've supped on lobster and Chablis. The whiskey we had together before leaving was good, but man cannot live on whiskey alone."

Now I realized why there was such stillness and emptiness in these smaller rooms; everyone was pouring into the larger ones to devote himself to substantial pleasures. And of course Schlaggenberg would not miss out. Without more ado, I replied:

> "Licentious brute, by your plump cream puffs blinded,
> Your gloating eye shall never be contented,
> Your grasping hand shall never seize its prey.
> The sign of that's been given you today,
> So while you're here don't act like one demented."

Kajetan, departing, and waving both hands in a motion of fending something off:

> "Deceit and cheating, from a chronicler
> Who's often borrowed my own pen from me!
> Selma's a phantom, a mere fantasy!
> But many a second reality has burst:
> I should have steered clear of them from the first!"
> (*Exit*)

No one had disturbed our nonsense. I was left alone. Almost, I felt, it had not really been Kajetan who had just left the dusky room, but a vanishing apparition, the kind which could suddenly bob up in front of me in one of those empty laundry rooms in my parents' house, where as a boy I had at the bottom of my heart always expected them—no less frightened, but nevertheless expected them. Here too was a new room that had opened up for just this once, as if a wall had slid away.

Levielle came in. He too appeared from the right, from the empty salon. He looked around indignantly; only then, as if by afterthought, did he regard me: with raised eyebrows taking note of a phenomenon which had the impudence to intrude upon his presence.

"Aha," Levielle said, "delighted to find you here, Herr—Herr von Geyrenhoff. I had been wanting to ask you something—namely, this: do you think it quite so eminently proper and correct to bring into Frau Ruthmayr's house a man who is known to have had a relationship with his own sister?"

"In the first place, Herr Levielle," I replied with perfect calm, "he never had a 'relationship,' as you call it, with her, and in the second place Charlotte is not his sister, as you yourself know better than anyone else, but the daughter of Georg Ruthmayr and Baroness von Neudegg, later Countess Charagiel. And in the third place I did not bring him into the house; Frau Ruthmayr herself expressed the desire to see him here. She admired him as a writer and asked me whether I happened to know him. To be brief, I had no choice but to request Herr von Schlaggenberg to drop his card here. He did so, and was invited. *Voilà tout.*"

"Naturally, and appears on the scene along with you," Levielle commented. "There is something else that I would rather like to ask you, quite by the by, and that is why you want to be constantly interfering in affairs which would take their regular and orderly course without your meddling. It must be a tic of yours. I've heard recently, too, that you are writing something." At these last words he smiled too frankly; the smile was a few millimeters too wide, was already an attack.

I had only a single shot left in the barrel, and that was really of too heavy a caliber for this occasion, and at such short range, so to speak. Nevertheless, I fired it.

"I interfere, as you call it, Herr Levielle, only out of concern that in the end you might after all be able to reach agreement with Cornel Lasch on the methods for obtaining the capital."

It was a direct hit. I saw that at once. Only the surface, the very outermost skin, held his face together.

He said: "You are indulging in fantasies. Oh well, you have become a writer after all. Good evening."

Exit.

Once again I remained alone. I thought of nothing. I enjoyed this room which did not really exist, in which everything fitted together. When, from the side toward the dining room, a cataract of white silk burst in, I knew at last why I was standing there.

Friederike was alone.

"Oh!" she exclaimed, and halted in front of the bookcase. "So here's where I find you, Herr von Geyrenhoff. Haven't you been to the buffet? There are such good things. . . ."

She fell silent; I might almost say her courage failed her. Perhaps she really recognized, during these moments, what state I was in; at least she said so later. Oddly enough, only now did I realize that her toilette was a bit behind the times. Or no, rather she was deliberately eschewing the prevailing fashion. The lower part of this full evening dress fell in a wealth of folds, somehow crinolinelike, and very wide; it had swayed as she entered. The great décolletage, the uncovered shining shoulders, forced my gaze down; it was as though it smashed to the floor at Friederike's feet, in front of the silver pumps she wore.

We greeted each other anew as though we had not yet met at all that evening, and since she—swimming closer to me, to the very wall of her crystal cage—extended both hands to me, I seized them, and at the same time tried (because the sight was simply too much for me) to direct my eyes so that they would not strike her shoulders. But I could not manage it.

"I was looking for you, Herr von Geyrenhoff," she said. "Because I have a great request to make of you."

"At your service, my dear friend."

"I want to discuss with you a matter that is very, very important to me and to ask your advice. Would you have the great kindness to come to tea here on Saturday—day after tomorrow, that is—at five o'clock? Of course we will not be disturbed at all then."

"Certainly," I said, bowing. A really painful, repulsive fear crept through me as I did so. She couldn't be going to ask me whether she . . .

"Incidentally, this unseasonal party tonight has a particular significance, which you may not be aware of." (Now fear froze me completely.) "Counselor Levielle is leaving Vienna; he is moving to Paris for good. Tomorrow is the day set for his departure. His household on Johann Strauss Gasse is being broken up. So that this is virtually his farewell today. . . ."

I swayed inwardly like a ship returning again to even keel. A truly frightful phantom which I had conjured up with lightning rapidity had as fleetly taken its leave.

I was still holding her two hands. "Until Saturday," I said, "and I am entirely and absolutely at your service. And now may I ask you to permit me to thank you and take my leave quietly?"

"What? You want to go already?"

"Yes," I replied. "Without attracting attention."

"Well, as you wish, dear Herr von Geyrenhoff, as you wish. . . ." She smiled. I kissed her right hand, and then, since I was holding the other, kissed that one also.

Striding along the dark street, which was damp and cool, I found after a while that I was violently hungry—I had, after all, disdained the "good things." And so I went into a large, almost empty café and ordered an eggnog. At the moment it was quite clear to me that I could not possibly have partaken of anything else.

It was too much; it broke off; the taut chain snapped. This evening suddenly became stripped of all meaning; it dissolved into atoms which circled around one spot like slivers of wood in the tiny whirlpool of a brook. Here I sat in my evening clothes, inspiring respect in the discreet waiter. Probably he knew where I had just come from. A waiter knows everything. The brook cadenzaed down the deep gorge in Wertheimstein Park. I had been walking there only recently. A few unimportant but obstinate fragments of the talk at the party whirled through my head. That had been right at the beginning, in the upper part of the hall. The transoceanic flyers, Chamberlin and Levine. They had arrived this past Sunday, in a pouring rain but greeted by an immense crowd nevertheless, at the Aspern Airfield, and this afternoon, likewise in the rain, had unexpectedly set off for Prague. The terrible storm in Payerbach at the end of last week.

The park there totally washed out, terrible landslides. Director Altschul had told us about it. He and his wife had been eyewitnesses of the catastrophe. Army engineers had been sent in. Now a vision of the almost empty hall as I took my leave. This time it had been Ludmilla who helped me into my coat. I was almost falling asleep. I ordered a taxi. . . .

On Saturday morning it was raining again. The day remained cool. At five o'clock I was with her, deeply moved when I saw that she was really glad I had come. On Friday I had resolutely crushed a whole gnat-swarm of illusions that had sprung up as the result of those minutes spent with Friederike in the library corridor. But now the marshes of my hopes, or rather of my dreams, were dried out.

"It is very good of you to have come, Herr von Geyrenhoff," Friederike said.

She was wearing the same high-necked, steel-blue dress I had seen on May 30, the day I walked on the escarpment for the last time. The glass walls had been closed and once again made the small salon into a separate room, and the genius loci addressed me gently, with a barely perceptible, delicate odor of camphor— on Thursday, passing through here, I had not noticed anything of the sort. So I was greeted by the fragrance of a new segment of life, which is always a hereafter in the here; it was as though a tiny, very faint, but penetrating little voice were speaking to me.

Almost immediately, however, it was drowned out by Friederike's voice. She spoke of what was uppermost in her mind. It was, as I now learned, a financial matter. With Levielle's departure from Austria she had lost her adviser, mentor, or, if he might be called that, the administrator of her fortune. "You see, I virtually inherited him from Georg" (she meant her dead husband), she said. "I really don't understand these things at all, haven't the faintest idea of them."

"Where is your capital, if I may ask?"

"Land," she replied, meaning by that the Land Credit Bank.

Today I was really hearing her voice at length, and undisturbed, in complete privacy, for the first time. This very soft, low, rather dark-toned voice emerged with a compelling force from her physical being; it represented Friederike; it reflected a perfect acoustic image of the optical impression made by her personality. It was a lonely voice, too. It seemed unaccustomed to talking at length in any connected way, seemed not really in control of itself. Fundamentally, she remained mute. She only floated close to the crystal wall of her cage, noble and beneficent in her essence, and moved her mouth; it was almost as if you saw it more than heard it.

And now she flatly asked me to help her in these affairs, to advise her.

But I shrank back. Was I to take Levielle's place at her side—perhaps as an elevated lackey with expectations? . . . The result was that I was plunged into an extraordinarily different predicament. I also learned that Levielle had had certain powers of attorney from her. As she spoke I gathered that these powers had been considerable. For example, when she was absent from Vienna he was empowered to carry out urgent transactions on the stock exchange without securing her permission. Though of course she had never been able to exercise judgment in such matters, and probably had always agreed to whatever he proposed. Had she received back these powers of attorney? I asked.

"Yes, of course," she said. "Here they are."

She handed me the documents. I was amazed. Levielle had exercised direct disposition of certain funds.

While I looked through the papers, I was again struck by the faint fragrance of camphor. This whispering voice decided me. The hurdle would have to be taken. I could not reject her request. It was impossible. And so I said to her that I was entirely at her disposal. All the while, I was feeling the most intense tenderness for Friederike. And I inwardly pledged myself to examine her affairs with circumspection and great care, to do the best I could in these matters. I remarked that I would not wish such extensive powers of attorney as Levielle had received and exercised, that these seemed to be unnecessary. Finally I asked permission to speak with Director Edouard Altschul about the whole matter.

"But he isn't with 'Land' at all," she said.

"No," I agreed, "but he was a director of the Land Credit Bank for many years."

"By all means speak with him if you think so, Herr von Geyrenhoff," she said. "After all, he's a friend of my house."

Then we fell silent.

She extended her arm, gave me her hand, and said: "I thank you." As I kissed her hand, I felt immoderately happy because now I would have the opportunity to see her more often, to be in constant touch with her. The bridge had been built.

Around the middle of the following week, while I sat going over certain financial records of Friederike's, I received a letter from Schlaggenberg—whom I had not heard from since the reception at the Palais Ruthmayr. I opened the plump envelope with some surprise, for it was postmarked Vienna. It was after all not very far from Kajetan's house to mine, and the telephone did exist.

My dear and most respected Herr von Geyrenhoff, false chronicler, repulsive mystifier, and crypto-Selmist:

Why did you vanish away in such hideous stealth on Thursday? I supped a second time on roast beef with mayonnaise and burgundy, because as you know I don't care for champagne, preferring whiskey and soda—the little man's champagne, you might call it. The buffet was magnificent. Incidentally, crypto-Selmism and chronicleering seem to be somehow connected down in their depths. Desist, my friend! Or better yet: just collect notes! [I was incidentally doing just that again, and was diligently at it; how otherwise could I put together this present text today, after twenty-eight years!] This scribble-scrabble ought to be done away with.

But to the point, *ad rem,* to the points, *ad res.* (Incidentally, and it serves you right—on Thursday, around twelve o'clock, I had a long talk with your star—would have given anything to sit on the floor at her feet, sweet feet, silver pumps, but it wouldn't do, so I stood with her for fifteen minutes, indescribable, because I'm after all somewhat bigger than the star, than this central sun, divinely fearful whitely shining gleam, kept looking desperately only at my own reflection all the time. She's read three books of mine. I'm an impossible person.)

Ad rem: prodigia et eventa simul inciderunt, as the captain would say; the omens arrived simultaneously with the events they foreshadowed. Yesterday they started giving me the sack at Alliance. I was asked to withdraw from my contract, and was offered something in the way of severance payment. I was satisfied. Five editors were fired at the same time, as I then learned. In other words, extensive changes. Cobler will no longer be editor-in-chief. Gyurkicz has remained as artist, but a certain Weilguny, his competitor, was likewise bounced.

No sooner had I left the soil of Alliance, which I did not have underfoot so very long, in all conscience, than Quapp came running to me, all agrin, with a letter from a lawyer, Doktor Philemon Krautwurst (*sic!*). Agrin because she suspected some good, since she had been to this selfsame Krautwurst in connection with the Neudegg bequest. We went there together.

Have a shot of whiskey, section chief and crypto-Selmist, and hold on to your chair.

Doktor Krautwurst had received the matter you know of into his care on June 2, charged by Financial Counselor Levielle to take care of the "rediscovered (!) military testament of Captain of the Reserve Georg Ruthmayr, killed by enemy action in 1914"; Krautwurst was appointed both curator of the legacy and executor of the will, since Herr Levielle in view of his impending permanent removal to France (did you know about that, by any chance?) would not be in a position to perform these duties. That is approximately what he wrote to the lawyer. Doktor Krautwurst showed the letter to me and Quapp. And do you know what I have seen, have held in my hand? The original of that "military testament" of 1914. Sure enough, one of the two signatory witnesses is an Anton Lach, corporal, bugler of the squadron. And there is express mention of the banking house in London in which Quapp's bequest is deposited, and the express statement: "in distinction to what my wife, as principal legatee, is to receive as soon as these securities are released, these being deposited . . ." and he mentions another bank in London. So you see how accurately your excellent sergeant informed you! When Krautwurst took over the affair, he wanted to see the original will, and Levielle gave it to him. The two must have discussed the affair in detail; that was evident from several remarks that Krautwurst made.

But now, as I have already said, have yourself a whiskey.

By the time Doktor Krautwurst sent for Quapp, he had already done a considerable amount of work in her behalf. Above all, he had verified the fact that the securities mentioned in Ruthmayr's supplementary testament are actually there in England. Along with the original of the will, Levielle gave the lawyer various deposit slips and lists. Now, after the London bank had answered affirmatively, Doktor Krautwurst immediately started the necessary procedures going in the Austrian Comptroller's Office, simultaneously requested a court decree, and only then sent for Quapp. So that it is already possible to obtain an approximate estimate of Quapp's inheritance—all the more so since at the time of the sequestration in England the whole sum was changed into English war bonds—just as in your case—and the current value is therefore easily determined. Naturally, Quapp too will suffer the usual losses that go with these transfers. But all in all, and with all deductions—at a pessimistic guess, Quapp will have at her disposal a fortune of at least 10,000,000 schillings by next year—disentangling the whole business will probably take at least six months, it seems.

Enough. By now you have probably fallen out of your chair, in spite of holding on tight, and I only hope that nothing has happened to your whiskey glass. But after all, you were the very person—you remember, don't you?—who *ex abrupto* guessed something like that amount. How in the world did you know?

Well, Quapp is taken care of for the present by the Neudegg legacy; besides, of late she has been displaying a tendency toward thrift—you could almost call it stinginess. Which, however, hasn't stopped the dear good girl from immediately placing 50,000 at my disposal. And I've had to promise her that when the torrent of wealth begins to flow, I will let some of it be diverted toward me. Nevertheless she goes on being thrifty. She walks half a mile—and you know Quapp has never particularly liked walking—to buy ham cheaper. She avoids restaurants altogether, and of late has been keeping out of pastry shops, for which she used to have a weakness. She's smoking cheaper cigarettes and claims they're far more satisfying because harsher. . . .

All this is a sign of something. To some extent it is a normal human reaction. Those who acquire substance live more cautiously; no one bounces around carrying a full vessel, but rather bears it carefully. But the accent is what counts, the emphasis, the overemphasis in this case. The signs suggest that the moon is about to turn on its own axis and show its alien other side. You understand me, no doubt. Quapp's preliminary life and preliminary biography have come to an end. All gifted women have one such; and never can a man be so profoundly, so annihilatingly, and so drastically unfaithful to the dreams of his boyhood as a woman to those of her early youth. Indeed, many a man transposes his preliminary biography into reality to the last iota, thereby proving that it was not his preliminary biography at all, but the actual one, though in the bud—so that in a sense it stood complete from the start. But Quapp has shown a gift for inheriting. Like her mother. That is a personal quality. It belongs to the same category as good or bad luck in gambling, as popularity or unpopularity. Those are the auspices under which a person's life stands. She has manifested her gift for inheriting. Now her life is really beginning.

Very well. I was bounced from Alliance. *Laus Deo.* I promptly turned around and wrote a letter to Stuttgart announcing my impending arrival—wrote to that eminent publishing house which is interested in having me finish a long manuscript—they've already read large parts of it. You may recall Quapp's mentioning the matter the afternoon I was at your place and met that fine fellow Alois Gach, to whom we owe so much. The negotiations in Stuttgart will not be difficult, since for the time at least I am independent and don't have to burden myself with advances; so I shan't ask for any. No more fragmentation for me! No more Alliance articles! No Selmism! It gives me devilish pleasure, though, that my novel, to which they gave such big billing in one of the Alliance sheets, will go on running there serially; they can't very well cut it off in the middle. I was supposed to receive the second half of the fee only after the last installment had been published. But by "special dispensation" they allowed me to draw it right away, together with their rather considerable (by my standards) compensation for ending the contract. Incidentally, everything was done in the most amiable manner; they were awfully sorry, even mentioned the thoroughgoing changes in the directorships of the entire firm, and so on—the usual things that are said on such occasions.

I am on the point of leaving.

I give you my regards, most honored and respected Herr von Geyrenhoff. My thanks go with your image, which quite often rises before me, with cryptic features and a Selmic smile.

So long!

Kajetan S.

P.S.
Glacial flow. An explosion. How do I feel?
In such cases one can only look at one's
reflection. She spoke of the books of a

person who nevertheless stood before her
as an impossible creature. The stars darken.
A fearful suspicion rises within me,
suspicion of a certain cryptic gentleman.

Naturally I went to the telephone at once. But Kajetan had already left, so his distinguished landlady informed me. For how long? She could not say; she only fancied that it would be some time, since "Herr von Schlaggenberg has settled the rent for three months in advance."

Settled—oh well. An unpleasant word, an offensively respectable word.

I did not feel easy about this precipitate departure of his, no matter what cogent reasons he might give for it. The whole thing looked like an emotional act.

I promptly telephoned Quapp, whose number in Hietzing I already had. Why, I mused meanwhile, had he not come to see me again? Why had he instead sat down and gone to the trouble of writing a long letter? That meant he was avoiding me, didn't it? Avoiding my protests against something, perhaps? But against what? The letter contained nothing, so far as I could see, that I would have objected to.

And so I sat once again over my lists of deposits, withdrawals, correspondence, books.

I knew the governor—this impressive title had been granted him—of the Land Credit Bank personally, and in fact should have met him at Friederike's reception, for he had been invited. But the day before he had sent his excuses; pressing affairs would not allow him to come.

This man was one of the few personalities who belong so solidly in the foreground of those years that the period can scarcely be imagined without them. I do not mean to assert that they were necessarily key figures of the era. The key figures never stand in the limelight. Rather, such persons as the governor were locks to the gate of the purely external future: locks into which destiny eagerly thrusts its crudely material keys.

I had a lay understanding of the role played by the Land Credit Bank in the economic life of those years. But this was not what figured in my thoughts at all. What figured there, rather, was the governor himself.

It must be remembered that I was seeking security, security for Friederike. Nothing else. Given this limited aim, I wondered about the personality of the governor. Here was a man who was all forcefulness and high position but certainly did not stand for security. In this case high position interested me not at all; I did not like the idea of a brilliant or dazzling personage at the head of an institution to which Friederike's weal and woe were entrusted. The governor's virtues, his stupendous career within a few short years—all such things lay outside of the narrow slit through which I viewed the problem. I was blind to all that.

I talked the matter over with a large number of competent and trustworthy people whom I knew. For days on end I ran about from one to another. But not one person said anything that quieted my uneasiness, nor on the other hand anything that would have induced me to make radical decisions or changes.

It was odd—the few times I had met the governor socially, he put me in mind of a man who was entirely different from him: that arch-journalist Cobler, until recently editor-in-chief of the Alliance firm, to whom I had once been introduced by Kajetan.

As I have said, I no sooner read Kajetan's letter than I telephoned Quapp. She appeared to be informed of his departure, laughed and trumpeted as usual on the telephone. I told her that I had heard the glorious news and offered my congratulations. With her dear, good, warm, exuberant manner she cried: "We owe everything to you, Herr von Geyrenhoff. Make believe my arms are around you!"

Now I made my request. Would she take me up to see Doktor Krautwurst sometime, just as an old friend, so to speak?—I would very much like to see the original of the will. "I've seen it myself," she said, and her voice darkened. "You know, when I read the name—to know that this is your father's handwriting . . . Imagine, Herr von Geyrenhoff, in his last hour . . ." She broke off, and for several seconds we were both silent on the telephone.

The visit to the lawyer took place the following week. By this time I had acquired a comprehensive view of the enormous fortune I was taking charge of. It had actually not suffered any significant diminution since 1914, aside from the fairly high subscriptions to the Austrian war-loan. But compared to the total funds involved, that loss was trivial. In addition there was the landed property. There were no mortgages at all on the estate, and it was rented out for ten years. That matter remained to be investigated. The investments in securities could be called masterly: a widely distributed portfolio in which the fluctuations would pretty well balance out. My hat was off to Levielle. I had, of course, already called at the bank and presented my credentials; and as I have said, I had already consulted with various people who might give me advice and information. There remained only Edouard Altschul; I wanted to hear his opinion, but not before I had heard everybody else's.

Quapp and I met at the very spot and at the very same time of day as we had before our call upon Doktor Mährischl on May 30. We were going to see Doktor Krautwurst together. This time, too, Quapp arrived on the dot. Was it true that our Quapp was undergoing profound changes and would become not only thrifty but even punctual? Had her mother, who had shot the castellan's canary, been a paragon of punctuality? Odd that Prince Alfons's story should come to my mind just then.

Fifteen minutes later, in the ever-punctilious Doktor Philemon Krautwurst's office, the navel of the whole affair lay before me on the table. Forgive this wild image. But it was really so. Here was Georg Ruthmayr's testament. The lawyer and Quapp had gone over to another desk. I read the neat running hand of a corporal of the Imperial Austrian Army. Gach had been more than circumspect with his: "My impression was that the captain, to come right out with it, had a daughter out of wedlock somewhere. . . ." For here there were no obliquities: Quapp was plainly named as Ruthmayr's natural daughter. All the facts were down. Concerning Quapp's mother also. At the end there was a typical little "dictation error," as documentary specialists call it: "This my last will and come my mission dear Financial Counselor." Of course it should have read: "This my last will and commission, my dear Financial Counselor." There followed signature with rank and regiment: "Georg Ruthmayr, Capn., D 7." On the brink of death, Ruthmayr had still been able to write legibly.

I was not following the murmured talk between Quapp and the lawyer at the back of the room, nor did I even hear it any longer. What lay before me on the desk represented the transformation of circumstantial evidence into a physical fact. It was like being back at school, when after calculating by formulas—a process I had always mistrusted—the correct result leaped out at me in the end. And suddenly there took place a change of planes, a breaking of the tension. Yes, it was really a kind of death. This was the end. The beginning lay on the path between the rows of bare wintry vines where Schlaggenberg had run into me again, before the beginning of the new year. There a constellation had risen for me, composed of the stars of other persons' lives, stars on which life was different from that on mine, a hereafter in the here: the curious constellation of my chronicling, which had led to nothing but had taught me so much. Now it was falling to pieces. And in its shattering, it was already casting this one and that one away, casting them out of their relationship to one another and into a state of unrelatedness. With Quapp's vast inheritance (was it indeed the beginning of her true biography?), with Kajetan's sudden departure, with—with my secret love which busied itself in the vain effort to forget itself—with all that, an era was vanishing whose beauty would smite me only much later. Though I felt something of this then as I sat over the captain's will—felt it coming as the full moon rising unexpectedly, silently and swiftly over the ridge of a hill. And so it is today, so it has come.

We talked of this and that with the lawyer. Quapp's French birth certificate had arrived: Kajetan had written his mother for it. Doktor Krautwurst commented that the will's turning up so late was a very curious matter. He said no more, and I too held my peace. For this affair which had occupied my mind so long— this affair was dead. It had reached its end in the "library corridor" of the Palais Ruthmayr on June 23. Quapp, too, made no comment.

Undoubtedly the promise that Levielle had given to Kajetan's father, Eustach von Schlaggenberg, would not have been considered a sufficient reason under the criminal code for Levielle's thirteen-year suppression of Ruthmayr's military testament. But it may well be that he pretended to himself that he was bound to keep Quapp's birth a secret until the death of Countess Charagiel. The shallow stupidity of so-called "clever" people cannot be approximated by the deepest thinker.

Levielle had made up a story for Doktor Krautwurst's benefit, of course. The original of the Ruthmayr testament had lain, it appeared, in a batch of documents connected with entirely different matters—and thus mislaid, could not be located, though it had long been sought. Recently, it seemed, for reasons entirely unrelated to Ruthmayr affairs, the file in question had been opened and the vanished will, together with the deposit certificates and lists, had been discovered. Doktor Krautwurst had accepted this story without any commentary—perhaps too pointedly without commentary. But Quapp and I did the same. The affair was proceeding smoothly and rapidly toward final settlement: why throw up obstacles, strew sand into the gears of the necessary formalities?

Just by the way: before the law it made no difference that the British government did not begin to release sequestered "enemy"

funds until 1926. Ruthmayr's last will should have been presented to the probate court at once—not even the existence of a
state of war should have hindered that. According to Levielle's
account, to be sure, the will had apparently been lost almost
immediately after it came into his hands, since there had never
been an officially accredited copy.

"Those arrogant faces—they ought to be smashed in like a
windowpane!" Schlaggenberg had said in reference to the financial counselor and his brother, the general staff surgeon ("pseudo-
Levielle"). "You really ask yourself how people like that do it,
who they think they are and where they get such brazenness."

I asked myself another question: how did Levielle explain
things to himself, when he was alone?

Not until fourteen years later did I obtain the key to this question. Halfway to the present day, that is.

During the Second World War, as an Austrian reserve officer,
I had been forced to join up with the Germans. In the uniform
of the German Air Force, I rode from Mont de Marsan to Biar-
ritz, where I was to take over the airfield. That was in 1941. As
my car passed the thermal spa of St. Pierre de Dax, it ran into a
jammed column of vehicles on a narrow street. The drivers were
all in an extraordinary hurry, probably more out of their motorists'
obsessiveness and self-importance than from any real cause (there
were scarcely any such at the time). Stopped in the incessantly
tooting column, I found myself looking directly into the show
window of a bookshop, and precisely in the middle of the display
I saw a new book by Paul Valéry, a paper band around it bearing
the legend: "*Vient de paraître.*" It was, incidentally, the last book
published in his lifetime: *Tel Quel.* I sprang from the car and
into the shop, breathlessly asked for the book, and received it
from the extremely friendly proprietress (who was perhaps
pleased that the enemy appreciated the literature of her country). As I rushed out onto the street again, the part of the column
in front of my car had already begun moving freely, but all

the vehicles behind were held up by mine, so that the concert of horns had reached a hysterical pitch. It sounded altogether silly and childish. I jumped back into the car, and off we went.

Out in the open country again, I had the car stopped and examined my treasure. The book was unwrapped; I had quickly taken it as it was from the proprietress while she just as rapidly handed me my change. Opening the paper-backed volume, I at once came upon some passages which answered my question about Levielle:

Le comble de la vulgarité me semble être de se servir d'arguments qui ne valent que pour un public—c'est-à-dire pour un spectateur ou auditeur réglé necéssairement sur le plus sot—et qui ne résistent pas à un homme froid et seul. . . . Il ne faut jamais user à l'égard de l'adversaire —même idéal—d'arguments ni d'invectives que soi-même, seul avec soi, on ne supporterait pas d'émettre, qui ne se peuvent véritablement penser, qui n'ont de force que publique, qui font honte et misère dans la nuit et la solitude.

It seems to me the height of vulgarity to make use of arguments which are aimed only at a public —that is, at a spectator or listener whose level is necessarily that of the stupidest—and which will not pass muster before a cool and solitary person. . . . We must never use toward an opponent— even an assumed one—arguments or charges which we could not endure to bring forward if we were by ourselves, which cannot truly be thought, which are only effective publicly and which would heap shame and misery upon us in the night and in solitude.

Levielle would no doubt have raised a great hue and cry about Kajetan's "breaking his word," had Kajetan ever taken action against him before the death of Baroness Charagiel. Just as he had lashed out at me in the "library corridor" for having introduced Friederike to a man known to have a "relationship" with his own sister. . . .

Such brazenness is made possible by a life lived on its own inner surface, with constant falsification of the ego's accounts. Such are the Levielles, the pseudo-Levielles, and the Charagiels.

They make things easy for themselves. The least one can do, in return, is not to let them get under one's skin.

But the height of brazenness, to my mind, was the visit that Levielle had once paid, together with his brother, to the Schlaggenberg estate in southern Styria. That had been during the lifetime of old Eustach. And Levielle had never said a word, then or later, to either of Schlaggenberg's parents about an existent, even if seemingly lost, will of Ruthmayr's. Apparently, too, the brothers had put on the dog at the time, as Kajetan had indicated to me. Here brazenness reached the altitude of the Cimborasso, that peak veiled in cloud so dense that it mocked any attempt at exploration.

Alongside Quapp, I walked down the old-fashioned staircase, and we stepped out onto Wipplinger Strasse, which in olden times had been called Wildwercher Strasse, because the furriers (*Wildwercher*) had had their workshops and booths there. (For such bits of information we were indebted to Stangeler.) Did I have anything to do right now? Quapp asked me. No, I said. "Oh, then we could go and sit somewhere together for a while, couldn't we? All right? Wonderful! Until half-past five. Because then I have . . ." She broke off.

"What have you at half-past five, Quapp my girl?"

I looked into her face. Her eyes were wide open, she was looking full at me, with a grin stretched from one corner of her mouth to the other; and then she burst out: "I have a date."

"Bravo," I said. We stopped off at a small and still entirely old-fashioned café called "Zum alten Rathaus." Here we had to discuss our visit to the lawyer. There was much that had to be gone into, much that had to be digested. Everything was still topsy-turvy, not yet fitted into reality.

She wanted to thank me; that was the view she took of what had happened—that it had been my doing. Whom else did she owe it all to? she cried when I protested. Without Gach I would never have come into possession of the facts, I said; and yet

Gach had not effectuated anything, had merely been a key which fitted into the lock of the situation. Into the lock of the present situation, which always simultaneously contains the future and shuts it away, because the future can scarcely ever be interpreted. All of us together had formed that lock, including Kajetan, including Levielle, including Lasch, including—I almost said "that Charagiel woman." But then I fell silent. At that moment I felt a hope in regard to Friederike; like a spring-green wing it rose up and down within me just once. Why now?

Quapp told me that her mother—"I suppose I really ought to say 'Kajetan's mother' now, eh?"—who had been enormously pleased about the Neudegg legacy, seemed unable to believe seriously in the impending new one. That was evident, Quapp said, from some lines she had tucked into the envelope in which she had sent by registered mail the original of Quapp's birth certificate. Nevertheless, she had first sent Miss Rugley, the English housekeeper and companion, to the nearest district court to have two certified copies made. They had even managed to dig up, in the little district town, a photographer capable of taking a photo of the document. Since she had gone to all that trouble, Quapp said, the following sentence in the letter had seemed all the odder: ". . . Of course I scarcely imagine that anything whatsoever will come out of this whole fantastic story, but still precautions must be taken in case this letter should be lost along with the unique document enclosed."

I said: "Your mother acted quite rightly. It is evident from all this that at the bottom of her heart she is far from thinking the whole affair fantastic. But when for a very long time something has been inside us, and we have kept it in like the contents of a tightly corked bottle, it rather drops entirely out of life, and then it cannot so quickly be patched onto life again. Life means communication, contact, partition walls between contents. Partition is painful, of course. Pain is the psychic manifestation of partition. . . ."

I broke off; I had been indulging in a monologue. But Quapp followed. Her eyes, big, far apart (ah, where are you, with your mute fishy look behind the partition, behind the wall of crystal?) —her eyes stared in fascination at me, as if out of a wholly irreparable, incurable solitude.

We fell silent.

Then she said: "You know, I don't really belong anywhere any more."

"But that's a wonderful situation!" I blurted out—a sudden wild alarm within me. "The only situation in which a person can ever learn where he really belongs."

Was she still here, my good old Quapp? Was she so lost already that there was nothing for it but for her to assume her destined life, shoot off into its orbit, to be forever ruled by the elements of that orbit? For a tiny moment I thought I could almost feel its tug upon her.

Then it was all right. Her gaze darkened, a velvety wave warmed her wide-open eyes.

"May I tell you a secret, Herr von Geyrenhoff? Do you know whom I have a date with? Nobody else knows."

"Please tell me, Quappchen," I said.

"With your cousin Géza."

I laid my hands on hers, with a hearty pressure. So, for a few moments, we sat looking the picture of a real pair of lovers.

Yes, constellations break up and fly apart, and almost improbable constructions or mere floating wish-dreams fall to the ground fulfilled, becoming simple facts. Now, of course, I thought of my meeting with Géza in the Hofburg cellar restaurant, of my distress that things were as they were—when, as I thought at the time, they might have been arranged so much better. Well, now they had been so arranged, though only a little earlier such an arrangement would have seemed inconceivable. But the constellation was gone. The configuration in the sky of Döbling was vanishing forever. And though there ought to be great cause for rejoicing—the genius loci out there was veiling its face in sorrow. Already the glowing rust color of things long past was appearing.

And the sorrow which I now anticipated—though I myself was hitched to the wagon of the future again, and so young once more, and full of secret dreams, not to say bold hopes—that sorrow at the moment overweighed all other emotions within me. And I looked into the dear face opposite me as if it were already a memory conjured up out of distant years, full of sweet melancholy—looked at that face then as I do now at the remembered image, twenty-eight years afterwards.

Right at the start, on the way to the lawyer's office, we had spoken of Kajetan's departure. As we spoke, it became clear that Quapp simply took it as a fact, accepting it respectfully and without comment, as an authoritative act. If anything, she felt admiration for her brother's powers of rapid decision, and rejoiced with all her heart that the time of uncertainty and divisiveness had ended for him, and that he was preparing to devote himself once again to work of size, coherence, and importance. I said nothing more on the subject.

Outside the café I quickly and softly wished Quapp much luck on her date, whereupon she laughed wide-eyed and clasped my hand tightly in bidding me good-by. I went along Wipplinger Strasse toward the Ring, Quapp's afterimage in my mind's eye; so that only now and with some astonishment did I realize how pretty she had looked; more than that, how harmoniously and tastefully she was got up, with her speck of a hat, her summer dress and gloves. Only now, too, did I become aware of her expertly made-up olive complexion, and smelled in remembrance her perfume, Bois-des-Îles. All through our meeting these externals had only signified for me the transformation that was taking place in her, the turning-point which she must be passing through. Now, however, this carefulness about her appearance seemed adequately explained by her rendezvous. Yes, she had moved—from Eroica Gasse in Döbling to Fichtner Gasse in Hietzing. And no doubt she would soon be moving much farther.

I arrived at the stock exchange, turned to the left, and walked down Ring Strasse. I had no further plans for the evening. The weather was quite ordinary: no excessive warmth; a slight breeze. The breeze brought with it the thought that after this conclusion had been reached, all my windows in truth stood open; that it rested entirely with me, if I so wished, to move to Paris or Italy or southern France, say the Côte d'Azur. There was that little mountain village of Cagnes-sur-mer where, so one heard, even persons of considerable distinction were settling down those days. The last I had heard, Kajetan's teacher was living there. (Kajetan should have gone to see him; that was what he should have done!) Should I go on here in Vienna acting a second Levielle, with or without expectations? Should I station myself in front of the crystal wall in order to look into Friederike's mute eyes? I did not understand the language of fish. But it appeared that she had no other. I had been with her several times recently.

My patience was giving out. My patience even with myself was giving out. And precisely because during the visit to the lawyer and then in my talk with Quapp I had just shaken off a good many obsessions, I felt for some minutes—still walking on the Ring and then along the park—as if I were accompanying myself, were someone else at my own side. And I was looking out through a number of perceptibly widened slits. Moreover, a stream of air was blowing in through them, what might be called the stream of happy prospects. Very well, I was distracted. But only in that manner which might better be called "collected."

As though emerging from between a pair of curtains momentarily pushed aside, Bank Director Edouard Altschul came toward me—by now I was walking along the wrought-iron fence of the Hofburg gardens. He was holding his cane behind his back, his head lowered, so that I could scarcely see his face. But now he looked up, greeted me, and at once stood still. It was plain that he was not going to avoid a conversation, might even be seeking one; at any rate, he made no attempt to pass by.

We lifted hats and shook hands.

"Are you in a hurry?"

"Oh no, not at all," Edouard Altschul replied. "I've just come from a conference at the Bristol with a British consignor—had to take over the thing myself, the man doesn't speak a word of German. We were drinking whiskey, which doesn't agree with me so well. I sent the car away, wanted to stretch my legs a bit and have a cup of coffee. Because I've got to go back to the office again."

In talking with me he had, I felt, pushed aside something that was troubling him—perhaps had been glad to do so—but I detected it; it was there in the timbre of his voice. This needed, I thought, a little probing, although I no longer seriously considered that anything could be wrong with the bank in which Altschul was one of the directors. I had in the interval learned enough to reject any such idea. Nevertheless, I was interested in the reasons for his depression, which I had noticed at Friederike's reception, and which I now detected even in his manner of walking. The cause, I assumed, was one and the same.

"May I accompany you for a bit?" I said.

"I'd be delighted," he replied.

We began strolling along at a deliberate pace. I informed him straightaway that I had taken over the administration of the Ruthmayr holdings and had various questions I wanted to ask him, of a professional nature. "But then your business is with the 'Land,' " he said. Nevertheless, I replied, I wished very much to present certain facts to him, as soon as it was convenient for him, and to ask him for advice—just for his personal opinion, that is.

"Why, gladly, Herr von Geyrenhoff," he said. "Here's a place for a cup of coffee." He indicated the tables of a large café set out on the street opposite one of the wings of the Burgtheater. "But let's go in," he suggested. "I don't like sitting in the noise of the street."

Inside the café a summery emptiness prevailed. "Yes, the 'Land,' " he commented casually as we sat down, "that's an industry bank."

"What precisely is meant by that, Herr Altschul?" I asked, for

I really wanted to know precisely, and in particular to have his explanation.

"Of course every bank can grant loans to an industry. That isn't the point here. When we say an industry bank, we are referring to a special institution which arose after the war. In order to permit the reconversion of industry to peacetime production, and to allow for modernization and reconstruction, long-term credits were needed. By and large these could not be obtained abroad after 1918. The function of the Land Bank was and is the transformation of short-term foreign credits into long-term credits, so-called industry credits. It's a type of bank which does not exist in the West—a kind of Austrian specialty."

"And what would be the direct opposite of an industry bank?"

"A commercial bank, of course," he said.

I had the impression that he was making his explanation as brief and simple as possible for the benefit of a layman, but was not thereby being superficial or offhand.

"A commercial bank can, of course, always participate in industries, to the extent of its capital reserves. In so doing it can suffer losses. That has happened. But the area of its liquidity is by its very nature far greater than for any institution of the other type."

Very well. This was a fair beginning. But I was still far from knowing what was troubling him; he had regained full equanimity in the course of this conversation. I tried another tack: "Have you been back to your venerable Frankfurt of late?" I asked.

"Yes, quite recently, in fact," he replied. "Incidentally, you wanted to consult me about the duties you have assumed. It occurs to me that I will be free now for a good hour or so. Unfortunately, this happens rarely nowadays. It might be a while before I could be at your disposal. If it's all right with you, we could go up to my office after the coffee. We can talk undisturbed there, whereas here somebody we know might sit down near us, or pass by. Do you have some notes on the questions you wanted to ask?"

"Yes, everything," I replied. "I have it all down here, in a

notebook. And thank you very much—it's more than kind of
you to give me time this very afternoon."

"Why, with pleasure," he said. "You were asking about Frankfurt. Well, as you know, I've been living in Vienna for more than
twenty years now. My wife—of course you know Rosi—is Viennese. I really can't say that I like everything so very well here,
that I accept Vienna without criticism. But on one particular
point, you know, a light has gradually dawned on me. I really
saw it clearly for the first time when I went back to Frankfurt
only recently. Out there, people are simply writhing and thrashing themselves to death. Not out of diligence, or efficiency, or
joy in work, or out of necessity, because they have to. Oh no,
that's not it, not at all. On the contrary. It's done out of weakness,
out of a kind of neurotic compulsion. Out of compulsion. Out of
sickness. Yes, that's it. That's the truth, the unvarnished truth,
no matter what rationalizations they have for it. As soon as they
start to explain it, everyone begins to wriggle. Wriggling isn't
rational. Well, that's how it is. Shortly before I left for Frankfurt
I'd begun reading a book by Kyrill Scolander, and in fact I took
it with me." He mentioned the title. "I couldn't make too much
out of it, too deep for me, I guess, but one sentence stuck in my
mind. That one sentence wasn't too deep. . . ."

To my amazement, he reached into his breast pocket, took out
a notebook, and read aloud to me the sentence he had copied
into it: " '. . . The much praised strong modern man, in truth
so much infected by his own efficiency that his weakness . . .' "

It was evidently not even a sentence that he had jotted down
but only a phrase, almost a formula in the mathematical sense.

"That's what it all comes down to," Edouard Altschul remarked,
replacing the notebook in his pocket. "There you have the source
of what might be called our habitual nausea. Quite aside from
any particular cause. In me, too." He was silent a while. Then he
amplified: "You see, Vienna has taught me that. There in the
West I would never have become conscious of this condition—
possibly I would not have understood that passage in Scolander's
book, either. But when you go from illness to health—though

only a very relative state of health—and then return again, as I often return from Vienna to Frankfurt, you see how things stand."

I now found myself looking across a gulf, but I was very keenly aware of what was on the other side. I recognized this disease as something alien to me: still, the possibility of acquiring it must have existed in me, or otherwise I would not have understood it. So that it nevertheless lay within my scope. To put the same idea another way: every man has a number of electrical outlets within him. Some of them may never be plugged in, but the means for conducting a current exists, even though that current may come from a veritable hereafter in the here. What is intelligence but conductivity, readiness to let currents flow? And nevertheless this disease of his was not my own; I was situated differently, being a permanent pensioner. Sitting there beside Altschul, I recognized "pensionism" as a true situation with its own special tasks and responsibilities. These were, to be sure, no easier than fighting that particular psychic disease of which Altschul had spoken. Still, I was safe from his disease—through no merit of my own. Pensionism, a form of life for which the Frenchman and the Austrian is specially suited, is in truth a severe trial. A man who has borne up splendidly in active service can fail at it. As a pensioner and chronicler I had already failed once. I must not let it happen a second time.

And so, taut with inner tension, I caught sight of him now—of Kyrill Scolander.

"There he is!" I exclaimed, laying my hand on Director Altschul's arm.

From the farthest end of the exceedingly long room, where he must have been sitting at one of the marble tables, a man came walking down the length of the café. The Basque beret on his head—unusual headgear in Vienna at that time—was thrust back slightly, and its dull black contrasted with raven, almost glistening hair. The jacket of his light summer suit was unbuttoned, revealing a bright-colored shirt and the hint of a substantial *embonpoint*. Above the collar and a small, negligently knotted knit tie, rose the tanned face of a southerner, taut and smooth, though not without fat, the nose, however, straight, knife-sharp, very pointed.

But all this seemed merely the holder for the candle, serving solely the purpose of supporting the eyes. I have never known anyone who could look so present and perceptive as Scolander. He manifested the extreme opposite of absent-mindedness and distraction, of preoccupation or daydreaming—traits which the average person so readily attributes to the artist. Readily, because the average man does not want the artist, with his superior resources, meddling in the mess of everyday affairs. In the case of Kyrill Scolander, there was no telling but that he might, and that may have been the ultimate reason for his being so widely unpopular. Scolander could have chosen for his device the well-known *oderint dum metuant*—let them hate me as long as they fear me.

Those eyes of his were presence itself. They were large, wide-open, empty, and well-ventilated shafts of apperception through which things, seen clearly and entirely unmodified, just as they were, could be poured into the mill of thought. Including the ludicrous. That sharp nose seemed indeed to specialize in the ludicrous, to take note of it even sooner than the eyes—eyes which then, precisely since they took in everything, made the ludicrous even more ludicrous still. There was, in fact, a touch of boyish rascality there which would astonish me anew whenever I beheld this otherwise so dignified a face.

Present, as he always was—moreover, his eyesight was very good—Scolander recognized Altschul and me at once. He turned aside from the central aisle and approached us. We rose at once from our chairs.

Our greetings were ceremonious, true to traditional Austrian etiquette, replete with cordiality and geniality, with expressions of delight and inquiries into each other's well-being. Yes, Scolander said, he would gladly sit with us for fifteen minutes or so; unfortunately he had no more time than that. And then he promptly vaulted the rails of mere convention. For even as he asked how we were, he was seeing us through and through; there was no concealing anything from him. Moreover, the tone of his question was just a shade more keen than is usual, and there was a certain tension even in the way he waited for a reply, as though he were really expecting an answer, as though he were prepared at any moment for his interlocutor to say something else besides the usual "Very well, thank you."

I let him know that he had just been quoted by Director Altschul, and the director whipped out the notebook and showed him the passage.

"It strikes me as simply amazing, Herr Altschul," Scolander said, "that a man as busy as you still finds time to look into my books."

"I have to," Altschul replied. "In Germany, especially western Germany, where I come from, you know, people are far more aware than they are here that books, if I may put it so, are as necessary as groceries. This is why the Germans will never quite submerge themselves in their enormous industriousness."

"No, I don't think they will either," said Scolander. "The Germans save themselves with their intellect, while the Austrians do the same with their vital juices. Each has his own way. Only the future will demonstrate who comes out better in this test; that is to say, who retains more of his humanity. In both cases the sources of error are inordinate, for only both forms of reaction taken together could really be called intelligence. . . . Herr von Geyrenhoff," he turned to me, "I'm fortunate in meeting you here for another reason, because I hope you will have the address of our mutual friend Kajetan von Schlaggenberg. I haven't heard from him for a very long time. He wrote me—that must have been at least six months ago—that he was on the point of moving, and since then there's been nary a word from him. I shall be here only a week—arrived yesterday from Cagnes-sur-mer, where I live—a little mountain village on the Côte d'Azur—involves an interminable ride through Ventimiglia to Italy, and so on. Next week I have to be in Munich, where I'm to direct a play for the *Kammerspiele*. That's that pretty little Riemerschmidt Theater on Maximilian Strasse. I was director there for three years once and now I've taken on the job again. But I want very much to see Herr von Schlaggenberg here in Vienna. In fact, I came here partly on his account."

I had to inform him that Kajetan had left for Stuttgart a little while before. Scolander wondered whether he could not meet him somewhere in Germany. But unfortunately I did not even know the name of the publishing house Schlaggenberg was likely to be going to see in connection with the big book he was planning. My mention of this project appeared to interest Scolander; he seemed very glad to hear about it. All he could do, however, was to take down Kajetan's address in Vienna.

What seemed to me at this moment significant was Schlaggenberg's trip, inauspicious insofar as it took him from Vienna on the occasion of one of Scolander's rare visits. No matter what favorable arrangements he made in Stuttgart, he evidently would be traveling on—instead of returning with his contract in time to see Scolander. For if Kajetan were returning, he should already have been back. But the rent had been "settled" for three months in advance, as his highly respectable landlady had informed me over the phone, and there was no knowing how long the Herr Doktor would remain away.

Possibly very long. Scolander's effect upon me was like that tincture which precipitates and clarifies a murky solution. Now I understood. That Kajetan's teacher should be here and that Kajetan himself should be absent at precisely this time (couldn't he have left a week later!) struck me as a bad omen. In my mind I saw Schlaggenberg starting out from Stuttgart, where he would have arranged everything very sensibly, on a journey of madness: to London. I saw him as in a crystal ball, standing at my desk when I re-entered my room, completely absorbed; and afterwards I had found Camy's letter turned over on the desk, with the back of it facing up—the back on which her address was written.

But was she still in London? This question flashed into my mind, bringing with it a sense of relief. Had she not written that she would be coming but would not stay in Vienna, would go out to the country somewhere with her father? No further word had come from her since then. Had I offended her by not answering her letter? Perhaps she was already in Austria, perhaps in Vienna at this very hour, and in that case Kajetan's trip would be taking place under fortunate auspices, at precisely the right time. . . .

In any case, I must reread her letter.

And perhaps write to her in London?

Warn her?

No, it was already too late. All these thoughts flashed through my mind at an extremely swift pace; they took only seconds. But I could not escape Scolander. It was plain that he could see something going on in my head. So could Director Altschul, no doubt. And yet it was almost uncanny that Scolander should instantly understand what it was, and know just where to pierce me.

"Herr von Geyrenhoff, have you heard anything to indicate that Herr von Schlaggenberg's marriage may be patched up?"

"No," I said. "His wife is living in London these days." And now, firmly resolved to properly conceal the thoughts which Scolander had already guessed (for hiding ourselves is our oldest heritage, the trait that marked the beginning of a real biography for Adam and Eve!)—I changed the subject. For if I was confronting so ambiguous a personality, a bearer of omens, perhaps a Pythia—then I was going to have information from it too, to extract an interpretation not only of Kajetan's journey, but also of things which at the moment were of greater importance to me.

"I deeply regret that Herr von Schlaggenberg is not in Vienna," Scolander said meanwhile.

"He will regret even more that he was not here to see you," I replied. That was by no means a mere politeness. I then turned the conversation bluntly, and without further ado, in the direction I wished. "Professor Scolander, I have a request to make of you," I said. "Namely, to ask you to be so good as to give me an opinion on a subject which is in all likelihood personally very remote from you."

"Gladly. Those are the only subjects on which we can have sensible opinions."

"But may I first—under the supervision of Director Altschul, so to speak—explain to you very concisely the difference between an industry bank and an ordinary commercial bank?"

"Go to it," he said. "But I must warn you that I know as much about such matters as a crocodile about the quality of parchment."

"Nevertheless . . ." I said, and repeated what the director had told me earlier. "Is that right?" I asked then. Altschul, who seemed amused by this council of laymen, said: "Quite right," with a confirming headshake.

Scolander made a remarkable sight. He leaned farther and farther back in his chair, as farsighted people do when they want to examine a picture or piece of writing which they are holding in their hands—as if their arms were too short for them. But then he leaned forward again, slightly closer to me. It seemed as if he were seeking the proper distance from the object, which in this case was me, my explanation, and my impending question, which I had not yet asked. And for some seconds, while his clear cold eyes rested upon me, I had the grotesque feeling that he was twisting himself like a pair of opera glasses, constantly adjusting his focus.

I concluded.

"I understand," he said.

"Now I come to my point. Let us assume that you possess a large private fortune"—the idea seemed to entertain him; a laugh like a rascally boy's spread over his whole face—"which of the two types of bank would you prefer to entrust it to?"

"The answer is self-evident," Scolander replied after a moment of silence. "Since I would not be interested in power or influence, but solely in the unostentatious grayness of mere security, I would carry my money to the commercial bank. Which undoubtedly— judging by what you have just said—has greater flexibility for weathering the various fluctuations of the economy."

I perceived that Altschul was regarding him with serious interest. The Pythia had spoken. Now Scolander took his leave of us in the most charming manner and strode briskly off between the tables, bearing his firm *embonpoint* before him.

We had sat down again, and called to the waiter for the check. "It almost seems," Altschul said, "that all capacity for judgment is based solely on taking the proper distance from a subject" (had he too interpreted Scolander's maneuvers with his body in this way?). "Only at the proper distance will the necessary detailed knowledge be found; in fact, it would be subject to a kind of law of gravitation, would fall into place given the successful establishment of correct distance. There is one of the mysteries of what is called universality. But the very people who are so fond of saying 'more Goethe' seem to have grasped very little of such elementary truths."

I must admit that I had not known Altschul from this, his intellectual side. I knew, of course, that as the son of a very old aristocratic Jewish family of Frankfurt he could not be considered newly hatched, so to speak, in the way that men like Lasch or Cobler were. Before this, the commonness of his wife had distorted my view of the man. I was glad—quite aside from my other purposes—of this opportunity for being with him alone for once.

We sauntered down Teinfalt Strasse and past the Land Credit Bank, which was installed in a kind of colossal afterbirth of the Palazzo Pitti. We now approached Altschul's own place of business.

The inner glass door swung shut behind us and the doorkeeper hastened ahead of us toward the elevator. Immediately, an almost perfect silence enclosed us, accompanied only by the faint singing of the lift. And that broke off as our cubicle reached the desired floor and stopped with a gentle recoil. The silence continued into the wide corridor with its green runner; very much the same kind of silence that prevailed in the ancient rooms of the nearby Schottenstift or in the baroque hall of the National

Library. But here it was artificial, supplied on order by the architect's soundproofing, further secured by the upholstered doors, cleanly and consciously severed from the noise of the surrounding world. This silence was not the result of patience, not the creation of centuries which had steadily enriched it, so that a single noise could no more destroy it than the woodman's axe-blow can shatter the stillness of the mountain forests. This was utilitarian, a product of engineering, and would have been broken by any unexpected loud sound like a pane of glass under the impact of a stone. Here any such sound would have seemed naked and scandalous.

We entered Altschul's office, settled down in easy chairs, and the director reached for a cigar case—cigars being more in keeping with his German habits than our cigarettes. I gladly took one. Childishly—I am aware to this day that it was childish!—I felt that one should smoke cigars when one discussed such matters.

Only now did it come to me that I meant something to Director Altschul. I was no longer and not merely a member of a different world from his (the world of the pensioner), but something more considerable: the administrator of the Ruthmayr fortune.

"Director Altschul," I said, "would you have the great kindness to glance over these lists and tell me what you think of the choice of securities."

"Many thanks for your confidence," he said, taking the big, hard-bound notebook. "Although on the whole I am pretty well acquainted with the matter, and have been for a long time—that's how things are in financial circles. Besides, I myself was at 'Land,' as you know. Still, this will refresh my memory."

He then fell silent for almost ten minutes, his face half hidden behind his cigar and the notes.

I was pretty well conscious of the decisiveness of these moments. The double accent that Scolander had given both to the state of Schlaggenberg's affairs and my own responsible concerns —that accent continued to dance within me like a bright little

wedge of light that had pierced this afternoon. It seemed to me
now that a very long time had passed since I had sat over Captain Ruthmayr's will.

"The placement seems very good to me," Altschul said at
last. "Did Levielle do this?"

"Probably," I said.

"Evidently he can do things well if he chooses," Altschul said, a
certain bitterness in his voice. "Well, you know, strolling on the
roof of a capital structure like this has its advantages, even if
none of it belongs to you. A great help on the stock exchange, for
example. I don't imagine the honorable financial counselor lost
out. Have you checked on the deposits?"

"Of course," I replied. "They were extremely cooperative over
at the Land Bank."

"I should think they would be," he said. "Well, these securities
are good, and I don't see—not at a casual glance, at any rate—
where changes need be recommended. It's remarkable how
both the speculation in the franc and the Lumber Bank crash
seem to have passed over this capital without affecting it in the
least; otherwise it would show some shrinkage from the account
with which I was familiar when I was at 'Land.' So Herr Levielle
refrained from playing any tricks, with this money at any rate.
Ruthmayr, incidentally, always was with 'Land.' Long before the
war. But now, my dear Herr von Geyrenhoff, what advice of
mine did you want? I don't see that you need any, as far as this
goes."

I spoke slowly, leaning forward, bowed, as it were, by what I
felt to be the importance of the matter. "Dear Herr Altschul," I
said, "the advice I wish is not in regard to the securities in which
the Ruthmayr fortune is placed, but rather the question of trans-
ferring it totally from the Land Bank to yours."

Altschul was silent for several moments. Then he said in his
most amiable tone: "You know that in my capacity as a member
of the directorate here I have no right to say and cannot possibly
say anything else to you than that our bank would be delighted
with such a transfer and would be at the greatest pains to prove

itself worthy of confidence by the most careful management. All this you may assume. But now may I be permitted to speak to you not as an official but as a private person—which really means, to ask you a question in turn?"

"Please do so," I urged him.

"The question is this: what has brought you to consider such a step? For obviously your questions in the café sprang from the same consideration."

"Herr Altschul," I replied, "let us disregard for the moment the verdict passed by Kyrill Scolander, which was a purely abstract one. All that aside, there still remains the real source of my uneasiness: the personality of the governor. To be perfectly frank, that is what bothers me."

For a full minute neither of us said a word. At last Altschul made the following statement: "Yes—Bismarck once said: 'Every man is worth as much as he can afford, deducting his vanity.' That seems to fit the case. I quite understand you, Herr von Geyrenhoff. Well then, you are asking me whether such a transfer is advisable, whether it is justifiable. Perhaps it will surprise you now if I respond to this altogether objective question with a few highly personal bits of information. Or to put it differently: I must unfortunately speak of myself, which in general people should not do. But we will come right around to the subject again. Please bear with me."

I was more than surprised. Was I to have fall into my lap the answer to the question I could not even touch on? Was he really going to confide in me? Would I learn the reason for those despondencies in which I had caught him of late, on the street and at Friederike's party? Or was I to take this merely as a figure of speech?

"On May 14," Altschul said, "we had a conference in this room which showed me the full gravity of my personal situation. Perhaps you know that about the beginning of the new year Financial Counselor Levielle suddenly came forward as principal stockholder of the Alliance General Newspaper Corporation. At about this same time he was brought to our bank by a friend of my

wife's, the wife of Doktor Mährischl, the lawyer. Brought first to
see me personally. Relations between the banks and the press had
been profoundly shaken by recent revelations of corruption in
the form of 'subsidies' which several newspapers, or rather the
editors of the financial sections of those newspapers, were said to
have received from funds which had been set aside by this or
that bank or industry expressly for the purpose—and so on and
so forth. I imagine you know about that. It was blown up enormously, all the more so since the Vienna Press Organization saw
fit to intervene, if only to cut the rumors down to size. What it all
came down to was that these dreadful practices had been going
on for some time, that they were time-honored customs. Customs
are never prescribed, never conform to written directives—they
simply exist. But if any one such custom is 'exposed,' completely
out of context, it looks crooked. That is how it is. The exposure
had been made—probably instigated by some malcontent—and
now we bank people simply did not know where we stood. You
are aware, Herr von Geyrenhoff, I am sure, of the tremendous
importance of press relations to a bank. Such was the situation
when Herr Levielle came to us, with both hands full of newspapers, so to speak, and offered to put himself at our disposal. All
he asked in return was the financing, or rather let us say the
refinancing, of several medium-sized firms which were distinctly
solvent, though not exactly overwhelmingly prosperous. . . .
Well, I argued that by means of capital investments which for a
bank our size could not be considered sizable we would satisfactorily and permanently solve the problem on an entirely different plane. Nor was it by any means clear that these firms—I
cannot give their names, naturally—would be bad investments
for us. At the time this matter was discussed, the directorate
voted with me—though by no means unanimously. Levielle was
mistrusted, the more so since the collapse of the Lumber Industry
Bank in 1925. Well, quite soon after we had made this agreement
with Levielle, two of the firms went bankrupt—or rather, they
would have gone bankrupt but for our bank's devising a reasonable compromise with the creditors. You can imagine that this

did not strengthen my position here. That was the state of affairs by the middle of May. The rest of the companies that Levielle brought to us are just about dragging along. But the main blow struck me only recently. Levielle suddenly cleared out of the whole Alliance affair—*sans dire un mot,* be it noted. And above all, without offering to sell us his holdings. Today it's no longer possible to say who's in control there. Probably the former Prague group again. All our bank has had out of this business—which I sponsored—is an assortment of rotten eggs."

Altschul fell silent.

I sat leaning forward, puffing on my cigar and doing my level best not to show too plainly my strained attentiveness. He was not telling me all this out of sheer desire to communicate. What, then, was the reason for his openness? For there must be a reason. To my shame I must admit that at the time my intelligence did not meet the test; I could not yet see the reason. The only thing I knew for certain was that he was not talking to ease the fullness of his heart. The emotional impulse and charge which we recognize at once was singularly absent from his speech.

"Well now, you see, my dear Herr von Geyrenhoff," Altschul continued at last in the same dry, informative tone as before, "that is the fix I am in. That is the reason why I am in Vienna right now and not vacationing in Bad Gastein as I ought to be at this time of year. I still do not see how this press affair is going to turn out. Articles and news items have appeared which are not exactly pleasant for us. Some of them affect more or less directly those firms of Levielle's which I brought into the bank. It almost looks as though we shall have to pay for the unpopularity of Levielle, who has now taken himself off to Paris. You might put it, if you will, that he has skipped out. Unfortunately, we are left holding the bag. On the other hand, his disappearance has another aspect, since you, Herr von Geyrenhoff, have fallen heir to his rather considerable position: namely, that of financial adviser to Frau Ruthmayr."

"So, already stamped as Levielle II," I thought. Aloud, I said: "In no way will I use this position to further my own ends."

"That is apparent in your case, Herr von Geyrenhoff, just as the opposite is apparent in the case of Herr Levielle. I beg you not to misunderstand me." Here, for the first time, emotion entered his tone. "And now I am coming back to the subject," he added tersely.

He shifted his chair a little so that he was sitting directly opposite me across the small smoking table, and leaned forward a little so that I could look directly into his eyes.

"A fortune the size of Frau Ruthmayr's belongs in a large commercial bank. That is what Herr Scolander said. I say the same thing, and do so quite aside from the personality of the present governor of 'Land.' I am speaking to you as an individual, for what I would have to say as a director of this bank I have already said right at the start. The Ruthmayr fortune was first deposited in the Land Credit Bank long before 1914. But the character of that bank has since undergone great changes; we have already touched upon its present functions in the economy. Ruthmayr was a large landowner—perhaps this was what brought him to 'Land.' But it is not a land bank any more, in any sense. We may generalize, by the by, and say that if the nature of anything drifts too far from the original meaning of its name, we should be on our guard. A prime example of that was the Austrian Lumber Industry Bank. But that is just by the way. Now I must ask you to pay the closest attention. For I am about to tell you the real reason why I spoke about myself and my personal situation, when you may well ask why I did so."

He paused long enough to look at me. His own expression was as calm and collected as it could possibly be.

"My position here is severely shaken," he said, "not because of the material losses incurred from the arrangements I advocated in connection with Levielle. Those losses are too insignificant to matter to an institution of our size. The harm is more of a psychological nature. It reached its height a short time ago when it became clear that my whole action in regard to the press affair was futile. Now then: if a client like Frau Ruthmayr were to be brought to the bank through me—not that the Ruthmayr fortune in itself could be of decisive importance within the framework in which we work—there is no doubt in my mind that this would restore my loss of prestige, repair the psychological damage, and reinforce my position. The upshot of my talk is this: the advice I have given you serves my own very personal interests. This fact should make me skeptical of my own advice. Nevertheless, I cannot in all objectivity give you any other. Skepticism on your part, however, is not only justified but obligatory. In saying this I am showing you the substantial basis for such skepticism. To do otherwise would not be honorable. We are speaking just between ourselves here."

"In truth, Herr Altschul," I said, rising and dropping the rest of my cigar into the ash tray, "we are just between ourselves here! In the most exclusive of all clubs, which at the moment has only two members. My decision is made. I shall recommend to Frau Ruthmayr that she transfer her account to this bank. She may well follow my advice. I will not conceal from her the fact that the transfer was initiated and arranged by you, Herr Altschul. You will hear final word from me within the next few days."

He too had risen while I was talking. We shook hands. As he closed the upholstered door behind me, he gave me one brief, cordial nod through the crack.

I walked in the artificial silence down the green runner of the wide corridor. Every really decent man, I mused, carries a kind of jewel within the housing of his personality; those are the rubies by which the watchworks of practical life run; and life would come to a standstill if these indispensable gems were to drop out.

It is well known that a few years later the Land Credit Bank collapsed. The crash, which took place with lightning rapidity, was started by a telegram which some person, who to this day remains unknown, sent to Frankfurt from a post office in Vienna's Third District. The news therein instantly became known on the floor of the stock exchange. The directors of the Austrian National Bank declared their willingness to undertake a supporting action, but changed their minds the following night. A bad half year followed for the clients of the Land Credit Bank. Finally it was decided that Altschul's big commercial bank would absorb the impact. The outcome was a *Fusion*, as it was called in those days.

Friederike was spared all this.

I decided, as I descended the broad staircase, not to call on her at once, not to see her at all for the rest of the day. The matter should be slept on once again.

But even then, there on the stairs, I realized that the scales had been tipped for me not by the competent specialist in banking, Altschul, but by the total outsider, Kyrill Scolander. His image was still present in my mind in the form of that small, sharp wedge of light which he had struck that afternoon. In 1932, when the whole affair was long past, I ran into him on the street one day and thought to thank him for his oracle. The idea seemed to amuse him greatly; he laughed heartily and said that this was something utterly new for him, to have played the expert in big financial transactions, for he knew considerably less about such matters than a cow about astronomy.

During the following days I gradually learned after all to understand the language of fish and to lip-read the meanings of a mouth that remained essentially mute behind the painful partition that separated us, the wall of crystal. She floats up to it, the eyes directed upon me; she speaks, and yet she remains mute. She is incapable of composed, coherent speech. And while a fine perfume of camphor presides like a pale ghost in the small salon with the wide glass wall, I see Friederike standing in the doorway to the terrace (or was it by the window?), late at night, confronting without alarm a band of men, some of whom had already climbed over the garden fence to the accompaniment of Beppo Draxler's guitar. A half-full bottle of cognac was handed up to her. Undoubtedly she only pretended to drink; but nevertheless she took the bottle and handed it back again. She was still in her silk dress (not brown, this time) which she had

worn to the opera; and behind her the light from the dead captain's room fell upon the terrace. And suddenly all were gone,
everything was gone, the guitar silent, and she heard a car starting away. No, the whole incident could be explained only by
two circumstances: a state of rebellion in which Friederike had
been that night, and her high degree of intuition (a product of
that rebellion and her solitude), which told her at once that this
was not a gang of hoodlums but a harmless party of tipsy gentlemen who would probably be a good deal embarrassed at their
own behavior afterwards, and who perhaps for that very reason
had vanished so suddenly in the midst of the prank.

No, my awareness of that ridiculous but remarkable scene,
during which for a moment the crystal wall had been shattered,
did not constitute a hereafter in the here between Friederike
and me. That existed anyhow. There was no need for this anec-
dote, for my knowledge of it, or for her innocence of my knowledge.

I came to her with my recommendation that she transfer her
account in a far more pessimistic mood than I had been in when
I discussed it all with Altschul. I was expecting to encounter some
insurmountable obstacle, and brought the whole complex subject to her attention slowly and with the greatest circumspection.
Her reaction was one of the greatest surprises of those days.

"Thank God!" she exclaimed, clapping her hands. "I have always been uneasy about this man Victor! But there was no saying anything against him to Levielle; the counselor thought
the world of him. Please do that, dear Herr von Geyrenhoff,
make the arrangement with Director Altschul. Now that you
speak of it, I'm glad that the governor of the bank did not come
to my party on June 23. You understand, I don't have any actual
antipathy toward him. He just makes me uneasy. Uneasy."

She fell silent.

I too held my peace.

She looked down into her lap and said: "Disgusting, really,
such a fat old woman, without a husband or children, and with
all that money."

She receded from the crystal wall, fled, deep into the greenery and the algae. I realized then that I had all along somehow felt that a moment such as this was coming. But now I for my part was incapable of speech, nor was it yet time for speech. More was yet to come. Her head remained bowed, and now a drop fell upon her dress, and then another. Perhaps I should have fallen to my knees before her. But no, I remained numbed. It was too horrible. What had become visible here was the floor of her existence, and below it the abyss over which that floor was laid: the helplessness of the rich, which in many ways can be more terrible than the impotence of the poorest. For their condition keeps them far more shut in by desolation and leaves them without companions, and without the slightest claim upon anyone's sympathy or aid, which the poorest of the poor frequently receive.

"Dear, dear madam, my dear lady . . ." I said. That was all I was capable of at the time. She composed herself, quickly took her small handkerchief. Then she looked up again.

So I beheld Friederike in such helplessness, in the misery of her existence—a misery which needed no immediate cause for breaking forth because its reason was always present. That, at least, was how I saw it at the time. Yet even as I so beheld her, I was for my part expecting help from her, awaiting her soothing hand. Recent events, inexplicably leading back again and again to my fifteenth year and to Countess Charagiel, née Neudegg, had renewed the sting of that small poisonous arrow she had left sticking into me. That was what I was constantly trying to convey to Friederike—but then I would also have to tell her about Quapp, and who Quapp was, for this was part and parcel of that memory of Countess Charagiel. This flashed into my mind, while Friederike was using her handkerchief and I was stammering out my helpless and senseless phrase. (Later on, she pointedly reminded me that in similar moments of emotion among men it is a kind custom for one to lay his hand on the other's shoulder.)

At the same time I also keenly recognized the weakness and mendacity in my thinking: "I want to have no secrets from her."

This was only a pretext for my need to communicate. I wanted to bring this matter up with Friederike for purely egoistic reasons; all those centrifugal impulses sprang solely from such reasons; that was why I was tempted into the error of wanting to tell her "everything" that Georg Ruthmayr had never told her—he who must have known her better than I. (To make matters worse, it now occurred to me that I myself had at one time been wont to think more clearly about Friederike, about her obstructed horizon and her habitual ignorance, which in a way was something like Quapp's. . . .) In his official will Ruthmayr had not mentioned Quapp at all, and yet he had already made arrangements for her legacy; probably that separate fund in London had been intended for Quapp from the start. But only in his last hour had he taken the necessary legal step, hitherto omitted—and done so in such a way that his wife would continue to know nothing about it. He must have had his good reasons for that. Only Sergeant Gach should not have been sent to his financial factotum, Levielle, in Vienna; Gach should have been sent to Eustach von Schlaggenberg in Styria. . . .

In 1914, however, the matter had looked quite different. At that time the Schlaggenbergs were rich landowners; and from all that Kajetan had told me about his father, Eustach had scarcely been the sort who from the start would have had an eye to a Ruthmayr legacy for Quapp. Which, to my mind, he should have done. I don't want to conceal that this is my opinion.

There I sat then, forced to see that anything I chose to tell Friederike about Quapp would be totally superfluous, entirely without rational grounds. If such information had any effect at all, it could only be harmful.

"Forgive my giving way so, Herr von Geyrenhoff," Friederike said. "That twenty-third of June was a key day in more ways than one. Everything has been different since. Also because Levielle is gone, of course. You cannot imagine what that means to me—really, his mere absence is a source of happiness in itself. Not to have to be docile and deferential. Not to be always told, silently: fat old woman, stupid, incapable of living, in need of protection, duty to deceased friend. I never tried to get rid of Levielle. The mere effort would have been beyond my strength. It was thirteen years ago that Georg was killed—soon the fourteenth will begin. During that time I've become an old woman without having lived. Since June 23 I want to return to life. Returning is painful. You have no idea, Herr von Geyrenhoff, how painful it is to return to life."

With that, she fell silent. For the first time, I had heard Friederike speak, not merely observed mute movements of the mouth behind crystal. Suddenly the thought seized me furiously —furiously, because a moment before my rage had been directed against Levielle—that there was no crystal wall, that nothing separated me from Friederike except the Charagiel woman— that she had been the wall all along, nothing else. . . .

"Perhaps it all comes from my having had no children with Ruthmayr. I am quite a simple person. Perhaps he did leave children—possibly even a number—he might well have. I always shut my eyes, but saw quite well through closed lids, if you know what I mean. I never interfered with him. I never loved him; that is the truth. I know it today. I never . . ."

She broke off.

The following day Director Altschul had tea with Friederike in the garden arbor. I too was present. We did not sit in garden chairs, but in comfortable easy chairs, between which Ludmilla pushed a tea wagon that rolled noiselessly over the gravel on rubber wheels.

There was little actual discussion of business. Altschul did not stay long. His personality seemed to have a profoundly reassuring effect upon Friederike. There was no missing that; she became almost gay. The airy shade, speckled with spots of sunlight, within this wide tunnel formed of sheer plant growth, suggested that we had been transported into another world, though we remained conscious of the sunny gardens surrounding this solitude. Friederike remarked that she liked to stay there in the summer, and that she had postponed her stay in Gastein because she wanted to make a small alteration on the house; however, the architect with whom she had to discuss the matter would not be returning to Vienna until the second half of July.

The director took his leave, and I remained with Friederike. As Altschul bade us good-by, something happened that was perfectly plain and yet can scarcely be put into words. He united us with a look; he performed a syn-opsis, and with palpable benevolence. It left me with a feeling of confusion. As I sat there beside Friederike, facing the now empty third chair, I was much closer than I was willing to admit to those recurrent moments when my fifteen-year-old self walked in the fragrance of Claire Neudegg to the garden gate, still before the poisoned sting and as if on the point of flying off into something unimaginable and never seen, probably into a hereafter in the here. Not only Friederike was returning to life; I too was doing so. We both entered it at the same moment.

She said: "If there were one such child who looked like Georg Ruthmayr, I believe I could be very fond of it. He was my husband, after all."

Only a perfect philosopher, possessing the iciness and the inhuman curiosity of his kind, and wanting to see whether this poor soul struggling toward life would manage things by itself, and how, could have held his tongue then. So I told her about Quapp. I explained the legacy entirely in Levielle's terms—"rediscovered" testament and all. I said that Quapp's mother was the Baroness Charagiel, and made it clear that the affair had taken place before Ruthmayr and she, Friederike, had ever met. And while I was thus letting the cat out of the bag, something altogether enormous and unexpected happened: it carried with it the sting that Claire Neudegg had left in my flesh. Even as I spoke I became insensitive, quite neutral, toward the whole matter. I could scarcely grasp it. My body, sitting in the chair, was healed down to its ultimate depths, down to the central core of life somewhere deep within.

"Yes, Georg was generous," she said. "Generous and negligent.

Always postponing things. Always doing things at the last moment, at the very last, God knows. Of course, I absolutely must meet her, this Fräulein von Schlaggenberg. To think that she's the sister, in a way, of your friend, whose books I have been reading for years. Yes, now I see it—I've begun to live again. Shall we walk a bit in the park?" she added vivaciously, rising. "And then you must telephone Fräulein von Schlaggenberg and ask her to come to see me. How many things have changed since June 23! But above all—I'm living again!"

Her dark eyes flashed. I saw that in her for the first time; previously, I would not have been able to conceive such a thing.

We left the arbor. The sun was melting everything in a crucible; the greens ran; the already slanting twilight gold overwhelmed the foreground. We crossed an expanse of lawn and stepped in between the trees. Somehow, it was like a triumphal march, and I remember to this day that Friederike seemed to me taller than usual. Between the scattered trees, the glitter of the sun at my back, I saw the angular profiles of the houses beyond the garden.

Inside, when I wanted to telephone, Ludmilla had to show me where it was—that telephone which had once played a part during Doktor Mährischl's vain calls, his frantic efforts to reach Levielle quickly. I understood now why I had not heard it ringing that time; the apparatus was far from the small salon with the glass wall. It was installed in a niche alongside the entrance to the dining room.

With Quapp I agreed on Friday, July 15; she was to come at six. It occurred to me that I had been invited to breakfast on the same day with Hofrat Gürtzner-Gontard. Nine-o'clock breakfast; that was the latest form of his invitations. He even had certain "methodological" reasons for this. But of that, more later. Friederike asked me to come to tea at five on the same day, and stay with her to greet Quapp.

People in the city make sacrifices to great Pan, the god of summer, with camphor and naphthalene. That is the cool scent of solitude that lingers in the deserted and shuttered houses, wafts like a pale ghost around the covered furniture, while the occupants of the houses go into the real woods, or stand in gardens, on narrow gravel paths between flower beds embellished with spheres of colored glass. The dark woods can be seen lying like a dropped garment at the foot of more distant mountains whose naked rock glows with a milky mildness in the high summer sky, here and there accented with the white of a snowy field.

The apartment in the Blue Unicorn where Kaps had lived and died was taken over in the spring by Herr and Frau Mayrinker. Their furniture and possessions now stood there, suitably distributed. Very fine furniture and household articles they were: an Empire commode; a baroque secretary with "tabernacle," as it is called; genuine old Czech and Viennese glass in small china closets. In short, Count Mucki would have been delighted and would have roused from his languor, which otherwise happened only when he was permitted to talk nonsense as he had done at Mary K.'s party when he driveled away to Dwight Williams, lovely Emma, and still lovelier Grete Siebenschein in English, Czech, and German all at once. The Mayrinkers had such a flair for décor that Mucki would not even have noticed that among the old things there were also new ones, pictures especially, regular blows below the belt, colored lithographs unrivaled for triviality. One, very wide and oblong in format, hung over the twin beds and represented the Flight from Egypt, with innumerable winged *putti* hovering above the heads of the holy couple much as dragonflies flutter over the Danube meadows in summer.

Herr Mayrinker was manager of a Vienna branch of the Austrian Credit Institute for Trade and Industry.

There was something absolutely perfect about this childless couple, like flowers preserved under glass (there were such *objets d'art* about their apartment), or as though they were floating precisely in the center of a soap bubble. Mayrinker's business life ended every Saturday at one o'clock and began again on Monday at half-past eight. Frau Mayrinker, bordering on fifty, about the same age as her husband—of whom she always spoke as "my husband"—was really a strikingly pretty, curvaceous blonde. But she did not attract attention because she did not play up her shapeliness, and also because she had such a good-natured little face, which always discreetly moderates the attractive overemphases of femininity. The couple's tender and vigorous marital relations throughout the twenty-seven years of their marriage were taken by both partners, not as any special and exceptional good fortune, but as something entirely appropriate to them, and theirs by right. No one considers—and the Mayrinkers were very far from ever considering—what twists and turns life, given its excessively wild and dangerous nature, must perform in order to skirt such a special Mayrinker area. Often it must act in the very last moment to throw back the besetting swarms of unhappy chances which want nothing better than to invade such a sanctuary. People give little thanks for that, little thanks for so unnatural and therefore difficult a setup. For people give thanks only for what happens, not for what never takes place. Horizons like that of Kajetan von Schlaggenberg are rare. For Kajetan's included also the uncommitted and unnamed, the anonymous and never-happened segment of life.

Herr Mayrinker, a kind and very modest man, also brought into the apartment, in addition to the old furniture and the new pictures, a hobby. He often spoke of it to his wife on Saturday evenings, when they sat out in the country somewhere in the summertime, over a glass of wine—in Nussdorf or in Sievering. And she would listen graciously to him, for she was in every respect indulgent. Moreover, the hobby received fresh impetus in midsummer of 1927, when the *Illustrated London News* published pictures and reports of Douglas Burden's expedition to Komodo—material which had previously been published only in the official organ of the New York Museum of Natural History.

In short, Herr Mayrinker was passionately interested in dragons and winged serpents. What the meaning of that may be is hard to say; but people grow accustomed to many things, and *nil admirari* has been pretty well drilled into some people. Others, on the other hand, possess it *ab ovo* (here was the place for Herr von

Geyrenhoff to use his favorite expression). Such a person, for example, was no doubt Castellan Mörbischer at Castle Neudegg.

Naturally, Herr Mayrinker was deeply stirred by the discovery of the dragon of Komodo; his wife had to listen to endless stories about it. He studied Komodo on the map; it was located below the eastern Sunda Islands, between Flores and Soemba, looking extremely tiny but in reality scarcely smaller than Lake Constance. This living giant lizard of Komodo was several yards long. It was not at all like the crocodile, for it lived on land and ran swiftly, had scales, a forked serpent's tongue, sharp teeth and claws, reared up on its hind legs when provoked, and spewed frightfulness at its enemies—namely, the pestilentially stinking contents of its own stomach. It is plain: the creature had everything that a dragon-lover's, or drakontophile's, or drakontomaniac's heart could desire. And so this new missing link replaced the native *Lindwurm,* concerning which Herr Mayrinker had always hunted down every dubious report. Likewise, the giant dragons of earlier ages, the saurians, took the back seat with him —although these pets were set aside only temporarily. As for the *Lindwurm,* pretty Frau Mayrinker had once summed up the problem with Solomonic wisdom. "There are three possibilities," her dictum had run. "Either it exists or it doesn't exist. But the third possibility is the most plausible: that you yourself are it, darling." Thus Frau Mayrinker at night, in the marital bed.

Sometimes a wild entanglement of writhing dragons' bodies took form in Herr Josef Mayrinker's mind. He would also see the giant varieties of primordial days thumping through the ancient forests, their tails lashing the waters of lakes or swamps into huge waves—the enormous *Tyrannosaurus,* say, bearing his mighty skull with its annihilating teeth twenty feet above the ground, or the ponderous saurian with the high ridged back, *Stegosaurus ungulatus.* Herr Mayrinker had never learned Latin or Greek, but he never forgot any of these names. *Stegosaurus,* in order to steer its monstrous body, needed three brains, one in the head, one above the front and a third above the rear extremities. (And the one in the head was by far the smallest.) He meditated also on the stocky *Triceratops,* with threefold horns and heavy armor plate of thick wide slabs of bone behind the skull. Herr Mayrinker envisaged this creature standing in an open, pampaslike region, among scattered tropical trees, in the intensely pure light of the early days of creation. The landscape would be primevally simple, descending in a gentle, shallow slope to a sea that no keel had ever parted. Out of that sea there frequently rose a long serpentine neck, twenty or more feet long, which the monster dragon held high: a plesiosaur, *Hydrotherosaurus,* belonging to the family Elasmosauridae. But the mosasaurs, like *Tylosaurus,* say, did not have boat-shaped bodies over which a swanlike neck and tiny head groped into the air; *they* were real serpent-dragons of the sea, darting swiftly along with a rush of water.

Herr Josef Mayrinker thought about these creatures as another man might think about his postage stamps or his garden.

And he pondered these writhing and twisting serpentine bodies, and looked up rather absently, to where wall and ceiling met, in the upper emptiness of the room where we seldom look.

But not long after the beginning of July the Mayrinker apartment was shrouded in cool camphor, in the twilight of closed blinds, through which every evening at a particular spot a rod of light entered, very thin but absolutely straight and several yards long; one end of it rested on the narrow side of the "tabernacle chest," approximately halfway up, as though intending to point out something there. The Mayrinkers were in Pottschach. That is still a long way from Semmering and the high mountains. Nevertheless, even there, the air as you step out of the train smells entirely different from that in Vienna, even while it is still mingled with the smoke from the locomotive. Sounds and echoes are changed too; you notice that as soon as the conductor calls out the name of the station.

This summer resort is situated in a countryside of low hills, almost in the plain.

Deep industrial canals flow quietly and rapidly, the streaked water almost noiseless in its passage.

It is very hot. In the garden the roses throw out strong scents. The colored glass spheres shine dazzlingly.

The Mayrinker household has been transferred here, with everything that goes with it. Sleep, by open windows, is particularly restful. The city has sunk below the horizon. In the heat it sinks into itself and becomes lonely, because so many have left it, and it will grow lonelier still above the shimmering asphalt, although hundreds of thousands of people are still riding and running around within it. The city inclines toward meditation. For that purpose it has many hollow spaces, caverns, cavities—the draped and coolly camphored rooms. At last the furniture comes into its own. But the meditations of the city take place not only in such closed rooms. In front of a small tavern on a side street the tables stand on the sidewalk. Shining beer mugs are to be seen. From the tavern comes a cellarlike smell, perhaps from the vats of wine and beer. Only now do we notice that the moon has risen over the street. The evening is very warm. The moon will be full on July 14.

A small red sphere appears suddenly above the summer-dense foliage of the trees at the foot of the hill. It rises rapidly, very rapidly. At once Renata von Gürtzner-Gontard and Lilian Garrique fix their arrows to the bowstrings, lift, draw, and the arrows are off. For a moment they whiz through the air like two long dashes. Almost in the same second the red sphere vanishes, wiped away. Fat little Bully rolls, running for all he is worth, down the slope, and plunges into the undergrowth between the trees.

"We got it," Lilian exclaims.

There was no saying which of the two struck the errant balloon. But the girls' exploit called for a short silence. The scout, leaning on his javelin, which had been thrust into the ground, clutched the shaft with both hands and gazed, overwhelmed, at Renata. Sylvia, the falcon, peered sharply ahead of her, as though expecting something to follow from the successful shot.

Something did. For just as Gaston Garrique volunteered the first remark: "Like Indian braves; really, there's something almost disgusting about it"—just then Bully broke through the swaying bushes and came running up the hill, holding high above his head both arrows, to which something clung; it looked as if they had been tied together.

Both shots had evidently pierced the balloon. The burst rubber clung like a ring just in front of the feathers—a withered, tough membrane binding the two shafts together. The resistance of the wind had stopped the flight of the arrows, and both had plunged to the ground, with Bully cleverly marking the place of their fall. Such was the conclusion arrived at by the investigating commission.

"These are our friendship arrows, Renata," Lilian said. "We must make a tiny notch on each shaft so that we'll know which they are. And we'll always keep them in the quiver. Or better still, back home we'll mount them on the wall on two nails and never use them again. But you take mine and I'll take yours. That is even more than blood-brotherhood."

The two girls exchanged arrows, each one slightly different in its feather and the color of its varnish. Then they shook hands energetically. No one laughed, not even Gaston Garrique.

They left the hill in the direction opposite from that in which they had shot their arrows, and soon reached the wall of a park-like garden, which they promptly scaled, with the aid of Gaston's back; Gaston then climbed up himself, with a helping hand from above. Bully had been the first up; on top of the wall he removed the pieces of glass which had been thoughtfully scattered along it to hamper just such feats as this. But of course Sioux warriors thought nothing of such obstacles.

The park, self-contained and self-absorbed in the midsummer day, perhaps lost in a few dreams wafted up from the city—the park received the Redskins not like their native forests, through which they were wont to creep stealthily, whether on the hunt or the warpath. Here there were no thickets; a well-groomed path led along the inside of the wall, and this they followed. The girls carried their bows, still strung and taut, negligently under their arms. After a few paces they caught a glimpse, far below, of the white gleam of a house. Otherwise there was nothing, no trace of life, only a receptive alien stillness.

However, where wall and path curved around a dense group of trees, they came upon a simple open garden hut, made of small logs and roofed with bark. Inside it, at a table on which lay books and open notebooks, sat a fat small boy with a grieved expression —so lost in his grief, which was probably connected with the notebooks before him, that he did not notice the approaching tribe.

They offered him the peace salute, then sat down around him and looked to see what he was doing. He seemed not displeased. Sitting between Renata and Sylvia, he soon made his plaint, which was chiefly concerned with the correct use of "shall" and "will" in English, and furthermore with his difficulty in grasping a simple fact: that a trapezoid might also be conceived as a rectangle with two added triangles, or as a rhombus with an attached equilateral triangle, and that therefore the area of the trapezoid could also be determined if the area of these figures was determined and then a simple addition performed. Such were the fantastic things demanded of him by his highly nervous papa at these private lessons, one of which was to take place the following afternoon. The worst of it was that you never dared ask about something you didn't understand, and asking never helped anyhow. And as for his not understanding about "shall" and "will"—that created torments of uncertainty, for Papa assumed that he was in full command of such distinctions.

Renata and Sylvia promptly attacked the matter. No doubt Papa explained things too abstractly; the two girls at any rate soon succeeded in clearing away these roadblocks on the path to higher education. The others around the table maintained a well-bred silence and listened. Finally the pupil was questioned by the board of examiners—excluding, of course, Bully. He was put through his paces in drawing with ruler and compass, and finally he was drilled in translation from German to English.

After an hour, all went swimmingly, and the boy eagerly set about making a clean copy of the answers to the problems his father had set.

The tribe set out once again.

All this had been only a pause, after all.

In reality they were on the warpath against a certain Baroness Haynau.

After once more scaling the wall and peering through the dense hedge on the other side, the warriors saw the baroness's house some hundred feet in front of them, its open wooden veranda parching in the heat. Keeping to cover, they held a council and carefully considered the possibility of firing from their place of concealment. Then the missile was prepared.

First the tribe's letter was written on a small sheet of paper. It read: "From this moment on, for two weeks, the strawberry-colored jumper will no longer be tolerated. If it is seen once more on the veranda during this period, it will be pierced by the arrow of the Sioux." This note was folded and tied behind the tip of a sharp arrow, with string which Bully produced from his pockets. It was fastened so that the arrow's length, and hence the draw of the bow, was not reduced by more than half an inch. Lilian and Renata drew lots to see who would shoot, and as it turned out, Lilian won.

She stepped forward to the predetermined spot and raised the bow. Next moment a low rumble came from the house, like the vibrating of a feebly struck drum, and the whole tribe, peering from their cover, saw the colored arrow sticking into the boarded rear wall of the veranda.

Now was the time to leave the neighborhood and to proceed stealthily from bush to bush, one Indian behind another. Once out of sight of the house, the two girls unstrung their weapons; the bows were slid into long linen cases, and quivers and arrows vanished into similar wrappings and were then stuffed into Bully's almost empty knapsack, for this contained only their bathing suits. The long wrapped arrows stuck up above his head.

Baroness Haynau—a tall gaunt woman in her seventies—

obeyed the tribe's menacing command without resistance, as she herself was to relate two years later. She raised no outcry, did not go running to the police; for two weeks she simply wore a green instead of a strawberry jumper. Perhaps her motive was partly superstitious. She may well have thought that wearing the strawberry jumper during the critical period might bring her some kind of bad luck, if not necessarily a second arrow. Everyone is equally prone to superstition, especially old ladies. The tribe, by the way, did not shadow her at all, in fact never came near the neighborhood again. So that the baroness could have worn the strawberry-colored jumper undisturbed.

After a quarter hour's tramp the tribe settled down at a "refreshment stand," a booth of boards with tables on trestles in front of it, where ice-cold lemonade and raspberry pop could be had. After their recent feats, the warriors' thirst was mighty indeed. "We have terrorized her," Lilian suddenly burst out, and her face, dissolved in laughter, fell forward against the rough wood of the table top. The conception of the old baroness's fright was contagious, and not even Gaston Garrique could refrain from laughing; ordinarily, the lanky boy was rather dull, although he joined gladly in everything and since Schlaggenberg's disappearance had really been the leader of the group. Bully alone did not really understand what the joke was about—namely the grotesque magic of the word "terrorized" in connection with so harmless and aristocratic an old lady.

Thirst quenched, they withdrew deep into the nearby woods —directly on the outskirts of Vienna there are still-dense, brushy, quite wild woods, which make for the charm and variety of the city's situation. Here they settled down to hold another council —after Bully and the scout had circled the spot to make sure they were safe from eavesdroppers. And while they talked they kept watch, so that no one could creep up on them.

For this council of war concerned the tribe's most important undertaking: one directed against Financial Counselor Levielle.

As soon as everyone was sitting cross-legged, the long-drink-of-water took the floor.

"Warriors!" he said. "We have to think what to do about this counselor, will-forger, fortune-hunter, or whatever the old stinker is—I didn't catch all the stuff on him exactly. Anyway, a crook. It seems to me that we have spent enough time scouting out the field. The chief's disappearance is no reason not to carry out our campaign. In the first place we can get into the garden through the neighbor's yard, because the little garden gate to that yard is broken and has no lock, it's just closed with a wire. But the glass door to the terrace will be blocked, of course. On the other hand, the door from the stairs into the apartment often stands open for long periods of time. Bully and I checked on that. We passed the second floor as though we wanted to go higher, and then looked down from above. A woman came out with a pail and went down the stairs. She left the apartment door open behind her. We waited upstairs for a while, then went down again. This woman was standing in the front hall with the superintendent's wife, whom we already know, gabbing with her. She'd set the pail down; it was full of rubbish. All that time the cleaning woman was talking with the superintendent's wife we could have sneaked in and got the thing out of the apartment. But by then it was too late, of course. Besides, there was the danger that there might be some people still in the apartment. People seem to have been working in there. Lilian and I saw several men go in with ladders and pails."

Gaston Garrique could not know, of course, that Levielle had had his apartment refurbished because he intended to rent it, except for that one room at the head of the hall into which Alois Gach had once had a glimpse, where the handsome baroque secretary stood. Levielle intended to set aside this room for occasional stays in Vienna.

"From what the old cavalry sergeant said, you go right from the vestibule into the room where the old-fashioned secretary stands. The chief described that to us in detail. Then you have to stand in front of the desk and run your right hand slowly down along the narrow end until you feel a small uneven place, a hollow or a bump, though it won't be much of a one, because it can only be felt, not seen. That is the secret button that makes the right front drawer jump out. We'll scram with whatever is there, because there won't be time to look through the papers. I'm going over all this so that each and every one of you knows what we're after."

"Right!" Lilian said.

"Now we'll hold a vote," Gaston said, "to see whether we want to start this campaign tomorrow."

There was no opposition; everyone agreed. "All right," the long-drink-of-water said in conclusion. "Now, just so that our parents or our aunts don't decide to take us to some castle or church tomorrow, I suggest that we mention tonight at dinner that we're planning a big swimming outing tomorrow. To—where to, Renata?"

"To Klosterneuburg," Renata said.

"Good, to Klosterneuburg. We'll say that it's just too hot in the city and that we want to start out early. If we stay around the hotel too long, somebody will think of something to do, or Uncle Franz or one of the aunts will attach themselves to us. That's happened before. So let's meet at half-past seven in front of Renata's house. Decently dressed, too—not the way we are today. That's important. We must look as respectable and well behaved as possible. That would be helpful in case we're caught, too. Naturally we go without weapons or tools."

They rose, picked up their things, and crossed the ridge through the brush in order to descend to the Danube and go swimming. Coming to a fire lane in the woods, they saw the river far below them. At this great distance, its flow was not discernible. It lay motionless, an outstretched ribbon, gleaming somewhat in the sun, bedded down in its expanse of valley.

On the afternoon that the arrow was shot into Baroness Haynau's veranda, René was not to be found in the cool library corridor of the Institute. He had completed his work there for the summer—not only the paper for Professor Bullogg, which he had dispatched to America before June 20, and not only his simplified version of the old manuscript for Herzka's use, but also his own Merovingian studies. In consequence, René was at home now. He had intended to go swimming. But he was suddenly swept by so palpable a sense of well-being that the prospect of glittering water, the noise of the bathhouse, the way down to the beach, all seemed to him superfluous. Such activity would merely trouble his peace of mind. So he stayed. It was relatively cool in his room, which faced north upon a wide yard surrounded by buildings—apartment houses with long rows of windows—and was about on a level with the tops of several old trees which reached all the way to his floor. In front of Stangeler's two open windows ran a narrow balcony with an iron railing.

René had spent many a summer in Vienna while his parents were off in their country house, in the Rax district. Luckily, they had held on to this house in spite of their personal financial collapse in the general catastrophe of 1918. Of course they would have liked to have their son there; but Stangeler often stayed in Vienna for weeks during the summer, making his way as best he could until his money gave out, often burdened and depressed by some task he had fallen behind on, with the overdue assignments and lack of funds combining to reinforce each other and his bleak mood. Added to that in the past few years, there had been a number of severe conflicts with Grete. Oddly enough, these had tended to take place during the summers. In short, there had emerged what one harsh judge of René had once called his "tattered way of life." A phrase which contained more than a bit of truth.

But now René looked back with a certain astonishment upon the tangled and jangled image of his very recent past.

Today, July 14, 1927, that image already seemed as alien to him as a landscape on the moon.

To think that he had once lived like that!

But the gulf which separated him from all that could not be

plumbed because it could not be named, could not be measured because it had not the measure or name of particular improved circumstances. It existed, really, only in the way in which he now looked at this room and the objects within it, or at the railing of the balcony outside and the big motionless treetops above the yard. It was there even in the way he listened to the distant tinkle of a streetcar's bell or a short muted automobile horn. Only through such things as this did the principal change and improvement come into René's consciousness: the fact that he no longer needed to worry about money. He could, for example, have gone to Venice at a moment's notice (Grete had proposed this). His passport had been renewed (again at Grete's suggestion, so that he would be ready if Jan Herzka wanted him to travel). But the trip to Venice would have been just as superfluous as the walk to the river bank now seemed. . . .

To all sides stood intoxicating areas of freedom—which remarkably enough accorded very well with his now fixed relationship to Grete. But his lordship René did not notice that there was anything remarkable in this.

The keys to his parents' apartment on the second floor had been left with him for some reason; there was something he had to do. Oh yes, that was it: he had to check once again to make sure that the gas and lights were turned off. René went downstairs and carefully went over the apartment.

Upstairs again, as he was entering the hallway, the telephone rang shrilly—it was like a dog's barking when a stranger approaches.

Stangeler lifted the receiver, and at once had the feeling that a tiny machine gun was being fired directly into his ear: "Doktor Stangeler himself, isn't it? This is Pomberger and Graff, publishers and printers, Director Szindrowitz speaking. Herr Doktor, a close friend of yours, Bill Frühwald, has recommended you to us and spoken highly of you, and our firm might possibly be prepared under certain circumstances and conditions to consider publication of your book on criminal secret torture in the Middle Ages, although of course you must fully realize, Herr

Doktor, that this would be an enterprise primarily for the promotion of scholarship, without reference to financial gain, and you must furthermore consider that publication would naturally be in your interest, designed to acquaint a wider public with your name. In the event that you would be realistic in your expectations of recompense, we would be prepared, in spite of the difficulties which inevitably arise with regard to such publications, to take the matter under our most serious consideration. Although the printing costs of a work like yours would be considerable, we are disposed to take the matter in hand immediately—that is to say, in the form of a preliminary discussion. Director Abheiter and myself—Director Szindrowitz is my name—are prepared to call upon you without delay. Your friend Herr Bill Frühwald has already transmitted your address to us, and we would like to pay our respects to you, in half an hour say."

"Good . . ." ("Good God, what ever gave you the idea?" Stangeler was going to say, but he was not given the chance.)

"Very well, then, we will be along in half an hour."

At this the telephone was hung up, and the conversation thus ended on this elegant note. At least Stangeler knew that in half an hour these two vulgarians, that is to say, the directors of Pomberger and Graff (a publishing house René had never heard of), would be descending upon him.

He tried to interpret the incident. He did not for a moment consider the offer itself. But he tried to summon back the oily and yet at bottom crude tone of the telephone monologue and to recall the details of that ghastly and offensive syntax. René committed the error, to which he was only too prone, of trying straightway to interpret the thing that struck him. It was as futile as ever. What remained was a profound uneasiness about the telephone call—uneasiness, rather, that such a call could happen to him, and had happened.

Half an hour later Directors Szindrowitz and Abheiter entered Stangeler's room. Both were men of around fifty, dressed in too up-to-date a style, smelling excessively of cologne; and they talked as the one had talked on the telephone, incessantly, either simultaneously or alternately, employing much the same language. They spoke standing, sitting, bobbing up and down; they never stopped talking, and belabored the point that any scholarly activity nowadays would be an altogether hopeless matter were it not for idealists such as themselves who were prepared to further the interests of scholarship. Gradually, and with a growing astonishment which thoroughly excluded any attempt at interpretation, Stangeler observed that both men were dressed virtually alike, and although their resemblance stopped there, their alternate delivery resulted in a likeness of voice; in the incessant flow of words the voice of the one passed smoothly into that of the other, so that Stangeler imagined Abheiter was still speaking when Szindrowitz took up the thread. Although the strophic mode was in itself deadening, this vocal identity gave the two an eerie air.

The alternating lecture had by now reached the subject of popular education, enlightenment, popularization of the results of science and scholarship. In this great cause, no stone must be left unturned and no field unplowed, they emphasized. And therefore a scholarly work which might bear fruit, from the historical side, for one of the most modern and topical branches of research, namely sexual science, ought to be made accessible to the widest possible audience, which of course would be possible only through the offices of "a publishing house experienced and distinguished in this special branch." At this point Stangeler was bombarded with the illustrated prospectus of an eight-volume "Library of Sexual Science" already published; the titles and texts as well as the sample illustrations made it plain that the firm of Pomberger and Graff truly deserved to be called an effective agent in this field.

On the other hand it must be said that Messrs. Szindrowitz and Abheiter had taken the wrong tack, from a commercial point of view, and hence were not very effective as potential acquirers of a highly important manuscript on criminal secret torture in the Middle Ages (had they known the contents of the manuscript, they never would have come). For they were far from grasping that their babble was spreading itself precisely on the border of a hereafter in the here, and they had not the slightest inkling of how it sounded from that hereafter. But the demonic force of vulgarity's push, pry, and urgency springs precisely from ignorance of the realm into which it is pushing its way; vulgarity fancies that everything else is exactly like itself.

The two men literally forced Stangeler out of the predicament into which he had got himself. The more they proved to be utterly and crudely impossible, the easier it became for René to master the situation, since he was spared the danger of saying anything. Abheiter and Szindrowitz talked so much themselves that they left no room for reply. At last, however, they paused for breath and waited a little to see what Stangeler would say. After having been so beaten down, René could scarcely rouse himself to speak at all, so oppressed was he by a sense of the folly of all words.

At last, however, he managed the casual remark: "I intend to publish the source I have discovered in America, not here."

"But my dear sir!" Abheiter cried. "How can you think of that? It would have to be translated into English first, which would leave very little profit for you."

"No," Stangeler said. "They would not want such a document translated in a publication of that sort. It would be for specialists, after all. At most my commentary might be translated."

"But then you could not possibly reach a wide public," Director Szindrowitz exclaimed.

"That is entirely unimportant to me," Stangeler tossed out.

This last sentence was dropped in so indifferent a tone that its genuineness carried across the barrier of the hereafter in the here and made contact with the two men's commercial and tactical instincts. They became aware for the first time that they had gone too far, that in fact they had attacked the whole matter from the wrong angle from the start.

In the light of that recognition Szindrowitz now said: "Discounting whatever you may do in America, Herr Doktor—that does not affect our interests. Nor should it hinder you from seeking to derive here, in the form of a more popular publication, the proper reward for your great labor and toil. When I spoke earlier of modest requirements in regard to recompense on your part, I was thinking in terms of a large publishing house like ours, whereas of course the sums in question would be quite substantial. Were we to conclude a publishing contract, we would be prepared to place at your disposal at once, as advance upon the per-volume royalties—calculated upon the basis of the unbound copy—up to 3,000 schillings."

Director Abheiter nodded agreement.

Just as Szindrowitz had finished, René heard in the hollow stillness of the hall outside the stertorous ringing of the telephone.

Later Stangeler candidly confessed that for the moment he had wavered, this in spite of his precise realization that such publication, even if not done under his own name, would sooner or later ruin all his chances in the world of scholarship (that much he was capable of understanding even then). But he wavered only during the few moments it took him to move from his room down the long hallway to the ringing telephone.

It was Grete, and she had news. Dwight Williams had just called her to say that Professor Bullogg was in town and wanted to arrange a meeting with Doktor Stangeler. "Could you come tomorrow between ten and eleven to the Hotel Krantz—it's called the Ambassador now—and if you can, bring the original right with you. And just think, René, Professor Bullogg said all sorts of nice things to Williams about your paper, and the exactness of your notes. He said you must be a first-class specialist, and that the introductory essay was absolutely magnificent, and so on and so forth. What do you say to that? Did you know you were so clever, my sweet . . . ?"

And so on and so forth. They arranged to meet down in the Prater, where it would be cooler, at the last streetcar stop. Grete's voice sounded very high and clear, at times like the cry of a bird. But in truth she was flying over the peaks of her life, it seemed.

Slowly, Stangeler returned to his room, and observed that

the two men were looking everything over carefully. But there was nothing to see. The desk was bare.

René expressed his regrets and his definite rejection of their offers, and sent them about their business.

Immediately the silence closed in around Stangeler again. And out of it there rose, round and pure and sonorous, without his attempting any interpretation, the real meaning of the whole incident. Hitherto he had received no such clear proof of the mutation that had taken place in the relationship between Grete and himself as he had just had in those moments during the telephone call. For the first time he realized what had really happened in the last two months, since his trip to Carinthia with Herzka. It was this: that she had joined with him like the waters of a river at its confluence with another. It was no longer that she lay in bed with him from time to time (he now looked back upon that as upon a primitive stage of his own history), but that she flowed along with him in one and the same river bed. And he realized also that no insight into his own self, no deepest prob-ings of himself, let alone his own feelings no matter how mighty, could confer that indubitable and tangible certainty which springs from the facts of external and material existence. These alone have real, unshakable, decisive authority. *Facta loquuntur.* Only facts speak. Depth is outside.

"Depth is outside." He murmured to himself this sentence of Kyrill Scolander's.

And began dressing to go out to the Prater.

When Stangeler got out of the streetcar at the last stop, it was still daylight. The tall treetops and the luxuriant greensward were streaked by the red-gold of the evening sun. Grete came straight toward him, for she had arrived on the preceding tram. She bore in his direction her entire feminine armament, but her peaceful intentions were unmistakable; these bastions were not to oppose him, these points not to pierce him. Rather, all the drawbridges had been let down, inviting entry. Two months had sufficed to make peace second nature to her. . . .

But that is putting it wrongly. Peace was her first nature. René recognized that now. This peace was the real thing. Whereas the war had been a highly artificial though perhaps indispensable stage in his relationship with Grete. Seen from the here and now that struggle for position appeared almost as primitive as their former occasional unions.

Nowadays they had something far more important on their minds. For Grete recognized more clearly than René the far-reaching significance of the business which had been initiated by Williams and which was now rapidly approaching realization— just as, a short while before, Mary K. had grasped more fully than Leonhard himself the importance of his arrangement with the prince. What was said about Leonhard might well be said of Stangeler also.

But let us center our attention on the couple now strolling slowly along the main boulevard of the Prater, toward "Constantine's Hill." Beyond the hill this low-lying part of Vienna's surrounding countryside spreads wide, determined by the course of the river: a landscape of vast open meadows in which here and there giant trees rise in splendid isolation. The meadows fade into woods whose branches hang low over threading streams, often forming a perfect vault above them. Where the surface of the water widens into a pond, one can see on its other shore the distant fine intricacies of an incredibly high crown of trees standing against the evening sky. This has nothing in common with the luxuriant undergrowth, with the deep, almost sonorous odor, the marshy exhalation of the water, and with the gnats which sometimes infest the place. It belongs to far distances, to the wind, the open windy expanses of the river, the gliding ships, the passing time, no doubt to partings and sorrows also.

On the main boulevard where Grete and René are strolling, there are no gnats. We hear Grete reporting that Williams actually thanked her for this chance to do a favor for Professor Bullogg, who was an important man to him at Cambridge—that is to say, at Harvard University. Williams had also said in his frank manner: "Your fiancé is an awfully fine fellow, Fräulein

Siebenschein, and enormously gifted; I have the greatest respect for him." Naturally words of that sort gladdened Grete's heart. Later, we see the couple crossing the vehicular roadway of the boulevard—which is several miles long and runs straight as an arrow. From the middle of the roadway you look to both sides as though through the wrong end of a pair of field glasses: distances recede. Later, we see the couple sitting in the garden of one of the Prater cafés, for this is their location, in this neighborhood which gradually passes over into the domain of the well-known Wurstelprater, the amusement park which at night drives a tremendous gouge of brightness into the meadows, a gouge whose walls crawl with innumerable colored lights, whirling and stationary, where there is a spinning and dinning of carrousels, some of which at that time were still very graceful, almost Biedermeier in style, although they had been built only toward the end of the nineteenth century; some had wedding coaches adorned with fairies and sprites. In fact, one colorful merry-go-round with a bridal chaise stands there and turns there to this day.

One of the Prater cafés boasted the Hornischer Ladies' Band, all dressed in white with colored sashes, all highly respectable. There were about twenty in the band, and they played very well. Nevertheless, for anyone who knew Vienna then, the name "Hornischer" has an unpleasant ring. The name is in itself crude and sounds embarrassing—even if you do not think of hornets; embarrassing as certain other names which in Vienna are common in every sense, like Rambausek. Hornischer, however, has in it an element of hidden violence and inwardly directed brutality; not even the twenty pretty ladies in their white dresses and vivid sashes could change that fact. The name made your hackles rise. At one point, when Grete and René looked up from their food, they saw something enormously big and yellow hanging very low against the sky between the trees; it took a second before they recognized it as the moon. It was the full moon of July 14. From the amusement park sounded the bell of a carrousel, then came the tune of the barrel organ that played while the carrousel rotated. Old-fashioned merry-go-rounds with fairy coaches and bridal chaises have a special music of their own, the tunes defined by the tinkling of little bells.

Grete and René went home early, shortly after nine o'clock, for there were important things in the offing the next day. At this hour Anny Gräven, who usually loved going to the Prater, was already very drunk. She did not go out. She lay in her room on the bed, fully dressed, with the light out, and in the darkness pondered organically, less with her head than with her body, whether she ought to get up to vomit over the pail, or whether she could still conquer her nausea by falling asleep, without risk of vomiting all over her bed. During these deliberations she tried to counter the whirling movement she felt by fixing her eyes on some distant blue lights from the railroad; these lights fell through the high bleached curtain, which had been drawn half aside. A glow from the street lamps also entered the room.

WHEN I lie down at night, I always sleep on my back, then the very moment the back of my head falls on the pillow the night before comes back to me. And it goes on, too. The way the boy didn't come and didn't come back from the toilet that time, it was so awful because I thought he'd been drawn down, sucked in. All that night I couldn't stop worrying, and Croaky didn't come in again until the next night. I feel life double, and I have double worries too. Not everything is double. Cubby was double. Fräulein Renata never. But the wine hoses were double. Till now the fire has been a single red pimple. The shears, too bad, I've never been able to bring it down, it's hard to believe.

Sometimes I lie there like under the surface of water, so deep down inside the city, but it isn't because the Danube has risen or anything like that. It's a violet fog, a sea of fog that covers everything. My husband was in the war against the Italians and took part in that big offensive at Flitsch-Tolmein when the Austrians in the valley below had to march waist high through the green poison gas when they advanced. They let it loose themselves and then it gathered down below. That's what this violet fog is like, but not poisonous, good and sweet-smelling, and everything is much prettier when it rises. Inside it you see everything much better, it's like a lot of lilacs have melted in it. Tonight there was nothing but lilac fog, I forgot all about them down below, didn't even look up to the ceiling to see whether maybe a Cubby box was up there. Croaky and I just floated along in the lilacs.

After I woke up, I remembered that he's dead. I didn't cry much, just a little. The lilac was so good.

I already know that I lived in a narrow street and that now big buildings are going up there, up to where it's very bright and always windy, you see the Hermannskogel or the Kobenzl out by the belt line. And it would have been better for Croaky. But the people didn't leave anything behind and moved into the bright houses through the white doors and dragged all their junk from the narrow streets right with them, chests and boxes and old wire and lamps. In the end everything looks like a clean plate flies have specked up. Moving wouldn't have done any good, they still crawl around down below here and splash in the mud. And yet here in Liechtental there are still a few good folks too, so that the ones down below can't win the upper hand entirely and can't come up, that would be too frightful, so naked and slimy in broad daylight, and the horror of it, before everyone's eyes.

I've often wondered that I have to live so far down below, and was born there too, not on the bright and dry upper slopes, like on Leopoldsberg, for example. I often thought that when my husband was still living and we went out there on a Sunday for a bit of country. Others have lived drier not only outside the city, but down below too, even my own husband, and that always gave me the willies, on account of myself, of course. We lived in the same chicken house but on different roosts. But I didn't mind that he was better off and that I myself had to live down below in the damp. Wouldn't anything reach up for him. I didn't mind. The streets here are my streets and I've got to be content. Only that business with the wine hoses wasn't decent. At the end one of them moved, I saw it plain. Yesterday I dreamt I went to see the professor, wanted to have them all cemented up, have him fill them with concrete. If no more wine came through, that would be the tavern keeper's worry. Up to a few years ago I was still a good-looking woman. Nobody can force such things on me right out on the street, not the tavern keeper either, they just hadn't ought to put the things out of the cellar hole, the horrid black creatures. That's like talking in broad daylight about the worst things, things that have got to be kept secret. And in the end, when the clock strikes twelve, they'll all come crawling out of every sewer grating at once, the wet black horrors, that will be what will happen. Of course everybody will start running then, every man for himself, and shooting won't do any good. That all comes from playing around with such things.

But when he sits up there in my room, just where the ceiling meets the wall, and holds his arms spread out to all sides, sticking there like a spider, I can't do anything against him, although I have got the scissors in the room. It isn't really exactly my room, and so I don't have the scissors right at hand. Of course I cannot cut Cubby down; even if I were to stand on a chair I couldn't reach him, because he's up there too high. Anyhow I'm much less afraid of him when he sits up there, so small, almost square, like a box, with a crooked nose like a parrot in the middle of his face. I can't do a thing to him on account of I'm still lying in bed. It's always very still when he's there, Cubby the box. Then, whenever I see him, I always remember that I've never really seen him down there in the caverns, luckily nothing has ever come out of the water. If anything did, it probably wouldn't be small like Cubby who maybe can't actually do anything to you, but very big, and not like a box but soft and snaky and full of slime. I would have died if it had really come out of the water, or even a part of it, a sucker arm. I would have died if it had come closer, I never would have survived it. Whenever the Cubby box is stuck up above me on the ceiling, the room looks like a cavern, all bare, or like a laundry room or the room next to it, the ironing room. And far away from my apartment. But yet I was lying in bed.

Often I feel so blue here in this neighborhood and wonder why should I live so low, almost by the Danube, all those things can get at us so much easier down here. Many people live brighter and higher. And that makes them faster. I would be ashamed if it came out, the kind of slow troubles I keep having with the box cub. Fräulein Renata says the name is cube, but what am I supposed to do about that? When he sits up there on the ceiling and has dug his wire arms in like a spider, he's nothing else but Cubby in the bare room.

Like a red pimple the fire starts up, a moment ago it was very small, just a piece of glowing coal glimmering at a single spot like a pimple on the nose. But it's ripe, it has to burst. Now they've killed Croaky. Can't undo that. There's no turning back. It wasn't them down there, and just a while ago I was always scared they'd come for Croaky and even reach up when he went to the toilet. But still it was that box Cubby who took him there where they shot him. And it was really box Cubby from down there too, but the horrible arms were made of wire, all of them of wire. Fräulein Renata said they all had to be left because you couldn't know which had current and which didn't. But they all should have been pinched off. Now he's caught the boy and brought him there, and that's how the misery happened, and not only for me. They never should have been allowed to kill the boy. Because now there's nothing to stop them. Now everything will have to burn, the fire will come, and I'd like to know what else is going to come out of there, because nobody can bring the child back to life.

ONCE the full moon had set, or more exactly, once it had vanished behind the high mountains, the night grew steadily darker
as morning approached, in spite of the stars, for in the deep forest they only rarely shot a flash of light between the branches.
A yellow leaf breaking from a birch tree could have been heard
distinctly in this perfect vacuum of noiselessness; even more so the
scurry of a small lizard out of a layer of decaying leaves in which
it had taken shelter for the night, only to be frightened by the
noise of the leaf. Nothing answered these sounds, and not a twig
stirred. The forest was silent as a burial vault. Darkness also lay
dense upon the path outside it, which ran along the slope, parallel
to the fence around the grounds of the rest home (here was the
small gate through which Leonhard had once stepped). Neither
fence nor gate could be seen; all that was visible were a few
stars overhead, where the branches did not roof the path
entirely.

But even without a watch, one who knew the forest would have
sensed the approach of morning even in this blackness. There
was a delicate breeze, though noiseless and short-lived. And
shortly afterward there sounded from the black depths of the
woods the first bird call. For a while it remained unanswered. But
if you now peered sharply between the trees on the grounds of the
rest home, peered eastward, a green tint could be observed already spreading over the sky beyond the mountain ridge.

Into Pokorny Gasse the daylight poured in long rods, poured from the stars; it cut sharply, with glaring rays, into a horizon clean as freshly laid-on lacquer. In these moments the blackbirds, and all the other trumpeters and drummers assigned to honor Apollo, made their usual general pause. Immediately afterwards there began such a racket that anyone who might be trying to conduct a conversation in the street at this early hour would have had difficulty doing so. A din of whistling, artful singing, prolonged cadences, cries, replies, and challenges began.

The newly risen globe of the sun disappeared for moments behind smoke and puffed-out columns of steam from the railroad yards. When the first white and still faintly reddish bands of light fell upon the "escarpment" and the small strip of park, the sun already stood considerably above the horizon, mathematically speaking. In Pokorny Gasse nothing stirred as yet. It is a quarter where people do not get up so early.

But in the gorge that falls away from the main street of Döbling down to Wertheimstein Park, a quacking and puffing of feathers had already been going on for some time, and water-fowl were producing that ridiculous raucous tone that comes naturally out of a broad beak. Some waded into the little brook and then out of it again, and finally assembled with a good deal of chatter at the brink of the pond. Soon they were moving in groups, with seemly gravity, over the surface of the water, tail-feathers coquettishly waggling.

Meanwhile God's missiles of light had penetrated the foliage and the gorge to the very bottom, hollowing out glowing green grottoes among the bushes.

For Quapp it had been a sweet time since she came to live in Hietzing, in a world without ghosts. Sweet except for the fact that she had been seized by an irresistible compulsion to occupy herself with financial affairs. Although she was at the moment without cares, cares beset her; the great prospects of which Geyrenhoff and Kajetan had informed her on May 29 had henceforth become the secret passion of her life.

She saw Géza almost every day.

And she no longer saw Gyurkicz.

She had moved, and moved on.

After the visit to the lawyer, and especially since Georg von Geyrenhoff had been to the lawyer's with her and they had sat afterwards in the café "Zum alten Rathaus" (for his presence had somehow set the seal upon the whole affair, as far as Quapp was concerned)—ever since then her entire previous horizon had been rent, had fallen in limp withered pieces, like posters that have become detached from a fence. Even the fence itself collapsed, and she saw herself facing a tremendously vast expanse of life, opened up for her solely by the fact that in the near future she could look forward to real wealth—measured by the modest standards of a young lady's private life, that is.

That was how she felt about it in today's morning quiet, a rosy quiet, for from the balcony of her second-floor room she looked down upon the garden in which stood one flowering rosebush alongside the next, dark and scarlet red, white and yellow and the color of tea. A spray of the latter variety of roses stood in a vase on the table.

It was the lack of cares, the vision of a wider area of life (which need not necessarily mean a wider horizon), the freedom to make decisions without the obligation to make them, that buoyed Quapp up just now. Not the least of the factors was the present lack of constraints upon her. She could await the coming wealth in comfort.

She did not miss the 50,000 she had given to Kajetan.

That had been carefully calculated in advance.

She had a financial plan.

Nevertheless Quapp whittled down, in small and large matters, the sums allotted her under that plan. She spent less than the budget both on her daily expenses and on her purchases—the latter chiefly concerned with her wardrobe. A few days before, she

had haggled with the milliner Pauli and got the price of a hat reduced by fifteen schillings. But she had filled out the gaps in her
clothing, all the way from underthings to shoes. . . .

She was looking forward to tea this afternoon with Frau
Friederike Ruthmayr. By now, of course, she knew who the
lady was; Herr von Geyrenhoff had followed up his telephone
call with a note, more or less briefing her on Friederike Ruthmayr: ". . . Quappchen, you are going to meet a very dear, good,
and beautiful woman who was your father's wife. . . ."

So she was a kind of second mother, Quapp thought.

In passing, like the beat of a bird's wing, her mind conceived
a quick suspicion, not entirely unfounded, about Herr von Geyrenhoff and the lady in question. . . .

Well then, she thought, pushing that aside. Toward one in the
afternoon she was to meet Géza at a restaurant in town. They
would have lunch and then perhaps spend the next few hours
together. And while Quapp was considering—with deepest satisfaction—what it meant to appear at the home of this Frau Ruthmayr not as the poor thing she had been but as an equal, completely free and independent and looking it—at the same time
she was vividly conscious of Géza's manner toward her. For with
the greatest sensitivity he left the guidance of their mutual relations entirely to Quapp herself, accepting every step forwards
or backwards as she directed it. . . .

She thought a good deal about Géza. But that pain as if the
fine threads of inner seams were being pulled, the pain of being
in love, was now familiar to her from twofold experience. This
third time she could almost treat the whole thing with detachment.

There was a flash that went to the very rim of her widened
sphere of existence. She placed Géza there, at the rim. Would he
do? Could she not expect something very different now?

Yes, he would do; he would stand up. Excellently, in fact.

Géza was being transferred to Berne as secretary of the legation. He had received the news only two days before.

Everything fitted in. She felt that. Géza fitted into the new horizon. He belonged there as though a place had been reserved for him.

She would have on the afternoon dress she was planning to wear for tea at Frau Ruthmayr's. She had already decided on the dab of hat she would wear. Perhaps a light coat also?

She might drop in on the violin-maker. Her Amati had been with him for weeks, for a checkup and possible repairs.

She also wanted to have the instrument appraised.

Quapp had not the slightest intention of selling the violin. But she wanted to know what she really possessed. Only an offer could establish its value clearly.

The quiet, the rosy quiet, was so extraordinary that Quapp kept feeling that it must be very early in the day. She had not yet looked at her watch. Her toilette was completed—except for the dress, which she would slip into at the last moment—and she had already breakfasted. She stepped out onto the balcony again and looked down at the rose garden. As she did so she made a mental note of something which, after these several weeks, she could no longer avoid recognizing.

Since she had stopped practicing, she had no trouble getting up in the morning, with the result that the day fell naturally into an orderly routine. She no longer faced her usual morning crisis when, in her resistance against beginning practicing, she could only sit and sit while sluggishness gradually filled her limbs with lead. Now she admitted this to herself. That admission was a significant moment for Quapp—given her character. Even while the thought came to her, she was intensely conscious of the densely packed quiet of the morning—of what she still thought to be very early morning.

At last Quapp looked at her wrist watch. It was well on in the day: fifteen minutes to nine.

Anny Gräven had finally succeeded in falling asleep on July 14, shortly after nine o'clock in the evening, without having to throw up. The bed remained unsoiled. Toward two in the morning she woke, found herself lying dressed in the dark room, and managed to get up and then go back to bed again properly. Her nausea had vanished. Her head, too, was no longer dull and heavy. She had drunk only wine, and obviously good stuff, with nothing else in between or afterwards. Mixing drinks is what really gets you down. Before going back to sleep Anny took a precautionary strong headache powder, containing a trace of codeine, to forestall a hangover the next morning.

She rose unnecessarily early; having slept almost eleven hours, she could not go on sleeping. After a few cups of black coffee, she felt quite chipper, walked about her small apartment smoking cigarettes, checked the complexion of her entire body in front of the big mirror, took a bath, rummaged among her lingerie, and looked over her clothes. On the night table beside her handbag lay a Punch doll, an absurd toy with wriggling rubber legs. Somebody had stuck the thing into her bag during yesterday's drinking bout. Anny made it wriggle, and laughed. She still laughed easily at everything, in spite of her really depraved state, which was caused not only by alcohol. The Greeks, Xidakis and Protopapadakis, scarcely drank. They had not taken part yesterday. And Anny had earned nothing last night.

She still laughed and was still unwary; that particular enchanting feature of her nature, which had once attracted Leonhard, had remained. Whatever her state, she was incapable of gloomy foreboding; whereas many people, when their way begins to be steep and slippery (as everyone's way is, to tell the truth), feel a kind of warning pressure of conscience, a kind of repentance for follies they have not yet committed. Which has never stopped anyone from plunging into these follies. But at least they were expected. Misfortunes often lie within people in the form of dark, anonymous dumplings; what particular forms and names they will assume remain uncertain. Which state is the better is a moot question. To Anny, in any case, such forebodings were alien. She was never warned, and so lived all the easier. To be sure, such carefreeness could be dangerous.

After she had made the bed, she closed the window again. The beginnings of heat could already be felt.

It is somehow touching to see how even in a second reality, in a regular hereafter in the here (which is where our Anny and all that pertained to her stood), all the familiar daily actions must be performed, just as in the most primary of realities. Matter does not give way so easily; it remains obstinately present long after its reason for being has been lost. Even the man dedicated to the most frightful forms of so-called idealism must brush his teeth in the morning before he smothers the world in the sawdust of its reconstruction, unless he sets fire to it totally, on the principle that nothing counts but the future. The tooth-brushing of the moment remains, though is only just tolerated.

With Anny Gräven, however, the obstinate presence of matter left over from reality quite sufficed. When someone rapped on her door, with the palm, not the knuckles of a hand, she knew it must be popeyed fat Anita. She opened the door and asked: "Whaddya want, Piggy?"

"There'ss a gang downstairss, c'mon, somep'ns up in town, we're all gonna go."

"Piggy" was tight. Anny spotted that at once. Her thick babble signified that in the tavern downstairs a party had gathered and was planning a stroll into the center of the city for some purpose.

It was almost half-past ten by now. And Anny was already bored. For that reason she welcomed the pretext to do something. In the tavern old Rottauscher and his pupil Zurek were sitting, and oddly enough the two Greeks, who ordinarily never came there. There were also several young men and women who did not belong to the "party" but likewise joined the expedition into town. Old Rottauscher greeted Anny cordially. She was handed a double slivovitz, crystal-clear, pure and fragrant in the shallow glass. It tasted wonderful. Some rolls and butter and a portion of ham satisfied her hunger, which she became aware of only after the plum brandy, and this was followed by another slivovitz. Anny had not yet discovered what was going on in the city. But she did not ask, nor did she listen to what people were saying. She ate and drank. When it came to paying, she found that old Rottauscher had already paid for her. Then Anny set out, walking with him and Zurek. Wide Prater Strasse was almost deserted. After the coolness of the tavern the heat was like a wall of feather beds around Anny. No streetcars were running. Zurek pointed this out. Anny had not noticed.

It was like gliding in a brightly painted boat over dark still waters; that was how it felt in the rooms Leonhard now occupied, which had been added on as guest rooms to the massive and extensive Palais Croix on Reisner Strasse. There were other rooms of this sort up here. Leonhard had two of them. In the one, with adjoining bath, he slept; the second was his study, which had an anteroom. Both rooms looked out upon the gardens, a little above the tops of the trees.

Perhaps it was due to the oxygen-rich air from the garden which Leonhard breathed here—at any rate, he slept especially soundly and well, so that he usually awoke very early in the morning. Immediately after waking he would step out onto the balcony, a very wide one, for the added-on guest rooms were, in their total area, far smaller than the huge flat roof of the main building.

When he came up here, from the library or the dining room, it was like leaving the house, ascending out of it. The Palais Croix undoubtedly dominated him, enclosed him with its ponderousness, emphasized at every step its width and depth. (Moreover, at the beginning Leonhard was constantly discovering new rooms—for example, two small salons reached by a corridor which led from the farthest corner of the second library room and which was almost hidden by the bookshelves.) Downstairs he had to defend himself; sometimes he felt almost oppressed and driven to the wall. But up here, among this new, smooth, hitherto unused furniture he felt himself in a vacuum, a hollow world which at once made him its natural center, and which modestly receded to form a mere setting for him. Downstairs he might be dominated; up here he was dominant.

The sun came out on the balcony. Leonhard stretched out,

completely undressed, in its warmth. The houses beyond the garden were low; he was screened by the treetops. The same feeling always overcame him up here: of a tremendous vaulting below him, as though this big building were lifting him up with overpowering force, gathering strength and rising like a wave. Now he became fully conscious of all that lay below him: the curving staircase of red marble, the first reception room, the library—not the smaller rooms filled with books, but the big hall. All of it very empty, having a deserted air. Most of the furniture was huge; there were almost no small pieces. The two salons to which the corridor led—a narrow, glassed-in corridor which looked out on the garden—were obviously never used. A cool odor of camphor lingered in them. In these salons, however, there were some smaller ornamental pieces, little chests, small tables, which utterly enchanted Leonhard. Rococo, they were called.

There was not the slightest resemblance anywhere to the Palais Ruthmayr.

To make oneself useful here, repair something or hammer around a bit—that was altogether out of the question.

This early in the morning the summer sky was of an absolute, lacquered, almost dead purity. The heat was already promising to be serious; it had not yet really begun, but it was ready to break into the awaiting vacuum, to raise the specific gravity of that dominant emptiness. Leonhard felt this, and hastened to take his bath, shave, dress, and get to his morning studies. There always remained, lingering from the day before and the hours in the cool library, certain unfilled gaps, unclarified, contradictory feelings, beginnings of thoughts. He reserved this early hour for the completion of all that—as one slips the fingers completely into a glove. An inner warning told him that he must keep well in advance of the heat of the coming day; once the mind had awakened fully out of an awakened body, and advanced to its fullest potentialities, the summer could no longer enclose it in dullness. Leonhard sat in the study. The room wore like very light clothes. The new, smooth-surfaced, simple furniture receded to the wall, became bright shadows.

This young man here, sheltered and alone, laboring to the best of his ability on his education, apparently with no obstacles in his way, was truly occupying a top cell in the honeycomb of life. The happiness of such a state is not generally praised loudly because it is a state so few are permitted to experience.

But what he could not really bring up out of the depths within himself was a curious disorientation, a constant temptation to be mistaken about the season of the year. All his concentrated daily studies, which were essentially exercises in concentration, did not overcome this. Midsummer had become equivalent, for him, to the second great segment in his life; that had already been accomplished, and therefore he felt that the season was over. Autumn was at the door. It was like being on the point of emerging from a sunken road into open terrain, filled with an extraordinary variety of color, backed by a cooler but purely blue sky. The completed season had begun with that night in whose stillness Leonhard had entered a new realm of language. Between that night (now more than a year in the past, though he did not date it thus) and the present day, lay the summer. The results of that summer, which now showed themselves, belonged entirely to the autumn—indeed, they constituted the autumn.

So, at any rate, it seemed at the central plexus of certain moments. The thing could not really be thought through properly. Leonhard had tried in vain.

At bottom it was much the same feeling with which, in childhood, one began a new school year.

He had his breakfast up here in his rooms, ringing when he wanted his tray brought.

Today the breakfast appeared without Leonhard's having pressed the button. There were steps in the anteroom, then a knock at the door. It was the prince's personal servant, a dignified old man past seventy, who was in actuality already on a pension but who continued to function as major-domo and reserved to himself personal attendance on His Highness—whom he had known as a boy. His name was Josef Schildelka; Croix used to call him "Papa Pepi," and when they were alone the old man tenderly called the prince by his first name, or rather his nickname as a child: "Fonserl."

"Good morning, Herr Schildelka," Leonhard said, getting up.

"Excuse my coming without your calling, Doktor," Papa Pepi said. He put the tray down on a table by the wall and moved a chair into position.

"For taking the trouble to come up in person!" Leonhard said. "I'm much obliged, Herr Schildelka." Usually a maid brought his breakfast.

The "Doktor" with which he was addressed in the household could not be escaped. All the servants conferred this academic distinction upon Leonhard, although at the beginning he had attempted to disclaim it. Perhaps the title even stemmed from instructions from the prince; in any case, it was stubbornly adhered to.

"It's because I have a message from His Highness to you, sir. The house telephone isn't working, nor the bells either, because we have no electricity, and none of the lights are functioning. And when I went past Heumarkt—I went out specially to find out what was wrong—I saw that the streetcars aren't running. It must be a big outage. And to make everything worse, our car isn't running either; it won't be back from the garage till this afternoon. His Highness must go to Metternich Gasse this morning, that's nearby, to see the countess, His Highness's aunt, on account of a family council today. So he wanted to ask if you would go to the university library in the course of the morning because there are four books in the reading room there reserved for His Highness, and would you ask for an extension on them and look through them if you like. They haven't been used for three days and otherwise would go back on the shelves today. I wondered why His Highness didn't have the books taken home here, I could have fetched them on his card, but His Highness wants to have them there because some professor is using them with him, they're reading together there. So would you take a look at these four books too, Doktor, sometime during the morning, and renew the reserve on them, because reordering them makes a bit of a fuss, as you know, sir."

Papa Pepi also explained that the prince would not be coming to the library today for the usual afternoon work session, and would probably have to stay to tea at Metternich Gasse, but in any case Herr Doktor had other plans for the afternoon and evening, or so he had understood from His Highness.

Whereupon Papa Pepi departed.

Leonhard sat down to breakfast.

At half-past five he was to see Mary.

Oddly enough, when the old man had spoken of the electricity outage, Leonhard's first thought had been of his visit to her. As if the fact that the streetcars were not running could have stopped him! He could walk, after all.

Leonhard knew that they would be alone today—in the evening too. Hubert and Trix were in Döbling, where friends were giving a party to inaugurate a new big private swimming pool— a water party, then, with boats and lanterns in the evening. Very nice in this heat. . . .

It must not be imagined that Leonhard gave no thought to the problem of Mary. He was fully conscious of the obstacles that would have to be surmounted there—obstacles for her as well as for him. But such thoughts meant nothing. The current was simply carrying him to her, and however rough the rapids, they would have to be run; there was no other way, for him, for her. Rarely, in our life-fearing age, which constantly sacrifices the present to the idol of a more and more dubious future, has a couple lived so entirely in the breathing and existing minute, in present happiness and unhappiness, without debasing and poisoning these by secret considerations of what was to come of it, where it would all lead ("this cannot lead to anything!")—considerations which at bottom mean a constant betrayal of one's partner. But no, Mary and Leonhard had taken up the unique wreath that life had tossed them, and them alone—had picked it up without looking to see whether it was made of roses, of thistles, or of both woven together, as is the usual way. Most lovers pick each other over; this won't do and that won't do (as in a shoe shop); and will we do for each other at all, and where will this lead? If one goes at it this way, heaven may have the brightest ideas and yet everything will remain patchwork. When you try to pick the nettles out of the wreath, the few little roses droop, and then the whole thing isn't worth the effort.

Our couple were providentially healthy. Like Dwight Williams, say. Yet how much simpler had Dwight's case with buxom Emma Drobil been. Stability had been there *ab ovo,* as Herr von Geyrenhoff would have said.

Leonhard decided to set off immediately after his extraordinary breakfast—extraordinary only because brought him by Papa Pepi. His morning exercises still pulsed through his limbs, quite literally, for his whole muscular body often worked along with the liberating thrusts of his mind. Only the autumn in July persisted, footlighted everything, insisted upon its chronological error as though it were the actual truth. It felt so in the red marble staircase, continued to feel so on deserted Reisner Strasse. Here and there a cooled strip of pavement was left over from the night; the sun had not yet come entirely through the morning mist; it cast a milky glow of light between coolness and heat, as it evaporated the last remnants of dew in the gardens. In the city park the sun had already blazed more harshly, especially on the nearer side of the Wien River, in the part reserved for children, with its wide playground, its sandpiles, and the more scattered younger and smaller trees. As he walked along, Leonhard still felt at his back his new home, which he was only gradually animating and occupying; gradually putting his impress upon this vast, ponderous building, upon the two small salons behind the library, where the cool camphor smell lingered in the corners, and upon the glassed-in corridor that looked into the garden whose smooth lawn flowed like pond water around the thick black tree-trunks. The new home was grief. Or perhaps it was still the grief of parting from his old life. For even in shifting from the lowest to the highest point of our fortunes we are never spared the grief of parting—it continues on into our arrivals. That little den of his on Treu Strasse—only now did he see its innate nobility. It had been the scene of his heroic struggles for freedom. A firing station—more than that, a splendid bow which had shot the arrow that now flew into the clear blue sky. But his grief was something else in addition, an expansive autumnal feeling, muted, milky. For having once crossed the boundary between a here—let it be what it might, in this case the boundary of the old "I'll do your prayin' for you"—and a hereafter in the here (in this case the big high house, the small salon, the delicate odor of camphor)—once that shift had been made, it became plain all at once that there were innumerable hereafters in the here, innumerable houses, palaces, villages, garden paths, swimming pools or ponds, innumerable squares and streets like Althan Platz and Treu Strasse.

He had come to the deeply sunken, wide, walled-in bed of the Wien River. On the bridge he looked down upon the two promenades on either bank. Here he attained to the feeling he had never been able to have with Anny Gräven: to long not only for the particular ecstasies, but for her, Mary's, hereafter in the here; to long for a place behind her delicate brow, for the ability to look through her eyes, seen for the first time from within. All morning she had been held off by the strenuous exertions of his intelligence. Now she was with him, all at once and overwhelmingly; she rushed in everywhere like water into a ship that has been forced below the surface.

Punctually, at half-past seven in the morning, Kajetan's gang —now under the leadership of Gaston Garrique—assembled in front of Number 2 Schmerling Platz, where Renata von Gürtzner-Gontard lived. Everyone turned up almost simultaneously. Sylvia Priglinger, already accompanied by the scout (in neat sports clothes and without his javelin), came from the direction of Lerchenfelder Strasse; Gaston Garrique, Lilian, and plump Bully Bullogg from the center of town; and Renata stepped out of her front door just as this group arrived.

At once the "tribe" set off, Gaston in the lead. This morning—
"without weapons or tools"—they did not look especially adven-
turous. Lilian was wearing a white, short-sleeved blouse; Renata
a pretty plaid skirt; and Gaston, the long-drink-of-water, paraded
a pair of light gray flannel trousers which had even been freshly
pressed, and an ocher-colored shirt with flap pockets. Bully, almost as wide as he was tall, had on short khaki pants. He alone
was carrying something, a sporty leather bag into which everyone
had stuffed his bathing suit.

To Gaston's mind the hour was still too early for their coup
against Herr Levielle; they had met so early only to forestall
possible other plans and instructions from the grownups. They
therefore walked slowly toward the Fourth District, Wieden,
but not yet to the vicinity of Johann Strauss Gasse. Then they
set up a kind of headquarters in a small café where it was still
cool and shady.

By then they had long since discovered that something was
going on in town that day. They had also observed the absence
of streetcars. Sylvia, in fact, had some precise information: there
was fear of labor demonstrations. She even said why, but no one
paid attention. Gaston seemed to regard such doings as favorable
to their own project. "A riot in town will be all right for us," he
remarked. It would certainly distract attention from them. Any
kind of disorganization can be helpful to a coup, whether large-
scale or small.

Around half-past nine Gaston set out alone with Bully, who
left his bag in the café with the others. They only wanted to
reconnoiter, Gaston said. They tramped through a large part of
the district to scout the general situation. By ten o'clock they
knew that it was by no means normal. There were few people
moving about the streets, and little traffic; on the other hand,
groups of people had gathered in front of doors, in an obvious
state of excitement. Bully caught talk of shooting reportedly taking place near Parliament (though nothing of the sort could be
heard here). In front of the house on Johann Strauss Gasse, they
observed several persons deep in talk. Gaston and Bully quickly

recognized among them the cleaning woman whom they had recently watched coming from Levielle's apartment, pail in hand, leaving the door open behind her. They could scarcely count on such a lucky chance today. They did not go past the group but swerved promptly at the adjoining house, where no one stood. They went under the archway completely unnoticed, entered the courtyard, had no trouble loosening the wire loop which held the gate to the Levielle garden, and closed it behind them. Now the decisive step had been taken; they felt like arrows that had been shot off and were already flying in a fixed orbit. They strode across the garden, which was not very big, and at once saw that the French door to the terrace was open.

They moved along quickly on the lawn, keeping off the gravel paths. Quietly, purposefully, they ascended the steps and entered a bright, almost empty garden room with an open door at the back. Pausing briefly, they listened, let the stillness simmer in their ears, and controlling themselves masterfully, forced themselves to remain almost perfectly calm. Then they crossed the heavy rug. In the next room they at once saw the imposing baroque secretary.

With Bully watching him in extreme suspense, Gaston went up to the huge complicated piece of furniture and ran his right hand along the side. Because his other hand dangled, unprepared to check the little drawer, it sprang out with an audible clack. The boys looked in at once. There was nothing inside but two copies of typewritten letters, on thin paper, and one original letter. Gaston thrust the papers into his jacket pocket, and carefully pressed the little drawer back until it snapped into place with a soft click and completely disappeared. A moment later they were beating a retreat through the sunlight of the garden. They looped the wire over the garden gate again and slowly went out through the neighboring house and off down the street to the right. A brief glance at the group in front of Levielle's house, still talking volubly, reassured them that no one had taken the slightest notice of them.

Once out on the street, though, Gaston and Bully were nevertheless aware of some uneasiness. They did not take the shortest route back to the little café. Two or three times, at street corners, they glanced behind them. But as was to be expected, no one was following them.

As he entered the back room of the café, where the rest of the gang were sitting—the only guests at the moment—Gaston raised his finger to his lips, commanding silence. Then he said in a terse murmur: "We've got it."

They paid and set off in the direction of the South Station. Not until they reached Maria Josepha Park, which the 1918 Republic had renamed the Swiss Garden, did Gaston make his report. Then the letters were examined. They seemed unimportant. The first were instructions to a lawyer named Mährischl, written at the beginning of the year, in regard to a legacy which the lawyer was requested to take charge of; the matter was roughly outlined in the letter. The gang did not read it through. The second was a copy of a letter concerning the same matter, and written in almost the same language, but dated May 30; this one, however, was directed to a Doktor Krautwurst (the lawyer's name greatly amused them). The third sheet of paper was an original letter from Doktor Krautwurst, dated June 1, declaring his willingness to handle the matter, and inviting Herr Levielle to his office for a consultation.

"All right," Gaston said.

"What do we do with the stuff?" Lilian asked.

Gaston took out his wallet, extracted a stamped, addressed envelope, and put the papers into it.

"We're sending them to the chief," he said. "Let him do what he likes with them." Gaston moistened the flap and using the sporty bag for support, sealed the envelope. They crossed to the railroad station and found a letter box. After Gaston had dropped the envelope in, he suggested that they take the train right there.

"To Klosterneuburg? No, we'd have to take the train at the Franz Josef Station," Renata replied. "And we said we were going to Klosterneuburg."

"It doesn't matter," Gaston said. "I want to telephone to the hotel anyhow. The folks may be worried because of this trouble going on in the city. I'll tell them that we're taking the train here and going out to—where to, Renata?"

"To, to—to go swimming in Vöslau."

"Fine, Vöslau."

"They'll ask what we were doing, staying in town so long."

"That's easy. We went to the Franz Josef Station, big crowds, couldn't get a cab, walked all the way over here. Now all of you stick to that story. Besides, I'll ask my folks to telephone reassurances around, to your parents, Renata, and to Sylvia's mother."

"That's fine!" Sylvia said. "She'll tell your mother right away," she added, turning to the scout. To Gaston, she explained: "We live in the same house."

"All right," Gaston said, and went to find a telephone. He was gone a long time; the others waited in the station near the ticket windows. At last he returned and informed them that he had put through the call but that it had taken a great deal of trouble and patience. The telephone was no longer working properly; there were constant interruptions. In fact he had had to use the office telephone which had been put at his disposal by a railroad official. The official had told him that, for all anyone knew, the telephone might not be working at all later on. ("They're very friendly to foreigners here.")

But they had carried out what they had planned, and done what there was to do. As things turned out, they did not return from Vöslau that day because in the meanwhile the transportation strike in the city had extended to the railroad. They therefore spent the night at the Hotel Stefanie in Vöslau quite like grownups ("without weapons and tools"), dining in the hotel restaurant, dancing in the bar. At a late hour Bully Bullogg very skillfully walked on his hands over the tables, without knocking over a single glass. Lilian and Gaston distinguished themselves in dancing, and in singing American songs, to the great delight and amusement of several ladies and gentlemen from Vienna. The texts of some of the songs were rather risqué. Next day a truck took the six young people back to Vienna.

When Leonhard reached Schottentor and wished to cross the Ring for the second time, he saw an immense crowd of people slowly approaching. They were still some distance away and looked like a moving wall, completely blocking the street. He could make out banners stretched on poles, but could not yet read the text. There was no noise; the procession or demonstration moved ahead quietly. Leonhard likewise had the impression that another such procession was coming down Ring Strasse itself, but he could not yet see this distinctly; perhaps the crowd in that direction consisted only of the curious, or passers-by held up by the traffic police.

That day was full of so-called "instinctive actions," sudden muscular decisions which arise quite independently, almost from outside the self. Usually they are highly surprising, even to the person who executes them.

What Leonhard instantly did was to run diagonally across the Ring. A policeman shouted something and turned toward him. But when he saw Leonhard running up the ramp of the University and disappearing through the door, he probably took him for a student late for a class, and looked away again, back at the approaching procession.

As usual, only one of the huge doors to the colonnaded hall was open; the others were almost always left locked and barred; they were blind, so to speak, and opaque as well with their heavy green wire-glass and wrought-ironwork.

Leonhard slowed down as soon as he entered. What he did was still not an action that came from himself, but perhaps for that reason it all flowed and followed effortlessly, moving precisely in the direction of least resistance. "I beg your pardon," Leonhard said to a small group of people who stood in the hallway—including the doorkeeper, Ernst Mayer, a small man with cap drawn down to his brows, and another university employee—"I beg your pardon, but are you aware that a large demonstration is approaching from Alser Strasse. It might be sensible to lock up."

Instead, the doorkeeper and several of the others stepped out onto the ramp to see what was happening.

"Are you a student?" asked a middle-aged gentleman who had remained inside.

"No," Leonhard replied. "Though I may be, starting next year. I am Prince Alfons Croix's librarian."

"Ah yes!" the other man exclaimed. "I've heard of you. Is the prince coming today? My name . . ."

He introduced himself. Leonhard, although he could scarcely make out the name, and heard only the title "Instructor," realized that the prince had mentioned this very person to him.

"No, the prince cannot come today," Leonhard replied. "That is why I am here."

He was still explaining the purpose of his visit when a din began to be heard, at first diffuse but rapidly swelling to a roar. The people who had stepped out suddenly leaped back inside and began closing the tall wing of the door. It moved ponderously; the instructor and Leonhard jumped forward to help. At last it was closed and barred. "Herr Fessl," the instructor said to one of the attendants, "it might be a good idea to close the small back door on Reichsrat Strasse also."

Fessl started off. At the same moment the noise outside rumbled up the ramp; the tramp of feet resounded under the high archway, and shadows and violent movements could be seen through the thick glass. Then came several heavy blows against the door. Bits of glass, first small, then sizable, rattled to the floor.

Only at this point did Leonhard break free from the fortuitous tracks of automatic action and speaking. And as this happened, there tumbled out of the disintegrating mechanism his real motivation—accounting also for his sudden dash across Ring Strasse a few moments before.

"The door should have been closed at once," he murmured to the instructor. And relapsed into disjunct fragments of thought: "The library—such treasures—Pico della Mirandola . . ."

The instructor betrayed nothing of the astonishment he probably felt. He scrutinized the glazed portion of the door from top to bottom, as though estimating its strength, and said: "Yes, of course, of course . . ."

The noise outside had meanwhile abated. Perhaps the leaders of the demonstration had intervened. Leonhard took his leave: "I must go to the library now."

"Of course, of course," the instructor repeated, shaking hands with Leonhard. "Do give my regards to the prince," he added cordially.

Leonhard went out toward the back of the portico, with the steps on his right, and entered the arcades. The court surrounded by these is immense, as is the whole building. At bottom it is nothing but a Renaissance nightmare on the part of the architect Ferstel (there are also no end of Gothic and Greek buildings of this sort), one of those specimens of art history uncritically applied such as still burden our cities nowadays; in the last century these were regarded as artistic, and the Ferstels, Schmidts, and Forsters were regarded as great architects. We do not think so now. And yet must we not grant that above such copies, such as the Loggia dei Lanci in Munich, or this Renaissance courtyard, the sky seems to grow bluer and warmer, as if the building had brought something along from the land of its origin? When we see such a sky suspended for decades over these pillars and arches, bordering these gables on summer days, we feel that a synthesis has arisen which is really beautiful. Not that we should ascribe such beauty to the genius of an architect who had none. Rather, time, memories, the blue summer sky, and the slight weathering which lessens the assertiveness of such structures, have in their sum gently added the beauty originally lacking. It was still in the big courtyard, and very warm. Beyond the green central lawn, where there was still some shade, students sat reading.

Leonhard was well aware of the wild words that had come to his lips a while before, emerging under stress from some deeper level of his past. He had used the same intonation as once before, when, walking along the Danube Canal with the bookseller Fiedler, he had attempted to explain the fundamentals of his own existence and had engaged in his vain gymnastics with German grammar, constantly repeating: "It remains to be proved, it remains to be proved." That had been long before Mary, far from Mary, in an incomprehensible prior life, one already strong and distant enough to breed a kind of grief or yearning—as had already happened once before, that morning.

But today would be the first time that he would be free to spend many hours at the university library (at least so he still thought at the moment), not the hard-won fifty minutes of the past. Leonhard had not been here since his change of fortunes, for he had been eager to become acquainted, as quickly and thoroughly as possible, with the prince's extensive collection of books. Now, as he paused for a moment in the high hall, which was filled with the pure emanations of mountains of books, a kind of alpine air of the intellect, the progress he had made in so few weeks of life seemed monstrous to him; it engendered a kind of agoraphobia, so vast and open to the sky seemed the new areas of his life. He walked along the railing to the entrance, gave the prince's name, and stated that four books were reserved under that name—he did not have to give the titles, nor did he know them. The books and a seat number were given to him, and he walked over the rather echoing stone floor, which imposed a quiet step, between the long reading tables to his place.

The first book was a work about Pico della Mirandola: Mortetoni. Unfortunately Leonhard did not know Italian.

The second contained texts of Pico in translation.

The third likewise contained texts; it was a collected edition printed in Basel in 1601, and Leonhard quickly found in it that passage he had once come across in Weininger's glorious book— in the very first parts of the treatise, or rather speech "On the Dignity of Man" (*De hominis dignitate*), on page 208 of the first volume.

It was as if the whole meaning of this new phase of his life had been compressed into a shorthand symbol. The weight of it literally bowed Leonhard down. He felt as if the place where he sat in the hall had an enormous weight resting upon it, as if his chair were sinking a little into the floor.

I awoke very early that morning, though not so early as I had at the time of my escarpment walks. The sun was already up. The clock read six. The first thing that occurred to me was that I was to have breakfast at nine o'clock with old Gürtzner-Gontard. He had invited me to such a breakfast once before, at the beginning of June. Obviously a crotchet of his, though of course he gave rational grounds for it, explaining it in humanistic terms, in fact. Only morning conversations could be first-rate, he maintained; you brought to them sharpened dialectic that had not yet been dulled by the pros and cons of a whole day. For all through the day people spent their time thinking in contradictions, suffering distortions and abrasions of the intellect, so that by evening impartiality no longer existed, or at least not to the same extent as in the morning. Only early in the day, he went on, did you have all your resources at your disposal; only then were you still untouched, virginal. Well, let him have his theories. I attended to my toilette, limited myself to a cup of black coffee, and resolved to freshen up my matutinal virginity and stretch my legs by walking. And so shortly after eight o'clock I set out at a leisurely pace into a brilliantly blue summer morning that made a fearfully hot day absolutely predictable.

During those days I was in a state of considerable distraction. When I examined myself, I became aware of a distinct slackening of energies—to the point of being mostly lost in reverie—from the day I had proposed to Friederike that she transfer her funds from the Land Credit Bank to Altschul's commercial bank and had been met by such astonishingly lively agreement. Since that matter had been decided—the transfer was already in progress— I had begun to slacken off. It actually seemed to me that my conception of my surroundings was becoming blurred, as though I were becoming the exact opposite of a man like Scolander. . . . .

Now, too, as I walked along, my state was curious. Not that I was tired or exhausted—why should I have been? But I felt immersed in a kind of milky aura that lay particularly around my eyes and ears, and within that aura were only rounded premonitions rather than the sharp edges of clear thoughts. I knew what knowledge I lacked, what I ought to have known, but this knowledge itself was something I could not grasp. Not only the external world, but my own inner world also had lost distinctness. My sole point of reference, if it deserves to be called that, was the fact that I was expected at Friederike's at five o'clock, to wait with her for Quapp, whose appointment was for six. It was to be hoped that Quapp would be punctual, in keeping with her new character. I had impressed upon her that she must be on time, even going so far as to send her a written reminder.

So I strolled along, in my slight haziness of mind, the warmth of the day already tangible. I cannot say that my new state disturbed me; quite the contrary. Rather, it afforded a kind of well-being that I had long missed, for I had too long been burdened with speculations, mental combinations, and decisions I felt obliged to make. Now at last I was shedding all that and returning to my own proper life.

The streets were empty and still. I plodded slowly along, again thinking that at six o'clock that evening I would be introducing Quapp to the Palais Ruthmayr. Here was an accent after the fact, a piquant detail in the science of life, which does not exist as a science except, perhaps, in the hands of novelists. A coda, nothing more. For all was over. Something new had already begun, or was about to begin, perhaps this very day.

It was not until I reached the end of Nussdorfer Strasse, by the big intersection, that I really began to miss the streetcars, became conscious of the tracks as abnormally dead. In such cases the word "outage" springs to our minds, as the normal key to the situation. I too used this key, without for a moment thinking that in case the electricity had suddenly failed a number of the red-and-yellow cars would be stalled along the tracks.

Content with my inadequate explanation, I slowly climbed the hill of Spital Gasse. Here it was plain hot; the asphalt threw waves of heat up into my face. Alser Strasse was deserted, completely deserted (at this moment, and especially for me, as it were; later I found out that shortly before I reached it, processions of workers had been marching down this very street: I just happened to be there in a hiatus). I plunged into the quiet old streets of Josefstadt. Ten minutes later I stood on the edge of the park which fills the greater part of Schmerling Platz with green lawn and trees. It was too early to go up to Gürtzner-Gontard yet, and too late to prolong my morning promenade any distance. I therefore sat down under the trees, looked at my watch, and whiled away the time. I cannot say whether I really heard anything from the direction of Ring Strasse—noise or sounds of movement. Perhaps I only imagined it afterwards. Finally I rose, crossed the street, and entered the house. It was two minutes before nine. The superintendent—a man named Waschler, whose officious expression always amused Gürtzner-Gontard—stood beside the elevator and expressed his regret at being unable to take me up; the elevator was not working because the current was off. I climbed the stairs.

I entered the big room which faced on Schmerling Platz, the room with the "old Turk" gazing intrepidly from the wall. Today he was looking down upon a table set for breakfast, which stood beneath the portrait. Gürtzner-Gontard came toward me in a flowing silk dressing-gown which he seemed to be inhabiting like an apartment—that was how it struck me—and greeted me warmly. "Punctual as in the army," he said. The tassel of the fez swung forward. "Everyone in my family was up early today. Our Renata is off on a day's outing with the Garrique children—they are relatives of my American daughter-in-law, who has just come over with Franz. You've met the young people already, Geyrenhoff—at Friedl Ruthmayr's reception. Franz mentioned that to me."

"Yes, and was enormously taken with them, I can tell you that," I replied.

"Glad to hear it," Gürtzner said, pressing my hand, which he was still holding. "Just think, my other boy is coming over for a visit too this year. Anatol."

The old man beamed. Again I was stirred by a deep feeling of gratification—as I had been at Friederike's reception—that some things had fallen onto happy paths. It wasn't absolutely necessary for things to go wrong. Here was proof of the opposite. For a moment I thought of Stangeler, of my last meeting with him on the "escarpment" on May 30. In his case, too, solutions had been found—actually been found for everything. Not to mention Quapp. In such moments as this I had strong hopes for myself.

"Yes, our baby, Renata, started off at half-past seven. The rest of the children were waiting for her outside the house. Very punctual, I must say, for young people. A whole troop of them. I saw them from the window. All of them decently dressed, which you can't always say for them. Most of the time they look like Indians, what with carrying spears and bows and arrows, but today even our girl left her 'weapons' behind. . . ."

We had meanwhile taken seats at the table. Eggs were brought in, and tea. I sat facing the window, and this time too the broad prospect struck me as a tapestry hung to form a background for Gürtzner-Gontard's long lean face under the red fez and black tassel: the blue-gray of distant blocks of houses, belonging to remoter quarters of the city, here and there interrupted by the green of isolated trees. In those minutes I comprehended distance and proximity simultaneously, in a strangely alternating interpenetration. Perhaps I was enjoying the peculiar pleasures and receptivities of that hazy state of mind which was mine at the time.

"You know," he said, "I was really quite touched by those young people. A real little troop. Young Garrique took the lead and the others followed behind him. They actually marched off. As I watched, the thought came to me that all people who are born into the same period—contemporaries in the strictest sense—can recognize one another. With the nose, so to speak, like dogs. Their communication is instinctive. Every era brings forth its own race, you might say. These young people, for example, didn't stand around and talk, discuss plans; they just trotted right off with Gaston Garrique, that long-drink-of-water, leading the band. It seems to me that when we were young and were going off on such an expedition, we would have first had to talk about it, at some length."

I agreed with him, but the subject did not really interest me. We had finished our breakfast and lighted cigars. By then the noise from the street could no longer be ignored; we had been hearing it for some time, perhaps, without paying attention. "Well, well," Gürtzner-Gontard said. I went over to the window with him. Not much could be seen. A few people were running through the little park on Schmerling Platz, going roughshod over the green lawns, and from Lerchenfelder Strasse crowds were pouring into the square. At the moment we saw no police. (At such times we always think, first thing, of the police; it is some kind of disease.) After the Hofrat had opened the window, the cries of an enormous throng welled up. These came from the direction of Parliament, but also from closer to us. There was good reason for our seeing no policemen, although we did not know it at the time; they were defending the main gate of the Palace of Justice against the mob. As yet the police had not used any weapons. Incidentally, they succeeded in holding the building only until near noon.

Around ten o'clock René Stangeler left the vault of the Austrian Credit Bank for Commerce and Industry. To the official who closed the vault he said pleasantly: "Kindly give my regards to Manager Mayrinker."

"Thank you, sir," the official said. "Herr Mayrinker is still on vacation; he's out in Pottschach."

René stepped out into the heat of the street and was instantly enclosed on all sides by it. Under his arm he carried the pigskin portfolio (a gift of Grete's) which contained Ruodlieb von der Vläntsch's manuscript.

He had to go on foot in any case. In the first place the route by streetcar was too complicated, involving many transfers, and in the second place the streetcars were simply not running. René easily deduced the reason. Very well then: across the bridge, with the tracks below, the rows of freight cars, and here and there a waiting locomotive sending up puffs of steam. All seen innumerable times. Every neighborhood familiar from childhood is comfortable, because familiar things function so smoothly, and depressing because worn too smooth; neither the eye nor the mind is any longer capable of grasping those small rough spots which are so necessary as stimuli and which any strange city, even any village or ordinary highway, can offer insofar as we are unfamiliar with them. To roughen again the images worn smooth from daily view, or rather, to smash those images in order to find new points of support among the glittering fragments—that requires an extraordinary effort of the mind. Many a person clings to his very first environment, stays obstinately within it, perhaps because he secretly hopes someday to summon up that effort, to find the magic word, Sesame or Mutabor, which transmutes a district known since childhood into the rugged landscape of its true reality. He renounces the refreshments of novelty in order to test his own potentialities against the dead background offered by birth and circumstance, to prove his own creative powers once and for all. *Exemplum docet, exempla obscurant.* Perhaps Prince Croix had really seen rightly.

Such was the case here. The sensations which followed in a particular succession—railroad smoke, open prospect to right and left down the walled bed of the Wien River, softly self-contained salient of green, the city park—in their recurrence these phenomena could sometimes fall into painful ruts and channels. Now, on his way up Wollzeile, things improved. Stangeler began to enjoy the situation which he carried under his arm, so to speak. He became capable of grasping it romantically. Yes, it was really romantic. Neudegg! He had ridden down there with Herzka on May 16. How much had changed since! Now he was entirely free. He could go to see this American, not as a student, but as a younger colleague.

The scene around him roughened up, became more granular.

At the desk in the Hotel Ambassador he gave his name, and was at once asked up.

He was received by Mme Garrique, whom he already knew; nevertheless, she again identified herself as the professor's sister. René once more heard the Hungarian accent in Mme Garrique's German, that intonation familiar in Vienna. He almost asked her where she came from, but something restrained him, as if the question approached unfavorable if not dangerous ground. Mme Garrique struck him as more likable than when he had first met her. What was more, the feeling seemed to be mutual, for she became animated, merry, and at the same time respectful toward René, in a womanly discreet way, as if he were a scholar of standing. She even dropped a remark paying him that tribute. Stangeler, drinking his vermouth and soda, suddenly had the direct impression that Mme Garrique was acting as her brother's delegate.

"My brother will be here any moment," she said. "He just went out to see what all the uproar in the city is about. . . ."

They had just begun to discuss this when Doktor Bullogg came in. He greeted Stangeler with the utmost cordiality. His glance instantly leaped to the briefcase, which René had laid on a chair, and he asked in a significant tone: "Have you actually brought the manuscript with you?"

"Certainly," René replied. "Here it is."

"Splendid!" Bullogg exclaimed, clapping his hands. "Doktor, I'm immensely obliged to you."

His German was somewhat less marked by the Hungarian lilt than his sister's, but no Austrian would have taken him for a native. René bowed slightly in acknowledgment. It struck him as strange that Doktor Bullogg in no way attempted to hide his vital interest in René's discovery—any more than he had done in his letter. René was only too familiar with the manner of specialists in his field, who always tried to belittle any accomplishment of others, especially a person young and still unknown. Even as they did this, they laid claim to the discoveries of such obscure scholars for their own advantage. In spite of Doktor Bullogg's letter, René had been prepared for such an attitude. That nothing of the kind took place quite overwhelmed our René. Moreover, he took an instant liking to the short stocky man.

Smooth-shaven, with thick horn-rimmed glasses, wearing a comfortable jacket under which he shifted his shoulders with visible gratification after he had sat down, Bullogg seemed to have entered completely into the euphoric and good-humored atmosphere of the New World in which he was now living.

The professor first reported on the situation outside. Rumor had it that the police at the parliament building were firing upon the demonstrators; some claimed they could hear the shooting all the way over to the hotel. He himself had heard nothing.

"Daisy," he said to his sister, "a lucky thing for Mamushka that she did not come. I dare say she will give up the idea entirely now. I am speaking of my mother-in-law in London," he added in explanation to Stangeler. "Mme Libesny. She was going to come to Vienna with a friend who is living with her, a young woman whose father is a doctor here. But now there's no telling what will happen next. No streetcars or buses are running; perhaps there will be a railroad strike too. The desk clerk says the telephone is already partly out of order."

At that moment the telephone rang. Mme Garrique went over to the small table in the corner of the room.

"Gaston!" she exclaimed joyfully into the apparatus. "Thank God. Wherever are you children?"

A lengthy conversation followed. Finally Mme Garrique transmitted the news that the children had gone on foot from the Franz Josef Station, where there was a fearful crowd, to the South Station, and were about to take a train out to Vöslau to go swimming. They would not try to return to Vienna until they heard that all was quiet.

Bullogg laughed. "I told you, Daisy, that the children would be safer out of town than here; in town they would be right in the thick of things, simply out of curiosity. Is my Bully with them?"

"Of course," Mme Garrique replied. "Gaston says that he's very proud to be carrying the bag with all their bathing suits. Excuse me a moment—I'll go across the hall to tell my husband and Peggy (she meant Bully Bullogg's mother). Then I'll try to telephone Hofrat Gürtzner-Gontard and Sylvia's mother."

With this apology to René, she vanished (to his regret, as he had to admit to himself). The adjoining room was the professor's. The two men moved into it, briefcase and all, to work together until lunch and, if need be, afterwards too.

Toward half-past nine the same morning, Herr Küffer—general manager, principal stockholder, and virtual owner of one of the most important breweries in Vienna, head of his family and many times a grandfather—drove up to Number 6 Althan Platz to take Mary's children out to Döbling; they had been invited for the entire day and evening to the Küffer house, which resembled a small palace more than a villa and had the requisite extensive gardens. Küffer clambered vigorously out of the car. He was in his mid-sixties, plump but not fat, and extremely agile. He had that capacity to be well liked which is inborn, and which in his case was sustained by enormous inherited wealth and a youth spent in the purple shadows of a great house; a youth in which, also, he had early employed his amiable manner to form all those connections which eventually serve so wonderfully to support a man's activities. The extent to which they so support and facilitate the life of maturity can be fully appreciated only by one who at first lacked such connections entirely and had to build them slowly.

Capping the charm was the freshness of the man (which he probably owed to an early and consistently happy marriage). Since now, at the peak of his life, he belonged to that relatively small class of people who want nothing of anyone, but who for that very reason are met more than halfway by others, he had ample opportunity to help people—and used it. Moreover, individuals with an inborn capacity to be well liked have an inimitable and unlearnable skill in making contact effortlessly, without a jar, even when their character is not essentially benevolent. Likability itself decides relationships a priori; oddly enough, such likability is compatible with a great variety of character traits. The paradox is that likability has no causes. It is not a product of this or that circumstance; all we can say is that this or that circumstance will intensify it.

That was very much the case with General Manager Küffer. Moreover, he himself did possess a benevolent character.

And finally, he had an incorrigible preference for young people and a kind of obsession for giving them pleasure wherever and whenever he could.

He also had a childish disposition. As far as possible he avoided men his own age. Perhaps he fled from their skepticism, their keener distinctions, their subtler judgments. Only toward the young did he display an entirely genuine cordiality. Some might be inclined to suspect that perhaps he was not very intelligent, and that he liked to compensate for this lack by an advantage in years. However that may be, his abilities were altogether adequate to his position. He was never known to have made any wrong decisions, to have taken the wrong track in business, or suffered losses.

His investments in luxuries were considerable, but carefully calculated and controlled. Such was the case with the new swimming pool in his garden, or rather his private park. For a private pool, it was simply enormous. Magnificently engineered, it was set in the level part of the park, turned away from the city and with a view of the open country. Moreover, the pool was connected with a system—conceived by Küffer himself in slow, loving stages of planning—of shallow concrete canals on which you could sail through the entire park on little two-seater electric boats, at one point traversing a natural pond where water lilies grew thickly under drooping willows. The swimming pool was to be dedicated today by a sports festival for the numerous young people of the Küffer household and their friends.

Küffer was very serious about this whole affair.

"Everything's been tested and works like a dream," he said to

Mary immediately after his exceedingly respectful greeting, with its almost tender overtone. He was among those people who highly esteemed Mary's achievement of the past year in Munich. Understandably enough: loving life as he did, he admired her way of surmounting a catastrophe which might have deprived her of a full life.

"Have the motorboats been tried out too, Uncle Benno?" (That was what Mary's children called him.)

"They work perfectly. You'll see. Late last night we charged all the batteries. They're marvelous."

Laughing, Mary clapped her hands. "The trouble you go to, Herr Küffer!" she exclaimed. "And all just to amuse these brats —and yourself too, I suppose."

"You really ought to see it, my dear," Küffer said, filled with pride in his project. "Why don't you come along too?"

"I'd love to, some other time," Mary said. "I have a caller this afternoon."

Trix glanced over at her mother. Her eyes seemed to grow darker, in that manner peculiar to her when she was stirred by some deeper emotion. Herr Küffer inquired with some concern whether Mary was to remain there all alone until afternoon; at least she had her maid there, did she not?

"No," Mary said, "Marie is back home in Moravia on vacation. But I have a good friend here in the house who's going to 'feed' me at noon, as she puts it, and keep me company a bit, and lend a hand when my visitor comes."

Trix looked down at the floor. Herr Küffer remarked that it would be wise for Mary not to go out at all that day. There were workers' demonstrations going on in the city. The streetcars were no longer running.

"There's no current here either," Hubert remarked. "What luck that you charged the boat batteries yesterday. Today that wouldn't have been possible."

"What's that?" Mary exclaimed. "I hadn't even noticed."

Hubert went to the door of the breakfast room and pressed the switch. In vain.

Heaven only knew what might happen in town later on, Herr Küffer said. "I would feel better if you were with us. But at any rate, do stay home all day. And then—there's something else. The real party starts this evening, and will surely go on until very late. I wouldn't want to have the young people's return disturb your rest, and so I would suggest that you allow me to keep the children overnight. We have plenty of guest rooms."

Trix said eagerly: "Oh wonderful! That would be sweet of you, Uncle Benno, if we could stay overnight. And not have to disturb Mama."

"When must you be at the office tomorrow morning, Trix?" Küffer asked. "I can take you over in the car."

"Not at all," Trix replied. "I have today and tomorrow off. That's why I'm home today; I wanted to be free for the party, and since tomorrow is Saturday and only a half day, they gave me the whole week end."

"Fine!" Küffer said. "And Hubert has no school. So we can all sleep as late as we like tomorrow morning and breakfast on the terrace. There'll be high doings tonight. I have a whole box of candles in the car—who knows whether we'll have electric light? —I bought them just to make sure. Have you candles, Frau K.?"

"I always have some in the house," Mary said. "I like keeping them in candlesticks on the piano—it reminds me of my girlhood."

Probably she had touched some hidden memory in Küffer. For a few moments he slipped away, as if into a space visible only to him. Then he returned animatedly to the sole subject that seemed to interest him at the moment: "At ten o'clock we'll shoot off the fireworks. Then we take our cruise through the whole park, by lantern light. There'll be dancing in the garden room, perhaps by candlelight—with real candles in the chandeliers— we happen to have some there. Certainly we're having wonderful luck with the weather."

This last was said in parting. Mary agreed with him about the weather. "I'm glad to have a reason not to go out in this heat," she remarked, laughing.

Really, everything was working out splendidly, everything fitting in. Except that the weather did not remain consistent. But that was not a serious problem. At nine o'clock in the evening, when the rain began, the program was rearranged, the fireworks and lantern sail canceled, and all sorts of entertainments were enjoyed inside the house (by candlelight). The band played and (this much must be mentioned) Hubert K. fulfilled his hopes, which he had twice attempted to do in the course of the day.

Now and then we heard a shot, and after a relative silence, a whole volley. Gürtzner-Gontard and I were standing at the window when there came a knock at the door. We had been looking down at the street, even using field glasses. These lay on the window sill. When Frau von Gürtzner-Gontard entered, I sped forward to greet her. Her parents were of the old nobility of Bohemia, and her German had those Slavic overtones which just slightly make mock of our language and which linguistic connoisseurs highly appreciate.

"There's no reason for that at all, Melanie," Gürtzner now answered her. "Let us be glad the child is out of town; the young folks must have reached Klosterneuburg by nine o'clock. They are safe there. Safer than they would have been here. A good thing I gave her a bit of money to take along. If young Garrique is sensible, and he is that, he won't come back to town with the children until everything quiets down, but will spend the night in Klosterneuburg or somewhere in the neighborhood. The news of what is happening in Vienna will spread like wildfire. No, Melanie, I'm not at all worried. On the contrary, I'm glad Renata is not here at home." (In the Hotel Ambassador, as we have seen, the same view was taken.)

"I suppose you are right," she said.

As she nodded, she looked a little like a sheep, which oddly enough emphasized her aristocratic quality. A certain hypertrophy of nose and lips can make a face look very strong and self-assured, as well as elegant. Such faces are frequently seen among members of old families. I wondered at her calm and apparent fearlessness. No clapping of hands, no fuss and excited talk. She had bearing, and the kind that is not merely the product of upbringing.

She quickly left us, understandably enough preferring to return to the rooms whence she had come, which did not face on the square. As soon as she was gone, I went to the window and again looked down at the woman with the milk bottles. She lay motionless, face downward, on the sidewalk near the little park. She was an elderly woman, probably an old woman, to judge by the obstinate way she had attempted to bring her milk bottles home just at this time. Obviously, she was dead. Perhaps she had been deaf, had not heard the shooting and only thought that some minor excitement was going on here and that she would make her way through it all right. I took the field glasses and looked at her. She was wearing clumsy, lace-up shoes and black stockings, and a skirt of some coarse material which had slid up to her knees. Her hair was covered by a shawl, and it was clear as day that she was dead. She lay in a wide splash of white that had hardened on the pavement and glistened: the contents of two large bottles of milk which she had been carrying in a net shopping bag. Her hand was still clutching the bag, with its shards of glass. Her arms had been thrown forward. Immediately after she had fallen (I had seen it)—whether from a bullet fired by the police or their opponents, was impossible to tell—the milk had radiated swiftly in all directions over the pavement. But then a great quantity of blood poured out beneath her, and soon the two liquids began to mingle. At first they appeared sharply separated: white and red, milk and blood. Milk and blood—in Austria and Germany the phrase connotes vitality and healthy youth. Here a single shot had converted metaphor back to its crudely material fundamental meaning. (And now the milk, together with the blood, trickled into the gutter.) But every metaphor that life shatters implies a loss of human freedom. For freedom can exist only so long as fictions and metaphors are stronger than crude reality, and thus uphold our dignity. In fact every shattered metaphor is nothing but the flag of human freedom trodden into the dust—in this case red and white.

Call it splitting hairs if you like, and say that I had associated too much with people like René and Kajetan—for me that fall of the colors, inextricably linked with the old woman who lay face down, shot to death—that was what brought home to me the gravity and irrevocability of what was happening on July 15, 1927. Only then did I feel the full weight of it—felt that weight bearing down upon far more than this day alone. My feeling was heavier than myself, I might say, as I still stood looking down upon the dead woman who lay there in her milk and in her blood, both by now completely intermixed and soiled. A long thin tongue of the liquid had groped its way along the gutter and was already far from her.

With shots still falling here and there, two members of the Republican Protective Association ran up, lifted the old woman, and carried her away. The stain on the deserted pavement remained. Only now did I recognize the obstruction at the entrance to Lerchenfelder Strasse as a manned barricade. Only now, too, did a sound of harangue penetrate to my consciousness. It was amazing: speeches were being delivered in the square. A revolver had been fired from the barricade only a moment before. The police had not answered the shot. Now there was relative quiet, and for that reason I heard the speakers, mostly women. The voices had a piercing but thin note as they reached my window; they sounded like the noises made by someone hiccuping. The men's voices rang out somewhat better, more resonantly.

I lowered the field glasses. There were three women and two men shouting into the tightly packed crowd that surrounded the Palace of Justice. Naturally I could not understand a word. (These speakers were urging the "mob" to hold off the firemen who were trying to reach the Palace of Justice to put out the flames, but this I learned only in days to come from the newspapers.) The women were dressed like ladies, not at all "proletarian"—and through the glasses I recognized the first of them. It was Rosi Malik, the poetess. She was standing about ten paces from the "mob," gesticulating wildly; at one point she flung both her arms over her head. She was wearing a green summer dress with white polka dots, and had no hat on her red "bobbed" hair. The other two female agitators, however, wore fashionable small cloche hats. There was one I could see very well; she was a frail, pretty little creature with raven-black hair.

I was also able to identify the two men. One of them belonged here every bit as much as a British ship's master belonged in a Polish village, or an occultist belonged at a rugby match. It was no other than our gentle editor Holder. So Alliance was honorably represented here—naturally. As a street-corner orator, Holder seemed thoroughly miserable. He had uprooted himself from his literary flowerpot and was standing by and squeaking. Now and then he attempted forceful gestures. But they were angular and embarrassed, not to be compared with Rosi Malik's, although hers too were fairly spurious.

The other man was Gyurkicz. He was doing far better than Holder. His voice carried well, whereas only an occasional squeak could be heard from the editor. I had the feeling that Imre was having the greatest effect upon the crowd; most of the roars of approval were directed to him. He alone was not standing on the pavement, but had selected an elevated point: the top of a large gray box which perhaps contained sand for strewing the sidewalks in winter, or gravel for the park paths, or gardening tools for use in the park. Whatever it was for, Gyurkicz stood on it and addressed the crowd, obviously with great success. It was plain to me that Gyurkicz was employing the shallowest and most commonplace means to work upon the crowd, and for a few seconds I was actually overjoyed that I could not possibly make out what he was saying; there at the window I felt protected against those platitudes. They were the means which corresponded with his own nature, as with that of his audience. An old cartoonist, commercial artist, and propagandist, he knew his audience because he was one with it himself. Imre too was playing a part. I knew that, with absolute certainty. He was taking over, lock, stock, and barrel, the "revolutionary orations" he had seen and heard, perfect models which needed no embellishments from personal experience.

The Malik woman was a termagant.

Holder's brazenness was artificial; he had to whip himself up to it.

But Gyurkicz's brazenness was genuine and naive, and for that reason effective.

Once again shots cut across the squeaks, rantings, and shouts of the orators. First one, then ten or twelve shots replied. From where I was I could not make out who was firing, nor at whom. In spite of the elevation—Gürtzner-Gontard's apartment was on the top floor—it was impossible for us to take in the whole situation. The façade of the Palace of Justice was turned away from us, and its narrow side blocked the view; otherwise I would later have been able to see the fire engines caught in the crowd. Similarly, the trees of the park concealed part of the scene. When the shots rang out, the speakers vanished. I cannot say that I actually saw them running or retreating into the crowd; I can only give my highly subjective impressions (such as I am doing throughout this whole account). I must say that never in my life, neither in war nor in peace, had I seen anyone vanish so abruptly as did those who had just been shouting: Holder, Rosi Malik, and the two other women.

Except for one person. That was Gyurkicz.

He remained standing on his box and turned slowly in the direction from which the firing had come. As he did so, he thrust his hands into the pockets of his trousers. So he stood upon his pedestal. I studied him through the field glasses and saw that he was well dressed, as always, this time in rather sporty clothes, his lightweight and light-colored summer hat precisely centered, inclining neither to left nor to right. What Imre was looking at was hidden from me by the trees of the park. I held him now in the circular field of vision of the glasses, and studied him; in magnification he seemed quite close. When more shots fell, he leaned forward slightly, jerked his right arm backward, and next moment lifted his arm, now holding a pistol, and fired. From behind him, where people were taking what cover they could, there were shouts of "Bravo!" Imre fired again.

He was using the big pistol I had seen in his room—one of his emblems, then, like the steel helmet or the skull of his "fellow-officer" (or "executed criminal," as the story of the moment might be) that stood on the chest. An emblem suddenly finding employment, plunging into the thick of utility. It gave me a pro-found scare. The woman with the milk bottles had opened my eyes. Seconds before, I knew what was going to happen. Meta-phors were crashing to the ground, emblems breaking through their false bottoms into reality. It could not help happening—to Gyurkicz too. Every such consistently played fantasy sooner or later explodes into life.

He was still firing when there came a crack that seemed to float across the square, and wrenched Imre backwards, off the box.

In this case too I realized at once that he was dead. What fell from the improvised platform was a lifeless sack that remained lying motionless, not outstretched, but somewhat bent in the middle, intercepted by the low paling of the park, which did not allow his head to fall quite to the ground.

It seemed to me in those clairvoyant seconds that Imre had been killed not by bullets but by the high-tension current of life itself, in which he had created a short-circuit. It is impossible to equip and adorn an inner surface, a false bottom, with many emblems over a period of years and then use one of the emblems to shatter it. The sudden contact with naked reality is fatal. Time-honored lies which play their necessary part in the econ-omy of the psyche cannot suddenly be replaced by truth. Every second reality that is abruptly displaced by first reality leads to death.

Here, however, sheer pose had been transformed from the shadow to the substance of real bearing. I was with him entirely; it was as if I were inside him; I thought of the old song, "I had a comrade . . ." Truly, a part of myself fell to the pavement with him. Those seconds were the actual result of my chronicling.

What I had just seen, and still saw, was the whole fruit of Imre's life. And it was good, it was sublime, even though he had harvested it only by his death. It was the restoration of his honor, the healing of his deepest injury, the elimination of his most secret shame. The man who lay there had had a right to call himself Imre Gyurkicz de Faddy and Hátfaludy.

A parallel for his accomplishment would have been for Quapp to overcome her compulsive tremor, to extirpate that blackest, innermost shame—which she never had been able to do. The rushing torrent of thought whirled that idea too through my mind, at the very moment I was being shown with what celerity the mechanism of life can conclude any biography at any time so that its center is cast up, the round hazelnut springs forth from the split shell and lies for a moment smooth and glistening in plain sight. Only for a moment. For I confess that the very next moment produced a countercurrent in me, the thought: "The true fruit of all my chronicling is Friederike." Today, when everything is in every sense over, I know different. My first thought had been true. Of all those who had known the man lying dead down there, perhaps still clutching his emblem (I could not see this too plainly), I was probably the only one who understood him, who grasped the honorableness of his miserable death, who was with him now. For that, and for no other end, I had begun my scribblings and learned from them, been shipwrecked in the course of them. *Primum scribere deinde vivere.*

I turned away. Gürtzner, too, who was looking out, gazed gravely down at the dead man. "He was a friend of mine," I said —for only now could I really say that. I laid the field glasses on the window sill.

"*Oremus*," Gürtzner answered and added the first two versicles of the *De Profundis*. I fell in at the third ("*si iniquitates observaveris, Domine: Domine, quis sustinebit?*"). After the last shots it had grown quieter in the square down below. Shortly after we finished the prayer, the noon bells began to ring. I felt a profound astonishment at the cold way these symbols of daily order seemed to comment on the scene.

Scarcely ten minutes after General Manager Küffer had taken Mary's children off to Döbling, Grete Siebenschein came upstairs to see Mary with the news that she could stay with her until five, for that was when René, who was working with the American professor, would be returning. Which, of course, would be no obstacle to Grete's looking in on Mary once again, if she wished.

"But you're expecting a visitor too, aren't you?" she added affectionately.

She knew all about it. Mary always told her the truth. Trix too knew all about it, though not a word had ever been said to her. Trix was the other extreme of habitual ignorance.

Grete was going to prepare a lunch downstairs in her parents' apartment, and then bring it up for the two of them.

"Today I have the privilege of serving you," she said.

Lingering over their coffee, the two women were very happy; they could talk their fill of what was chiefly in their hearts. The outside world introduced no disturbances. No members of the Siebenschein family had gone out. No one called. The only tidings of anything abnormal in the city had been brought by Küffer. Mary and Grete scarcely gave the thing a thought.

Mary had been moved by the way René had asked her pardon, some time before. Then she had heard a great deal about his latest professional successes, and of his better treatment of Grete. That had been enough. René was rehabilitated in her eyes. Mary was too sensible a person to have let her judgment of young Stangeler calcify. Moreover, since she had met Schlaggenberg she had taken a different view of all these matters, had recognized that a person can be preceded by an image of himself which exists independently of the person's reality, has been conceived and propagated by others and is separated from the real person by so deep a gulf that the absurdity can be recognized only by one who stands at least at an equal distance from the image and the object.

"We will wait," Grete said. "That is a woman's main occupation."

This adage had fallen from her lips more than once. Nevertheless, in spite of all the waiting she had done, our Grete had never achieved any mastery of the art of waiting. For no one who truly knows how to wait expects to summon up what he is waiting for by worrying it. Rather, he remains passive. That is what waiting means.

After five o'clock, Grete kissed Mary and discreetly left.

One of the two windows of the room stood half open. Professor Bullogg and René Stangeler sat over Ruodlieb von der Vläntsch's pages. Both men were smoking, the professor a pipe made after his own lines: short and stocky. They were going through several portions of the original manuscript, René helping here and there to decipher certain paleographic idiosyncrasies. At one point he stepped to the window and looked down from the fourth-floor height into Kärntner Strasse and then, leaning forward, peered toward Ring Strasse and the Opera. The gorge of the street ran straight as an arrow, asphalt-paved, under the cloudless blue of the sky; it was far less trafficked than usual at this time. René suddenly thought of Castle Neudegg, of the lens-shaped chamber under the tower, and of that curiously intensified sympathy for Herzka which had come to him there. It had been an insight into the other man's personality, into his intense isolation, while he himself had won down there, for the first time, that supreme sense of freedom. The two states existed in himself, cutting him through down the center, like a painful interval, a partition wall. And he had also thought of Lord Achaz, who had expressed something of the sort to Ruodlieb on the round-way above the drawbridge, after the Lord High Steward and his men had ridden off: "And me seemeth I have ben made ayen whole oute of two halfe men, and the one half was of wode."

Now René heard shots, far away and feeble, yet quite distinct. Professor Bullogg seemed to notice nothing. Was not this partition between what was life and what was wood constantly shifting, backwards and forwards, killing life when it pressed forward? It seemed to him that he knew now what reality was, and knew that its degree was constantly shifting, the degree of coverage between inward and outward. Had he not experienced such a shift this very morning, in walking up along Wollzeile, when all the emptiness roughened up, became more granular and hence more animated? People who wished to see the rigid concrete channels of their lives extended into the infinite future were in fact doing nothing but stalling the continual delicate vacillations of reality. And the moment that vibrant equilibrium was halted, a second reality came into being: the rigid, isolated second reality of Herzka and Lord Achaz, and of all those others who knew precisely how things should be and whom they ought to shoot at, and why. Out of such a second reality came the distant low popping sound, the last dying reverberations of shots, which could be heard across all the intervening roofs.

What was the sense, René thought, of examining variant readings unless one also accepted and absorbed into oneself the truth hidden in the manuscript which now lay on the desk in front of the professor, under his thick eyeglasses? For a few moments Stangeler violently wished that he were already through with this work with Bullogg and could leave. Had he been with Dwight Williams, he would have tried to explain all these insights. But here, he could not even begin, though he did not understand why. Turning back to the desk with a last glance down into the street and at the irregular, old-fashioned ornamentation of the façades—they looked like dirty wares that had stayed too long in the window of a pastry shop—turning back to the desk, the secret of this period lay like a ripe berry in his mouth. His lips were closed upon it, but he did not bite into it.

The bathhouse in one of whose cubicles Frau Fraunholzer, née Küffer, the consul-general's wife, changed into her bathing suit, was painted white. It was considerably larger than such cubicles usually are, and was nicely equipped with a large wall mirror and other amenities. It was unbearably hot inside, although the bathhouse had been erected in the shade of old trees to one side of the big swimming pool. For on that July 15, 1927, the temperature reached eighty degrees, by no means a maximum for Vienna, but enough to start the perspiration flowing from Frau Lea in the closed little place as she stepped into her yellow suit.

There are cases, and these have become increasingly frequent in recent decades, in which the consciousness of an unfashionable appearance has enormously intensified women's modesty.

So it was with this virtually oriental beauty, who at forty-two stood in substantial splendor under her crown of black hair—in splendor and altogether out of tune with the creators of fashion of 1927. She donned a golden-yellow skirt that fell to the knees above the bathing suit (such skirts were still available in those days for the maturer woman), and was closed at the waist by a narrow white belt. Although in this costume the lush but uncontemporary gifts of nature were somewhat lost under the wide loose pleats, Frau Lea hesitated to step out of the bathhouse. Laughter and outcries beat against the white door, the sound of bare feet running, then splashes and a tumultuous uprush of the water in the pool, and simultaneously the low plunk of a dive.

She crossed her arms over her high bosom and stood for a few moments against the inside of the door with head bowed. A brief wave of ideas splashed through that head—for us a sample of the extraordinary respectability of her inner life: the rehabilitation of her marriage as a result of Etelka Stangeler's tragic decease two years before; the happiness she had since enjoyed with her husband Robert, whom the other woman had taken from her for more than five years; their life together now in Belgrade. . . . She was here on a visit to her parents. How young her father still was! Here he had gone and built a big new swimming pool in the park solely for the pleasure of young people, and now he was giving this party to celebrate its opening. She had watched the diving and waited until now to undress; there was no evading it any longer, for everyone was in the water, even Papa.

It may be noted here that the ladies' breast-stroke race had been won with ease by plump Lilly Catona, amid general cheers. To the accompaniment of enormous acclamation, Herr Küffer had presented her with the prize, a set of elegant silver accessories for the toilette table.

Lea stepped out.

The shouting and laughter at the big pool were deafening.

Beyond, one looked into the expanse of greenish-blue hills upstream along the Danube.

After the heat of the cabin, it felt cooler outside, in spite of the blazing sun. From each of the cubicles of the bathhouse a path of stone slabs set into the close-clipped lawn led down to the concrete edging of the pool. Right beside the end of Lea's path stood Hubert K. He was brown and slender as a pencil, more boy than youth. The upper part of his body was feebly developed. He had crossed his arms over his chest and was looking at Lea, without making the slightest movement, or smiling, or attempting to make any contact with her as she approached him down the path. He studied her. His eyes wandered slowly down along her body. She suddenly became aware that earlier, when she had been fully dressed, during the races—in which Hubert had not taken part—he had stood beside her the whole time, and that even when she walked around the pool to watch the diving and swimming, or to look up at the hills, he had managed to be near her. Now he looked first at her shoulders, which were as white as her arms, then at her hips, and finally at her bare knees and legs. What Hubert succeeded in doing would have been extremely difficult for a young man differently constituted: he remained completely outside the situation, so that in fact no situation at all existed between Lea Fraunholzer and himself. He seemed to feel no need to establish a connection. By this coolness he converted the partly undressed woman on the flagstone path to a pure object. It was a monstrous performance. Lea could not endure it. She crossed her arms over her bosom again, as she had done inside the cabin. At that moment Fella Storch came by, thin as a rail, fragile as an insect. Hubert calmly turned his gaze away from Lea, took Fella's arm and sauntered to the pool with her. There he unexpectedly threw her backwards into the water, and plunged in himself.

Trix, who had observed the scene by the bathhouse, felt deprived of one further hope. For now Fella was lost to her for the second time; her deeper understanding with Trix's brother seemed, in spite of everything, to be proved anew. Trix had also observed, of course, the greedy craving with which Hubert had devoured the consul-general's wife when she first appeared, still dressed. Did she no longer attract him? Too fat after all? But even so, did he have to treat her that way?

With justification Hubert would have replied to her that he had treated her in no way. He would have been able to say: "I haven't done a thing to her," just as he had that time he made Fella stroll about in front of the café in Nussdorf, on that false tryst, to the amusement of the whole party he had brought with him.

Moreover, good little Trix completely misunderstood her brother. He was very much concerned about Lea Fraunholzer. For that very reason he was applying indirect methods.

Prince Croix, of course, would never have denied that he had deliberately, if altogether casually, chastised Hubert. Not that it was likely that he would ever have cause to mention the little scene in front of the door at Althan Platz, after the party at Mary's. But Trix had fixed secret hopes upon that very incident, hopes which she admitted to herself, for they were wholly benevolent and hence admissible. The reproof from Croix had seemed to her terribly sharp, and she had hoped that it would teach her brother a lesson.

That he would at last refrain from indulging in a certain type of behavior.

That he would change.

Here we see how young people are incapable of fully grasping one of the hardest facts of life: the absolute constancy of character. Pedagogues too are unable to grasp this; hence their pathetic belief in the possibility of education. Pedagogues have themselves never passed through intellectual puberty. Instead, they take physical puberty in the objects of their educational efforts all the more seriously and self-importantly, and investigate it by the methods of psychology.

Trix turned away from the noise of the swimming pool and walked across the close-cropped lawn under the high trees.

She walked deeper into the park, white-skinned and red-haired, her bare feet in the soft grass, in her blue bathing suit, her small, child's belly bulging slightly. She knew everything (and yet not everything, as we have just seen; she still lacked knowledge of some fundamental things, which would have to be hammered into her at some later date). Among other things, she knew whom her mother was expecting this afternoon. And she also knew what her mother was unresistingly expecting. All would be quiet, at home. Here the festival was due to reach its height this evening—with boats and lanterns.

She walked on. It grew quieter around her. There were tall bushes. The view opened out to a different side, also into open country, vineyards in the foreground, a sky already pallid from heat above the marching rows of stakes that supported the vines.

Hubert and the problem he signified stood like a wall before her.

That came first. Only beyond that wall was what would be happening at home this afternoon. Everything was muted. Once again she thought of sitting by the river with Leonhard. Sucking candy.

Fella, too, was a part of Hubert.

Everywhere, hard walls.

She turned back into the woods of the park, among the bushes. Here the channel ran, the water clear; you could see right down to the smooth bottom, for it was scarcely a yard deep. She wanted to step in, splash about, duck under, cool herself, wet her suit. A loud humming came from behind a bend in the concrete channel. Trix stepped back. One of the small electric boats glided by, a trim, brightly varnished brown vessel. At the wheel sat Hubert, leaning slightly to the left and just touching Frau Fraunholzer, who was staring rigidly straight ahead, with an expression of despair on her face. Almost at the same moment something sprang with whoops and laughter from another bush. It was Fella Storch. She jumped into the canal beside the boat, held on to the rim, and let herself be drawn along, kicking her feet as in the crawl. Trix drew back. She fled. Almost ran. She reached the edge of the woods again, where she had been before, and gazed into the greenish-blue distance. Like billowing clouds, the chiming of the bells rang in her ears. It was twelve noon.

Dust hung in dense clouds above the leaping, running people, and Anny Gräven stood in the midst of the tumult, watching, without any feeling of gloom, but also entirely without amusement. Since she did not know what it was all about, the whole affair did not concern her. No instincts were set going. Our Anny, then, was not very susceptible to excitement. Meisgeier's bold climb had given her a shock; this mere turmoil could not.

The situation so beyond Anny's ken had grown critical. The police had been forced to withdraw from Stadion Gasse—which runs off from the Ring along the narrow side of Parliament. The previous day road repairs had been in progress here, so ample material for missiles and barricades lay around. Cobbles were already piled on the torn-up street. This was why the police had been particularly anxious to seal off Stadion Gasse.

Now a hail of smaller stones flew after the retreating police, accompanied by howls, whistles, and cheers. The larger stones, and the wooden barriers left by the workmen, were used to erect barricades, so that police cars could not pass through.

The band which had left Prater Strasse after eleven o'clock to join in the excitement was now largely scattered, each following his own devices. Pop Rottauscher, for example, promptly plunged into the thickest of the crowd. According to his own statistics, he did well that day, picking no less than twenty-seven pockets, including those of two policemen. His pupil, Zurek, could not boast of such professional stamina. Herein lay his crucial weakness, rather than in that lack of reliability and respectability, or the faculty for looking so, which Zurek had named as the great asset of the older generation—in a talk with the novelist who gave his name as Doktor Döblinger (!). We will remember that Zurek had considered that he could catch up to old Rottauscher in technique, but not in decisive virtues of the personality. . . . Alas, no. The right appearance is never really of principal importance, and was not this time either. The main thing is a real love of one's profession; out of that love flows the unshakable discipline that Pop Rottauscher demonstrated on this day as he went about in the thickest of the tumult, paternally emptying people's pockets. Did Pop Rottauscher bother his head as to the causes or merits of this whole uproar? Not a bit of it. Whereas Zurek was taken in by the imbroglio. He participated in expressions of social antagonism by steadily throwing stones at the retreating police—did so all the more enthusiastically since at this time they were not yet armed with carbines and made relatively little use of their pistols, perhaps because they were beginning to run short of ammunition.

Behind Zurek, who was shouting in a highly unprofessional manner (for his occupation was essentially a noiseless one, after all), stood drunken Piggy. She too was shouting, and to add insult to injury was blowing a piercing whistle that she had picked up somewhere, perhaps taken from one of the wounded and then beaten policemen. To the credit of the two Greeks, let it be said that they were far less prone to abandon their normal parts in life and plunge head over heels into politics. They were only frisking civilians who lay about, more or less severely wounded. One of the two Hellenes was caught when he applied himself to his fourth victim. The police then gave him a beating, in our opinion quite rightly.

Anny Gräven suddenly decided she had had too much. She gave her friend Piggy a good kick in her fat behind and stalked off before Anita was done bawling her out. It turned out that it was not difficult to leave this inferno, if you wanted to. Anny made her way through the Rathaus Park—though in parts of this park the police were shooting it out with isolated demonstrators—and even passed the University. Now and then she had to run. Once on the Ring, however, she sauntered along. It was hot. The avenue was on the whole empty under the blue sky. Prater Strasse, particularly, was deserted. She marveled at how she had suddenly become mixed up in the riot, and how easily she had got out of it again. It occurred to her that she still had something to drink back home, wine and brandy. The thing to do was to go straight home. To have nothing to do with all this, certainly not with the police. Her room. Drink and smoke cigarettes.

Reaching her apartment at last, Anny felt something that really approached happiness. She closed the curtains and took off all her clothes; she wanted to have a good scrub and get rid of the horrible dust. No, no, all that was not her sort of thing. Whatever was she doing there? First drink. The wine gurgled into the glass. She inhaled her cigarette, stood beside the night table by the bed, and made the little Punch that lay there kick his legs. She laughed.

Quapp spent the entire forenoon in that same state of stillness and separateness she had enjoyed early in the morning, accompanied continually by the feeling of never before having experienced such a pitch of noiselessness. It is curious that she attributed this partly to her own mood, partly to the emptiness of the apartment, when in truth the phenomenon was an objective fact in the city around her. Those hours from nine to twelve had a quality of extraordinary disengagement; she was also disengaged from all plans or postponed duties. With enjoyment, she dipped into one of her brother's novels, and believed that she was really understanding the book for the first time. But all sorts of things can go on in people under the cloak of reading. While she read, Quapp was mostly returning by roundabout routes to a time and aura that had existed "before all that": before her first stay in Vienna, before that young musician, before "our crowd," before Gyurkicz, and long before Eroica Gasse, which last episode in her life seemed altogether astonishing and alienated from her. It was a return to the aura of a substantial and refined home of the past, and that return held within it the resolve to enter such an aura once more, having created it herself, and never to leave it again. From next year on, moreover, she would have the means for it.

With that decision, everything that had happened to her since she left or was forced out of her onetime home fell into the category of foolishness and error.

She suddenly recalled a tiff she had had with her mother's companion, the Englishwoman, Miss Rugley. It simply wasn't possible for anyone to reprove her in her own home. She saw the garden room of her parents' house, the green light from the tree-tops creating a mossy and subaqueous atmosphere, and on the heavy old sideboard the huge punch bowl with its host of green glasses. And in the same momentary vision she felt that Géza von Orkay was like a gate, the gate to her own house. She saw that house in its hilly landscape, and it came to her that Géza was perfectly suitable to form such a gate. That was Quapp's literal thought: the word "suitable" actually came to her mind.

These musings affected her strongly. She dropped the book and turned toward the balcony.

Now, as she stepped out onto it and looked down into the rosy stillness, she saw at once, as though through inverted field glasses, deep into small and remote Eroica Gasse. It was as though her gaze probed a deep hollow in the green street, as if Eroica Gasse were not illuminated by the sun, which did occasionally fall through the tops of the trees there, but were glowing from within. For the fraction of a second Quapp still felt, in this suddenly given perspective, the agitations and struggles of the first part of her biography. How faraway that struggle had become! And then it subsided below the surface forever. The breath of recollection, the message from the recent past, had brought with it an echoing afterpain. Already, it was over with.

Everything was over with. While she stood on the balcony looking down into the roses, the church towers in the vicinity began striking twelve o'clock. She could hear the bells of the parish church of Hietzing, of Penzing, and even the tiny bells of Ober-St. Veit. Quapp already was well acquainted with her new neighborhood, having taken many an exploratory walk.

She turned promptly back to the room and began her preparations for going into town. At eighteen minutes after twelve she slowly left the apartment, after checking the gas stove, kitchen taps, bathroom taps, lamps, ash trays. . . . During Quapp's first days in her new apartment, her landlady had often observed her new lodger going through this routine, and perhaps the good lady had left for the country the day before that much easier in her mind.

Quapp went down the old-fashioned staircase. Such unrural stairs, in a villa quarter or garden suburb close to the actual countryside, were ostentatious reminders of a period that was always ostentatious, even in the midst of rusticity: a period of cravats and detachable cuffs, top hats and flounces.

She walked down to the main street of Hietzing to take the streetcar. The summer heat was intense; Quapp realized it only now, for all morning she had been protected by the coolness of the shady apartment and, at the last, the amply scented water of her bath. No one was waiting at the streetcar stop. That must mean that a tram had just passed. Quapp stepped into what shade she could find, under the branches of a tree reaching over the sidewalk from a nearby garden. But there too it was hardly shady; the asphalt sent up shimmering waves of heat in a positively alarming manner.

Quapp stood there for some time. It was approaching half-past twelve. At last a link formed in her mind between two empirical facts: that there had been no electricity in her apartment, and that no streetcars were moving in either direction. That was why no one had been waiting at the stop. (As usual, Quapp was one of the last persons to discover the obvious.) So the electricity must be off. That too explained the marked silence of the morning. The whine of the streetcars, which habitually rode very fast along the long straight main street of Hietzing, had been missing: that characteristic rising chromatic scale when a tram came speeding up, and the tinkling of its bells.

But Quapp was in such wonderful equilibrium these days that she was not discomposed. She began walking at a deliberate pace toward Hietzinger Platz. By cab she would arrive too early rather than too late. The thought that the trip would be expensive touched her mind, but produced only a faint vexation. The first cab stand to which she came was empty. She walked slowly on, determined to avoid all violent movement in order not to become overheated and upset—so composedly did she look forward to her rendezvous with Géza. After another thirty steps a cab came rolling slowly toward her around the corner near the Park Hotel; it was obviously returning to its stand. She stopped it and said to the driver, a cross old man who reached back to open the door: "To the Opera Restaurant." The man mumbled something under his breath that Quapp, sitting in the back, did not make out. Then he turned around and drove very fast toward the city. The vehicle was old-fashioned and jounced heavily. Quapp was thrown back and forth on the seat.

They drove down the suburban portion of Mariahilfer Strasse, which has a market at a lower level than the street itself; from the car Quapp looked down at the roofs of the booths. They passed the vicinity of the West Station, with its dreary expanses —that most unattractive part of the city. Then uphill along Mariahilfer Strasse, between rows of houses coated with an ever-varying mange of advertising posters and business signs. Now they were on the last stretch, dropping down even more sharply than they had climbed, toward the center of town. The cab suddenly braked abruptly. Several men stepped forward. They had on something like the khaki lumber jackets which Quapp had seen on skiers. They were young men, and Quapp's first impression was that they had very decent faces and were looking grave. One of them opened the door of the cab and said to Quapp: "Please get out; this car is needed to transport the wounded."

Quapp looked at him and blinked her eyes. Here, in this harmless little scene, her habitual ignorance reached its zenith.

"But the lady's got to pay first," the grumpy cab driver said. Quapp paid and found herself standing on the edge of a traffic island. One of the members of the Republican Protective Association had swung into the seat beside the cab driver and ridden off with him. The others were already stopping another car. It was a large elegant limousine. "Extraterritorial vehicle, Royal Hungarian Embassy," Raymond Szilagi said in his mellow, calm bass. Géza sprang from the car, went up to the leader of the paramilitary troop, and said: "Legation Secretary Orkay." He produced identification. The leader did not look at the identification; he had just caught sight of the CD (*corps diplomatique*) on the car's license plate. Géza had already reached Quapp's side. "Why, Quappchen, Quappchen . . . . get in quickly!"

"Let them pass," the troop leader said, and signaled to his men to step back.

"Out of the city, Raymond!" Géza called in Hungarian to the chauffeur. "Drive up Mariahilfer Strasse and then turn right and work your way through the little streets, to Neubau, to Grinzing and up Kobenzl."

Raymond Szilagi turned the car. Quapp briefly explained her difficulties. Géza said that the ambassador had dispatched him to see what was going on in town; the car's plates would protect him, and if things grew too ticklish, so that he could not return to the embassy, he was to drive out to the suburbs somewhere and wait until the city quieted down. The ambassador hoped that he could by these means bring in a report on the general situation by evening. He could already have had it, for Géza had by that time driven up and down in the city. But now he took particular pleasure in following the second part of his superior's instructions, to wait out in the suburbs. "No sense in having bullet holes through the car," he said, laughing.

"Why, is there shooting . . . ?" Quapp asked, wide-eyed. But —of course, she had heard it herself. Now she realized that. She had only not grasped the meaning of the sound. While she stood on the traffic island she had heard, far off in back of her somewhere, small pattering, chattering sounds. Only now did she become fully aware of this earlier sense-perception. Géza leaned forward. "Stop a moment, Raymond," he said. "Fräulein von Schlaggenberg wishes to hear shooting." The car stopped on the right side of almost deserted Mariahilfer Strasse. Several of those reverberating, pattering, chattering noises could now be heard over the tops of the tall buildings. They sounded like small boys' cap pistols.

Quapp looked wide-eyed at Géza. "Why—what has happened . . . ?" she burst out.

"I'll tell you all about it some other time, Quappchen. Salvos in honor of a dead boy."

That was entirely beyond her understanding. The car started up again, left wide Mariahilfer Strasse, and worked its way around many corners through the Seventh District. Quapp noticed small groups of people gathered in front of doors. Géza sat facing her, and she him. With absolute irrationality, Quapp had the feeling that she had left her violin case there on that traffic island at the beginning of Mariahilfer Strasse. Today too she was riding away from everything, escaping from difficulties into the open country. Géza was radiantly happy about this encounter. Now they gathered speed, roared uphill. The main intersection. Szilagi stopped, although there was scarcely any traffic here. They had long since passed beyond earshot of the shooting. Billroth Strasse opened before them, wide and empty, and led them up toward Döbling.

In the afternoon Meisgeier turned up just in time to catch Didi, for she was already in full harness (and carrying her swollen briefcase), prepared to go into town to see what was going on there—despite the protests of old Freud, who did not like being left alone at such troubled times. Besides, he would now have to stand in the shop, instead of taking his nap in the back room.

"Coming with me?" Meisgeier said.

"Where to?" Didi asked.

"You'll see," he replied. "We're going to give the cops an eyeful."

Within the hour it was going to seem altogether incomprehensible to her why she had followed him without further question.

They walked down Alserbach Strasse, then across the square in front of the station and as far as the bridge. Here Meisgeier turned to the right and went down the steps. Down below, he led the way quickly further down the embankment and dived into a huge opening, very wide and high, the overflow outlet of the Als River, which runs underground. At the moment it was perfectly dry. Once upon a time, in the Middle Ages, the Als had been a clear stream coming down from Neuwaldegg and running through a pleasantly green valley in which only a few rural houses stood, and one relatively large building, a hospital.

Now, however, Meisgeier hustled Didi into a vast long corridor with a stone floor, stretching on into darkness under the belly of the city. Cold, depressed air wafted into their faces, not exactly stinking air, but the extreme opposite of a living, vital atmosphere. It quickly became dark. Meisgeier, who near the entrance had clung close to the wall so as not to be seen from the bridge, now walked more slowly in the center, his footsteps echoing. Anna Diwald followed close behind him. Once she turned around and looked back toward the bright light of the exit.

Ordinarily this great hall would shake at regular intervals with thunder from above: the trains of the "city line" (as the elevated and subway trains of Vienna are called). At one point their viaduct formed part of the ceiling. The heavy steel piers could be seen. But today no trains were running.

Meisgeier paused in the darkness, slipped off his rucksack, and a moment later the big electric lantern he had strapped around his waist flashed dazzlingly. In its long cone of light an elevation appeared, reaching from the right into the great hall and crossing it diagonally toward the left. They walked toward it. It was the raised, walled-in bed of the Als, with its weir and spillway for high water. Iron rungs led up to it. Here the underground river makes a bend and then runs parallel to the Danube Canal as far as the so-called "spillway chamber" under the end of Ring Strasse, where that street runs into the Franz-Josefs-Kai.

Meisgeier turned to the left.

What he dragged out, scraping it along the stone floor, was a small skiff, almost new, freshly calked, a boat that could well hold two persons.

Now the possibility of protest came to Didi's mind. Had she known that it would be her last, and that from here on she would be completely in Meisgeier's claws, she would probably have seized this opportunity and returned through the underground corridor back to the light of day. Perhaps Meisgeier sensed the importance of the moment better than Didi. He helped her over her momentary scruple with a: "Lift. You're a plucky girl."

With extreme effort they raised the skiff to the level of the water and placed it on the dark, rapidly moving surface, Meisgeier first fastening ring and chain to the iron railing. There had been no necessity to lift the boat over this railing. At the top of the ladder was a gap in the railing permitting direct access to the water, for the trained crews of the city sewerage department used skiffs to get from place to place in the underground system. The chief difficulty here was the slipperiness of everything, especially at the edge of the channel. A whole mess of poultry intestines, for example, had washed up on the rim, and there was other filth from the household sewers that emptied into the underground river. Didi had to climb down once again. Meisgeier gave her a pair of rubber boots from the rucksack and rags for stuffing them. With these, the boots were fairly tight, although they were far too large. Later on this particular footgear proved a considerable hindrance to Didi. The boots reached over

her knees and kept her dry. But Meisgeier with his leather soles
was to have better footing in the underground shafts.

"How'd you get the boat in here?" she asked while she was
tugging on the boots.

"Took a man t'help me," he said, and that was all. Now came
the perilous operation of getting into the boat. At last it was
done. Meisgeier had a short oar. He did not drop the limp
rucksack into the boat but put it on his back.

Then ring and chain were loosed, and the skiff immediately
glided off, but at a slower pace than would have been imagined
from the appearance of the rapidly flowing water. Didi could see
almost nothing. She sat in the front of the boat, her back to the
direction of their motion, and was blinded by the glaring light of
the lantern Meisgeier had strapped around his waist. The Claw
peered attentively ahead, moving the oar now and then. Didi
too wanted to see ahead, and turned around slightly on her
bench. But she could see nothing but the rushing water, and
felt as if she were in a tube that extended no farther than the cone
of light. She could not have said whether the tunnel was high or
low, narrow or wide. Her sense of isolation, in fact of utter displacement from her normal life into an entirely different world,
was so intense that she felt almost no fear. At the moment she
had not the slightest recollection of the bright upper world;
there was no partition or interval between her present situation
and her true self, and hence no pain, no anxiety, no longing to be
back. Nothing of the sort. The boat glided on. Perhaps they had
already been there half an hour.

In reality they used the boat only eight minutes, debarking
from it in the quiet, deep waters of the spillway chamber. To get
out now was not so simple. They had to scramble up to a kind of
small mole which was at most two feet wide and divided two
basins. They had to walk twenty or twenty-five feet along this
ledge. Meisgeier gave Didi a hand. Under the sharp light of the
lantern they climbed a number of slippery steps in a winding
staircase.

The Claw was no habitué here. He knew the place only

casually, had never been a sewer rat (and would have resented any such imputation—but then he would never have proclaimed that he had worked as a second-story man either). Under Ring Strasse run two tunnels. The one on the right, reckoning from the direction toward the University, is concrete-lined and has a walkway. That is to say, the current runs in a sunken bed, and along it is a continuous raised platform, so that it is possible to walk dry-shod. This sewer leaves Ring Strasse before the University and turns off toward Alser Strasse. The left tunnel—which is by far the older—is brick-walled and has no walkway. To follow it, it is necessary to walk in the water, which runs swiftly in the opposite direction and splashes up to the knees, while the feet vainly seek firm footing on the slippery bottom. This old brick sewer leaves Ring Strasse later and leads directly underneath Schmerling Platz. Didi and Meisgeier followed it.

It was hard going, in running water and against the current. Meisgeier suggested that Didi keep her hands on his shoulders as she followed along behind him. That helped her keep her balance. From one arm her bag hung suspended by its leather handle. So they marched along in step, like a pair of soldiers.

In such tunnels beneath the roar of the street traffic there are niches opening out to the side, provided with iron rungs leading up to sewer gratings. Through these some daylight falls. Ordinarily, every passing motor vehicle casts a brief thunder, a gush of noise, down into the sewer, and under such a main artery as Ring Strasse such shudders would normally follow one another in ceaseless succession. But there was very little of the sort today, and during the last part of this march under the street, nothing at all. But as they again approached a niche in the branch away from Ring Strasse, another kind of roar sounded from above: the noise of innumerable running and tramping shoes, and a tremendous wave of screaming, women's voices rising to the highest falsetto notes, crying again and again: "Shame, shame!" Then came a momentary silence; not a sound seeped through the grating. This silence was replaced by a rhythmic pounding that approached, passed directly over the grating, and was gone. Immediately afterward the heavy multiple beat of a salvo of rifles crashed down, and against this the wave of screaming surged from farther off.

Meisgeier entered the niche and climbed up to the grating. Didi likewise emerged from the water and stood below him.

During the tramp through the sewers, stirrings of protest had risen in her again, restrained only by her increasing suspense, which had now become a raging curiosity centered on a single point: what was this close-mouthed Meisgeier going to do, what had he in mind to express his fervent hatred of the police. Only for the sake of seeing this, of finding out, did Didi keep going. By now anxiety was welling up within her, as though filthy water were incessantly rising in the narrow shaft. Didi wanted to get out of there. Side by side with the suspense, something within her was preparing to burst out, something frightful and destructive, a mute roar of desperation.

Above her, the Claw unslung his rucksack and produced an object which he examined carefully. Didi was completely mystified. It seemed to be a long thin steel rod, about three feet long, or perhaps an extremely strong wire. There were narrow firm handles at either end. She saw Meisgeier compress the tool and thrust it through the grating, so that the handles came directly under it. He stood this way, on the ladder, arms raised high above his head. A moment before there had been fresh running and trampling, a screaming roar above the grating. Now, after a brief silence, came the marching tread of the police. Just as a shading of the sunlight indicated that they were passing overhead, Meisgeier threw all his weight on the handles, then released one end and in a flash drew the whole rod back through the grating, while his other hand clung to the rung for support. Above him came noises of a fall, thumping and scrambling, a police carbine hitting the ground. But soon this was followed by the rattling spatter of a salvo.

Neck thrown back, eyes staring upward, Anna Diwald saw this maneuver repeated three times. She held her precious briefcase pressed against her chest and barely choked back the roar of desperation and rage which was gathering in her. For now she saw her situation in its true light: she was immured in this shaft with a childish lunatic, with no possibility of retreat or flight through the hissing darkness behind her, without a light, without knowing the way. Like a spider, the horrid creature above her clung to the iron ladder. Her breath gave out. Now she managed to fill her lungs again, and her self-control was gone: she screamed piercingly. At that moment a shadow again passed over her, and a fearful crash followed that seemed to shatter the entire lower world with thunderous reverberations.

By one o'clock it became relatively quiet around the huge building, from which the flames were already snapping and crackling. From our window we could smell the odor of burning, although not a breath of wind leavened the sultriness of the day. The ominous stench gradually permeated the Hofrat's study. What was burning over there was largely paper—it could already be seen rising in sprays of sparks and sifting down in innumerable flakes of black ash. Stacks of documents dating back decades were aflame; soaked with kerosene, they had been used to start the fire. Among other things, the property registers of Vienna were destroyed.

Men of the Republican Protective Association had carried off Imre von Gyurkicz's body before the shooting stopped. This party guard, trained to be a fighting group, had taken over the duties of a medical corps, rescuing the wounded and administering first aid, piloting women and children out of the zone of fire (although most of the women present were active demonstrators who shouted slogans louder than the men). From medical corpsmen they soon became scapegoats. Uniformed as they were, but mostly unarmed, they made prominent targets for the rifles of the police. At the same time they aroused the ire of the crowd, which had already changed its composition. The original demonstrators had been workmen. Now the crowd was only rabble. "Swift as the louse and the arrow," says a Turkish proverb; but indeed the rabble is even swifter, and it hears every rumor. The rabble wanted a riot; the paramilitary troops wanted to quiet things and restore order. They wanted to help, and helped everyone, wounded police as well as citizens. But they could not beat a path for the firemen to the burning Palace of Justice.

That day I saw two mysterious incidents. The first of them occurred just below the house, shortly before Frau Gürtzner-Gontard called us to dinner. By half-past one the street between the house and the park was almost deserted. Fewer and fewer policemen had been coming by, and now they seemed to have disappeared altogether. I observed two boys of sixteen or seventeen busying themselves at the foot of a tall street lamp which stood in front of the house, its curved swan's neck reaching up to the third or fourth story. The young people were carrying tools, including an iron crowbar such as is used for prying up cobblestones. They set to work with all deliberation. I had time to see them remove the paving from around the foot of the street light, exposing sand and earth. Then Frau von Gürtzner called us to table.

We went through the wide dark vestibule and through a salon with china closets and armchairs and a large oil painting of an interment—perhaps belonging to the mannered school of Guido Reni. The atmosphere here was still and solitary, slightly perfumed by the leather of the chairs, and exuding a delicate hint of camphor. As we passed through the door into the adjoining room I became aware, with a physical pain, that a whole rioting city separated me from Friederike, with whom I was supposed to be by five o'clock. All the while we were dining, it was as if a clock were ticking inside me, warning me that I should use the relative calm of the moment to leave, to get out to Wieden, to the vicinity of the Palais Ruthmayr.

Later events proved that I would have done well to heed this inner command.

We remained sitting at table for a long time. We had had enough of what was going on outside. Frau von Gürtzner was by now easy in her mind about Renata. Toward eleven o'clock the

clerk of the Hotel Ambassador had managed to put through a telephone call (probably one of the last of the day) to her, and Mme
Garrique had transmitted the news about the children.

Here in the dining room, as we were taking our black coffee, I
became conscious again of that cool, delicate odor of camphor. Oh
well, it was midsummer now. That scent could be detected in all
apartments that had shut themselves off from the heat and noise
of the streets. It was almost as if the scent were giving tidings of
a salvation inherent in isolation, inviting one in more deeply. At
one point Gürtzner-Gontard and I went to the front of the apartment again to see what was going on. But nothing was going on.
A chain of unarmed members of the Republican Protective Association had surrounded the Palace of Justice, by then partially
hidden by flames and smoke. I looked directly below, toward
my two young people near the street light. They were still there
and had made good progress. No one interfered with them. The
square was deserted at that point. Around the pole was an open
pit, exposing the conical pins, several yards long, which hold
such street lights in the ground. As I watched, the boys seemed
to decide that they had done enough, for they laid their tools
aside. At their call, others came running up, and with rhythmic
cries of "Push-pull!" the pole was shaken loose of its last grip
on the ground. Soon it began leaning toward the roadway. And
suddenly it "gave," as woodcutters say of a tree. It was exciting
to watch. "Now," Gürtzner-Gontard said. Down below all the
young men had jumped several yards away from the foot of the
pole. As if a man had drawn back a long arm to strike and were
now delivering the blow, the tall slender column began to fall,
faster and faster, until it met the asphalt with a thunderous
crash, while at the same time its base leaped entirely out of the
ground, tearing up still more pavement and throwing earth into
the air. The top of the fallen iron tree lay across the road near
the park railing. No smallest fragment of the shattered lamp
could be seen.

It did not occur to me that this mighty trunk made a wonderful base for a barricade, and that even as it lay, long and gray

amid the smell of burning, it would block all police cars. I did not consider the purpose of the action at all. It seemed to me entirely apart from purpose, not the product of deliberate intent on the part of those who had felled it, but proof of a profound instinct in them. What had been felled here was part of the street lighting, and as such represented the continuity of daily life. That street light had been a feature of our ordinary ways, helping us to see. . . . Now no one wanted to have any part of those ordinary ways; at least the young people who had felled the pole did not. They might equally well have destroyed the church steeples after the ringing of the noonday bells; only the street light was more easily reachable.

"Productive activities of revolution," Gürtzner-Gontard said behind me; he too had been watching the felling of the pole.

He excused himself for a few minutes, saying that he wanted to go down to the front hall: Waschler, the doorman, would certainly have some news. I was left alone.

Meanwhile, the flames about the vast building opposite rose ever higher and brighter—Justitia in flames, producing relatively little smoke, but the glow of the fire was beginning to dart about behind windows that had not yet been shattered. Other windows, already black holes, had serpents of rushing smoke writhing out of their upper halves. The chimneys on the roof, which was already partly aflame, looked like red-hot barrels of cannon.

I looked down again at the fallen iron tree. It lay quite abandoned now; no one paid any attention to it. It flashed through my mind that the street light was blocking the very path I had taken exactly two months before, after visiting my former superior here, the path that had led to the solution of almost all pending questions, for later on the Graben I had run into the pseudo-Levielle, he of the surgeon-general's staff, or whatever he was; and then into Sergeant Alois Gach; and then, to top it off, we had met Quapp. . . . Now the iron tree lay here, truly a fallen symbol of the age, marking its passing, closing a stretch of life's track like the arm of a semaphore. And during the conversation with Gürtzner-Gontard I had looked down upon this same street light with its curved swan's neck, just as darkness was falling; the glass globe had already been illuminated, but the glow had remained compressed around it, since it was still daylight. . . . Afterwards, I had stood for a long time in front of the door, as if under a heavy overhang of contradictory thoughts. I once more had a vision of that embryo with its hands over its eyes: the embryo that refused to see the light, that did not want to see life and the continuity of every day. And for that reason it had just uprooted a street light, erecting at least for passing moments a second reality in which felled light poles were determining. For brief moments I thought I knew why I had stood so long in front of the door on May 15; that seemingly ponderous projecting roof of the gateway had been only my consciousness of my own burden as I stood looking out at the asphalt of the street, which some settled moisture had made shiny as fish skin.

I started suddenly, turned away from the window, and left the Hofrat's study. Now I thought I detected a faint trace of camphor in the anteroom (not unlikely, since it contained hunting trophies of his grandfather and a handsome tapestry on the wall). As I passed the salon I devotedly submitted to the greeting and caress of that scent, let it reach into my heart. And then I sat down again at table with Frau von Gürtzner-Gontard and gratefully accepted a second cup of coffee.

After a while I went downstairs, partly out of curiosity, partly to see where Gürtzner-Gontard was. The first person I saw in the ample entryway was Kajetan's former father-in-law, Dr. Schedik, who of course lived in the building. He had set up a kind of first-aid station, and was running about in a white, blood-stained smock, assisted by his nurse. The hallway was full of wounded people, including two policemen who had been badly beaten, and a member of the Protective Association with a bullet wound in his arm. At the rear several persons lay on mattresses that had been brought in from somewhere; they were wounded in the legs, though luckily not severely. Chairs had been provided for others. One of the ladies of the house had made a pot of coffee and brought it down, along with a supply of cups. The superintendent and doorman, Waschler, managed in all the confusion somehow to remain the principal personage, the *spiritus rector*. He was constantly issuing orders. Later, when we were upstairs again, Gürtzner-Gontard told me with great amusement how Waschler had dealt with a gang of rowdies who were hunting for police stragglers. They were getting ready to force their way into the house when Waschler opened the big gates a crack and peered out. Whereupon he had drawn himself up to his full height and announced in an officious tone: "No admittance here. Oh no! This building is the property of the city of Vienna, and I am responsible for it." Perhaps his words turned the trick, but more likely it had been Waschler's authoritative tone and official manner. Used properly (and Waschler knew how to use it), such a manner has magical powers in Austria, even in the midst of killing and arson, and even in the face of underworld characters.

Waschler learned something from the incident. He locked the big front gate. But since there was no peephole in the two huge wings at the entrance, he hit upon another arrangement which served his ends as well. There was a tall stepladder in the house which was used for cleaning walls and ceiling lights. By perching himself on the top platform of this ladder, Waschler could look out through the semicircle of glass at the top of the doors. Here he had a full view of the square, and thus was the only person who knew what was going on outside. From time to time he condescended to issue a bulletin—speaking from above, surveying the whole area of his authority and dominion. Unquestionably his situation was unusual for a superintendent, and he exploited it to the full. Herr von Gürtzner-Gontard was vastly entertained.

Gürtzner-Gontard had taken the two beaten policemen, whose heads were partly swathed in bandages, up to the apartment, where they could wash up and have coffee and sandwiches. The two officers, both decent and well-bred men, were visibly downcast. They could not understand what had been happening, were completely exhausted, and spoke little. One of them had been terribly beaten up by a gang of some twenty young louts. "I'm a Social Democrat myself," he said to Herr von Gürtzner-Gontard. "I don't know what got into those people. They weren't workers either, they certainly weren't workers."

"Hardly," the Hofrat said. "That sort of thing has nothing in common with socialism." (It may be noted here, by the way, that on that day a number of apartments which had taken in wounded and fleeing policemen were stormed, completely devastated and pillaged. However, we knew nothing about this, and thanks to Waschler all went well.)

We were still sitting around the table at three o'clock when the firing became so intense that the Hofrat and I hurried to the study window. In spite of our elevated position, our view was not so clear that we could form a picture of the situation and grasp what was really happening. In general we observed feverish running—hordes of people were sweeping through the park— and heard concerted shooting that steadily approached from a nearby street. The firing, moreover, was military, one salvo after another. This was the most important moment in the history of the Vienna police force since the First World War. The police had necessarily become armed troops (an irreversible process), closed formations which advanced in order, firing and driving everything before them. People jumped and ran, vaulted the fallen street light and the low railing of the park, and dashed through the shrubs, leaving a trail of whipping branches.

Later we learned from the newspapers that early in the afternoon the police had returned to their barracks on Marokkaner Gasse and been armed with carbines. Never before had the First Republic used them. It took fifteen minutes to find the key to the room where they were stored. Or so it was said. How much can be precisely known? During and after such occasions there are always people who wish to throw sand in the dreadful eyes of life; in order not to see those eyes, they prefer to spread rumors and tell anecdotes. Nevertheless, if the story of the key was true, that quarter hour would have represented a stumbling-block that life had placed in its own path, to delay its own pace for a few minutes.

It had nothing to do with all that, and yet for me it belongs here and nowhere else: that in those few minutes while we were making tracks for Gürtzner's study, I thought of Dr. Schedik and it occurred to me that I might have asked him where Camy Schlaggenberg was. But no, it was not possible; he had been far too busy. . . .

Standing at the window, using the field glasses again, we gradually formed a better picture of what was going on in the square. The turmoil now had all the look of an upheaval of the elements, an "act of God," as the phrase goes. . . . We no longer saw only the fleeing people; in running the crowd dissolved into innumerable individual dots; the scene became "pointillistic," and the intensely glaring sunshine emphasized that illusion. Now too we caught sight of the first victims; suddenly the square was spotted here and there with them, dark bundles in the sunlight. The troops of the Protective Association had to run too; their chain around the burning Palace of Justice vanished. We saw the first row of police appear, steadily firing their carbines. Their fire was answered; now both sides made liberal use of their weapons. I think the answering shots came from the barricade in front of Lerchenfelder Strasse. That barricade was soon taken by the police, and we heard an incessant barking of guns moving slowly away.

Now we observed the first fire-engine company at work by the burning building (had it been there before?). A number of motor-driven pumps had been brought up, and long lines of hose were laid out from the hydrants; there was one near us. Words were flung at the firemen; apparently the crowd wanted to strike up conversations with them. We had a good view of one group of this sort below us, to the left. Two firemen were engaged in attaching one of the huge hoses to a hydrant. Shielded by the group of bystanders, three boys of about fifteen made a dash at the hose. Immediately, a tremendous fountain of water burst from it; evidently it had been cut. The boys vanished almost as swiftly as had Rosi Malik and Holder earlier in the day.

In general, even after the police had swept the square clear with their incessant rifle salvos, the crowd did not disappear for good. People gradually drifted back; individuals pressed forward. That amazed me; more, it impressed me. More shots were fired, then more salvos. I stood dazed at the window. My state of the morning seemed to have returned: there was a kind of milky haze around my eyes and ears. My mind, despite all the stimulation, was clouded. I saw the men of the Protective Association on the square again. They were, it appeared, the passive sufferers of the day. They gathered up the human bundles that lay, some motionless in the sun, some thrashing about. They hurried forward with stretchers and ran into the lines of fire from the police, who did not hold their fire on their account. When the stretcher-bearers had carried someone away, only the red pool remained on the pavement—always very red at the start, far, far too red. I moved away from the window. Outside, the scene was quieting again. Gürtzner-Gontard and I left the study and returned to the salon. Frau von Gürtzner-Gontard had withdrawn completely.

But I could not stay here now! We sat behind closed doors, in wordless silence. Into my nostrils, filled with the feeble but raw and menacing smell of burning, entered the delicate scent of camphor. And it was the stronger power. I must get out of this daze, out of this roll of absorbent cotton in which I was wrapped, out of this haze around my temples and eyes. I wanted to reach Friederike. I wanted at least to make the attempt. Let the facts decide. This second lull in the rioting had to be utilized. It was approaching half-past four. I told the Hofrat that I intended to risk it. I would go now. Herr von Gürtzner-Gontard hesitated a moment. "Well," he said finally, "I scarcely think the police will take you for a demonstrator or a rowdy."

Those words gave me an inkling of how fundamentally he still misunderstood the situation. What a person thinks possible or impossible places him both in society and in his age. But whatever the case, there was no turning back for me. He accompanied me downstairs to tell Waschler to let me out. Dr. Schedik was not in the hall at the moment. The wounded people were feeling better, and talking quietly. The warm air smelled of medicaments. Waschler carefully examined the situation from his vantage point. The square in front of the house was clear and quiet at the moment. He descended, quickly unlocked the door, let me out through the crack, and immediately I heard the key turn twice in the lock behind me.

On Thursday afternoon Frau Mayrinker had ridden into Vienna with baskets of fruit—mostly berries. In Pottschach, Herr Mayrinker had accompanied his wife to the railroad station, carrying the baskets for her. The day was one of perfect radiance; the sharp light brought out every wooded crest, all the colored glass spheres in the garden, the signs over shops, and the remoter high mountains, serenely blue. The assault of such a multitude of excessively defined objects could not possibly be taken in all at once. The attempt to do so would have worn anyone out. In those days people did not wear sunglasses at every least opportunity; sunglasses were largely reserved for ski tours in the high mountains. The Mayrinkers did not even own a pair. There was nothing for it but to blink.

The railroad station was pervaded by the cool smell of beer kegs from an innkeeper's cellar, and the hot dust of the street. The railroad smoke was not something that came from outside, but constituted the very aura of the place. You stepped into it.

Making preserves is a compulsive activity of housewives. Come what may, jam must be made, with the result that most people eat jams that are four or five years old.

At the South Station in Vienna, Frau Mayrinker was aided by a porter, who put her and her baskets into a cab.

It was not really too hot. She had expected worse. Of course, she did miss the good air of the country! The city swarmed and roared.

As soon as she reached her apartment in the Blue Unicorn, Frau Mayrinker set to work. She scarcely took time for supper (she had brought everything with her and did not need to go shopping). The preparation of her apparatus—topped by a thermometer that looked down like a governess; the washing of the glasses, which next day would in addition be sterilized by hot steam; but above all the painstaking work with the fruit itself, the picking over of the currants, the removal of long stems and clinging leaves from the gooseberries—all this took hours. The quantities of crushed paper and bundled straw that emerged from the baskets of fruit and spread itself all over the floor drove Frau Mayrinker to undertake a general cleanup of the kitchen. Almost every job takes longer than we expect. When Frau Mayrinker at last went to sleep, it was long past midnight. She made her toilette, depetaling herself so that all her white rotundities were revealed, white shoulders and arms, quite like a baby's. These explained her husband's strong attraction to her. At last she clambered clean into bed, in a long fresh nightgown she had taken from the cupboard, its sharply ironed creases here and there forced out of the province of plane geometry by distinctly spherical shapes. She lay on her back, suddenly opened her tiny child's mouth as wide as possible, and yawned deeply. The novel lay ready on the night table (every year she chose with infallible instinct the stupidest of all the new books, and shunned all others with the certainty of a bat avoiding a stretched wire—her husband, of course, read only writings which tied in with his beloved dragons). But tonight she was too tired to read. She switched off the light and rolled herself into a smooth white egg under the nightgown, an egg of rejection of apperception from which she never emerged. She remained *ab ovo in ovo* (Herr von Geyrenhoff has a few phrases of this kind, but variations on them never occur to him [1]).

---

[1] I am letting this passage stand unaltered, for it is characteristic of Kajetan's impertinence—quite aside from that *"Chronique scandaleuse"* which as we know proved to be almost entirely unprintable. *Sunt certi denique fines.*

Next morning Frau Mayrinker awoke early, although she had not set an alarm clock. Like a proper housewife, she made the coffee with religious care, but then drank it hastily, after an equally hasty toilette. Immediately, she set to work, still in her dressing-gown. Some of the fruit still remained to be cleaned. By the time this had been done, and the glass jars were ready to be filled and placed in the cooker (only the first batch, for there was not room for all at once), the fire crackling in the stove and the sun already glaring outside had produced such heat in the small kitchen that Frau Mayrinker stripped off everything but her briefest chemise.

By noon the situation had clarified somewhat. A row of jars, already labeled, stood sealed with glass lids and rubber rings on the kitchen table. (The labels, incidentally, demonstrate the compulsive nature of this housewifely activity, for the date is always on them.) The third batch was ready. She had to keep adding fuel to the stove, for it held only a few of the oblong briquets which dissolved in the fire into extremely hot, long-lasting, glowing particles; if the door of the stove were opened too quickly, a bright, granular lava could leap at you. Some of it would fall upon the sheet metal beneath the stove door, and some would scatter here and there. In the course of one such operation Frau Mayrinker felt, as she knelt in front of the stove, a sudden flash of heat and light behind her, and a moment later came a crackling that had nothing to do with the fire before her eyes.

She banged the stove door closed, leaped to her feet and to one side. The flames were already flickering as high as a fire of potato vines in the fall; but in the tiny kitchen this was a gigantic bonfire, a pillar of flames that seemed about to reach to the ceiling. The crackling grew louder. Two of the fruit baskets were of painted wickerwork, and perhaps a highly volatile paint had been used.

So we may explain the physics of the matter. But Frau Mayrinker sought no explanation; she at once proceeded with re-markable fury to attack the fire.

There were two wet straining-cloths beside the stove. She spread one out like a shield and beat at the fire with it. The fire cowered only for a second. Then the second rag. The flames leaped up again. The pail. It was empty. She turned the faucet on full, let the water roar in. Before her eyes the fire grew. The curtain. Not there yet. The many berry boxes and cardboard cartons up on the kitchen cupboard. She emptied the pail. The fire shot up alongside it, as fluid as water that has encountered an obstacle. She struck out again and again with the two wet cloths. Smoke and steam rose, then the flames again. The third basket was already crackling away. She pulled it away from the curtain, saw it flare up brighter and brighter while the pail was filling for the second time. With furious energy she turned the pail upside down over the basket, from which a high tongue of flame was licking out—the burning straw and paper inside. The pail fitted the basket, covered it. While she was filling the pail for the third time, there were only small flames close to the floor. She did not need to empty the pail again; instead, she soaked the rags in the water and beat the fire to death wherever it showed its head. It did not come back. Pools of water were all over the floor. She had won.

She had won just a few inches away from the curtain.

For a second she thought of what would have happened if she had lost her courage, had run out of the apartment to seek a telephone and call the fire department.

The fire would have spread and enveloped everything. So painful was this idea that it immediately burst and vanished.

Now nothing was burning. Frau Mayrinker at once set about restoring order. She worked adroitly, steadily, without a moment's pause, her astonishment mounting all the while. With four fresh cloths she sopped up the wet spots in the kitchen—repeatedly wringing the cloths out over the pail. Then she gathered up all the burned and wet remains and deposited them in the steel garbage can, carefully checking for sparks. But there were none.

For greater safety, she poured water into the garbage can and moved it both away from the stove and far from the curtains—a compulsive excess of caution that seemed to her slightly suspect. She would not have liked being observed at this activity. In the midst of it she checked the thermometer of the canning apparatus, in which the third batch of preserves was still cooking, checked it with the greatest care. Slowly and cautiously she added fuel to the stove, even holding her metal dustpan under the door when she opened it. Though really, what could have happened now had a glowing grain tumbled out? There was no longer anything burnable on the stone floor of the kitchen. As she cleaned up the floor with broom and polishing cloth, she glanced occasionally at the rows of shining jars with their fresh preserves on the kitchen table—gleaming consolation. When she was finished, she became aware of an altogether astonishing state of affairs, which had begun to dawn on her even while she was restoring order, but which now struck her in all its undeniability: nothing was damaged. There was nothing ruined, no losses had been suffered. She herself had not received even the slightest burn. She went over to the curtains to look for damage there. But these too had not so much as been seared by the fire. The kitchen was spic and span, the fire in the stove burning quietly, the thermometer showing the prescribed temperature, and the third and last batch of jars would soon be finished and ready to be set on the kitchen table to cool off.

Only she herself, Frau Mayrinker, stood in the midst of all this quietly shining cleanliness soaked with perspiration, hair untidy, hands black, and in a chemise streaked with dirt. But this kind of damage, too, could be dispelled as swiftly as it had come. She aired the room thoroughly and set a kettle of water on the stove. (Before opening the window she had slipped into her dressing-gown, since people could see in from across the street.) During the airing, she took care of the third batch of canning jars. The sum total covered two thirds of the kitchen table and looked very serious indeed; there pertained to these crimson jars that gravity which belongs to even a single molecule of "gross national product"—for they were part of that, viewed from the higher "plane" of the national economy. The cooling supply of preserves on the kitchen table would, at a conservative estimate, cover the Mayrinkers' consumption until 1931 or 1932. At present the Mayrinkers were breakfasting *ex anno* 1923.

The canning apparatus had meanwhile been returned to its storage place.

The water on the stove appeared to have heated. Now, at last, she could allow the fire to go out.

Frau Mayrinker fetched a basin and set it on a kitchen stand provided with soap, brushes, and washcloths. She then closed the window, drew the curtains, and stepped into a small tin tub. There was no bathroom in the Blue Unicorn. She drew her dirty chemise over her head and tossed it aside.

Only now, after washing and dressed only in slippers, as she went into the bedroom for fresh underclothes, was she really overcome by the happiness of her momentary situation, the fruit of her victory over the fire. The daylight in the bedroom was muted; the green Venetian blinds were still lowered. Frau Mayrinker opened the wardrobe. The left side of it was divided into compartments in which her lingerie lay. The right-hand section was almost entirely filled by a large bag. This contained Frau Mayrinker's heavily camphored fur coat, which she had not been able to insert in the chest devoted to rugs and woolens. Moreover, the precious piece seemed to her safest here, for this oak wardrobe was of solid construction and could be closed perfectly tight.

The big doors of the wardrobe opened on noiseless hinges into the relatively cool room.

Only then, as a wave of the hitherto contained fragrance of camphor washed into the room, did Frau Mayrinker become fully aware of the stillness that prevailed about her.

She let the compartments of lingerie be for the moment and stooped, leaning the upper part of her body so deeply into the wardrobe that she had to support herself with her hands against both sides of it.

And here, in this odd position, she enjoyed her good fortune, her return to her happiness. Only now did the fire completely vanish, did its last traces flee from her nostrils, driven away by the cool scent of the camphor. Now she felt safety; now the fire could not return; it receded over its hair's-breadth boundary, withdrew from the realm of possibility deep into the impossible, from which it had so shortly before burst forth, crackling and leaping.

At last. She had almost vanished into the wardrobe, like a photographer diving under his black cloth. And in the camera obscura she had found again, seen shining, the little light that now as always illuminated her Mayrinker area.

When she emerged, her white knees almost gave way beneath her from weakness: hunger. There was a great emptiness in her abdomen, surrounded by body walls that seemed to have become exceedingly thin. She had had almost nothing since her quick breakfast, only snatched two pieces of bread and butter about half an hour before the fire. There were still some provisions in her traveling bag, but she must have something warm. She would eat in the "Flight to Egypt" over on Alserbach Strasse. Suddenly she could smell the clean odors of food characteristic of that restaurant, and her appetite was stirred to a high pitch. She would have beer too. So that she would sleep better after all the excitement.

The kitchen smelled only of soap now, no longer of burning—not at all. The stove door was closed; the briquets must still be glowing, for it was fearfully hot. Returning to the bedroom, she chose a summer dress, and after completing her toilette and removing the washstand, she opened the kitchen windows wide. The darkness poured in, and with it a few raindrops. It had become somewhat cooler.

At last she was ready. She took her pocketbook, a light raincoat, and her umbrella. Feeling quite hollow, she checked the stove once again, made sure the door was firmly closed. In the garbage pail the charred remains lay half under water. Frau Mayrinker closed the lid down and pushed the pail still farther away from the curtains. Now it was a good six feet from them. She stepped up on the white-painted kitchen stool and examined the cartons on the kitchen cupboard, lifting them one after another. Not a spark. Her hands shook with weakness. Now she closed the kitchen windows again and glanced around at all the spic-and-span corners. When she was locking up the apartment, her hands trembled so that she could scarcely find the keyhole. The operation took a long time. Now the door was properly shut.

Umbrella open, she walked along Liechtenstein Strasse, gazing at the ground. Her appetite had vanished, but the weakness remained, and she wished that she were already sitting at the set table in the Flight to Egypt. It was hardly raining now. She hesitated, closed her umbrella, and walked on. As she entered Alserbach Strasse she stood still and looked up the street and into the sky.

The sky was aglare with flames. She started with terrible fright; for a moment, in her weakness and exhaustion, all her happiness collapsed, the achieved rescue and victory vanished. Something had happened. She must have overlooked something. Irrationally, she could not for some time separate that fire over there from the little fire in her kitchen, which had long since been extinguished.

Toward noon, at the philosophy faculty's buffet (full meals were not served there but one could have a ham sandwich and a kind of coffee, though nowhere else in Vienna would the honorable name of coffee have been applied to it), Leonhard learned for the first time what was going on in the neighborhood. There was no shooting to be heard at the moment, even outside under the arcades. Leonhard spoke with no one, but he picked up the rumors being bandied about. All around him there was talk of nothing else.

Thus he learned that it had been the electricity workers whose oncoming procession he had dodged by racing across Ring Strasse. Their decision to strike that morning, taken independently of the union leadership, had drawn all the other events in its train: the stoppage of the streetcars because they had no power; the cessation of work at innumerable factories for the same reason (the Rolletschek webbing factory was also closed). The workers were marching into the city to protest the verdict of a jury which had acquitted the murderers of a workman's child and of a one-eyed war invalid.

Leonhard now recalled having seen this very man down in the Burgenland, and even recalled where he had seen him: in the tavern, far at the back, within that inclusive triangle which had Elly Zdarsa, Malva Fiedler, and Trix as its apices.

How much shorter than his life was his real past. And yet there were things in it that had already become incomprehensible, and certain points that were gently being moved into a new radiance, as had happened that very morning. The return of that one-eyed man did not strike him so hard a blow as today's second encounter with Pico at the library, along with some of the identical books he himself had used there and had now renewed again in the prince's name. The one-eyed man drew only a weak flash of lightning toward himself and toward the past, briefly flaring here and there like sparks from a damaged electrical conductor.

But what baffled Leonhard was why that first procession should have made that abortive attack on the University. In the general discussion, the true meaning of the attack was already being blurred. The group responsible for the brief action might be called "undisciplined, reckless elements." But call them what you would, they had committed one of the really remarkable "instinctive actions" of the day. Their assault was by no means directed against the intellectuals—as was assumed by the people talking in the buffet, who thereby shed some mild light on themselves. Rather, at bottom, the provocation had been a smell. For no sphere of the senses reaches so far into the hereafter in the here as that of smell; often it is no longer perceived with the nose, and yet it exists, and it is a veritable smell. In this case, the hostility of the workers was directed toward the regional stable odors in the University, toward the "provincialism" of those who studied here, toward a conservative temper held not because it had been sought and rewon, but which was "held" because it had been hung on to and never lost. Such a hold on traditions can be a source of a host of respectable errors, and the more respectable the errors are, the worse they are; compared to such errors, all vices (which, after all, being marked with filth, proclaim their nature) are mere harmless scribblings by the hands of fools. The "intellectuals" foregathered here had already descended, from that platform on which the historically acting man stands, precisely as many steps as those assailants outside when they plunged into the vat of the masses, which dissolves everything and breaks all chemical ties, sending some to the right and others to the left, as the customary classification goes. All roads of descent lead down, but never do people hate one another so passionately as when they choose different downward paths. Such downward paths may not even run together in the void, in nihilism; for then something would be revealed for all to see which must be concealed—or at least, the concealment of which seems to be the sole and ultimate goal of the struggle.

Leonhard had never entered the seminars and lecture halls. He was familiar only with the bookish, alpine atmosphere of the dignified library.

Therefore, for all his intelligence, he did not grasp what a clumsy blockhead like René Stangeler had ultimately been compelled to understand, from innumerable bitter experiences.

Leonhard left the buffet.

He did not believe that the electrical workers had battered at the door out of hatred for the intelligentsia. But he felt depressed because he did not understand the matter at all.

He sat down in a shady place on the steps under the arcades. The library had meanwhile been closed because in many of the rooms and corridors electric light was indispensable, even by day. The prince's books had been set aside and marked with the present date, so that they would lie ready for use in the reading room at least until Tuesday.

Here silence prevailed. It prevailed not only as a figure of speech; it was truly prevalent here, masterfully questioning intimate moments. Blueness crouched down over the edges of the roofs, leaned in over them, and simultaneously looked out into the far distances, as far as Wertheimstein Park in Döbling, as far as the Bisamberg, soared over all the fears of examinations that haunted the arcades in July, even made familiar contact with the foothills of the Alps, with the first fir forests rising in tiers up the withers of the mountains, tree mounting above tree, like an angular running script, till at the end a single line is left and then comes the gnarled low growth and then the silent crags, the naked rocks rearing into the sky and the torrents of scree dropping away from them like the garment of arrogance from the shoulders.

Leonhard's thoughts followed the blueness out to those hills, and to the rest home with the little door that led out through the back of the park. Meanwhile, after all that he had heard, a dull pressure like a growing lump, a tumor, spread through his breast. A mountain—that separated him from Mary. Had the stoppage of the streetcars, of which Papa Pepi had told him in the morning, actually grown into an almost insuperable obstacle?

How long had he been sitting there? And what was piercing him so painfully?

A loud, clear whiplash snapped into the Renaissance courtyard.

It was the first of those rifle salvos which the police began firing toward five o'clock in the afternoon and continued for a while almost without pause.

A rifle salvo, heard at such a distance, over a number of intervening roofs and blocks of houses, does not sound very loud. Nevertheless, it is far more penetrating than revolver shots, which at a few blocks' distance sound no louder than boys' cap pistols; they make no real report, but only a slapping noise, as if they were merely small bright spots in the ears.

This sound was like a sharp line, the snap of a lash.

As it struck him, Leonhard suddenly realized that he had been expecting something of the sort, and that the very lack of any obstacles in his way during recent weeks had been a source of anxiety. That venomous arrow shot from the nearest bush in Brigittenau—that arrow aimed by Malva Fiedler—had seemed almost a reassurance. Anyone moving steadily along his way must be aware of such snipers at his back, and ahead of him something looming up, some sort of obstacle, no matter what. . . . Not only for him, for Mary too. . . . Now here it was: he was locked in!

It is curious that Leonhard took it for granted that he was locked in there at the University. He was not altogether wrong. Everything had been closed up tightly, and during the shooting it is scarcely likely that anyone entered or would have liked to leave the building.

Locked in there, Leonhard was simultaneously locked out of everything that was happening outside. Only now did the diaphragm within him stretch taut, and on it the drumsticks of harsh facts beat their resounding roll. Now the pain came; it too was a fact; and once again the whiplash whistled and snapped into the Renaissance courtyard, and it was not difficult to imagine who was being fired on out there.

"No one separates himself from his natural places and persons with impunity," Scolander says somewhere.

Once more the lash snapped down.

Leonhard jumped to his feet.

He turned into the arcades.

From the direction of the aula, someone slowly approached under the echoing arches. Leonhard recognized the attendant who had helped close the big gate against the insurgent mob. Even the name, though he had heard it only once, came to him. "Herr Fessl," Leonhard said, "would there be any possibility of my getting to Reichsrat Strasse by way of the small exit? I have somewhere I must go and simply cannot delay any longer."

"Well, we'll have to look, Herr Doktor," Fessl replied (the title had already been conferred upon Leonhard at the buffet; it seemed to be quite general here). "If it's quiet outside and there's no danger of anyone's trying to break in, I can certainly let you out."

Leonhard went with Fessl, who seemed to be a calm and intrepid sort of person; at least he had demonstrated those qualities in the morning. A small stairway led down to the rear exit. The doorway was of rippled glass, which made it impossible to see the street outside. Fessl listened. The air here had that rather spent, nether-worldly quality it had had in the hallway of Leonhard's old house on Treu Strasse, when the door to the concierge's apartment had stood open for a while. Fessl took out a key, opened the door, peered out, beckoned to Leonhard, and let him slip out through the crack. After the coolness of the building, the heat above the pavement flung itself at Leonhard's face. Behind him the key turned twice in the lock.

From the terrace of the "dairy" café near Kobenzl Castle the fire in the city was visible. It lay in the middle background of the gray-blue mass of buildings which spread out like a lake down below, and the powerful sunlight made it seem small, compressed, confined to itself, like an electric bulb burning in broad daylight. But the fire did dart and lick out now and then, and clouds of smoke could also be seen, which somewhat obscured the flames themselves.

Otherwise, deep peace prevailed up here. Peace and above all the heat of the sun, which did not feel sultry as it did on asphalt or granite pavements. The air was warm, but light and free. It was like standing on the roof of the city, on the roof of events themselves, even. Nothing remained of the happenings down below but a dully reddening and occasionally flickering dot close to the horizon.

A sizable group of persons was standing on the terrace. Among them were a number of ladies and gentlemen who owned the automobiles drawn up outside the café. After these people had looked a while at the glowing dot down in the city, the "red pimple," as Herr von Orkay called it, there was nothing much more to do. So it happened that while the Palace of Justice was already burning vigorously—for it was two o'clock by now—some of the spectators settled down on the terrace for dinner. The proprietor had to improvise somehow, for the café at Kobenzl Castle was not really organized for anything much in the way of meals, especially not on a weekday. An old waiter darted hurriedly but still with ceremonious courtesy hither and thither, and negotiated with the guests. He must beg the ladies and gentlemen to be patient a little, he kept saying; things were a bit rushed today.

On the whole, the café managed well, and Quapp and Géza also had their dinner while the Palace of Justice went up in flames.

It must have been between three and half-past three when Géza and Quapp finished their black coffee and turned their eyes away from the outspread view—it extends to the left, whence comes the blue ribbon of the river, all the way down toward Nussdorf, and is restricted somewhat on the right by a rise which is called "Am Himmel" (At the Sky). This picture, with the blue lake of the city below, receding as far as the eye can see, is a favorite of everyone who comes up Kobenzl; in fact, to take in this particular view is virtually a must for all who visit the spot on outings. Perhaps they enjoy the obvious perspective upon their own lives which they obtain by ascending to this height, knowing that ordinarily their destined course is run down below there amid the blue mists. Today, however, such meditations and inspirations were considerably hampered; the view had acquired a highly unidyllic focal point which now and then displayed mutations, flickering more dully or more brightly, with or without swaths of smoke. Some of the watchers up here were using binoculars. More automobiles arrived from the city, and their passengers had all sorts of tales to tell.

Quapp and Géza left.

They strolled along the road which led to Am Himmel, and then turned into a path which, broad at first, soon narrowed, leading the couple into the woods above Sievering.

For some time they walked in silence. The cuckoo cried in the cool spaces under the forest's solid roof of foliage. Even at table, things had begun to reach a pitch for Quapp and Géza. Once they had arrived up here, both seem to have felt that this second rapid drive out into the country after a chance meeting had ripened everything between them more swiftly than they could have anticipated during the drive itself, with the motor roaring its way up the serpentine curves of the road. Now, there in the woods, everything was already on the brim, on the brink. This second so curious meeting—curious because it was a repetition, and for Quapp a renewed liberation from an uncomfortable situation, the first time an inner one, the second time composed of outer difficulties—this second meeting created or confirmed a tie between them. In a sense did so far more intimately than any caresses might have done—for no caresses at all had been exchanged between the couple.

The path grew steeper as they approached the so-called "Cross Oak."

The silence of deciduous woods is lighter, less formidable than that of the deep fir forests in the mountains, whose gravity silences the pipes of Pan and from whose surmounting craggy cliffs rises the hunting cry of the buzzard. Here, the sun's rays fell in clusters upon ground flecked with the shadows of leaves, and amid the smells of bushes and smaller plants the tang of wild garlic could already be detected; whole patches of these woods are covered by its grasslike leaves.

A short distance from the Cross Oak, Géza stood still and made a first grab at the rudder of the ship of love, which he was henceforth not to let out of his hand: "You ought to be my wife, Quappchen," he said. "Do you want to?"

"Of course I want to," she said.

Then they sat by the Cross Oak and made up for missing caresses, which were very sweet because long overdue; this tree of kisses needed to be shaken only very lightly, and promptly sent down a delicious hail.

She told him that at six o'clock she had to see a Frau Friederike Ruthmayr in Wieden.

"I'll drive you out there, of course," Géza said. "But first we must go back to the dairy. It's just possible they might have some champagne. And this is the time for drinking it."

On the walk back, details were gone into. Géza wanted the marriage to come off as soon as possible, so that he would be able to take Quapp with him to Berne when he transferred. "A bit unusual," he said. "But I'll arrange it. I'm supposed to leave in the middle of August. Monday I'll telephone the Foreign Ministry in Budapest—I have a good friend there. It will work out. You must go right with me to Berne. Where will the wedding be?"

She replied that probably they would have to hold the wedding at her mother's estate, down in Styria.

"You'll write your mother all about it right away, won't you, before this week is out? All right? And say I throw myself at her feet, all right?"

"All right, Géza," Quapp said. "But I must be at this Frau Ruthmayr's in Wieden on the dot of six o'clock. It's important. Sometime soon I'll tell you who she is."

"Yes, Quappchen, certainly," he said. "We'll leave here in good time."

Thus a number of explanations were postponed: who Frau Ruthmayr was, and why a public building had been set afire in Vienna and why guns were rattling so murderously. Meanwhile they were still walking downhill through the woods. Quapp said: "It would be a great advantage to your diplomatic career if you were to marry a really wealthy woman. . . ."

Géza stood still and looked at her in horror.

"Yes," Quapp went on undeterred. "Certainly. It's all very fortunate. From the beginning of next year I'll have a legacy of more than ten million schillings. I've just inherited it. It's connected with this lady I have to see at six on the dot. . . ."

"*Bászama!*" Géza burst out. "I don't give a damn. I have enough for our needs!"

"It isn't unimportant," Quapp replied with perfect calm.

"Don't say that. I know better. When a diplomat has enough money to entertain properly, he moves up in a very different way."

"Certainly that's true," he said conciliatorily. They walked on, reached the wide sunlit path, and then followed the road for a while. Soon they again came within view of the fire in the city. It had grown, was flaming mightily. At the brink of the terrace some thirty men and women stood watching it. Géza and Quapp went into the dining room. A Viennese waiter is hard to surprise. This one showed no sign that he considered their request unusual. The champagne was brought; the bottle slid about noisily in the ice-bucket. Quapp and Géza leaned forward, their faces close together as glasses touched.

I had left Gürtzner-Gontard's too early, and realized that too late. The lull had been only apparent; it did not last long. I turned to the left, although for half a second an inner warning told me that I ought to avoid a route which was marked by an obvious token as blocked, belonging to the past. Disregarding that warning, I jumped over the fallen street light. I ran. Almost immediately I found myself running toward an advancing line of police who held their carbines at ready. I shrank against the wall of the house. The man nearest to me pointed his weapon threateningly at me but went on past. I watched the company rapidly moving forward in step. One of the men in the center of the line suddenly fell forward on his face, but quickly picked up himself and his weapon; obviously, he had only stumbled. I remained pressed against the wall. The compact troop swung left, then raised their carbines, and the salvo snapped and roared. Already a new detachment was coming behind them. Again they marched forward, again one man fell, picked himself up, and took his place in the line. Opposite, by the park, stood a young police officer who shouted "Squads left!" to the men. They swung left, fired. Then the officer looked at the spot where the men had stumbled. I looked there too. There was nothing to see but a sewer grating. The next salvo from the next advancing line was fired when the men were twenty paces before me along the street. Only then did they move forward and pass by, and I watched them go. Again one of the men in the middle stumbled at the sewer grating and picked himself up. Immediately afterwards the officer, with two veritable tiger's leaps, sprang across the street and thrust the muzzle of his pistol into the sewer grating. He fired half a dozen shots straight down.

I pulled myself together and ran on. Then I succeeded in composing myself and walked along at a normal pace, thinking of Gürtzner-Gontard's comment—the thing was to make it clear that I was a peaceful, ordinary citizen. There were other people near me now, and perhaps they likewise were experimenting with the same conduct; having ventured out into the streets by necessity or mistake, they were now concerned with getting through with a whole skin. Instead of avoiding the police, they went straight toward them, possibly imagining that safety awaited them in the ranks of these guardians of the city. Next moment a salvo almost lifted the hats from our heads. Someone screamed. A police officer, sword clenched in his fist, came charging along the sidewalk. I had fled around the corner, and made off as swiftly as possible. Suddenly I was in a void of relative stillness. But I continued to walk rapidly along. In the middle of the street I saw a young policeman lying on his back, arms outstretched along his sides, as if on a bier. He was clearly dead. I recognized him as a policeman although he was wearing only shirt, trousers, and shoes. Someone had folded his dark green tunic and placed it under his head. His pistol belt was missing.

Still striding along, I unexpectedly found myself in streets that seemed perfectly normal. I had walked far, and walked on still farther. For a long while my mind was completely taken up with what I had just seen and experienced. Like two superimposed pictures, I kept seeing that young policeman lying in the middle of the street—a tousle of dark hair over his forehead—and that officer firing down into the sewer grating. This was the second incomprehensible sight of the day, far more mysterious than that of those two young people who had found time to dig up the base of the street light. Here, among the old houses of Josefstadt, I felt remote from all these events. I had got out of the inferno more quickly than I had dared to hope. Not until the following week did I learn that riots had raged in this district too; the office buildings of two conservative newspapers had been wrecked.

It had been relatively easy, though risky, for me to get out of the tumult. Now I found myself looking through open entrances into houses where people stood peering out anxiously, into arched entrance halls and spacious gardens beyond them, such as are often concealed behind the grimy and unprepossessing fronts of low houses in the older quarters of Vienna. The people in the entryways seemed on the point of vanishing and locking everything up again. I reflected that almost anyone could have left the scene as I had done; those who remained wanted to remain, though perhaps not to fight; they were held by interest and a sense of identification with the riots. I had reached Neubau; I walked down lower Mariahilf and descended a stairway to Wienzeile.

Here, on the steps, I was literally overwhelmed by bliss at the thought that nothing now was likely to keep me from Friederike. For here her quarter of the city began. And no obstacle came along. I was able to walk peacefully ahead. When I was fairly near, I entered a small café, washed up, combed my hair and straightened my tie, then sat bowed low over the fragrant coffee, inhaling a cigarette with deep pleasure. After all I had just seen, the café seemed like a palace. Life, violently driven by a nameless power out to the edge of the horizon, returned, danced up to me, greeted me.

I continued on down the street, in the heat. When I reached Friederike's house, the doorman greeted me with real delight, and immediately Ludmilla came running up: "The mistress didn't want to believe you would really be coming, sir, but I said you would certainly come. The mistress is waiting for you up in the hall, she didn't want to sit on the garden side because you can hear the shooting from there. . . ."

She ran ahead and opened the door wide.

At that moment I knew—from Ludmilla's gesture—that all had long since been decided, and that I was at home there.

So I went up the red-carpeted stairs.

At the upper end, Friederike appeared. I ran, taking two steps at a time. She raised her arms slightly when she caught sight of me. During those seconds on the stairs I was conscious of the delicate odor of camphor, perhaps because of the carpets and the wine-red brocaded furniture below. Friederike retreated to the background of the room; I could no longer see her; she awaited me somewhere there at the back. I leaped over the last step, hurried to Friederike, took both her hands, and promptly enclosed her in my arms. She pressed my shoulders hard, and with closed eyes held her mouth out to me. The suction into a hereafter in the here was so mighty that it swept me away like snowflakes. Then, hearing Ludmilla coming from the lower part of the hall, we took our seats like good children at the tea table. When Ludmilla had gone, we did not proceed to drinking the tea; we held hands. So far we had not spoken a single word.

Neuberg had taken a new room after his final break with Angelika. That seems to be the manner in which many people cast their skins after the collapse of a love-affair. His new situation was more favorable in several respects, since his quarters were more comfortable and more private, and had moreover two extra amenities: a bathroom and a roomy balcony all his own which could be entered from the hallway. The house was situated in one of the higher parts of the city, upper Josefstadt, and was loftier than any of the other buildings in the vicinity. Neuberg lived at the very top, so that he had a fine view all the way to the center of the city. Only from the balcony, however; the windows of the room looked in a different direction.

It had been a real collapse, though, a zero point; and inherent in that concept is the stopping of all tension, and therefore the possibility of a new beginning. Nevertheless, there were still

stirrings under the ruins—frequent stirrings. Daily, in fact: up-
heavals and wild rumblings, instead of gradual subsidence into
the leveling earth of the past, out of which the archaeology of
our memories may ever so much later excavate the debris, and
arrive at astonishing conclusions—for example, that the women
of a certain period, of certain strata, were all alike, which only
makes the original fiction that each was unique all the more incomprehensible. For all the grief lies in that fiction. "*Exemplum
docet, exempla obscurant*," Prince Croix once remarked.

There were, then, convulsive rumblings inside Neuberg.
Hands shaking and knees quivering, he could scarcely manage
to take advantage of the happy things that now began to happen. For it may be said that good fortune started to pursue him.
Had some stopper (Angelika?) been removed, which hitherto
had kept him corked up?

Yes, it was so, he knew everything. As yet he could not do
what he might have been able to do, but he already had the
necessary knowledge. This is a dangerous situation, for it divides
a man in two. If the two halves separate entirely, if the mere
knowledge becomes a kind of second reality from which no
bridge leads to the first, then all is lost. However, an incomprehensible displacement in his interior, virtually in the interior
of his body (Neuberg could never have produced the change
voluntarily), had carried him over a threshold. It was a small step,
but it put an end to that perilous separation. He had patiently
endured the state of absolute inability to do anything, suffered
it as a preliminary stage to regained abilities. The reward was
rich. The end of that stage had come shortly after the five-o'clock
tea at Grete Siebenschein's, where he had met the American
and his fiancée. Departing rather heavily lit, our friend Neuberg
had dropped into a bistro for a few more drinks. Back at his own
apartment, he had had a spell of terrible nausea. Ever since then
the faintest smell of alcohol had aroused in him a violent repulsion which ruled out wine and hard liquor as possible pleasures,
did not even allow him a glass of beer, and even extended to
Cologne water. Neuberg was not aware that he was being held

back from the brink of an abyss far less by the sensitivity of his stomach than by his pure Jewish ancestry; his remote forebears had fought and won the battle against all intoxicants, and left behind a serum in the blood against it.

At any rate, in his tipsiness and in the sleep that followed, Neuberg crossed the small threshold, as Odysseus landed in his sleep upon Ithaca and Leonhard Kakabsa in a state of semi-somnolence crossed the dialect frontier—for we never find our way home when fully awake. Beyond that displacement which had come to him as a gift, beyond the absolute inability to do anything, gentle allies came to the aid of our doctor of philosophy and practiced introspector. (A marginal note: if the author were, for example, president of an international league of women—for which role he is fortunately totally unsuited!—he would propose to the parliaments of all nations a bill forbidding the male of the species to meditate. When menfolk engage in such practices they can too easily hit upon an Archimedean point where they will be simply invulnerable—where, in other words, it will be impossible to soft-soap them. Women therefore would be empowered to defend—in highly concrete fashion—the supremacy of the winged and pink-backsided god. Though, alas, the members of women's clubs are poorly suited for this duty—and other types of women carry it out incessantly and successfully in any case; in fact, essentially they do nothing else—hurrah!)

Gentle allies, then, came to his aid. At the time Neuberg was alone in the apartment; the people from whom he sublet his quarters were enjoying a summer vacation. His experience after his bout of drunkenness had proved to be mere anticipation, a single tone of a still incomplete chord in a new key. But the onset of the new key by no means coincided with his change of quarters, much as Neuberg had longed for this and even assumed that it would be so. Far from it. No one is allowed to swing the baton and beat time for his own life, to determine how long a sequence lasts. Or perhaps a great composer may, but not a petty conductor. Here in Josefstadt, Neuberg still felt thoroughly miserable for a while: head burrowing into the pillow, weak-

kneed, unsteady, pressure around the heart (though the lad was
as sound as a bell)—in short, all those symptoms of poisoning on
which barkeeps and women make their living.

But just at this point the gentle allies intervened. One day
Neuberg began to feel acutely uneasy in his new room. And
since he knew that he was alone in the apartment and would
encounter no one, he employed the hallway as a run, and fled
out there. (A solitary man often does not feel able to cope with
the street and the indifferent crowds in it, and therefore does not
want to escape outside. Yet the presence of his mute surroundings
can suddenly become a threatening sword directed at the unfortunate's heart. And there is no shield against such a mood, because a bookcase, the afternoon sunlight in the window, a bath-
robe hanging on a hook, offer no room for interpretation—while
at the same time hidden but incontrovertible knowledge tells him
the opposite and transforms all those objects into visible strands
in the basic fabric of his own life.)

Neuberg, then, entered the hallway, running, and ran past the
glass door of the balcony. Across the hall, on the left, were
three closed doors to the rest of the apartment. The family must
have taken many precautions for their rugs or furs, or whatever
they had, for as Neuberg stopped, the delicate perfume of
napthalene or camphor cooled everything deep down within
him. Everything dropped away from him, as though his inner
floor were vanishing, and whatever happened to be around him
at the moment rushed in to fill the momentary vacuum. What entered was no terrifying phantom world, but substantiality that
filled the senses, gave them something to grind, stocked the mills
of the mind with grain. And so for the first time he saw this
hallway, light green and in the *art nouveau* style or Jugendstil,
as it is called—around 1907, say. The scent of camphor formed
discrete, self-contained geographic units, peninsulas and foothills
of an extensive, cool hinterland. Neuberg saw more than many a
person sees on a journey to Naples or Apulia. At the same time
he could feel almost physically, as one feels food sliding down the
gullet, that the center of his own being was returning to its

proper place, after having been dislodged. In another moment it was there, in place again.

That happened on the morning of July 15. Neuberg was quite conscious of the relative importance of these moments. As he went back to his room, the seal of facts was stamped upon the completed act. He had been aware of those facts for more than two weeks, but all this time they had lived a kind of ethereal, batlike existence within him. Now they rushed to his own replaced center: from January 1 on he would have a position in the government archives. From September 1 he would be helping to edit the most important publication of source materials of our time, the *Monumenta Germaniae;* this project had been interrupted by the war, but was gradually getting under way again. In the long run, he could not keep both jobs. But the two offers had arrived simultaneously. He realized that he had been suffering of late from a form of minor paranoia concerning "origins" and everything connected with them. For since he entirely lacked connections, since he was no one's protégé, it was obvious that these jobs had come to him solely on the basis of his professional qualifications.

Back in his room he immediately reached for the rope that had been thrown him and knotted it firmly around his chest. He had only one desire: to resume the work he had been partly neglecting. He threw himself into this with tremendous energy, as though his life were at stake (was it not?). He expected stubborn resistance. But there was none at all—for which the reason was partly technical; all his materials lay in good order on his desk; he had brought them from the Institute because he had not been able to work there any longer. Moreover, his Carolingian studies had reached an advanced stage, and had been abandoned at a point where they could be easily taken up again.

After three hours he was smitten by terrific hunger.

Neuberg did not recall having once had the slightest appetite during the last few weeks. Certainly never in the morning.

But this breakfast, taken almost at noon, turned into a veritable gluttonous orgy; he devoured everything he could find in the

house. Only after he had eaten did his inner situation really become consolidated. Once he looked up over his desk in the manner of those who wear spectacles and with lowered head will
look up over the tops of their glasses. That way of looking seems
at once searching and somehow irreverent, or at least implies a
doubtful wariness. In just this way, though he wore no glasses,
Neuberg looked up over his books and papers at the bridal
couple—namely, Director Dulnik and Angelika Trapp. He suddenly saw the whole affair as an undignified, ridiculous business.
Thank goodness he was out of it.

After two more hours of work he was clubbed on the head; all
the sleepless nights he had spent of late had gathered together
to deliver this ponderous blow.

Perhaps he sensed in the depths of his soul that no one can
enter wholly into his Ithaca except through the gate of sleep. As
if to carry things to extremes, he finished a bottle of beer (which
had been standing untouched in the corner for two weeks); he
had to cool it first by putting it in the bathtub and letting the
cold water from the nickel-plated shower hose run over it for a
good while. This time the beer aroused no repugnance in him.
It tasted fine. Then he kicked off his shoes, loosened his suspenders, and stretched out on the couch. Lying on his back, he felt
his ship casting off from the shore and quietly setting its course
for the homeward voyage.

When Neuberg awoke, it was dark in the room, and at first he
imagined that it was early morning. Quite often during the
nights of the past few weeks, when after hours of pacing back
and forth he had thrown himself on the couch, he had awakened
in his clothes early in the morning, sliding into a day that flowed
like viscous lead. Those had been only pauses in a decisive struggle whose end had already been sealed; he had been seeking
understanding and avoiding acknowledgment of a decision already taken. Today, however, as soon as he awoke he saw freedom glinting like a glorious lake, and he plunged into it like a

young frog. Immediately too he realized the actual time of day, and was eager to resume his work. What a pleasure it was to be in this room. He filled it and it fitted him like a comfortable jacket.

Especially now, with darkness falling. When he tried to turn on the light, however, nothing happened. At the desk too the lamp switch made no change in the darkness. Still a little sleepy, perhaps, Neuberg groped his way over to the washstand; his electric hot plate stood on its marble top, and he felt defiantly determined to make his coffee—damn it all, he needed some coffee right now!—even if he had to do it in the dark. But without electricity he could no more heat water than he could switch on the lights.

The thing to do was to see whether the short circuit had affected the whole apartment, for a recent experience had taught him that there were two separate circuits.

He started out, at a deliberate pace, becoming conscious as he did so of a coolness spreading through his body, in spite of the warmth of the room. He recalled having had a similar feeling after swimming for a long time in the Danube.

Passing by the glass door of the balcony, he saw a red glow outside. He stepped out into the relative coolness, felt the wet balcony railing under his hands, and gazed into the portals of the fire that loomed up like a structure of spires and red walls. The scattered thunderclouds in the sky cast back its reflection. The distant burning of Troy, seen from Neuberg's Ithaca; and beautiful Helen, or in this case Angelika, went up in smoke— which surely would have been a better thing in those days too.

Leonhard stood for a few seconds in front of the small back exit of the University—and suddenly recalled that he had left his hat lying on the steps by the arcades. With an excessive clarity that startled him, he saw the path to the right, the one leading into Universitäts Strasse. The street itself was clear and deserted: no obstacles anywhere. He scarcely looked to the left, though he heard a few isolated shots, screams, and observed out of the corners of his eyes the reddish glow of the fire and a kind of enormous hat of smoke above the roofs. Nevertheless, when he moved, he turned to the left. That was more than strange; in those moments he was estranged from himself. But the opposite direction, the street to the right, to Mary, remained with him as a possibility that he could choose when it pleased him.

Once you are estranged from yourself, nothing will be strange to you for long. When we roar through the switches of our mind's destiny, the action is violent and occupies us fully, but the switches themselves are not recognized as such. Neither when one lies in bed and crosses the dialect frontier (a second Odysseus, who also landed upon Ithaca in his sleep) nor when one suddenly realizes that one already knows Latin.

Not that at this time he considered anything, thought, imagined.

He turned to the left.

Already he was at the corner of the Rathaus.

He walked along the whole front of Schmidt's Gothic nightmare.

In a dream we take everything for granted. We wonder at nothing. Perhaps that circumstance is the sole criterion by which we distinguish between dreaming and waking. In the dream world we cannot wonder because we lack perspective, have not that distance from the object, that crack between ourselves and life, which constitutes wakefulness. Across that crack our arrow of criticism flies. Here no arrow flew. Not even when Leonhard saw that policemen, drawn up in a line, were using the butts of their carbines, whether from lack of ammunition, lack of space, or lack of forbearance, he could not determine.

His leisurely walking became a mad dash. He did not know that he was running, tearing along. His body made no comment, no objection; why should it have, when he had the heart of a three-year-old horse and lungs such as the Greeks at Marathon must have had, when under Miltiades they threw the Persians into the sea?

Only now was Leonhard practically cutting off the possibility of taking the right fork, to Mary; but he did not realize that, for he kept that other possibility in his heart and in a sense under the soles of his feet, which were in fact hastening in an opposite direction.

But his dash was stopped—although this too he scarcely noticed. A wave surged across his path, first in front of him, then behind him. The lashing salvos had ceased, but isolated shots still made bright accents in the roar of the crowd. The noise seemed to carry Leonhard outside again, to cast him out like surf, and even while he still thought that he saw beside him a young man with a big oily face who was throwing stones, and beside that young man a fat sluttish woman incessantly blowing a shrill whistle—even while he still thought he was in the midst of them, he found himself in an almost deserted street, in the middle of which something had been laid out—not thrown down but laid out, for the object seemed to be lying parallel to the sidewalks. Leonhard walked rapidly toward it.

"Leo, Leo!" voices called behind him. He did not refer the cry to himself. Then again—the shouting went on—then rapid trampling of feet, and then his arms were seized from either side. Niki Zdarsa and Karl Zilcher literally clung to Leonhard, dug their fingers into his arms, hung on to him, while they matched his rapid pace. Their sweat-drenched faces were much altered from the faces that he knew. They stammered something to him. He did not understand. His relief at seeing the two again, at having escaped the whiplash blows of the salvos of the carbines, for the moment deafened his ears, and while Niki and Karl clung to his arms, in fact he was finding support in them. They were saying again and again in their thickest dialect: "Lead us outa this, Leo, we can't stan' the sight of it no more. The soot are out, all the soot from the Prater. You don't see no more workers. You must know how to get through, you know." ("Soot" is a splendid slang expression in Vienna for the lowest of the low, the bottommost layer of society, whom you cannot even graze without soiling yourself as you would on a sooty stove lid.) Why

Leonhard, of all persons, should know the way out of this chaos, was not clear. But the leadership that the two were thrusting upon him forced him to a higher plane, to an elevated position from which he could survey the situation. They themselves were no longer capable of taking such a wider view, and therefore it was for him to take it. He had to take it, if only to show his gratitude that the two had come along at this moment, that they were there. And so the three young men, arms firmly inter-locked, strode rapidly down the deserted street toward the object which lay precisely in the center at the end of it, aligned with the sidewalks. The raging of the "soot," the Prater whores and their pimps, was left behind.

They soon recognized the object laid out on the street as a dead man. He lay on his back, arms stretched along his body, eyes closed. Under his head was his folded police tunic and cap. Over his brow a tousle of black hair. The horror lay in the young man's fineness. The chest still looked as if the lungs were filled with air, and Karl Zeitler's rather stubborn, boyish face still be-longed entirely to this day, only turned somewhat inward, emptied of some of its energy. This was no wretched bundle, cast down in a heap by the violence of the shot, twisted and distorted by the death-agony, only the remains of a man. Where it is so, you do not bid farewell to the body, but to the living man as you had known him. But Police Corporal Karl Zeitler lay here like a still-living man, behind a perfectly pure, clear crystal wall be-tween time and eternity. Who could say who had so neatly laid him out here? Perhaps the very persons who had stolen his service pistol.

Leonhard knelt on the pavement beside Zeitler.

Incomprehensible, beyond all else, that Zeitler had been taken from him.

He was still looking into Zeitler's close, wholly unchanged face, when a heavy trampling reached his ears, though he paid no attention; he was still enclosed within the ring of his sorrow as in a magic circle. Then someone shouted: "You bastards! You've killed him!"

Niki and Karl Zilcher were standing with hands raised, staring into the mouths of the pistols pointed at them. A pistol was pointed at Leonhard too. But he did not raise his hands. He remained kneeling beside the dead man, and only looked up. Along with his sorrow, the truth spoke from his face. No words were needed. The whole group—Niki and Karl with arms up, Leonhard kneeling, the dead man, the elderly police inspector and his two patrolmen, all three with pistols in their hands—the whole group remained motionless like figures in a waxworks.

At last Leonhard said: "Karl Zeitler from the Brigittenau precinct. My best friend. We used to study together."

The inspector stooped over the body. "My Lord, yes," he said then, and snapped in the safety-catch of his pistol.

The other two did likewise.

"Then you must be Herr—what was that name again, it begins with K . . . ?"

"Leonhard Kakabsa."

"Yes. He often spoke of you."

Leonhard had got to his feet; Niki and Zilcher lowered their arms. No one spoke; there was a moment of silence; not a shot was being fired anywhere.

When the inspector spoke at last, his words came out woodenly, oddly unsuitable to the occasion.

"Can you give us any information? Were you eyewitnesses?"

"We just found him lying here like this."

Leonhard had completely forgotten about the conciliatory animal warmth of the dialect at this moment.

"Are you workers?" the inspector asked, turning to all three.

"Yes," Leonhard replied. Any other answer, in regard to himself, did not even occur to him.

Suddenly the inspector's face changed as he dropped out of his part. In a kind of anguish, he demanded: "Can any of you tell me how this happened? How all this could have happened?"

The two younger policemen, who had been gazing with weary, exhausted expressions at the dead man, looked up. Their faces, dulled and grief-laden, showed the terrible effect of this day.

Leonhard was looking at Zeitler's head—the pale face still showed traces of mingled sweat and dust, while the black tousle of hair seemed to be sticking to the forehead. He felt his eyes grow hot, and then the tears welled out like a foreign power that could not be resisted.

"I do not know," he said.

At the end of the street the patient sufferers of the day, the Republican Protective Association, appeared in the form of three uniformed men carrying an empty stretcher. Perhaps they were here only to catch their breath a moment; shots could be heard again, and screams. At any rate, the inspector called to them, beckoned them to approach.

"Inspector," Niki said, fighting a lump in his throat, his voice already giving out, "I haven't seen any workers at all these last hours. The soot are out, all the soot from the Prater."

The police officer nodded. The stretcher-bearers had come up. "Would you please take our comrade with you?" he said to them. The men of the socialist paramilitary troop raised Zeitler and laid him on the stretcher. Leonhard went up to the dead man once more and brushed the hair back from his forehead. Then the stretcher was lifted. "I hope to see you again in better times," the inspector said, shaking hands with Leonhard. "In better times!" Niki and Zilcher said. Then the little convoy started off.

At the back end of the bier walked a young member of the Protective Association who was obviously weeping; probably his nerves could no longer stand up to the rapidly changing situations of the day. And so Karl Zeitler was carried by those who had been transformed from a party paramilitary force into ambulance corpsmen and pallbearers. It was as though someone were throwing open a red cape which proved to be lined on the inside with gleaming white velvet. Such were these men: *anima humana, natura autem christiana,* though they themselves would scarcely have admitted it. The funeral procession disappeared around the corner.

Our three young men were as yet far from being out of the danger zones. Shots and cries were again resounding close by. But it was as though the dead man had opened a wide breach for them, through which they walked as in a dream, keeping to the right now in the direction of the District Court (from which the whole affair had started) and toward the Alser. Arrived on Schwarzspanier Strasse, they marveled at how easily they had escaped from the inferno in which many another person was trapped. (But it was already growing quieter around the burning Palace of Justice.)

The gates to freedom often stand wide open, and no one sees them.

So they went on, through Währinger Strasse and Bolzmann Gasse, past the building of the former Imperial-and-Royal Consular Academy—a dead hereafter in the here. All three, and not only Leonhard, felt as if they were really carrying the dead man with them. Going downhill, their clothes and hair soaked with sweat, they marched through the horrible sediment of this day. Every day has such terrible sediments, only today a howling wind had whipped them up. Yet Leonhard felt a real happiness because these two were walking at his side; their presence was like a bandage over the recent wound of his parting from them, and under the bandage the wound was already healed. The two routes, moreover, the routes to right and left, now coincided; he trod both at once, for this led to Mary. Swiftly and willingly, Leonhard glided along the aqueduct which guided him there, and toward the inevitable cataract which he had known he would meet since early that morning.

It was like a green valley in deep peace, as it must once have been many centuries before when the little river, the Als, still flowed in the sunlight between meadows and fields down to the Danube, far on the outskirts of the city. Today it flowed within the city, in fact under its belly, in a rushing, splashing darkness out of which rose creatures which the purling stream of older times would not have nourished.

Some touch of that freer air seemed to be blowing around

Leonhard now, and perhaps it really came from the old days, wafted by the tales Karl Zeitler used to tell, out of his delvings into history.

They reached Alserbach Strasse and followed it, walking, as it were, in the valley bottom of this day, which to either side still reared wildly fissured spires into the air. At the corner where Porzellan Gasse turns in, Leonhard stopped. He had just caught sight of René Stangeler walking along, carrying a briefcase, but not by its handle; he had it tucked under his arm and pressed against his chest. Now René turned the corner and walked along Althan Platz to Number 6. To see his girl, of course. Leonhard waited a little until René would be far enough ahead; this was not the time for a meeting and the inevitable civilities it would involve. Niki and Karl Zilcher likewise stopped, to either side of Leonhard. They did not ask what this halt signified. There is a state of overstrain and overburdenedness in which people no longer react in response to minor stimuli.

Stangeler walked along as deliberately as if he intended to march several hundred miles. The incomprehensibility of the fellow's behavior seemed to Leonhard at the moment to border on sheer horror. His hand flew to his hair. It was damp with sweat. The thick hair between his fingers seemed to him the very same that he had brushed back from Karl Zeitler's forehead. For a moment he felt as if his brain were stirring beneath his skull, and his grief over Karl hit him so hard that he was frightened. Stangeler had entered Number 6. They walked on. In front of Mary's door Leonhard stopped again. "This is where I'm going," he said. Niki and Zilcher awoke from their daze. Perhaps they understood now why he had gone this way with them. It had completely slipped their minds that Leo no longer lived in Brigittenau. "You'll be coming around to Rolletschek's after quittin' time one of these days, won't you?" Zilcher asked.

"Yes, I'll come," Leonhard answered.

"Be sure to come," Niki said. In his voice was that same anxious overtone that had been audible in their farewell, when Leonhard crossed the Rubicon in a cab. Both men smiled now. In shaking

1297 / The Fire

hands they added an extra affectionate pressure. They turned away. Leonhard watched them go the short distance they remained within sight. However, the two did not turn; they thought he was already inside the house. Now they vanished around the corner. Leonhard entered Number 6, passed through the pompous hallway, listened at the elaborate staircase. Nothing stirred. Stangeler was by that time in the Siebenschein apartment. Now Leonhard gathered himself as if to jump, and then he flew up the winding stairs so rapidly that he had to lean inward as he ran, once, twice, around the shaft of the elevator. Then he braked and controlled himself. His running was too loud. At a proper and dignified pace, he passed the Siebenschein-Storch floor.

The abstracted state of mind of René Stangeler on this July 15, 1927, was quite unlike the daze in which Quapp was wont to live, with her habitual ignorance. René knew precisely why the workers were demonstrating, and later was able to construe approximately why and how the shooting had come about. But he lacked a certain facility and elasticity of apprehension which is essential if a person is to see clearly and to know what is going on. Someone in whom perception itself is subject to fluctuations will only at rare moments really take hold of the outside world (as René had done under the arcades of the University in conversation with Herzka, and later at the Carinthian castle).

It is true that those rare moments had been multiplying since the days René had spent at Neudegg. They were already so frequent that the individual points were moving closer together, on the verge of becoming a line, a real continuity. It is true also that René's condition today might well be called good, and was already adding one more point to the continuity. But in spite of that, he had felt a burden to himself. Underneath the bright and —in spite of everything—serene surface of this day, for the most part spent at the Hotel Ambassador, he had lain under the weight of that burden as at the marshy bottom of a pond alive with all sorts of dark fauna, with the sunny surface far above.

He had taken his leave shortly before Professor Bullogg, Mrs. Bullogg, and the Garriques had settled down to tea. He really should have stayed to tea, and had foreseen the obligation. But he had finished his work with the professor half an hour before. And René had had enough of that company. It was true also that no telephones were functioning, and that Grete would be worrying about his whereabouts. But that was not his primary reason for leaving. Rather he had simply had enough. But with his new-found social skill, René had learned to borrow from others those emotions of consideration which they would probably have felt in the given situation; he did so now to make his actions understandable, to give no offense, and to win approval for his conduct. We have, after all, observed him once exerting himself to be nice toward Frau Storch, who has since vanished entirely from our ken (and had not the effort been amply repaid?). Here too the method proved its worth. Clever Mme Garrique, whose eye had rested upon Stangeler with maternal benevolence more than once in the course of the day, thought it so touching that he could not bear to have his fiancée worry, and was setting out to see Miss Siebenschein even though all sorts of things were still going on in the streets. Thus Mme Garrique, immediately after Stangeler's departure.

He took "Ruodlieb von der Vläntsch's" manuscript with him. (With the professor, too, he had insisted that this could not be the author's real name. Bullogg could not see his point; he thought the name Ruodlieb not at all unusual for southern Austria at that period.)

René was taking the manuscript with him, then. On a day full of such disturbances it was not exactly advisable to go marching through the city with such a unique document under his arm. It was on the tip of the professor's tongue to issue such a warning and Mme Garrique very nearly said it outright. But it was not spoken. Stangeler was only invited to dinner at the Ambassador for Tuesday; they could then take up any questions that might meanwhile occur to the professor.

Why Professor Bullogg and Mme Garrique let René go march-

ing off into danger with the treasure remains an ambiguous matter. On the one hand they did not want to exact a confidence
which was not spontaneously granted. On the other hand, Stangeler emanated a somnambulist's sureness (so René's native idiocy
struck them), and perhaps the worst thing to do would be to wake
him. At any rate, as she later admitted, that is how it seemed to
Mme Garrique. Moreover, Professor Bullogg had already noticed
that this generally well-bred young man was given to a peculiar
obstinacy about minor details. He therefore withheld comment
when René, for the tenth time, questioned the genuineness of
Ruodlieb von der Vläntsch's name and affirmed that it must be a
cryptogram.

Moreover, the professor rather liked his young colleague's stub-
bornness. He did not regard it as childish, but rather as a childlike innocence, a total identification with the subject that filled his
mind, such as is shown by children when at play.

René trudged off. At that same pace with which he had
marched 300 miles on his flight from Siberia, across the Omsk
steppes and over the Urals. He kept to the right, not only because
his destination required it, for he did not take the shortest route.
This was an outflanking march. From the Hotel Krantz-Ambassador he had listened attentively to the shooting, had estimated
distances and localized the battle, and had determined from the
sounds that this was not even a "middling show"—in the war he
and his friend Ensign Preyda had used this phrase for skirmishes
that tended to spread beyond mere patrol actions. Especially
night skirmishes; when a "middling show" developed, you put
your boots on. Preyda—he and Stangeler had bunked together in
a dugout in the front-line trench—knew parts of the Iliad in both
Greek and Czech, and used to recite them for René's amusement.
"Well then," René thought, "it isn't even a 'middling show.' The
salvos don't sound like much. There can't be any great stir
throughout the city." It is almost incredible that our friend René
could make use of so absurd a standard and thereby reassure himself. He apparently did not consider that five rifle shots in the
streets of a peaceful metropolis are a far more significant fact than

half a crate of ammunition shot off in the trenches. And so he trudged peacefully along, Planken Gasse, Dorotheer Gasse, Graben, Trattnerhof, Bauernmarkt, Wipplinger Strasse. The only way to get about was to walk; nothing to be done about that. It vexed him that all the while with the Bulloggs and Garriques he had felt unhappy. In fact, he still felt so. Devil take it, why should he feel unhappy! The professor had virtually made firm commitments concerning things which Stangeler a little while before would never have dared to dream of: publication, dollars, Harvard. . . . Then why unhappy? Simply because those people in the hotel were each and every one more sensible than he himself, lived better and easier, more rightly, so it seemed to him. . . . They accepted with tranquillity and ease all that they possessed: professorship, money, car; they considered it all their due. For himself, he was not yet even capable of grasping the fact that Jan Herzka had actually given him 1500 schillings, now carefully put away in a bank account and increased each month by his regular salary check, also from Herzka. He could not comprehend his unhappiness, his apartness from all these substantial facts which Grete, in a way acting as his deputy, understood so much better. She rejoiced. He really did not. It all seemed a void, stupid, lightless abyss.

But Ensign Preyda—long since dead, killed in a counterattack—now fished something up, drew up in his net a silvery burden, something never seen before! Shortly before Preyda's death Stangeler had come home on his first leave, which was to be his last as well, for after his return to the front he was taken prisoner and shipped off to Siberia. That leave had been at the beginning of June 1916. He recalled the ride to the nearest railroad station, a thirty-minute gallop on a beautiful pony. In Lemberg, as Lvov was then called, he had taken the express train to Vienna. It actually had a dining car. René was then an ensign—in the Austrian Imperial Army that rank was equivalent to second lieutenant. Arrived in Vienna, his first act was to take a bath. Before he was out of the tub, little E. P. telephoned—he was in the Thirteenth Regiment of Uhlans, which occupied an entirely different sector of the front from the infantry regiment to which Stangeler was then assigned. René had written him that he was coming home on furlough—and here was E. P. calling already. A few days later they went on an outing to Sievering. E. P. brought along a young lady who had made no particular impression upon Stangeler, a pale girl with raven-black hair.

That had been Grete Siebenschein.

Of course René had already realized that he had known Grete since then—after his return from Siberia his break with E. P. had taken place on her account. Nevertheless, the fact struck him as utterly new. For eleven years it had remained part and parcel of the basic grating of actualities which sustain us, but of which we are scarcely aware. Only when we lie, and tell things differently from the way they really happened, or concoct outright fables, does this basis expand and contract a little, and a kind of swelling is formed, a tumor of mendacity which isolates the lying mouth from its sources and its real language. At such times many people tend to use bombastic phrases, behind which, of course, the truth completely vanishes. No one feels quite at ease about doing this. Many people—those who are more clear-sighted— suffer from a hangover afterwards. Only types like Imre von Gyurkicz lie without ill effects.

Stangeler, however, had never thought about his encountering Grete as early as 1916; through E. P. he had met her anew—in every sense—in 1921.

Now he suddenly saw her as having had a place in his life five years earlier (and in youth five years is a very long span of time!). And although at that time she had shone pallidly and shallowly upon him, like mother-of-pearl or the waning moon only glanced at, the memory now fitted her into that immutable fundamental "grating" composed of all that was once sacredly present. And it is no wonder that she became even more sacredly present now, acquired for René a kind of intensified validity.

For now that fundamental grating, which with advancing years disappears more and more under the growing ash-heaps of burned and consumed actualities, sent up into René's consciousness more than an indication of its existence. A part of the grating itself glowed to life, yielded light like a piece of white-hot coal that has fallen into the ash-pit of the humming samovar and now lies beyond the slit, sending out heat. Ah yes, that was what it had been like in Siberia, evenings, when he was studying, or talking with friends—that happiest period of his life, René now recognized. A time of stillness, of perspective, of pure learning, of taking to himself the things of the mind. Years of discipleship. And nowhere any staggeringly self-assured people who thought themselves entitled to automobiles or professorships. His tiny chamber in East Siberia, with its dim, yet penetrating light that shone all the way to Vienna and to Wipplinger Strasse—what noble origins it had had!

But beyond, what is that, what steps upon the scene behind it as if entering into the brightness of day itself? A meadow sloping up to the edge of leafy woods. E. P. wanted to take snapshots, first of her, then of René. There she stood now. Now—but it was now, this present day! Her hat had a broad rim and was transparent; perhaps that had been the fashion in those days; transparent as organdy or a dragonfly's wings. She smiled. René was certain of this: she had smiled. Her big lovely mouth smiled. High above her the treetops foamed into the summer sky.

It had been cloudless then, as it was today. On the way back, by a weather-beaten statue of St. Nepomuk, she had bought strawberries from a fruit seller who stood there with his baskets.

With that recollection, the fundamental grating became iron-gray once more; the white-hot glow departed; ashes fell upon ashes. There was one last flicker: that he still had her, the girl of that memory in the present girl, the girl of that time whom he had seen today for the first time. She had not departed into the void, stupid, lightless abyss.

With that thought, everything dissolved. René walked along Porzellan Gasse. He fell into that stream of details into which everyone plunges in whom tension has relaxed and who therefore becomes a world without a center, swamped by the drifting plankton of association which psychology considers the secret of life itself and therefore describes with enormous gravity and exactitude. We will fish out only a sample: apparently Professor Bullogg was not so learned in paleography as he might have been, for he did not know that especially at that period there had been several different ways to write the letter "s"—in fact, he had taken this as a peculiarity of the author. Moreover, he had not understood the genitive plural symbol for pounds of pennies: lib. ♌. Nor did he seem to be aware that shillings and pounds had not been coins, of course, but units of account. "Studied in Budapest, after all. Guess they don't keep after them there as they do at our Institute in Vienna."

Amid such reflections he turned the corner, where he was seen by Leonhard.

Arriving (with his briefcase) at the Siebenscheins', Stangeler was given an extraordinary reception. Grete flew toward him down the hall. Perhaps at that moment she reached the very height of her beauty, a flame hovering freely, entirely apart from the wick—smokeless, pure fire. She threw her arms around René and rested her head on his shoulder. "Sweet!" she exclaimed, and nothing else.

To our mind, Doktor Ferry Siebenschein was the hero of this scene.

He had peeked out of his door, but closed it again while the two were engaged in the greeting just described. He did not reappear until, by the sound of René's and Grete's voices and footsteps in the hall, he could judge that it was over. Then: "Ah, there he is, our *historicus*. Have you been wearing yourself out all day with the American, René?" It was the first time he had ever addressed René so familiarly, and he now spontaneously took him by the shoulders. "Don't tell me you've got the thing right there with you in the briefcase!"

"That's right," Stangeler said.

"We must have a look at it."

"I've never seen it either," Grete told her father.

"Into the bathroom with him!" Ferry ordered. "Have a shower, get out of those hot clothes, make yourself comfortable. Grete—about fifteen cups of tea for him. I'll take charge of the briefcase. But we'll all look at the treasure together."

So it came about that shortly afterwards Stangeler, wrapped in a violet dressing-gown and provided with slippers (all from Ferry Siebenschein's wardrobe), sat in Grete's room, crawled into the teacup, then drank the cigarette smoke, or both simultaneously, or vice versa. Fortunately, Frau Irma appeared only after this most intense proceeding. She blinked like a rat that has taken the whim to peer over the rim of its cellar hole into the sunlight. There are moments when the beatification of charm falls even upon things really *méchant;* and this was the case here, as far as possible, anyway. Later, after familial examination of Ruodlieb's work, René and Grete were left alone again, and Grete bent once more over the manuscript. "Imagine," she said, "he has actually entered our lives. When did he die?"

"In 1518, in Augsburg," René replied.

"That makes . . ."

"Four hundred and nine years," Stangeler said.

Before this little exchange, however, René had sat for some time at the tea table, while the manuscript was handed around and the expert contributed casual explanations. They sat around him with considerable respect. For these moments the poor fool had become something of a pasha, a pasha in a violet dressing-gown. But away with all of them now. We have more important matters at hand.

At five-thirty Mary K. moved into a chair in the hall which Grete Siebenschein had placed there for her, that she might practice a woman's principal occupation. For Mary wished to open the door almost as soon as Leonhard rang, so that he would not have to wait long; and she could not, after all, actually run down the length of the apartment.

Even during the last half hour that Grete had spent with her,

Mary had been prey to a curious feeling. It was as though deep within her, bubbling into an ample basin, the whole previous flow of her life were accumulating, uniting under the sign of this day and this hour. Everything was there, but this hour remained the great fount in which everything else gathered.

For a few seconds only, while Grete was slipping out the door, the brief impending solitude almost crushed her, and she was on the point of calling her friend back. Out of weakness. Mary knew. She knew everything. Not only what was impending now, when Leonhard arrived; but everything that would come much later, that remained inevitable. To be sure, this sorrow was something only known, as a thing sure to come, just as we always know of our eventual death but do not feel it as existent, cleaving, raging. Who can measure the vastness of such a difference! Mary too did not attempt to measure it, although she knew in advance all that she had to know. Knew also that no man had meant much to her other than her husband Oskar, who had died in 1924. That thought too was utterly present to her now, along with everything else that poured into this imminent present, this coming hour. She felt her situation to be unique, first because of her impediment, and second because this represented the crown of her great struggle in Munich the year before. And that situation was illuminated by an imperious accent, a decisive sharp wedge of light that excluded all possibility of retreat. For the first time in her life, perhaps, Mary found herself ready to enter, without hesitation or resistance, into a decisive relationship which had absolutely no rational future.

From her seat in the hall she looked out on courtyards, walls, the green top of a tree, and many rows of windows that stared darkly into the world like the ends of giant pipes. Everything seemed numbed to a greater stillness by the hot sun—this was the sunny side of the apartment; the rest of the long series of rooms were almost entirely shaded, except for the bedroom at the end of the long hall, whose windows likewise opened on the rear. Right now, wide beams of sunlight must be cutting across that room.

Though there, she remembered, the curtains were tightly drawn.

She straightened up, sat with the small of her back strained and concave. Now, with her whole being, she drifted swiftly toward the cataract. And in these moments she heard Leonhard's running footsteps on the stairway, loudly breaking the silence. Her heart pounded, not faster, but more powerfully. She rose slowly, with dignity. The running stopped. Once again, for the span of a breath only, everything gathered toward the possibility of a conceivable decision—but the decision had long since been taken. The more deliberate footsteps approached outside. The sound of the bell tore through Mary's body. Leonhard came through the opened door, threw himself down before Mary, and kissed *both* her feet.

At this hour two onlookers had left the theater of war, after only casually entering its periphery. Now they were ambling along side by side out to the garden suburb: Eulenfeld, long and gangling, and Körger with arms dangling like sausages. They reached Döbling dry, late in the afternoon, long before the rain began to fall—it started with isolated showers about nine o'clock in the evening. Neither was the kind of man who allows himself to get drenched. They felt a virtually total superiority toward the events they had seen in town—hardly a feeling entertained by people who can hear the grass grow. The captain and Herr von Geyrenhoff's nephew, on the other hand, were hearing the mills of the gods; they even thought they knew how to speed up, someday, that slow process of grinding.

They were approaching the end of their walk, somewhere along the length of Grinzinger Allee, when Eulenfeld turned to the left, said: "Think I'll have a slug here," and entered a small café where he dropped in fairly often on his way home from the city. Körger followed him in. It may be that he felt the need for a cup of coffee after all he had seen (though it had not been very much) and all he had discussed with the captain on their walk

("*habeant sibi*"—such had been the substance of his remarks—
"let them knock each other's heads in. All the better for us. *Tant
mieux pour nous. Duobus certantibus, et cetera, et cetera*"). But
aside from any desire for coffee, Körger usually followed the captain, who almost always set the direction and tone when the two
were together. And perhaps not only because the captain was the
elder. The bourgeois-looking Körger followed the aristocrat who
was already beginning to look far from aristocratic. He followed
Eulenfeld with an expression of tense doglike fidelity that had
nothing of fawning submissiveness about it; rather, he seemed to
have borrowed his face from a bull terrier. There was only one
respect in which Körger did not follow the captain: in drinking.
Many people drank for the captain's sake, the better to enjoy his
company—Stangeler, for example. Association with alcoholics is
extraordinarily difficult for those who do not join in the drinking,
and calls for endless patience. But Körger was successful at it.
Moreover, he never dampened the captain's enthusiasm by his
own abstinence. On the contrary, Körger actually encouraged
Eulenfeld. That is not so easy for one who does not tip the glass
himself, does not with constant "cheers!" work himself into a
cheery mood, and yet watches his companion's mood grow
steadily cheerier, and listens to his speech growing thicker.

The only explanation was Körger's extraordinary callousness;
he actually enjoyed watching Eulenfeld drink himself under the
table. For which reason he kept a bottle of whiskey at home
solely for the captain's benefit, and would constantly press it on
him. Here in the café he raised no warning protest against
Eulenfeld's frequent reorders.

In their political judgment of the day, both men were agreed,
as we have seen. Eulenfeld shook himself after every glass he
downed. Körger watched this too with interest. It seemed each
time as if this body, originally of such solid stuff, were twitching
under each new assault of the poison.

Gradually, and faster and faster after the fourth drink, Eulenfeld began to disappear, to become a feeble, blinking little star
in the dense mass of a nebula. Körger looked around the café,

which was bright and pleasant. They sat in the rearmost corner, in a kind of private niche, and at the moment were the only patrons of the place. This stage in his association with the captain was always the most rewarding to Körger. This was what he waited for. He had a term for it, "the cavalry captain's petrifaction" (*magister equitum petrificatus*). For only when the captain was completely stoned was Körger liberated from a sense of the other man's superiority. Otherwise that feeling was there at every step, in the choosing of a route or a café, in the decision to walk fast or slow, however Eulenfeld might set the pace. The feeling was located deep within Körger, and he had never yet permitted it to rise to the surface of consciousness and be verbalized. But when it vanished, he felt at once the absence of its constant light pressure.

Today too Körger enjoyed that sense of relief. His hour had come again, liberating him completely from Eulenfeld; and as the other went from bad to worse, he felt actually tender toward him, and wished him joy of every drop of his liquor. His real tie to Eulenfeld consisted of this special little torment, only a slight discomfort actually, as though a hand were lightly clutching at the bowels of his being. His real reward was the dispersing of that weak sense of disgrace when the captain was thoroughly drunk.

When that point was reached, Körger was in the habit of pushing the captain around in his thoughts, dealing with him as a mere means to an end. And so he placed the captain where he liked in his sketches of a new order, those sketches which were with him constantly and within which he strolled as in a second reality; they provided an elevated platform for his callousness, from which he could shrug his shoulders at the temporary structure of the surrounding world, like an architect looking down at a barracks. (Körger still made his little architectural drawings of one-family houses, two-family houses, villas, and so on.)

"Old swine," he thought now, regarding the captain, who had, he thought, fallen asleep (in which he was wrong), "of course people like him are done for, useless for us. But we have to pick

their brains a little, because, say what you will, they have front-
line experience and military knowledge and general education
and all that stuff. Which we don't. Let them be teachers. Then,
when the time comes, away with them. They can never understand us."

Now the captain spoke, right out of his absolute stupor: "Let
them bash one another's brains out. For all I care, they can both
stick it, the one lot and the other. Security—the one lot's or the
other lot's. That's it. Sooner or later the whole intellectual
manure-heap will go to the dogs, the kind Kajetan shovels out,
and the Ensign's too. Along with all damned security—a new and
weird kind of uprising will begin. *Vivant sequentes.*"

"Undoubtedly," Körger said.

The captain cleared his throat thunderously and grunted.

No one paid attention. The proprietor and the old waiter of the
café knew their baron.

Now Körger contemplated Eulenfeld, who seemed to have
fallen asleep at last, still sitting upright in a totally dignified
posture on the upholstered bench. As always, Körger's expression
changed—even as it changed when the captain drank in company and Körger watched him approach one of his "states." The
tense look vanished. Now Körger had a serene, contented, and
benevolent expression. When he had enjoyed the spectacle to
the full, he left. As a prank—so he thought—he left it to the captain to pay for his coffee; the little item would vanish into insignificance in Eulenfeld's much larger check. But it was no
prank. It was something far more serious—an eternally alert
frugality. In departing, Körger confided his friend to the waiter's
care. But this proved unnecessary.

"No need to be concerned, Herr Doktor," the waiter said. "The
Herr Baron frequently has himself a little nap here. We take the
liberty of waking him gently when it's nearly closing time. Usually the Herr Baron likes to have a couple of franks at that hour."

At three minutes before six o'clock we heard the sound of a car
driving up in front of the Palais Ruthmayr, and simultaneously

with the delicate chiming of a clock somewhere in the salon, Quapp came up the red-carpeted staircase, utterly charming in her dress and dab of a hat. She looked extraordinarily pretty. Friederike had risen. Quapp proved, as always, to have a chivalrous spirit. When she caught sight of the beautiful older woman, she dropped a low curtsey. "Good Lord!" Friederike exclaimed at the sight of her. She raised this Fräulein von Schlaggenberg to her feet, embraced and kissed her, drew a chair up close to hers, and sat Quapp in it. "It's unbelievable how she resembles him!" Friederike said to me. And then to Quapp: "How could you possibly be here so punctually when . . . ?"

"I came in an embassy car," Quapp said. She looked at me, and I smiled. Her eyes were very wide open.

"Shall we tell her?" I asked Friederike. She nodded. "Just half an hour ago this lady and I became engaged," I said.

"Oh, that's—that's—glorious, marvelous!" Quapp exclaimed, seizing my hand with her left and Friederike's with her right hand. Then she burst out: "I've become engaged too today. With Herr von Geyrenhoff's cousin, Géza Orkay."

I explained to Friederike who that was. Then turning to Quapp, "Quappchen," I said, "we're practically related now and you must call me Georg."

"Oh, how gladly," she exclaimed, "*Gyuri-bácsi!*"

"What a day!" Friederike cried, clapping her hands. "Really, no day for celebrating, but still we're going to celebrate." Her eyes flashed again, large and dark, as they had in the garden that time.

"So now, besides my mama, I've got myself another pair of parents . . ." Quapp said merrily.

"I want that to be really so!" Friederike said. She drew Quapp into her embrace again.

"So I shall be your stepfather," I said. "And my cousin's father-in-law. Complicated kinships. Heaven knows what will come of it."

Well, nothing but good came of it, nevertheless.

But around every peak of life there hover, like heavy black

clouds, the absentees and the dead—who are sometimes almost equivalent. In this case they were Levielle and Gyurkicz.

"Drink your tea and have something to eat, my child," Friederike said.

We stayed to supper with her then; in fact, with such turbulence in the city, Quapp was not allowed to set out for home.

After dining—by candlelight, for there was still no electricity—we drank a bottle of champagne. We were terribly aware that this was not a day when one should celebrate, and yet how could we not, with all our reasons? It was Friederike, then, who wanted to look out once again at the fire, from the terrace facing the gardens. We went down into the salon and out the back door. The rain had stopped, but every leaf was still dripping. The glow of the conflagration was enormous. In the darkness it was reflected from a number of thunderclouds that still hung in the sky. I took a deep breath of the damp air, perfumed by luxuriant plant growth —still with a lingering consciousness of the cool camphor fragrance of the lower part of the salon, through which we had just passed. But the smell that followed immediately afterwards, borne on a barely palpable breeze, came from the towering red flames: the implacable smell of fire. We stood on the wet terrace and looked out upon it like people on a pier gazing out at a wildly churning sea.

Thus ended for us the day which quite incidentally signified the Cannae of Austrian freedom. But no one knew that at the time, we least of all.

It may be added here that the bodies of Anna Diwald and Meisgeier were pulled out of the sewer shaft on Monday, July 18. They lay one atop the other, Anna with her body up to the waist in water. She might easily have fallen toward the center of the current, and would then have been floated away down to the overflow chamber at the lower end of Schotten Ring, near the Danube Canal. In that case the big briefcase would probably have been lost. As it was, Anna held this bag (which had once attracted Editor Holder's attention) pressed close against her even in death. Since it contained all her papers, photographs, letters, and other valuables, identification of the body was easy.

There was no doubt that both the man and the woman had been killed instantly. The shot which had blown out Meisgeier's light had penetrated his skull in a perfectly vertical line from above. At the autopsy it was discovered that the force of the shot, at such close range, had caused three completely symmetrical cracks in the brainpan. The bullet had penetrated Anna's head from the temple; moreover, there was also a steel-jacketed bullet in one chamber of her heart; it had smashed its way in right through her collarbone.

The police needed no papers to identify Meisgeier; they knew him well.

The following day, at seven o'clock in the morning, the police came to Anny Gräven's apartment.

They went to no unnecessary trouble with her. "Look here, Gräven," the official said to her at the first interrogation, "don't make things hard for us. Don't make a fuss. Look what I got." He showed her the few words which Hertha Plankl had scribbled shortly before her death and which Anny Gräven had sent on to Didi with a note of her own.

"Come on now, Gräven, give us the story."

Well, she told it.

"All right, then," the detective said when Anny had signed her statement. "We can start the proceedings right off, so you won't have to sit around here too long." (He meant in the police lockup.) "It looks like a Paragraph 6, complicity after the crime's committed, or maybe a 211. The penalty'll be by 213. It won't be too bad, Gräven, just six months in the clink is what it'll amount to."

It amounted to that. But the large number of petty criminal cases which resulted from those July days delayed Anny's case so that she did not come to trial before the second half of January. She had already served six months awaiting trial, so that soon after the verdict was pronounced she was released.

When she came out, she experienced a number of surprises.

Standing in the cold, gray, clattering street—it was a hard winter, although that particular day was relatively mild—Anny Gräven was overcome by an unwonted depression. Especially at the thought of her apartment (logical enough, at that season!), for the rent had not been paid all those six months. How could she have kept up the rent when she had nothing put by, having always ignored Leonhard's well-meant advice about that? She shivered. Also she was not dressed for winter weather. There was nothing to do but to take the streetcar home, although for all she knew she no longer had a home. Arrived at the Prater Stern, she did not enter the sprawling old structure through the Franzensbrücken Strasse entrance, but through the hotel and bar on Prater Strasse. As she crossed the barroom toward the rear, the man at the counter greeted her as though she had been there yesterday and the day before, in fact as though she had never been gone. That was a first small encouragement. Still, it did not mean anything. The place where fortune, good or ill, awaited her, was the loge of the concierge, who was also the desk-clerk of the dubious hotel. Anny entered his den for the sole reason that she was frightfully cold, could feel nothing but how cold she was. The concierge's box was so intensely overheated that Anny literally shuddered.

"Well, how are you, Frau Anny!" the concierge said. "So you're back again—lived through it, eh? Well, well, things are always happening, things are always happening."

His cigar smell made her uneasy, reminded her of the police; one of the officials had also smoked cigars. Exhausted, she dropped down in a chair beside his. After some moments in the reviving warmth, she felt capable of taking this bull by the horns. "Tell me, Herr Ladstätter, what about my apartment now?"

"What should be about your apartment?"

"I haven't paid nothing for six months."

"All settled," Herr Ladstätter said. "The gentlemen took care of that right away. You know, Frau Anny, the ones as used to be your regulars."

She felt a kind of dissolution, a dispersion and melting away.

Now that she no longer needed energy, the last remnant of her forces ebbed away. To Anny Gräven's knowing ear, the concierge's tone plainly indicated that the gentlemen in question had not only generously provided for her but had known how to arouse a proper respect in Herr Ladstätter. That was as certain as cash in hand—as certain as the cash gratuities that had been placed in Herr Ladstätter's hand.

Herr Ladstätter quickly pushed up his window and called through it to an elderly creature shuffling past: "Frau Anny is here, Frau Rambausek. Will you go on up and get her room good and warm. Everything's there—wood and coal." And then he said to Anny: "Stay here for a while, Frau Anny—the place is still ice-cold. You'd catch your death up there. I've got some mail for you too."

He turned to his cubbyholes and dug out something altogether astonishing. Meanwhile Frau Rambausek came in for a moment and greeted Anny Gräven with a torrent of words. She was deeply moved and commensurately loquacious.

Frau Rambausek had various things to bring up to Anny's warmed apartment: three bottles of red wine, one bottle of cognac, five packs of cigarettes, a large box of chocolates, a gift basket containing all sorts of preserves and imported fruit, and a box containing perfume and cosmetics. The bar sent up a complimentary bottle of wine. There were also the four letters which the concierge had handed to Anny. These had all been delivered by hand, not sent through the mail. Each contained money, one of them a very sizable sum.

As soon as Anny was left alone in her bedroom, she stepped first to the big mirror.

She studied her image in surprise. Certainly her summery suit no longer looked very smart. But the youthfulness of her own appearance amazed her; she thought she had never yet seen herself like this. Her face was smooth, though rather thin. Here was what half a year's regular living without staying up all night, without abuse of alcohol and cigarettes, had done for her.

She took a little of the bar's wine and smoked. The combination of alcohol and nicotine affected her so powerfully that she let the half-emptied glass stand, and laid the cigarette aside. As she sat in her armchair, looking out at the viaduct between the open curtains, and only faintly intoxicated, the time before her arrest leaped to her mind with extraordinary vividness. It took the form of a valley that she could look down into, or an open hollow, and then of a womb gaping wide. On the farther verge was the night she had watched Meisgeier from the washroom window, as he climbed like a spider up the airshaft. Thence the deep valley opened up, sank down as into a dark womb, since that night she had spent with a gentleman here in this very room, one who was so much like her other "regulars." She still remembered that story he'd told of the sister who had been cheated out of her inheritance. . . . Thereafter she had become more and more indifferent to such gentlemen; she had begun to neglect that sort of clientele more and more. . . . And yet they had taken all this trouble for her. There had been a Herr Doktor among them, a lawyer. For a while she had not wanted any of them. As little as she now wanted ever to see those Greeks again, Xidakis and Protopapadakis, and Zurek and all those other punks. . . . Today she would have known how to please the gentleman who had that hobby about witches, and who'd unfortunately slipped through her fingers; he would have sent her a whole basket of wine now, that was the kind he was, and a thousand schillings besides. But she'd let him go, just to oblige Anita, that slut. . . . With this lie to herself, Anny dropped off to sleep.

For lying is inescapable necessity. The chair was comfortable. She slept soundly. When she awoke, it was dark in the room. She saw the blue lights over by the railroad toward the Prater, and once again thought of Schlaggenberg.

In the course of the evening one of her old clients came to look in on her. It was the one who had put the large bills into his envelope. Anny changed into her best and went along with the gentleman in his car, to dine at Schöner's. Thenceforth, all the local cafés of the vicinity were extinguished from Anny Gräven's thoughts, except for the one in which she used to go to have sausages and beer with Leonhard. Now, as the car drove along and the gentleman sat beside her at the wheel, she thought of Leonhard with great intensity and affection.

THE PRINCE wrote from Paris: "My stay here will continue for quite a while. You would do wisely, my dear friend, to go out to the country now, for in the fall we will have a great deal of work ahead of us." In Paris, it seemed, a society was being formed to finance an authoritative edition of the complete works of Pico della Mirandola (including the ones on the Cabbala and astrology), there being, as Leonhard well knew, no such edition. Some excellent scholars were prepared to collaborate. "You can stay at Jaidhof any time you please," the letter concluded. That was the prince's hunting lodge in Styria.

The sense that a chronologically impossible autumn had invaded midsummer was now stronger than ever with Leonhard. He was living entirely alone now, floating in his brightly painted boxes above the brown depths of the Palais Croix. For meals he descended to the dining room. Papa Pepi daily inquired after Leonhard's well-being and wishes. Often, after dining, Leonhard would vanish—from the spacious library into the rearmost of the rooms filled with books, and from there through the narrow, glassed-in corridor overlooking the garden into the rococo salon with its faint fragrance of camphor. A green glow fell through the windows from the gardens, where the lawn flowed like a pond around the old black trunks of the trees. The light itself seemed moist, especially in the first days after mid-July, when the weather was distinctly cloudy. After it improved, Mary went out to Semmering again for a week. Trix was to join her on the week end. But for the rest of the time she would be alone. Now, when Leonhard looked out into the gardens from the glassed-in corridor, the light no longer seemed so moist and green; wide slabs of sunlight lay scattered over the lawn and rose to the eye in dazzling golden sheets, like the sound of brass rising suddenly out of an orchestra.

The rest home, where Leonhard still had a whole vacation coming to him, was in the vicinity of Semmering; if he were there, he would be separated from Mary only by a tramp of two and a half hours.

It must be observed that this was the obvious reason for his preferring the rest home to the prince's hunting lodge (which he planned to visit later on in the summer). It was the logical and substantial reason, but not really the decisive one.

For returning to the rest home meant going back to his beginnings, back to Pico della Mirandola, to put the matter in the language of Leonhard's own spiritual dictionary. It was not that he thought he had forgotten anything or left anything behind in the rest home, or in the dark woods beyond the fence, on the side of the estate that extended into the mountain. What, after all, could he have left, as Quapp once in imagination left her violin case standing on Kärntner Strasse, and once again at the beginning of Mariahilfer Strasse? No, he had not left anything behind; but while he was there something had been ahead of him, like a duty to be performed.

And so the girls again sunned their legs in the steamer chairs on the terrace, and the pond basin was still dry, and in the middle of it stood a structure of tufa, monument to a fountain that had once plashed there and whose outlets still stuck out from between the spongelike stone.

Leonhard informed the concierge that he wanted to start out before dawn to walk to Semmering. He was told where to place the house key after having locked up again from outside. When he awoke—without an alarm clock—a spicy and ambrosial night had entered through the open window and settled everywhere in his room. Everything was quiet. Feeling fresh and clean, he donned his good new sports suit.

The little door leading out of the gardens and into the woods was locked at night; the concierge had forgotten to tell him that. In the deep darkness Leonhard clambered over the fence. Then up the embankment. The woods were silent as a burial vault.

He stood for a moment on the path that traversed the hill-side, but this time he turned to the left, not toward the trees and the cliffs of Mount Rax. He set out approximately eastward. His eyes, accustomed to the darkness, caught the growing rents in the black velvet of the night, the slow emergence of details. The tree trunks separated. Now powerful pipings slashed the dark woods, made them resound, revealing their spaciousness, making plain that all was not an unbroken, black plane surface. At a bend in the path a greenish hint of the sky appeared, and while Leonhard was looking at it, the first bold and artistic cadenzas began from the depths of the woods and were almost immediately taken up close by. The concentrated, inexorable process made Leonhard stand still for a long time, breathing deeply. It almost lifted him up. His still-anonymous potentiality lifted him—who was still half in the chaos of the night. He wished intensely that he could compress that potentiality in a single decision as one takes and presses something in the fist. . . . Ah, but what is it? The beginning of the beginning of the beginning, the sketchy project of heroism at which all lives aim. In early youth all men feel the potentiality for great actions.

Now the birds halted their song, leaving space for a mightier, soundless paean.

During that general pause the sky broke open like the husk of a fruit, giving birth to the glowing god. And already he was there, above the dark ridges of the mountains, his strength concentrated as it never is in the later hours of the day, which he illuminates in a more disperse fashion. Now, however, an eye appeared, an eye like an arrowhead, aiming straight to the heart.

Out in the garden suburb the whitish dust is already settling upon the streets, and a single window in a farmyard suddenly leaps into flame, gathering all the white-hot glow into its pane and flashing it far across the plain over corn fields and crop lands as far as the first curving hills and the higher, veiled mountains.

The city sinks into summer as into a dissolving bath of acid. The nights arch their backs high: masses of stone looking up into the brightness of the moon seek the keystone of the arch, growing, climbing, escaping that close confinement that was their nature all the gray winter. A wild uprush of life, emanations and fragrances of vegetation, has broken out everywhere among the stone buildings, thrusts and sways in the gardens around colored lights and music, runs down the broad streets with the interlocked shadows of trees under whose dense foliage a moonlit night can be transformed into blackness enclosed within a glittering armor. Most nights are bright and thin; they do not surround people densely enough for sound sleep; the people become like the houses, whose windows are all thrown open, and so streets and gardens are full of nocturnal animation.

But I slept soundly.

Even with open windows.

The morning's brightness flowed into the room very early.

I turned around, still half asleep. An invigorating fresh smell greeted me. Maruschka had been busy in my rooms, had taken action against the moths, for the sake of my fur-lined coat, my ski things, my woolen gloves, sweaters, sealskins. . . . I lay on my back. The room grew bright.

Friederike was in Bad Gastein.

I would soon be visiting her there.

At the Palais Ruthmayr the alterations were already in progress.

In order to report to her about these, I rode out to Wieden that morning, and came to the quiet street which was now so familiar to me that it passed through me like a wave of honey when I entered it. "Good morning, Herr von Geyrenhoff!" Ludmilla called and came running toward me, kerchief over her hair and otherwise equipped with that armor which maids must wear when artisans invade. She guided me. In the small salon and in the big one behind the glass wall, everything had been pushed aside and covered. The furnishings stood in resigned sadness, with heads shrouded.

Then I stepped outside and saw the sky, and against it two pairs of legs: masons standing on a small scaffolding.

Here where the dark library corridor had once been, an enormous battering-ram of light descended. I took two steps forward. Fragments of masonry lay about. Everything was opened up. I looked into the gardens. All was airy. For seconds I had the feeling that the whole mansion lay broken open, shattered, turned inside out. In the salons with the muffled furniture I had missed the camphor smell. As I looked out into the gardens, with a strange feeling of expansiveness, as though I myself had been opened up, I was obsessed by a deep-seated error—a chronological one. I imagined that it was autumn. The feeling could not be shaken off. It was as though I were stepping forth out of a sunken road into open terrain of extraordinary colorfulness and variety, although the foundation color was a chilly, pure blue.

I have just laid down my pen and gone out to Wieden again, twenty-eight years later, and walked down the same street where the Palais Ruthmayr once stood. It was destroyed during the war. Now a housing project of the City of Vienna stands there. Friederike did not live to endure the Second World War. Her heart gave out. Perhaps she had become too immovable, too strong. But her end was exceedingly gentle. This should make it clear why I am living and writing in Schlaggenberg's "last studio," and not in that mansion in Wieden where I was permitted to spend the happiest period of my life.

Ah yes, I was already a happy man in midsummer of 1927 (we did not marry until the fall), alone in Vienna, inspecting the alterations upon Friederike's beautiful house, and on the point of going out to Bad Gastein to join her as soon as the work was well along. Ah yes, I was a happy man. But perhaps I did not know then, as well as I did later, how to breathe in happiness, how to inhale it deeply. That too is a skill and an art.

Time seemed to stand still that summer, like a tiny cloud forgotten by the wind, floating alone, high in the sky. Shortly after the middle of July the heat descended again; the period of cloudy coolness had lasted only a few days.

For a certain reason I was actually pleased that Friederike and I had postponed our nuptials. It seemed that a veritable thunderstorm of banalities was descending on us. Every day the mail brought more: Herr Jan Herzka and Fräulein Agnes Gebaur had entered the married state; Herr and Frau Trapp wished to announce the engagement of their daughter to Director Dulnik; Mr. Dwight Williams and Emma Drobil also seemed suddenly to be in a hurry; and as we have seen, my cousin Géza was in the greatest hurry of all. This wedding was to be celebrated at the beginning of August in Styria—the guests would include a large contingent of the Orkay family, and even Géza's chief, the ambassador, but not Kajetan, who had vanished from everyone's ken. And not me, either. I had excused myself on the ground that I could not leave Vienna because of "alterations on my fiancée's house." Meanwhile, the newlyweds had themselves returned to Vienna and were staying at the Hotel Krantz-Ambassador, as was only proper for a diplomatic couple. They had reserved a sleeping compartment on the train to Basel, where they were spending a few days before going on to Berne. They were to be house guests of some rich acquaintances or other, probably for exuberant celebrations on the soil of the Helvetian Confederation.

Friederike and I were content to remain outside all this pomp and circumstance, or at least at some distance in time from it. What we had in mind was, after all, also banal. But in this sort of banality people do not like to be accompanied by large numbers of others. Any crowding makes it virtually impossible to sustain the fiction of the uniqueness and singularity of the event; and that fiction is, after all, part and parcel of the whole thing.

So it was. The forgotten little cloud continued to float tranquilly in the blue sky. I did nothing, unless learning to be happy can be considered an activity (and for my part I think it a very serious one). The fragrance of camphor wafted through all my rooms, inner and outer. The windows stayed open. Faintly, I heard the tinkling of the streetcar bells on the main street of Döbling, and then the string of cars ascended with a rising chromatic scale up to the Hohe Warte. I lay on the couch. On the desk my blank note-pad riffled in a slight breeze. Camy's letter no longer lay there. I had put it away.

During this period I also took a few long walks in the nearer portions of the Vienna Woods, and as a happy man gazed upon a happy landscape, still living with it, still embracing its riper, more rounded greens of midsummer, seeing no invading brown rust of the past and of late fall. Oh no. For I was in love! And today? What most deeply connects an old man with life? What a question! And yet I venture to answer that question, though only for myself, out of my personal experience.

It is melancholy. "Beauteus Melancolia," as Ruodlieb von der Vläntsch calls it. That is the last, indestructible connection, the finest thread, stitched deep into the heart.

I stand in Schlaggenberg's "last studio," the afternoon sun entering. The doubly glazed skylight makes a roof of brightness above me; and now my hand flies to my heart, though that organ is perfectly sound and beats normally, and was never ill, or at most metaphorically so—twenty-eight years ago, when the crystal wall parted me from Friederike and I did not yet understand the language of fish.

I also took a long walk on the day that Quapp and Géza were to depart. About five o'clock I reached that district where the

Kamm and Mugl rise to their highest point between Agneswiese and the Jägerwiese.

This is one of the momentous points in the Vienna Woods; standing there, it is easy to feel that you are on a real mountain. The unusually steep sheering of the land down toward Weidling, the wild growth of the forest, the exposure to the wind, which has bowed many of the trees on the slope—all this plunges the walker suddenly deep into the self-willed, obstinately silent sublimity of forestland, far from his accustomed boulevards and streets. In winter, too, traversing this place on skis, meeting the stiff wind, you lost for the moment all reference to the great urban agglomeration that is nevertheless so close.

At the ridge stood a man. He had been standing there motionless all the while, looking out into the distance from the precipitous rims of the peak.

When I came closer, I saw that it was Kajetan.

Although we had not seen each other since June 23, we were not cast into that state of embarrassment in which people find themselves who basically have nothing in common, even though they occasionally meet and attempt to bring each other up to date, to sketch a picture that the other can never really see. We had no need of anything of the sort. I told him only that Quapp and Géza were in Vienna and were going to leave that day (and that we could take a cab together to the West Station).

"I know all about it," he said. "Went to the Hotel Ambassador this morning, right after my arrival. Heard the whole story. Heard about your engagement too, you dreadful mystifier." (Was that his idea of congratulations?)

"And how did you know where the Orkays were staying?"

"On the way back I found a letter from Mother waiting for me at my publisher's in Stuttgart—I stopped off there. Mother's furious with me. Because I wasn't at the wedding and didn't send congratulations. Naturally not. I didn't know a thing."

"And where were you 'on the way back' from when you stopped off at Stuttgart?"

"You know perfectly well," he said. "Incidentally, everything is arranged with the Stuttgart people."

A warm wind passed over the ridge. The woods shook and rustled. We walked down toward Jägerwiese.

In London, Kajetan related, he had stayed at Sloane Square, and the morning after his arrival had walked along King's Road and then turned left, in toward Chelsea.

"Do you know the neighborhood?" he asked.

"Yes, quite well," I said.

He had never expected to run into her the very first day—had in fact thought it quite possible that he would not meet her at all. As he was crossing from Chelsea to Battersea, on the right side of the Albert Bridge, he saw her coming straight toward him. She almost passed by without recognizing him. He lifted his hat, bowed, and went up to Camy.

"Her eyes flew wide," Kajetan said. "She literally turned white with rage, and had a numbed look. Then with her whole arm she beckoned to somebody who was apparently on the other side of the bridge, behind me. I did not turn around. I lifted my hat once more, made a short bow, and then I turned and walked swiftly back in the direction from which I had come. Not a word had been exchanged. Only as I was walking away did I see whom Camy had beckoned to. It was a bobby. He was walking toward Battersea, on the other side of the bridge, looking down at the ground. Perhaps he wasn't on duty. By day there isn't any patrolman in that vicinity. The bobby hadn't paid any attention to Camy and me. The whole thing took place shortly before eleven o'clock in the morning. Around two o'clock I took the train at Victoria Station and met the boat at Dover."

"How long were you in London, then?"

"Barely a day. Actually, only overnight."

"And when was that?"

"Four days ago."

"And all the rest of the time? Where were you before?"

A grim and gloomy look settled over his face. We had stopped on the rough path down to Jägerwiese. In the sunlight we could see out over the broad expanse which sloped, glittering here, there dull green, toward the woods of Hermannskogel.

"Aside from Stuttgart . . . I was . . . I was also in Paris for a while. I was still hesitating to make the trip to London. I drank heavily."

"You look it, Kajetan," I said.

"The reptile wanted to have me arrested!" he burst out.

We stood facing each other on the path. I knew that I must not flinch or shirk now, and said in a calm tone: "Kajetan, you are going to spit out the word you have just used."

Our eyes met and held.

"Yes," he said. Then he actually turned his head aside and spat.

We were silent. Finally he took up his story again, his voice very low.

"I crossed the bridge, kept walking ahead very rapidly, because I imagined I would fall down if I stood still for a moment. For some reason I did not go back toward Chelsea, the way I had come, but kept to the right and reached Cheyne Walk. Here, in that clear, inviting neighborhood with its fine greensward—it's almost like Döbling, you know!—my pace slowed, and finally I stood still. Deep beneath me, but as though I were resting all my weight entirely upon it, and as though I had a right to rest there, I felt something like a green strip of lawn in the middle of a crossing. It was as if I had slipped off that green strip some time before and was now finding my way back to it. Getting back on took the form of an observation which I made in retrospect—I hadn't made it at the proper time. Oddly enough, it concerned a child. Little Renata Gürtzner-Gontard—she's a child to us, after all—whom I had in my gang, along with her friend Sylvia, and the scout, and the Garriques. Only now did I realize—that's really being slow on the uptake for you!—that she was the same girl we'd seen once when we were skiing in the woods, and then at 'our crowd's' plenary outing—you know what I mean, when I was standing up there and she passed by. . . . And I instantly recognized the condition in which I'd lived for so long. That condition now dropped away from me. Camy had amputated it for me. It was a condition in which even facts ceased to convince. Because they were not even perceived. That was how I had been living. Immediately after those moments on Cheyne Walk, I felt in amazingly good spirits. I took the train to Stuttgart and signed the contract which had meanwhile been drawn up."

"Good," I said. As I spoke now I looked out across Jägerwiese into the milky glare of the sun. "So you finally set down your second reality and left it lying there on Cheyne Walk. Sooner or later you had to. Hold firm to your strip of green lawn now. Your future will be sprouting from it. Think composedly of Camy. Right this minute you are going to—not forgive Camy, but recognize that there is nothing to forgive—that at most it is for her to forgive. And you are going to do something else which will be decisive for the whole of your life: namely, stop absolutely and finally dismissing Camy by—well, let us say, by the Körger-Eulenfeld method and using a term borrowed from them. There is nothing lower and more vulgar than to communicate with oneself in language and in invective that is chosen on the basis of its plausibility to others." (At that time I had not yet read the already quoted passage from Valéry—I really don't know what bee of illumination stung me at the moment.)

"You are a monster," he said.

"Call me that if you like. If that's so, it's up to you to produce a monster and let it loose on yourself, in order to become a human being."

Again I fixed my eyes sharply upon him. He swayed a little (almost as he had done once before, on that traffic island, when the bottom had dropped out of him).

"Yes," Kajetan said. He exhaled audibly. His chest subsided, his head slowly drooped.

After our supper on the terrace of that former dairy, now a café, which belongs to Kobenzl Castle—it offers a splendid prospect of the city—Kajetan took a number of papers from his wallet and shoved them across the table toward me. "Yes, yes," I said, after I had looked them over, "always within the law and covering his tracks, Financial Counselor Levielle. But on May 30 he gave up the ghost, so to speak. Where did you get this trash?"

"My gang got hold of it for me. They rifled the old secretary desk that Gach spoke of."

"Marvelously clever idea," I said. "But don't throw the stuff away here; put it in your stove back home."

Twilight fell. The first feeble earthly stars down below began blinking in the inky lake of the city. We drank more wine and sat in silence. At last we set out. We had far to go, after all.

At the railroad station I saw them all assembled once again, the whole of "our crowd." Only Angelika and Grete Siebenschein were missing. Laura Konterhonz had turned up with Höpfner. "Well, well," Kajetan must have thought. That was another new development he became acquainted with here. She greeted him, incidentally, in a very ladylike manner, and with a certain condescension. He seemed well content, which of course only made her air all the more ridiculous.

Our crowd stood around the fancy couple—Quapp was dressed in a really distinguished outfit. She found a moment to escape from the ring of well-wishers, and we walked back and forth together a short way up the platform. She told me about her wedding, but cast scarcely a glance backward at the past half year. I was oddly affected to hear that Mama Schlaggenberg had considered it part of the wedding preparations to have all the high trees in front of the garden room cut down. "A whole new block of brightness stands right inside the house now." (I noted Quapp's description at the time, and have not forgotten it to this day.) "Then there was a kind of gigantic green punch bowl with innumerable glasses there. It was used at the wedding, but hasn't been returned to its old place. The room looks altogether different." Evidently Mama Schlaggenberg also possessed the talent of marking eras by altering external conditions. However, Quapp could scarcely have inherited that from her.

She did not ask me about Gyurkicz.

She spoke of Basel, of a number of eminent families there, the Burckhardts and Ehrenzellers and others. Here and now was the last chance for Quapp to learn of Imre's fate. Or did she know it, and did she deliberately refrain from mentioning the dead man? I examined her face, and it seemed to me that her habitual ignorance had persisted there, *in extremis,* so to speak.

I said nothing to her about Gyurkicz.

Two men had prayed the *De profundis* while Imre's body was still warm, his blood still flowing. How did that concern Frau Legationsrat Orkay? For me she was no longer one of our crowd. To be sure, I too had known—how to inherit. But I did not possess the memory of a chicken and a heart of stone to go with it. And so I held my tongue, and rigidly guarded within myself the epitaph I had written for my friend, who had truly become that only in the very last moments of his life. Guarded it against the otherwise inevitable contamination by the empty words she would speak.

The conductor called "all aboard." The train was drawn forward somewhat; it did not stand entirely in the station. Behind the sleeping car, in which the Orkays had their compartment, was another first-class car. The two now stepped upon the rear platform of this car, and so could look back through the glass of the door at us, at the group of our crowd. We, for our part, saw the young couple standing there as in an illuminated frame. With that creeping noiselessness and slowness with which every express train leaves the station, only to roar along shortly at sixty miles an hour, this train too glided away. The picture withdrew into the darkness of the night, while the waved handkerchiefs fluttered in the air like cabbage butterflies. I could still distinctly make out Quapp, small, occupant of a spark that was vanishing in darkness. In those seconds it seemed to me that I would never again see her or any other member of the group who stood with raised arms and waving handkerchiefs upon the nearly deserted platform—never again in this life.

List of Characters

(Principal characters are starred)

Abheiter, *director of Pomberger & Graff, publishers and printers*

*Edouard Altschul, *a bank director*

*Rosi Altschul, *his wife*

Anita ("Piggy"), *a prostitute*

Professor Bullogg, *medievalist at Harvard University, son-in-law of Mme Libesny*

Peggy Bullogg, *his wife*

Lilly Catona, *schoolmate of Fella Storch*

*Countess Claire Charagiel, *daughter of Baron von Neudegg*

Cobler, *editor-in-chief at Alliance*

*Prince Alfons Croix

Mathias Csmarits, *disabled war veteran with one eye, brother of Frau Kapsreiter*

*Anna Diwald ("Didi"), *barmaid, underworld character*

Beppo Draxler, *a "troupiste"*

*Emma Drobil, *a beautiful stenographer*

Dulnik, *manager of a paper factory, suitor to Angelika Trapp*

Ederl, *painting contractor, gambler*

*Captain von Eulenfeld, *leader of "the Düsseldorfers," former hussar*

Fiedler, *a bookseller and classical scholar*

Malva Fiedler, *his daughter, friend of Leonhard Kakabsa*

Lea Fraunholzer, née Küffer, *daughter of Herr Küffer*

Freud, *owner of a brandy shop*

von Frigori, *a haughty baron*

Bill Frühwald, *pianist and "troupiste"*

*Alois Gach, *commissioner of markets, former sergeant in Ruthmayr's regiment*

Garrique, *former wine dealer from Bordeaux, brother-in-law of Professor Bullogg*

Mme Daisy Garrique, *sister of Professor Bullogg*

Gaston Garrique, *the Garriques' son*

Lilian Garrique, *the Garriques' daughter*

Agnes Gebaur, *Jan Herzka's new secretary*

Geiduschek, *student at the Gymnasium, one of Mary K.'s admirers*

*Georg von Geyrenhoff, *the narrator, a retired civil servant*

Minna Glaser, *Irma Siebenschein's sister*

Glenzler ("Father"), *member of the editorial staff of Alliance*

Hedwig Glöckner, *head of a gymnastics school*

*Anny Gräven, *prostitute, friend of Leonhard Kakabsa*

Etelka Grauermann, *René Stangeler's deceased sister*

Pista Grauermann, *Etelka's ex-husband*

Frau Greilinger, *Dwight Williams's landlady*

*Josef Grössing ("Pepi," "Croaky"), *a boy, Frau Kapsreiter's nephew*

Magdalena Güllich, *Jan Herzka's former girl friend*

Gürtler, *a Viennese lawyer*

Anatol von Gürtzner-Gontard, *the Hofrat's son*

Doktor Franz von Gürtzner-Gontard, *the Hofrat's son*

*Hofrat von Gürtzner-Gontard, *Geyrenhoff's former superior*

Melanie von Gürtzner-Gontard, *the Hofrat's wife*

Pris von Gürtzner-Gontard, *wife of Franz*

*Renata von Gürtzner-Gontard, *the Hofrat's daughter*

*Imre von Gyurkicz, *newspaper cartoonist and painter, friend of Charlotte von Schlaggenberg ("Quapp")*

Jan Herzka, *head of Rolletschek's webbing company, heir to Neudegg Castle*

Hirschkron, *a bookbinder*

Holder, *editor at Alliance*

Robert Höpfner, *advertising executive*

Jirasek, *a tailor*

*Beatrix K. ("Trix"), *daughter of Mary K.*

Hubert K., *son of Mary K.*

*Mary K., *a widow who has lost a leg in a streetcar accident*

Anna Kakabsa, *Leonhard's sister, servant of Mme Libesny (in London)*

°Leonhard Kakabsa, *a young factory worker who educates himself*

Ludmilla Kakabsa ("Mila"), *Leonhard's sister, Friederike Ruthmayr's servant*

°Frau Anna Kapsreiter, *widowed sister of Mathias Csmarits, keeper of a dream-book*

Franziska Kienbauer, *secretary at Alliance, mistress of editor-in-chief Cobler*

Laura Konterhonz, *a mistress of Kajetan von Schlaggenberg*

Herr Köppel, *head bookkeeper for Jan Herzka*

Doktor Kurt Körger, *Geyrenhoff's nephew*

Doktor Philemon Krautwurst, *lawyer for Baron von Neudegg*

Krawouschtschek, *a carpenter*

Egon Kries, *Clarisse Markbreiter's son-in-law*

Lily Kries, *Clarisse Markbreiter's daughter*

Herr Küffer, *wealthy general manager of a Viennese brewery, a friend of the younger set*

Corporal Anton Lach, *bugler in Captain Ruthmayr's squadron*

Count Mucki Langingen, *hunter of antiques, friend of Prince Croix*

°Cornel Lasch, *brother-in-law of Grete Siebenschein, associate of Levielle*

Frau Titi Lasch, *sister of Grete Siebenschein*

Oskar Leucht ("Oki"), *a "troupiste"*

°Financial Counselor Levielle, *the villain*

Mme Libesny, *Professor Bullogg's mother-in-law, Dwight William's landlady in London*

Lilly Likarz, *an artist and a friend of Mary K.*

Doktor Mährischl, *a lawyer*

Frau Martha Mährischl, *his wife*

Rosi Malik, *poetess and popular playwright*

Clarisse Markbreiter, *sister of Irma Siebenschein*

Siegfried Markbreiter ("Purzel"), *her husband*

Frau Mayrinker, *later occupant of Frau Kapsreiter's apartment in the Blue Unicorn*

Herr Josef Mayrinker, *a banker and a student of dragon lore*

°Meisgeier ("the Claw"), *a murderer*

Mörbischer, *caretaker of Neudegg Castle*

°Hans Neuberg, *a student of history*

Baron Achaz von Neudegg, *father of Claire Charagiel*

Achaz Neudegker, *ancestor of Baron Achaz von Neudegg*

Oplatek, *a member of the Alliance directorate*

*Géza von Orkay (the "bird Turul"), *a Hungarian diplomat, cousin of Geyrenhoff*

*Alois Pinter ("Pinta"), *son-in-law of Franz Zdarsa, a pro-Hungarian conspirator*

Hertha Plankl, *a prostitute, friend of Anny Gräven*

Thomas Preschitz, *a socialist leader*

Ensign Preyda, *René Stangeler's wartime friend, killed in action in 1916*

Sylvia Priglinger, *a friend of Renata von Gürtzner-Gontard*

Protopapadakis ("Prokop"), *a gambler, Anny Gräven's friend*

Frau Thea Rosen, *a fat female*

Pop Rottauscher, *a pickpocket*

Rucktäschl, *a typesetter*

Miss Rugley, *formerly Kajetan and Quapp's governess, now housekeeper for Kajetan's mother*

*Frau Friederike Ruthmayr ("Fritzi," "Friedl"), *an immensely wealthy widow*

Captain Georg Ruthmayr, *her late husband, killed in action in 1914*

Dr. Schedik, *Kajetan von Schlaggenberg's father-in-law*

Scheindler, *author of Leonhard's Latin grammar*

*Frau Camilla von Schlaggenberg ("Camy"), née Schedik, *Kajetan's estranged wife*

*Charlotte von Schlaggenberg ("Quapp," "Quappchen," "Lo," "Lotte"), *Kajetan's sister, an aspiring violinist*

*Kajetan von Schlaggenberg, *novelist*

Frau Schoschi, *owner of the Café Kaunitz*

Kyrill Scolander, *Kajetan's teacher*

Doktor Ferry Siebenschein, *a lawyer, Grete's father*

*Grete Siebenschein, *René Stangeler's girl friend*

Irma Siebenschein, *Grete's mother*

Alexander Alexandrovich Slobedeff ("Sasha"), *a composer*

*René von Stangeler ("the Ensign"), *a brilliant young historian*

Frau Selma Steuermann, *Kajetan's ideal of womanhood*

Dolly Storch, *Professor Storch's daughter*

Felicitas Storch ("Fella"), *Trix's friend*

Käthe Storch, *Professor Storch's wife*

Professor Oskar Storch, *professor of anatomy*

Captain Szefcsik, *a pro-fascist Hungarian*

Raymond Szilagi, *driver of the Hungarian embassy car*

Szindrowitz, *director of Pomberger & Graff, publishers and printers*

Hofrat Tlopatsch ("Uncle Fritz"), *the "pope" of music in Vienna*

Angelika Trapp ("Angi"), *Neuberg's fiancée*

Doktor Trapp, *Angelika's father*

Doktor Trembloner, *a financial manager at Alliance*

Frau Tugendhat, *an employee at Alliance*

Ruodlieb von der Vläntsch, *author of a late medieval manuscript*

Waschler, *superintendent and doorman of Gürtzner-Gontard's apartment house*

Herr Weilguny, *an artist, competitor of Imre von Gyurkicz*

Frau Risa Weinmann, *former owner of the Café Kaunitz*

Fräulein Wiesinger, *Quapp's accompanist*

*Dwight Williams, *an American lepidopterist*

Frau Lea Wolf, *a fat female*

Xidakis ("Kaki"), *a gambler, Protopapadakis's friend*

Elly Zdarsa, *Pinter's sister-in-law*

Franz Zdarsa ("Old Goatbeard"), *a vineyard owner*

Nikolaus Zdarsa ("Niki"), *a friend of Leonhard Kakabsa*

Sergeant Karl Zeitler, *a policeman and local historian*

Karl Zilcher, *a friend of Leonhard Kakabsa*

Zurek, *Pop Rottauscher's helper*

A *Note on the* TYPE

The text of this book is set in Caledonia, *a Linotype face designed by* W. A. Dwiggins, *the man responsible for so much that is good in contemporary book design and typography. Caledonia belongs to the family of printing types called "modern face" by printers—a term used to mark the change in style of type-letters that occurred about 1800. Caledonia borders on the general design of Scotch Modern but is more freely drawn than that letter.*

Composed, printed, and bound by Kingsport Press, Inc. Paper manufactured by S. D. Warren Company, Boston. Typography and binding design by George Salter.